ALSO BY MELISSA GOOD

Dar and Kerry Series
Tropical Storm
Hurricane Watch
Eye of the Storm
Red Sky At Morning
Thicker Than Water
Terrors of the High Seas
Tropical Convergence
Stormy Waters
Moving Target
Storm Surge: Book One
Storm Surge: Book Two
Winds of Change: Book One
Winds of Change: Book Two

Partners Series
Partners: Book One
Partners: Book Two
Of Sea and Stars

Of Sea and Stars

Melissa Good

*Silver Dragon Books
by Regal Crest*

Tennessee

ISBN 978-1-61929-298-7

First Printing 2016

9 8 7 6 5 4 3 2 1

Cover design by Acorn Graphics

Published by:

Regal Crest Enterprises
1042 Mount Lebanon Road
Maryville, TN 37804

Find us on the World Wide Web at
http://www.regalcrest.biz

Printed in the United States of America

Chapter One

THE BOOMING ROAR sent a shuddering wave through solid rock, causing dust and bits of stone to fall from the ceilings. Jump-suited figures hastened to cover their heads.

"Son of a bitch!" Jason Anders knocked a piece of granite chip off his shoulder. "What are they doing out there?"

"Blasting," A tech supervisor told him, heading for the food line. "Again. I know we needed the updates but we need some sleep, too."

Jason ruffled his hair and observed the rock dust floating down from it. "Nice." He was brown haired and good looking, with a squarely built head and a lean, muscular body encased in black fabric with teal blue piping at the neck.

Here in the Citadel he wore no weapons, but there was an edge to him that suggested he might want to. In the hairline on the right side of his head there were healing blaster scars, still vivid and red.

He looked around and spotted a tall, dark haired woman entering the mess. "Hey! Jesslyn!" He waved her over, half standing and sweeping the dust off the top of the table. "C'mere!"

Senior agent Jesslyn Drake ambled over and picked up a chair at his table, dumping the debris off it onto the floor before she sat down. "What?" Like Jason, she was also lean and muscular, in the same gear but the rank pips at her neck had bars — his didn't.

"What's the racket?" Jason asked, as his partner, Brent, came over with a tray. "They blowing up the cavern?" He waggled his eyebrows at her. "Figured they might have told you, at least."

"Finally decided to put a forward facing dock load in," Jess said. "Closing up the roof. One of the donks said we were idiots for having an opening that let rain in every time we opened it."

Jason grinned a little. "Got a point."

"Got a point," Jess wryly agreed. "Lot of things just get to be how they get to be, you know?"

"I think they just like blowing stuff up," Brent said, forking into his seaweed. "Couldn't sleep for a week when they put in those new guns." Burly and bull necked, with his crew cut freshly shortened, Jason's tech shook his head in annoyance. "Jerks."

"It'll be over soon," Jason said. "It will, right?" he asked Jess.

"Two more intake tunnels, but after that, yeah," Jess replied. "Need the power to run all those new fitting bays."

A double bong sounded overhead. "Drake to Ops."

"Crap." Jess pushed herself to her feet. "Now what?"

"They can't take a crap without you, Jessie." Jason chuckled and gave her a slap on the leg. "If you're going up there see if El's called in. She's late reporting."

"Sure." Jess regretfully bypassed the chow line and wound her way through the crowd and out the door. She turned right and moved down the long arched passageway deep inside the Citadel's rugged mountain structure.

The hallways bore signs of new construction, and she passed newly set doors that would lead into newly blasted and cut chambers, glad at least the corridor that held her quarters was on the other side of ops and not up for any mods.

Construction group members were busy all over, sanding and smoothing the new walls and openings, and moving jet pads around with piles of building material on them.

The freshening up was nice, but she, like the rest of the agents and techs stationed at Base Ten was more than ready for it all to be done.

She cleared the crossroads and went down the passage to ops, walking through a solid blue ring that laid a tickle over the surface of her skin and then through a second before she reached the door, the extra security added just recently after a more than embarrassing breach.

The rings passed her mutely though and she palmed into ops. She stepped into a lock filled with sensors, and at the quadrants, raw and powerful blasters that could turn a person her size into plasma gooked dust in under a second. She didn't even look at them, but merely waited for the inner door to slide aside to let her on her way.

"Ah, Drake." Commander Bensen Alters turned from the main console. "Thanks for coming up."

"Problem?" Jess asked. "Jason asked me to ask if Elaine logged in."

"Nothing yet, no. But we received this." He handed her a plas. "Sit down, take your time reading it."

Jess did, resting her elbows on her knees as she regarded the plas. "Mini transport?" she muttered. "An enemy team inserted."

"Mmm." Alters took the seat next to her. "Right at the edge of Drake's Bay." He watched the angular face of the woman sitting knee to knee with him. "Familiar territory."

Jess looked up, then back down at the sheet. The digital signature of the transport was blurry, but clear enough to be identifiable. The ridge line it was tucked behind on the borderlands between Drake's Bay homestead and the processing center next door. "Could be going to the center," she said. "They're not stupid enough to try and get into the Bay."

"True," Alters said. "But with a mini trans, it's one, or at most a team." He leaned back in the console command chair. "There's some contention there. Might be an incursion against you."

Jess considered that. "Could be. I pissed a lot of people off. Not giving up the shares screwed them up. They could make a pitch to knock me off."

There was no particular emotion around the words and her face didn't display any. "After all, who else are they gonna ask? Maybe that's how they got my dad."

Alters nodded in approval. "Was thinking that myself. Given you were supposed to go to the quarterly sector meet up next week—it seems like good timing. Glad you don't have any illusions about the possibilities."

"Mmm." Jess put the plas down on the console. "Maybe I'll go over a day or so earlier and flush them out. Put a kill in. If that's how it went down, someone deserves it," she said, matter of factly. "Sure beats hanging around here."

Alters shifted forward a little. "They've been quiet. You put a hurt on them. Two birds with a stone they're figuring. Maybe take a team with you. I don't want to waste the opportunity, and you've got a message to deliver to the sector they probably won't much like."

They exchanged grimly wry looks. "It's a mess," Jess said. "They won't like it is putting it mildly. Sucks to be them."

Alters smiled at her. "Sucks to be them."

Jess smiled back. "Home sweet home," she remarked dryly, standing up. "Thanks for the heads up. I'll run a book on it and pick a backup team."

He nodded. "Good. Listen, Drake, I know this is a big political mess. I get that it's cramping your ability to assign out and probably long term affecting your career with Interforce."

She shrugged. "Dying would do that, too, and that's where I'll be heading eventually. Don't worry about it. Worse things have happened than having to be a knife in the side of my birthplace. My father's probably somewhere laughing his ass off."

"Probably." He lifted a hand as she turned and headed for

the hatch, slipping between two incoming people and causing a belated but distinct motion as they cleared space for her, regardless of the relaxed body posture and smile.

WILDCARD. NO ONE wanted to mess with her. Alters sighed. Even with the senior grade and the accolades, there was never a sense you knew which way a Drake was going to move, and this one was no exception to that rule.

And the damned political mess forced by Justin Drake's machinations was putting a cramp in more than his daughter's career, since they now had a senior agent who couldn't be sent across the line and left a major homestead in limbo.

"Anything for me from Central Legal?" He turned his head and asked comms. "They better call soon."

"Nothing yet, sir," comms reported. "Do you want us to ping them?"

"Yes." He rested his elbow on the console and pushed the plas into the recycler as the shift change happened, incoming staff nodding respectfully in his direction, but their respect had a different edge to him than they'd shown to Jess.

He was old. Alters regarded them dryly. He was past being crazy. Or at least, that's what they thought.

"Sir." The comms on staff turned. "Coded call for you, from West three, encap, eyeball."

"Send it over." He slid an ear cup on and faced his console. "Next crisis."

JESS WENT BACK to the mess to get her delayed lunch. Jason and Brent were still there, and April had joined them. All of them looked up as she entered and went to the line, all of them ducking as another boom sounded overhead.

"Holy crap," Brent groused.

Jess cocked her head. "That wasn't a blast. That's a carrier coming in at speed." She turned and regarded the food processor, tapping in a code with an impatient gesture. "C'mon."

The bio alt behind the counter, a tall, curly haired, fresh-faced man, leaned forward. "Is it all right, Agent?"

"Yeah." Jess glanced up at the bio alt, his neck encircled by a tracework collar above the edge of his pale blue jumpsuit. "I'm just hungry."

The man nodded and stepped back, paying careful attention

to the machinery his set was designed to manage.

Jason leaned on the railing and watched the line. "Bet I know which carrier it is," he teased Jess. "I heard they were doing engine tests on that new pod, and there's no doubt who'd have called dibs on the first run," he said, but there was a grin on his face. "Rocket for sure. Can fricken drive a boot at mach two."

Jess put her tray down and took the last seat at the four top, not without a sigh. "Well, since I'm effectively grounded, she's got to do something to polish her rep. At least she'll get to show off for the grounders next week when I go piss off the entire coast."

"Can't they just shift over your shares to someone else?" Jason asked. "What a pain in the butt, Jess. What was your pop thinking?"

"He was thinking he didn't want the Bay to go over to shitheads, some of which he spawned." Jess munched her fish stew stolidly. "He just wasn't figuring on me screwing that all up while I was still in active service."

"Freak chance," Jason said.

"Story of my life." She paused as the comms link clipped to her jumpsuit chirped and put the ear bud in. "Drake."

"Hello, Jess, it's Dev," a warm, slightly burring voice answered. "We just finished testing and the new pod is excellent."

"We heard you arrive," Jess said. "C'mon over for lunch."

"Be right there."

Dev disconnected and Jess removed the bud from her ear, aware that she was smiling for no apparent reason. She cleared her throat. "With any luck legal will pull their heads out of their asses and figure it all out soon."

"About as soon as med clears me," Jason commiserated. "Poor us, stuck here doing centops duty." He got up and gathered his tray. "Let me clear space for Rocket." He winked at Jess and made his way out of the mess, dropping his empties off in the bin on the way.

Brent shook his head. "My run's up next." He got up. "See ya."

"Does Dev care if they call her that?" April asked, after Brent disappeared. "It's sort of stupid sounding." She was a woman of relatively small stature, but with a muscular body and a way of moving that made people tend to get out of her way.

Jess shrugged. "Nah, Dev doesn't much care what she's called. I had to pull up the comic in archives to explain the raccoon part, though. She thought that was pretty funny and she likes cute looking animals."

April eyed her, but continued eating in silence.

The mess door opened and two techs entered, wearing dark green flight suits, carrying comms helmets. The one in the lead was short and female, with straight blonde hair. Following her was a tall, red haired male with an ambling gait.

Dev came right over to the table and put her helmet down on the empty seat next to Jess. "The new entrance is going to be excellent," she said. "Did you see the hole?" She ran her fingers through her hair, which was mussed from the helmet and a little sweat stained. "It's gigantic."

"Not yet. Maybe you can take me on a tour after lunch." Jess winked at her. "We might have two hours clear weather today."

"Absolutely," Dev said at once. "It appeared to be getting better as we were coming in. No lightning or anything like that."

Doug, the second tech, put his own helmet down next to April. "Hey, boss."

"How was the testing?" April asked.

"I like the new mods," Doug said. "But really, we were all there just to watch Rocket fly." He grinned at Dev, and moved over to the line to get his tray. "With those new power boosts? Booyah."

Dev cleared her throat in a diffident sort of way, then joined him in line.

April continued to clear her own tray. "Been quiet anyway," she said to Jess. "You haven't missed much. Just that one patrol down near Picchu."

"Haven't heard from them," Jess said. "Hope it's just a tech screwup."

Dev came back with a tray full of edibles and sat next to Jess. "The acceleration of the new engine is amazing. At least ten times better than the old ones."

"Oh, no." Jess propped her head up on one fist. "I'm screwed. They're going to have to bungee tie me into that damn chair. Or put me in a rubber padded suit."

Doug and April laughed, as Dev regarded her partner with a look of perplexed concern. "Do you want more restraints? I can ask the rigging technicians to adjust your position."

Jess reached over and patted her hand. "Relax. It'll give me a chance to work on my biceps." She lifted her arms and tensed them as though holding onto a console. "Ahhh!"

Dev realized she was being razzed. "Maybe we should have

them put in a three hundred and sixty-degree gimbal for you."

Doug grimaced. "Hey c'mon I'm trying to have some lunch here. Don't make me think of that upside down stuff you do."

April chuckled and shook her head. "So," she eyed Jess, "I heard through the grapevine you were going out to the seaboard council in a couple days. Want a watch on your back?"

Jess stared at her as she thoughtfully chewed a mouthful of water grains and krill. Of the agent teams now at the base, there were only a few she felt completely confident of.

Most were new, fill-ins brought from other bases after the near disaster that caused the destruction of North base, and almost all of Ten. Of the older ones, there were some who so fiercely resented Jess's promotion to senior it was hard for them to work under her.

Even all the heroics hadn't changed that. Jess swallowed her mouthful. She'd changed some minds, and it was good to have some of her worst adversaries dead in the conflict, but there were some who still felt she'd scammed her bars and didn't deserve to be over them.

Maybe even had a point.

But April was different. A newly graduated agent from field school, who'd been with Jess through the trials they'd recently faced. She stayed out of the politics just keeping her head down and her weapons ready.

Feral, almost, as befit her nomad heritage and Jess liked her as much as she could like another agent. "Sure," she said, after a long pause. "Didn't learn from the last time? Crap happens to me."

"Exactly why I'm asking." April produced a brief grin. "We're bored." She indicated herself and Doug, who was listening in silence. "Besides, this is the big roundup. Some of our elders are going to be there and I thought I'd take the op to say hello."

"Fair enough," Jess said. "Figure we leave in five days, late afternoon." She picked up another fish roll and bit into it. "Spend a day or so at Drake's Bay, then go to the conclave."

April nodded. "Sounds good. Thanks." She finished eating and got up. "Let's go, Doug. We've got sims in ten."

They left with brief waves, and Jess waited for them to go before she turned and regarded her tech partner. "We need to leave a little early," she said, lowering her tone, even though most of the tables around them were now empty.

"I see." Dev was chewing her seaweed salad with intense

concentration. "To go to your birth place first?"

Jess nodded. "I'll try to keep them from being assholes to you." She sighed. "But they're not going to be happy to see me, that's for sure."

Dev made a face and reached over to put her hand on Jess's. "I'm sure it'll be okay, Jess. It's really not your fault what happened. I mean, you said your father did all that. Right?"

Jess chewed her roll, giving Dev a wry look.

After a moment, Dev returned her attention to her tray, picked up a little cake and bit into it.

"Yeah, it'll probably be okay," Jess said, after the silence had become awkward. "They know I'm likely to shoot people if they piss me off. That's what usually keeps the peace. I'm just in a down mood."

Dev eyed her. "I have a swimming session scheduled for after lunch. Would you like to attend?"

Jess's lips twitched.

The mess door opened and a squad of bio alts entered with re-supply. They were walking a gyro and as they passed the two of them, they gave a nod of acknowledgment. "Agent Drake, Tech NM-Dev-1," the bio alt in the lead said, a comms link settled over his left ear. "Greetings."

"Hello, Geebee," Dev responded. "Is that from the shuttle today?"

"Yes," the bio alt responded. "Some of the boxes were from the crèche. Some went to distribution, NM-Dev-1, I think one was for you."

"For me?" Dev looked and sounded surprised.

"Bet it's from the Doc." Jess stood and picked up her tray, holding a hand out for Dev's. "Gimme. Let's go gear up and do some gym."

"Thanks, Geebee." Dev handed her tray over, aware that the bio alts were watching Jess take it, and go to the disposal. She picked up her helmet and joined her at the door, and they moved from the quiet of the mess into the busy hallway beyond.

At the end of the passage past Centops were the ops quarters. The last two in the hall were theirs. Jess's was the first and they entered using her doorway, remaining silent until the doors slid shut behind them.

Jess went to her work desk and sat down behind it, while Dev went past her to the inner door that separated their quarters. It opened at her approach and she went inside, going to the gear locker and stowing her flight helmet.

She stripped out of her pilot's jumpsuit and put it on it's holder, then she turned and made her way into the sanitary unit, already looking forward to the hot blast of water hitting her skin.

A soft bong sound made her stop and reverse her course. She looked back over at the stores locker and saw a faint glow behind one section of it.

"Provisioning complete," the mechanical voice said.

Dev walked over to the locker and opened it again, glancing briefly at the mirror in the back that reflected her slight, yet muscular body in her under wraps, and the metallic illuminated collar that went all the way around her neck.

In the suit it wasn't visible. Even in the light off duty jumpers she wore it wasn't, unlike all the other bio alts in the base. She was one of them, and not. Born from an egg on a space station like the rest of the biological alternatives, and yet, she held natural born status in the base.

Complicated, and somewhat disturbing to them, and occasionally to her. The rest of them designed and programmed for specific tasks, to fly shuttles, or fix machinery, or to clean and maintain the base.

Dev wasn't like them in that regard. She'd been designed to fill the role of an operations tech, and that meant she lived and worked, not in the dorm downstairs on a regulated schedule, but like all of the other techs who had a more conventional origin and were natural born.

A more than successful experiment that now had the administrative section of Interforce in a tailspin because not only did Dev perform the role of operations tech, she excelled at it. That meant the future of their recruitment program was now in question.

Along with throwing into question the difference between bio alts and natural borns.

With a faint sigh she turned her attention to the package in the locker, lifting it out and examining it.

Thoughtfully, she went and put it on her workspace, then returned to the sanitary unit and continued with her shower. "First things first," she said to her reflection, as she removed her under wraps and turned on the shower.

Steam and mist filled that end of the sanitary space and she stepped under it, breathing in the now, to her, familiar scent. She felt the water heat her skin and took a handful of the soap, that smelled a little spicy, and scrubbed her body with it.

The air in the room compressed a little and she faintly heard the door opening. "Jess?" she called out.

Jess's dark, shaggy head appeared in the entryway to the sanitary unit. "You were expecting someone else?"

"No." Dev applied some of the soap to her head. "But you never know really. In the crèche everyone but us had the keys." She stepped under the water and let it rinse her off. "You couldn't really tell proctors not to walk in on you."

"Hmph. Well, no one but me better be coming in here without your say so." Jess said. "Is that your box on the table? Can I look at it?"

"Of course." Dev turned off the water and got a towel to dry with as Jess disappeared back into the outer room. She wrapped herself in the towel and poked her head out of the opening. Jess was seated behind her workspace idly twirling the box in her fingers.

Dev dried her hair off and exchanged her towel for fresh underthings, then she emerged into the main room and went to her locker. "You can open that." She got a lined jumpsuit out and put it on, running the fastenings up as she walked over to where Jess sat.

Jess pushed it over to her. "Nah, it's your box."

Dev sat next to her, ignoring the box. "Are you upset?"

Jess's pale blue eyes flicked to her alertly. "Me? Why?"

"You seem...uh..." Dev searched her memory, "ticked off."

Jess scowled engagingly at her. "I am, a little. Pissed off all this stuff with the Bay is cramping me." She regarded the neutral expression on Dev's face. "Everyone else gets to go out in the field and I'm stuck here," she clarified to save Dev the need to look up the slang.

"Oh." Dev took her hand. "I'm sorry, Jess. Is there anything I can do to help?"

Jess sighed. "I wish." She stared dourly at the table. "All this legal garbage. By the time they sort it out I'll be retired and they won't need to."

Dev absorbed that. "Excellent," she said. "Then can we go on a boat and see seals and dolphins again? Or maybe a whale?"

It forced Jess to laugh and she did. "Ah, Devvie. I guess that might not be a bad thing, huh? I'll end up not croaking and you and I can have some fun together." She pulled Dev's hand over and kissed the back of it. "What would I do without ya?"

Dev smiled at her. "I wish all this legal stuff was done, too. My contract's in question and that's a little uncomfortable." She picked up the box. "I'd rather have that sorted out." She undid the catches on the box and opened it, noting the origin. "It's from the crèche."

Jess scooted her chair up to watch. "From the doc?"

Dev removed a square translucent piece and put it on the table. "Oh! It's so pretty!" She found a bit of plas inside as well and opened it. "It is from Doctor Dan!"

She put the plas down where they could both see it, it's surface covered with an untidy scrawl.

```
Hello, Dev!
    We've worked out a new process here on station
and it let us create these little squares of
compressed gas with star images inside them. I
thought you might like one to remind you of us.
Hope you and Jesslyn are well.
    DJK
```

Jess picked up the square and peered into it. Though it seemed clear, when she got her eye up close it turned into a silky black with pinpoints of light in it. "Wow."

Dev got next to her and peered inside. "That's amazing," she said. "It's so nice of him to do that, isn't it?" She moved her head a little. "I think that's the back view from station, opposite from downside. I remember looking at those stars there, with the hook shape."

Stars. Jess inspected them intently. Something she'd never seen in her life. The view of them from planet side blocked by the impenetrable layer of clouds that covered the earth. "Nice." She sighed. "The doc's a good guy."

"He is." Dev smiled in delight at her present. "I miss him."

Jess bumped her on the shoulder. "Bet he misses you too. But listen. We're leaving a few days early because ops caught a mini transport landing near the Bay."

Dev's expression went serious. "From the other side?"

Jess nodded. "So I get a little action." She smiled wryly. "Either they're trying to get into the processing center or they bought one of my family."

"Oh, Jess." Dev had no idea how to feel about that, having no family, but she had to assume it must make Jess feel bad. "That's terrible." She paused, seeing the noncommittal expression on Jess's angular face.

Jess shrugged. "Peh. Anyway, we get to use the council as an excuse to root around, and maybe draw out whatever it is." She stood up and ruffled Dev's hair. "Swimming?"

"Yes."

"Then maybe surfing?" Jess asked, in a hopeful tone.

"Yes," Dev answered firmly, repressing a shiver. "Absolutely."

THE GYM WAS busy, all of the operational teams getting in some extra time since they weren't out on assignment. Jess and Dev made their way into the changing room and Jess exchanged her jumpsuit for an exercise one. "One good thing about being stuck here, I got time in this place and got my ass back in shape."

Dev paused in the motion of sealing her own suit and regarded Jess in a moment of reflective silence. Then she cleared her throat. "Was it supposed to be a different shape than it is?"

Jess put her hands on her hips. "You're such a little punk sometimes."

"Is that good or bad?"

"You make me laugh. That's always good." Jess bumped her toward the entry. "I'm going to go into the pit. Come rescue me if you hear me screaming. I'll meet you at the pool when we finish our warm-ups."

Dev followed her into the main area and watched her as she ambled off toward the hand-to-hand combat arena, where there were already a handful of agents sparring with each other. It was Jess's favorite exercise, even though she often came out of it with lurid purple bruises, and once, a broken finger.

With a faint shake of her head Dev moved purposefully toward the exercise machines, stopping at the first empty one and setting it to conform to her body. She settled into the support surface and positioned her arms and legs. "System, start."

"Ident?"

"Dev."

The machine considered that. "Starting."

Dev nodded in satisfaction and felt the pressure come against her grip. She closed her eyes and started the exercise, a core strength routine she was very familiar with. At least now the machine didn't argue with her when she asked for more contracting weight than it thought she should use.

JESS PAUSED AT the edge of the sparring area and looked back over her shoulder to watch Dev in her routine, a look of intense concentration on her face. She chuckled and undid the catches on the heavy net that surrounded the sparring area and walked inside.

The net sealed behind her, and she walked along the rock wall toward the warm up line. She paused to pick up a pair of gloves and slip them on her hands, the magnetic closures tightening around her wrists.

She approached the heavy, old style, hanging bags of beach sand and started a rhythmic tattoo on one of them, alternating punches and kicks to get her body warmed up.

It also gave her a chance to see who was in the pit and might be up for a match. Jess worked her way around the bag, looking past it to the floor. Three transplants, an old buddy of one of her long time adversaries, and Mike Arias, one of the recently graduated agents.

Mike was fighting Harrison, and two of the transplants were going at it, which left her with the other one, Jorge, as a potential opponent. He was currently just standing around, waiting for one of the other bouts to finish.

Jess recalled his history as she continued her warm up. Jorge and his tech partner, Sal, had come from the west coast. He was a little older than she was, a little shorter, with a body that looked like he spent a lot of time keeping himself in shape.

He was neutral, stayed out of the politics like April did, and so far he'd kept his mouth shut. His partner had been poking warily around Dev, having heard about this odd prodigy, but reserved judgment about her so far, at least in public.

Jess felt her body loosen up and she finished her drill, then walked down the steps to the lower level where the rest of the agents were, pausing to make eye contact with Jorge and raise an eyebrow.

He held up his hands and nodded, then they both sidestepped into one of the padded rings and faced each other.

Jess gave him a little nod of respect and then dropped her arms, moving her center of balance over the balls of her feet, giving him first go.

He didn't hesitate. He came forward and engaged her with fast, rapid punches, one going right at her head.

Jess moved with him, shifting and avoiding the blows with a peculiar, sinuous grace as she stepped closer and tapped him in the ribs, moving past him as he turned and snapped a fast kick at her.

He was good. Jess smiled, aware that she was likely going to enjoy herself this bout. She ducked the kick, then uncoiled from the slight crouch she'd taken and came right up off the ground, tucking her legs up and then launching them out to hit him in the chest.

He flew backwards, eyes opening in surprise, then tumbled and came back up again and back at her, with a grin of his own.

Jess landed and came to meet him, exchanging punches in a crack of glove against glove. She opened her left hand and let him target it, then blocked a roundhouse from his right hand, hopping backwards just in time to miss a kick to the ribs.

She felt her breathing slow, and the color leach out of her vision, batting aside his powerful right hand and getting her left in to impact his chin.

She saw the madness rising in his eyes and knew in a moment they would both go past the line, and it would move from a friendly spar to something else. She savored that as she felt the change, and then they were going at each other in earnest.

Someone, in the distance, yelled in alarm.

Jess shifted into high gear, her hands moving with flickering speed as she got inside his defenses again and again. Then she was in the air again, one foot hooking his knee, the other slamming him in the gut, the combination dumping him on his ass.

She dropped into a crouch, aware of the low growl issuing from her throat. He paused, went still, and lifted his hands palms out toward her.

"Smart," Harrison spoke up. "Don't mix with the animal."

Jess straightened up, staring steadily at him.

"No problem." Jorge got up and smiled. "I like a good mix up. 'Specially with a captain in the ass kicking business." He blinked a few times, clearing the haze, and extended a gloved hand out to Jess. "Hai, Drake."

Jess's body relaxed and she returned the bump. "Back at you," she said, after a brief clearing of her throat. "Go another round?"

"Oh, yeah." Jorge shook himself and took up a position again. "Let's go."

"Hey, I'm next," Mike Arias said. "I want you to show me how to do that kick."

Jess flexed her hands and smiled, dismissing Harrison with a brief twitch of her lips. She went back to the center of the pit and cleared her mind, considering she might have gotten a point or two out of the exchange.

Heh.

Animal?

DEV WAS HALFWAY across the pool, swimming with careful, determined motions that abruptly became a flail when a large body landed in the water next to her, ducking her under. She scrambled for the surface and shook her hair out of her eyes, spluttering. "Whoa!"

"Devviie!" Jess warbled under her breath. "Whatcha doing?"

Dev dog paddled, keeping her head above water, and looked around. "Swimming?" She watched Jess roll lazily over onto her back. "Was your session successful?"

"Yes." Jess hooked one hand around Dev's bicep, then she kicked her legs in a scissors motion, pulling both of them effortlessly through the water. "Ended up in a two on one the other two regretted."

Now in the shallows, they both stood up and let the water sheet off them. Dev saw new bruises on Jess's body and a long scratch down her left thigh. "Are you injured?"

"Nah." Jess didn't even look down. "Felt good."

Dev eyed her doubtfully. "Well, that's excellent then."

Jess chuckled. "I know you think I'm nutty. It's okay." She raked the dark, wet hair off her forehead. "They train us to like being kicked around."

Dev tried to imagine what that was like. She reviewed her programming and tried to think of something so profoundly unpleasant that she'd been geared to enjoy and couldn't. "Okay," she said. "I'm glad you're happy about it."

Jess slid down in the water and stretched herself out, enjoying the gentle buoyancy. "But you lucked out. I used enough spare energy to not want to go surf the rest of the day." She watched the muscles to either side of Dev's mouth twitch. "You're such a good sport about that, Devvie."

Surfing was difficult. Not only difficult for her, but occasionally dangerous and often painful. Dev nevertheless participated when Jess wanted to, driven by her urge to make her natural born partner happy.

Programming, yes, but also a deep inner emotion that supported and surrounded that programming, reinforcing it to cause her to subvert her own comfort willingly.

Was that like Jess enjoying being struck?

Dev frowned, then applied herself to the water again. "I'm almost done with this session. Would you like to get some sun replacement after we finish?"

Jess leaned against the wall, a mildly distracted look on her face. She glanced up at Dev. "I would. C'mon, race ya!"

Dev good naturedly started forward, having no illusions whatsoever that she could keep pace with Jess. She'd gotten much better at swimming, but Jess moved through the water like she was part of it.

They reached the other side of the pool and started back, swimming shoulder to shoulder as Jess alternated between strokes, her head turned to watch Dev, the translucent eyelids that protected her eyes underwater glinting faintly.

She kept her breathing air-based though, and they continued a dozen more laps before they hoisted themselves out of the pool and stood dripping together for a moment, as a crowd of others moved past from the weight bearing area.

They were aware of the looks they both got, brief and shifted quickly away. Jess ignored it and led the way over to the changing area, grabbing a towel as they walked inside and tossing it to Dev. She wiped her face off and roughly dried her hair, then let the fabric drape around her neck.

April and Doug entered. "Hello, there," April greeted, as she went to a set of lockers across from theirs.

"Hello," Dev answered, as Jess lifted a hand in acknowledgment. "How was the new sim set, Doug?"

"Eh." Doug waggled his hand, as he stripped out of his jump suit. "I don't like the new autonomics much. Feels laggy."

"Everything feels laggy to you, rookie," one of the older techs told him. "All you do is bitch about the gear."

Doug held both hands out. "Can I help it if this stuff is older and draggier than school?" He half turned. "You try it, Rocket. See what you think."

Dev toweled her body off before getting back into her work suit. "Well, I haven't had much to compare it to, but I will be in them this evening." She paused, noting the older tech was staring at her neck. "So we'll see."

The tech jerked around straight and faced his locker, and Dev glanced behind her to find Jess relaxing, her glare moderating to something more normal.

Deciding she had nothing to add to the conversation, she did up the catches on her suit, covering her collar, and took her towel and the wet exercise suit to the recycler.

Brent caught up with them as they exited. "Hey. You hear they're opening up a senior track?" He said to Dev, coming up on her right side.

"Yeah?" Jess peered past her. "You should try for that, Devvie."

Thankfully, programming supplied the information promptly. "Do you mean a senior technician position?" Dev asked.

Brent nodded.

"I don't think so," she replied in a mild tone. "I don't think they'd like a bio alt applying for that. People already have discomfort. Are you?"

"Tried twice. Ain't got the brains," Brent admitted. "Bet you could do it." The difference in Brent's attitude and the older tech in the gym was striking.

"How about if I assist you to study for it?" Dev said. "I would like you to achieve that if you want to."

As much as his naturally morose expression allowed, he brightened. "Sure."

"Excellent." Dev lifted a hand in goodbye as Brent split off from them and headed for the simulators. Then she glanced up at Jess, who was frowning. "It would be nice to help Brent, don't you think?"

"He's a rock head, for a tech," Jess said. "You're wasting your time. You should go for it yourself. You'd ace it."

"Possibly." Dev followed her along the corridor toward their sun replacement rooms. "But I would rather avoid the discomfort," she said. "I have noticed there is a lot of that in the new teams who came here after the attack."

"Hm." Jess palmed her room open. "C'mon in with me."

"Of course."

They entered the rad chamber and removed their clothes. Jess went to the console and coded in a session for both of them.

When she re-entered the main room Dev was relaxing on one of the two translucent lounges and she paused to regard her before she took a seat on the opposite couch. Dev was short and compact, but visibly muscled just under her skin and that always seemed a little at odds with her calm and polite manner.

"That cut looks like it is causing you discomfort," Dev said. "Would you like me to put a bandage on it?"

"Nah." Jess lay down and let her body go slack, feeling the distinct ache of hard use and now the faint sting of the cuts she'd gotten. "Not unless it starts spurting blood," she added, as an afterthought.

Dev half sat up and peered at her.

"Just kidding."

Dev lay back down and folded her hands over her stomach.

"Have jackasses been bothering you?" Jess asked, after a moment of silence. "Giving you a hard time?"

Dev considered her response for a bit before answering. "It's just things I hear that people are saying, but not to me." She glanced at the other couch, seeing Jess's pale blue eyes looking directly back at her. "Generally when you are not present."

Jess's nostrils flared a little.

"So, thank you so much, Jess, for being so nice and thinking I should try to achieve that new grade, but I think it will just make people even more uncomfortable."

Jess sat up and swung her long legs off her couch, resting her hands on the side of it and leaning forward. "Screw them," she stated flatly. "Dev, you're as much an ops tech as any of them are. You've got full status. You've done more than most of them have and they're just jealous of you."

Surprisingly, Dev nodded. "Yes, I understand that. It has to do with status, and that's very important to natural borns."

Jess's brows lifted.

"And bio alts, too, actually," Dev admitted. "We always want more status."

"But it also makes you a target." Jess's expression shifted to pensive. "Don't I know it." She rested her elbows on her knees and laced her fingers together. The reddish gold light of the rad darkened her skin, but the burned in designs on both arms were still visible.

Dev resisted looking at her own arm, which had a handful of the designs as well. "Let's wait until we do a few more missions, Jess," she said. "Then the next time maybe I will try that. I think it's better if a few others get it first, since they told me it's been a long time since it's been offered."

"Yeah, okay." Jess sighed, and stretched out on the couch again. "It just pisses me off."

Dev got up and went to kneel down by Jess's couch, putting a hand on her arm. "Please don't be upset, Jess." She leaned forward and very gently kissed Jess on her ribcage, then put her cheek down on the spot and looked up at her face.

For a brief moment, it remained a stony mask.

Then the grim tension dissolved, and Jess's expression softened as she smiled a little, one hand reaching to stroke Dev's cheek. "You're so good to me, Devvie. Everyone else thinks I'm just a grumpy maniac, but you never do."

"You're not." Dev smiled, glad she'd done the right thing. "You're amazing, Jess."

Jess smiled back, and edged over. "C'mon it's big enough for both of us up here." She surrendered to the peace she knew was there, hovering at the edge of her own insanity, wrapped up in this mutual affection.

"Absolutely." Dev got up on the lounge and curled up against Jess, winding her arms around her in contentment, glad to let the rad lull them both to sleep.

DEV STOOD NEXT to her carrier, the sounds of ongoing construction in the cavern almost overwhelming. She resisted the urge to cover her ears and continued her walk around the pad, checking the newly installed engine pods and moving past the open hatch to run her hand over one of the joints.

Overhead the sound of rain on the recently finished roofing thundered, but the giant new forward doors were half open and she could see other carriers on slow patrol, watching it.

Clint came up onto the pad from the diagnostic station. "Hey, Dev, everything okay?"

"It seems so," Dev said. "And, also, I would like to say congratulations on your new promotion." She indicated the insignia on this collar.

Clint grinned, looking around before he leaned an elbow on the carrier. "Thanks, Dev! I was trying for this one a while. Nice they put it all through after all the last mess. Bumped my allocation up, too."

Dev grinned back. "Excellent. It's good to be successful."

Clint returned the compliment with a wink. "You should know. I heard they opened a senior track. I know you'll make it on the first go."

Dev drew breath to argue, then paused. "Thank you," she merely said. "Actually I am looking forward to taking this carrier out and getting some longer range metrics on the new engines."

He nodded and shared the contents of his readout pad. "Well, you're ready, so if you want to start checks have at it." He indicated some of the contents. "I'm interested to know if this torque upswing works out."

Dev glanced up as she spotted Doug heading for his carrier parked on the next pad. She lifted a hand as he called a greeting, almost completely unheard in the overriding noise.

"You taking the kids with you?" Clint asked. "I have their rig on standby."

"Yes, they will accompany us." Dev patted the engine pod and turned. "Let me get things ready to fly." She walked up the ramp and passed the skin where her name and Jess's were stenciled and paused. "Oh, Clint?"

He hurried over. "What's up?"

Dev glanced around. "Please do me a favor?"

"Anything."

"If someone has some idea to change this to that Rocket thing, please don't let them. I'd rather it be my designation." She pointed at the skin.

Clint regarded the block letters. "Don't think they mean that as an insult, Dev. I heard one of the other techs talking more like it's," he paused, "...kind of a your one of us sort of thing."

She considered that. "I don't mind them calling me that. It's just this is my designation. It's who I am, and I would like that accurate on my...um...our vehicle."

"No problem, Dev. I get it," he said. "I got your back."

"Thank you." Dev waved a little and went inside, bypassing the quiet and dark weapons station and slid into her pilot's seat up in the nose. The wraparound cockpit showed new and freshly installed modules everywhere and she paused a moment to look at them.

She folded her hands over her stomach and considered a somewhat new sensation as given programming was overlaid with learned experience gained as she had installed most of the new components, and in some cases, gotten a suggestion or two in on their design.

She tried to compare the two different sets of knowledge, but it was hard, as they'd now integrated to a reasonable degree and she had to remind herself what she'd been given and what she knew of her own self.

With a soft grunt, she slid forward a little and started bringing up the carrier's systems. She reached out and picked up the comms and settled it in place, hooking it into the carrier pilot suit she was wearing.

The big machine came alive around her, boards lighting and the talkback whispers starting in her ear cups as she prepared to bring the engines online.

She glanced to her left, out the big window, and spotted Jess entering the cavern, walking alongside April.

The former nomad was taller than Dev, but Jess towered over her, one of the tallest female natural borns Dev had yet met. Both women had on their half armored suits, weapons seated at hard points. They casually crossed the floor in conversation with each other.

Dev could see others watching them. Some of the cavern techs in brief interest, some of the bio alt techs in serious consideration.

That was complicated. The bio alts in general in the Citadel tended to regard Jess positively for a number of reasons, not the least because of how Jess treated Dev. They didn't tend to have the wary fear of her that some of the natural borns did.

But Jess seemed to be in a reasonably good mood today, even laughing at something April said as the other agent angled off toward her carrier, leaving Jess to come onto her own. She looked up as she did, meeting Dev's eyes through the plas.

Dev smiled and waved, and her smiled broadened as Jess waved back, giving her a little salute as she walked along the grated floor on her way to the carrier entrance.

In preparation, Dev lit up the weapons console, bringing all the boards online as she heard Jess's steps on the ramp. The carrier rocked just slightly on it's skids as Jess entered. "Hello."

"Hey, Dev." Jess settled her long blaster into its clips and dropped into her chair. "We ready to go?"

"Just about." Dev watched the reflective panel over her head, and in a moment Jess's pale eyes met hers in it. They both smiled in reflex at each other. "I'm glad we can go and do some good work."

"I was bored, too," Jess said. She pulled her restraints around her and secured them then triggered the hatch closure. "Let's get flying, NM-Dev."

Dev triggered her own restraints and settled herself as her seat rocked and shifted forward. "BR270006, comm check," she said. "Standby for systems regen."

"BR270006, clear comms," the voice from flight ops answered. "Standing by."

Jess heard the soft whine of the engines spooling and whistled softly under her breath as she commissioned her systems.

She felt the faint twitch as the power systems exchanged, and the pop and thunk as Dev released the feeds. Jess was aware of a distinct sense of relief, glad indeed they were headed out. She cracked her knuckles and checked that her restraints were all the way retracted. Very glad.

Chapter Two

DEV SET COURSE and trimmed the engines before she looked back over her shoulder. Jess was sprawled in her chair, her boards quiesced at least for the first part of the short flight home. "One hour flight time," she said. "The other carrier is behind us, slightly to the left."

Jess nodded. "This is going to be interesting since I didn't warn them I was coming, or that I was bringing guests."

"Is that going to cause discomfort?"

"Oh yes."

Dev spent a few more minutes getting the carrier all sorted before she turned in her chair to face Jess. "Is that a good or bad thing?" she asked. "It is difficult for me to determine what we're seeking to achieve in this effort."

Jess's expression was wry. "Ah, Dev." She sighed. "Where do I start? Remember I told you the last time we went to the Bay it was different?"

"With the scans and everything. Yes," Dev answered. "But since it was only the second or third place I'd been it was hard for me to tell the difference. But it seemed more like...more like a base than the Quebec place or the other places we went."

"It is more like it." Jess wriggled into a more comfortable position. "Back in the day, after everything went to crap, it took a little time for it all to fall apart," she said. "The governments fell apart last because they had the most to lose."

Dev folded her hands and just listened, programmed history surfacing.

"Last thing that went to pieces, was the armed forces." Jess went on. "And parts of those forces were...well, let's say they'd been working for a while to get the basic human being and goose them a little."

Dev's brows creased a little.

"Not too different from you, really," Jess said. "Some things don't change, I guess. But there were forces that were being genetically tweaked. Bigger. Stronger. Hardier." She picked up a cup from her console and drank from it. "Remember I told you my mother paid some quack to mess with her eggs? That was what was left of all that after all this time."

"Oh," Dev said. "I didn't know that."

"They leave that out of most histories," Jess said. "Anyway, back in that day there were a couple of those guys who decided, after they weren't getting paid anymore, to find a place and set up shop for themselves, and take all their buddies with them."

"I see."

"Their names were David and Brian Drake." Jess smiled. "They had two sisters named Sally and Jess."

"Oh!" Dev sat up a little. "Like your name?"

"It's a family name," Jess said. "All of them had been in that special program." Jess's blue eyes twinkled a little. "So they took the last of the transports they could steal, and they found Drake's Bay, just a bunch of caves in a mountainside on the edge of the sea."

"So all of them were soldiers?"

"All of them were," Jess confirmed. "And they were mostly mean and aggressive sons of bitches, and didn't get along either with each other or the people left in the area, who they beat up and pretty much enslaved."

"Oh," Dev said. "That doesn't sound good."

"Wasn't," Jess said. "That's why that's never told in the history books. Anyway when the regional governments finally bribed and scraped enough together to get things going again that's who they went to."

Dev frowned again. "Went to for what?"

"Muscle. They cut a deal with them. They hired them as mercenaries," Jess said in a cheerful tone. "Promised them food and support if they'd join what was going to become Interforce."

"Oh."

Jess took another sip. "But after that they realized there was something wrong with them."

"Something wrong?"

"All the fiddling had made a lot of them psychos, and that bred," Jess said. "Not only in the Bay, but other places. You know what a sociopath is, Dev?"

"Yes," Dev said. "I have programming on that, and other psychological anomalies but..."

"You've got real life experience with one, too." Jess tapped her chest.

Dev blinked and her eyes widened a little.

"One of the things they had to screw around with was taking away all the emotional stuff. Guilt, compassion, all that crap. Messes up your ability to kill things at random and on command," Jess said. "So I'm a highly functioning sociopath. No soul searching. No wringing of hands. Give me a mission and I execute it. No mental stress about blowing people up."

Dev's jaw actually dropped. "They did that on purpose? Really?"

Jess smiled, just a little. "I minded more about killing a seal than my instructor, remember?"

"I remember. But..."

"Seal was an innocent bystander. Jackass wasn't." Jess tapped her head. "All in here, nothing in here." She tapped her chest again over her heart. "No feeling."

"Wow," Dev said, after a moment's thought.

"Kind of kicks your ass when you find out," Jess agreed quietly. "But in this business, it makes it a lot easier, Dev. We get our heads blown off, but don't have much post traumatic stress anymore." Her eyes had a humorous glint in them. "That's why they take us at five or six. They get to us, and structure us, and we have time to intellectually figure out it's a pretty good life, even though it might be a short one at the end of it. Only one in a hundred refuses to go into service from school."

Dev remembered her human interface classes, and she could almost hear Doctor Dan's calm, gentle voice explaining things she now understood he'd known from a personal perspective in a unique way.

"It takes a lot to screw us up here." Jess pointed at her head. "Something like what happened to me before we met. Before, that would have nixed whoever it happened to. For me it just sent me to psych for a while. Now I don't even think about it."

Dev blinked again.

"Of course, you did help with that." Jess smiled at Dev's nonplussed expression. "Crazy, huh?" She swirled the beverage in her cup and drained it. "So anyway, over the years it meant more Interforce came from the Bay than pretty much anywhere on the east coast, and since they took a lot of us, the rest bred cleaner and it's gotten less crazy I hear." She leaned back. "But Drakes...all of them had it. All of them bred it. We end up with more of it than most and most of us turn out assholes because of it."

Dev couldn't think of anything to say to that, so she changed the subject slightly. "Did Doctor Dan know all this?"

"I'm sure my dad told him, especially if he took him to the Bay, and he did," Jess replied. "He's no dummy and neither was my pop, and it's not a secret inside the family, at least not those of us who went."

"Wow," Dev repeated again.

"My dad was the first of us for a while who lived long enough to retire and come into shares at the Bay," Jess said. "When you do that, go inactive, you're supposed to be old enough to leave the crazy behind, but people still looked crosswise at him. I realize it now, thinking back."

Dev watched her face, seeing nothing more than reflection there. "Will it eventually not be like that?" she finally asked. "If it goes along enough?"

Jess remained silent for a few minutes. "They tell us there've been fewer of us over the years," she said. "But I don't know. Someone once told me it's a black and white, off or on thing. What they flipped." Her eyes were a little unfocused. "Maybe the doc would know."

"Doctor Dan knows a lot," Dev said. "Maybe we can ask him sometime."

"Maybe," Jess said. "But until then, just keep all that under your hat."

Dev just looked at her.

Jess had to laugh. "Don't tell anyone."

Dev smiled then. "Jess?" she asked, after a few more minutes of silence. "Is that why they don't like bio alts there? Because of what happened to them before?"

"Nah, I don't..." Jess paused and her eyes shifted to the floor. "I never thought about that," she admitted, with a frown. "Just was a thing you knew there. Or maybe they had to fight so hard to keep the place going...I don't know."

Dev sensed the discomfort and she turned, settling back in her seat and running a set of checks with automatic motions. The weather had slacked off a little, and she could see the deep greens of the sea rolling gently against the cliffs that bordered its edge, ruffled with only slight caps of white.

The new sensors were reporting and she checked the scopes, seeing the depth soundings repeating back to her showing the sea life underneath the surface. She tuned them, knowing a moment of self pride in the knowledge that the programming for them had come from her.

Clint had gotten the credit for it. She'd just suggested it, then turned over the code module from her own scanner to him and he'd taken it to the modders from there. Excellent, really. Now all the carriers had it.

She heard Jess release her restraints and move around behind her. "They put in a new dispenser, Jess. I brought some tea for it."

"I see." Jess's voice had a smile in it. "Want some? We might as well get as much pleasure out of this as we can before we get to the homestead."

"Yes, please." Dev checked the nav. "Forty-five minutes."

"At ten minutes out, send a call," Jess said. She put cups in the dispenser, poking around in the new compartments. "You brought honey, you little bunny."

Dev just smiled. "BR270006 to BR34066, sideband, sendit," she said into her mic, and watched the sideband connection come up between her carrier and Doug's.

"Check," his voice echoed softly into her ear. "You there, Rocket?"

"Yes. Please keep this pinned up. We will make contact in thirty-five local minutes."

"Gotcha," Doug responded. "So, hey, Chester's so torked they didn't get to go with us like last time. I'm super glad April asked."

Dev had no idea how to respond to that. "Please stand by," she compromised, shaking her head a little, then looked up as Jess took a seat on the low jump bench next to her position and offered her a cup.

They sipped their tea in silence, Jess's hand resting casually on Dev's knee, her legs extended along the floor of the carrier in what had to be cramped discomfort, content to simply sit there instead of her comfortable padded position in the back.

Dev had noticed Jess seemed to like to do that. She pondered having something done to her raw jumpseat to make it more comfortable, then put her cup in the holder and picked up comms as it crackled into her ear. "We're being hailed."

Jess chuckled soundlessly. "They're on their toes this morning. Send our ident." She remained where she was, leaning back against the console as Dev shifted channels and sent the transmit.

"Drake's Bay control, this is Interforce flight BR270006 inbound, with escort," Dev said into her mic. "Senior agent Jesslyn Drake in command," she added, seeing the gentle twinkle in her partner's eyes.

There was a long moment of silence. "Keep on course, aim for the landing bays," Jess instructed. "They don't open up for us land it right on top of the damn roof."

Dev hoped sincerely they wouldn't have to do that, but she trimmed the course and changed their angle slightly, still twenty minutes out from the homestead. She drew in breath to repeat her request then paused when she heard the crackle of comms opening.

"Interforce flight BR270006 and escort, please use landing bay six, pads one and two." The voice came back, without any negative inflection she could detect. "Control sends greetings, and welcome."

Dev looked quickly at Jess, whose eyebrows were almost up into her hairline. "Thank you, Drake's Bay. We copy and will comply." Dev closed comms. "That sounded relatively optimal."

"It did," Jess said, in a surprised tone. "Huh."

"You weren't expecting that," Dev said, as she relayed the landing instructions to April and Doug. "Is it not correct?"

Jess got to her feet and went back to her station, put her cup in it's holder and dropped into her chair, pulling her restraints as she activated her screens. "Really good question, Dev." She switched her inputs to receive and started to analyze the results. "Really good."

DEV SLOWED HER forward speed and dropped her altitude as she made her approach to Drake's Bay homestead. It was situated in a half circle of cliff walls around a roughly round bay, the outer edge dropping down into the water via a series of descending spires.

The stone itself was layers of grays and blues and greens, and to Dev's eyes, the place had an eerie and majestic beauty, combined with the deep blue, green and gray of the protected bay before it. Fishing vessels were crossing toward the sea level caverns below.

Overhead, above them, a flyer was drifting lazily, in a circling pattern.

One side of the circle had a series of openings and she headed for one of them, it's metal bay doors standing open to receive them.

As the carriers flew slowly overhead, a sea bell rang beneath them, audible in the sensors she had open, and Dev glanced quickly in the reflector, watching Jess's face for a reaction, reassured when it was only a raised eyebrow.

After a moment Jess reached up and touched a control, and her station went dark, spooling the power back to Dev's batteries. Then she returned her hands to their folded position on her stomach and twiddled her thumbs in the slightest of nervous twitches.

Dev went back to her piloting, sliding the carrier a bit sideways to straighten her approach, cutting the mains as they cleared the cavern entrance and using her residual momentum to land on the pad on the right side of it.

Not even a touch of the landing jets. She felt the skids settle to the pad and secured the engines, opening the power link hatch as a tech outside approached them.

Jess unfastened her restraints and stood up. "Nice landing, Dev. April in?"

Dev peered to her right. "Yes, they're fine." Dev secured the carrier's systems. "This seems nominal."

Jess fastened her suit up. "Yeah. They keep things pretty square here." She pulled out her backpack and Dev's, already loaded with changes of clothes and their kits. "Open the door."

Dev got up, triggered the hatch as she collected her scanner, and walked back to get her pack from Jess. She closed the fastenings on her sharkskin jacket and settled the pack over it, waiting for Jess to do the same.

The jacket was non reg sharkskin, and lined, a set of her tech insignia fastened to the well fitted collar. It had a silvery green and blue sheen to it that reflected its different colors depending on the light.

Dev liked it. It was both less bulky and warmer than the reg issue and fit her well, and Jess repeatedly told her she looked good in it. All excellent.

"Okay." Jess settled her pack. "Let's go, Devvie. See what insanity we have in store for us today." She paused, regarding the weapons rack, then regretfully palmed it closed before she led the way down the ramp to the pad.

The tech who had connected them was securing the line and he looked up as they approached, giving Jess a respectful nod. "Drake," he said, as he stepped out of their way. "Welcome."

Jess paused. "Hello, Reggie. This is my partner, Dev." She indicated her companion. "Dev, this is Reggie. He's a cousin of mine."

"Hello," Dev responded. "It's nice to meet you."

The bay tech regarded her seriously. He was shorter than Jess, and had curly dark brown hair and hazel eyes. He didn't resemble Jess even in the slightest. "You're a bio alt?" He asked, after a pause. "Really?"

"Yes, really." Dev wasn't sure what to make of the response. "Biological Alternative, set 0202-164812, instance NM-Dev-1," she said. "But most people call me Dev."

Jess waited with unusual patience as she watched her cousin process this. He wasn't one of her brighter relations, but on the flip side of that, he didn't have that edge some of her closer ones did.

Ten years her junior, he also wasn't likely to be a smart ass and get his head taken off by her to start the visit off on completely the wrong foot.

Reggie extended a hand. "Welcome, tech Dev."

Extremely unexpected and somewhat excellent. Dev took his hand and returned the grip. "Thank you very much." She released him and he went back to his work. She turned and looked at Jess. "That was interesting."

"That was interesting." Jess repeated, shaking her head. "Might have been the nicest thing to happen to us all day," she added with a sigh. "Let's hope it wasn't."

"JIMMY'S OVER AT the processing plant," Jess's younger brother, Jake, said. He had met them as they crossed from the landing chamber into the main section of the homestead. "We didn't know you were coming over. Domestic ops are finding you some space."

Dev took advantage of Jess's conversation with her brother to look around, appreciating again the great central staircase of Drake's Bay. They were at ground level of the roughly round interior space so large it could hold most of the Citadel inside it.

There were hallways leading off in three directions, and a ramp-like iron staircase circling up along the wall with landings on levels that again branched off in all directions all the way up to the top level, just under the thick transparent panels that allowed the outside light in.

Beautiful, in a rough and stark kind of way.

Underneath her feet, she felt the rumble of hydro tunnels, and unlike the last time she'd been at the Bay, everyone was busy going about their business, at least pretending to ignore the visitors in their midst.

They weren't really, she knew. She was standing just behind Jess, and just ahead of April and Doug, and she could plainly see all the people furtively watching the four black and green clad bodies in the middle of the floor.

It was hard to tell what the feeling was behind the looks though. Dev folded her arms over her chest and let her gaze slowly range over the interior of the space, lit by the dull gray from outside, but also from fixtures in the walls all the way up in a mixture of silver and gold illumination.

She could smell a lot of things around them. Some food in preparation, oil and mech somewhere nearby, and to her immediate right, from a half open door obscuring a hallway, the salt washed dampness that came from the sea.

A man appeared from one of the first level halls and trotted down the steps. Like most of the rest of the people in the space, he was dressed in overalls and boots, with a high necked sweater in an indeterminate color.

Jess had her hands in her jacket pockets, and she removed them as the figure came down to their level and arrived where the small group was standing. "Hello, Brion."

"Jess." The man gave her a brief nod. "Welcome home," he added. "We've got a section in four west you can have, if you don't mind. No space for all your team in the family quarters." His face was studiedly non-emotional as he looked up at her.

Jess smiled without any humor. "That's fine," she said. "Hasn't been home for me since I was five." She half turned and inclined her head a little. "I'll get my team settled and then do a recco. Don't need any guidance."

Brion nodded in response. "Door's keyed." He glanced at the rest of the group. "Welcome."

April stood in a relaxed pose, her hands behind her back. She merely nodded in response, as did Doug.

"Thank you," Dev said.

"Go on back to whatever you were doing, Jake," Jess said. "We're fine."

Jake looked uncomfortable. "Okay," he said. "When Jimmy gets back, maybe we can meet up. I think he had some stuff he wanted to talk to you about."

Jess chuckled dryly. "I bet he does." She edged around him and headed for the steps. "Tell everyone to stay the hell out of my way."

"Sure." Jake sighed, as the rest of the group skirted him and followed her.

FOURTH LEVEL WAS guest quarters. Jess got to that level and went counter clockwise to the first hall and proceeded down it. Could have been worse, could have been better. She passed under the embedded lights in walls shaped from the raw stone into smooth precision.

Doug broke the silence after a moment. "This place is amazing. Not even the Juneau Loft is like this."

"Can't take any credit for it, but thanks." Jess glanced over her shoulder. "It was built by a bunch of people who really knew what to do with plasma cutters."

April chuckled dryly. "My tribe was in shelter here when I sat the battery." She commented. "They took me that day. Figured otherwise my people'd pull out and me with them."

"Here, really?" Jess headed toward the set of doors that had light blue lamps lit outside them.

"Here, really," April said. "Not sure who was happier about it. I'd just gotten the shit kicked out of me by the mater. I remember that first night sleeping warm and dry and fed." Her eyes went a little unfocused. "Pretty sweet."

Jess paused and they all paused with her. She indicated the doors, going to each one of the four and palming it open. "Put your hands on it. It'll rekey," she said. "Don't trust anything inside," she added. "Do a class one scan soon as you get settled."

Dev put her hand on the panel of the accommodation next to the one Jess ended up in front of, watching as it turned purple, then blue again as she felt that deep itch in the chip under her skin. A moment later, the door opened and she proceeded inside.

The walls inside, as outside, were squared and smoothed. There was a small sanitary unit in a recessed area, a space to hold things carved into the stone and, to her surprise and mild delight, a hammock swung on the other side of the door instead of a bed.

Very plain and very utilitarian. Dev nodded in approval as she removed her pack and set it on the rock shelf, divesting herself of her jacket before she removed her scanner and tuned it, glancing around as it started up.

There was inset lighting in the roof and a comms panel was set in the wall near the sanitary unit.

It wasn't different, really, than the transient quarters she'd spent the night before leaving the crèche in, and she spared a smile for that now distant time, and the hours she'd spent unable to sleep, wondering what her new contract would be like.

Her scanner beeped gently, and she went back to it, hitting the key to let it start its work as she turned slowly in a circle.

It picked up the four of them at once, already keyed, already marked as friendly. She caught the blip that was Doug doing the same thing she was as their scanners saw each other and then went past.

The level they were on didn't have much to tell. A lot of

voids in the rock that were shaped like the chamber she was standing in, then onward past that to other levels and larger returns.

Dev's brows lifted as the scanner passed over large energy returns that refused to resolve and then security rings of what she recognized as the kind she was used to in the Citadel, protecting spaces deep inside.

Then a brief blast of power as a scan came back at her, and she felt the tickle against her skin before it disappeared.

Interesting. Dev put the scanner down on the flat surface and then sorted out her things, leaving most of them in the pack but removing the small sanitary kit she usually took in the carrier with her. She went to the unit and inspected it, a little surprised to find a square shower area virtually identical to the one in her Citadel quarters.

She even found hollows in the stone with fabric in them. She picked up a piece of the fabric and sniffed it, the scent matched the sea foam spiciness she knew from there as well.

Well, Jess said a lot of people at Interforce had come from here. Perhaps they'd brought these things with them.

She heard a faint knock at the door and returned to her pack. She picked up her scanner and jacket and moved toward the entrance, pausing a moment to make sure the person outside her quarters was Jess before she pushed the unlock.

It seemed this place was somewhat incorrect. She poked her head outside the door to find Jess and April there, packs still on their backs. "Hello."

"See anything?" Jess asked.

"Many things," Dev replied. She reversed the scanner and handed it over. "I sorted them by relative correctness."

Jess inspected the scanner and April edged around to look at it, while the other door opened and Doug emerged, rubbing his head. "Did they do this just to piss you off, Jess? Smacked my noggin twice already."

Jess glanced at him with a smile. "Something like that," she said. "Most of the time visitors were shorter than we are. The ceilings are higher where the family sleeps and on the lower levels."

"So at least half of us are safe here," April remarked. "I noticed in the entrance there you have a lot of tall people around." She looked at Dev. "Right?"

Dev made a little face. "Pretty much everyone's taller than me. I didn't actually notice that."

"Mmm." Jess handed back the scanner. "Let's go take a walk." She pushed the door open to Dev's space. "I'm going to drop my stuff in here. That okay, Devvie?"

"Of course." Dev got out of her way and reset the scanner, restricting it to near in readings, mostly standard returns moving around but not approaching them. After a moment, she retrieved the stored record that was her partner and applied it as a filter.

Doug peered over her shoulder. "Whatcha doing?"

"Figuring out which persons share bio with Jess," Dev said. "It's interesting."

April emerged from her assigned space and a moment later Jess joined them. "We'll start at the top," Jess said. "Might as well climb those long ass stairs to start with." She led the way back toward the landing.

"No elevators?" Doug asked.

"Only to move freight. Everyone else is expected to use the steps." Jess seemed mildly amused. "Old customs." She started the climb upwards. "Family quarters were on the second level though. The higher you ended up the lowlier you were considered."

April chuckled.

Dev admired the iron railing on the steps they were climbing, sturdy, but decorative in whorls and shapes that gave her something to look at while they were walking. The exercise itself didn't bother her and it was interesting as they got higher and higher, closer to the roof.

"How long did it take them to build all this?" April asked, after a moment or two of silence. "Generations must have."

"A lot. They started off below and built up." Jess reached the top landing and looked up at the hazy view of clouds overhead through plexi so thick it was taller than she was. "Story was, someone back in the day said they did this so when the rain finally stopped and the sun came out again, we'd see it."

They all looked up at the sky light in pensive silence. "Can't even imagine what that would be like," April finally said. "The sun I mean."

"I think I saw a vid once," Doug said. "Or maybe that was a bonfire. I don't remember."

Dev, being the only one present who had actually seen the sun, remained quiet.

"Anyway," Jess said, indicating the level. "This is actually storage. They don't hate anyone enough to make them live up here. The big lifts are along the west backbone." She led them over to a large, central opening and looked inside.

Doug stared at the huge space with it's arched ceiling. Inside were barrels and crates and bags of pretty much everything, all stacked in areas, all marked. In the distance, two men were moving a floating pallet along, with boxes on it. "Wow."

"Yeah," Jess said. "I used to play up here." She turned and started back down. "Then they finally roped the stairs off so my little punk self couldn't get to it."

"Jess, I can't imagine —" Dev started.

"Me as a little punk?" Jess seemed amused. "You've seen pictures, Devvie." She paused on the next level. "Want to see the armory?"

April perked up. "For sure. Got any old timey stuff there?"

"Oh yeah." Jess started down another hall. "Think they even have some cavalry sabers."

"No!"

"Yeah."

IT WAS DARK by the time the tour was over, and Dev had swapped out her scanner memory twice to capture all of it. They'd used the cover of Jess's apparently random showing off of her birth home to poke and pry and inspect, ending up in the food hall, almost full at that hour.

There were no food dispensers, Dev noticed as they claimed a back table. Just a big island in the center of the hall with basins of edibles in them, attended by workers who cycled back and forth into an inner chamber, taking out empty basins and bringing them back full.

It smelled good. She slung the scanner around to her back and followed Jess to the island, aware of her stomach rumbling. Jess handed her a plate and she took it, aware suddenly of the workers all watching her.

It went quiet, a little.

Jess seemed to realize it and paused, resting her wrist on Dev's shoulder as she let her eyes travel from worker to worker in a grim, silent threat. They dropped their gaze and started back into motion, grabbing some empty pans from the other side of the island.

"Try this." Jess went on as though nothing had happened. She reached over and scooped up a thick, stewy substance and deposited it on Dev's plate. "Clam stew. One of the only places on the seaboard you'll find it."

"Thank you," Dev said. Jess pointed out this and that, and Dev ended up with a full plate as they made their way back to the table.

"If you could sell that look," April said, as she put her plate down and sat. "You'd be able to buy Interforce, y'know."

Jess chuckled humorlessly.

"What's their problem?" Doug asked, lowering his voice. "They've got a problem with Rocket?" He glanced at his fellow tech in some puzzlement.

"Yes," Dev answered before Jess could. "Doctor Dan explained to me that this location doesn't approve of bio alts." She paused to ingest a mouthful of the stew, chewing it curiously and swallowing. "Unfortunately there's nothing I can do about that since I can't stop being one."

"Neither can they, so they better get over it," Jess added, raising her voice a bit so it would carry. "Unless they want to go scrape rocks."

When she looked back up and across the table at the crowd, no one looked back. Jess grunted in satisfaction and went back to her plate, hoping that would be the end of it.

THERE WAS A small area just past their assigned quarters where the hallway opened up and provided a space to gather in. There were some chairs around a heater, with a utilitarian drink dispenser on one side and a water tap.

Dev and Doug were seated side by side, comparing notes. Jess was reviewing the scans with April, and they all had hot cups of tea by them as they worked along in relative silence. The lamps in the walls gave them decent light, and far off they could hear the faintest rumble of thunder.

The rasp of bootsteps made them all look up, and both Jess and April got up and faced the opening. After a moment though, Jess relaxed. "Hello, Jimmy."

James Drake entered and pushed back a hood of waxed fabric from his head covered in rain. "Jess," he said, and gave the rest of them a brief nod. "Just got back. Sorry about the quarters." He looked around. "If you'd have given us a few days notice—"

"Shut up, Jimmy," Jess said, in a mild voice. "There are a half dozen rooms free down on two. Someone decided to be petty enough to irritate me but not enough to make me snap their neck." She went back to regarding the notes from the scanners. "Next subject?"

Jimmy visibly reddened.

"Get everyone in the business office tomorrow after first chow." Jess looked up at him again. "I've got questions, since I've got some time and I'm here."

"Jess, look —"

"Look nothing." She cut him off. "Until Legal sorts this, it's my gig. I know someone's running scams so get everyone in there, let's get it on the table."

"Jess."

"Yes?" She folded her hands and stared at him.

Her brother sighed. "I came over here to ask you to come talk to us," he said. "Just family."

She studied him in silence for a long moment, then shrugged. "Sure." She turned to regard her little group, all of whom had the same more or less identical noncommittal look on their faces that told volumes about what they thought about the idea.

Jess actually found it sort of charming and she smiled a little at them. "Keep an eye on things," she said. "Call me if you need me." She touched the comms clipped to her jacket and then she turned back and gestured at Jimmy. "Lead on."

He waited until they were on the stairs before looking at her. "You could have let us know you were coming."

"I could have," Jess said. "But I'm under ops and it was a better idea not to." She let her eyes scan the hall as they descended. "So what was up at the processors?"

He stared at her for a long moment. "Not much. They were just asking if we could up our output. Two of the uprange homesteads died out."

"Just left?"

"Something like that. They stopped sending product and when we went to go find out why the places were empty, they weren't there." They reached the second level landings and Jimmy turned, making her stop walking. "The whole rooms thing wasn't on purpose, Jess."

She gave him a sardonic look.

"If it was just you, wouldn't have been a problem," he said. "Don't blame Brion. He did the best he could. No one wanted strangers in the family area."

"No one wanted a bio alt there," Jess countered. "Even one with Interforce creds."

Jimmy looked away and half shrugged. "You said it, I didn't."

"Jimmy, it's fine." Jess took a step toward him, forcing him forward. "I'm a lot happier bunking with them where we are. As I told Brion, this isn't my home. Move. I've got dockets to review."

"You're really going to go through with this? You're going to the conclave?" Jimmy didn't move. "Really Jess? It's not your home, but you're going to screw us all over whose home it is?"

Jess shoved him hard, sending him flying against the wall. She walked across the landing after him and grabbed him as he bounced back. "Listen, moron." She held him against the rock surface. "Get it through your thick skull that I'm just following the damned law. I have no choice. Until Interforce Legal gets it's head out of it's ass and figures out how to get me out of this, I'm in it. You want to blame someone? Blame Dad."

"You can just turn it over, Jess." He squirmed against her hold.

"I can't." Jess thumped her forehead against his. "I'm not civ, you idiot."

He went still. "What?"

"I. Am. Not. Civ," Jess repeated. "I'm active duty Interforce. I won't have access to my civ profile until I retire." She thumped him in the head again. "It was a fluke, Jimmy. No one planned this."

"Ow. Stop it," he muttered. "Shit. Are you kidding me? The legal comp here said...you really can't do anything?"

Jess sighed, and shoved him down the tunnel that led to what she'd once called home.

"CAN YOU SEE her?" April perched on the arm of the chair Dev was sitting in.

Dev watched the wireframe. "Yes, she's in the second level area we identified. It seems relatively nominal," she added, evaluating the speed of Jess's motion.

"Mmm." April got up. "I remember where the chow hall was. I'm going to see if I can get a fishroll out of them. C'mon, Doug." She glanced at Dev. "You want to stay here?"

Dev nodded. "Jess is expecting me to remain in this location. Please be careful. There are many areas we couldn't fully scan here."

"Right." April motioned to Doug. "Bring your rig." She waited for him to gather his scanner up before she led the way up the passage toward the stairs.

"I'll bring you back a snack, Rocket," Doug called over his shoulder. "Hang tight."

Dev watched them go. "Hang tight to what?" she murmured under her breath, going back to her scanner and its readouts. She was relaying through the carrier so she had that system's far greater range and storage, but even that couldn't get through some of the security. "Very interesting."

She adjusted a setting and reviewed the results, flipping back and forth to the wireframe to keep an eye on Jess. She seemed to have stopped in one area now, and the wireframes in the space seemed to also be stopped and seated.

"Hm." She shifted the sensors, and regarded Jess's outline. Her skin seemed cool and she appeared quiescent, so Dev decided all seemed well and she went back to her bio scan, tracking April and Doug as they climbed up to where the food place was.

A soft scuffing made her look up, and she retargeted the scanner in close and found a wiremap moving toward her. It wasn't doing anything to hide its presence, and she detected no energy based weapons on it, so she closed the scanner and waited.

It didn't occur to her to call Jess.

Yet.

JIMMY LEFT JESS in the family room and went to get the others. She walked over to the structure that had once been a fireplace, and still had a mantel and heating element inside it. She looked up at the wall it was set into.

The memory wall, they called it. All the generations of her family who had died were listed on it. On one side those in the cause, on the other those outside it. Hand hammered metal, the Interforce dead including their rank and accomplishments.

Last of all on that side, her father's. She stood quietly, studying it.

"Hey there, Jessie."

Jess turned her head. "Hey, Uncle Max. Didn't know you were in port."

He chuckled and ambled over to her. He was a tall man with a limp and snow white hair, a full beard and moustache to go with it. "Came in yesterday. Hella catch. Needed an offload."

"Nice."

"So." Max hitched up one strap of the waxed overalls he was wearing. "Justin cocked us up some bad, hah? Make you the Drake? What the hell?"

"I don't think he did that on purpose." Jess demurred.

"Fishballs. Of course he did." Max shook his head. "Too smart for his own damn good, always said that. Wasted his ass all those years in service. But now what?"

"Legals trying to sort it out." Jess knew there wasn't much point in arguing with Max. Her father's eldest brother, with a full share of Drake assholery and the independence that came with being a ship captain to go with it. "Meantime I've got to do the dance."

Max laughed. "Bet they're all pissing." He poked her. "What's I hear you brought a jelly bag here? Didja? Piss 'em off all the more?"

Max had been at sea during their last very brief visit, Jess recalled. "My tech partner." She said, succinctly. "So yes."

"Say what?" Max stared wide eyed at her. "Those people over the hill out of their minds? You out of yours?" He put his gnarled hands on his hips. "The hell?"

Jess heard footsteps approaching. "It's a longer story than we've got time for right now, unk. I'll introduce you later. It's not what you think."

The door opened and the rest of her family entered, most looking like they'd been sprayed with seagull splat from the expressions on their faces.

Jess went over to one of the chairs and sat down. "Siddown," she told them all. "Let's get this over with."

THE FIGURE THAT emerged into the open space was dressed in overalls and a thick woven sweater in blues and greens. His face was covered in a black and white haired beard and gray liberally laced his dark, straight hair.

He paused and regarded her. "You the thing?"

Dev cleared her throat gently. "If by that you mean, am I Jess Drake's tech, who is a biological alternative, the answer is yes. My name is Dev." She looked to one side. "We have some fresh seaweed tea here, would you like some?"

"No." The man sat down in a chair across from her. "I got some questions."

Possibly excellent, possibly not. "I will try to answer them if I can," Dev responded politely.

"If you can I'll eat my boots," the man said. "What's the rating of a thirty centimeter intake socket?"

Completely unexpected question. Dev blinked at him.

"Twenty seven and six fifteenths, but the thrust is dependent on the velocity of throughput. And it can be torqued."

"Resistance per meter of twenty gauge?"

"Fourteen point seven per meter, with standard attenuation," Dev supplied.

He studied her. "What's the exchange rate of battery to online systems?"

"Eighty two percent for ours," Dev said. "I cannot say for sure for yours here, but scans indicate they are either eighty percent, or seventy five point four." She was finding this very unusual inquisition agreeable, based on her expectations. "Though I think I did see one at suboptimal sixty percent near the entrance to this facility."

"I just replaced it." The man regarded her. "You actually know some of this shit." His tone was surprised.

"I actually do," Dev agreed. "I know that biological alternatives are not liked here, and it's difficult. I'm sorry about that," she added. "Would you like to continue? I have some time until Jess returns from her meeting." She smiled a little. "It's enjoyable."

He took a breath then they both looked up as the lighting changed color, from a standard yellow white to red. "Not now." He got up swiftly, as there was a deep bonging sound overhead.

Dev also got up. "Is there something wrong?"

A deep voice emerged from the overhead speakers. "Attention, attention, defence groups six and eight, report to the perimeter west gates. Incoming fire in progress."

Dev closed up her scanner and swung it to her back, moving toward the small space assigned to her. "Excuse me." She put her palm on the lock and the door opened. She ducked inside and picked up her pack and Jess's.

"Where do you think you're going?" the man asked, watching her. "Probably just some scavengers."

Dev headed down the passage before he could get in her way. "Landing bay, actually. Chances are Jess will want to observe whatever that is." She touched her comms. "Ack ack."

"Bay six," Jess's deep voice came back at once. "Tac."

"Ack, en route." Dev broke into a run, turning and heading up the stairs, dodging bodies moving in a hurry the other direction. She realized at the entrance to the landing bay that the man had kept up with her and was at her heels.

No real time to analyze that. She triggered the remote unlock for the carrier and it responded as she raced across the stone floor.

There was noise all around and the slow bonging sound was pervasive. Dev tossed both their packs in the open hatch then went to the power intake and manually disconnected it, throwing it clear as she doubled back and bolted up the ramp.

The man was inside. "You really can't be in here," Dev told him. She slipped past and went to her seat and started the boards. "Jess will be onboard in a moment."

"S'okay." He was perched on the back shelf. "She wont mind if I take a ride," he said confidently. "We're cousins."

"I see." Dev dismissed him as she heard the distinctive sound of Jess's running bootsteps coming across the stone floor, the carrier coming into status around her as the boards powered up and she brought the engines online and balanced the leads.

She got her comms helm in place and strapped in, testing the landing jets as Jess entered and closed the hatch. "Jess, there is an intruder inside," she said. "A relative of yours apparently."

"Chris what the hell are you doing here?" Jess yelled, as she got into her position.

"Enjoying the show," he responded. "Relax, Jessie. I ain't hurting nothing."

"You're going to hurt yourself if you don't get strapped down," Jess said. "Dev, go."

Instantly the carrier shifted and rotated on it's skids, boosting up on it's landing jets. Dev tuned the forward sensors as she spotted April and Doug shove people out of their way as they rushed to their carrier.

Chris grabbed at the struts on either side of him. "I got a grip, g'wan. See if you can fly this thing, ya thing."

Jess took comms and hit external. "Get that door open!" but the big external door was already opening, and they could hear the alarms ringing. "I mean it, Chris, get in the jump kit."

Dev was already heading for the opening, as people dove out of her way in all directions.

"You're going to hit the wall, you idiot!" Chris yelled, then let out a yelp of shock as the carrier suddenly inverted sideways as it went through the opening gap. "Shit!" He frantically grabbed hold of the internal spars as he slid sideways.

"Toldja." Jess got her boards in sync and pulled down the two handed triggers. "Dev go around to the right and down between that ridge and the next one. Someone's shooting."

"Yes." Dev leveled the carrier and cut in the mains, shoving them both into their chairs and Chris against the back wall. She turned on the external sensors and the rain shield. She powered through a blast of wind and got through the gap.

She could see plasma fire, and she sent the sensor output to Jess's station as she picked up speed and started to level. She felt a pleasant chill as the carrier systems responded, preparing for battle.

"Gimme a run right up that path there, Devvie," Jess said. "See that white line?"

"Yes." Dev let the carrier lose altitude rapidly and lined up with the line that seemed to lead to a cavern on the next ridge. The outside sensors shielded the glare as Jess's plasma guns let loose.

"Want to put one right in that cave," Jess called up. "Then come up and around, mkay?"

"Yes." Dev increased power as she felt smaller blasters come up against the bottom of the carrier, none large enough to damage their shields. She held course, almost at ground level, their engines blasting sand in every direction until she was out of space and out of time, and she felt Jess release the big forward guns.

"Go!"

Dev cut the mains and flared the upper jets to shove them upright, then cut the mains in again as they missed the cliff face by inches and she had them going straight up, feeling the new power of the engines with some satisfaction.

Excellent.

Dev inverted, and they flew upside down for a moment as they got distance from the cliff. She then rolled them upright and they headed back toward the homestead again.

Sensors showed the energy blasts were gone, and she slowed, turning on the forward floodlights and tipping the carrier nose down a little to direct the light on the place where the attack had been.

The path was gone, replaced by huge holes, and as she checked the aft sensors, she saw smoke pouring out of the cavern Jess had blasted into.

Doug's voice erupted into the cup on Dev's ear. "Check check," he said, as the sideband came up between them. "Rocket, you there?"

"Yes," Dev responded. She ran a set of routines to see if they'd taken any damage. "Is everything all right there?"

"Booyah," Doug answered. "April got one of the guys who were shooting. We got him tied up here. She thought Jess might want to talk to him."

"Excellent." Dev saw Jess's thumbs up in her reflector. "Please return to the landing area," she added, interpreting the next hand gesture, as Jess circled her hand. She secured the console and put the carrier into a gentle turn, boosting their altitude to pass through the crags on either side.

"Holy shit," Chris said. "I think I broke a rib." He clutched his side. "You were not, by Neptune's left testicle, lying."

"I warned you." Jess secured the weapons boards and pushed her triggers up over her head. "Dev doesn't mess around." She pulled down her own comms. "Let me tell med to meet us."

Chris eased carefully upright, his legs braced against the carrier floor. "Tell them to stop and pick up a pair of my damned boots," he said, with a wry grimace. "And some hot sauce."

Dev smiled, but didn't turn as she prepared to put the carrier back into the landing bay. Doug and April hovered off to the left, waiting their turn.

They had, she thought, done well. Perhaps it would help Jess with her family.

Perhaps the Chris person would tell everyone about her answering with excellence and that might also help.

"What did that boy call you?" Chris asked. "Rocket? Holy fishcakes."

DEV LANDED BACK on the ground in the bay, noting that it seemed a lot more crowded than when they'd left. There were lots of men and women in thick clothing. They carried hand weapons and waved their arms around, making quite a lot of sound.

Jess was on comms with April, so she quietly shut things down. She opened the power port as one of the techs ran forward to reconnect them. Once the boards were secured she released her restraints and got up, looking back at Jess in question. "Should we open the door?"

Jess glanced out the window then straightened in some surprise. "Half the damn Bay's out there." She frowned. "Something happen? They get hit inside?"

Since Dev had the answer to none of those questions, she remained silent with a quizzical expression.

"Yeah, it'd be easier to just go ask them, wouldn't it?" Jess hit the unlock. "Let me let med in."

"Much obliged," Chris grunted. "Holy crap that was stupid." He edged out the ramp first, as several men in dark red came forward. "Easy there, vampires. Just cracked a rib." He waved them back and then joined them at the foot of the ramp. "Worth it though!"

Jess went out after him, intending on heading for April's carrier but stopping short when sight of her was greeted by a booming roar from the crowd in the cavern.

Dev came bopping out behind her, eyes wide in alarm. "Jess! What's going on?"

"No it's okay. That's a good noise." Jess lifted her hand in acknowledgment. "We just fought for the old home team, Devvie. Don't worry." She waited for Jimmy to push his way forward and for the yelling to stop. "It's fine."

Dev eyed all the fist pumping. "All right if you say so."

"Nice one, Jess," Jimmy said, with a wry smile. "If there's any left of them they're still running out through the lower pass."

"That's how we do what we do," Jess said. "I've got to interview one of the skanks before we resume our family fun." She pointed to the other carrier. "Want to witness?"

He nodded. "You kick Chris in the gut?" he asked, as the meds lead the bearded man away. "Didn't think he had a beef with you."

"No. He didn't strap in when he was told. Devvie has no respect for gravity and he was in free fall when we went upside down." Jess waved Dev forward. "Get your recorder ready."

"I saw that," Jimmy said, slowly. "That was her? Really?"

Jess nodded. "Oh, yeah. I sure can't drive that bus like that. She's an animal. Right, Dev?"

An animal. Her blonde eyebrow lifted. "Well," Dev said. "If I have to be an animal, can I be a bear? They were more attractive than the seals or dolphins." She looked around and realized a lot of the crowd were looking at her. "Did we do something incorrect?" she muttered to Jess under her breath.

Jess looked out over the milling crowd of bay residents and sensed the excitement. She noted their admiring glances at the carriers that were still offgassing a little on their pads. "No. They liked it." She put her hand on Dev's back and gave her a little scratch between the shoulder blades. "All good."

Jake caught up with them. "That was kickass," he said. "That's what reg Interforce can do. Little bastards deserved being blown to hell."

Jess caught the slight flinch on Jimmy's face. "Well, let's go talk to one of them and find out what made them so suicidal today." She started through the crowd for the now open hatch on the other carrier.

April stood in the opening, her blaster casually cradled along one forearm. "Good run," she said. "'Specially that dive up the cliff. My toes curled just watching."

Dev smiled, following Jess up the ramp and into Doug's carrier. He was seated in his pilot's station out of the way, but he waved at her when she entered. She waved back, went over to him and claimed his jumpseat, and got her scanner ready to record.

"That was nutso," Doug said. "Did you know how close you were to that rock?"

"Yes." Dev gave him a mild look. "Our sensors are functional." She glanced at the weapons station, where a scruffy looking man was seated, his hands and legs secured to the chair. He had a cut on his head and was covered in sweat and dirt and scrapes everywhere.

He was angry and desperate looking, and he ignored her and Doug, staring instead at Jess and her brothers who leaned against the outer skin of the carrier. "Bastards."

"Unfortunately for you, no. Legitimate Drakes." Jess crossed her arms and regarded him. "What were you looking for?"

The man jerked his head toward Jimmy. "He knows. Little fucking liar. Made a deal then broke it. We was just looking for what we was owed!" He looked at Jimmy. "You sic them on us?"

Jess turned her head and looked steadily at her brother, who refused to meet her eyes. "Want to talk about the deal?"

"No. Not here," Jimmy muttered.

Jess turned to the man. "What was the deal?" she asked, as he just glared at her. "Cough it up, or I'll break your arm."

His expression shifted a little, darting between Jimmy and Jess. "Who're you?"

"Jess Drake," she answered.

Jimmy cleared his throat. "My sister is the majority stakeholder of Drake's Bay," he said, succinctly. "I'd answer her if I were you. One more body's not going to matter."

The man stared at him for a long moment. "You lied."

Jimmy shrugged. "You took the deal."

"We was to bring all our scrounging here for food," the man said. "Took all we had, didn't give us nothing. That's why we came. Take what was ours."

Dev saw Jess was getting angry. Her fingers twitched a little and her nostril flared.

April caught it, and shifted to bring her blaster around, her eyes going to Jess's face as she waited for signals and Jake seemed to realize it, too, as he took a step back away from his brother, closer to the ramp to outside.

It was quiet for a moment, save for the raucous noises from outside drifting in. Jess finally drew in a breath. "Did you make a deal with him, Jimmy?" she asked, in a gentle, mild tone. "What were they scavenging that you wanted?"

Dev stood up to get a better angle with her scanner.

Jimmy sighed and rolled his eyes. "The processing center wanted pea gravel and slate," he said. "I decided what we got wasn't worth the food we offered to them."

"I see."

Dev sensed what was going to happen. A moment later Jess turned and grabbed Jimmy's cloak front, yanking him toward her, slamming her elbow into his jaw with so much force it snapped his neck.

He dropped without a sound at her feet.

"Fuck, Jess," Jake whispered.

"You get that on scan?" The rasp in Jess's voice was very audible.

"I did," Dev said, quietly.

Jess turned and looked at Jake. "The only currency we have worth anything is our honor. Ever hear that saying?"

Jake had no idea where to look, his eyes flicking from his brother's body to the visibly furious operations agent standing brace legged in the carrier. He obviously realized he could be the next victim and lifted his hands up in reflex, palms out, chest high. "Heard it," he muttered.

"Our contracts and agreements are based on our bond, which is dependent on the trustworthiness of our promises. Do you know what he did to us, Jake?" Jess could barely speak she was so angry. "He made that worthless."

April nodded to herself. Doug just watched, wide eyed.

Jake looked briefly at Jess. "They were just scavengers."

"He made a deal. He spoke for us." Jess bit out the words. "Didn't daddy teach either of you anything?"

"No. Not really," Jake answered with bleak honesty. "He never thought either of us were worth much. That's why he did what he did with you. I guess."

Jess exhaled. She turned and went to the door of the carrier and glanced around. "Brion." She found their domestic ops chief nearby. "Got something for you."

Brion eyed her warily as he came to the door of the carrier and looked inside. He looked at the limp body on the floor then exhaled. "Okay." He pulled his body back. "Let me get a med stretcher." He had gone a little white, but his voice was steady.

"Thanks," Jess said. "You know we're always a double edged sword."

"Both sides are razor sharp," Brion acknowledged. "I'll get the details squared." He disappeared and Jess went back to her interrogation.

Her target now watched her, wide eyed. "Y'killed him." He stated the obvious. "Fuck."

"I did," Jess said. "Just like I killed a whole lot of the people you brought with you. So we're both responsible for a lot of blood today, huh?"

The man exhaled, all the anger drained out of him.

"So we all lost," Jess continued, in a grim sort of tone. "But maybe some got lucky. You're going to get taken out on a flyer and see if there are any left. If there are, I'll turn over what he promised you."

He stared at her.

"What's your name?" Jess asked, after a moment of silence.

"Don't got one," he mumbled.

Three men in overalls appeared at the opening, carrying a stretcher. They looked at Jess for permission and then entered when she nodded. One of them paused as they got the stretcher arranged and looked back at Jess, giving her a little nod back.

"So," Jess said. "Get someone who can pilot a skid and take this guy out. Get me a count." She stared hard at Jake until he shook himself and scrambled out of the carrier, stepping gingerly over his brother's outstretched legs.

The bearers followed him, taking Jimmy's body out with them, replaced by two other bearded, pony tailed figures, who wore raggedly woven flight jackets. "Need some wings, Drake?" The nearer one said, in a deep and gravelly voice. "That the one there?"

"Yeah." Jess stepped back to make room for them. "Take him back to their camp, if there's anything left of it. Need to know how many are out there."

"Got it." The two of them untied the scavenger from the chair and pulled him upright, then carried him out between them with little effort.

Jess sighed and leaned against the wall. "What a mess."

April went to the door of the carrier and peered out, then she looked over at Jess, raising one hand and circling it. "That got props."

Dev eased up next to her and put a hand on her elbow. Jess took a breath then glanced down at her. "See?" she told Dev. "Toldja you should be glad you don't have sibs."

Dev sorted through all the responses she could have to that and settled on what she hoped was the least offensive. "He was incorrect?"

"Yes."

"I see."

"Families suck sometimes," April said, with a humorless smile. "Mine does, too."

"That's not my family," Jess countered. "My family wears black and green. These are just people I share blood with who are more often just a huge pain in my ass."

April held up a hand. "Taken. But you were right about the cross. Word gets out you can't trust a homestead, no one goes there." She seated her blaster and put the safety back on. "That one felt sketch."

"Jimmy?"

"Yeah."

Yeah. Jess straightened up. "Let's close down and go get some chow and rest." She glanced at the blaster April had holstered. "Keep that with you. I'm going to stop for mine. Screw the regs here."

April gave her a thumbs up, then she went to her rack and started adding to her hard points. Doug swiveled around and started shutting down the carrier.

"C'mon, Dev." Jess waved her toward the door. "Let's see what three-day-old cod we're going to get dumped on our heads next."

Chapter Three

ALONE IN THEIR own carrier, Jess dropped into her seat and rocked back gently, her eyes going a little unfocused. "Set up a deep scan," she said. "Alert on bio mass and energy."

"Yes."

Jess remained quiet for a few minutes. Then she turned her seat around a bit to face front. "Did that bug you, Dev?"

Dev paused and turned in her seat. "Excuse me?"

"What I did in there. That bother you?" Jess repeated, watching her face.

"Oh. You mean when you made that person dead?"

"Yeah."

Dev pondered that. "No," she said, finally "I didn't really understand what was going on. But my programming says the whole making dead thing is part of this work."

Jess tilted her dark head a bit. "The doc really knew what he was doing," she said, in a slightly surprised tone. "He really got it. Takes some techs time to eject that stuff."

"Yes. He told me before he left the base that he, in fact, made someone dead because they had done incorrect things to your father," Dev said, matter-of-factly. "And that he'd changed my programming to allow me to perform correctly if someone tried to do incorrect things to you."

Jess got up and came forward, crouching down next to her seat. She put her arms around Dev in an uncomfortable and awkward hug. "Thanks, Devvie. Despite everything, I do feel crappy about breaking my brother's neck. Can't take all of that out of us, I guess."

Dev had no idea what that feeling was, but hugging Jess was always excellent and so she tightened her grip. She felt the muscles in Jess's face move as she smiled. "You're so amazing," she told Jess. "You do even the hardest things excellently."

Jess chuckled wryly. "Ah, Dev." She reluctantly released her and backed off a little so she could look at Dev. "Something's going on here. Maybe that was part of it. Keep your eyes open and don't trust anything here. If I didn't have enemies before, I damn sure do now."

"Because of making that man dead?"

"Yeah."

"I see." Dev reached up to brush the hair out of Jess's eyes. "So more people might be incorrect?"

"Yeah."

"Suboptimal," Dev said. "I will try to make sure no one is attempting to make you dead, Jess," she added in a serious tone. "I don't want that."

Jess leaned forward and kissed her on the lips. "No, me neither." She braced her hands on the chair and kissed Dev again, feeling the welcome gentleness of the touch of Dev's hand on her cheek, and the even more welcome burn in her guts.

It flushed out the odd regret and brought her a welcome warmth that allowed her to put aside the discomfort. She eased forward as they continued to explore each other, safe in the confines and privacy their carrier provided.

IT WAS VERY dark outside and raining, the thunder audible through the bay door as Jess and Dev walked along the flight line toward the inner corridor.

"Hungry?" Jess asked.

"Yes, actually." Dev had her jacket on and her scanner over her shoulder, having sent the memory contents into the carrier's systems. "The meal before was excellent."

Jess scanned the area around them as they walked, the caverns mostly empty now save a few techs working on flyers. "Yeah, grubs not bad here." She reached up and touched her comms as it beeped. "Go ahead."

"All's quiet," April reported into her ear. "Looks like there's about thirty some of those scroungers left."

Out of probably a hundred fifty, according to Dev's count. "They giving them rations?"

"Yes. No one seems eager to go against your orders." April's tone was definitely amused. "We secured the area they gave us and we're heading to dinner, if that fits your plans."

"Does," Jess said. "Meet you there." She clicked off, and they started up the stairs side by side, climbing up past the second level to the third and moving into the hallway where the echo of voices gathered to eat could be heard.

So far they hadn't met anyone, and Jess took a breath and straightened her shoulders before they cleared the entrance and paused, looking for April and Doug.

The sound level immediately decreased, registering with Jess just as she spotted the other ops team at a table on the left hand side near the wall.

She fought the urge to flinch a little as all those eyes, and all that attention, fastened on her, and she let her hand rest on the grip of her blaster as she walked between the tables. She swung her head from side to side to meet the stares.

Dev walked quietly behind her, lifting her scanner in one hand and adjusting it, coming up short and stopping as someone rose in front of Jess and got in her way.

"Drake."

"Yes?"

Dev edged to one side to see who was holding them up. She saw April start to come toward them, and then Jess lifted her hand and made a sign, and April halted and retreated back to the table where Doug was seated.

The man in the way was as tall as Jess, but had curly red hair and interesting freckles on his face. "What's the score with you?"

Jess smiled a little. "C'mon, Ben. Ask at the table, we're hungry." She started forward and gave him the choice of moving along with her or being slammed into.

For a moment, she thought he was going to stand in place and let her hit him. But at the very last minute he turned aside and then started walking with them, now part of the focus from all the other eyes around them.

April had seated herself next to Doug, and they both stood as Jess arrived. "They told us they'd bring trays around," she said.

"They will." Jess took a seat at the head of the table and patted the left hand side, where Dev slid into place. "Sit," she told Ben, pointing to the last chair. "You elected?" she asked him. "April, Doug, Dev, this is Ben. He's one of the operations managers in the power station here."

"You remembered," Ben said. "I'm flattered." He glanced at Dev then looked back at Jess. "So what's your deal? You staying here? We heard you made some domestic rearrangements after the fight before."

Some of the workers came around and put down bowls of some liquid substance, smaller empty bowls for them, and a platter of pressed seaweed cakes.

Jess waited for the motion to end then she put her elbows on the table, lacing her fingers together. "I'm active ops service," she said. "Interforce is working on straightening the paperwork all out."

Ben studied her. "But...you going to council for us though?"

She nodded. "Tell everyone to relax. Jimmy skunked us and

paid for it. I'm just going to keep things clean until they can get me out of this."

Ben ladled himself a bowl of soup, then handed around the utensil. "Okay." He picked up the smaller bowl and drank directly from it. "But there's a wide range of opinions on all that. Know what I mean?" He produced a brief grin. "A lot of us miss Justin."

Ah. Jess merely shrugged a little, but smiled back. "I miss him," she said after a pause.

"It was good to be able to talk to someone who just knew."

Ben nodded silently.

Jess dipped herself a bowl and then paused before she put it down in front of Dev instead. "There ya go Devvie, before you start chewing the table." She handed her a cake. "I know all that super star driving makes ya hungry."

"Thank you," Dev replied with a brief grin. "Other activities also," she added, before taking a bite of the pressed seaweed and chewing it.

This brought a rakish smile to Jess's face as she dipped herself a bowl before handing off the ladle to April.

Ben was staring at Dev and she returned the look mildly until his eyes shifted back to Jess, then she inspected the bowl. It smelled of the substance she'd experienced as mushrooms back at base, and a spoonful of it proved quite delicious.

"So is that her?" Ben asked.

Dev put her spoon down and extended a hand. "Hello. Yes, I'm NM-Dev-1, the operations technician assigned to Agent Drake." She waited for him to reluctantly extend a hand back. "And also, a biological alternative who was born from an egg in space."

He gripped her hand and released it. "No way," he said and shook his head. "You're no bio."

Doug chuckled, but remained focused on his soup.

"Yes, way." Dev went back to her own bowl. She looked up as footsteps approached to find her unexpected visitor, Chris, coming over. He was wearing a sling, holding one arm close to his body. He circled them and grabbed a chair from a nearby table.

"Hey." He studied them. "Move over greenies." He squeezed the chair in between them as Dev moved closer to Jess and Doug to April. "I want to have dinner with my new friend, Rocket."

Now they had pretty much the attention of most of the people around them. Chairs turned around and all pretense at looking elsewhere abandoned.

Chris got himself settled and reached for the ladle, handling it a bit awkwardly. "Agree with Benny there though. Ain't no bio." He looked at Dev. "No offense intended, ma'am."

Dev politely held his bowl until he finished pouring into it. Then she casually undid the fastenings at her neck and opened her suit up, exposing the chased gold and tracing of her collar. "No, really. I am," she said, in a matter-of-fact tone. "The NM and the Dev stand for new model, developmental."

It went a little quiet and she was able to continue consuming her soup, which she did after fastening her suit back up.

"Holy shit," Chris said, after a moment.

"That's what we all said," Doug added, unexpectedly. "Serious rock star."

Jess cleared her throat. "Can we get through dinner?" she asked, making a pushing back motion with her hand. "Food can't get here."

People eased back so the servers could get to them, but the attention didn't diminish. "M'kay." Chris studied his seatmate with interest. "Someone made some hella breakthrough then. Cause you ain't no jelly bag brain."

"No, I'm not," Dev said, observing the platters now landing on the table. "Oh, Jess! Those are shrimps!"

"I knew I came to the table armed for a reason," Jess drawled. "Nice!"

"What are those?" April asked, curiously.

The circular pink animals were swiftly divided, and Dev was glad to see she'd gotten a sizable portion of them for herself. She smelled the spicy scent coming off them, just the same as in Quebec. "They're shrimp," she told April. "We had them on one of our first missions."

"Quebec?" Chris asked. "Jontons?"

Jess nodded. "Had to convince her not to eat the shells." She leaned back a little in her seat, letting her peripheral vision take in the scene and analyze it, watching the range of reactions to the bio alt in their midst.

Big mix. Chris's acceptance had helped, though, the senior operations tech at the stakehold carried both acknowledged and unacknowledged status. He'd gone through field school up to the point of pairing then backed out.

Some said, flunked out. Jess had never bothered to find out either way. So he knew Interforce, and didn't, enough to be skeptical but not enough to lose the inbred respect for the service that was a commonplace at the Bay.

Dev picked up a shrimp and twisted it's head off. She looked past Chris to where April was watching her. "You suck the heads out," she said knowledgeably, reversing the head and putting it to her lips and inhaling sharply.

The expected goo hit her tongue, and she mouthed it before she swallowed, finding it a little different than at Jontons but just as delicious. "It's good."

April imitated the motion, her head jerking back a little as the substance entered her mouth. Then her brows contracted. "Wow," she said after swallowing. "That's the most bizarre thing I've eaten since Polar base."

Doug was already ripping the legs off one of his. "Landies." He sighed, shaking his head.

Everyone chuckled, and the energy around the table eased slowly, the sound of discussion just as slowly rising around them. Jess sucked a shrimp head out, casually letting her eyes drift around the surrounding crowd.

Some were still watching Dev, and she watched them carefully, but discerned more curiosity than animosity there. Good sign. She bit into the shrimp's body as the tension in her guts retreated, able to enjoy the spicy taste.

"You were at Polar?" Ben asked April. "Thought it was long closed?"

"Was," April said. "We recommissioned it."

"Dev recommissioned it," Doug reminded her. "We were just there to boost the batteries and keep the snow off her head."

"That is not accurate at all," Dev disagreed immediately. "Everyone participated."

Everyone's eyes shifted to Jess. "She's right," Jess said. "Even me. I picked the lock on the front door." She divested another shrimp of it's head. "They had some crazy old freeze drieds in there. We ate 'em."

"Can't even imagine," Ben said, with a more relaxed smile.

"They even had coffee," Doug said. "That was weird." He held up a shrimp. "This is way better."

Chris was managing his meal one handed, and he bit the head off a shrimp. "Love to see that." He put the body down and prepared to suck the head. "You keeping it open?" He looked over at Jess. "After all the craziness?"

Jess merely nodded. "Keeping a lot of options open," she said. "We rode the edge up there."

Ben leaned on the chair arm nearest her. "We figured when

we got the alert from you," he said, his voice now serious. "We halfway expected to become Base Eleven."

There was a moment of silence. Then April spoke up. "No." She studiously ripped the shell off a shrimp. "Wasn't going to let that happen." She glanced up. "No one at Ten was. Everyone got all in that, mechs, techs, bios."

"Scientists from the bio station," Doug added, with a slight twinkle.

"Doctor Dan was amazing and brave," Dev said. "But no one was more amazing than...mmfp." She looked up in surprise as Jess covered her mouth with one hand, and the rest of the people around the table started laughing.

"We heard you got the star, Jess," Ben said, waving a shrimp head at her. "C'mon, it's props for us, too. You're a Drake from Drake's Bay, after all."

"The Drake right now," Chris added. "Probably got half the legal between here and the coast shitting starfish over that."

Jess removed her hand from Dev's mouth, aware of a wash of strong and complex emotion. A quick scan told her the hostility around her had faded and been replaced by something odd and unexpected.

She'd done something right here. Jess lifted her cup and in response, cups lifted all around her, a touching of that dark and edgy energy she'd always been aware of, once grown, here at the Bay. A ferocity that rode just below the surface.

"Hai!" The yell went up suddenly, making her skin prickle in response. Jess raised a fist and heard the stomping boots, as the servers started to come around with pitchers, and she smelled the rich and pungent scent of the dark beer they held.

Unspoken celebration. Jess let out a breath, seeing Dev's steady regard of the room, the faint nod of her head as she picked up and understood it with her bio alt's intense awareness of her surroundings.

Something was in flight.

JESS SAT BEHIND her console on the carrier, her comms helmet connected as she waited for the secure link to base to come up. Up front, Dev was busy running scans and reports, sorting out all the information she'd retrieved so far and bundled it for transmit once Jess was done.

Jess still felt buzzed from the beer. "That was cool, huh, Dev?" She asked, watching the countdown for the comms link.

"That everyone thought you were amazing? Yes." Dev glanced over her shoulder. "And I think they are not so upset about me. At least, I hope not."

Jess held up a hand as the comms synched, and she felt the scan hit her eyeballs. "Drake, J.," she muttered into the mic.

A moment later the small screen came up, and she was looking at Bensen Alters. "Sir."

"Evening, Drake." He was in the small command room off Ops, as secure and private as was possible on base. "How are things there?"

Jess issued a short, wry chuckle under her breath. "They were right. Something irregular is going on here, but it's linked into my family, not general ops," she said. "Stake was attacked by scavengers earlier. We went out and did what we do."

Alters nodded. "Any reason?"

"Yes. They were promised something then double crossed." Jess kept her voice even. "By my brother, James."

The commander's eyebrows lifted. "Unusual," he said. "Not at all Drake like."

"No."

"I'll let legal know. He was in the mix they were reviewing." Alters sighed. "We don't want that kind of result."

"I killed him."

He folded his hands and studied her. "I see." His expression lightened a bit. "Hm."

"And a hundred twenty some of the scavengers," Jess said, after a moment of silence. "Dev's bundling the vid for you, she'll send it momentarily."

He nodded at this. "Good job, Drake. I was just trying to figure out if the stakehold was going to make a claim on it. Have no idea what the legal position on it is since it's never been an issue before. Guess I'll send it over to them, too."

Jess shrugged. "Haven't talked to the rest of my family since. I'll let you know if anything bubbles up."

"Good. Well." Alters cleared his throat. "Something did come in earlier. A request from the science station."

Dev's ears perked up visibly, and she turned in her chair.

"From Doctor Kurok?" Jess hazarded a guess.

"Yes. He said he's finished the initial structure for our tech project. He'd like you and your partner to pay them a visit so he can make sure it's a fit." Alters leaned forward. "I let him know you were out on assignment, but I think it's in our interests if you comply."

"Hm."

"And since we can't assign you out," he reminded her.

Jess sighed. "Yes, I know. "She glanced up at Dev, who had a very noncommittal expression on her face. "Let me talk to Dev about it, and we can figure it out when we get back."

"Good luck at the council tomorrow," he said. "Try not to kill anyone there. I'm pretty sure that would be a legal problem for us." He gave her a wry look. "Oh, and by the way, we finally got signal from Elaine."

"Everything okay there?"

"No. But you can't do anything about it, so it'll hold. Jason's working it. Thanks for the report, Drake. Keep your head down."

"Yeah, thanks." Jess cut off the connection and pulled her comms link off, tossing it on her console. "That's a bucket of fish shit."

Dev made a face.

Jess sighed. "Send the vid. We'll worry about the station when we get back. Probably have to take the shuttle from there anyway." She saw the frown get deeper on Dev's face. "Won't make you go if you don't want to, Devvie. I get it."

Dev got up and came over to her. "I want to do excellent work for you, Jess." She crouched down and rested her hand on Jess's knee for balance. "So if it's required, of course I'll go." She took a breath. "And I would like to see Doctor Dan."

Jess gently brushed her fingers through Dev's hair. "Don't worry. I won't let them mess with you. The Doc knows that." She saw the smile return. "Anyway, we've got to finish this mess first. Maybe by the time we get back, they'll have moved on to something else and not waited for us."

The thought seemed to comfort Dev. She stood up and straightened her jacket out. "That's true." She moved back over to her station. "Sending now."

Jess swiveled in her chair as she heard a knock on the outside of the carrier door. "Who's outside, Dev?" She glanced up at her screen as the image from the external sensor was driven to it. "Ah. Uncle Max."

"Is he going to be incorrect?"

"Let's find out." Jess hit the hatch unlock and let one hand drop to her blaster, just in case.

Because with Drakes, you just never knew.

APRIL SETTLED INTO one of the hall chairs, positioning

herself to face the opening. "Wish this hallway had a lockable door. There's just a lot of stuff going on here."

"No joke." Doug had his input pad on his knee and was working with his scanner. "Busier here than at the base."

"Well," April extended her legs out, "they do more stuff. Collecting and fishing and all that. We concentrate on one thing."

"Hmm. Some areas won't return," he said. "Let me try that phase shifting Dev came up with on it."

April smiled and shook her head. "Scary smart. She's right to be careful about claiming cred — doesn't want to be a target."

Doug had half an ear on the conversation. "Stupid of anyone to make her one. Not with Jess around. Holy crap that guy never even saw it coming."

April smiled and stared off into the hallway with unfocused eyes. "I did. I saw her breathing change like it did when she gutted Bain. Didn't understand it then, but the Doc did. Saw it in his eyes."

"She's pretty freaking ferocious," Doug said, then grunted a little. "Hey, April, come look at this, will ya?"

April got up and came over, circled his chair and peered over his shoulder. "What is it?"

He traced a section of the screen, moving it to his pad and expanding it. "It's a biological return, but I've never seen one like this before."

"Biological like in people?"

Doug shook his head. "No, it's not rock, not sand or water. It's some substance that gives carbon and traces back. I thought I saw something a little like it when we were on the other side in that science center."

April studied it. "Is that in a cavern? Looks like it's down around the intake level. Maybe it's seaweed? They could be growing it there."

"No, this is seaweed." He indicated a second area, smaller and at the rim of the stakehold. "It's partially exposed to the sea, see? It's a different profile and the scan recognizes it." He tuned the scanner a little. "Those phase shifts are creepy good."

"But it doesn't recognize that," April said. "And that cavern wasn't on the tour earlier."

"New since Jess hung out here, maybe," Doug said. "Should we go check it out?"

April leaned on the back of the chair, her eyes narrowing thoughtfully. "Be a good time for it. Everyone's heading off to bunk time here now." She straightened up, then paused as she heard the faint scrape of boots against the stone floor. "Someone's coming."

Doug tuned the scanner. "Rocket," he said, immediately. "That's an easy peg."

April chuckled. "Yeah, only bio here. Let's show this thing to her."

A moment later Dev arrived, scanner in hand and two backpacks slung over her shoulders. "Hello," she said. "Jess is conversing with a relative of hers. She'll be back here shortly."

"She's got nothing but relatives here," Doug said. "That DNA marker you filtered for is freaking everywhere."

"Yes." Dev opened the door to the chamber she'd been assigned and put the two packs inside, then closed the door and joined them by the heater, undoing the fastenings on her jacket as she sat down. "In my human interface classes, we learned that there are some recombinate mtDNA components that can become pervasive." She put her scanner down on the table. "Doctor Dan called them — sticky — "

"You had classes with him?" April asked. "I mean, you had classes where he talked about making you guys?"

"Of course," Dev said. "We know what we are. At least some of us, anyway." A brief smile appeared. "And the advanced sets had classes on why natural borns were different because it helped us interact with them."

Doug got up and came over to her. "Can you use your advanced skills to look at this?" He showed her the returns from his scanner. "It's a cavern down at the lower lev..." He paused as Dev took the scanner from him and peered intensely at it, with a slight, indrawn breath.

April leaned forward, watching the shifting expression on Dev's face.

After a long moment, Doug cleared his throat. "You know what that is?"

Dev tuned the filters intently. "Yes I do," she finally said. "That's vegetation." She looked up at them. "Plants."

"Plants?" April said. "Is that like what they were trying to do over the other side?"

"I don't know," Dev answered honestly. "There is no indication around them of the machinery involved in that instance. But that bio mass is growing plants that this scanning program does not recognize."

They were all silent for a moment, digesting the implications of what Dev just said. Then Dev shook her head and manipulated the scanner. "I'm going to sync to my device and see if I can relay it through the base systems."

"What will that do?" April asked.

Dev looked at her. "I have a copy of the dataset from the science station there. I will attempt to match it." She regarded April. "It would be good if you could communicate with Jess, please. I think she will want to know."

"Puh." April touched her comms link. "Want, yes. Like? Doubt it."

THEY WERE OUT on the ledge, looking out over the sea. It had stopped raining and the air carried a rare dryness as Jess regarded her uncle, both of them seated on the cold stone wall.

"He screwed up," Uncle Max said. "He never told the council. Never told any of us."

Jess shook her head. "Wasn't living here enough?" she asked. "Having all this? What was he trying to prove?"

"That he was a better man than your father," Max said. "He hated Justin. But then, most everyone in the family did."

Jess sighed.

Max chuckled. "He saw through all the bullshit, Jess. He was smart, the way you're smart, the way your brother wasn't." He regarded the sea. "Interforce takes the best and brightest of us, always has."

Something clicked about that in Jess's mind, and she nodded after a pause. "And most of us die young because of it," she murmured. "Except he didn't."

"He was Drake both sides," Max said. "He knew something about that the rest of us didn't. He wanted to pass it. Wanted to have kids. He told me before—well, before they got him—how glad he was that he had."

"Well he definitely passed it," Jess said, in a droll tone.

"He did," Max said. "And the Bay as well, unfortunately."

"Unfortunately?"

"You're active, Jess. When Justin retired, we found out he'd somehow gotten enough shares to his civ profile to claim majority. Big squabble. No one's really sure how that happened."

"Huh."

"Even now," Max said. "Maybe the service? Maybe your grandfather? We don't know. He was the first in service to retire in a rock's age. No one knew what to do with him but we figured he'd just code everything into the family pool."

"But he didn't."

"No. Most of us think he just wanted to be a jackass about it. Justin could be."

Jess smiled. "He passed that, too." She let her head rest against the rock. "Jimmy was convinced I could just hand it all over to him. I just wonder why, if Dad did what he did, that he'd think I would." She regarded the faint light reflecting off the sea. "Of course, I don't think it came down like anyone expected."

Max shrugged. "Freak chance."

"Yeah." Jess said thoughtfully. She looked up at him. "Family must be boiling. But the stakehold? I got the sense there's something else there."

He took a breath to answer, then went quiet as the comms chirped in her ear.

"Drake," she answered, hearing April's voice on the other end. "What's up?" She listened to April's terse report, her own brows creasing. "Okay," she finally said. "Let me come take a look." She got up. "Sorry, uncle. Duty calls."

He stood and walked with her back inside. "Ship's leaving tomorrow dawn," he said. "Anyway, good luck, Jess. Hope it all works out."

"Glad you're leaving?" she hazarded.

"Always." He smiled at her. "It's why I understood Justy the way I did. That being in charge Drake thing's full up in me. Ship's a good place for it." He paused. "Sigurd Rolaffson sends regards, by the by."

Jess chuckled dryly. "Bet he does."

"Story there, no doubt."

THE BIG, HAMMERED metal doors that led off into the family compound were firmly shut as Jess climbed up past them, not even giving them a look as she continued on her way.

The big hall was mostly dark and empty. She was the only one on the stairs and as she got up to the fourth level she paused and looked down and saw nothing but rock and steel and the steady illumination of the lamps on it below her.

They were fully inside. There was no reason they needed to keep that diurnal rhythm and yet, just as at the Citadel, they did. Sometimes after the night meal there was entertainment, then all would go off to bed, save the ops watch.

That, buried deep in the mountainside, kept up around the clock, listening and relaying messages and watching sensors just as they always had. Drake's Bay control, where a few channels were up to restricted frequencies.

Jess smiled and headed into the hallway that went to their quarters.

She sensed the motion before seeing or hearing it, hand pulling the blaster and unsafing it, aiming, fingers tightening between a breath and a second.

"Hai!" A dark figure blending into the darker walls, hands outflung at shoulder level, palms out. "Friendly!"

"Friendly but stupid." Jess tilted her blaster up. "What do you want, Ben?"

He lowered his hands and looked around. "Got something to tell you before you go out to the regional. Something they should have told you, on two."

"C'mon." Jess holstered her blaster. "Does it have to do with a cave full of veg?" She waved him to join her.

"You knew?" he said in a shocked tone.

"No," she said. "But my team just found it." She led him to the open area, where April was standing to one side, her long blaster out and aimed. "Relax," Jess said. "Whatcha got?"

Everyone looked at Dev, who got up and brought her data pad over. She glanced at Ben, then displayed it to Jess. "This facility here," she said. "There's obscuring scan over it. It appears to be a large open cavern that has class one and class two plants growing in it."

Jess looked at it, then at Dev. "What kind of plants?"

"Consumables," Dev responded. "I believe several types of beans, beets, and these are peas." She regarded the readout. "There are also root vegetables."

Jess looked at Ben. "That what you wanted to tell me? What is this, Ben?"

Ben took a step back away from her. "That's more than I knew," he said. "Just that something was being done down there, and Jimmy was behind it." He looked at Dev and the pad. "Is that true? What she's saying?"

"She'd know better than I would. I've never seen any of this stuff." Jess regarded the data. "This what they do on station, Dev? Those kind of plants?"

Dev nodded. "They do. They grow all sorts of things, and I believe it's exchanged."

"For what?"

"That I don't know." Dev said regretfully. "They tested it on us. I've eaten most of this." She looked at her pad. "Except beets.

I think though a portion of it is given to the natural born on station."

"Or sold to anyone with the cred for it," Jess said, after a moment.

"But how are they doing it?" April asked. "Some rig? Like the other side?"

Jess looked at Ben, who shook his head. "I don't know," he admitted. "They've been using that cavern for a workshop since forever, then one week they had all the machinery moved out, and it was put off limits."

"They used to do a little rice in there, like at Ten," Jess said. "Never could grow much, took too much power for the rad for it, and half the time it died anyway." She handed the pad back to Dev. "Square that away, Dev. Let's go find out what this is."

"It's protected," Ben said. "No one was supposed to know about it. I think they even had people in there from somewhere else."

Jess stared at him.

"It was a big deal, Jess. They were talking about this changing everything for the Bay. If that's all what she said, imagine how much it'd be worth!"

April leaned against the wall, her blaster cradled in her arms. "Imagine how every single person on the planet would want a piece of it. It'd be different all right. As in, you'd lose every damn thing you had here."

Dev put away her equipment and walked over to stand by Jess. "People off the planet as well," she said. "The DNA profile chains in that material match what I had in the database from the crèche."

Jess looked at her. "You mean, they came from there?" she asked, in a surprised tone.

"It appears so." Dev folded her hands in front of her. "But most of them are more successful than the results from station."

Doug joined her near the entrance. "Oh, boy. This is gonna be interesting."

"And maybe not in a good way," April said. "You were right, Jess. Things do happen to you."

Jess took Ben by the arm. "You're coming with us." She started down the hall. "Let's not give them any warning."

DEV PRIVATELY HOPED that whatever it was they were doing would be concluded soon. It had been a long day, and she was a little tired.

They walked down another long rock hallway, this one pitched downward, with a finished stone floor that showed signs of a lot of wear. She saw pits in the surface, and in some places it seemed to have been patched.

They went around a gentle curve, and she felt the brush of air across her face, and with it a scent. "Jess."

Jess turned to her. "What's up?"

"I can smell dirt," Dev said. "Synth dirt. I remember it from the lab."

Both agents had their blasters out, and now they all slowed. Jess motioned for the techs and their unwilling guide to stay behind.

Dev had her scanner in her hand, and she tuned and re-tuned it, watching Jess and April slide forward down the hall toward a large set of metal doors. Besides the bio behind the door, she wasn't picking up any returns that could be people, or weapons, or people with weapons.

Excellent. Hopefully. There was no scan or potentially disruptive energy, and she caught Jess's signal to come ahead. "This all seems correct."

"I don't get it," Ben muttered. "They've been guarding this since forever."

"Maybe guarding it against random people is different than guarding it against us," Doug suggested, with a brief smile. "Have you seen what's in there?"

Ben hesitated. "No."

"Bring that up here, Devvie." Jess touched the door, feeling along the fold between both of the leaves of it. "I don't want to blast this if I don't have to."

Dev and Doug came over and started scanning the locking mechanism. It was huge, the bolt roughly the size of Jess's arm, and they could see ones the same size buried into the rock floor beneath.

Through the gap, they could all smell the odd, nose tickling smell that Dev had called dirt, and when April pressed her ear against the door, she reported hearing a repetitive hissing sound.

Dev leaned close to her. "I think that's irrigation," she said. "Watering the plants," she clarified. "But it's hard to tell."

"Can you open the doors?"

"No, Jess." Dev looked disappointed. "It's not an electrical system. It's mechanical."

Jess regarded the door. "Ben, how else can we get in here?"

"Don't know," Ben said, glumly.

Jess stepped back. "Get away from that opening." She drew her heavy blaster and braced herself, triggering the blaster and squinting as a blue beam emitted from it and impacted the metal.

At once, a loud alarm started flaring, echoing off the rock. April immediately drew her blaster and turned. "Get down!" she yelled at them, bringing the big rifle up and aiming it back down the still empty hallway.

Dev and Doug dove for the ground and pulled Ben down with them, moving into a small angle to get some protection, leaving the air clear for April to shoot as the nomad braced and aimed, going off safety with the gun, taking on a brief flare of pre-aim.

Jess finished the center lock and dropped to one knee, aiming at the ground and sending the blaster fire under the door.

The alarm cycled and grew louder, then softer, then louder again, echoing and echoing through the rock. April had her eyes pinned on the last curve they'd come around, her finger tightening on the triggers.

The hallway remained empty.

Jess finished cutting the bolts, and then she stood up and walked over to where April stood, peering past her. "What the hell is the point of that alarm?"

Ben scrambled to his feet. "There were guards here," he said "And more should have responded. You know the drill, Jess."

Jess peered at the emptiness, then shrugged as Doug and Dev joined them. "C'mon." She turned and went to the doors and gave them a shove. They rocked back and then unexpectedly opened forward.

"Crap!" Jess somehow got out of the way, and the rest of them ran for the walls as a blast of air rolled out, with a cloud of gritty substance behind it.

Jess bounced off the wall and started back inside, with April at her heels, both agents hauling their rifles up and around as they disappeared into the cloud.

"I don't know what the hell's going on but I'm outta here." Ben started running in the other direction.

"Let him go," Doug said. He got his scanner out. "Let's go before we miss the fun." He took off after April, raising a hand up to shield his face from the particulate in the air.

"Yes." Dev was already on the move, blinking her eyes as the dust from the explosion faded. She brushed the dirt off the screen and drew in a breath full of organic smell as she came around the edge of a tall plastic wall and almost crashed into Jess's back.

The two agents were standing at the edge of a platform, looking up. The cavern roof overhead was full of phosphorescent illumination, a rich yellow-green color that bathed everything inside. On the platform, across the entire length of the cavern were trays and trays and trays of plants in a rising series of levels.

Outside the alarm was still going off.

Jess turned and looked at Dev. "What the hell?"

"I don't know." Dev had her scanner at her side, amazed at the cavern. "The other man ran away, Jess."

Jess put her blaster on it's points and walked over to the platform. She heard water and she peered into the side and blinked as a gentle wash of liquid hit her face. She licked her lips experimentally then grimaced and wiped the back of her hand across her face.

"Doesn't taste good?" April guessed.

"Chemicals," Jess responded.

Dev came over and touched the nearest plant. "This is...um..." She leaned closer and inspected a leaf. "I think this is corn."

Doug edged up next to her and reached over, touching the leaf with a look of amazement. "No kidding, really?"

"Really." Dev peeled down the sides of a roughly obloid item, exposing rows of small nubs. "See?" She turned to Jess. "Those are seeds, and you cook them if you want to eat them. They served them to us once or twice in the crèche. Everyone liked them."

Jess leaned over and sniffed it cautiously. "Huh."

April walked slowly in an aisle down the center of the platforms. She looked from side to side, her rifle cradled in her hands. "Doug, make sure we're clear," she called back over her shoulder. "I'm going to try and find that alarm to shut it off."

Dev tilted her scanner up and was studying the readings from the roof of the cave. "What is that, Jess?" She pointed at the glowing substance.

"No idea." Jess regarded it. "I mean, well, I know there were some glow rocks around back in the day. But not like this."

"No one else is in here," Doug called out to his partner. "We're clean."

Jess held her hand out and watched the yellow-green light bathe it. "Is this like rad?"

"Something like. Yes." Dev regarded her instrument. "Not

exactly like, and not like some of the growing chambers on station, but it's a light frequency that allows for photosynthesis." There was a distinct tone of awe in her voice. "Jess, this is amazing."

"It's what the other side was trying with that crazy thing that blew up, isn't it?" Doug asked.

"Maybe." Jess walked along to the next section and stopped to regard the thing growing in it. She reached out and took hold of the small, green hanging pods and carefully twisted one off.

"That's a pea." Dev reached down and felt the substance it was planted in, bringing back her fingers covered in damp brown. "This is dirt. The cloud that came out when the doors opened was also dirt, only dry."

They were covered in it.

"A pea." Jess experimentally put it in her mouth and bit into it.

"No, Jess you..." Dev grinned a little at the face her partner made. "You don't eat the outsides...here." She took the pod and prised it open, exposing three perfect, round green beads. She selected one and put it in her mouth, then offered the pod to Jess.

With a doubtful expression, Jess took the second and ate it, chewing it slowly. Doug took the third pea and bit it in half, mouthing it before he swallowed.

"That's weird," Doug said.

"A little like some of the round things on seaweed," Jess said. "Not bad."

The alarm cut off abruptly, and in the silence that echoed afterward, they all heard hissing and the drip of water and a soft fluttery sound all around them.

It was odd, and suddenly to Dev, familiar. She drew in a breath and released it, then followed Jess and Doug as they walked along the pathway toward where April stood, rifle braced against her hip.

As they crossed a path, Jess stopped and brought her gun up, moving sideways and putting herself between the opening and the two techs as they spotted a lone figure moving toward them.

Dev scanned it. "It's the man who went with us, Jess. You said he was called Chris?"

"Yeah." Jess rocked forward, putting her center of balance over the balls of her feet. "Maybe he can tell us what's going on here."

April arrived at a lope and joined Jess in the crossroads. "This place is crazy."

"You turn off that alarm?"

"No."

Jess cradled her rifle as Chris arrived, his arm still strapped to his chest. They faced each other in a tense pensive silence before he looked around, then exhaled.

"What?" Jess finally asked.

"I turned off the bell," he said. "No one's going to respond. Everyone's glad you found it." He shifted a little in discomfort. "No one felt right about it, Jess."

"No one?" Her dark brow arched.

He shrugged a little. "Jimmy's gig," he said. "Yes, a few were in it with him. Some of the bright kids, they put this together and were jazzed up about it until..." He stopped.

"Until what?" Jess asked in a surprisingly gentle tone.

"They thought it was for us," Chris finally said. "As in, for the stakehold. New stuff, good stuff, new foods, for all of us."

"He was probably going to sell it," April said. "No crime in that."

"No. Was going to make real good money on it he said, to Quebec and the like," Chris said. "Then they came asking."

Jess went still. "They?"

"Someone told them." Chris looked uncomfortable. "They heard, you know they do, Jess, and two of them came one night to talk to Jimmy." He paused to take a breath. "That was before the big blow out. Then we thought it was all over with, after the fight."

Jess watched him closely. "But they came back."

"I think so. Don't know really," Chris said. "But I think he met with them in the rough."

"Today."

Chris nodded. "He said he was at the processors. We know he wasn't."

"He made a deal."

"Maybe. I don't know, Jess. You should ask the family."

Jess looked around, at the space. "You're right," she said, after a pause. "Let's go." She circled her finger to include her group. "Someone has answers."

Dev followed Jess back down the hallway, with Doug at her side. "Interesting," she said.

"This night's going to end with blood." Doug predicted. "Massive amounts of not coolness."

"Non optimal."

"That, too."

"SOMEONE'S GOING TO tell me what the deal is," Jess said, facing a semicircle of relatives, most a little foggy with sleep, all looking at her with undisguised apprehension.

As they should. She and April were armed with guns without safeties on, and after all, she'd killed Jimmy earlier. They all knew the Drake temper. They all knew what she was.

Dev was seated at a console in the corner of the business room in the stakehold, her scanner out, her eyes shifting from it to the board she was working at. Doug was seated next to her, just watching.

Jimmy's wife was missing, and his other two kids. No one seemed to know where they were.

Jake was the only one with slivers of guts. "Jess," he said, after a very long silence. "It's not what it looks like."

Jess rolled her head and looked drolly at him. "Really?"

"It was an accident." Her brother stood up and put his hands in his overall pockets. "Finding out about the glow, I mean. We were just messing around with some stuff."

"You were messing around with seed stock and proto soil obtained from Biologic station two," Dev said. "Are you certain you don't have access to this system? I don't want to damage it."

Everyone turned around and looked at her. After a moment, as if sensing that, Dev looked up, "I come from there," she said into all the silence. "I do know what the substances are."

Jake exhaled. "Fuck."

Jess and April exchanged glances. "Go back to your carrier," Jess said. "Send a request for an investigation team. They need to get over here ASAP."

"Right." April scanned the room, shook her head and left.

"You'll get points if you tell me what the story is before they get here," Jess said, sitting on the edge of the table behind her.

"Or you'll shoot us?" Jake's wife spoke up, in a bitter tone.

Jess shook her head. "I'm not going to shoot anyone, unless someone starts shooting at me. I'm going to hand you all over to Interforce Security and let them deal with the collusion issue."

"Bio Station two is on our side," Jake said. "That thing comes from there!" He pointed at Dev.

"I know," Jess said. "But if you'd done a legit deal with them, we'd know. Look, people. The stakehold didn't buy in to whatever this was. Someone broke honor. They know it, I know it. You might as well spill it."

"No one here knew but me and Jimmy," Jake finally said. "I mean, we all knew something was being done, but only Jimmy and I knew who we were talking to."

Jess looked at him.

"So, yeah, we did a deal with a guy. We didn't know if he was the other side, but he could get us what we needed, and that was stuff to test those glow rocks with."

Dev went back to the console, attaching the leads from her scanner to it and tuning it carefully. It all sounded very incorrect and non optimal and she felt a discomfort in her guts just thinking about it.

The screen came back with a challenge, and she studied it, then called up a program of her own from the scanner and set it to run.

"So it worked," Jake said. "Aren't you glad, Jess? Do you know how much that stuff's worth? We could make it big. Why are you acting like this is something criminal? Jimmy was going to sell this whole new crop to Quebec. We finally got something to make the place independent."

"Because a mini transport from the other side landed on our edge two days ago," Jess said, in a quiet tone. "And Interforce wondered what they were looking for."

Now the silence had a completely different flavor to it, and Jess smelled real fear. "They thought maybe someone was arranging for a hit on me." She smiled. "I thought that's maybe how they got to dad."

Uncle Max stood up. "Jesslyn, do you know what you're saying?

Jess got up off the table and walked over to him. "Yes."

A small bleep and a muttered grunt from Dev distracted her, and she turned and detoured over to where Dev was seated instead. "Whatcha got, Dev?" She peered at the screen. "That's the filestore."

"Yes, I am decrypting it," Dev said. "And I...JESS!"

Jess felt the pressure in the room change and she turned and brought her gun up and fired with literally no thought involved. "GET DOWN!" She bellowed at the rest of the family, who dove for the floor as two armored figures entered and fired back.

"Oh, not good!" Doug grabbed ahold of Dev and dove under the console, hitting the recall key on his comms that linked him to April. "Tac! Tac! Tac!"

JESS DODGED THE blasts and dropped to her knees, firing up into the chest armor of the two attackers, who aimed past her and swept the room.

She saw the closer one's rifle move in Dev's direction. A second later she let out a booming roar and lunged at him as she fired at the second man. The rage came on so fast she had no control over it, the view going black and white as she ripped the gun out of the hands of the enemy soldier, then reversed her motion and slammed him in the head with it.

She heard a crack and a popping sound, and she threw the gun away from them against the wall, her fingers curling into the broken piece of his armor, yanking hard.

The other soldier was abruptly shoved forward and then was gone out of her peripheral vision, and she could concentrate on the opponent who was grabbing for her.

She could see a skin suit now and she reached inside the armor, evading his grip and bringing one boot up to shove him backward, growling all the while. Her fingers got a hold of his throat and she started squeezing as he hit the wall. She straightened up, shoving his much larger body against the rocks.

She heard a shocked male scream behind her, but had no time to wonder what April was doing as she shoved her weight against her adversary's arm and pinned it to the wall. His body started to jerk as she closed off his airway.

She clenched her fingers with all their strength and felt the windpipe crush as she got her boots up against the wall and exploded backwards, taking the front of the enemy soldier's throat with her, air and blood and all.

She flipped upside down and landed, sweeping around fully with her rifle aimed in one hand and the other dripping with red stained cartilage.

April stood over the second soldier, or actually, half standing on him, the curved knife in her hand likewise bloodstained.

The doorway was full of Drake's Bay staff, all armed, with nothing left for them to use them on.

Jess's opponent slid down the wall with a rattle of broken armor, his body shuddering helplessly as he bled out and died.

A moment of silence. Then Jess let her rifle drop a little. "Everyone okay?" She looked over at the console as Dev's blonde head appeared, and then Doug's, and she blinked in relief as she let her gaze continue around the room.

"Might have gotten a hangnail," April said reflectively before she got off the soldier and kneeled to pull his helmet off. "Doug, need an ID."

Jess released her grip and let the bits of flesh and cartilage drop to the ground, shaking her hand a little to get some of the gore off it. "So." She regarded her family grimly. "Someone have something they'd like to tell me now?"

Her body was still twitching. She was still seeing in that colorless, flat monochrome. Still in the zone, and they saw it. Though Interforce was an integral part of the life of Drake's Bay they didn't often get to see it this up close and personal.

That was the whole point, wasn't it? You gathered everyone like her up and pointed them at the enemy. Home became an abstract, something agents kidded each other about over drinks when one of the regional differences surfaced.

"Well?" she prompted. "That second shot was for you, not for me. And they came up through the family quarters, not from the main hall."

"How do you know that, Jess?" Max got slowly up, looking shaken.

Jess tilted her head a little. "I used to live here. I know where that back door goes to, Uncle Max."

"No, I..." He lifted a hand. "I mean, how did you know they were shooting at us? Could have been the console, or the rest of your lot. Or maybe you were right and you were the target."

Reasonable. Jess nodded at him. "Because I saw his eyes, and the angle of inclination on the igniter in that blaster," she replied. "He couldn't see the techs from where he was standing, from his height." She looked over at the console. "Dev, get his scan please."

"Yes." Dev came around the console with her scanner and went to the other soldier, pulling the remains of the helmet aside and regarding the twisted look of terror frozen now on the man's face. The armor was hardened resin, meant to block blaster fire, and it had, the surface covered in char.

But she had seen Jess attack him, close in, using his own weapon to smash the armor directly and she understood why their side, her side, had an advantage in all this fighting. She captured the chip scan from his hand. No matter how armored and how much larger these soldiers seemed, Jess was stronger than they were and absolutely fearless.

"No," Jake said. He was sitting on the floor near the wall where he'd thrown himself on Jess's warning. "She's right it was us. They never would have sent just two if they'd known she was here." He let out a long, shaky breath. "Jess, we don't know."

Jess went over and crouched down next to him. "Don't know or won't tell?" she asked in a conversational tone.

"Don't know. It got too deep too fast," he admitted. "We thought we knew what we were doing, then it just went south and Jimmy stopped telling me stuff. Said it was too much."

Sounds in the hallway behind the watching guards brought Jess up to her feet, and both she and April moved toward the door, bringing weapons up.

The guards parted, though, and three big men in black overalls entered, carrying a limp figure in gray and blue. They shoved the figure forward and let it land on the ground, it's head cracked and covered in blood. "Think we found who let them in, Drake." The first of the three said. "His cred's on the back door out there. One of Jimmy's boys."

Jess studied the figure. "Thanks, Mike. Did you crack his head or did they?"

"Wasn't me, but I woulda," he responded promptly. "Sorry I missed all the drama, Drake. I was cleaning up the backyard."

"Jess."

Jess turned on hearing Dev's voice. "What's up?"

"I have access to this system now if you wish to see it," Dev said, once again seated behind the console. "I have started a dump to the carrier."

"Hey." Mike started forward. "What's she doin' there!"

Jess was already at Dev's side, sliding into the seat next to her. "She's cracking into the Bay's systems for me." She put her gun down and peered at the screen, then paused and sat up. "You know something? I'm an idiot."

Dev eyed her. "Excuse me?"

"I could have just logged in for ya," Jess muttered. "I have creds here." She glanced at Mike as he came over. "But hey, this made you look better." She reviewed the data coming into the screen. "Mike, this is Dev. My partner."

Mike braced his hands on the console. "So that's the bio alt."

"Yes. Hello," Dev responded.

"Mike's the head of security for the Bay, Dev." Jess flipped through the pages on Dev's tab. "He's supposed to make sure no one can get into their systems or anything else."

"Gee thanks, Drake," Mike said. "Since they locked me out of half the crap around here, I don't guarantee anything."

"Locked you out?"

"Said it was need to know, and I didn't need to know. Business stuff," he responded in an indignant tone. "Bullshit."

"I relayed the IDs through my rig," Doug said. "Got a squirt. They want to talk to you, Jess."

"Bet they do." Jess propped her chin up on her fist. "Dev, can you rig a relay here, so we can do vid?"

"I think so, yes." Dev put her hands on the control surface. "I'll have to import the crypto keys from the carrier, it will take a few minutes." She glanced at Jess. "Wouldn't you rather go there and do it?"

Jess drummed her fingertips on the console. "Would you rather I do that?" She asked, after a pause.

"Yes."

"Let's go." Jess stood up. "Everyone else stay here." She headed for the entry. "We'll be right back."

IT TOOK THEM almost fifteen minutes to get to the carrier. Jess kept getting stopped on the way, people in the overalls of the Bay going out of their way to greet her and get a word in.

By the time they opened the hatch Jess was making faces, and she immediately hit the door seal as soon as they cleared it. "Shitcakes."

Dev breathed a sigh of relief as she settled into her station, swinging the chair around to face Jess. "I'm glad we're here."

Jess sat down in her seat and regarded her. "You are?"

"Yes."

"Because you wanted to be alone with me?" Jess asked, hopefully.

Dev leaned her elbows on her knees. "Of course," she said. "But also, something I saw in the console was incorrect and I wanted to talk to you about it when the others weren't listening."

Jess sighed.

"And also, I did not want to import our keys into that system. I will get your communications arranged, and then perhaps we can discuss the incorrectness."

"Or we could just kiss each other," Jess said mournfully. "Because I've got a feeling I'm not going to enjoy the communication or your critique of my homestead's records keeping." She hoisted herself to her feet and racked her rifle to charge before she came over and dropped onto the jumpseat next to Dev.

Dev studied her. "It has been a difficult day."

"Yeah." Jess let her head rest against the pilot's console. "But this isn't making it shorter. Spool up the comms." She sighed again. "Let me get that over with anyway."

"Yes." Dev put her ear cup on and started up the

communications board, tuning in the frequencies to the satellite far overhead. She got sync, then sent out their ident. "BR270006 to Base Ten. Requested comm sync."

There was a moment's silence, then she saw the link come up. "Base Ten copy. This is centops. Sec comms request for Agent Drake."

"Yes, stand by please." Dev set it up, then glanced at Jess. "Do you wish this at your station?"

Jess debated just sitting where she was, then realized she'd need to authenticate with her eyeballs, and reluctantly got up and went back to her chair, settling into it and pulling the comms board toward her. "Gimme a sec."

"Please stand by," Dev repeated into her comms, waiting to transfer the request to Jess when she came live on the board.

Jess got her comms kit on. "Send it back." She waited, then adjusted the board as it lit, and the identiscan hit her. She blinked, then forced her eyes still as the pupil analyzer did its work, the screen pausing before resolving into the image of Bensen Alters. "Sir."

"Drake." He glanced around. "Are you alone?"

"Just me and Dev."

He paused and Jess wondered if he was going to ask her to make Dev leave, but then he cleared his throat and went on. "I hear you found the insertion."

"They found me," Jess said. "Though, I don't think they expected to find me since there were only two of them and they didn't look like they were figuring on dealing with anything other than my crap ass relatives."

He nodded. "They were a lower level team. Intel thinks they were there to interact with someone at the Bay."

"Probably my late brother James," Jess said. "Probably they were delivering something and realized something had gone south, and tried to erase evidence, as in, the rest of my family."

Alters studied her. "Do you know what they were delivering?" he asked, after a moment.

"Seed. Got a cavern full of all kinds of stuff I don't know the names of but Dev does, since they came from the same place."

Both of his eyebrows shot right up. "What?"

"You should come look. Got no idea where this is going to end. Apparently there's some kind of glowing rock here in the Bay that lets plants grow."

"What?" His voice lifted in both volume and tenor.

"So they were probably here to collect samples," Jess said.

"Because I'm betting no one around here had money to buy that stuff from topside and give it to my feckless sib."

"Drake, are you serious?"

Jess propped her chin on her fist. "Unfortunately, yes. I even ate a...what was that, Dev?"

"A pea."

"A pea," Jess repeated. "Sorry. Wasn't expecting to find this here."

Alters leaned back in his seat and looked at her, visibly dumbfounded. "All that chaos on the other side with blowing things up and you just have it naturally there?" His voice rose in amazement. "Drake, are you kidding me?"

Jess grimaced, spreading her hands in a resigned shrug.

"Holy shit. We're on our way." He signed off, and the screen went blank

Jess exhaled, letting her forehead bang against the console. "Crap."

Dev decided she thought Jess needed some hot tea and comfort more than she needed to hear about the incorrectness she'd found. So she quietly assembled a cup and brought it over to her, setting it on the console.

Jess looked up and studied her, the mist of steam from the tea rising between them. "I didn't expect to find something world changing here, Dev."

"Is that what this is?" Dev perched on the edge of the weapons console. "Because they could grow plants?"

"Sure. That's what the other side was trying to do when we blew everyone up."

"No, I know...but what if that's the only place it can happen? There's something special in the rocks, isn't there?"

Jess shook her head. "Have no idea. The research team from the base'll tell us." She picked up the cup and sipped from the tea. "Thanks for the drink."

"You seemed in discomfort," Dev said. "And it's been a long day."

"And it's not over, and we've got to go to the council tomorrow," Jess groused. "If we're lucky we've got an hour to chill before the goons get here."

Dev stood up. "Should I prepare the bed area in this vehicle? We could get some rest. I think if you go back to the other space, you won't get any."

Jess thought about all the people back in the family chambers with those dead enemy, and April randomly pointing guns at them, and smiled. "Y'know, that's not a bad idea, Devvie." She stood up and ruffled Dev's hair. "But first off, tell me what you saw in the rig."

Dev went and got her scanner and brought it back over. "It was this." She displayed something on it and turned it around so Jess could see it. "These traces. I think they..." She paused, as Jess grabbed the scanner from her and peered at it. "They appear to be from the other side."

"They are," Jess said. "That was a full data link."

"Yes," Dev said. "I didn't want to import our keys there."

Jess handed back the scanner, then leaned over and gave her a kiss on the lips. "You're such a rock star. I'll have the team take that apart when they get here. No telling what they sucked down because of that idiot."

Dev smiled in quiet contentment. That had been an excellent result. "I am going to relay that to Doug, so they don't do anything unfortunate while we are gone." She took the scanner back to her station and sat down, resuming her ear cup.

Jess watched her, then picked up her tea and settled back in her console chair, rocking it back and allowing her body to fully relax as she let her head rest against the padded surface. The color had leeched back into her vision, and she felt calm, able to eject the buzz from the fight as she considered the situation they were in.

So many possible vectors. So many possibilities. She tried to remember if she'd spent any time in that cavern, and found nothing in her memory about it. So was it new? Something they'd found recently?

And what were those rocks? Jess studied the roof of the carrier. She didn't remember seeing any glowing rocks growing up there. She'd been in enough underwater caverns to know.

So where had they come from?

Unexpectedly, hands touched her shoulders and started a warm, steady kneading pressure, and she looked up to see Dev looking down at her with a gentle smile.

To hell with it. "Let's get that bunk set up," Jess said. "Probably be the only nice thing to happen to me for the rest of the night. "

Chapter Four

IT WAS LATE, and they were back in the cavern, this time with a dozen other people in Interforce uniforms, including Bensen Alters.

Jess was getting tired and bored, having answered the same questions over and over again since the team arrived. It was long after midwatch, and she'd sent April, Doug and Dev to bed, and her family as well now that Interforce security was guarding the halls.

"Drake," Alters said. "This is unbelievable."

Jess sighed.

The commander laughed shortly and gave her a slap on the arm. "I mean it. We're going to take some samples, and send it up to Juneau for them to analyze. I talked to HQ about twenty minutes ago and they're having a fit."

"I bet," Jess said. "Maybe it'll encourage legal to get my ass out of here because I'm going to be the biggest target this side of a shrimp harvest once word gets around." She folded her arms over her chest and frowned.

"Drake, do you understand what this means?"

Jess eyed him. "As in, do I get it that there are plants growing here? Sure. What if this is the only cave on the planet it'll do this in? So we've got a cool cavern. Extra cred when we sell it to the ritzy boys, or finally a decent salad in the mess."

Alters pursed his lips and regarded the glowing ceiling of the cave. "Bet some of the lab boys can figure it out," he said. "Feels a little warm." He held his hand out. "Maybe I'm imagining it...what did you say you ate in here?"

Jess steered him over to the peas and plucked one off a stalk, splitting it open as she remembered Dev doing. She presented him with the round balls. "Peas. Dev knew all about 'em."

Gingerly, he took one and put it in his mouth, chewing it with a thoughtful expression. "Not bad. So what's the temp here? Your family up in arms?"

"With us here? No. Family's scared shitless. Residents are clapping behind their back. There's a lot of hardliners here who didn't much care for Jimmy doing a deal with the other side."

Alters took another pea, and strolled along the corridor motioning to her to follow him. When they had progressed to the other end, away from the rest of the busily scanning team, he paused. "We sure that's what happened?"

Jess inspected a section where a bushlike plant had round, fuzzy objects on it. "What else would it be?" She reached out and took hold of a large sphere, tugged it off the stem, and brought it to her nose to sniff it.

"With the attack? We know they're involved." Alters watched her with interest. "But are they the instigators, or did they just hear about it and do what we'd have done?"

Finding the scent sort of nice, she bit into it, surprised to find it juicy and sweet inside. "Oh." She licked her lips and reached out without looking, pulled off another one and handed it to him. "Better than those peas."

Agreeably, he took it and bit into it.

"I'm wondering myself. I just can't make myself believe Jimmy solicited them," Jess admitted. "Even before the shares transitioned, he knew better."

"Huh." He examined the sphere. "That's good." He looked around. "People here we already talked to were pissed off because they humped a lot getting this place setup, then didn't get any of the results."

"Yeah."

"You can always depend on personal envy. They think your brother was a shithead. Most of them are glad you offed him," Alters said. "We just need to find out who his contact was."

Jess had sensed that. The undercurrent of glee that greeted her on her return and the intense concentration on them in the mess hall was clear. The essential "they" that was the collective feeling of the stakehold had been against this.

If they hadn't found the cavern, they'd have been led to it. Jess understood now what the undercurrent was and why she and her team had been given the unspoken welcome. "Yeah." She nibbled the round thing. "Just stings."

"Unexpected, here," Alters said. "That whole cock up with you and the shares, though, is going to work to our advantage."

Jess sighed.

"Maybe to your advantage, too, Drake," he said. "I had an idea on the way over. We'll put a force here, you in charge of it. Going to have to defend this place until we figure out what the end game is."

Jess drew breath to protest, then paused.

Alters smiled, seeing it. "You're learning. Even politics can be strategic, Drake. It's not all just blowing things up."

DEV WAS CURLED up in her hammock, the room darkened around her save the glow from her scanner screen. She was sorting and consolidating all the data she'd gathered, putting it into segments and transferring it to the greater storage of the carrier.

The hammock was comfortable but she was halfway wishing they were still in their space, wanting the comfort of the familiar surroundings and wishing Jess were there, to make this area seem more correct.

The people here were becoming more curious about her. She'd found them going out of their way to make eye contact, not at all easy since they were tall as Jess was and she wasn't. The man Chris had brought over some other techs to talk to her, and that had worked out all right, she thought.

The finding of the plants had shocked and distressed her. She had the seed lots and there was no question that they'd come from the storage lockers on the bio station, a quick search of her database in the Citadel had confirmed it, but the transfer had happened before she'd even been sent downworld.

She drummed her fingers on the sides of the scanner. Would Doctor Dan know how they'd been sent? Who they'd been sent to? She grimaced in some discomfort. Would Doctor Dan have been involved?

After all he knew this place. Had been here. Had seemed silently delighted over the present Jess had given him that had come from here, the shirt he'd taken back to station with him.

It made sense that he might be interested in something that involved this location, the place both Jess and her father had come from.

But nowhere in all the data could she find his details, so that was a comfort at least and all the work kept her from thinking about what Jess had said, about going back to station.

Her stomach clenched even thinking about that.

She was afraid they would have to, that this trail of the seeds would lead them there, and Jess would want to find out how they'd gotten to her home place. And where Jess went, she would go.

But she didn't want to.

The door opened, but her scanner had identified the body approaching minutes ago, and she looked up to find Jess looking back at her as she came over and put her hands on the hammock Dev was curled up in. "Everything correct?"

"No." Jess regarded her. "Everything is crap in a basket. Got room in that hammock for me?"

"DANIEL?"

Dan Kurok turned to find Randall Doss standing there, apparently having called his name more than once. "Yes, Randall?"

They couldn't be more different men in appearance. Doss, the director of the science station was tall and a little rounded, with a large, moon shaped head and dark, curly hair in perpetual disarray. He wore glasses and usually had an expression of slight bewilderment on his face.

A scientist risen above the work, now mostly concerned with pacifying both those above and below him.

Kurok, his chief genetic scientist, was a head shorter, with a compact body and thick blond hair sprinkled with silver gray and a gently twinkling pair of green eyes that nevertheless held a sharpness the director's brown ones didn't.

"It's time for the meeting," Doss said. "Are you sure you're ready for it?"

"Yes," Kurok said, putting his hands in the pouch pocket of the woven outershirt he was wearing. "More than ready, Randall. Come along." He eased around the taller man and headed for the conference space on the uppermost level of the space station.

The executive level, where the most senior members of the station had their offices, and also spaces available to meet with guests and notables.

It was one of these that they went to, a room made from curved clear flexible plas, shielded from the shifting path of the sun. It contained an oval table and comfortable chairs and there was a surface on the outside wall that could be darkened for projection.

There were six people inside, five men and one woman, all dressed in space jumpsuits. All of them shifted and swiveled in their chairs as Doss and Kurok entered, and the casual chatter trailed off.

"Hello, everyone." Doss went to the head of the table and took a seat. Kurok sat down at the far end facing him, leaning back with his hands still tucked inside his pocket. "Thank you all for coming here today, I appreciate the promptness."

"Well, Randall, hope you have good news for us," the man seated next to him said. "We've been waiting a long time for the two of you. We're busy people, you know."

"Us, too," Kurok said.

Doss looked uncomfortable. "Well, Charles, you know this sort of thing takes time sometimes. It's a new process."

"So you keep telling us," the woman said. "None of us wants to wait eighteen years for this project to be profitable. So what's the story?"

Doss cleared his throat. "Daniel?"

The people in the room turned to face Kurok. He blinked mildly back at them, the wash of deflected and filtered sunlight splashing across his chest. "Certainly, we have a new schema that will be the basis of a set that is currently about to go into production, pending one last test."

"Another delay?" The woman sighed. "For crying out loud, Doctor Kurok."

"Not so much. I want the prototype to come in so I can do a synapse compare," Kurok said. "So that has been requested. Always better to tweak before we commit the eggs than after."

"So you're bringing the demo unit back up here?" Charles Tennit asked, propping his head up on his fist. "I thought it was assigned."

"She is," Kurok replied. "I've asked the contractor to release her back to me for a few days. With some luck her natural born partner will accompany her, and I can get a full set of metrics."

"Is that important, or necessary?" Charles asked, with a touch of impatience. "We had nothing to do with who it's assigned to."

Kurok looked at him in silence, until he looked away, a faint flush appearing on his face. "Have any of you ever met an Interforce agent?" he asked. "Since this contract directly affects them, maybe you should before making nonsensical statements like that."

They looked a little horrified and shifted in their seats. "We've heard all we need to about them," Charles said, stiffly.

"And then?" the woman asked. "After you make these tests, Daniel?"

"And then, Auralia, I can release the set. We already have the gel base set up to receive them."

She nodded, pursing her lips, their surface painted a permanent coral pink. "A few more days can't change the commit, of course," she said. "Sorry, Daniel. There's been a lot of interest over this advance, and not just from Interforce."

"I know." Kurok tilted his head a trifle. "But what you really want to know is, can I take the advances I did with Dev and put them into currently grown sets to get money for them before the new set matures."

"Yes," the woman said. "I don't want to wait eighteen years for results. You tweaked this one in a few weeks, why not others?"

"Not that easy. Dev was different..."

The woman rolled her eyes, and Charles slapped his hand on the table.

"She's an experimental unit. NM Dev. New Model, Developmental," Kurok said, with a touch of sharpness in his voice. "Her synaptic structure is different. That was the whole damn point."

Charles stood up and started pacing. "How different could it be, Daniel?" he asked. "What changes did you make to make her so successful a unit?" He leaned on the table and stared down at Kurok. "Or is the truth you really can't duplicate it, and it's a fluke?"

Unruffled, Kurok laced his fingers together and produced a faint smile. "It's true that Dev succeeded at a higher level than originally anticipated, and it's also true I'd never tried that complex a design before. But relax, Charles, I know why she ended up as advanced as she did, and yes, I can duplicate that."

"What did you change, Daniel?" Auralia asked, leaning toward him.

"If I start quoting nucleus counts you all will be asleep in a heartbeat." He smiled at her. "You know this is a highly technical science."

A subterfuge of course. Kurok knew exactly what it was he'd changed but saw no advantage to anyone if he revealed it to these financially focused individuals in terms they could understand.

Yet.

"We just don't know if we can divert an existing set," Doss said from the other end of the table. "We're trying some things. That's all we can say."

"Not good enough, Randall." Charles turned and stared at him. "We need profits. We're not making enough on the sets you have in production now." He stood up and spread his hands out. "This station's expensive."

"Charles, please chill out," another of the men said. "This was a freak chance that worked. Don't harass them because of that."

Charles rounded on him. "Interforce wants this now, not in twenty years. It was a success, Steven. Yes, awesome. Now they want more." He glanced at Kurok. "And word's out to more than them."

"Are you all done pontificating?" Kurok asked, regarding the curved ceiling. "I have work to do that you all constantly tell me is both expensive and urgent."

Doss sighed. "Daniel."

"C'mon." Charles waved at the rest of them. "We're getting nothing as usual. Let's go see what lies we can come up with for the investors in this place."

They all left, leaving Kurok and Doss alone in the room, the door shutting behind them with a sucking hiss.

"Daniel, must you antagonize them? They're the board's representatives. You don't make things any easier."

Kurok got up and went to the outer wall and looked outside. The turning of the station brought the stars into view and he regarded the velvety black of space. "It's not my job to make things easy, Randall," he said. "I'm a scientist, not a politician. You know that."

Doss sighed again. "When the unit comes here, will you be able to do something to duplicate the success? Will it help?"

"She," Kurok said. "When Dev comes here, I might get some hints from how she integrated that could give me some ideas to tweak some other sets. Maybe." He turned to look at Doss. "If she lets me look."

Doss stared at him. "What do you mean by that, Daniel?"

He shrugged and smiled. "She's got a mind of her own. She's lived independently since she left here and I don't really know how that's all going to play out when she gets here. I'll ask her. There's nothing that says she'll agree."

"Daniel!" Doss looked almost horrified. "But she's a bio alt. We control her. She's a construct! What are you saying?"

Kurok turned again to face the stars. "I'm saying these changes I did that make this new model so valuable for you all might end up someplace we didn't expect, that's all Randall." His breath fogged against the surface. "They are human beings."

"Legally they aren't."

"Scientifically they are." Kurok turned and leaned his back against the outer wall, something almost no one else on station would do. The clear surface unsettled them, like they were perched on the edge of a drop.

But then, Kurok had spent more time downside than most, doing things that would horrify his colleagues if they knew. "And as a scientist, you know as well as I do that's what really matters."

"Well of course that's true." The director came over to him. "Daniel, this could be so important for us. Please don't antagonize the board. Please? They don't like it."

Kurok smiled unexpectedly, a twinkle appearing in his eyes that wasn't all humor. "Of course they don't. But I do. And the truth is they're dependent on me to replicate this." He started for the door. "So they better chill out."

Doss watched him leave, shaking his head and retreating back to the front of the room to get a cup of tea.

DEV WALKED QUIETLY through the doorway into the landing bay, producing brief smiles for the people inside who looked up to watch her pass.

They seemed more curious than unfriendly, not bothering to hide their stares. She detected no danger from them, which was a little surprising given that Jess told her how much her kind was disliked here.

She wondered if it was the fact that she had her collar covered that made them less incorrect. After all, with her jumpsuit on, there was no obvious difference between her and anyone else in the cavern.

She triggered the unlock for the hatch and watched it open then made her way back to the pilot's station. She sat down in her station and started up the flight sequence. She glanced out the window and saw Jess's tall figure enter from the hallway.

"Hey," Jess said.

She regarded Jess in silence for a moment. "You look very attractive in that clothing."

In the act of drawing a breath, Jess paused, one eyebrow shifting upward. "I do?"

Dev nodded.

Jess glanced down at herself. Instead of her usual black jumpsuit, she'd put on a thickly woven pullover in Drake's Bay colors and a pair of sharkskin pants tucked into her regulation boots. "They told me not to freak out the civ council more than I had to," she said. "So I found this in a drawer in one of the store rooms."

"I like the colors," Dev said, swiveling around in her seat and preparing the carrier for flight

Comms crackled. "Tac two to Tac one."

Jess pushed her comm link into place. "Tac one. Go ahead."

April and Doug were on patrol outside, searching for the

downed mini transport. "Tac one, target spotted, endit."

"Stand by we'll join you." Jess got her restraints in place. "Let's fly, Dev. We'll check out what the kids found first and then head over to the meeting." She settled back as she felt the carrier shift under her, watching the forward view in her screens as Dev prepared to take them out.

She felt a bit uneasy with all the change and at the prospect of staying here at the Bay for a while. It felt like things were slipping away from her, and though Alters had confidently sold her on commanding the small force he ordered up, she wasn't sure how that all was going to turn out.

She wasn't sure she was that kind of leader, outside being responsible for herself and Dev, or maybe just the kids.

A lot of other agents were going to get a chance to move ahead at base now. Jess scowled. Just when things were going really good for her, too.

"Jess?"

"Mmm?" Jess looked up as they exited the cavern and into free air, a morning of only drifting mist lacking a storm for a change. The wind was only thrumming gently against the hull as Dev banked around and started for the outer edge of the half circle Bay.

"I can stay here with you, correct?" Dev asked, after she finished the maneuver. "You said you were not going back to the Citadel."

Jess went still for a moment, her mind racing, going over what Alters had told her. What had he said? He was sending a force, she'd be in charge. Had he inferred anything at all about Dev? That he'd want her to go back to the base with him?

The sudden gut clench relaxed as she replayed the conversation and confirmed to herself that nothing had been said about Dev, one way or the other.

"Yes," she said finally, aware of how stiff Dev's body had gotten. "You're my partner. That didn't change just because they want me to be a boof head here for a while. And he didn't mention anything again about us going topside."

"Excellent," Dev said. "I was worried about that this morning."

That made Jess smile. "That why you skipped breakfast?"

Dev glanced in the reflector, a sheepish expression on her face. "Yes."

Jess put her hands behind her head. "I'll make it up to you when we get back. Don't worry, Dev. You ain't going nowhere. You're mine."

That was excellent. Dev got her course set in and maneuvered through the pass, spotting Doug's carrier on the horizon. "There they are." She boosted a little, increasing their speed as they skimmed over the rocky ground.

It was rough, and wet, and there were layers of moss spreading on either side of the blast area that they'd fired the night before. There were small figures out there working, and she was low enough to see them stop and look up as the carrier went over. "What are they doing?"

"Scraping lichen." Jess glanced into the screen. "Something I never wanted to end up doing, tell you that. It's hard work."

Dev considered that. "Isn't what we do hard?"

"Different kind of hard," Jess said. "That's hard, and boring, and potentially death making." She paused thoughtfully. "Well, maybe it is a little like our jobs," she admitted, with a wry smile. "Not so much boring I hope."

"With you I never feel bored at all," Dev reassured her. "No matter what we're doing."

Jess grinned to herself. "Aww thanks, Devvie. Back atcha."

Dev slowed the forward momentum as they came in range of the other carrier. Doug backed off so they could see what the rookies found. There was a small outcropping of rock, and just past that, nestled behind the ridge, was a compact craft.

She scanned it warily, one hand on the throttles in case the object decided to react to the energy sweep. "This is a model 245B, standard small transport," Dev said.

"Yeah." Jess had the specs on her console. "New."

Dev backed and went sideways around the craft, giving Jess a 360-degree view. The transport had no energy readback, naturally, since it was supposed to be stealthed and invisible to common land based searchers.

But not to airborne ones, and certainly not from Interforce craft. Jess checked the outline. "You getting anything from it?" she asked. "Get closer."

"No, nothing." Dev cautiously lowered the carrier, watching her scanner intently. The transport was blended into the rock much like theirs would have been and as she got closer, she saw the energy return spike and abruptly boosted them back up, hitting the jets hard.

Jess grabbed her restraints as they lifted. "What was that fo— oh crap."

"Ware!" April's voice came through the tie line, urgent and sharp, and Jess felt the carrier jolt into motion, the mains cutting in and driving them up between the ridges toward the sky a moment before a blast hit them on their lower shields and drove them farther and faster upward.

"The craft exploded," Dev explained somewhat unnecessarily, since the outer screens were still awash with energy flare. "It sensed this vehicle, I think."

"Oh yeah." Jess was recording everything, watching the shield power and damping the return. "Anything left?"

Dev arched around and started down again, seeing the visual of the scorched rock and shattered bits scattered now over the ground. Where the transport had been was mostly rubble, and a few shards of twisted metal flung across the ridge. "I don't think so."

Doug's voice came through the comms. "Bugger blew up! Reminded me of those guys who were chasing us from the Pole."

Jess shook her head. "No. I've seen these do that. They're programmed not to be found or searched, like ours are. If someone came near this thing and it knew it was one of them it would have blown up, too."

Dev glanced at her in the reflector. "With us in it?" she asked. "That might be suboptimal."

Jess chuckled. "No." She finished her scanning. "Well, no sense in hanging around here. You two want to land and see if there's anything to be found? We're heading for the council."

"Will do," April responded. "You don't want an escort?"

Jess paused, then exhaled. "They asked me not to cause a ruckus. It's not that far. If we need backup, I'll call. Till then watch everything."

"Got it." April clicked off.

Jess settled back in her seat. "Okay, Dev. Let's go."

Dev recalibrated the route and turned the carrier in an arc, boosting up to rise past the mountain ridge that housed Drake's Bay and continued further inland.

Ahead of her the ground was craggy and uneven, bare mountains with valleys between them mostly filled with rock rubble, and sometimes water.

It seemed vast and unfriendly. "Do people live here, Jess?"

"Define live." Jess watched the screens. "Nothing really to live on. Most of the scavengers live on the coast, picking up shore leavings that the processing center leaves behind. Or they hide in the hills and try to pick up scraps from places like the Bay."

"That sounds unpleasant."

"It is," Jess said. "When I was going to bust out, I'd have

ended up in one of the bunkers near the shore collecting seaweed and shellfish for the processing center. I might have gotten decent bunk room at the Bay though, since I am a Drake."

"I see."

Jess regarded the ceiling for a moment in silence. "Actually given what my dad did, I'd have gotten better than that, though I didn't know it at the time. Woulda been a shocker for everyone, especially me." She sighed. "Glad it worked out like it did though. I got to meet you." She looked up to see Dev watching her in the reflector, a small, delighted smile on her face.

Jess felt a little warm spot inside her seeing that. She winked at the reflection and saw Dev shift her attention somewhat guiltily back to the controls and suddenly had to wonder if spending some time at the Bay with Dev wasn't going to end up being kind of okay.

Since she didn't have a choice anyway, right? Find a bright spot? Should she get them some better digs?

Dev interrupted her musing, having spotted a line of moving figures far ahead of them. "Oh, Jess, look!"

Jess bounded up next to her and knelt on the jumpseat, peering out the window. "Nomads," she said. "Big caravan of em."

"Like April?"

Jess nodded. "They travel between the homesteads, trading. They pick up stuff in Quebec, trade it in the Bay, then they move off to the next place. I remember liking them when I was small. They usually had candy." Her eyes twinkled a little, and she got up and went back to her station, starting a capture.

Dev magnified the view, examining the moving line. There were big, square vehicles being pulled by smaller ones, and walking people surrounding them. Most had sticks, all were wrapped in layers of fabric.

The carrier caught up rapidly to them, and she saw the ones in the back turn to look at them, then slowly the whole train stopped and watched as they overflew it.

"Got the shields on, Devvie?"

Dev glanced back. "Yes, but do you think they will try to injure us?" She sounded surprised. "We haven't done anything to them."

"Nomads are only friends to nomads. The rest of us are marks." Jess nudged one of the controls on her board and took a scan. "They'll steal you blind if they can. We had to put a watch on them every time they stopped at the Bay."

Dev filed that away for future knowledge. "But April seems pleasant."

Jess chuckled. "Only you would consider a nomad ops agent pleasant, my friend." She saw nothing else in the scan to concern her and let her head rest against the chair as she closed her eyes. "She's nice to me because she figures I'm her ticket to elevation. She's nice to you because she knows I'll wipe the floor with her if she isn't."

"Would you?"

"Absolutely."

Dev didn't think so. Not that Jess wouldn't make someone hurt if she thought it was necessary, but that April only acted in a pleasant way because she was forced to. She thought April liked Jess and interacted with them because she enjoyed it.

But there was no sense in being contradictory. It was already shaping up to be a somewhat incorrect day.

THE COUNCIL WAS held in the remains of an old stone construct, perched on a ridge amidst the rubble and destruction of what was once a city where people lived, back when there were people and cities.

As they approached, Dev slowed the carrier, pitching it forward just a little so she could see what they were flying over.

The pattern of the city could still be seen. Roads and buildings, some collapsed into bits, others partially standing, filled the horizon.

In some of the buildings, she could see signs of life. Bits of cloth fluttering in the wind and motion in and out of doorless doorways. "What happened here, Jess?"

"Huh?" Jess opened one eye and peered through the window. "Oh. Same thing that happened everywhere. Everyone croaked. Or left and went to the coast."

"But there are people there."

"Uh huh," Jess said. "Trade for some scraps from the nomads, trap a bird now and then. Some of them sitting on old caches of freeze drieds. When they run out they'll croak, too." She shifted a little. "Some of them scrape up moss and lichen from the rocks, eat that, and bugs. Usually they show up when council's due, and beg."

That sounded very incorrect. Dev grimaced a little as she maneuvered. They were heading up a short slope to the ridge where she could see flyers parked and the far off moving dots of people at the entrance.

"That used to be a bank," Jess said. "You know what that is?"

"Yes." Dev slowed again and started studying the ground for sufficient space to land. "I had that in basic history."

"At the end, it was just digital bits. But they used to build these huge vaults to make everyone believe they were permanent and untouchable. Morons," Jess said. "But at least they built them from stuff that wouldn't degrade."

And, in fact, the building they were heading for did seem complete. It had steps leading up from the rubbly ground that appeared functional, and behind the overhang she saw two doors flung wide open.

Even with the bottom of the steps was open ground. "Put it down over there," Jess said. "Try not to squash anything. Those flyers are expensive."

"Yes." Dev located a flat area past where the flyers were parked and aimed for it. It was not quite even, but the carrier landing systems could handle that and she cut the mains as they drifted over, aware there were figures standing outside staring at them.

Jess chuckled. "Bet most of them never saw one of these close up before."

The carrier landing jets fired as Dev set them gently down, sending up a cloud of steam as the jets heated the ground water. She extended the skids and felt them level underneath them with a gentle rock. "So, what occurs here now?" she asked, securing the engines.

Jess unhooked her restraints and stood up. "Have no clue. Every quarter year all the stakeholders meet up and talk about crap. I've got word from Interforce they suspended the rule that keeps us from being stakeholders, and that's going to piss them all off, but beyond that I'm not sure what's going to happen."

"I see. "

"Stakeholders are not supposed to bring outsiders but screw it. You're coming with me," Jess said. "So put your snazzy jacket on and let's go cause a riot."

Dev was pleased at being included but not so much about being in a riot, which according to her programming, was both uncomfortable and possibly dangerous. Nevertheless, she shut down the carrier and retrieved her portable scanner and outer garb and joined Jess at the hatch.

Jess stowed a hand blaster in her belt at the small of her back and pulled the woven fabric over it to make it unobtrusive. Then she brushed the sleeves down and hit the hatch, pausing to let the ramp unfold before she led them both out and onto the rocky ground.

Dev realized as she stepped on it that it wasn't natural rock, but something like the ground inside the landing bays. "This is made stone," she said.

"Concrete," Jess said. She put her hands in the pockets of her pullover and started across the landing space, already aware that they were collecting attention fast. "C'mon."

A group of people was standing at the top of the stairs leading into the old stone building. All of them half turned to watch the two Interforce operatives approach.

They walked past the flyers. Figures crouched on the lee side of them watched them pass, staring at them intently.

"Pilots." Jess strolled along ignoring all of them. They got close enough to see the faces of the people on the steps, and she grinned a little, understanding the looks of anger there.

Being the senior stakeholder of a homestead was a big deal. There were only, probably, two dozen of them scattered up and down the eastern coast, all of them under the nominal protection now of Base Ten.

Some were larger, some smaller, but all of them were centers of humanity, and each of the stakeholders were the ones who controlled the commerce between them. Were responsible for collecting valuable items, running fishing boats, making deals with nomads, whatever it took to take control of resources to feed their residents and gain cred.

Drake's Bay was one of the largest homesteads, and being right on the coast, had access to resources some of the others didn't. Jess understood that her family had a relatively privileged existence and were more comfortable than many.

Died more often than most in the cause, of course, but still. Though her own life would have been one of hard labor up until she'd grown into the shares system if she hadn't gone for Interforce.

People worked hard at the Bay. Everyone got something out of it, housing, food, med if they needed it, but the people who got the most were Drakes. The shares were all tied to the family, passed down between the generations hopefully to those who had the best chance of keeping things quo.

But in the family, everyone wanted to be—the Drake. The one who made the decisions. When there wasn't a clear senior stakeholder, it went by committee, so at least some of the family got to rule the roost. There wasn't a contingency for what had happened with her.

Interforce took you. You were gone. No participation in the stakehold until you retired and went civ. After you stopped getting paid by them, and supported by them, when you were fully back in the fold and could be expected to make decisions based on what was best for the family without a conflict of interest.

Justin made them uneasy. He'd brought an outsider viewpoint back with him, and Jess remembered the fights behind those kitchen doors when she'd made her brief visits after he'd been to council and pissed everyone off.

Hadn't played the game with them, hadn't been a deal maker, hadn't backed down from any of them in the big arguments, because after all, he was not only the Drake, but an inactive ops agent.

Everyone knew that even retired, Justin had that edge and that temper, and it usually only took one of those flat looks to end almost any fight.

Jess chuckled without much humor.

"Are you going to tell these people about the plants?" Dev asked, suddenly. "My research indicated this meeting involves commerce."

"No," Jess said. "They told me not to say anything."

They reached the bottom of the steps and started up them, as a thin, brassy bell rang. The people on the steps above them turned and started to move inside, a few lingering at the entry until they reached the top and joined them.

The largest of these stood squarely in their path and obviously meant to intercept them. He was tall and broad shouldered, with a thick beard and tawny colored hair pulled back into a knot at his neck. "Drake?"

Jess paused and regarded him, their eyes on a level. "That would be me, yes."

"Dan Furstan, Niagara Holding," he said. "What's the deal at the Bay? We've heard all kinds of stories."

Jess held up a portable comp chit. "I'd rather only go through this once," she said, but in a mild tone. Niagara was one of the stakeholds they were relatively friendly with, according to the brief, crabbed notes she'd dug up. "But it's good to meet you."

That got a tiny, wry smile from him. "Justin was a friend." He turned aside to let them walk on. "And he didn't have many."

"No." Jess returned the smile. "We never do." She glanced to the side. "This is my tech, Dev."

Dan studied the slight figure standing next to Jess. "Not sure she's welcome."

"Not sure I care."

"You're definitely Justin's get." His smile broadened a little. "Going to be an interesting council for a change."

DEV SPENT SOME time examining the chamber, as she perched on a seat next to the bigger one Jess was sitting on.

The room was filling up with people, who were spread out across the large, round space that was empty in the middle, and surrounded by chairs separated by dusty dividers that went all around the perimeter.

It seemed that each space was allocated to a stakehold, and they had carvings in them in the stone that indicated which one belonged to which homestead. The one they were in had the image of the snake like thing she recognized from Drake's Bay. It had space enough in it for about a dozen people, with seats of various sizes and construction.

The other sections were the same, and all of them were more full of people than theirs was. Overhead there was a dome. In the dome the clear surface let in outside light.

It was quite attractive. The railings around them were the same substance as the table in Jess's kitchen and they felt warm to the touch. The chairs were also the same, but in the other areas some were covered in a thick covering. "Jess..."

"Those are bearskin, yes," Jess answered as though reading her mind. "Sorry about that."

Now, how did Jess know she was going to ask about it? Dev peered at her with interest. Could Jess read her mind? "I understand the need to use all resources, Jess. I am wearing the skin of an animal myself."

Jess looked at her. "So you don't think they're cute anymore?"

"I did not say that."

Jess chuckled. "It's a sign you've got cred," she said. "Those things cost like crazy." She stretched her legs out and leaned her elbows on the chair arms that were bare of any fuzzy substance. "Never got much traction at the Bay."

"Because the animals are attractive?"

Jess tilted her head a little. "Boats bring in the skins sometimes. I think the idea was, you sold it for hard cred, you didn't keep it to use."

"I see."

"Sorry about that, Devvie." Jess reached over and patted her on the leg. "Having seen those cubs, I couldn't use one now either."

Across from them was a section with rather more people than the rest of them. They filled the space completely and took up all the seats.

Jess nodded at them. "Quebec City. They're the biggest group in council. Only major town on this side of Atlantia."

Dev studied the group with interest, since that was one of the few places she'd been to. The people who filled the section were all dressed in colorful garments and made a show of dusting off the chairs before they sat down.

"Maybe we can get started now," Jess said. "I think that was the last bunch they were waiting for." She straightened up a little. "Looks like they're bringing around some drinks."

Without being asked, Dev scanned the tray, running the results through her biologic analyzer. "Jess, that is leaf tea." She paused as the man offering the beverage stopped in front of them, and Jess stood up to retrieve two cups.

The man looked at the two of them, then at the cups. "Council members only," he said gruffly.

Jess smiled. "Going to take it away from me?"

"We have rules here." He returned her stare boldly. "Everyone follows them, even Drakes."

Jess turned and handed a cup to Dev, then she turned back to face him. "Ever had an active Interforce ops agent be a council member?" She watched him frown. "Here's a clue. We come as a pair. We put our lives on the line for you rockscrapers every day. Don't grudge someone I regard as family a cup of damned tea."

Her voice was quiet, but serious, and lacked its usual mocking tone. After a brief moment, he nodded and turned away to take his tray on down the line.

Jess resumed her seat, inspecting her cup with a suspicious sniff. "Did you mean this is real, old timey tea?"

"Yes." Dev took a sip of it. "I'm sorry if my being here is incorrect and is causing discomfort."

"I'm not." Jess took a swallow of the beverage and licked her lips thoughtfully. "It's okay. I think I like sea grape better."

"Me too," Dev said. "I have had leaf tea before but it was a different kind than this."

"Wants some honey in it." Jess glanced around the chamber,

with a slightly mocking smile, their almost empty section now almost awkwardly obvious. "Rest of them bring guards, and spongers. They shouldn't say a word about me bringing you."

A silver haired woman in a lined over-tunic went to the middle of the open space and held up a little device, moving it and producing a tinkling tone. "To order."

Comp had very little information on the council, so Dev sharpened her attention, ready to learn something new. She saw some of the others watching Jess, and in the section next to them the man who had spoken to Jess was laughing at something.

The silver haired woman put the device down on the wooden podium she was standing next to and put her hands on top of it. "Eastern Seaboard council, fourth quarter, year three hundred fifty-two."

Jess put her tea down on the small table at the edge of their section and sat up.

The woman looked directly at her. "First order of business, let's get this straightened out. I'm told there's a change of stakeholder at Drake's Bay?"

"No bullshit. I like it." Jess got up, went to the rail, put her hand on it and vaulted over. The round section in the middle was a body length down and she landed lightly, walking over to the podium and extending her hand with the comp chip in it. "Jesslyn Drake."

The woman took the chip gingerly. Then she walked over to an old console in the center of the back of the circle and inserted it.

One of the men in a section stood up and faced her. "You're active Interforce. Not allowed by reg."

Jess stood with her hands folded in front of her and shrugged slightly. "They're our regs. We can change them."

A low murmur went up around the circle. Dev watched everyone carefully and kept her scanner tuned for energy flares.

"Not fair, Drake," the man objected. "You've got an elected stakeholder there."

She smiled. "Not anymore. Jimmy's no longer with us." She folded her arms over her chest, rotating a little to scan the circle. "He made one bad deal too many."

The woman behind the console looked up and cleared her throat. "This seems in order." She sounded profoundly surprised. "You have the legitimate number of shares."

"Dad was a stickler for details," Jess said. "That was Justin Drake. He coded his shares to my civ profile."

The woman looked at the screen. "They were transferred. I see that."

"She's Interforce," the man said. "Active duty!"

"They, as in Interforce, have released the sanction. It's their sanction, not ours," the woman told him, sounding even more surprised. "Authorized by the directorate in Pichu." She looked back at the records. "Their intent is for Agent Drake to remain in control of the stakehold."

A lot of voices now rose. Dev set her device to record them, in case Jess wanted to inspect them later. Jess returned to the railing, then leaped up and grabbed it, hauling herself up and over it and back into the chair she'd started from in an easy motion.

"These individuals are not pleased," Dev said.

Jess folded her hands over her stomach and watched the rest of the room stand and mill around in their sections talking loudly, fully aware that no amount of discussion could actually change the facts she'd just recorded.

They couldn't vote her out, couldn't lodge a protest, couldn't even legally draw a suit about it, and any of them who might want to do something more direct and physical had the simple fact that she was, in fact, active Interforce to deal with.

The rest of them had brought guards. Big, bulky figures with clubs at their belts and old, well cared for blasters in holsters at their hip. Murders weren't unknown, and more than one stakeholder argument had ended in bloodshed, or gotten into trouble either coming or going to the council.

The closest thing they had to law was Interforce Security and their own guards, and even Interforce Security would think twice before crossing Jess.

Jess was more trouble than most of them wanted to deal with. So she smiled benignly at the crowd, and relaxed, waiting for all the chaos to die down so they could start plowing through whatever the agenda was. She glanced at Dev, who was busy watching everyone around them, finding her profile unexpectedly engaging. "Hey Dev."

The pale, sea colored eyes went to her at once. "Yes?"

"Whatcha doing?"

Dev scooted to the edge of her chair and shared her scanner screen, still holding it down low so it couldn't be seen. "I was recording this for you, and also, running some bio scans on these individuals. None of them seem related to you."

Jess laughed. "Did you expect them to be?"

Dev started to answer, then paused as the woman in the center of the room rang the tinkling device again.

"Show me later." Jess patted her knee and returned her attention to the council. "Bet most of them are related to sea cucumbers."

Sea cucumbers. Dev frowned and sent a quick search into the scanner's memory, then relaying the request to the carrier. She looked at the picture it returned, then looked at the people, then looked at Jess.

IT WAS NICE to get back outside. The weather had turned colder, but the clouds seemed to have thinned a little, and there was less moisture in the air than there had been.

Jess leaned her arm on Dev's shoulders, watching the pilots with slightly narrowed eyes. "Time to get back to the ranch. C'mon." She nudged Dev toward the carrier.

"Drake!" The rep from Quebec waved a hand at her.

"Got a call. Need to move." Jess escaped into the carrier. "Send comms." She hit the hatch control and dropped into her seat, growling a little. "Stupid crap." She slapped her restraints in place. "Get moving, Dev, before another idiot tries to bang on the door."

Dev obediently got the engines going, hitting the landing jets and boosting the carrier up and off the concrete. There were still two flyers on the ground, and she saw the man who had been talking to Jess and the tall man from Quebec talking to each other near one of them.

She turned off the external sensors as they rose up out of audible range and she gently drifted over the big building, circling it before she laid in the course back to Drake's Bay.

"What did you think, Dev?" Jess asked. "Bunch of crap ass, huh?"

Dev glanced at the reflector. "I was confused. I wasn't really at all sure what was going on."

"No, me either." Jess sighed. "Furstan suspects something."

"About the plants?"

"About something. He wants to come visit." Jess shook her head. "And Quebec City. Jostar hinted they had a signed deal with us for something." She released the belts and got up, moving restlessly over to the drink dispenser.

They headed down the slope from the ruined city, and Dev could feel the wind rising as it tugged against the profile of the carrier. Ahead of them was a flat rocky stretch with jagged hills on either side and a large body of water in the distance.

It was dark and light grays, greens and the flat black blue of the water, and as they started over it the rain started coming down.

Jess came over and claimed the jumpseat, handing over a cup of kack as she extended her legs out along the floor. She tipped her head back and regarded the wash of water cascading over the forward shield, the faint rumble of thunder coming through the plas. "Ah, Dev."

"Yes?" Dev said. "You seem upset."

"I am. I don't like all this. I don't like the politics and the yakking. I want to go back to the Citadel."

Dev decided that fit how she felt as well. "It would be good to be in our space," she said. "It's more comfortable than the quarters they assigned us at your place."

Jess remained thoughtfully quiet, her brows twitching a little.

"And I kind of miss the pool," Dev concluded. "I thought my last session was pretty successful."

Jess finally sighed. "I forget sometimes that I've spent more time there than I ever did at home." She paused. "At the Bay, I mean. Crap I left when I was five. I think I spent a total of two months there since then."

Dev watched her from the corner of her eye, the turned up collar of the pullover giving her a different profile. "Are you in discomfort over it?" she asked.

"Yes," Jess answered. "Well, no. I mean..." She made a low noise in her throat. "I don't know." She cradled her cup in both hands, drawing her knees up and resting her elbows on them in oddly cramped discomfort. "It's weird."

Dev trimmed the engines, her eyes flicking over the boards. "I think I understand. It would be weird for me if I had to go back to the crèche," she said. "It would cause me discomfort, because I'm used to something different now."

Jess was glad to shift the focus from her squirminess to Dev's. "We treat you like one of us."

"No." Dev shook her head faintly. "You don't really, Jess. You always know what I am, and so does everyone else at the base. What is different is that I have the ability to interact with you freely. You don't know how I'm expected to react."

Jess puzzled over that for a few minutes. "What does that mean?" she finally said.

Dev turned her head and regarded her. "What I just said to you. If I had said that to a proctor in the crèche, I would have been taken in for some adjustment. They do not want me to understand as well as all that."

Jess blinked at her. "What the hell?" she said. "They make you super smart and then get mad when you are?"

Dev smiled wryly. "Doctor Dan did that. I'm not entirely sure everyone knew," she admitted. "He told me once, when I wanted to ask some questions about programming, that it was okay for me to ask him anything, but not my regular proctors." She adjusted their course. "He said it would cause them discomfort."

Jess felt slightly enlightened. "You really are different," she mused. "NM-Dev."

Dev was about to answer when the scanner alerted, and she focused on the screens, since the forward shield was awash with rain. "There are people ahead," she said. "Some kind of conflict."

Jess got up and went to her station, stripping off the pullover and hanging it over the back shelf, then exchanging the trousers she had on for a jumpsuit from the hatch against the back wall. She seated herself and belted in, then pulled her screens closer. "Give me some juice."

Dev shunted power to the weapons and activated the boards behind her, adjusting their course to approach and trimming the engines. The scanner showed use of energy weapons, and she boosted the power on the shields in case someone decided to direct them at the carrier.

She studied the wiremap coming back. "Jess, here is the outline." She sent the image back.

"Nomads," Jess said, after a brief pause. "Looks like a wagon train on the road." She scanned the energy pattern. "Someone's shooting at them. Turn on the recorders, let's fly over again and get a capture before we move on."

"Aren't we going to assist them?" Dev asked.

"No. Not our business," Jess responded briskly. "Just want to gather some intel." She looked up after a relatively long period of silence greeted her words to see Dev watching her in the reflector, a studiously noncommittal expression on her face.

She knew what that meant. She knew Dev well enough by now, after four months of service together, to know that she wanted to stop and help everything in her path, including limping starfish, and therefore thought Jess should do it, too.

Wasn't in the cards. Wasn't her gig. She met Dev's eyes in the reflector. Interforce wasn't a rescue service.

She drummed her fingers on the weapons console, wrenching her gaze from her partner's with some effort and studying the wiremap instead. "Must have been the group we overflew earlier," she said.

"They appeared to recognize this vehicle as we went over them," Dev offered. "Could they be part of April's family?"

Possible, not likely. Carriers were extremely distinctive lumps of metal and it would have been smart for anyone traveling to make note of them. She didn't even know what tribe April had come from, never thought to check, didn't actually care.

Didn't matter, after all.

"I wonder if they might have heard about the plants?" Dev said.

Jess tried not to smile, but after a moment, she gave up. "You're a sneaky little bugger, Devvie." She sighed. "Okay, take us down and let's see who they are." She pulled down her targeting rigs and got her hands into the trigger gloves.

The carrier responded immediately, as they went into a dive and she felt the grav on her, watching the scope as it showed them heading groundward at a slightly alarming pace. She tapped comms. "Tac two on?"

Almost immediately Doug's voice came back. "Tac one, Tac two on station."

"Mark loc," Jess said.

"Marked." Doug said.

April's voice cut in. "Ops?"

"Jess, one minute," Dev said.

"Ack," Jess said into comms, then disconnected and got herself ready, watching the wiremap change to visual with enough clarity for her to identify what she was looking at. "Standby for targeting." She identified the blaster sources from a rocky outcropping off the flat surface that was once a road.

The nomad train, which it was, had their vehicles in a square and themselves inside it, firing back with hand weapons.

Their attackers were using long range blasters, much higher power, and as she watched, they took out the side of one of the cargo wagons, sending it in pieces up into the air. "Get between them and the nomads, Dev."

"Yes." Dev sounded happy.

"Let's hope they have no limping starfish."

"Um...what?"

"FASTER." APRIL WAS in her rig, thigh muscle jumping as she watched the screen, anticipating the fight to come. Doug was in the pilot's seat, giving the throttles a nudge as they shot between two craggy ridges and closed in on Jess's last position.

"Not too fast, boss." Doug had his eyes glued to the scan. "Last thing I want is to come around a corner and find Rocket coming right at us."

"Boards'll pick them up," April said.

"Want to make book on that?" he responded. "Or that my rookie self can outfly her?"

April grunted as an answer, acknowledging the thought. She'd sim'd pretty much every single flight and fight scenario comp had come up with, but nothing quite matched the way Dev flew, they hadn't been updated yet to accommodate her space born acrobatics.

Crazy weird. After the run over to the other side, they'd learned to keep well clear of their airspace and never to assume the bio alt would react as per the sims.

Never.

Dangerous, to anyone in the area, and on top of that she had hair trigger Drake on the guns, who apparently didn't have to think before shooting and trusted her instincts as to who was friend and who was enemy.

April thought that the outline of her carrier would mark them as friendly, but you never knew. "Time?"

"Two minutes." Doug adjusted the pitch and moved a bit forward, getting his boots on the side thruster pedals and adjusting his grip on the throttles.

It was raining, and misty, the clouds descending down between the hills and making visual almost useless. He depended on the scan, and now, ninety seconds out, he got wiremap and picked up Rocket's motion ahead of them. "There they are."

A ripple of energy went through the boards as April brought her guns live.

"They've got target." Doug saw the blaster flare and adjusted their trajectory to arc in the same motion, leveling and dipping toward the ground. "That escarpment, to the left. Big energy."

"Got it." April was aware of the road, and the outline of the caravan, but she disregarded it, assuming that Jess had defined friend and enemy accurately, and they weren't about to get shot in the ass.

Always a possibility though. "Watch our rear shields."

"Bumped."

Doug held his throttles ready, concentrating on the other carrier that was heading toward the rocks at top speed. The enemy fire had come off the road and was focused on Dev's machine, the forward shields splashing diverted energy to either side.

Dev had her hard shield down and was flying blind, just on her scan. Doug shivered a little, glad they were on a vector and not yet being targeted so he didn't have to do the same. April was used to targeting on the boards, but he didn't like not having true vision out the front.

Dev's voice cut into their comms over the sideband that had come up when they'd come into range. "Tac two, stand by for overshot. We will reverse course."

Doug was relieved to hear the warning. "Tac one copy, taking hard cut south," he answered, getting ready to change course. "Hear that, boss?"

"Got it," April said. "Glad she warned us."

"No joke."

With a shuddering boom, Dev's carrier came over the escarpment hiding the enemy and cut both speed and power, the energy beams flying past them into air as she tumbled and rotated a hundred eighty degrees.

Doug took his craft to a sharp right, blowing by the gun emplacement as April let loose. He saw Dev flash past them, releasing plasma bombs into the protected space the enemy was hiding in.

"Ware," Dev's voice cut in unexpectedly. "Energy release."

"Oh crap." Doug hit the landing jets and boosted them up as he heard the crackling boom of an explosion so loud it vibrated through the skin of the carrier. "They had a power sink."

He hit the engines and sent them rocketing skyward, turning to the right and skimming over a rock wall then ducking down behind it as the explosion turned the air to fire.

Rocks tumbled down the walls, and the top edge of the crest disintegrated, rubble flying and impacting the outside skin of the carrier with pocks and pings as Doug flew them through it.

"Get back there," April said. "Though I'm guessing not much is left."

"Nope." Doug shifted the scan output to her boards as he slowed down and moved into a turn, now between two narrow canyon walls as he headed back to the battle area. "Hey, look!" He saw a small flyer speeding away.

"Follow 'em." April brought her guns back up as the carrier

bent around in another turn, and sped up. "Tac one, Tac two, in chase."

"Tac two, ack."

DEV STARTED DAMAGE routines, getting alerts from some of the systems stressed by her flight maneuvers and the explosion they'd flown through. They were high over the road now, coming back in a curved descent.

"That was nice." Jess rubbed one shoulder. "I need to get padded straps though."

Dev chanced a glance behind her. "Did you take some damage?"

"Better than us getting hit by that fireball," Jess said. "That was a big one."

"There was a lot of energy." Dev returned her attention to the controls and did an overfly of the explosion site, the rocks scarred deep black with a significant ejecta that reached past the road. "The scanner shows no biologic signs."

"With that boom? I bet it doesn't." Jess studied the output the screens. "Go ahead and land on the road." She replayed the explosion with some sense of satisfaction, the two plas bombs she'd placed landed with pinpoint accuracy.

Nice.

"We'll need to do a scrape once the temp drops," she said. "Need to find out who those suckers were." She adjusted the straps again. "Unless that's what the kids are chasing."

Dev brought the carrier around and dropped to ground level, slowing the mains as she approached the road that the wagons were still huddled over. There were figures in motion, but they were behind the bulk of trucks as the rain started to come down harder.

She got the landing jets going, cutting the main engines as she slowly lowered the carrier to the ground, raising the hard shield up from the curved front nose, the sound of the jets covered by the rumbling thunder overhead.

The carrier settled onto it's skids, and she shut the external systems down, making sure the recordings were spooled to memory and switching from battle scans to the systems that would watch their surroundings. "Secure."

"Mmm." Jess relaxed, her eyes going to the front shield. "They staying in their box?"

"Yes." Dev switched the forward scan back to Jess's station.

"This storm is quite extensive." She twitched a little when a lightning blast came out of the sky and slammed into the ground to the west of them.

Jess folded her hands over her stomach and leaned back in her seat. "We'll wait then. Let's see what happens."

DOUG LEANED FORWARD a little as the carrier wove through the canyon, the scanners locked on the flyer struggling to stay ahead of them. "Can't be many of them in there." He repeated a sweep. "Two I think."

"Two is two more than none." April carefully tuned her forward weapons. "Get directly behind them, and level."

He complied, dropping in behind the flyer and increasing power to the engines as they closed in. "No markings. Unregistered," he said. "Local though."

"Local," April agreed. She lined up her guns and took careful aim, dialing down the power as she got off a shot and hit the flyer in the engines. It lurched and tumbled, and she let off another shot, scorching the top of the craft as it slowed.

"Nice." Doug slowed with it and followed them down as they headed for the ground, lights starting to flash on the tips of the flyer's wings. "Scared."

"Should be."

He kicked in the jets and hovered as the flyer landed. He turned on the lights on the bottom of the carrier to bathe the craft in a flat, silver glare.

The hatch on the side popped open and two figures tumbled out, holding their hands up.

April chuckled audibly. "Okay, I'm going out there. Keep it hovering a little just in case they're squirmier than they look." She got up and went to the weapons rack, seating her long rifle and putting handguns in both side holsters.

Doug lowered the carrier to the ground and watched in the reflector, triggering the hatch when April gave him the hand signal to. April hopped out, ignoring the lashing rain as she crossed the rocky ground. Both of the figures were taller than she was, but Doug saw the apprehension in their eyes as his partner approached, full of that dark energy that was typical of the field agents. They liked scaring people, he decided. He opened the scanner and started up the recorders.

April stalked them, glowering at the two of them as they took hesitant steps back. Doug tuned the scanner higher, so he could hear what was going on.

"D...don't shoot us!" The closer one stuttered. "We give up."

April paused and regarded them, seeing the lanky, angular frames and wide eyes. "Who are you?" she asked shortly. "Why were you shooting?"

The closer one cautiously lowered his arms, then lifted one hand to shield his eyes from the rain. "Cooper's Rock Holding. We were just guarding the road. They shot first."

"Bet they didn't," April said. "There's nothing here for a caravanserai to shoot at."

His nostrils flared. "They saw us getting in the gun cache. Shot at us," he said. "We were just getting back at them."

April studied him. "What's your name?"

"Jack."

She glanced up as the thunder rolled over head, and a lightning blast turned the sky to silver. "Both of you, come with me," she ordered. "My senior'll want to talk to you."

"Who's that?"

"Jess Drake." April smiled at the look of sudden apprehension on their faces. "She's the one who blew that emplacement to hell, so if I were you I wouldn't bother to lie to her." She drew a handgun out and motioned to the carrier. "Move it."

Jack looked behind him. "We can't leave the flyer here," he said. "Scavengers'll strip it. We'll follow you back."

April looked skeptically at him. "You willing to risk being blown out of the sky if I think you're lying?"

The other boy edged up. "We'll come witcha, Agent. No screwing around. I want to go home to dinner."

She let them wait for it, the rain pelting down on all of them. "Where'd you get those big blasters?" she asked, finally, watching their eyes closely, especially the corners of them. The faces slacked and relaxed a little as they exchanged glances.

"Don't know," Jack said. "Been there a long time. My daddy used to come out here and shoot rocks for fun with 'em."

April fired her blaster at him, clipping his ear as he let out a shocked yell. "Don't lie. I don't have time for it. I'll just blow your head off if you do it again."

The other boy waved his hands at her. "Homestead and Progets Cliff bought 'em. Had to beat off those damn pirates somehow. Stealing everything they get their hands on. Been in like three months."

April nodded. "That's better. They weren't here last time I

came through here and that was a year back or so. What pirates?"

"Traders." Jack had his hand over his ear, and he was glaring at her sullenly. "Didn't have to do that."

"Traders. Like nomad tribes?" April asked in a mild tone. "Like the ones you shot at today?" She watched the other boy nod hesitantly. "Okay. Follow me and we'll go ask them about that." She holstered her gun. "Tear off in another direction, we'll take you down."

"Okay," the younger boy said. "C'mon Jack."

"Fuck that," Jack muttered. "I'm going home."

April removed her gun again, and this time shot him in the head. He dropped to the ground, steam rising from the blast, face obliterated. "Sorry. He was really too stupid to be allowed to breed."

The younger boy had jumped aside. "Shit! You kilt him!"

"I did," April agreed. "Now get in the flyer and follow me unless you want me to knock you over the head and bring you to the Drake naked."

He turned and ran for the flyer. "Okay!"

April shook her head and headed back to the carrier, aware of Doug's eyes watching her through the plas. She gave him a slight wave, went to the hatch, and hopped up into the craft. "Morons." She hit the hatch close. "Mater always said Cooper's mated with starfish."

Doug prepared the carrier to fly. "Seem like kids."

"They are."

"I was kinda stupid as a kid," Doug said.

"Good thing we didn't cross paths until you grew up then." April seated her restraints. "Make sure the little bastard follows us."

"Mmm." Doug boosted on the jets and rotated, then started on a course back to the road.

JESS SLID INTO her issue jacket and put her hood up. "I'm going to go talk to them. Tired of sitting here."

They'd only been sitting for a matter of five minutes, but Dev just nodded. "Shall I come with you?"

"Nah. No sense in both of us getting drenched. Just keep an eye on them for me and let out one of those cute yells of yours if they do something sketch." She punched the hatch door and exited without waiting for Dev to answer.

Dev sighed and returned her attention to the wagons, which

were still tightly shuttered and blocked any sign of their inhabitants. The rain was coming down sideways and in waves that flowed over Jess's tall, angular form as it made its way across the road's rubble strewn surface.

Just shy of the front wagon Jess stopped and stood, her hands in her jacket pockets, head down a little, protected by the hood, being relentlessly pelted by the weather.

It seemed somewhat non-optimal.

Dev glanced behind her at the weapons station, then she returned her attention to the windscreen. Her fingers were on the comms key as she leaned on her console a little, ready to yell a warning into Jess's ear.

Comms crackled in her ear. "Tac two, Tac one."

"Ack," she responded.

"Target one, en route."

"Ack." Dev reached over and triggered the outside comms. "Jess."

Jess, who had merely been loitering and waiting for the wagons to burp up someone, half turned and looked back over her shoulder, reaching up to touch the comms key in her ear. She held up her other arm, shielding her face from the rain. "Go, Dev."

"The second carrier is on the way back. They have a captive," Dev said. "There is also a wave of much heavier precipitation coming down the road. Perhaps you should return?"

"Ya think?"

"I do, actually. You appear to be in discomfort."

Jess regarded the sky, then she turned and retreated back to the carrier. "No movement in there, huh?"

"No."

Jess was dripping all over the floor of the carrier, and when she pushed her hood back, raindrops trickled from the point of her nose. "I should have kept my ass inside." She shed her jacket and hung it up. "Why did you let me do that, Devvie?"

Dev looked over at her. "Excuse me?"

"Next time just tackle me." Jess got up and retrieved the pullover, settling it over her head. "Don't let me be stupid."

Dev checked the long range scan, then got up and went to the dispenser, removed some towels, and walked over to dry Jess's face, with a serious, intent look. Jess's cheeks were chilled, and she gently put her hand against one of them, staring down into her eyes. "You're never stupid, Jess. You're the smartest person I know."

Jess stuck her tongue out, making a face when it was wiped with the towel.

Chapter Five

DAN KUROK SAT quietly in his office, a soft rumble of computer generated thunder echoing softly in the background. He studied a tablet propped up on his desk and made notes into a console just to the side of it.

A soft knock on the door panel made him pause and look up. "Come in." He triggered the lock and sat back as a tall figure dressed in a white lab coat entered. "Hello, Halley."

"Hello, Doctor." The woman came over and sat down. "Pardon me for interrupting you, but I have some directives here I'd like to discuss if you have a moment."

Kurok sat back and folded his hands over his stomach. "Go ahead. It's time I took a break from this anyway."

Halley smiled. "Thank you, sir." She looked down at her pad. "The arrangements for the visits from NM-Dev-1 and the Interforce person. I see you countermanded the housing?" She looked up in some confusion. "Was there something wrong?"

"Yes," Kurok said. "You placed Dev into crèche quarters."

Hally's brows creased. "Yes, sir, I did. Where else would I have assigned a biological unit?"

"Guest quarters. Preferably right next to Agent Drake's. Which is where I put her." He watched the proctor's face twitch. "And I locked that down so no one could imagine I made a mistake and change it back."

"I don't understand."

"Dev is our guest," Kurok said. "Just as Jesslyn Drake is. They are coming here to assist me at some effort and disruption to themselves. I want them treated with courtesy."

The proctor studied him. "But, Doctor, NM-Dev-1 is a bio alt. The only place she should be housed, outside the crèche, is in transient quarters. You know that. It's the rules."

"I know." Doctor Dan smiled kindly at her. "I wrote most of those rules you know."

"Everyone will get upset. And it will cause a problem for the other bio alts," Halley said, seriously. "Think of the precedent it would set, and all the questions."

"I know. I have. However, I also thought about how difficult it's going to be for Dev to return here, given she's lived as a natural born for almost six months, and how unhappy it would make her if we put her back in the crèche."

"But she's a bio alt."

"I know, and she knows that. But she's not lived as one since she left here. They don't treat her as one," Doctor Dan said, with a note of finality in his voice. "So since she's doing me a favor, I'm going to make sure she doesn't suffer unhappiness because of it."

"But, Doctor." Halley looked distressed.

He interrupted her gently. "And, of course, we're all going to respect the presence of Senior Operations Agent Drake, who I suspect will break the neck of anyone intentionally making Dev unhappy. I'd rather not lose valuable scientific personnel including, of course, yourself."

Halley shut her jaw with a tiny, audible snick.

"So if you want to give that as the reason I've made such a radical exception to the rules, feel free to do so. Everyone should also understand that our rules, as we know them, will quite possibly not be respected by Agent Drake, and there's also a good possibility that we will not be able to do anything about that."

"Doctor, that sounds terrible. The agent sounds very dangerous."

"She is." Doctor Dan smiled his gentle smile. "Jess is a quite classically presented amoral sociopath, and she's spent most of her life practicing her brutal and significantly homicidal talents with great success. But all in all, I quite like her, and I think you all will find her engaging and somewhat entertaining."

Halley merely stared at him.

"She's also rather attached to Dev. Let's make sure that doesn't get anyone killed, all right?"

Uncertainly the proctor stood up and retreated, escaping out the door and leaving him once again in peace. Kurok chuckled a little and went back to his screen, pausing again as a note presented itself to him on his pad.

He tapped it and read it through, drumming his fingertips on the desk.

APRIL STOOD NEAR the back of the carrier, long rifle cradled in the crook of one arm. Their hapless captive stood near the hatch dripping rain on the floor, while Jess relaxed comfortably in her padded seat.

Doug sat on the jumpseat near the pilot's, his head close to Dev's elbow as they both hovered over the controls.

Outside the storm had gotten worse, raining so hard you

couldn't see the wagons from the carriers, though Dev was monitoring them through her scanners.

The kid had his arms wrapped around him. "Two, maybe three weeks back we all got plundered, the stores, you know? Took everything they could get and ran when the alarms done went off. Ran back to the road."

Jess glanced over at April, who shrugged. "Could have been a tribe. They do that," April said. "I remember some raids, back in the day."

"You one of them?" The boy asked, after a pause.

"I was," April responded. "Now I'm Interforce."

The boy refocused on Jess. "So we weren't gonna let them do it again. Why'd you get all up in the biz?"

Why? Jess rolled her eyes in Dev's direction. Dev returned the look noncommittally. "Didn't look like a two-sided fight to me," Jess said. "When we came over the horizon, we saw wagons getting blown up by high power blasters."

The boy looked down at his boots.

"Unlicensed blasters," Jess said.

"Had to get something," the boy muttered. "Anyway we paid for it. Was six of us in there."

Jess stood up, towering over him. "Where'd the blasters come from? Who'd you buy them from?"

He shook his head. "Dunno."

Jess had her hands in her pockets, and she stood there in silence, regarding him. He was thin and weedy, reminding her a little of her youngest brother. "Dev, contact Cooper's Rock holding. Ask for whoever runs the place. I want to talk to them."

"Yes." Dev put her cup in her ear and turned to comms, adjusting the frequencies as she called up the local civ list. "Cooper's Rock stakehold, this is Interforce flight BR270006 calling. Please respond."

The kid swallowed.

"They know you're out here?" April asked.

He shook his head.

Dev waited, then repeated her hail, her eyes glancing over the scanning results as she did. The wagons remained in place outside, and her wiremaps showed no moving life around them. No doubt the nomads were sheltering from the rain just as they were.

"No answer?" Doug asked in a low voice.

Dev shook her head and repeated the hail a third time.

"That's some stupid people," Doug said. "Let me tell ya,

where I come from? They teach you to answer an Interforce hail even if you're tied up and dead."

"Hm."

"Or having sex," Doug added, as an afterthought. "You just don't blow 'em off, you know?"

None of that really made sense to Dev, so she concentrated on comms, fitting her ear cup a little more firmly and tuning the receiver a little as the faint sound of a carrier opening came to her. She unconsciously leaned closer to the console, half closing her eyes to concentrate.

There was the sound of activity in the far off background, then a strong, female voice answered in her ear. "This is Cooper's. Who's calling?"

Ah. That seemed more correct. "Cooper's Rock this is Interforce flight BR270006. Flight leader requests to speak with person in charge there." Dev settled back in her chair.

Momentary silence. "You're speaking to them. This is Darana Cooper."

"Please stand by," Dev half turned. "Jess, we have the person you requested on comm."

Jess nodded. "Gimme." She indicated her board.

Dev transferred the comms back then started a deep scan on the nomad wagons. "There seems to be a good deal of energy weapons inside those vehicles," she commented to Doug.

"Oh yeah." He squirmed around to look at the screens. "Those guys are crazy vicious. They'll shoot ya and not even ask."

Jess cleared her throat a little. "This is Jess Drake," she said into comms. "Who's speaking?"

"Dee Cooper. Hello, Jess. Long, long time no talk."

"Has been," Jess acknowledged. "When I'm done you'll wish it was longer. We flew right into a firefight over here near the old west road."

Cooper cursed under her breath. "Those fucking guns."

"Those fucking guns," Jess agreed. "Which I blew into particles along with a half dozen trigger fingers."

"Shit! I knew that would end like crap. But with all the stories we heard about you bunch being overrun we had to put something in," Cooper said. "I heard about North, and all the damage at Ten."

Jess listened in silence. "Hm," she finally responded. "That's now the third story I've heard around those guns. Wonder when I'm going to hear the real one." She felt a mental tickling. "We'll drop the surviving punk over there."

Cooper sounded surprised. "Don't know what you're talking about there, Jess. But it is what it is. C'mon by. You on patrol?" she asked, curiously. "I thought I heard you made senior."

"On my way back from council," Jess said. "Surprised you weren't there."

"What the hell?"

"You're behind in the gossip, Dee." Jess smiled. "I took over at the Bay. Shares screwup."

Cooper snorted audibly. "You're kidding, right?"

"Nope. Found out my brother was running dark. We processed him out yesterday," Jess said. "C'mon by some time. It's been a while."

There was a brief silence. "Well, crap, Jess. You're right. I should have gone to council. I just had a sitch I had to take care of. I will swing by. We should talk."

"Drake out." Jess cut the connection and swung her seat around. "Take him with you," she told April. "We're going to chase this seal hair poking my neck." She tapped on her board. "Sending you coordinates, Devvie."

"Yes." Dev took them and plotted their course, as April grabbed the kid and Doug stood up to join them. "Jess, there is someone approaching this vehicle."

"Now they decide to move their asses," April muttered. "Figures." She shifted her rifle. "Want me to put them off?" she asked Jess. "Might have some cousins in there."

Jess stood up. "No. Take him to your rig, wait for us. I'll talk to them." She put her jacket on and pulled the hood up, moving to the hatch. "Open her up, Dev. This shouldn't take long."

THE NOMAD LEADER had a heavy sealskin overjacket on, with a fur lined hood that protected his face. He stood in an aggressive stance halfway between the wagons and the carrier, and Jess took her time walking over to meet up with him.

Behind her she heard the kid being dragged over to April and Doug's bus, and she knew if she looked over her shoulder she would see Dev's face in the window, watching her with serious intent, the sound of the open link between them echoing softly in her ear. "Anything happening in there, Devvie?"

"There are two persons on the other side of the wagon who appear to be watching us," Dev answered. "There are another two who are trying to move the damaged vehicle."

"No one pointing anything?"

"No."

Good sign. Jess slowed her pace, stopping a body length from the nomad and waiting.

"Agent," he finally addressed her, taking a step or two closer. "Don't want no debt to you. What that cost me?"

"Cost you the truth. Who started it?"

The man smiled, a flash of white inside his thick, black beard. "Cheap enough." He studied her face. "You local?"

"Drake," Jess said. "Drake's Bay," she added, somewhat unnecessarily.

"Ah." He sobered. "You coming back from council then? Heard the Bay got take over something like."

"Who started it?" Jess countered, but with a smile.

The nomad chuckled under his breath. "You know already, Drake. We bare had time to put the defense on. We were thinking of shelter when my scout bike got blown out of the air with a kid on it." He indicated the ridge. "We heard 'em laughing."

"Kids," Jess said. "We caught two of them. From Cooper's Rock."

"Yah, figures. Woman there let's 'em run wild. I should file a suit against 'em for it." the man said. He redirected the conversation. "The Bay going to be an outpost now, Drake? Tit for tat."

"Something like." Jess responded. "What family are you?"

"Brogan," he said. "We were at the Bay two weeks back. Heard lots of things there." He watched Jess's face intently. "Lots of things."

Jess shrugged. "I've only been back there a couple days." She lifted a hand and started to back away. "Got work to do. Good traveling."

"We're good traders, Drake," the nomad said. "If you've got like to trade."

"Heard that." Jess headed back to the carrier, hearing the low whine of the engines spooling as Dev saw her approach and opened the hatch. She jumped up onto the deck and hit the close, taking the time to take her jacket off as she felt the carrier move under her. "Let's go, Dev."

"That person seemed in discomfort," Dev said. "There was another individual behind the first conveyance with a weapon."

"Yeah. I saw him." Jess sat down and exhaled. "We need some intel. Got the feeling everyone around here knows more than we do." She pulled over her screen and triggered comms. "Tac two, Tac one."

"Ack."

"Fast run, just drop," Jess said. "Recon."

"Ack." Doug sounded somewhat relieved. "Stand for lift."

"Go." Jess closed the channel and belatedly fastened her restraints. "Go back to the Bay, Dev. Something's going on here."

Dev boosted up without comment, shifting the carrier up and over the wagons and gaining altitude quickly. In her screen she saw the aft sensors still capturing the solitary figure of the nomad standing in the rain watching them.

Then she cut in the mains, and he was left far behind as they swiftly accelerated through the speed of sound, a soft boom trailing behind them.

IT WAS STILL raining hard when they came through the pass and circled around to the landing bays. They found the upper bay open to receive them, and inside a senior transport was visible.

"Alters is still here," Jess said, as they braked. "Don't see anyone else yet."

"No," Dev said. "Just the one transport and the two carriers that accompanied it." She aimed for the landing bay, her eyes flicking to the scanner. The bay operations comms hadn't seemed unusual or wary, but you never knew.

She'd learned that in her short time at Interforce. Things you trusted and things you expected could turn completely around when you least expected it. "BR270006 to Drake's Bay control. We are inbound to pad two."

"See ya there, BR," the casual response came back. "Glad to see ya back."

Were they, actually? Dev cut the mains as they came into the landing bay, hovering a little as she moved to one side around the transport and settled onto the steel layered pad. She secured systems and opened the power hatch, hearing the slither and thunk as they were hooked up to the Bay's batteries.

Jess got up from the jumpseat, patting Dev's leg as she stood. "I'm going to go talk to Alters. See where his plans got to. Those eggheads he brought with him should be done with their review by now."

Dev nodded. "I think I will do some work on this vehicle. There is not much to do in the space they assigned us, and we did take a little damage in that explosion." She got up and went to the equipment locker, opening it to reveal her comprehensive toolkit.

"Yeah, that's kind of a crappy spot, huh?" Jess opened the

hatch, but paused in it to watch her.

"I'll see if they can find something else for us, now that we're gonna be around for a while." She ducked outside and headed past the transport.

Dev sighed and opened up a console, taking a seat on the floor and sliding inside. The last adjustment was almost done when she peeked out to see Doug enter with a circuit board in his hands. "Hello."

"Hey, Rocket." He sat down. "You got any spare A2s? I blew mine when we had to pop off from that boom."

"I think so." Dev squirmed out and opened the lower cabinet. "We took some damage as well."

"Hey, so I was talking to the transport driver on the way here." Doug leaned closer and lowered his voice. "There's some seriously funky stuff going on here. Like besides all the stuff we saw, there's some people missing from the guy Jess offed's family."

"Really?"

Doug nodded. "His wife and two kids," he said. "The reason we know one of the kids is really missing is he didn't turn up to be taken in."

Dev propped herself up on one elbow. "Tayler," she said. "The little boy."

"That his name? You seen him?"

"I did," Dev said. "He showed me a starfish when I was here last. I showed him a vid of a bear I saw in the north."

Doug twirled the card in his fingers. "Driver said he heard base talking to the commander. Some mucky mucks are headed here to check it all out."

Dev sighed. "I don't think Jess is going to like that."

"Not much she can do." He gave her a sympathetic look. "But hey, maybe they'll decide to take over and we can go back to the base. I hope so. I get the creeps here, a little."

"Me too." Dev located the replacement card and handed it over to him. "I would rather go back to the base myself."

ALTERS INTERCEPTED HER on the way down the steps, and they moved aside into one of the storage rooms on the fourth level.

"How'd it go?" he asked, as they sealed the door behind them.

"Not bad," Jess said. "Council was pissed, but they realized pretty quick they couldn't do anything about it so they just moved on." She took a seat on one of the boxes. "Bunch of pointless crap after that, but Jimmy must have spilled to a lot of people because all of 'em wanted to talk to me."

Alters nodded. "Figured that." He sat down across from her. "This is a mess."

"Wasn't intended."

"No one said it was," he replied, mildly. "Some of the science derps from base are due here any minute to try and figure out what that glowing rock's all about." He glanced aside. "See if this is a single source for it."

"What if it is?"

Alters looked a bit uncomfortable. "Well, let's see what happens first. No sense in speculating. Anyway it's pretty obvious though that the materials for this came from topside."

Jess nodded. "Dev thinks so. She recognized the seed stock."

He smiled. "Except that no one official there will admit to doing a deal. Not with him, not with anyone. We asked. Sent them the material scans. They say they know nothing about it."

There was a little silence. "Someone's lying," Jess said.

Alters nodded. "Intel thinks so. They think it's possible something's going on up there, and HQ suggested we need to find out."

Jess knew where this was going. "Yeah."

"Since they already want to see you and your partner, it made sense to me to tell HQ you'd be the ones we'd send up to check them out," Alters said. "So there'll be a shuttle here tomorrow."

"Thought I was supposed to be in charge of something here," Jess said, after a pause.

"Plans change. HQ wants answers," Alters said. "This place and the resident squad'll be here when you get back." His voice took on a slightly conciliatory tone. "C'mon, Drake. We both know you'd be the one they'd send anyway."

She shrugged. "I wasn't looking forward to getting stuck here," she admitted. "I'd rather be out in the field."

Alters smiled. "Glad you see it that way, Drake. I know this is crunchy. So get you and your driver ready and go fly in space for a week. I'll do my best to get this sorted out here before you get back."

Jess eyed him. "You?"

He made a slight, knowing face. "I don't really want to hang out here either, so nail them, wouldja? HQ doesn't want me to leave until the science people weigh in." He had the grace to look a bit apologetic. "No offense to you, Drake."

On the verge of being offended, Jess paused and thought. "None taken. I'm field ops. I'd never have been in the line if this hadn't been my homestead." She got up. "Let me go ask Dev what she wants to do."

Alters cocked his head. "What do you mean?"

"She really didn't want to go back up to station," Jess said, evenly. "So I'm not gonna make her."

The commander blinked. "Drake. That's a bio alt. She's got no choice in this."

She nodded slightly. "My partner. My pilot. Base Ten still stands because of her. She doesn't want to ride up to where they may treat her like what she is? Not gonna force her."

Alters got up and walked over to her, studying the still, angular features. "They want to see her."

"Don't give a shit."

He smiled a little. "Drake, you're a piece of work, you know that?" He sighed. "This is not going to make you any friends. No one likes ops who refuse to take orders. Understand?" He lifted his eyes to meet hers, and then looked away again. "Don't screw things up for yourself."

Jess just nodded and left the room before the temper she felt building got her in more trouble. She headed for the steps and was halfway down another flight when she spotted Dev trotting up to meet her.

Determined looking, a tiny frown on her face, body moving as smoothly as she had that carrier's systems running.

It made her smile grudgingly and took away the gnawing in the pit of her stomach. She sped up her own pace so she ended up on the first level just as Dev reached it. "Hey."

"Jess," her brother Jake interrupted the reunion, appearing from the family quarters with a harassed look on his face. "Hey listen."

Jess almost ignored him. Then she turned. "What?"

"Okay so, not to be an asshole, but can you tell your watchdog to stop shooting at staff? They're just trying to move you to nicer quarters."

Dev exhaled. "That's why I was trying to find you," she told Jess. "Someone was in the space we were assigned, moving our things. April did not think that was a good idea."

Jess regarded her then looked at Jake. "Eleven generations of us in service and someone thought that was a good idea?"

Jake sighed. "They were just trying to show some courtesy."

Dev handed Jess a comm link, and she put it in her ear and tapped it. "Tac two, Tac one."

"Tac two," April answered promptly.

"Stand down," Jess said. "My idiot family is trying to do something nice for us."

"Ack."

Jess clicked off. "Next time ask first," she said. "Where were you thinking of?"

He motioned her to follow and they went down the hall and through the entryway into the family quarters. They passed the kitchen and the clusters of common rooms as well as two hallways Jess knew led to where Jake and the late Jimmy had lived. They came to a right hand hall and Jake pushed open a slightly ajar door that blocked it. "Here."

It was at the skin of the mountain wall, and there were periodically cut out windows in the rock that let in the light from outside. On the other side of the hall were doors to quarters, and Jake stopped at the last of them. "These haven't been used for a while."

Jess put her hand on the lock and it opened, and she pushed the door ahead of her as she walked inside. "That's fine." She glanced around at the large chamber, which included a food service area and granite faced sanitary unit. "It's good, Jake."

"Great. Let me go make sure no one else's been shot." Jake stomped off.

Dev eased inside and looked around. "This is pleasant. Nicer than the other location."

Jess perched on a table. "Should be. It's the stakeholder's digs. My father and mother used to have it." She smiled. "Close the door."

Dev did and walked over to Jess. "Is something incorrect?"

"Yeah," Jess said. "It's getting more and more fucked up. Alters told me the brass wants him to stay in charge here."

Dev frowned. "Aren't you supposed to be?"

Jess shrugged. "Anyway, he needs someone to go up to station and find out what the score is with the seeds." She watched Dev's face go carefully noncommittal. "I told him I would go, but you don't have to if you don't want to."

Dev's expression went still, only her pale eyes moving a little as she studied Jess's face. "I told you, Jess. It's okay. I want to go where you go," she said after a long pause. "I don't want to stay here without you."

"You could go back to the base. Honest, Dev. I don't want to freak you out. I get it." She cleared her throat a little. "I want to do right by you. I mean...you're my friend, right?"

Dev sat down on the table next to her, shoulder to shoulder, and they both remained silent for a few minutes.

"You are my friend, aren't you?" Jess finally asked.

"Yes." Dev answered at once. "In as far as I understand what that is, I am," she added, somewhat disconsolately.

"Aw." Jess rested her head against Dev's. "You're the best friend I have, Devvie."

"Mmm. I think you're the only friend I have, Jess. Would leaving me here make you happy?"

Jess straightened up and frowned. "No."

Dev exhaled and nodded. "Well, you leaving me here wouldn't make me happy either. It's okay, Jess. I want to go with you." She sounded positive. "Even if it's hard, or makes me feel sad or incorrect, I want to go with you and show you the stars and the sun."

Jess let out a relieved sigh. "That's a damn good thing, Dev. 'Cause I really wanted you to go with me."

"I can be helpful," Dev said.

"No. I just don't want to be without you," Jess replied, simply. "That would bum me out." She stood up. "C'mon let's look around our new digs and get our stuff. "

Unexpectedly, Dev threw her arms around Jess and hugged her in a fierce, intense way. After a brief, startled breath of inaction, Jess responded, happy just to be there in the moment. Even though everything was going sideways, after all, she still had this.

Whatever this actually was.

"OH, DANIEL." RANDALL Doss hurried over to the table in the quiet restaurant, where his colleague was stolidly munching through his food. "I'm glad I found you."

"Were you looking for me?" Dan Kurok put his fork down and took a sip of his drink. "We have a paging system, Randall, and I do carry a comms link. And lastly, you could have asked my admin to find me."

Doss sat down across from him. "Daniel, have you seen the shuttle schedule? The one due in tomorrow?"

"Yes," Kurok said. "We'll have our guests here tomorrow evening. I've checked all the preparations, and with any luck we won't horribly embarrass ourselves or get someone's neck broken by accident."

"Do you think it'll be all right, when they see the prototyping?" Doss looked worried. "Daniel, so much is riding on this project."

"I think it'll be fine." Kurok picked up his fork again. "Randall, either order and eat with me, or go away until I'm done. This protein doesn't do well when it's cold."

"Oh. Yes. Of course." Doss signaled to the server. "Sorry, Daniel. I'm just so frazzled about this, and that investigation. Horrible."

"Investigation?"

Doss placed his order then turned back to his reluctant tablemate and lowered his voice. "We haven't bothered you with it, you've been so busy. But it seems some of the product from the labs was found downside."

Kurok stopped chewing. "Eh?"

"Exactly." Doss took the glass of wine from the waiter and took a swallow. "Interforce. It seems they found seed product in a cavern, and Daniel, it was growing."

Kurok blinked and put his fork down again. "Eh?" he uttered again. "What are you saying? Growing inside a cave? You know that's not possible, Randall. We've only had the most limited success using artificial light."

"Exactly," Doss said. "That's what I told them. I asked them for details, but they wouldn't give me any, just the stock numbers, and, Daniel, they were ours."

The waiter returned and put a plate down in front of Doss, giving him a little bow of respect before retreating.

"Thank you." Doss dug into the plate, and for a moment they were both silent.

Kurok slowly took a drink from his glass. "Did they say where they found it?"

Doss shook his head. "You know Interforce." He cut a piece of the protein cake. "This is quite good, Daniel. I'm glad you asked me to sit down with you."

Kurok sat back with his glass, swirling its contents thoughtfully. "Well, maybe Jesslyn will know more about it. I can ask her when she gets here. Maybe it's just a small pot after all."

Doss nodded. "It could be, yes." He took a sip of wine. "They didn't seem too excited about it. Just a query, you know? That's why I didn't bother you or the other staff with it. Didn't seem like that big a deal, but still. I don't like it being our seeds."

"No," Kurok agreed. "You know there still are some rogue genetic hacks down there, Randall. Maybe someone did some meddling."

The director shook his head disapprovingly. "So dangerous." He chewed and swallowed. "Thank the stars that doesn't go on much downside. Could turn out anything!"

Kurok smiled. "True. Humans with gills, for example."

"Ugh!" Doss shuddered. "I can't even imagine what that would look like."

"I can." Doctor Dan went back to his plate. "And in less than twenty-four hours, you might as well."

"What?"

"THAT'S SKANK." APRIL folded her arms. "Shift you off like that. It's your place."

They were seated at a table in the mess, Jess perversely avoiding the kitchen space in the family quarters, preferring to eat with the common masses instead. "Meh." She leaned back in her chair and picked up a big mug, taking a sip of local brew. "Honestly? I'd rather go back to base."

"Me too," Dev agreed at once.

"Me three," Doug chimed in.

April settled lower in her seat grumpily. "It's all BS. Someone realized how much cred is up for grabs here."

Jess nodded. "Why I want out. Money always means trouble. I'm glad we're going topside to chase down what the game is there." She glanced at Dev, who was chewing stolidly through a thick fish stew. "Devvie promised to show me stars."

Doug sighed. "Yeah that's kinda cool. You get to see all that weightless stuff and all that, and the sun!"

Dev nodded and swallowed. She still didn't want to go, and parts of her were all tied up in knots. The more she thought about getting on the shuttle the more unhappy she felt, but she was also smart enough to realize she had no choice.

No choice, because Jess had to go, and she didn't want to leave her. The thought of being left behind while Jess went to the station was causing her more discomfort than the thought of going along.

A little crazy. It was like being pulled in two directions and not really sure which direction was the right one.

"Is that going to be weird for you, Dev?" April asked suddenly. "Going back there?"

"She's fine," Jess responded immediately. "I'm going to make sure they treat her right." She braced her elbow on the chair arm and rested her chin against her fist. "First time they look crosswise they're going to get my boot in their ass."

Dev grinned a little, imagining it. "I think Doctor Dan will make sure everyone is correct to us, Jess. I am looking forward to seeing him." She nibbled a slightly sweet seaweed cake as the servers came over and brought around a bowl of something.

Jess seemed surprised. "Pudding!"

"Yes, ma'am." The server's eyes twinkled. "Someone said they made it just for you, Jesslyn. They heard you liked it, and we don't get it often."

"Gimme." Jess pushed her dish forward, and closely inspected the large spoonful of dark, jiggling substance. "Mmm."

Dev leaned over and examined it, sniffing the scent. "It smells like the brownies."

Jess took a spoonful as the server went around to the rest of the table. "Mm." She scooped up another spoon and offered it to Dev, realizing a moment too late that it had made everyone stare at her.

Her body twitched and she felt a sense of confusion, but she was too far into the motion to retract it without embarrassing them both, and so she just kept moving.

Screw it.

Dev took a bit off the spoon and mouthed it. "That is excellent." She shifted back to her own dish as the server finished depositing the substance on it. "Really good."

Jess dug into her dessert and enjoyed it, bringing back to her mind memories of being a child and sharing it with her brothers. It made her smile to think they'd made it for her, then the smile faded as she realized word would get out soon enough that she wasn't really in charge of anything.

A dis, April had characterized it right, since stakeholds were at least nominally autonomous, and she was human enough to feel more than a touch of shame and anger over Alters pushing her aside like that.

Then warn her not to make waves?

Jess's eyes narrowed, but then a gentle touch on her knee made her look up and over at Dev who was watching her with that adorably intense concern on her face. Her anger slid off it's tracks unexpectedly and she exhaled. "Glad you like it."

"I did," Dev said. "But I thought for a moment you did not. Is all correct?"

"Yeah." Jess went back to her pudding. "I was just remembering something that pissed me off. All better now." She licked the spoon, enjoying the sweet taste and stolidly bypassing the melancholy. "So here's what I want you two to do while we're topside."

April and Doug leaned closer. "That's what I said. We're not part of the parade," April said. "That's not our gig."

"Not your gig." Jess agreed. "But those guns out there."

"Hah. You were right." Doug poked April in the leg. "You said that was sketch."

"It was. Those were big ass high power rigs. Not something you pick up at market." April looked pleased at the grin on Jess's face. "Either they got them from our side, or they got them from their side, and if they got them from their side, why?"

"And they were new," Doug added. "I ran the profile before they blew up, and it was twelve gamma."

Dev looked at him with interest. "Really?"

He nodded. "I got it on scan. Still on the bus since we don't sync here."

"Makes no sense to have them there. Just to blow up a caravanserai?" April scraped the last of the pudding off her plate. "They weren't carrying anything like that. Just hand weapons."

"Right," Jess said. "So we have those. I want you to visit Cooper's Rock and talk to them there, see if you can get an angle on the guns. I don't believe either story those kids were spilling."

"It might be useful to know if there were more of those weapons," Dev said

April nodded. "I'm going to hook up with that van tomorrow and angle my connections to try and see if they've seen this stuff before. I know the leader of that bunch. Used to camp with my tribe."

"Okay, good." Jess stood up and stretched. "Let's go try out our new beds. Tomorrow's probably going to be a long ass day."

Doug joined her. "Better than those hammocks. Almost as nice as our quarters on base."

Jess smiled. "Almost."

April caught up to them as they walked between the tables and headed for the entrance, shrugging off the watching eyes of the sparse diners. "I'm glad it has an outer door. Makes me feel better. They put Alter's bunch in that kind of barracks space near the cave."

Jess chuckled. "Did they? I missed that." Her humor was restored. "Glad I don't know most of them. They're the newbies.

The teams Alters brought in from the west coast."

April looked at her, one brow cocking in question.

"They leak." Jess's eyes twinkled. "And the enviro doesn't work. Cold as crap in there and close enough to the wall for sea lice to infest."

"Oh, wow." Doug made a face. "Did you tell them to do that?"

Jess shook her head.

"Maybe they don't like you being dissed either," April said. "Like they got a 'tude."

Jess considered that as they walked through the halls, aware that she was already starting to get used to being here, her steps becoming automatic as she led the way to the first level and the section that had been assigned as theirs.

Jess palmed the outer door open and held it, then followed the three of them down the outer walk, passing the windows set in the cliff wall. She paused and looked out one, the inky darkness broken by the working lights of the Bay and the tiny sparkles of boats moving in and out.

"Hmph." She turned and went to the inner door, pushing it open and walking inside, then coming to a complete halt as her skin prickled and her battle instincts flared.

She turned and ducked as a whisper came over her head, and then she just let her body react. She dove at the shadowy figure in the corner of the room and caught them by the back of their jacket as they bolted for the door, hauling them around with her momentum to slam them into the rock wall.

They cried out in pain, and she lifted them up in her grip and got her hand around a fabric covered throat and squeezed.

Fingers grabbed at her wrist and pulled, but she just squeezed harder, staring into the eyes framed by a dark blue harbor hoodie.

She smelled fear. The person on the verge of blackout. She released the throat she was choking and put her hand against her attacker's chest instead, pinning them to the wall. "Now."

The outer door opened and Jess came close to overreacting before she recognized the body heading her way. "Get the lights on, Devvie. Let's see who we got."

"Yes." Dev went to the old fashioned lamps and turned one on. "Are you all right?"

Jess studied the body pinned to the wall. "Sure." She released her hold. "So, who are ya?"

The figure licked its lips. "Someone who loved your brother."

A shaking hand swept down the hood, revealing a young, female face with an oval shape and curly blonde hair. "And wants to take revenge for you offing him."

Jess regarded her. "If you haven't bred yet, don't. Gene pool doesn't need that much stupid. Plus you suck at killing."

Dev circled the room and turned on the other lamps, then she came over to stand next to Jess, regarding this short, slim invader. "I am going to parse into these systems and see why this location allowed her to enter."

"Shut up, you rag doll," the woman said.

Jess whacked her in the face, feeling bone crunch under her knuckles, sending the girl slamming back against the wall. She grabbed her as she bounced off then picked her up and put her over her shoulder, heading out the door as she whistled lightly under her breath. "Lock 'em out, Devvie."

With a faint shake of her head, Dev sat down at the stone carved desk in the room and put her portable scanner down.

JESS TURNED THE punk over to security. "Who is she?"

The on-duty chief rolled his eyes. "Name's Kacey. She had a full out hard on for Jimmy, no matter he was married and had the kids."

Jess's mental train switched tracks. "And where are Mary and the kids?" she asked. "Heard from Alters that Tayler never showed up for school."

The chief looked around, then back at her. "Can't tell for sure, but one day they were here, the next day they were gone. We were told not to ask any questions."

"By Jimmy?"

"None other, and since he was the elected head of, we didn't ask."

"When?"

"Three weeks back."

"No one saw them go?" Jess asked, in a skeptical tone.

"No one saw them go, but everyone heard a flyer come in and land up on the top bay. That didn't make it into the logs."

"A flyer," Jess mused. "So everyone hears a flyer, and no one sees a mini transport from the other side come in and land. Really, Chief?" She crossed her arms over her chest and regarded him.

He shrugged. "You know the drill."

Jess shook her head. "Maybe I don't. Last time I spent any

time here I was five. A lot of things can change."

The security chief leaned against the doorjamb and folded his muscular arms over his chest. "Yeah. Like a Drake making book with a jelly bag." He watched her closely. "Not everyone appreciates that."

Jess leaned against the opposite side of the door frame, crossing her ankles and lacing her fingers together. "I took convincing," she said. "So I won't take offense at that, this time. Dev's not a jelly bag."

"Not a bio alt?" He looked at her in surprise. "They said she was."

"She is. Just not a jelly bag brain," Jess replied. "She's smarter than both of us combined. New kind of bio. "

The chief frowned. "All the people out there, scavengers and all that, and they make bios now who can even take our jobs? Mine? Yours? What's the payoff in that, Drake? The one good thing about them was they were dumb as rocks."

"Don't think they'll ever make any that can take my job." Jess smiled. "Those skills you don't want to code spirals for." She flexed her hands, then lifted her eyes and looked right at the chief, who, after a brief inhale, took a step back.

He lifted his hands, palms out, facing her. "I remember Justin. Don't need a reminder."

Curiously, it cheered her up. "So anyway. Jimmy had an admirer. Keep her out of my way." Jess pushed off from the doorjamb. "Dev and I are taking a shuttle out tomorrow. The two with me are friendly." She looked back at him. "Can't vouch for anyone else."

He lowered his hands. "Heard that," he acknowledged. "Good flight."

DEV GOT HER gear settled in the big space she'd been assigned, then stood with her arms folded regarding her things, deciding what to take with her to space.

Interforce uniforms, yes. She set them aside. Her sharkskin jacket, yes, and her pack and sanitary kit that she took on the carrier with her. Though she knew they would have necessities up on station, she wanted to bring her own.

They were different, and she wanted to be seen as different, especially in crèche housing. Uncomfortable as that would be, she wanted some of her own things with her. Though Jess promised to make everyone be nice, and she had every faith in her partner, she knew what the rules were.

She was a bio alt. Even Doctor Dan couldn't change that. At best, they'd put her in transit quarters, down near the shuttle bay, but at least there she'd have a little privacy.

There was a tap on the outer door, and she went over to open it, reasonably sure who was on the other side. "Hello."

"Hey, Devvie." Jess rambled into the room, bumping the door shut behind her. "Like your new digs?" She peered around, then went over to poke at the bed. "Not bad." She sat down on it and rested her elbows on her knees. "Know what?"

Dev came over and sat next to her. "What?"

"I could use a nap," Jess said. "It's been a long ass day."

"Me too," Dev said. "I would like some rest, especially before our trip tomorrow." She kicked out her feet a little, bumping her heels against the base of the bed. "I wonder if I'll have to sleep in a pod tomorrow night."

Jess regarded her. "You're sleeping in whatever bed they put me in tomorrow night," she said. "And let me tell you, Dev, I ain't sleeping in no plastic egg."

Dev let her head rest against Jess's shoulder. "I don't think you'd fit," she said. "Most of us are shorter than you are."

Jess put her head down against Dev's. She thought about things she could be doing, places she could be poking into, and somehow it all just seemed pointless.

Boring.

It made her feel better just to sit here with Dev, rocking them both back and forth a little together as she listened to the mechanical sounds of the Bay around her.

"Tomorrow morning, I'm going to take you down to the beach I used to swim off when I was a kid," Jess said. "It's not crazy waves like at the base. It's just a nice piece of sand. We can scrounge."

"I'd like to see that place. Was it where you have that picture of you?"

"Where I look like a wet piece of seaweed? Yes." Jess smiled. "We can go swimming. Maybe we'll see dolphins." She watched Dev from the corner of her eye, seeing the tension slowly relax across her face. "Maybe we'll see a turtle."

Dev nodded a little. "I'd like that." She reached over and took hold of Jess's hand. "Jess, could we practice sex tonight?"

Jess blinked. "Sure. Nice big bed to do it in, not that crappy little hammock." She picked up Dev's hand and put a kiss on her knuckles. "Want to get a shower first?"

"I'd love to." Dev soaked in the moment, gathering it to her, intent on savoring all the human experience it offered, because once they went back to station tomorrow, you never knew what would happen.

DEV LIKED THE beach very much. She ruffled her hair dry, tasting the rich saltiness of the sea on her tongue as she walked across the soft, moist sand.

This was much nicer than their surfing space. The sand was a semi circle tucked against one of the extruded cliff walls of Drake's Bay, with a tumble of salt washed boulders behind it.

A portion of the rocks were altered, making a space that was sheltered from the weather that contained a place to cook with control surfaces that ran under the ground back into the big caverns in the cliffs.

Jess was in there, wet and disheveled, busy preparing a fish she'd caught in the water they'd just recently come out of, aligning it on the electric grill, along with some crunchy seaweed and some mussels.

The swimming had been successful as well, since the half circle of beach fronted a shallow, protected bit of water that wasn't very deep and had no real current, perfect for her to practice and for Jess to play around in, doing flips and dives and other odd acrobatics.

It had only rained a little and now was not at all, the air a little dry and cool and the breeze enough to dry them. Dev felt a sense of animal comfort that was a little surprising but good.

Also, the fish Jess was cooking smelled great. Dev went over and watched the process, determined to push aside her anxiety at their pending trip to space in order to enjoy the treat.

"How's that, Devvie?" Jess regarded her work. "Lucky to find that big a grouper this shallow."

Dev studied the split opened animal currently grilling. "It seems very appealing. I like this space as well." She indicated the beach and the rocks. "Thank you for bringing me here."

Jess grinned. "Used to spend a lot of time here." She poked the fish. "Nothing really like it near the base."

Dev put the towel she'd been drying herself with around her neck and found a chiseled rock bench to sit on. She got herself settled only to jump up a moment later. "Oh Jess! Look!"

Jess grabbed the knife she'd used to clean the fish and jumped around the grill, raising it as she got around the rock edge enough to see what Dev was looking at. "Oh." She relaxed. "Devvie, don't do that to me, huh?"

"What is that?" Dev asked as a large animal lifted its head and looked at her, strings of seaweed hanging from it's mouth.

"That's a sea turtle." Jess regarded the beast, whose back was easily as wide as the width of her reach. "Hey, buddy!"

The turtle chewed reflectively then went back to the pile of green the water had washed ashore. Behind it, Dev saw the track in the sand it had made as it came up out of the water. "Were we swimming with that? I didn't see it." She edged forward.

"Don't put your fingers near it's mouth," Jess warned. "They lay eggs on the beach. Never knew them to do it here though." She returned to the grill and sorted out her bounty onto old, scarred plas plates.

The turtle ignored Dev as she came closer. Its body was hard, she noted, big and oval shaped, and she tentatively reached out to touch it, finding it slightly rough and a little slick. The animal moved forward on its short feet and munched steadily on the same type of seaweed that Jess was cooking inside.

She knelt down to observe it, keeping her hands far away from its beak like mouth. It paused and looked at her, its eyes deep and black, and very inhuman.

Jess came out with two plates and sat down on a rock. "Here." She offered one of the plates to Dev, who scrambled to her feet and sat next to her. "They live longer than we do." Jess indicated the turtle.

"Really?" Dev ingested some of the fish that freshly grilled and dusted with spice was delicious. "What is the hard part for?"

"Protection. Like our carrier," Jess said. "It pulls its head and legs in and nothing can get at it." She regarded the turtle. "It's a living dinosaur. You know what that is?"

Dev considered. "No. I'll look it up when I get back to my scanner." She paused to chew and swallow. "This is really good."

Jess seemed pleased with the compliment. "Dad taught me to make this. Said it was good for an agent to be able to fend for themselves, out in the beyond." She looked up and around the little cove. "We used to come down here when I was on leave, just the two of us."

Dev tried to imagine what that would have been like and failed. She just had no reference. "It sounds nice."

"Yeah." Jess looked off into the distance, eyes a little unfocused. "He said he and I were family in a way the rest of them weren't," she said, in a thoughtful tone. "I think I miss him."

More things she really didn't have referents on. Did she miss anyone? Dev didn't think so. Her most interesting relationship was sitting right there next to her. It was like whatever had happened to her before in her life was just...just really nothing. Dev frowned and wondered if that wasn't a little incorrect. "If you were no longer here, I would really miss you," she said. "That would be horrible."

Jess chuckled and bumped shoulders with her. "Aw, you sweet talker you." She nibbled a mussel out of it's shell, then glanced up sharply as her ears picked up the soft shift of boots against sand. "Hope we're not going to have our lunch ruined."

Dev looked around, unsure. "What?"

"Someone's coming, around the rocks there." Jess wolfed down the rest of her fish and set the plas down, dusting her fingers off and standing up as two figures came around the bend and onto the beach. "Hold it."

The two stopped and looked at her, uncertainly. They were in Interforce jumpsuits, but with science piping and the typical side packs, and unknown to her. "We were just taking some samples," the one in front said.

Jess walked casually into their path. "What kind of samples?"

"Commander Alters said we had free range," the second one said. "Can you just let us get on with it?"

"No." Jess felt her posture alter, and she took a step toward them. "Alters doesn't own this place, and you better not bring your jackasswardness out here and annoy the person who does."

They took a step back, recognizing the change. "Sorry," the one in front said. "You must be agent Drake. No offense intended, Agent. Hard to know one of us here, half the folks here look like they belong."

Jess relaxed, but only a little. "Lines a little thin between in and out here," she said. "You'll live longer if you assume we're all a little screwball." She indicated the bags. "Now, what kind of samples are you taking?"

They hesitated. "We're not supposed to talk about it," the second one said. "It's restricted."

Jess felt her temper flare and knew they knew it.

Dev's voice came from behind them as she walked up and joined Jess, her scanner in her hand. "It's two segments of phosphine bearing mineral, with interjections of what appears to be volcanic sediment. There are no radiant qualities to the samples they have."

There was an uncomfortable silence when she stopped

talking, broken by Jess's low, wry chuckle. "Thanks Dev." Jess rested her elbow on Dev's shoulder. "My tech," she added. "Take your rock collection and go somewhere else. This is my beach."

They backed off. "We'll just come back later," the second one said. "And we'll make sure the commander knows."

Jess sighed, waiting for them to leave, and then going over to sit down next to the turtle, giving his head a light scratch with her fingertips. "Ain't going to end well, Devvie. I better talk to Alters myself."

"Perhaps he will decide to not have us go to station."

"Don't count on it."

DEV DID UP the catches on her backpack and set it on the chair near the old, rock surfaced desk in the space she'd been given.

Her skin still tingled from the shower she'd taken, finding the water pressure here in Drake's Bay significantly more powerful than what she'd known in the Citadel.

Interesting. The soap smelled like the type at the base, but it was just a little different, a little spicier and the scent just a bit stronger. She'd taken the time to fill one of the empty tubes from her kit with it to take it up with her.

That was good. Not only was it different from what the rest of the bio alts would have, it was from her partner's homeland. Dev patted the outside of the pack, which already had her scanner and her toolkit inside it.

She went over to the dispenser and retrieved a glass of fizzy something, not the kack they had at base, but something lighter and with a different, sharper taste. It wasn't as intense, and she'd decided she liked it.

The furniture in the room was odd and also a little strange, the chairs and one of the tables made out of the organic substance like the table in the private kitchen. She sat down on one of the ones near the bed and leaned back, waiting for Jess to knock.

She'd heard the arrival of the shuttle earlier and now that it was time, she just hoped it all worked out.

There was an inner door to her space, and a few moments later it bumped open and Jess poked her head in. "Hey!" She came in carrying her own pack. "Ready?"

"Yes." Dev stood up and put her cup down. She picked up her pack and swung it onto her back. "Are you?"

"Mmm." Jess closed the door and they left from Dev's main

one, going down the corridor and emerging into the first level of Drake's Bay.

Surprisingly the halls were full of people, and it took them some time to make their way through the crowd and down the long passageway toward the distant pad the shuttle had set down on. This was past the main part of the stakehold, but there were people lining the way from the time they left the family quarters to the entrance to the pad that the shuttle was on.

No one said anything. The Drake's Bay personnel were just there, sorting ropes made of seaweed and moving boxes around, apparently randomly at work and justified to be there.

Jess knew better. She kept a smile on her face all the way down, lifting a hand and returning casual greetings until they went through the last big metal doors and exited into the raw, bare stone space that was the shuttle pad.

A half dozen Bay guards were there. "Drake." One of them gave her a tap on the chest salute. "Good flight."

Jess paused and regarded him. All six of the guards looked right back at her, braced, in Bay colors. "Keep an eye on things," she said. "We might have land crabs in the kitchen."

The lead guard smiled at her, without any humor at all. "Heard that."

Jess touched her forehead in a return salute and walked out from the overhang of stone into the open.

Not like at the base. Nothing guarded the pad. It was just a large, flat stone plateau that now held the big, tube shaped shuttle with its gently pointed snout and the wide wings jutting out to either side.

A shuttle loader was waiting for them. "Jesslyn Drake?"

"That'd be me," Jess said. "And NM-Dev-1."

He nodded. "Come with me. Station arranged quarters onboard for you."

They followed him across the empty pad and up the ramp and into the entryway of the shuttle as wisps of rocket fuel tainted the air. They turned to enter the main cabin as they came to the hatchway, but the man waved them forward. "Private cabin."

They got a glimpse of the main room, half full of bodies in seats, most of which bore bio alt collars and had eyes fixed on the far wall. Dev remembered being one of them and met the eyes of one near the end of the row of hard seats.

He stared at her, then looked away, and the door shut as they moved into a smaller chamber, with wider, padded seats. "Here you go. Have a good flight." The loader shut the door behind them, and they were alone.

They stowed their packs in the small cabinets, then took seats in the plush, comfortable couches, fastening the restraints as the engines rumbled into life below.

Jess tightened her seat belt and looked around. The smaller cabin was very much like the one she'd first faced Bain in, a bit of plush that had indicated to her his status.

Now she and Dev shared the space with its sanitary unit and both drink and snack dispenser. "Nice," she said.

Dev settled into her seat and licked her lips. "Different. I was in the main cabin when I came downside with Doctor Dan."

"So what happens now?" Jess asked. "Never been on one of the space ones before."

"First the rockets will light," Dev said, "and then...oh."

The rockets lit and there was no point in speaking as a rumbling filled the space and they were being shaken violently as the shuttle took off, first moving slowly and then accelerating.

Jess felt an itching buzz in her ears and she grimaced a little as grav increased and she felt herself being shoved down into her seat, a pressure that increased steadily along with the rumbling for long minutes. "Ugh. Supposed to feel like this?"

Dev opened one eye and regarded her. "I really don't know. I've only come in the other direction."

Jess closed her eyes against the discomfort and flexed her hands, taking deep breaths until she felt the pressure slacken and then the sound did, and the next thing she knew gravity was gone and she was lifting up just a bit off her seat against the restraints. "What the..."

"We're in null," Dev said. "There is no grav until we get to station."

Jess absorbed this information. She lifted her hand and watched it float in space as an announcement clicked on with the same information and warning about removing restraints.

At once, she released her belt and let it drift free, then let go of the chair arms and pushed herself up. "Whoa!"

"Jess, be careful." Dev released her own belts, getting ready to assist.

Jess straightened out her body and relaxed, drifting up near the ceiling of the cabin. She reached up and pushed her finger against it, inverting and going downward head first. "This is cool," she said. "I like it." She felt her entire body re-aligning as her joints appreciated this lack of tension.

It felt great. She turned herself around slowly and watched Dev watch her, Dev's short hair lifting around her head.

After a moment Dev released her hold and pushed upward, and they floated together in the middle of the cabin.

Jess tucked her knees up and rotated so they were facing the same way.

"Null can be fun," she said. "It takes a while to get used to."

Jess did another tumble in the air, then rotated and stretched her body out as though she were flying and extended her hands toward Dev, who caught hold of them.

She pulled Dev to her, and as they met in mid air, she accurately aimed and kissed Dev, keeping that up as the momentum rotated them together. She let out a chuckle as they parted slightly, then leaned in for another kiss. "Let's see if I can take your mind off where we're going."

It was a new experience, and Dev more than welcomed it.

Chapter Six

IT WAS ALWAYS interesting to watch the shuttle come in. Dan Kurok leaned against the outer wall, appreciating the gentle dance of the big craft as it nosed carefully closer, aiming for the docking connector between two struts of the station.

It was quiet. The station was in night shift, and most of the staff and bios were in quarters and crèche respectively, leaving only a few people loitering about.

Doss, of course, and a half dozen of the scientific administrators, two of the station ops, and near the far edge of the docking ring, three security guards.

Kurok watched them in some amusement as they shifted from boot to boot eyeing the shuttle. He had no earthly idea what the guards thought they were going to get to do in this little scenario, but he was half tempted to just let them find out the hard way the difference between station and downside.

"Daniel." Doss came over. "They're almost here."

"Yes, I see the shuttle." Kurok indicated the big craft settling its nose in to the docking ring. "Now, suppose you get rid of those two proctors, and the guards, and let me handle this." He stepped around Doss and headed for the lock.

"But, Daniel, don't you want them to take care of the unit?"

"No."

Doss hurried after him, and they joined the small group of administrators. "Daniel, I must protest."

Kurok rounded on him. "Please don't bother, Randall. You're asking for trouble, and if something stupid and lethal happens there's a limited amount I can do about it."

One of the other administrators sighed. "Dan, c'mon. We know this is your super special project but the bottom line is it's a bio unit. You can't pretend otherwise."

Kurok shook his head and folded his arms. "Fine," he said. "It's not me that's going to end up either dead or horribly damaged. I'll just stand back out of the way because you all can't be bothered to remove your heads from your asses and listen to me."

"We have security here," the man answered, stiffly.

Kurok just chuckled without humor.

The inner lock opened, and as he expected, Jess and Dev were the first ones out. Jess was in front, her very tall figure encased in the solid black with green piping of an Interforce drop suit, head sweeping back and forth, body thrumming with energy.

Her eyes found the security guards, and she grinned, meeting Kurok's gaze next. Behind her Dev was keeping up with her longer strides, dressed in her deep green tech jumpsuit, but over that she had on a beautiful and shimmering greenish blue jacket that was obviously not Interforce issue.

Both had regulation packs on their backs, and Jess had done them the courtesy of not having any visible weapons hanging off her, though Kurok fully expected the pack to contain them.

Dev looked wary and anxious.

"Wow," the administrator next to Kurok muttered. "I didn't expect the agent to be that big."

Kurok chuckled again then went forward, leaving the group behind. He got smiles from both visitors and then a moment later he gave them both hugs, spending a long moment embracing Dev and patting her on the back. "It's going to be okay," he whispered into her ear. "Just relax."

Dev responded with a powerful squeeze and a real smile, then she stepped back diffidently as Jess gave him a hug.

"How was the trip?" Kurok asked as they started toward the welcoming committee.

"Interesting," Dev said, eyeing her partner. "I think Jess enjoyed the null a lot."

"Oh, I did," Jess said. "Thanks for arranging for the private bunk. Woulda probably freaked out the civs in the main cabin."

"Let's save that story for later," Kurok said. "Please be patient with the idiocy you're about to encounter. We'll get through it and go have some dinner."

"Mm," Jess rumbled low in her throat. "I promised Devvie I'd make sure no one got jerky on her."

"I figured that." Kurok smiled at the group they were approaching. "Please try not to shoot the walls. Vacuum disarranges everything and is tedious to fix," he added in a low tone. "Well, everyone." He raised his voice as they arrived. "Let's make introductions."

Everyone, including the proctors, was staring at Jess, who, after a moment, seemed to find this funny. She casually draped her arm over Dev's shoulders and waited, making a point of reaching over to brush some nonexistent dust off the tech insignia at Dev's collar.

Kurok saw the motion and stifled a smile. "This is senior

agent Jesslyn Drake, of Interforce, and her tech partner and pilot, Dev," he said. "As you all know, Dev was born here, and is a prototype for the Interforce tech service that's been extremely successful."

"Yes, hello." Doss edged forward, bravely extending his hand to Jess. "You are most welcome, Agent Drake."

Jess took his hand and clasped it, staring hard at him after she released her grip.

"And of course, welcome back, ah...Dev," he added belatedly. "We were very gratified to hear of your excellent work."

"Thank you, Director," Dev responded. "Thanks to Doctor Dan, I was well prepared for this work and have had excellent programming to assist me in performing it."

Kurok smiled at her. "Dev is far too modest. But we can all discuss that later. I'm sure our guests want to relax after their journey from downside." He glanced at the two visitors. "Let me walk you to your quarters, hm?"

"Well we..." Doss paused, finding those cold and unnerving blue eyes fastened hard on him again and noting the uneasy and nervous expressions on everyone else's faces, most especially the proctors. Even the other administrators were completely and unusually silent, leaving all the talking to him. "I mean, you see we do have some protocols, Daniel and—"

Jess shifted a little, straightening up to her full height. "Hey," she barked, getting everyone's attention immediately. "Dev's us now. You better treat her like one of us. First one who doesn't is gonna get my fist in their face. Got it?"

The administrators looked at the security guards, who stared back, wide eyed.

Kurok merely stood and waited. He could smell the fear, and though he knew Jess was putting on a show, the potential for violence in the tall figure next to him was real.

"Oh, of course, no!" Doss recovered first, and stepped up, gaining himself points if he'd only known it. "Of course Dev is our welcome guest, as you are, Agent Drake! We're very thankful you could take time from your busy schedule to come up and assist us in moving the project forward."

"Great. We done posturing now?" Kurok said. "C'mon you two. Let's get you settled." He put a hand on Jess's back, feeling the silent laughter as he guided them through the crowd toward the portal from the shuttle bay into the main part of the station.

Dev glanced at the proctors as they moved through, giving

them a polite smile as they backed up out of the way. They looked troubled. Everyone looked incorrect. But she had Jess's arm over her shoulders, they were with Doctor Dan, and for now it all seemed like it was going to be all right.

They cleared the dock doors, and then Jess just stopped, tipping her head back and staring up. "Are those stars?" she asked after a brief pause.

Doctor Dan gently guided them to the side of the passage so they didn't block traffic. "Yes, those are stars," he said. "I forgot you wouldn't have seen them on the shuttle."

The station had clear panels and Jess was under one, looking up at the speckles and pinpoints of light against a silky black background. She hadn't been sure of what to expect, and now she wasn't sure what to think when Dev took her arm and pointed down. "That's what downside looks like from here."

She refocused and looked out a second panel, seeing a huge gray surface rolling below them, bathed in shadow and darkness. At the very edge, she saw a slice of brighter light. "What's that?"

"Ah. That's the sun about to come up," Kurok said. "Does that a dozen or so times in an orbital day." He could hear, in the edges of his hearing, the servos in motion to move the solar panels, and the motion caught Jess's attention. "Let's get you in quarters. You'll have plenty of time to sightsee, I promise."

Up until the time they'd left the shuttle, it had seemed routine. Jess reluctantly started to move, letting her eyes scan everything. Station was very, very different. Walls were clear or visibly metal.

The air smelled strange and sterile, like the depths of the systems storage bunkers in the Citadel.

Her balance felt odd.

And there were stars overhead and the world below, the dark surface punctuated by flashes of lightning that rippled across it.

She had no connection to the surface. The comms didn't reach up here.

She felt Dev take her hand, and she was glad. She focused her attention on the walkway and set aside the wonder for a little while as she listened to the bumps and low, subvocal thumping around her as they walked across some main corridor and headed for a large, vertical clear tube.

There weren't many people around, she noticed, and no visible bio alts.

"Okay, we step in here, and kick upwards," Kurok said. "Remember how to do this, Dev?"

"I do." Dev took a firmer hold of Jess's hand. "Jess, this is null."

The tube seemed like a complete drop to the bottom, but Jess felt the lack of gravity as soon as they cleared the entrance, and like Dev, she pushed upward and then they were just drifting up past other levels, mostly darkened.

It felt amazing, just like the shuttle had once they were out of the earth's gravity. It was almost like being underwater.

Then light blasted them, and she jerked in reaction, turning toward the source and seeing a ball of white fire come up over the edge of the world, laying a silver surface over the tops of the clouds and bathing the inside of the station.

"That is the sun," Dev said. "A star, close up."

"That's cool." Jess watched the light move in fascination. "It just burns in space?"

"It does," Doctor Dan said, as he guided them to a landing platform. "Here we go. This is the distinguished guest quarters." He led the way back into gravity, and they walked along a plush corridor whose roof was open to the stars. "I assigned your rooms personally."

"Mmm." Dev made a low sound. "I think that possibly caused some discomfort."

Kurok chuckled. "It did. I won't lie to you, Dev. There was some idea of putting you in crèche quarters, but I refused to allow it."

Jess eyed him. "Good idea. Cause I wouldn't have gone for that."

"Yes, I know." Doctor Dan paused before a door, and then opened it with a touch. "Let's go inside and have a talk."

"Good idea," Jess repeated with a wry expression. "Got some grog in there?"

Kurok paused. "Do we need some?" He watched both heads nod in response. "Ah. Let's go to my quarters for our chat then. I'm more prepared there."

KUROK'S QUARTERS WERE on the other side of the ring level they were on, and his were the last in the section. They met no one on their quiet walk, the hallway lights dim save the spears of sunlight that darted through panels at regular intervals.

Kurok palmed his door and waved them inside. "We'll keep this short. I'm sure it's been a long day for you both."

Had it been? Dev didn't feel particularly tired. Especially

now that she knew she wasn't going to be spending the night in the crèche or in transport quarters. She smiled a little as she felt Jess bump against her and looked aside to see the brief grin on her face.

"We're fine," Jess said for them both. "We got to relax this afternoon on the beach."

"Ah, I think I know the beach you speak of." Doctor Dan smiled as he closed the door. "Are you also a cooker of fish?"

"I am."

His quarters were, for station, spacious and included three rounded bubble shapes in a mixture of clear plas and brushed metal. The front one included an area to sit, and the walls were mild and translucent, a soft non-color that had a number of framed images on them.

Dev stood quietly and waited, but Jess went to the images and looked at them with interest as Doctor Dan retrieved a bottle and some glasses from a cabinet. "I think I've been to a few of these places," Jess said.

Doctor Dan smiled. "No doubt you have. That underwater cavern is just up the coast from Base Ten."

It felt very strange to be there. Dev thought she knew what it would be like to come back to the station, but things turned out very differently than she'd expected. It was interesting to her how that made her feel inside.

Maybe it was that they had started from Jess's home. Had spent the trip in a private cabin so different than her journey downside.

Now here they were in Doctor Dan's private space, which she'd never seen before. It was nice and she noticed the Drake's Bay shirt Jess had given him hanging on a notch near the door. "This is a very pleasant space," she said after a moment.

Doctor Dan looked up from pouring the drinks. "You think so, Dev? It's all right, I suppose. The porch has a nice view." He indicated a sealed door. "We can go out there later if you want."

Jess detoured over and peered at the door. "Airlock?"

"Safety." Doctor Dan brought a tray with him back to the seating. "All of these subsections are designed to self seal in case of cracks or punctures. The shields are good, but micro meteorites get past them sometimes and a break in the surface will really ruin your day."

Jess looked at the opening and then at him. "Nice, but a little creepy." She walked over and took a seat in one of the chairs, sprawling at her ease as she took a glass. "Thanks."

Unfazed. Completely at home. Doctor Dan remembered that was a hallmark of most of the agents he'd ever met and certainly had been one of Justin's.

Even though she was now in a station in space for the first time in her life, Jess had that air of commanding the circumstances he remembered so well. "Here you go, Dev. I think you might have had this before."

Dev took a glass and sniffed it. It was honey mead and she smiled. "I have, yes." She took a sip and relaxed a little in her seat next to Jess. "I like it."

"So do I." Kurok sat down and regarded them. "First of all, thank you both for coming up here."

Jess grinned. "Interforce is as interested in this project working out as you all are. They want more of Devvie."

"They do," Kurok agreed. "Which is quite bemusing to me, of course, since my thoughts of being able to structure a set that could do what I myself had done seemed, more than once, to me to be self satisfyingly gratuitous."

"That really what you were after?" Jess asked, swirling the mead in her cup. "Seemed crazy to me that you brought that out right when we needed it."

Dev felt a bit self conscious, listening to the conversation, since the it in question was her. But the mead was good and she just sat quietly sipping it, content to let Jess do the talking.

"Mmm...not exactly," he admitted. "What I was after was something a bit more radical." He relaxed back into his chair, regarding the liquid in his glass. "Something I'm only willing to discuss with you here, where I know we're in private."

Jess's brows lifted a little.

Kurok winked at her. "Because I know every inch of these walls."

"That a problem here?" she asked. "Thought this place was full of high minded scientists."

"Hopefully that was as full of Interforce drollery as I remember."

Jess chuckled in acknowledgment and lifted her glass in his direction.

"One of the things we'd always done here in creating bio alt sets is limit them," Kurok said. "Limit their intelligence, especially in the area of self determination and independent thought. You can do that, you know. There's an area of the brain where that develops and you just fill it with null matter and it never does."

"Mmm. So you did intend them to be servants." Jess said, but in a mild tone. "That's what the Bay always thought."

"The Bay, being what it is, with the history it has, would naturally think that." He smiled at her. "Since it's as much an incubator as anything I have up here." He paused, then exhaled. "Anyway, it wasn't so much they were designed to be servants as they were designed to be content with what they were asked to do."

Dev drew in a breath, memories of conversations in the crèche echoing in her head. Hadn't they been convinced every assignment would be a good one? She considered that. Or had that just been what they'd said, knowing it was what the proctors wanted to hear?

"Humans, natural born ones, are not ever naturally content," Doctor Dan said. "And no one really likes taking out the garbage. So if you're creating human beings who are intended to do that, or to shuck shellfish or whatever, for me as a scientist it made sense to make them want to do that and be happy as a result."

"Huh." Jess grunted softly. "Sometimes that doesn't work out. I've seen it." she said "The be happy part."

"At the Quebec City place," Dev said. "But I told you, Jess, they also program us to accept being treated badly. We're okay with that. Really."

They both looked at Kurok, who lifted his glass in acknowledgment. "Part of the being content."

Jess considered that for a minute. "That's fucked up."

Kurok didn't look offended, even though Dev looked like she wanted to protest. "It is," he agreed. "It's part of the scientific principal known as the law of unintended consequences, or sometimes alternatively the end justifying the means."

"Uh huh."

"Or lies you tell yourself to justify what you want to see done," Doctor Dan amended, with a quiet smile. "We all do it."

"Truth." Jess acknowledged. "Like taking kids from their families before they end up killing their sibs or old annoying aunties. Just the right thing to do." A faint smile appeared on her face. "It might sometimes even be the truth."

He studied Jess. "Truth is very rarely black and white. So your next question of truth, if you want it answered, will include you in a very small group of potential traitors to humanity."

A small silence fell. "Small, because it right now includes only myself, a few of my staff, and since she will very quickly recognize it in herself, Dev," Kurok said. "So think carefully before you ask, Jesslyn. You come from a very, very conservative thinkers."

Jess swirled her mead in it's cup and drank it ṣ. watching Kurok over the rim in silence for several long moments. "Y'know," she finally said, "my dad left me a note after he bought it. Told me if I went rogue to look you up."

Both of Daniel Kurok's eyebrows lifted sharply.

"Said he knew you would give me a hand," Jess added. "That I would be something to you."

For a long moment, he went still. Then he lifted his glass and grinned wryly at her. "He was a clever man, your father."

"So bring it," Jess added with a lazy smile. She lifted her free hand and made a little come ahead gesture. "Maybe I'll surprise you."

Now it was Kurok's turn to ponder, and he did, taking his time before he set his cup down and hiked one ankle up onto his opposing knee. "I was a young idiot when I started working with bio alts here on station," he said. "I didn't originate the program, they were already working with basic models when I got here, mostly to do tasks here on station in space."

"They didn't want to have to clean up after themselves?" Jess asked.

"Not really, no. It wasn't that. They had a sense that because they lived here up on station, doing all this urgent, needed science, they should have people to do the things that weren't scientific in nature." He cleared his throat. "And they could do some basic modifications, to allow adjustment to null, and that sort of thing."

Jess chuckled humorlessly.

"Splitting hairs, yes," Doctor Dan acknowledged. "They didn't want to bring up downworlders, ergo, the bio alt program. Originally just for station, but then, when word got out, very lucrative for those downworlders who needed trustworthy workers, whom we could customize for their needs."

"Slaves," Jess stated.

"Because they had no choice in any of it, yes," he said. "That was where the program was when I got here."

Dev felt so wide eyed her eyeballs were sore. This was, maybe, too much truth for her to comfortably absorb. She had her cup in her hands, still half full, and she felt the solid weight of it as she waited for what was going to come next.

Doctor Dan seemed to realize her discomfort. "Now, Dev, this seems incorrect to you. I know basic school presented this ıformation in a very different way."

Dev put her cup down. "Yes," she said, "but...we knew. The sets in my classes, we understood the truth behind what that was, we just didn't talk about it much because we knew it would make the proctors unhappy."

Kurok smiled.

"You knew they were bullshitting?" Jess asked her, in a tone of surprise.

"No, well." Dev gave her an appealing look. "Jess, I don't know what a bullshit is. But we knew things about us that we knew the proctors didn't. We didn't think it was incorrect, we just thought it was sort of funny."

Now Doctor Dan laughed, a light, surprised sound.

Jess leaned forward. "That's what you did. You did that." She pointed at Dev. "Had nothing to do with her being a tech, but that smart stuff. That. They get it."

"Yes, actually, I did that," he said. "When I became first an advanced, then the senior geneticist here, I put in a macro level change to the overarching biological alternative programming." He laced his fingers together and put his hands behind his head. "I wasn't trying to make a better bio alt. I was trying to make better human beings."

Dev made a small sound of surprise.

Jess leaned her elbow on the arm of her chair, looking intently at him. "When I first met Dev, I knew she was different." She held up a hand when he started to answer. "We have bios on base. I'd dealt with them as mechs. They're simple."

He nodded.

"Dev was different." Jess looked over at her. "She was complicated."

"Yes," Kurok said. "Dev, like her year and near year mates, understand what they are. Who they are. What we are. How we're different." He paused. "So when they asked for a bio alt that could be an Interforce tech, the foundation was already there."

They both looked at Dev. "I am a developmental unit," she said. "So that does not really surprise me."

"And Dev was yet again different from the rest of them because what I added with her, was a very high level of intelligence," Doctor Dan said with a faint smile. "The 'New Model' part of what Dev is. A potential we deliberately had avoided before now."

NOW THEY HAD tea. Three cups of steaming, honey sweetened, real leaf tea in front of them as moving light reflected against the outer walls from the passing sun.

Dev had forgotten all about being hungry, or the trip, or being in the crèche. She found the matter of fact explanations Doctor Dan gave them to be breathtaking, though she mostly kept silent hardly knowing what to ask.

It was one thing to tell yourself something inside your head. Dev exhaled a little. Totally another thing to have someone like Doctor Dan saying it because Doctor Dan had actually done it.

But Jess had known all along. Even without Doctor Dan telling her, she'd known that Dev was different. Was smart. Was like her, a natural born. Even when they'd only just met because Jess was herself very smart, even though she often said she wasn't.

"If they find out about this they're gonna lock you up in one of those plastic eggs," Jess said. "You realize that, right? Even the security chief down at the Bay realized making smarter bios didn't mean anything good for the average yonk down there."

"Actually, they'll just space me," Kurok said. "It's much cleaner, and one more piece of debris out there won't matter. I've had to be extremely careful about the DNA patterns I've used." He sipped his tea reflectively. "But I know someday they'll figure it out. I'm not that arrogant."

"That's a little crazy."

"Mmm." Kurok nodded. "More than you know. Staff's already saying that the latest sets seem to have an understanding of status and advancement." He sighed. "They compete for attention and want to excel. So far everyone views that as a positive."

Jess got up to stretch her legs, rambling around in a long oval pattern. "That's why they were so jazzed to get on comms on base," she said suddenly, looking around at Dev. "Right?"

"Well, yes, sure," Dev answered. "To do that means better tasks and more responsibility. That means a better place." She put her cup down. "It was...Jess, do you remember when we were in the base and you all were up outside and I was down in the bio alt quarters?"

"When we were going to be splatted? Sure." Jess went over and peered out the airlock door. "When you got that door opened."

"Yes. I was able to get into systems when I logged in with my operations credentials," Dev said. "I told the rest of the sets that it was not optimal for the enemy to leave that avenue open, and they said the enemy hadn't expected one of us to have those credentials."

"Yeah? And?"

"They said I was the first. And I was. But they did not want me to be the last."

Jess walked over and leaned against the back of the chair that Dev was sitting in, looking over her at Kurok. "If they figure out what's going on, those bio alts are probably in trouble."

"That's why only very few people know," Doctor Dan said. "To anyone else, we're just working on making bio alts more useful. You saw the reaction to Dev's success."

"Yeah." Jess watched him thoughtfully. "But what's the end game, Doc? Bios take over the world? How does this make anything better?"

"Fair question." Kurok smiled his gentle smile at her. "And I'm not entirely sure if I have the answer to it yet." He looked around as the door announcer chimed. "Ah. I believe that might be dinner." He got up and went to the door, pausing to study the panel beside it before he opened it and stepped back. "Hope you enjoy what I ordered."

"Agents eat anything," Jess said. "And Dev eats anything except spicy crabs."

"And live animals," Dev muttered. "But I know we won't get that here."

Jess chuckled and gave her a little hug from behind then released her and straightened up.

A bio alt entered, pushing a small cart with trays on it. "I hope it's all satisfactory, Doctor Dan." He glanced into the room, then quickly returned his attention to Kurok.

"Thank you, Ayebee." The doctor indicated the small preparation space. "Just leave it there." He stepped back out of the way. "I appreciate all the things you brought here for my guests."

The bio alt looked pleased at the acknowledgment. "Thank you." He looked over at them again. "Hello, NM-Dev-1. Welcome back. We have heard of your excellent work."

"Hello, Ayebee," Dev responded cordially. "Thank you. I've done my best so far." She glanced at Jess. "This is my friend, Jess."

"Hello." The bio alt gave Jess a somewhat nervous look. "Is it all correct, Doctor Dan?"

"Yes, thanks. I'll take it from here." Kurok let the bio alt out, and then returned to the cart. "Come over here, my friends. There's too many plates to carry them."

There was a small counter near the preparation area with little seats next to it, and for a moment the three of them were silent as they sorted out the contents.

Once they were settled, Kurok regarded them. "Let's change the subject while we eat. Tell me about this whole seed thing, hm?" His voice was casual. "Doss told me someone from Interforce called up here about it?"

Jess was curiously tasting the contents of the plate, but she looked up sharply at the question. "What did he tell you?"

He chewed a few times and swallowed. "Just that someone found some of our seed stock downside. No one seemed to know much about it," he answered. "Or did they?"

Jess studied him intently. "That's all he said?"

"Should there be more?"

Jess regarded her meal. "Alters told me they asked about how an entire cavern full of plants from those seeds could end up in Drake's Bay." She looked up at him. "Where apparently some rock can make them grow."

Kurok's jaw actually dropped, and he stared at her in open astonishment. "What?"

"What what, what about the seed, or what about the glowing rocks?" Jess looked a bit amused. "Just my luck, right? They find some damned crap at the Bay that does what that big ass machine we blew up did. Figures."

"Glowing rock?" Kurok repeated slowly. "What kind of glowing rock? There's no type of phosphorescence anyone's ever found that can trigger photosynthesis on a large scale. We'd have regenerated half the damn planet. I mean, what the hell?"

Dev got up and went over to her pack, opened one of the pouches in it, and removed something. She came back over and put the item on the table next to his hand. "Here you go, Doctor Dan. I brought a little bit of this here for you to see. I thought you might want to."

He put his fork down and picked up the rock and turned it over in his fingers. It emitted a soft glow, peachy yellow in color, just under the surface of it's rough exterior. "Are you kidding me? This was in the Bay?"

Satisfied, Jess went back to ingesting her meal. "That was in the Bay. Someone did a deal with my brother." She forked up a bit of yellow substance and chewed it. "There was some of this down there." She pointed at the substance. "What is it again?"

"Peaches?" Kurok said. "Your brother was growing peaches?"

Kurok hadn't known. Jess felt a sense of relief in her guts. Unless his acting skills were beyond her ability to detect, the bewilderment not only on his face and body language but in his voice rang true. "Peaches," she said. "I like 'em."

"Randall said it was no big deal," Doctor Dan said. "No big deal. Son of a bitch! So now who in the hell was lying?"

"I have some vid of the cavern, too." Dev sat back down. "It was really nice, Doctor Dan. It reminded me of the grow chambers here. It smelled excellent."

"I'm sure it did," he muttered.

"Base sent some of the research team over," Jess said. "I get the feeling there's lots of cred in this."

"You told them?" Kurok's voice dropped almost an octave.

Jess looked back at him and shrugged. "I'm active duty," she said. "Sure I told them. After I told them I offed my sib for doing deals with what I suspected then was the other side."

He covered his eyes with one hand and leaned on the table. "Son of a bitch."

Jess merely chewed, a look of wry bemusement on her face. "And here you thought you had news, huh?"

"Son of a bitch."

FINALLY, THEY WERE in their quarters. Or to be more precise, they were in Jess's quarters, seated on the bed together. "He's freaking," Jess said, resting her elbows on her knees and looking around the space.

"Doctor Dan?"

"Yeah."

Dev cleared her throat. "He does seem quite discomfited. I think we really made him incorrect with our report. I have never seen him so surprised."

Jess chuckled soundlessly. "You doing okay, Devvie? About being up here I mean?"

Dev nodded. "It's not like I thought it was going to be," she admitted. "I'm actually feeling sort of excellent at the moment."

"Aw, c'mon you didn't really think me and the doc were gonna let them take you and put you back with the rest of them, didja?"

Dev smiled a little. "Honestly? Not really, but I was trying to psych myself so in case it did happen I was okay with it." She looked around. "But I also know my being here is going to upset a lot of people on station, and the Ayebee is going to tell everyone I was in Doctor Dan's quarters."

"Screw 'em," Jess said.

Dev's brow creased a little. "How would that help?"

Jess snickered. Then she got up and wandered around the space, looking out the panel near the ceiling to see the stars outside. The sun was behind the earth again, and it was darker than dark out there, a richness of black she'd never seen before.

"I think I will go get some rest." Dev stood up and lifted her backpack. "Doctor Dan said he would meet with us in the morning." She moved to the door, aware of the tall, silent figure at her back. "Good night, Jess."

"I might come visit," Jess said, as the door opened. "Don't get freaked out."

"Of course not." Dev left the room and went to the one right next to it, pausing before putting her hand on the pad. She felt the faint tingle as it processed the chip in her hand then the door slid open to admit her.

It was dim and quiet inside, the lights coming up a little as she entered and put her pack down on the bed. She opened it and removed her sanitary kit and her sleep clothes. She took both into the small sanitary unit and set them down, pausing to review the facilities.

Water, yes, as she'd expected, though there was a sign pleading for economy with it. She ignored two small tubes of soap and set out the ones she'd brought with her. She used a little to wash her face then exchanged her jumpsuit for her sleep clothes.

Then, at last, the sight of her collar made her twitch a little, the first time it was visible since she'd come on station. Dev exhaled. She didn't hide it on purpose. It was just how the Interforce uniforms were made after all.

But the sleep clothes, the sleeveless shirt and shorts, exposed the bio alt device along with the dark brown lines patterned into the skin of her shoulder.

She folded her arms and regarded her profile somberly then she turned and went back into the main area of the room. She detoured to the courtesy station to retrieve a small cup of tea, just as she would have done in her quarters at the base.

She took the tea back to the bedside with her and put it down on the plas table, sitting down on the bed and bouncing a little experimentally.

Reasonably comfortable. She pulled herself up and leaned against the inflated pillow, the surface just a bit yielding as she stretched out and picked up the tea to sip it.

So here she was. Dev looked up at the ceiling, which partially revealed the stars and partially was opaque to the level above. This was far and above the fanciest place she'd ever been in on station, and it was hard to lie here and think about all the bio alts in the dorms below or in their sleep pods rotating along station edge.

That had been her life. Six downworld months ago she'd left here and that had been all she'd known, and now?

And now. But Doctor Dan said they'd wanted to put her back in the crèche, only he'd not allowed it. Dev could feel the truth in that, and she'd seen the discomfort in the admins' and the proctors' faces. In fact, she suspected the two proctors had been there to take her away.

Doctor Dan had thought ahead about that and made sure it was okay. But Dev knew that even if he hadn't, Jess would have. And now she knew for sure that she'd always felt a little different because she was.

Doctor Dan had made her different. Had made her smart, and brave, and able to think with excellence so she could help Jess in a very good way.

She smiled at that and squiggled down a little into a more comfortable position, sipping her tea in contentment.

JESS SPENT A little while watching the stars, thinking about what they'd learned so far. It was good to spend a little while just reflecting, something she didn't often get a chance to do in an insertion. Usually that was like their attack on the other science base, all action and violence, not so much time to stand quietly and think.

But now she could. For a while. And after that she would grab her pack and go over to Dev's room, where she would curl up with her in bed and be able to relax as much as she ever did, content that she'd be able to protect Dev in case anyone got any crazy ideas.

She went over to the chair near the far wall and sat. Arranging her long limbs so that she could just look out the panel as she saw the streaks of light from the sun start to gild the station.

It was cool. Jess folded her hands over her stomach and just watched. Being in space was cooler than she'd thought it would be, full of interesting things to see and null gravity to enjoy.

Now she would have to carefully hunt down who the target was and make sure no one messed with Dev. A fairly easy assignment she reasoned, and maybe Alters would be done screwing around by the time she got back.

She wanted him to be. She wanted them to decide the cavern was just an isolated freak and leave the Bay to grow some stuff in it to sell and move on. Let her move on. Let her go back to regular duty, maybe name a placeholder for her there to keep an eye on things.

Maybe Alters would. He was getting close to retirement. Jess gazed thoughtfully out the panel, seeing some motion in the background, a white faint streak moving across her plane of vision.

Did she care if Interforce took over the Bay?

Jess's nose wrinkled a little as she made a face. She did care. Even though going back there hadn't ever occurred to her. There was a part of it that was a part of her deep in the gut, a wash of old memories of being a child there, of her parents.

Of her brothers.

Of swimming with her father in the bay she'd brought Dev to, herself a little kid squealing with laughter.

She was the Drake of Drake's Bay right now, and there was a connection to the old place that made the thought of Alters and the Interforce group rummaging around rub her raw.

"And I was the idiot who brought them there." Jess sighed, twiddling her thumbs. "I should have kept my stupid damn mouth shut."

She wanted to go back in time and not kill Jimmy and leave him in charge since he'd been elected head of the family committee in the absence of any clear legal stakeholder. Go back in time and not find the damn cavern. Go back in time and not tell Interforce.

Too damn late for that. She hadn't even thought twice when she'd told Alters.

Idiot.

Jess stood and lifted her pack up, trudging out the door to her room and going to the next door over. She knocked on the surface, ignoring the annunciator, and waited, hearing the soft sounds of motion inside.

The door opened, and Dev was there. She looked tousled and adorable in her shorts and tank. "Hi."

"Hello," Dev responded. "Would you like to come inside?" She backed up a step.

"Yeah. I was bumming myself out in the other room." Jess moved inside and dropped her pack near one of the chairs then sat down. "You scan this place?"

"Yes." Dev sat down in the chair next to her. "It's possible there are devices here our scan won't pick up," she added, apologetically. "The systems downside are a lot less sophisticated."

Jess looked around the room pensively. "You think the doc'd let them put bugs in?"

Dev had to think about that, and she did. They sat there together in silence for about ten minutes then she cleared her throat gently. "I would like to say no."

Jess smiled wryly.

"But we were asked to come up here, and I do not know why," Dev continued. "They do not need us to look at the set metrics, Jess. Neither of us really know what we'd be looking at. I took some basic DNA classes with Doctor Dan, but I didn't get a chance to do anything advanced."

"Mmm." Jess nodded.

"Do you know why?"

Jess pulled her pack over and removed a small slate from inside it, setting it on her knee and flexing her fingers. She started it up and began typing, scrounging over a little so Dev could see what she was doing.

Jess typed:

    Don't think it has anything to do with the new
    bios. Something else going on. Could be about the
    stuff he said tonight, could be the seed stuff.

Dev nodded a little. "I see." She went shoulder to shoulder with Jess and took over the keyboard.

    But he sounded like he didn't know anything
    about the seeds, and I didn't find anything in the
    logs showing that he did.

Jess took back the slate.

    I know. That rang true to me, too. I don't
    think he knew about that, but what if someone else

```
here did, and made him ask us to come?
```

Dev typed:

```
    I don't think anyone could make Doctor Dan do
anything he didn't want to do. Just like with you.
```

Jess chuckled softly.

```
    Not on purpose. What if they came up with a
good reason to ask, but it was a scam? They could
want to get us out of the way if they were sending
more seed or whatever.
```

"Oh," Dev said. "That could be true."
Jess bent over the slate again.

```
    Can't trust anyone but us, Dev. We go along
with the game, but always keep your eyes out for
something that doesn't click. Doesn't seem right.
You know this place, I don't.
```

She waited for Dev to read it, and nod, then she deleted the
page and turned the slate off. "You know what?"
"What?"
"I'm hungry."
Dev blinked at her. "Didn't you enjoy the meal at Doctor
Dan's?" She reached for her pack. "I have some crackers."
"Yeah, it was okay." Jess leaned back. "It was just...that was
all vegetable, wasn't it?"
"Yes."
"I want some fish."
Dev scrunched up her face. "Oh, Jess, I don't think we have
any of that up here. I know there are some tanks, but that's for the
director and people like that. We never got any." She frowned.
"Maybe we could get some protein bars from the night desk."
"Night desk." Jess sounded interested. "Where is it?"
"Downlevel, near the labs. It's for the natural borns who
work the late shift and a few of the sets who clean. They usually
had the bars plus some tea always available."
"Sounds good." Jess stood up. "Get your togs back on. Let's
go snooping."
Dev eyed her "For a snack?"
"Sure. For a snack."

DEV WASN'T SURE at all if it was a good idea to go snooping. She was back in her jumpsuit, her scanner slung over her shoulder as she and Jess walked down the quiet, darkened hallway.

She hadn't gotten out much in the late shifts. Once or twice when she'd gotten out of lab later than usual, and the night she'd eaten dinner with Doctor Dan right before she left. She looked down the passage and saw a guard near the drop tube right at the edge of the level. "Jess."

"Yes?" Her partner was sauntering along, dressed in her off-duty blacks. "Ah. I see."

As they approached, the guard half turned to face them, but kept his hands resting on the belt around his waist. "Evening," he greeted them courteously.

A natural born. Dev gave him a brief smile. "We're just going down to the ops center."

The guard amiably moved out of the way to let them pass. "Please be careful of the drop tube. They were doing maintenance on it."

Jess regarded him. "What's your deal? You keeping an eye on us or what?"

The guard looked puzzled. "Ma'am?"

"What's your job?"

"Oh." He indicated the hallway. "I make sure no one bothers the people who live up here," he said. "The admins and scientists. And guests." he added. "Priv."

"Uh huh." Jess moved forward again. "Nice." She touched the tube entrance and watched it light up, the translucent door sliding open. "We'll be back."

"Yes, ma'ams."

They stepped inside the tube and started dropping. "Now that's interesting, Devvie." Jess rotated as they drifted down, amusing herself. "Does he not know who you are? Someone forget to tell him?"

"My collar is covered," Dev responded. "It is possible he does not know since I am the only member of my set and he is a natural born. I don't think I have seen him before, since bio alts are not allowed up on that level."

"Uh huh." Jess tucked her knees up and did a somersault. "I really like this."

Dev steadied her as she completed rotating, and they approached the bottom of the tube. "Yes, I see that." She was aware of her voice echoing and how quiet it was around them. "I don't think you should do that during the day. There are too many other people in the tube."

They settled on the bottom, the door slid open, and Dev led the way out and turned to center.

There were four bio alts there cleaning the floor, and as they spotted them, it was obvious that they at least knew who Dev was. They straightened up and looked at her with undisguised interest, watching them as they passed by and headed for the desk visible at the center of the hall.

"NM-Dev-1," one of them called out.

Dev paused and turned. "Yes?" She waited for him to approach.

He smiled at the recognition. "Are you well? They said you did excellent work downside." He motioned the rest of his setmates over, and they eagerly complied. "It's good to see you."

The BeeEff's were tall, had brown curly hair, and a spattering of freckles across their noses. Jess studied them briefly, putting her hand on Dev's back.

"Thanks, BeeEff. This is my partner, Jess Drake. We work together, downworld."

"Hello," The BeeEff said, timidly. "You are a natural born."

"I am," Jess said. "And Dev here is a rock star."

The nearest one regarded her. "That is good?"

"The best," Jess clarified for him with a smile.

The BeeEffs all looked at Dev with approval. "It's good you have done such excellent work, NM-Dev-1," the one who had spoken before said. "It's good for all of us."

Dev drew breath to speak then paused as a proctor approached with a slate. "I think the proctor is looking for you," she said, almost apologetically, as the man paused. "Nice to speak with you."

"Yes." The BeeEffs nodded. "Good night." They went back to their cleaning task, and Jess and Dev walked on, aware of the eyes of the proctor fastened on them.

THE PEOPLE AT the night desk had their shorts in a twist. Jess recognized that immediately. She leaned on the counter as Dev politely requested some snacks, watching the supervisor on duty try to figure out a way to deny the request with her listening.

"Is there a problem?" Jess finally asked. "We had a long day and we're hungry."

"Oh, no. It will just take a moment," he finally said, reluctantly. "I'm sorry for the delay. You are Jesslyn Drake?"

"I am Jesslyn Drake," Jess confirmed in an amiable tone. "The hungry homicidal maniac. Cough up the grub."

"Jess." Dev put a hand on her arm. "The JayCee is coming with it. See? Over there." She pointed at the hallway behind them where a bio alt was visible, heading their way pushing a cart. "It'll just be a minute."

"Citizen Drake, you could have made the request from your assigned quarters," the supervisor told her. "It would have been delivered to you."

"I didn't make the request. Dev did," Jess said. "But she can get goodies delivered to her bunk, too, right?"

The man looked at her. "Ah, well—"

"Because I sure wouldn't want anyone here to diss my tech," Jess cut him off in a flat tone. "I'm sure Dan Kurok warned all of you I'm easily irritated and like to hurt people who make me that way."

The supervisor's eyes widened a little. "We were told to treat you as our guest, with courtesy," he said. "But NM-Dev-1 is not a citizen. She is a biological alternative, and we have regulations regarding how they are to be managed here."

Brave of him, really.

Jess put her hands on the counter and boosted herself up, leaning forward. "She's an Interforce tech. With credentials," she said. "You realize that makes her a citizen downworld, right? And we agents don't put up with desk wonks insulting our partners."

The man turned his head slightly and looked at Dev, who was standing just to one side, hands folded in front of her.

Dev remained quiet. She knew the super was really mad. Behind him she saw the bio alts on shift, the ones straightening the ops center and doing some data entry, and knew they were listening closely to what was going on.

Jess would get points with them. Dev glanced aside as the JayCee arrived. She broke up the uncomfortable tableau as she went and retrieved the plas case he had on the cart. "Thank you, JayCee."

"You are welcome, NM-Dev-1." The bio alt smiled at her. "It was my pleasure to bring it."

Dev smiled back then half turned. "This is my partner, Jess," she said. "Jess, this is JayCee. I was in class with his set."

Jess waved. "Hi there." She straightened up. "We'll head

back to our bunks now so you can relax," she told the supervisor. "Don't let me catch anyone being a jackass, okay?" She pushed away from the counter and held her hand out. "Gimme that, Devvie. I'll carry it for ya."

Dev eyed her. "If you are going to tumble in the null tube again, I'd better hold onto it," she said. "You'll make a mess."

"Point made. Let's go." Jess let her eyes travel around the group, seeing the stoneface expression on the supervisor and the imperfectly hidden delight on the faces of the bio alts. She winked at them, then sauntered after Dev, letting out a low whistle under her breath.

"Are you causing people discomfort on purpose?" Dev asked, as they walked down the now empty hallway.

"Yes."

"Why?"

"Because when you knock people off balance they don't have time, sometimes, to think about how they react, and you learn things like that," Jess said in an unexpectedly serious tone. "And, I don't want them to be comfortable with the idea of treating you like you belong here. You don't."

"I see," Dev said, thoughtfully. "The sets here seem to find that interesting. I think they like you."

Jess chuckled, bouncing a little as they approached the tube again, looking forward to the drift upward. "This might end up being cool, Dev." She palmed the tube entrance open and kicked away from the pad, zooming upward with a low rumble of delight.

"It's going to end up being something." Dev closed the door and kicked gently up herself, unable to stifle a chuckle of her own.

JESS FOUND AN encrypted squirt waiting for her the next morning, delivered to her on a slate. "Thanks." She took the slate from the bio alt who delivered it, moving back into the room she'd been assigned and sitting down to open it and read.

Dev was sitting in the open area, waiting. They were due to meet Dan Kurok shortly, and he'd told them he'd come to get them and lead them to breakfast.

"Now what?" Jess presented her eyeballs to the slate and waited for the message to decrypt. "We've been up here less than a day."

The slate cleared, and April's image appeared. "Good

morning," she said, clearing her throat. "Science team just left. They took samples. We scoured the back beyond and found two more gun emplacements, but they were empty. No one wants to take cred."

"Hmph." Jess grunted.

"We deactivated them," April continued. "Doug parsed the records comp here and extracted transport movement. It's embedded. Two trips didn't have point of origin."

"The seeds, I guess," Jess muttered. "Would they take an entire transport?" She looked up at Dev.

"No. The other was probably the synth dirt," Dev said. "That's quite bulky."

"Ah, sure." Jess triggered the message to continue.

"We also found a script. I embedded that, too." April looked troubled. "I think it's code, but I'm not sure. Maybe Rocket can look at it." April looked around then back at the screen. "That's all for now. Hope your trip's profitable."

She signed off, and the slate went blank. The attachments bubbled up, and she brought up the script first, leaning to one side as Dev came over to look at it. "Whatcha think, Devvie?"

Dev looked at the letters on the screen for a while. "There seems to be a pattern, but I am not sure what it is. I would like some time to study it."

The annunciator chimed.

"That must be the doc." Jess stood up and locked the pad, slipping it into her backpack and locking that as well. She set it down next to Dev's and went to open the door. "Morning," she greeted Doctor Dan.

He looked slightly amused. "It is, and a relatively amusing one for me, having to read the night operations report."

Jess smiled and shrugged. "We were hungry. Those vegetable things don't do much for me. "I kept thinking about Jonton's jumping shrimp."

Kurok had his Drake's Bay overshirt on and he leaned a shoulder against the door opening, his hands in the front single pocket of it. "Well, I can't promise breakfast will be any better, but let's go get it over with so I can give you a tour and then get my programming review with Dev done."

Dev settled her scanner over her shoulder. "Doctor Dan. I don't think I'm qualified to review anything you have done," she said. "I only just barely got out of the basic class."

"Tch tch tch." Kurok made a clucking noise with his tongue as they joined him in the hall. "Dev, that's not at all true. If you hadn't ended up being assigned so spectacularly, I had you marked down for a place in the lab with me."

Dev caught her breath in surprise.

"What did you think? That I was going to let you work in the kitchen?" He smiled at her expression. "Come on now. You knew you were an advanced student."

For a moment, Dev took herself out of that space they were walking through, her mind throwing her into the sudden question of which she would have liked better. Staying at station? Working with Doctor Dan?

That had been her dream of dreams.

Now? Dev glanced at Jess, who was blinking into an errant beam of sun, a brief flash of it lighting up her pale blue eyes as they never did downworld.

"But I'm sure you're glad things worked out as they did," Doctor Dan said placidly. "Am I right?"

Dev cleared her throat gently. "I really like my assignment very much, Doctor Dan." She saw Jess's lips curve upward. "But thank you for letting me know about working with you."

He chuckled. "Well stop being so modest. You've got no reason to be."

Jess grinned at him. "I'm trying to talk her into going for the senior rank they just opened. She thinks it's going to piss them all off."

"Well, she's got a point," Kurok admitted. "But I suspect they'll get over it." He eyed Dev. "After all, they did with me."

"Hah!" Jess chortled. "She tell you what they all call her?"

Dev felt her skin warming. "Jess."

Doctor Dan's eyes twinkled at her. "Now, Dev. How bad could it be if Jesslyn puts up with it?" He clapped his hand on Dev's shoulder. "I want to show you the structure outline for what will become your colleagues some day, and I very much value your opinion about it, since you know how it feels from the inside."

Dev didn't deny how excellent that made her feel. "The other techs refer to me as Rocket," she admitted, as they moved down the passageway. "I don't quite understand why."

Doctor Dan muffled a laugh. "Really?"

"Rocket Raccoon," Jess said. "I think it's cute as hell." She eyed Dev. "Just like she is."

Dev sighed. "I don't think I look like that animal, Jess."

Kurok patted her shoulder again. "Did your cohorts give you this name on their own, Dev? They came up with it?"

"Yes."

"That's excellent," he said in a serious tone. "That really is, Dev. It means they accept you as one of them." He led the way past the drop tube and around the curve of the station, toward the center. "I remember when they started calling me DJ, you know? After I came to Interforce."

Dev listened with interest. "Really?"

He nodded. "You could of course use my first name, Daniel, or Dan, which is a short version of it, but they found something completely different to call me, and it took me a while to realize what that meant."

"Hm." Dev glanced at Jess. "I remember you asked me what I wanted to be called."

Jess nodded. "I liked Dev. It's short and sounds good. But Rocket is a lot of fun."

Dev dropped a step or so behind her companions as Doctor Dan explained the parts of the station they were passing. They were on the residential level, and most of the people they passed were natural born, often turning to watch them go by.

"So, up at the apogee of station, we have the classrooms and the common areas," Doctor Dan said. "All the children learn up there. I'm sure Dev has told you about it."

"She did," Jess said. "All the kids?" She sounded skeptical.

"Actually, yes," Kurok said. "Until they're around six or seven, all the children learn together. Why make separate classrooms? They all learn to read the same way."

"We all don't read, Doctor Dan," Dev said, as they came to a cross path and turned. "I remember some of the sets in my classes couldn't."

"Well that's true." Kurok led them into a clean, brightly lit cafeteria that wasn't too different than the one at Base Ten. "Come, let's get some breakfast, and then we can finish talking." He took a tray and they followed him, taking a selection of items and moving along the line.

Doss saw them and hurried over. "Good morning, Daniel. I see you have our guests with you."

"Incredibly observant of you, Randall." Doctor Dan smiled gently at him. "Will you join us? I was just explaining to agent Drake how our school framework is set up. Doctor Doss developed the class structure, Jess. His specialty is developmental sciences."

Caught between pleasure and a suspicion he was being made fun of, Doss managed a slightly plastic smile. "Well yes, of course." He followed them to a table near the wall of the café where they had a good view of the outside of the station. "I hope the accommodations were acceptable, Agent Drake?"

Jess settled into her seat next to Dev, pausing to look outside as she caught sight of motion. "What's that?" She pointed at a vehicle moving past the plas panel with mechanical arms extending from it.

Dev glanced past her. "Maintenance. I think they're cleaning the exhaust vanes."

"Huh." Jess watched a moment then focused back on Doss. "Bunk's fine." She studied his round, moonlike face. "So you the guy in charge?"

Kurok chuckled, but kept his attention on the toast he was putting jam on.

Doss sighed. "That's the theory, you know. I'm the director of the science part of the station, of Bioforce." He took a sip of his tea. "Is this your first time in space...ah..."

"Call me, Jess." Jess bit gingerly into the protein cubes on her tray. "Yeah, so far it's pretty cool with all the floating around stuff. I'm not so crazy about the chow." She swallowed then shrugged and forked up another cube.

"Is it so different downworld?" Doss seemed very glad to be on a safe subject. He was dressed in a space jumpsuit, pale blue in color, with the soft space boots everyone on station wore. "The food I mean?"

"Very," Kurok answered. "Jesslyn is far more accustomed to fungus, seaweed and animal protein." He munched his toast. "I actually prefer that myself."

"Really?" Doss studied him. "I've never heard you complain about the food here, Daniel."

"What would the point of that be?" Doctor Dan inquired. "This is where I live." He glanced at Dev. "Which do you prefer, Dev?"

Dev didn't even have to think about it. "Downside. Jess has introduced me to some really excellent meals." She straightened up a little in her seat. "And at the base, they make special things called brownies."

"Oh!" Kurok broke into a grin. "They still make those?"

"They do," Jess said. "Only on special occasions, but they do." She scooped up more of the cubes and swallowed them without chewing much. "These don't taste like anything."

Dev had to admit that was true. She had always enjoyed meals on station, but now that she had downside to compare it to, the items did seem bland. "I had clam stew at Jess's birthplace. That was really excellent."

"It is," Doctor Dan said, with an easy smile. "One of the few places they make it with all those shallows to clam in." He glanced at Doss. "Drake's Bay has all sorts of surprises, you know."

Doss eyed him warily.

Jess regarded her now empty tray. "We done here? What's next?" She leaned on her forearms. "Gonna show me how you grow stuff up here?"

Her eyes were on Kurok, her senses were pinned to Doss, and her ears picked up the increased breathing and the shift of his body against the chair.

"If you like, sure." Kurok stood and picked up his tray. "But first, if you don't mind, I'd like to get a scan of you into our analyzer, with all your specialness." His eyes twinkled at her. "I'm going to enjoy scaring the living daylights out of every colleague I have."

Doss stood up as well, glancing from him to Jess. "Daniel, what do you mean?"

"You'll see." Kurok waved them along. "Let's go, you two. Maybe I can figure out how to get this damn machinery to cough up some brownies later."

DEV SAT ON a stool behind the genetiscan console. She watched Doctor Dan tune the leads for the sensors poised above Jess's relaxed body as it lay on the examining table. "Just a moment more."

"What's Doss's background?" Jess asked, her eyes studying the machinery over her head.

"Eh?" Kurok looked up from his fiddling. "Early brain stem development. I wasn't kidding. He did design the class structure." He paused. "Why?"

"He got family downside?"

"I have no idea. Never thought about it. I've known Randall for many years, and he's got the imagination of a sea slug." Kurok finished his calculations. "Just lie still for a moment, would you?"

"Sure." Jess closed her eyes and to all intents and purposes went to sleep.

"Perfect." Doctor Dan started the scan, leaning forward and watching in fascination as the advanced heuristic device parsed through Jess's biology. "Look at that bone structure."

Thus invited, Dev hopped off the stool and came closer, peering past her mentor's shoulder at the screen. "Is it different?"

"Oh yes, look." Kurok traced a pattern on the display. "It's five or six times denser than average, and do you see this structure here? In my knee, or yours, Dev, we'd have far less of these arches." He traced another line. "And there are ten times more ligament attachment points here."

Dev looked over the console at Jess, who had one eye open peering back at her in some amusement. "That's amazing."

Jess closed her eye and shook her head.

The scan moved up Jess's body, slowing a little as it came over her chest and recorded the double lung structure that allowed Jess to breathe water. "Just amazing." Doctor Dan shook his head. "I've been wanting a look at those since we were in that water."

"My gills?" Jess queried.

"Exactly." Doctor Dan came around the console and approached her. "I don't know who did the work, but I will tell you, as someone who has done a bit of this, they were good." He leaned on the table, regarding her. "That's not an easy change."

Jess folded her hands over her stomach. "Always surprised me it worked as well as it does," she said. "First time I got my head held under the water to force it, I thought I was going to croak."

Kurok studied her. "She did that?"

Jess shook her head. "My father did. It got picked up in a scan, and he had to prove it had a purpose."

"Hm." Doctor Dan frowned. "No way was that a random mutation. It's far too specific."

She shrugged slightly. "I tested in the year after that so it just became a note on my med."

A soft sound chimed overhead. A female voice followed it. "Doctor Kurok please contact the Director, Doctor Kurok, please contact the Director."

"All right I heard you." Kurok went back to the console and pressed a few keys, putting a commlink into his ear. "This is Dan Kurok."

Dev moved away from the console so as not to appear to listen, even though she thought Doctor Dan probably did not mind. She went over to Jess and put her hands on the surface of the table.

"Hi," Jess said. "Like my insides?"

"I like all your sides," Dev readily responded. "Does this

make you be in discomfort?"

"Nah." Jess stretched out a little and then relaxed. "Doc's okay. And I don't mind, my guts are what they are, you know?" She twiddled her thumbs. "I got over them being a novelty a long time ago, though I gotta tell you it was worth the look on the medic's face the first time I got sent to the tank."

"Okay." Kurok put the comms link down and went back to the console. "We're invited to lunch with staff." He rolled his eyes slightly. "I think he's just anxious to get the sign off on Dev's design to tell the truth, and he knows if he keeps annoying me I might speed that up."

"Make 'em wait," Jess said. "Dev promised to show me the floating place up top."

"Ah, the null grav gym." Doctor Dan lauged. "You do enjoy the null, don't you?"

"I do. It reminds me of being under water," Jess said. "Only less wet."

"That knife wound finally completely healed I see," Kurok commented, his eyes on the screen. "Bet that was a relief." He glanced up over the screen. "All done."

"You're faster than the meds at base." Jess levered herself up off the table and got onto her feet. "Now what? We get to see your side of the business? I wanna see where Dev came from."

Kurok was typing on an entry pad. "Absolutely." He finished and saved the dataset, sending it to his privately coded storage. "I even have pictures of Dev as a baby. Interested?"

"Hell yes," Jess said cheerfully. "She's seen my snotty infant shots."

"Yes, I have, too." Kurok's eyes twinkled a little. "So let's go give you the backstage tour, shall we? And, Dev, I got a note from your friend Gigi that she'd love to meet up with us to have some tea."

"Excellent." Dev put her hands behind her back and rocked up and down a little in her issue boots, glad she was in her Interforce uniform, with its dark piping, her insignia neatly polished on either side of her neck. "I would like to see Gigi. Is she still assigned to the Director?"

"She is." Kurok marshaled them out the door and led the way down the hall. "She's anxious to hear how you've been doing." He glanced at Dev. "You're free to tell her what you like, but I'd go a little light on the details if I were you."

"The gory details?" Jess asked. "That'll be a short conversation."

"Mmm."

"I can tell her about the bear," Dev commented. "That should be pretty safe."

"Except for the two-inch-long fangs."

THE CRECHE MADE her squirmy, Jess realized in relatively short order. She paused inside the door to a large, light hued chamber, full of rows upon rows of small mechanized units, where workers wore white jumpsuits and headcovers as they moved down the lines.

"So, these are the incubators." Doctor Dan led them over to the nearest set, peering inside one. It was full of a rosy colored fluid and contained a small, twitching form. "That's a pre-natal bio alt."

Jess's eyes got wider as she regarded the thing inside. "A what?"

"A baby, before it's born." Kurok muffled a smile. "When they're close to birth stage, we transfer them into a birthing unit for their last month of growth before being born."

Jess gave Dev a sideways look. "Is that the egg thing?"

Dev nodded. She'd been in here many times, of course, and it was a little funny to see Jess's somewhat alarmed reaction. "I told Jess I came from an egg in space and she thought I was making a joke."

"This is weird," Jess said. "Can we see an egg?"

Kurok motioned them on along. The tenders turned to watch them as they passed, the pale walls and floors making the dark jumpsuits Dev and Jess were wearing a startling contrast. "There are a thousand individuals in here, representing fifty different sets." They passed the last row in which the units were empty. "And those are waiting for Dev's successors."

Jess peeked inside one. "So that's supposed to mimic a uterus?" She sounded dubious.

"Mmm...except the fluid is artificial amniotic and the embryos are fed artificial nutrients." Kurok palmed another door and gestured them past him. "And it accelerates the process. Only takes three months instead of nine."

They went through a connecting passage and into a second chamber, this one quiet and dimly lit, and full of rings in motion, with plastic ovals turning slowly as they rotated. Each one was roughly arm length in size, and here the minders sat at consoles full of screens they intently monitored.

One of them got up and smiled as they approached. "Hello, Doctor Dan."

"Hello, Seth," Doctor Dan replied. "This is Jesslyn Drake, from Interforce, and you will remember her partner, Dev."

"Yes, of course," Seth said. "We were told you would be visiting. Welcome back, Dev."

"Thank you," Dev replied. "Jess was interested in seeing a hatching chamber processed."

"I wouldn't go that far." Jess muttered.

"We're about to open one," Seth said. "Would you like to watch?" He didn't wait, but led them over to a table surrounded by technicians. They'd removed one of the ovals from the moving rings and had it cradled in holders.

"You moved around like that before you were born?" Jess whispered, pointing at the rings.

"Yes," Dev said.

"Explains your flying style." Jess made sure she was well behind the rest of them. As they clustered around the egg, it was popped open. She warily eyed the interior, which seemed to be a large ball of goo, quickly wiped down by a technician to reveal a small, naked, gasping baby.

They washed it down with a faintly steaming liquid and it opened its eyes, stuck it's tongue out and hiccuped.

Jess regarded it. "Messy."

Doctor Dan gave her an amused look. "Not nearly as much as a natural born. Which I don't guess you've ever witnessed."

"Nope. Only seen a whale deliver underwater," Jess responded as she watched them wrap the new baby up in a piece of fabric and attach a plastic band around it's tiny arm. From where she was, Jess could clearly see two letters printed on it and a set of numbers.

"That's a KayDee," Dev told her in an undertone, as they moved the halves of the egg away. The baby vanished to another chamber and they prepared to unhook a new egg from the ring. "They do station maintenance."

"Ah huh." Jess was glad Kurok was leading them elsewhere. "So he'll stay here then, I guess?"

"Or go to another station," Dev said.

They followed Kurok out into a hallway, and then they were in the main part of station again, heading for a lift tube. "We'll take a look at the play gym then get some lunch." He saw the grin on Jess's face. "Much more to your tastes, I'm sure."

"Not much for babies," Jess said. "Once we graduate to field school, we never go back to the areas where they bring the kids into."

"No, I suppose not." Doctor Dan kicked off in the tube and they floated upward, along with a flock of others.

This was the first time they were with a lot of people, and Dev quickly noticed they were being watched by everyone. She folded her hands in front of her and ignored the looks as they passed any number of proctors and staff, and on the edges of the tube, other bio alts.

As they passed the mid levels up to the upper section, there were fewer people around them, and Jess took advantage of that and went into a series of lazy tumbling motions. There was a fluidly graceful way she moved that was different, and she quickly drew the eyes of the few onlookers left.

Kurok watched with a faint smile on his face. Not what the staff had expected, he was sure, this Drake, with her aerobatic antics. He half turned and caught Dev's expression as she too looked at her partner, the unfeigned affection clearly showing.

"Seems like a natural spacer, eh Dev?"

"Yes. Jess is so amazing at everything."

"Did I just hear that?" Jess was upside down, eyeing them.

"I said you were amazing," Dev repeated. "And you are!" She reached up to take Jess's extended hand, as her partner rotated around to normal attitude. "Do you know how long it takes most people to know how to tumble in null?"

Jess rolled her eyes and looked over at Kurok.

"She's right," Doctor Dan said. "Some never learn. At least not without throwing up every other minute."

"I had more than enough practice with my ass over my head with her flying," Jess said. "I had to get extra restraints put in so I'd stop banging my head on the bus floor."

Dev turned an appealing shade of pink, while Doctor Dan merely laughed.

Then exited on the top level and were now at the outer rim of station, heading along a passageway that had classrooms on either side of it.

"Do you ever keep the kids separate?" Jess asked, unexpectedly. "The bios and the rest? I know you said not in basic but after?"

"We don't have many natural born children up here," Doctor Dan answered quietly. "In a year, maybe ten or so. They attend basic education classes with the sets who they match in terms of standard intelligence."

"Ah."

"Then after that, they take a set of tests and are sorted out to various areas on station for specialized classes."

Jess smiled at him. "A battery."

"Of sorts, but academic in nature," Kurok responded. "Not quite like the one downworld." He gave her a sidelong look "We have more control over the genetics, you see."

They came to a wall, the thick translucent surface curving under their hands as they watched the activity beyond. There was a heavy set of lock doors and beyond it, bathed in sunlight, a host of children tumbling in null gravity.

Jess looked charmed. "Is that what you remember?" she asked Dev. "What you told me about?"

"Yes." Dev remembered well being one of those children. If she closed her eyes she could feel again the freedom of floating and the giggling of her classmates. "It was fun."

"That looks really cool." Jess watched the children playing a ball game, bouncing off padded surfaces and laughing in delight. "Can we go inside?"

"You can," Doctor Dan said, dryly. "I've lost my taste for null. That trip on the shuttle was enough for me to remember why."

He went to the edge of the lock and palmed the door open, waving them in. "Have at it, kids."

Jess bounced right in, and Dev joined her, the two of them standing side by side as the portal shut and sealed.

"Stand by for zero gravity conditions," a woman's voice, the same one they'd heard before, chimed. "In ten seconds. Nine. Eight."

"C'mon." Jess went to the front of the chamber, waiting impatiently for the inner door to open. "Let's go, Dev."

The door opened, and Jess leaned forward, then shoved off with both feet, heading upward swiftly as Dev followed her.

It was an amazing feeling. Jess reached one of the padded surfaces and turned in mid air, kicking off again and savoring the sensation of flying as she reached out and caught hold of Dev, pulling her around and then releasing her.

They both spun into a ray of sunlight, brilliant though buffered by the shielding on the outer skin of the station. Jess spread her arms out to savor it, this light she'd only ever seen the dimly reflected faintness of.

At the far end of the space, a thick and padded net was spread, curtaining off the play area, and most of the children were down at that end, batting colorful rubber balls at each other. They were unaware of the two dark clad figures moving around above them, and Jess flipped over and floated on her back.

Chapter Seven

RANDALL DOSS CAME up behind Kurok. "What are they doing? Daniel, you let them in there with the children? What's wrong with you?"

"Watch them." Kurok leaned against the wall. "They're not doing anything. Watch Jesslyn in the null, Randall. As natural as she'd been born here."

Doss peered at her. "She terrified the night staff. They came and complained to me." He sighed. "I don't know if we should take that other contract, trying to reproduce something like her, Daniel."

"No harm. We can't," Kurok said. "The manipulation they did, the mutations they encoded, it's far too dangerous to try. I'll send you the report and the scan I just did."

Doss looked shrewdly at him. "Can't, or won't?"

"Can't. We don't have the skill for that level of manipulation anymore. Thank goodness." Kurok watched Jess push gently off a surface and roll into a somersault, moving past Dev who reached out to catch her. "We barely touch the surface of that kind of thing, and frankly, I wouldn't want to try to program that kind of amorality."

Doss looked relieved. "After seeing her, I'm glad to hear you say that. So we should just agree to do the study? Can we get that much money out of it?"

"Study? Sure," Doctor Dan said. "But we can't reproduce something like her, and even if we could, I wouldn't."

"Really, Daniel?"

"Really." Kurok turned and looked him full in the eye. "Matter of fact I'd kill anyone who tried."

"What are you saying?" Doss said, after a long pause. "Are you serious?"

"Very."

Doss's eyes narrowed a little. "Daniel, consider your position. You should not say things like that. I'll do you the courtesy of forgetting I heard it."

Doctor Dan smiled and went back to watching the two dark figures.

JESS FINISHED A lazy flip in mid air, reaching out to grab a padded strut as Dev drifted up next to her. They paused together, watching the children play down the curve from where they were floating. "This is cool."

Dev smiled. "I'm really glad you are enjoying it."

"Are you?"

"Yes. I find null really relaxing. We didn't get to experience it a lot after we left the basic school, but every once in a while you could come in and play catch or something if you had a few free minutes."

Jess regarded the children. "They kept you pretty busy, huh?"

"They did. Some of us...not very many, got to do what we wanted in between class and lab, or lab and meal. We could spend ten or maybe twenty minutes doing what we wanted."

Jess digested this in silence. "That because you were a superstar?"

"No, well." Dev frowned a little. "Maybe. I was always sort of advanced in class. Gigi was, too. We had a little assigned crib down by the dorms. I would go sit in there and do a lab, sometimes, or read a few pages of my book."

A scream drew their sharp attention, and Jess curled her boots up and got them up against the padded strut as her body tensed, ready to launch. "What was that?"

Dev hand over handed along the support, her head turning right and left to locate the sound. Another yell rang out, and from the corner of her eye she saw Doctor Dan bolt away from the glass and start running down slope. "Something's wrong."

"Yeah but what?" Jess searched the area herself, but the outline of the station and the angles defeated her instincts. Then she saw the net spread below the children, springing free and opening. "That a good thing?" She pointed.

"No...oh no!" Dev's eyes widened. "That open space, if they fall through there and grav cuts back in they'll fall!"

Jess uncoiled her body and launched herself toward the net, wishing now that this null grav was water, since there was nothing to continue pushing against to make herself go faster, and she wasn't equipped with wings.

Beneath her she saw the children tumbling toward the opening. "Not good!" She suddenly felt the faint tug of gravity against her.

"Not good!" Dev yelled back.

She could see the edge of the net and angled toward it,

lunging past several bio alt kids, who goggled at her in frightened alarm.

No time to worry about that. She caught the edge of the net and saw a strut coming up, curling herself up in the air and kicking out as she reached it to zoom off in a different direction, the net caught in the clenched fingers of one hand.

She heard a klaxon and saw moving figures from the corner of her eye as she shot across the open space, dragging the net behind her as she saw the loose fastening the net had come off of.

She got a hand on that then quickly got her body twisted around in time to fend off another strut, pulling her arms together to catch the net around her.

Gravity went weird, and she felt forces pushing and shoving against her from directions she never expected them to. She felt pressure against her lungs, and a sudden headache, but she clasped her hands around her opposite wrists, coming to rest in mid air as the net tried to pull her grip apart.

She gripped harder, resisting the pull and arched her back, closing her eyes in concentration.

"Hang on, Jess!" Dev reached her side and was now climbing up the net as children bounced against it, wide eyed in eerie silence. "Hang on!"

"Hanging." Jess opened one eye as a small body hit her. She looked down to see a tiny moppet with curly red hair clutching her jumpsuit. "Hey."

The bio alt child looked up at her. "Ma'am," he burbled as another child bounced against him and took hold of her. "Scared!"

"Ever hear of going from a boat into the water?" Jess inquired, but got only incomprehensive stares back. "Never mind. Don't pinch me."

The first child wrapped an arm around her leg and stared through the net as the gravity fluxed again and they were shoved downward.

Dev got ahold of the loosened line and climbed up into the rigging, putting the line over her shoulder and pulling it forward as she climbed up the supports toward the control panel. She paused as the pull increased and took a better hold as she was almost yanked free.

"Whatever you're doing, Devvie, hurry it up. I'm collecting limpets," Jess said, tightening her grip again as the pull became intense, making her muscles suddenly stand out under her jumpsuit. "Getting crunchy!"

"Yes!" Dev saw the issue, the huge hook that held the net had disengaged and was drifting. She looped the line over the hook and secured it, then she bounced over to the control panel. "It's lost power!"

"Can ya fix it?" Jess closed her eyes again as the strain increased. "Before my shoulders come out of their sockets?"

Dev turned around and looked across the open space.

There was a jet pod making its way toward them, far too slowly. She could see technicians on the walk, watching. The children were all falling against the net in confusion.

She felt grav fluctuating again.

Not correct. She turned back and got to the panel, unlatched the front and yanked it open. Inside, she let her eyes scan over the boards, and without hesitation, reached inside and tripped the reset relay, pulling her hand back as the boards re-energized.

With a growling clank the hook started to retract, pulling Jess with it toward her along with the five or six children who had latched onto her. "It's okay, Jess!"

Jess relaxed her hold and moved herself away as the mechanism pulled the net taut again, and the odd stresses and pulls against her vanished. The children started drifting again, and after a moment, they started laughing as though it had just been a big game.

"Good!" One of the children who had grabbed onto her said, kicking away from the net and turning a somersault. "Where's da ball!"

Dev shut the panel and drifted down to join Jess as the hook retracted completely, and the games started up again. "It's an excellent thing you caught the net, Jess," she said. "With null grav fluxing, the children could have gotten really hurt."

"Mmm." Jess still hung onto the net fabric, watching the kids move off, their fright gone. "That sort of thing happen a lot?"

"It happens." Dev scanned the area intently. "But not a lot. It's quite a coincidence it happened just then."

"Mmm," Jess repeated the low sound. "How much of a coincidence?" she asked. "You knew that system in there, Devvie?"

"No," Dev answered, after a moment. "That is not something I was specifically programmed with. But really systems are systems and there are always similarities. Power might have fluctuated and made it go offline." She considered. "There wasn't any overlay though."

"You just figured it out," Jess said. "Like I just did what I do."

"Yes."

Jess saw a group of white lab coated figures watching them. "Or the whole thing could have been arranged to give them something to look at." She started down the net. "Let's go find out."

Dev pulled herself along behind her, the null area no longer seeming so lighthearted.

KUROK HAD STOPPED mid walkway and gone to the glass, seeing Jess catch the net and secure it with her powerful grip. He could see the surface fluctuate and the children tumbling, but the con that handled grav in the gym was on other side of the ring from him and out of reach.

A safety pod was on the way, maneuvering cautiously, but Jess's quick response kept the net mostly in place, and the gap that threatened to open to let helpless children tumble down to deck had closed.

There were klaxons sounding though, and he saw by the motion of the net that gravity was threatening to take hold, pulling the synth webbing taut against the hold Jess had on it. He saw her body flex in response.

Doss caught up with him. "Oh my goodness, what's going on, Daniel?" He was gasping. "Oh! The agent! The children! Look!"

"The agent." Kurok repeated. "Demonstrating the utterly contradictory quality of sacrificing self to the greater good." He watched Dev climb up to the equipment panel, the fluctuating grav making her somewhat unsteady. "The only thing that ties Interforce together and keeps it going."

"But..."

"Watch." He leaned against the glass. "There must be several thousand kilos of force pulling on that grip. Can you fathom the engineering that went into that?" He watched Jess in fascination. "Imagine the strength there."

"Well...yes." Doss pressed his hands against the glass next to him. "Is the chamber malfunctioning?"

"So it seems."

Doss spotted Dev's moving form. "Oh! What's the unit doing? Daniel!"

Kurok eyed him dourly "Dev? Probably she's fixing the problem."

Doss frowned. "But that unit never received station

maintenance programming." He looked at Kurok. "So how would she know what to do?"

"What do you mean, how would she know? She's a tech," Kurok said in a testy tone.

"Yes, of course, but not for our systems. That's a very specific set." Doss stared at him. "I saw the programming schema for the unit, it had nothing in there about station."

Kurok carefully controlled his breathing. "How would you know what to do, Randall, when faced with some unknown parameter in a class structure? You'd figure it out, based on experience, right?"

"Well, yes of course."

"Dev does the same thing." Kurok turned and started down the tube again. "Not really that remarkable actually. Humans have been doing that for twenty thousand years." He sped up to a jog, wanting to get away from Doss's questioning eyes.

"But, Daniel!"

"We can discuss it later," he called back over his shoulder. "I want to make sure everyone's all right." He got around the curve of the ring and sped up, breaking into a jog again.

He heard the klaxon stop blaring and glanced through the glass, as the sound of mechanical motion cranked through the air, and the safety net curled back properly into place. At the top of the net he saw Dev close up the equipment panel and hurry to join her partner, and he had to wonder.

Coincidence?

He triggered his commlink. "Kurok to mech ops."

"Mech ops here, sir." The voice was quiet and respectful, not surprising since it was bio alt and knew well who he was.

"CueTee, please give me a report on the malfunction in null space one alpha. It has just occurred, and there was fluctuation in null as well as a release of the safety restraints. Complete diagnostics."

"Yes, Doctor Dan," the CueTee responded. "Is there damage? Do you need a mech team? Should we alert medops?"

"No," Kurok replied. "NM-Dev-1 resolved the problem, all is well. I just want to know what happened."

"That is excellent, Doctor Dan. I will get the report for you right away. Mech ops out."

He dodged several running technicians and got to the main airlock at the center of the null area. Without much thought he keyed the door open and went inside, the two techs following him. "Easy there, boys."

"Hello, Doctor Dan," the nearer one said. "Is there trouble? We got called down here. They said there was a malfunction."

"Who sent you, lads?" he asked in a casual tone.

"The security desk," the DeeDee answered earnestly. "The director's office called down, I heard them."

"The security desk?"

"Yes, Doctor Dan. The supervisor there told us to come here right away. Is it correct?" The tech's voice took on an anxious tone.

"It's fine. You're all correct," Kurok said. "Let's go."

The outer door sealed and the mechanical voice sounded, warning of the grav change. Kurok took hold of one of the padded bars near the inner door and exhaled, feeling the shift as weight came off his spine and only his hold kept his feet on the ground.

The inner door opened and he pushed off the bar, drifting into the null and onto the viewing platform just inside.

Above the net, the proctors were gathering in the children, getting them sorted by set and grouped together, the children holding each other hand to wrist in circles.

Jess and Dev were coming across the net to the platform. "Wait here," he told the techs. "NM-Dev-1 might be able to tell you what the problem was."

"Oh!" The DeeDee caught hold of the spar next to him. "Excellent!"

Jess came barreling over the rail, flipping over and hitting the glass wall of the airlock with some force. "Hey, Doc. Any idea what that was all about?"

"Not yet." Kurok eyed her, reaching out a hand to steady Jess as she came around to land. "Waiting for Dev to tell me what she found."

Dev hitched herself over onto the platform more decorously. "Hello, Doctor Dan," she said, as she got her feet settled. "The panel went into overload. It was amazing how Jess got the net to stop until I could reset it."

Jess grinned, then hooked her legs over the top of the support and hung upside down, rocking gently side to side. "You owe me a shoulder massage for that."

Dev smiled. "Of course."

"So there was no power inside?" Doctor Dan asked her. "These techs were sent to look at things, but it seems there's nothing for them to do."

"No." Dev looked at them. "It was the retraction hook panel, in the subsection. Completely de-energized. I reset it. But you should inspect it and see if there is something that caused it to go offline."

"Yes." The two techs nodded, then started off the platform, using belt hooks to fasten themselves to the net lines as they started across.

The three of them exchanged glances.

"What's the chance of that happening?" Jess asked, folding her hands over her stomach.

"It happens," Kurok admitted. "It's all mechanical systems in there, the net and all that."

"Doctor Dan, I don't remember hearing of that happening at the same time grav had an issue," Dev said. "The children could have really gotten hurt."

"Mmm." Doctor Dan drummed his fingers against the rail. "Let's go get some lunch," he said. "We can discuss this later." He triggered the lock door and led the way inside, dodging at the last minute to avoid Jess's tumbling form. "Jesslyn!" he barked out in mild exasperation.

Jess chuckled as she turned upright and took hold of one of the poles. "Sorry." She landed next to him. "Gotta take my fun where I find it."

LUNCH WAS AWKWARD. Dev was aware that Doctor Doss and the people with him were in a lot of discomfort, and the fact that not one but two bio alts were seated at the table in the senior scientists dining room wasn't helping.

She was glad to see Gigi, though. She was waiting for the general talk to get louder, so they could share a private word or two since Jess had ignored the seating plan and steered her to a seat right next to her friend.

"Ah, ah." Doss cleared his throat. "Agent Drake, let me first say we owe you a big thank you for being so forward in helping out in the null gymnasium earlier."

"Yes," the man sitting next to Doss said. "My name is John Akerson. "I'm one of the financial directors here at Bio Station Two."

"No problem," Jess responded. "You all are supposed to be so super scientific up here, it kinda surprised me to have it all go tits up like that."

"What does that mean?" Gigi asked in a whisper.

"She thinks it was strange the malfunction happened," Dev

whispered back. "It seemed incorrect to have the board lock up at the same time grav was in flux."

Gigi frowned.

"There was a power surge," Doctor Dan replied in a careful tone. "Mechanical operations reported that one of the solar arrays over provided the grid."

Jess looked up and to the right, where one of the arrays was clearly in view. "That?" She watched in some fascination as the array shifted its angle, following the course of the sun they were moving past.

"Not that one, but yes," Kurok said. "I suppose that must interest you, Jess. Nothing like that downside."

"It's useful, like the hydro tunnels are," Jess said. "Seems to provide you with enough power."

The scientists relaxed a little, and one of them leaned forward. "I haven't been downside. Tell me about that. One of my brothers worked on a turbine station in Quebec City."

The chatter rose a little, and everyone focused on their cups, turning attention away from their unwelcome table guests for the moment as Jess amiably described the tunnels they used for power.

"So, how is it going for you, Dev?" Gigi asked. "Everyone says you have done really excellent work."

Dev grinned a little and blushed. "That is what they say. I just used the programming they gave me and did the best I could. It was Jess who really did some excellent things and got very good results." She considered. "But I was glad I could help her in that."

"They sent a vid up with you flying a vehicle," Gigi said. "The proctors of the pilots, you know, the KayTees, have been studying it."

"The carrier. Yes," Dev said. "I have done quite well with that, actually. It's a lot of fun to fly, and they have just installed some new and more powerful engines. I like them."

"Excuse me NM-Dev-1."

Dev looked over at Akerson. "Yes, sir?"

"I heard you went right to the control panel and fixed it, in the null," he said, in a somewhat accusatory tone. "Without being instructed to."

Dev was aware of Jess reacting next to her, and instinctively she reached out and put her hand over her wrist. "Of course, sir. My programming is in tech. The entire point of the advanced level was not to have to wait for instruction."

He stared at her.

"Dev is correct," Kurok said. "That's precisely why she received the programming I designed."

"Do we want bios who make their own decisions?" Akerson asked. "I'm not sure."

"That's exactly what was requested, John. Please. You've read the contract. Now stop."

Akerson frowned at him. "That wasn't what it said."

"It was," Doss replied firmly. "Now please stop, or leave. These are our guests." He turned his attention to Jess. "Now what were we talking about? The turbines, wasn't it?"

"Do you," Gigi asked under her breath, "make your own decisions, Dev?"

Dev saw that Jess's eyes were still narrowed, but her body relaxed a little. Dev waited until she saw her lean back a little, then she settled back herself. "Of course," she responded to Gigi. "It's what the work is. We go outside the base and stop bad things from happening. Jess depends on me knowing what to do."

"She doesn't tell you?"

"Sometimes. Where to go, and what course to put in, things like that. But the rest of it, no. She expects me to do it on my own."

"Wow." Gigi smiled a little. "That's amazing." She glanced around then back at Dev. "There are more of us at the Interforce base, isn't that correct? A lot more? One of the proctors said they were sending two more full sets downworld."

"There are." Dev forked up some of the protein cubes. "Ten or twelve different sets."

"Do you stay with them?" Gigi asked, in a curious tone.

"No." Dev smiled. "I live next to Jess. I have to be ready to work at all times with her." She took a sip of the tea they'd been served. "All of the techs and agents live in one area."

"But they're natural born, the rest of them?"

"Yes."

"Is that difficult?" Gigi asked. "I can't imagine having to live with all natural borns around me. It would be uncomfortable I think."

Dev considered that. "It isn't difficult at all." She was suddenly aware of the slight twitching of Jess's ear and knew her partner was listening. "It was a little uncomfortable at first, but after we did a few missions, it was fine. The other techs are mostly very nice. They call me Rocket."

Gigi paused uncertainly, but then she smiled a little. "Do

they? Is that good? Why do they call you that?"

Jess leaned past her, addressing Gigi directly. "Because she's the best pilot we've got, and the queen of the wrenchers." She reached a hand over. "Hi. I'm Jess."

Gigi took her hand and then released it. "Hello." She paused, then smiled a little timdly when Jess did.

"Agent Drake," Doss distracted her. "Excuse me, but is it true? I mean, are you from the Drake's Bay homestead?"

"What clued you into that?" Jess asked with a deadpan expression.

"Well...." He frowned. "Someone said it." He looked accusingly at one of the other scientists.

Jess leaned back in her chair and regarded Doss. "Yes, as my name might indicate, I am in fact from Drake's Bay. Why?"

Doss nodded. "It's quite strange that you're visiting us here, and we've heard from Interforce that there seems to be some issue with product from here at that location."

Jess folded her arms over her chest. "Someone sold my brother a bunch of stuff from here, yeah. What of it?"

"How do you know it was from here?" Akerson asked sharply.

"The seed lots had designations from here, sir," Dev said. "I recognized them."

Akerson looked like he was thinking of being mean to her, Dev thought, but after a quick look at Jess he decided not to, which wasn't surprising since Jess was glowering at him, and even sitting down she was taller than he was.

Taller than everyone was actually.

"It could have been stolen," Akerson muttered.

"Yes, that's possible," Dev said. "But regardless of how it arrived downworld, it came from here. There were twelve to fourteens species, including fruit plants, grasses, mint and sage, corn, peas, and some beans."

"And peaches," Jess said.

"They were grown using a bioluminescent mineral based photochemical reaction," Doctor Dan said. "Dev was kind enough to bring me a sample of the phosphine bearing mineral," he added with a faint smile.

There was a little silence. "Daniel," Doss said, after a moment. "That's very unusual."

"Yes," Kurok agreed, shortly. "We need to send a team there to review it. The implications, if the mineral is producible, are somewhat profound."

Akerson leaned forward. "They grew seed with it? You're sure?"

Jess leaned forward as well. "I ate the peaches. Didn't much care for the peas. However it worked, it did."

"How could they think this wasn't of great importance?" Doss sat back in his seat. "My stars."

The bio alt servers came over and removed their plates, and a second set of servers came in with small dishes with a ball of frozen confection in their centers.

Dev's eyes widened a little, and she got a poke from Gigi, who indicated the plate. They gave each other a thumbs up and quickly started in on the treat.

Jess watched Akerson. "Sure someone from here didn't do a deal with Jimmy?" she drawled a little. "That was my brother's name. James Drake." She watched the faces, senses made sharp from years of playing this game, alert to twitches around the lip, the shift of shoulders, the sudden motion of hands washing each other.

Doss looked the most uncomfortable. "We'll check the records, certainly, but there was no transaction in these goods that I knew of," he said, stiffly.

"Nor I," Akerson said. "But I won't lie and say we wouldn't be interested in working with you on that kind of project. But of course," he drew back a little, "you're Interforce. You can't speak for them."

"Of course." Jess smiled at him without any humor.

"That's not quite true," Kurok said in a mild tone. He was busy finishing his meal and kept his eyes on it. "Jesslyn is, in fact, the current Drake of Drake's Bay, due to an odd confluence of intent and happenstance."

Awkward silence. Kurok waited a moment, then looked up in mock innocence. "Sorry." He eyed Jess. "Was that a secret?"

"Not downworld it ain't." Jess's eyes twinkled at him in somber appreciation. "Just an uncomfortable truth." She let her eyes lift up and pin Doss. "But that's why Interforce is there, at the Bay, poking around in your seed beds. I called them in."

Akerson put one hand on the table, fingers curled into his palm. "The rest of these white coats may not know about downside, but I do. Active Interforce can't be a stakeholder."

"Mmm." Kurok wiped his lips. "Drakes don't always go by the rules. Jess's father often didn't." He let the waiting bio alt take his plate. "Thank you, AyeBee."

Jess's eyebrow twitched. She'd never heard any rumors of

Justin being a rule breaker. The opposite, in fact. She took a breath to protest, then paused as Kurok gave her a swift, sideways glance, along with the faintest twitch of his lips.

Huh.

"You're welcome, Doctor Dan," the AyeBee said. "Can I bring you a tea?"

"Yes, please, along with some of that ice cream." He put the napkin down. "Jess is in fact the controlling stakeholder. More importantly, she was the controlling stakeholder when those seed lots were delivered over. I checked the lot dates. That means whoever did the deal really did it with Interforce and now they're very, very interested." He looked around the table. "So if anyone here does know about this, you might want to speak up."

Akerson glanced at Dev and Gigi. "We should discuss this in private," he said. "As I told Doss, I don't know squat about this. But I can see profit in it, just like Interforce can." He got up and shoved his chair into place. "Doss, your office, ten standard." He walked quickly out of the dining hall.

Doctor Doss sighed in exasperation. "Daniel!"

"Yes, Randall?" Kurok gave him one of his kinder smiles. "Please don't be stressed. The man is an ass, and the whole station knows it."

Doss got up. "That's not the point. Must you prod him like that? The council is upset enough already." He pushed his chair in. "He can cause us a lot of trouble." Doss started off to follow Akerson.

After an awkward pause, the rest of the scientists got up and left the table, muttering half hearted goodbyes.

Kurok watched them leave then he edged his chair around to the side. "Now, you lot." He lowered his voice. "Gigi, it probably would be best if you pretend you never heard any of this."

"Of course, Doctor Dan," Gigi answered promptly. "I pretend I never hear anything in the Director's office."

Jess chuckled. She prodded and then tasted the ball of ice on her plate. "Hey. Finally something I like." She mouthed the substance. "Your kids are smarter than you are, Doc. They're clued."

"Mmm." He grinned. "You have no idea."

Gigi looked around "But...could you come down to the crèche for a moment? Everyone really wants to say hello to Dev," she said. "They asked me to ask you because they knew I was going to have a meal with you today."

Doctor Dan smiled. "Is that okay by you, Dev?"

"Yes," Dev said, after a moment. "As long as Jess goes with us," she added unexpectedly.

"Like I wouldn't?" Jess said. "C'mon. I still want to see your baby pictures." She got up and waited for them to join her. "Let's go see how the other half lives."

"Quite more than half."

THE TRIP TO the crèche involved another grav tube, which made Jess happy. She resisted the urge to tumble in space as they drifted down, slowly shedding the proctors and staff of the station as they gathered isolated bio alts along the way.

It was obvious to Jess that all the bio alts both knew who Dev was and had their attention glued on Dan Kurok. She saw them watching him, waiting for him to look their way, hoping for the recognition that indicated.

Dev had her noncommittal expression on, and Jess casually rested her hand on her shoulder, feeling the tension under her fingertips. "Relax, Devvie."

Dev gave her a sideways glance then smiled a little and looked down.

"So, here we start going into the living quarters of all the bio alts," Doctor Dan said. "They have a meal hall, recreation, and so on that's exclusive to them."

Jess studied the decks they were moving past and thought about the areas in the Citadel that served the same purpose. Were the corridors bleaker and more utilitarian? They didn't seem to be here. They were still the same smooth curves and mild, milky colors.

The bio alt halls at Base Ten were more roughly cut, but Jess considered that most of the lower areas of the Citadel were like that, including the passages she took daily down to the power turbine tunnels where she surfed in the backwash.

Bio alts in the lower halls. Here. At the Base. Jess cocked her head slightly to one side. There were no bio alts at Drake's bay but there...

No. There, lower levels were better. "Huh."

"Something wrong?" Doctor Dan asked.

"Just thinking." Jess returned her attention to their surroundings. "So what was all that about my dad being a rebel?"

Kurok chuckled dryly. "Had to say something," he said. "I was trying to see who knew what there and failed rather miserably I'm afraid."

"Someone knew something," Jess said. "I could smell it." She fell silent as they caught up with a larger group of bio alts, some of whom waved timidly at Gigi.

Here the floors were plain metal, and the doors had no ornamentation as they had on the upper levels. There was no soothing weave on the walls, it was bare and faintly reflective, and there were no pictures or random art anywhere.

They reached the next to last level and left the tube, emerging back into gravity in an area bounded by security doors with portals where they could see guards working at consoles. The guards looked up as they came into view, but relaxed when they spotted Kurok, who was apparently well known to them and expected. "Hello, Doctor Kurok," one called out and gave him a wave.

"Hello, lads." Doctor Dan returned the wave. "Just here for a visit."

Each had a space jumpsuit on, with a tool belt that held several canisters and one rectangular device mounted prominently on the strap that came across their chests where they could slap it with one hand.

"No problem, sir," the guard said. "They always love it when you come down." He glanced at Dev and Jess and nodded at them.

Jess watched the guards thoughtfully. Gigi could have been a walking floor mop.

The doors to the interior were open and they walked through into a wide, busy space that held the soft murmur and echo of many voices.

Dev moved closer and lowered her voice. "This is the dayroom. And there, where the ramp goes up? That goes to the sleeping pods."

"Hmm." Jess looked around. The space was full of bio alts, all dressed in various color jumpsuits, some blue and red, some light green, some dun colored. All of them wore visible collars, and as they entered, a ripple ran across the room as the bio alts noticed them.

The black and dark green uniforms were unique and drew their gaze.

Then they all recognized Doctor Dan, and some reacted to seeing Gigi. Then they put two and two together as they realized the shorter of the two strangely dressed women was known to them.

Was one of them.

Jess easily felt the electric result. Excitement and interest as bodies straightened up and turned toward them. She sensed the response to be positive, her own body relaxing as her senses understood the people moving toward them to be friendly, or at least not dangerous.

There was a central desk, staffed by other bio alts, and they came to a halt near the oval structure as many sets moved toward them.

"Hello, Doctor Dan," the closest of them behind the desk greeted them. "Hello, Gigi5 and NM-Dev-1." He looked uncertainly at Jess.

"This is Jess," Gigi supplied. "She's a friend of NM-Dev-1's, and also, of Doctor Dan."

The bio alt behind the desk looked reassured. "Hello, Jess," he said. "I am CeeEm245. I am on duty today here in the hall."

"Hi," Jess responded amiably.

Doctor Dan put his hands on the table. "We heard everyone wanted to say hello to Dev, so we stopped by to visit, and also, Jess wanted to see the crèche."

Several proctors came over and paused uncertainly. Kurok glanced at them then turned and leaned on the counter. "Jess works for Interforce, who holds Dev's contract," he explained to the now clustered masses. "Dev now also works for Interforce as an operations technician, the very first of her kind to do so."

"An excellent assignment," the CeeEm said in an impressed tone.

"A very excellent assignment, and what you all might not know is that I, myself, was once an operations technician. I worked for Interforce just like Dev now does." Doctor Dan acknowledged the murmured interest with a slight wave. "So I was very happy and very proud that Dev was able to do this."

Dev maintained a prudent silence, merely standing next to Jess with her hands clasped behind her back.

Doctor Dan smiled. "I'm sure all of you have lots of questions," he said. "Am I right?"

One of the BeeEffs stepped forward. "Yes, Doctor Dan, we do. We want to get such excellent assignments, too."

The proctors looked unsettled and a bit nervous. They shuffled their feet as the crowd very gently eased around them toward the console. "Doctor Kurok," one of them said, "are you s—"

"Good lads. Go get yourself some tea," Kurok told them. "I can handle this."

"But—"

"Go." He shooed them off. "I want everyone to feel free to ask whatever questions they want and not be embarrassed. Go on."

The proctors looked reassured and nodded. "I understand. We'll be back in a while."

"There." Doctor Dan leaned over the console and tapped on an input pad. "Now, let's have it, everyone. Ask away."

There were a lot of questions. But first, Doctor Dan got behind the console, took over one of the positions and put vid on the screen. "This was Dev's very first mission," he said. "So you all can see what she does for her assignment."

Jess chuckled.

"Hmm." Dev muttered under her breath. "Isn't that supposed to be restricted?"

"C'mon, Devvie. You're a rock star." Jess patted her back.

The screen lit up and then audio cut in, and they heard Dev's voice on comms, requesting flight clearance. The KayTees were gathered near her and watched with deep interest as the carrier lifted out of the docking cavern and into the weather.

"We have programming for that location," one of the KayTees said. "I recognize it."

"It's Interforce Base Ten," Dev said. "It's where we are assigned. There are KayTees there who fly from that cavern also."

Gigi inhaled as the vid turned in a complete circle, showing first the craggy ridge line that the base was built into, and then the endless expanse of sea. "Oh! Is that downside?"

"That is downside," Dev confirmed. "The substance hitting the window is called rain, and it happens a lot." She sat on a stool next to the counter, and Jess leaned on it behind her. "It's water," she added. "Everything almost is water downside."

"What is that you are flying?" One of the KayTees asked.

"That is BR270006, a Bantam class heavy armored carrier," Dev said. "I am the pilot, Jess is the flight leader."

"And the gunner." Jess lifted her hands up and wiggled her fingers.

The carrier moved into flight and went through the speed of sound, the cracking booms echoing through the big space, making the bio alts jump a little.

"That's a sonic boom," Doctor Dan said into the quiet that followed. "You KayTees would have had that in programming also, since the courier craft you fly can go that fast."

"Yes," the nearest KayTee said. "We know that."

"We have heard that in the sim," a second said.

Dev's voice came again from the vid, seeing a target. Then the carrier went into evasive maneuvers and the bodies all around them jerked in reaction, eyes glued to the vid screens as the POV from the carrier swirled and rotated, going up and over the incoming rogue carrier.

Then Jess's voice, battle clipped and warning, and flashes of blasters coming past the nose of the carrier to blow the other one out of the sky, the implosion resounding through the screen as pieces of it went in every direction.

"That vehicle was empty. But it was dangerous," Doctor Dan said. "Dev, did you find your programming useful during this event?"

Dev was quiet for a moment. "Knowing what controls to use and how to make the craft fly was excellent," she said. "I knew exactly what to do."

"My first experience in flying upside down," Jess added. "But not my last."

The screen now showed the approach to Gibraltar and Dev took a breath, knowing what was coming since she'd had to suffer watching it endless times in the operations lounge. "This was a bit more...um..."

The room went quiet as the carrier sped up and then went into battle, blasts coming past them and impacting them, rocking the carrier from side to side, the chaos an odd counterpoint to Dev and Jess's calm voices in call and response to the situation.

"Here comes the big boom," Jess said as the carrier went right at the mountain face, turning at the very last second as chasers zoomed past them and crashed into it, and then the rumbling thumps as Jess put plasma bombs into the slim opening going sideways across the rock.

A flash of the rear sensors as the firestorm erupted and then a shudder as the blast caught up to them and blew them sideways, the carrier tumbling almost at the edge of control, falling powerless down and down until the energy overload faded and Dev could start up the engines again.

She did, and then they were shooting over the ruffled waters. "That is the ocean," Dev said. "There is a lot of it."

"That is also water," Gigi said.

"Yes," Dev agreed. "I swam in it."

Everyone nearby turned and looked at her.

"Jess taught me how to surf," Dev said. "And when we collected Doctor Dan, we had to swim to get away."

"Rescued me," Doctor Dan gently corrected. "But that is another story."

Jess pointed at the screen. "You don't want to miss this next part."

The heads swiveled back as Dev outraced the enemy, taking them down to the surface and then zooming through the big round wave. Many of the sets gasped and then gasped again as the carrier barreled at top speed at the rock wall, tip on it's edge, and rocket straight upward at high speed right up into the clouds with enemy fire thundering at them on every side.

Only to tip and fall and circle, and then the mechanical voice noted the squirt from Jason and they heard Jess's voice yelling for her to run, run, run, that it was over and they'd done it. And she put the engines into full, remembering that solid thump as it had driven her back in her seat and the restraints retracted.

As always, Dev felt her heart race, remembering that. Now she took a breath and lifted her head as a thick silence fell and she found a sea of eyes on her. It felt like it might be a little incorrect, those looks and all that quiet as the flares receded, and all you could hear was the alarm and the warning beeps.

She remembered breathing hard and feeling exhilarated.

Jess broke the silence, casually straightening up to her full height and draping an arm over Dev's shoulders. "Best pilot in Interforce," she said, "and a kick ass wrencher."

Dev's nostrils flared a little and she glanced back at her partner. "Jess."

Doctor Dan chuckled. "And of course, that was just Dev's first flight, so you see, with the programming track we developed for Dev, she was able to be quite successful at her assignment."

The KayTee nearest them turned fully around and looked intently at Dev, then at Kurok, then back at Dev. "What is the thing on your uniform?" he asked. "The green thing?"

"That is my technician's insignia," Dev answered. "I received it when I arrived at the Interforce Base number ten and keyed in." She half turned and looked up at Jess. "Jess has one as well."

The KayTee examined it, the crowd moving closer. "Do the gold lines mean you are a natural born?" he asked Jess, a little timidly.

Jess shook her head. "Those mean I'm a senior operations agent. Dev'll have those soon enough." She glanced over at Kurok. "Just like the doc did."

Gigi edged closer. "They're pretty."

"They are attractive," the KayTee agreed, looking from Dev

to Jess. "The green means you are a technician?" He touched her sleeve, briefly.

Dev understood the underlying question. "Yes, all techs wear green with black edging and agents wear black with green, when we are on duty."

"All of you?" the KayTee asked. "You and the natural borns?"

"Yes."

The bio alts looked at each other then up at Doctor Dan, who leaned against the counter on the inside of it, watching them.

"So you can see," Doctor Dan said, after a moment of charged silence. "We have developed a very successful programming set. That's why Interforce has asked for more resources like Dev."

A CeeEff edged closer. "Could you give us that programming, Doctor Dan?" she asked. "We would like to be excellent and successful at our assignments also."

Murmurs rose, and then there was a stir as some proctors emerged from the staff break room behind the ramp to the sleep chambers, coming to a halt as they saw the crowd. "What's going on here?" one asked, loudly.

Doctor Dan straightened up. "It's all right. I was just showing them a vid."

"Oh." The proctor looked a little embarrassed. "Sorry, Doctor Kurok."

"No problem. All right everyone, that's all for now," Doctor Dan said, as the bio alts started to move off in every direction. "CeeEff, that's a good question you asked," he added, to the young woman who had stayed, watching him. "You already have some of the programming, you know. It was in the advanced B12 section."

A faint smiled appeared on her face, and she nodded. Then she turned to Dev. "Congratulations, NM-Dev-1. You have done some excellent work."

"I had a lot of assistance," Dev responded modestly. "It was really Doctor Dan's programming.

"Tch tch." Kurok came around the counter as the proctors approached them. "We can discuss it all later, hmm? I think it's time for us to finish our tour and go to the lab." He casually eased between the proctors and Dev. "Something I can help you good folks with?"

"Oh, no, Doctor Kurok," the proctor who'd spoken up before said. "We were coming to see if there was something you needed. We heard the reports of a crowd in here." He glanced at Jess, who still had her arm draped over Dev. "Security told us."

"Well, nothing to worry about. I was just showing off Dev's first mission," Kurok said. "I knew everyone would want to see it. After all, she's one of them."

The proctor nodded. "Of course. I'm sorry. I didn't mean to..." His voice trailed off. "Anyway, is there anything we can do to help?"

"No." Kurok patted Dev on the shoulder. "Now it's time for Dev to see what we've developed for her successors. Excuse us." He waited for them to move out of the way, and they did with some reluctance.

"Can we see the vid, Doctor Kurok?" The second proctor asked as they started to move away. "Is it in the library?"

Kurok looked over his shoulder, a bit of his sandy hair covering one eye. "You can. If you need any explanation of it, come see me later."

All of them looked relieved. "Yes, Doctor," the first proctor said. "Thank you."

He smiled. "Not a problem, lads. Enjoy."

Gigi gave them a little wave as she left, returning uptube to her station in the outer office of the Director.

JESS ACKNOWLEDGED THE shift as they walked, her honed senses moving from a benign watchfulness to that inner tension of being in enemy territory. Something was in work around her, something other than the seed scam, which she reckoned was probably nothing more than a grab for cred.

"So," Doctor Dan indicated a direction, "these are the genetics labs, where I spend most of my time on station."

"This where you design people?" Jess clarified as they went down a long, long corridor, which curved up at its far horizon. "Cook up the spirals?"

"Yes." Doctor Dan palmed into one of the side doors and stood back to let them enter. "This is my development lab." He followed them inside. "Dev was born here, in fact, in this room."

Dev suppressed a faint smile as she glanced around. The room was a large space with a curved outer wall that displayed the stars. There were comp stations in different locations, and one long wall was a workspace, now displaying genetic scribblings.

She had spent time in this lab, working on her final project for genetics class, but that had just been because the largest of the historical repositories was here, and Doctor Dan had made it so it could only be accessed from inside the space.

She hadn't thought to ask why, then. She'd just been very glad to be allowed to use the systems here in Doctor Dan's very own laboratory.

Jess strolled around the lab, peering into the screens. "All just phosphor to me," she said with a smile. "I haven't even seen my own scan, or if I did, I wouldn't have any idea what I was looking at."

"No, I suspect you haven't and wouldn't." Kurok went over to the main station, sat down and pulled over an input pad, keying it on. "It's an esoteric science, and you lot downworld don't have much use for it."

"True," Jess said.

"Now, Dev." He motioned her over. "Let's start with your design."

That got Jess's immediate attention, and she joined them in front of the screen. Kurok called up a sequence and displayed it.

"Still nothing but phosphor to me," Jess said. "I was hoping for baby on the bathrug shots."

Doctor Dan chuckled. "Later." He picked up a light pen and traced a line on the screen. "This is the complete structure for the technician programming, you see that Dev? It fits here, along the Satlut promontories, and curves around inside the section here."

"What does that mean?" Jess asked.

Surprisingly, Dev was the one who answered. "Programming goes in different places in our heads," she said. "Sometimes they just put it in some empty space where they find it, and you have to hunt around for it. But this wasn't like that."

Doctor Dan nodded. "Right."

"This was put in this place here, and that's right between the general area, and the part where you don't have to think about what you're doing." She leaned closer to the screen. "It makes it easier."

"Instinct," Jess guessed.

"Mmm...artificially induced instinct," Kurok said. "So the specifics, like about the carrier, the controls, and so on, that's in general." He touched an area. "You can overwrite it if you need to, with newer data, and that kind of thing. But this here..." He touched another. "That's a little magical."

Jess's dark eyebrows hiked up.

"It's not data, exactly. It's a methodology that blends a framework with a natural inclination."

Jess stared at the screen, thoughts shifting through her mind with a jittering rapidity. "So...you take something like the natural ability to problem solve and give it a specific structure."

Both Dev and Doctor Dan looked at her in some mild surprise. "Yes," Kurok said. "I designed Dev to have a flexible, powerful mind, and then shaped that with technical detail." He paused. "Very good, Jesslyn. I didn't realize you had that background knowledge yourself."

Jess shook her head. "I don't. You know perfectly well I don't. It just makes sense." Her eyes took on a darkly humorous glint. "After all, that's exactly what they do with us, isn't it? They take a natural twist and give it a purpose."

Doctor Dan grunted.

"Isn't that where you got the idea?" Jess asked. "Watching my dad?"

For a moment, she thought he was going to get mad at her for saying it. She waited, seeing the tensions shift, as his eyes lifted to meet hers, in a fine intellectual fencing, probing gently with respect.

Then he smiled, with a touch of sheepishness. "Not consciously," he said. "But there's probably a grain of truth in that, Jesslyn, even as I see where you see that in hindsight."

"So Jess was right," Dev said. "She told me we were not that different."

Doctor Dan chuckled under his breath and shook his head. "Anyway," he pointed back to the screen and shifted the input, "this is what the design is for the new techs. I shifted some of the integration into general because we'll have more time to give them specific information."

"So they won't have to guess all the time," Dev said. "That will make them be in less discomfort."

"Exactly." He paused. "Was it terribly uncomfortable for you, Dev? We just had so little time."

"Not really, Doctor Dan. I got used to it. It made me work harder, but in a good way."

Jess wandered off, roaming around the lab and peering at the tridimensional models integrated into the walls, all genetic representations marked with cryptic symbolism. She studied one of the models, seeing different colored pathways marking out something apparently relevant, branching into this area and that area.

It was the most intricate of the models, and Jess circled it curiously, leaning over to read the cryptic label, already sure of what she would see. "Hey, Dev. It's your head." She peeked past the model to see Dev looking back at her.

Doctor Dan smiled. "Yes. That's the developmental new model. Hidden in plain sight as it were."

The doors to the lab opened, and three men entered, two of them with the belts the guards had worn in the crèche. "Doctor Kurok?"

Jess circled the model and got between the men and the table Dev and Doctor Dan were at, standing squarely in their way. "Stop," she commanded them.

"It's all right, Jess." Kurok gently eased past her. "What's the problem, boys?"

"There's a missing person, Doctor." The guard in the lead looked nervously at Jess. "They would like your help in finding them, with genetiscan," he said. "It's one of the children. We think they might have gotten lost during the malfunction."

"Absolutely. Give me the designation," Doctor Dan said. "Sit down, friends. This won't take long."

Jess moved aside and went back to the table as the guard handed over a plas to him. She saw his eyes drop to it then jerk upward in confusion to stare back at the guard.

"This is a natural born," Kurok said, watching the guards nod. "And you think they're lost?"

The guards nodded again. "Doctor Doss is asking."

Kurok sat down behind another console and keyed it on. "I see." He started tapping in data. "Or at least, I hope I don't see."

DEV LOOKED UP from the screen she was studying, sensing motion. She watched the guards, who had retreated to the far wall, and saw one of them fingering the device on his chest. "Jess."

Jess eased in next to her. "Yeah?"

"The thing those guards have," Dev said in a low tone. "That is what they use to stop us." She watched the man. "Remember I told you?"

"I remember." Jess leaned against the table, tilting her head to keep the guard in her peripheral vision. "That square thing on his chest?"

"Yes."

"They use it often?"

Dev's eyes narrowed. "We think it's more often than they should," she said. "There are different levels. Some of them hurt."

"I figured." Jess leaned on the counter. "Hey, Doc?"

Kurok looked up from his task, visibly irritated. "Yes?"

Jess raised an eyebrow at him, and after moment, a faint grin appeared on his face. "Wanna dump the badges?" she mentioned casually. "They're making me twitch."

He glanced at the guards. "Boys, you can take off. This'll take me a while. I'll call it in to operations."

The guards looked uncomfortable. "Sir, they told us to stay."

"And I'm telling you to leave," Doctor Dan said, "unless you're here to arrest me."

The nearest one's eyes widened. "Oh no, Doctor Kurok! We're here to um..."

"Protect me?" Kurok's eyes twinkled. "From these two, huh?" He gave Dev and Jess a sideways look. "You dangerous characters you."

Jess chuckled audibly. "Can't decide which is funnier. That I'd do something to you, or that they think they can stop me from doing something to you."

The guard frowned. "Hey. We have a job to do here. Doctor Doss sent us."

"And Jesslyn's point is, if she decided to break my neck, there's not a damn thing you could do about it." Kurok shook his head and returned his attention to the screen.

Dev now regretted saying anything. She started toward Doctor Dan, ready to offer her help in the search. "Can I scan that for you?"

"Hey!" The guard started forward. "Stay away from him."

Doctor Dan looked up over his screen. "Please don't be an idiot," he said just as Jess started to follow Dev over.

"Hey!"

Jess sensed the change and her eyes widened as she saw the flush on his face. Then too many things happened at once. He slapped at his chest, Dev jerked and cried out, then dropped like a rock, and then it all went black and white for her.

Cold.

Hot.

Rage swept over her like a wave in the ocean, and she let instinct take over and surrendered to it.

Before anyone could draw another breath she was over the console, reaching for him, batting the other guard out of the way and booting the third across the room in one long rippling motion that ended with her and the guard who had zapped Dev nose to nose.

"Dev!" Kurok dropped to his knees on the ground. "You bloody idiots!" he yelled. "What in the hell was that for!"

The guard tried to bring his hands up between them. "Hey I—"

Jess's right fist hit his jaw, and a moment later he was dead on the ground. Just like that, just that easy. She turned, grabbed his body, lifting it up and throwing it against the wall with a sodden, heavy crunch.

She went for the next one, and as her hands touched him she heard two sharp, staccato syllables and went still. She held him in a grip and turned her head to look at where the sound came from.

Shocked, a little, when she realized it was Kurok, looking slightly shocked himself.

The stop code. Probably written in the quirk of his brain somewhere, a reflex trained bone deep inside the techs that went through field school who had to be paired with an agent and knew when they were in the zone together they might need it.

Nothing exotic. Just a code that was just as deeply drummed into the predatory spirits that lived just under the skins of people like Jess.

Kurok looked at her, one hand lifted in her direction. "She's only down, not out," he said, in a gentle tone. "And we need to find out if they did that on purpose." He pointed at the guard Jess had her hands on. "Mind asking him?"

The guard in her grip had the sense to stay still, breathing hard, staring at her. Jess looked at him, and his heels rattled against the floor as he pissed himself in fear.

"Did he?" Jess rasped, feeling her fingers twitch against him.

His teeth chattered. Jess held him up with little effort, barely keeping herself from breaking his neck, and he probably knew that, could see it in her eyes and in the vibrating tension in her body.

"Did he!"

"Okay, maybe I should ask." Kurok stripped off the harbor jacket he was wearing and wrapped it around Dev's quiet, still form. Then he stood up and walked over to them "Albert, please don't be stupid. You don't want to die or get hurt, and there's a very good possibility of both if you don't tell us."

"Nnnno." He managed to get out. "Told us to guard you." He turned his head so he could avoid Jess's eyes. "Said they were dangerous."

Doctor Dan sighed. "Yes," he said. "But what would make Edgar use his controller? Dev wasn't doing anything to me." He reached over and grabbed the man's jaw, turning his head to look into his eyes. "Albert?"

A mediocre man, a guard because he had no other use. His face was twisted, and his nose had been broken before, and now he just shook his head. "Dunno."

Jess shifted her grip and put pressure on him, bending his back into an arc and he screamed in fear. "Cough it up," she said. "I can hurt you so badly you'll beg me to kill you, and buddy?" Jess tightened her fingers, "I promise you it'll just make me laugh because that's just the kinda gal I am."

He stared at her, shaking, into those ice cold blue eyes.

"You can't even make charges. You injured an Interforce op," Jess said. "I'll cut you in pieces, slowly. Leave parts of you all over the station."

One more moment of resistance, and then he broke. "No no no...just...didn't mean to take her down. Swear it! Just stupid! Just mad about her!" He was babbling now. "One of them!"

Kurok sighed.

"Not fair!" Albert squealed. "Make it better than us!"

Jess dropped him and watched him bounce off the hard steel ground with no expression on her face. "Idiots."

"Yes." Kurok looked over at the dead guard, and the unconscious one, and the puddle of stinking, shuddering coward at his feet. "Sorry, Jesslyn."

"For what?" Jess turned and went to one of the specimen sinks, releasing cleanser over her hands before she shook them free of the residue and went back to where Dev was lying.

Then, in a breath, it was color again and she felt her guts clench and she dropped to one knee as the other refused to hold her up. "Hey, Devvie." She braced one hand against the floor and touched Dev's face, which was still and blank. "Hang in there, huh? Doc'll fix you up."

She was suddenly scared. An uncertain terror filled her, and she could barely keep herself propped upright. "She's gonna be okay, right Doc?"

"Yes." He came over and patted her shoulder. "Do an old man a favor hmm? Can you carry her over into that room on the far side there? I have a programming table I can use to bring her back up."

For a long moment Jess was afraid she couldn't do it. Her body was shaking inside and she had no real idea why, but after a few breaths she leaned forward and gathered Dev's slack form up and stood, cradling her body against her.

The room to the side was quiet and had no star windows in it. It was roundish as most of the spaces in station were, and there was a console on a raised platform on one side and a rectangular table on the other.

Jess very gently laid her burden down on the table, as she heard Kurok come in behind her.

Kurok joined her and then pulled down an overhead rig. "I locked the outer door. Last thing I need is some wig head stumbling in here to ask me a question and tripping over a corpse."

"She was scared of those zappers," Jess said, moving aside a little. "What are you going to do?" After a little pause, a hand reached out to touch Dev's without conscious thought.

"I'm going to connect up and make sure they didn't do any damage." Doctor Dan undid the uniform at Dev's neck and eased the dark fabric aside, exposing her collar. "Then I'll bring her up." He glanced up at Jess's face. "She'll be fine," he added, in a gentler tone.

Jess went around to the other side of the table and rested her hands on it, facing him. Her fingertips were still twitching. "That going to cause you trouble?" She jerked her head in the direction of the outer chamber.

"Probably. But I did warn them." Kurok carefully attached the programming rig to the jacks on Dev's collar. "We scientists tend to be really obtuse at times." He shook his head absently. "We think what we want to think and never stop to remember the important details."

"You managed to remember the stop code."

"Mmm." His face creased into a smile. "Remind me to tell you later the first time I had to use that with your father." He went to the console, sat down behind it, and brought up the screen. "This doesn't have an input to station systems. It's standalone."

"Good."

Kurok looked at her. "Got that prickly feeling, do you?" He ran the calibration automatically, watching the tall figure across the room. "I never lost it," he admitted. "As long as I've been here, I've been looking over my shoulder."

Jess found herself distracted by Dev's quiet, pale face. "Doc?"

"Hmm." He glanced over the console at her.

"Can you take the collar off her?"

Doctor Dan waited for the program to boot up, his hands

leaning on the metal of the console as he regarded her with a serious expression on his face. "That will limit her," he said. "There's a lot left for me to give her that way."

"Could also save her life," Jess responded. "Anyone finds out about that zapper, they got an angle I can't counter."

Kurok grunted in acknowledgment. "We all have weaknesses, Jess. Not to mention it should be her choice." He concentrated on the screen a moment, pausing to look back up at her. "But yes. I can."

Jess curled her fingers around Dev's, convincing herself that she felt a return pressure, even though there was no motion at all other than a steady motion of Dev's chest.

Doctor Dan peered intently at the screen, his hands still on the input pad. "My god."

Jess stiffened. "What?"

"No, it's all right. Just way more synaptic growth than I expected."

Jess reached over and moved a bit of hair out of Dev's eyes. "Yeah okay. Can you wake her up and then look at all the googlies?"

"Give me a minute." He started inputting. "I will."

Chapter Eight

SHE HEARD WHISPERING in her head and at once became aware of being down and knew she was being programmed.

Her heart pounded and she tried to move, but part of being down was being frozen still. So instead she tried to force herself up.

She felt the insistence of the programming and panic started to take her over. She was aware of a hand on her and voices, as she fought the hold of the rig and against the paralysis. Then the release came. She was up.

Her eyes snapped open and everything was blurry. Then a face came close and she saw sparkling blue, and it was Jess. She gasped and reached out, her hands finally freed. Jess caught them and pulled her into a hug.

She was sweating and breathing hard, but the hammering in her chest was easing as Jess patted her on the back in awkward comfort. "Jjjjess."

"Yeah it's me. Take it easy, Rocket," Jess said. "You're freaking me and the doc out."

The doc. Dev straightened up on the table, half turning in Jess's arms to see Doctor Dan there, his hands leaning against the surface. He looked upset. "Oh! Was that you, Doctor Dan? I didn't...oh, I'm sorry."

"It's okay." Doctor Dan still looked upset. "One of the guards put you down, Dev. I was just taking the opportunity to put in some updated data before I brought you back up. It's me who should apologize. I should have asked you first."

Dev felt herself calm, a very quick search finding all of her recent memories firmly in place.

And Jess was here, and there, in her heart, in that special place. She leaned her head against Jess's arm then got herself sorted and sat up, blinking sweat out of her eyes. "I didn't mean to...um."

"Freak out?" Jess asked. "I was hoping you'd have all your eggs scrambled when you woke."

Dev laughed faintly. "You know, the morning before I found out about going downside I had eggs for breakfast." She exhaled. "Gigi and I."

They were all silent for a moment. "Now I'm hungry," Jess

said. "Doc, the food up here sucks."

Kurok leaned back against the console, running the fingers of one hand through his hair. "Yeah, you know that's one thing I did enjoy being downside the last time. I'd forgotten how bland it is here." He studied Dev. "I didn't intend on getting you so upset, Dev."

Dev felt a little embarrassed, sitting there. "I just didn't want to lose anything," she said after a moment. "I think if I'd known it was you, Doctor Dan, it would have been okay. I know you won't hurt me."

Jess put her hand on Dev's damp back. She sensed her fear and felt Dev's body shiver. She gave her a little scratch with her fingertips, wanting to help but not entirely sure how.

Doctor Dan came back to the table and leaned on it, studying her. "No, I would never knowingly hurt you, Dev. But I can't vouch for everyone who has the skills that I do." He looked up at Jess then back at Dev. "Will you trust me once more, Dev? I'll make it so you don't have to be afraid of anyone doing anything like this to you again."

Jess made a little grunt of approval. Dev looked up at her. "What are you going to do?" She looked back at Kurok.

"I'm going to put you down and remove the synaptics," Doctor Dan replied in a gentle tone. "Jess asked me to do that, you know, and I said it needed to be your decision. So it is. Let me know if that's okay."

Dev blinked. "Oh."

"You can think about it for a little bit. I'm going to go and get some protein bars for us to snack on." He patted her hand. "I'll be right back."

He left, and they were there in the quiet of the programming room, its dim, calming light bathing them.

"You okay?" Jess finally asked.

"Yes." Dev ran her fingers through her sweat dampened hair. "That was really uncomfortable. I knew I was down, and I felt someone in there."

"That would creep me right out," Jess said. "I think the Doc's okay, though."

Dev nodded. "He is. I can feel the parts where he was, and it's just a little bit of tech loading. He didn't have a chance to do that much."

"Like I said, that would creep me out. But you're right, he didn't have time to do squat because soon as he was in there all sorts of alarms started going off on this thing."

Jess indicated the programming rig.

Dev grimaced.

"He said you had a lot of good stuff in there. I'm sure he wouldn't have messed that up, Devvie. He wants you to be a super wrencher."

Dev stared at the far wall. "I didn't care about that," she said after a long pause. "I don't care about that. I..." She exhaled. "I don't want anyone to go in there and change the things I feel."

Jess hitched herself up on the table and sat next to her, her hands clasped between her knees. "Feel?"

Dev nodded. "The special feeling I have for things. For people." She looked sidelong at Jess. "For you."

"For me?"

"Yes."

Jess pondered that. "I don't think the doc would have done that to you. He knows what that is, that whole feeling thing." She leaned her shoulder against Dev's. "But honest, Dev. If anyone tried to mess with you like that, I'd rip their hearts out through their chests."

Dev looked at her from under her pale bangs.

"Even the Doc," Jess said, "and he knows it. He knows what I am."

That kind of stunned Dev. Not that Jess would do violence. She understood that part. But that she would do it on Dev's behalf to someone like Doctor Dan, who she knew Jess liked.

That seemed strange and somewhat incorrect. Then another thought occurred to her. "The guard..."

"I killed him," Jess said placidly. "I broke his neck and nearly did that to another of them. So maybe now the rest of them know what the doc does." She smiled. "It's good to have me as a friend and crappy to have me as an enemy."

Yes. Dev exhaled. That was true. "I'm really glad you're my friend."

"We're like a directional explosion. Point us in the right direction and it's all good." Jess sounded almost cheerful. "Otherwise, not so much."

The door opened and Doctor Dan returned and pulled some wrapped items out of his harbor shirt front pocket. He dropped them on the console. "Help yourselves, my friends." He sat behind the console and regarded them. "Had a bit of a complication. Some of the DeeArs came in to clean the lab."

"Found the mess?"

Kurok nodded. "Mmm. For some reason they seemed to think

I'd done it." He looked vaguely bemused. "But in the end it worked out as I had them tidy up and take the two living ones to med."

Jess chuckled. "Bet that adds to your mystique."

There was a little silence, and then Dev cleared her throat. "Can we do the collar now, Doctor Dan? I'm ready."

"I think we should, Dev. Because after word gets around about the guards, I'm sure there'll be some degree of confusion here, and I might not get a chance."

Not for the first time, Jess found herself impressed with this man's casual courage. She understood what he meant, even if Dev perhaps didn't. "Hey, I pulled the trigger." She got up off the table to give Dev some space to lie down. "Let them be pissed at me. You warned them."

"Oh, I don't think so, Jesslyn." Doctor Dan came around the console and pulled the programming rig down over Dev again, this time with those trusting eyes watching him. "Now, Dev, you understand this will mean you can't get any further enhancements."

"Yes," Dev said. "I'll have to do it all myself."

He smiled. "And there's never been a mind that came out of this lab more suited for that." He gently attached the rig then touched his fingertips to her forehead. "Go down, Dev," he said. "When you come back up you'll be one of us."

Dev blinked, faint moisture appearing on her lashes. Then she closed her eyes and her body relaxed.

Kurok turned his head. "Prop that door open, will you, Jesslyn? If anything in the outer area stirs, warn me."

Without a word, Jess went to the portal. After it slid open, she leaned her body against it, crossing her long legs casually and folding her arms. The outer lab was quiet, the guards were gone, even the smell of urine replaced with a gentle floral scent.

She looked back into the inner chamber. Kurok had settled back behind the console and was staring intently at the scan screen. His fingertips moved over the input surface, but this time Dev remained quiet and still, and there was no flare of alarms.

Jess remembered how uncomfortable Dev had been talking about the collar. She nodded a little, glad Dev made the logical choice to get rid of it. "She doesn't really need that thing anymore, does she Doc?"

Kurok smiled. "It's always useful to be able to be given what you need with little effort," he said. "Imagine being able to be given an entire deployment briefing, with pictures and diagrams, in minutes without having to study it."

Jess made a little sound under her breath. "Never thought of it that way."

"No, most people don't. They usually consider the negative parts of being a bio alt, never the positive ones." He completed a rapid fire set of inputs and studied the results. Then he flexed his fingers and typed in a shorter series, the last few taps slowing until he stopped.

For a few moments he just stared at the screen.

"Something wrong?" Jess finally asked.

Doctor Dan sighed. "No. I just didn't think this would be as hard as it is." He glanced up at Jess. "But I better get on with it." He turned back and pressed a final input, and a moment later the rig attached over Dev flickered and then retracted, removing itself from the set of connects on either side of her neck

"That's it?"

"When you know exactly what you're doing, it doesn't take long." He got up and circled the console, pausing to pull out a drawer and remove a small case that he brought with him to the table. "Now there's just the mechanical bit."

Jess watched him open the case and remove a set of hand tools that glittered faintly in the light overhead. He pulled one of the panels down and positioned it, and then he gently moved Dev's head to the right.

Very far off in the distance, Jess heard the faint echo of a klaxon. She straightened up a little then looked back into the room. "Hear that?"

"Yes." Kurok had a tool in one hand. "Probably nothing good." He worked deftly at the glittering metallic surface wrapping Dev's neck. "Hopefully it won't be utterly bad."

"Let me go find out." Jess left the door and let it slide shut behind her, moving across the lab at a lope. She reached the outer door and it opened. She darted out into the hallway, sweeping her senses right and left.

She heard the klaxon more clearly now. It wasn't the same as had been sounding in the null gym. This one had more urgency to it. A sound of running footsteps drew her attention, and she turned a corner to find one of the bio alts coming toward her at speed. "Hey!"

The bio alt skidded literally to a halt, panting, and stared at her. "Where's Doctor Dan?" he asked. "Please? I must find him."

It was one of the ones who had spoken in the big room. "Why?" Jess asked.

He looked behind him then at her. "I have to tell him. They sent me from operations. There are bad people here."

Uh oh. Jess took a step nearer to him. "What kind of bad people? People like me?"

"I don't know. They told me to find Doctor Dan and tell him there are bad people here, and we are in danger," the bio alt told her. "You're Doctor Dan's friend. They told me that, too."

"Who's they?"

The bio alt stared at her. "A KayTee," he said. "They were in the crèche, this morning. They said you were there. You are Jess."

"Okay, c'mon." Jess pointed back the way she'd come. "He's in his lab."

The bio alt looked completely relieved. "Thank you!" He hurried past her and turned the corner. Jess debated continuing, but then some instinct grabbed her and she whirled around and bolted after him, catching up to him as he got to the lab door.

He jumped, startled, but put his hand on the pad and waited for the door to open.

It didn't. He put his hand on it again, but the door stayed shut and the pad itself remained pink. Jess nudged him aside and put her own hand on it, feeling the tickle as it scanned through her skin, activating the chips embedded under it.

The pad turned teal and the door opened. "G'wan." Jess pushed him forward, and as they passed through she turned and palmed the internal panel. The door slid shut and the pad turned pink again. "Hey Doc! We got problems!"

The bio alt looked around. "Doctor Dan?"

Jess loped to the door of the programming room and hit the latch. The door opened and she got inside before it fully retracted. "Doc."

"Sh." Doctor Dan was bent over Dev, his hands moving in a slow, cautious motion. "Terrible time to make me jump, Jesslyn."

"One of your boys is here, saying we've got bad people in the joint." Jess spread her arms out to block the door as the bio alt crowded in back of her. "Not sure what that means since he doesn't seem to think that means me."

"Oh, dear." Doctor Dan finished his cautious task and straightened up with a grimace. "It probably means we have an enemy shuttle locking on."

"Enemy."

"Other side." Doctor Dan hurried around to the other side of the table. "I have one more probe to remove. Give me five minutes."

The far off klaxons suddenly got louder, and the lights flickered overhead. "Make it a one minute five minutes, Doc." Jess pushed back from the door, bumping the bio alt backwards. "I'm gonna run to our bunks and grab my gear."

She let the door close. "Stay here," she told the bio alt. "Or better yet, go get some of your friends and bring 'em back."

The bio alt nodded. "Yes."

"Everyone's gotta help the doc, right?"

"Yes."

JESS RACED THROUGH the tube shaped hallways, bowling over no fewer than three panicked bio alts who got in her way. She reached the tube their rooms were in and got to the door, slapping the pad with her hand and lunging at it.

Fortunately for both her and the door, it opened and she scrambled in and grabbed both her and Dev's packs and threw them over her shoulder, feeling the weight and heft of her hand blaster whack her in the ribs.

She got out the door and back into the hall and was two steps down it when the lights flickered and went from pale white to an annoying shade of yellow she disliked intensely. She blinked against it as she broke back into a run.

The guard at the entrance was gone. She turned the corner and moved into the wider hallway again, hearing a booming thunk echoing off in the distance. A crackle sounded over head and as she reached the tube where the doc's lab was, a metallic sounding voice erupted.

"Emergency stations. Emergency stations. All security to lockdown."

She felt a shudder go through the floor and saw tube sections closing off. She redoubled her speed, sliding through a closing panel as it almost caught her, in order to get into the section with the lab in it.

The area was full of scared bio alts. Jess could smell it on them, and they turned agitatedly as she approached the door. "Hang on, kids." She bumped her way through them. "Gimme some space."

"Where's Doctor Dan? The door is locked," A BeeAye protested, his palm against the panel. "They told us to come here!"

"Relax." Jess got her hand on it and the door slid open. "Don't shove."

She bounded into the lab with the crowd of them after her. "Close that door behind ya...Hey Doc!"

Jess felt the agitation before she heard it and turned, setting down Dev's pack as the door filled with security, all with stun sticks and several jumpsuited figures behind them. She got herself squared to the inner door and got her blaster out and into her hands as everyone else came to a halt.

It went quiet. Jess released the safety on the blaster and cradled it, legs spread. "Stop!"

Doss was in the lead, two other of the administrators behind him with several proctors. "I'm sure there's some misunderstanding here, we just need to speak to Daniel."

"He's busy," Jess stated, flatly. "Why not go see why all the alarms are going off? Ain't because of him."

"Oh, no, it's fine." Doss held up a hand. "Really there's nothing going on, just some maintenance." He licked his lips. "Really, we just need to ask Daniel a question. Can you ask him to come out here?" He glanced to either side at the security guards. "Everyone just settle down. It's going to be fine."

He was lying. Jess was actually a little surprised it wasn't printed across his forehead, which was shiny with sweat. The administrators behind him looked scared. They were watching the bio alts with a surprising amount of nervousness.

But the bio alts responded to his words and they all sorted themselves out and lined up along the lab tables, watching the displays with curiosity, used to the scientist's direction and programmed to obey it.

One of them peered at the model of Dev's brain.

"He's busy," Jess repeated. "So that was maintenance, huh?" She glanced up at the lurid yellow lights, still glaring. "Your systems don't seem to think so. When lights change like that where I come from, we get the guns out."

"It's just maintenance," Doss insisted.

"What's he busy with?" One of the other scientists asked. "We don't have any routines running."

Jess shrugged. "I'm an enforcement agent. I don't know what all that stuff is. I just know he's busy, and I'm not gonna bother him." She smiled. "Neither are you."

The metallic voice sounded again. "Emergency stations. Corridor twelve A, minor breach."

Doss inched forward. "Now, I'm sure you'll let me contact Daniel. I'm in charge here."

"Nope."

"Look, here, Agent..." The other scientist pushed past him. "I don't know what kind of game you're playing but we've got to talk to him so—" He got within range, and Jess casually kicked him backwards into Doss and two of the security guards.

"No," she said, placidly. "I'd go see what's falling apart on your thing here if I were you. I'll tell the doc you were here."

One of the guards lifted his stun stick, and Jess shot it out of his hand with a light touch on her blaster. It clattered to the ground and bounded off, the bio alts jumping out of it's way as they stared at Jess.

"Don't do that." Jess shifted her grip on the gun. "I know the doc's told you what I do for a living."

"Agent, please." Doss bravely moved toward her. "It's urgent! We need to talk to Doctor Kurok right away!"

"Why?" Jess felt the motion behind her as the door to the programming chamber opened.

"Yes, why?" Kurok came up next to her, wiping his hands on a piece of fabric. "It's all right, Jesslyn. Why don't you just go and keep your partner company while she wakes up."

Wakes up. Jess smiled a little. Wakes up, not comes up. He'd done it. "Sure you want me to do that, Doc?" she asked. "All those zap sticks don't look too friendly." She regarded the guards with a squint eyed look.

"It's fine." He patted her on the side, a gentle and natural motion she didn't resent somewhat to her surprise. "Let me find out what all the fuss is about." He edged past her. "Everyone settle down now, BeeAye, can you bring me that folder?"

"Yes, Doctor Dan." The bio alt trotted over to the desk, and the anxiety in the room lowered noticeably as the bio alts relaxed, some of them settling down on the benches near the walls.

The security guards, though, were still focused on the tall, dark clad figure behind him, nervously fingering their stun sticks. The two guards who had been knocked down were back up, watching Jess warily.

"Daniel, we must speak with you." Doss looked meaningfully at Jess. "It's important. And urgent."

"I gathered," Kurok said, dryly. "What's the emergency? I see the comp systems are offline."

"Well..." He looked again at Jess. "Let's go into your office so we can speak privately."

Doctor Dan glanced casually around and met Jess's eyes. "Why don't you join us after Dev's ready?"

"Daniel..." Doss objected.

Jess smiled. "Sure, we'll do that." She lifted her hand and let the gun rest against her shoulder, not missing the twitching from all the security guards in the room as she shifted again and picked up Dev's pack, getting the strap over her shoulder.

Jess let them wait, then she stepped back and into the chamber, allowing the door to shut in front of her before she safed the gun and turned to regard the table. "Hope he knows what he's doing," she muttered. "That's a bunch of three-week-old dead fish there."

As she said it, the lights changed color and went back to the normal off white shade, and the overhead speakers made a little clicking sound. "Operations to normal," the voice announced. "Return to standard stations."

Jess regarded the speaker thoughtfully. Then she walked over to the console Kurok had been working at and tapped the input, watching as the screen stayed at a static screen with "SYSTEMS OFFLINE" on it. "Huh."

Dev was still out, lying on the table that now had all the mechanical bits retracted, her slim form covered with a light blanket. Jess went to her side and peered down, putting her hand on her shoulder. "Hey, Devvie."

She saw marks just under each ear, and she tilted her head to inspect them, small cuts that had been swabbed with antiseptic she could just smell. They seemed closed and just had a tinge of rust red around them.

"Deeevvvvie," Jess warbled, blowing into Dev's ear gently. "C'mon, rock star. Wake up."

Dev's breathing changed a little, and after a moment, her pale eyes flickered open, blinking in a little confusion. She looked up at the ceiling then turned her head. "Jess!"

"Hey," Jess responded. "You're a people." She touched the small wound, then peeled the neck down on Dev's Interforce uniform to find a distinct lack of a collar beneath it. "Doc did a good job." She inspected the skin, which seemed a little lighter than the surrounding surface but had no mark on it.

In reflex, Dev reached up to touch her neck, her fingers pausing as they felt only smooth skin. "He did? It's done? Where is he?" She sat up. "It hurts a little."

"He had to take something out." Jess peered at the cuts. "Those things in your head I guess."

Dev's gaze went inward and her eyes unfocused briefly. There was a difference, but she was hard pressed to describe exactly what it was.

She knew it was there, though, and it made her smile, and suddenly she was so glad they'd come to station. "Oh, Jess. He really did it."

Jess ruffled her hair. "Glad that worked out, but we'd better get ready to do stuff because something's going on out there. I got your gear." She unshouldered the pack. "They just announced everything was cool, but I don't think so."

Dev sat up and shifted around, hanging her legs off the table. She took a deep breath and released it. "Where is Doctor Dan?" She hopped off the table, took her pack and opened it, removing the jacket she'd folded inside.

The cuts on her neck stung. She felt a soreness up along the line behind her ears to the back of her neck, and if she turned her head she felt a twinge. "He really did it." She carefully settled the jacket over her body and tugged the sleeves straight.

Jess took a step back to watch her. "He's in his office. He wanted us to come over after you got up." She put her blaster on it's holster at her side. "There are a bunch of your buddies outside and some of the other docs."

Dev moved her jaw around and rubbed the back of her neck.

"Sore?" Jess asked.

"Yes," Dev said. "I think it will take some time to adjust." She came over next to Jess and looked at the console. "Oh!" She reached out to touch the input pad. "That's unusual." She put her hand flat on the embedded square, but it didn't react.

Jess tightened her pack and put her hand on Dev's shoulder. "Yeah, let's go find out what's actually going on. Doc may need our help."

"Yes," Dev said. "We should go find him. I want to say thank you."

They headed for the door, pausing as the surface under them shifted a trifle, and Jess felt heavy, then not.

"Suboptimal," Dev responded without prompting. "Not good at all."

KUROK WENT BEHIND his desk and dropped into his chair. Doss and his retinue followed, and the door slid shut behind them. "Now, what's going on?"

One of the men with him pulled a blaster out and held it. "We've got problems."

Kurok gave him a withering stare. "Put that away. If you think that's supposed to intimidate me you've got the wrong idea, Charles."

Doss came over to the edge of the desk but stayed standing. "Daniel, there's a shuttle locked on. They want the seeds and the system. The one we sold to the homestead."

Doctor Dan put his hands behind his head and leaned back in his chair. "Did we do that?"

"Don't act stupid, Daniel," the man called Charles said. "You know perfectly well what we did. Don't pretend you don't."

"Well, except I don't," Kurok replied in a mild tone. "If someone was supposed to tell me, they didn't, so sorry, Charles, I wasn't a part of that stupidity."

"It wasn't stupid," Doss said. "Daniel, it's a breakthrough. You know it is. That was the only place they found that mineral, and they were glad to work with us on it. Don't disparage that."

Kurok regarded them. "And now we have the other side here, ready to take it from us at gunpoint because they know damn well they can't take it from Drake's Bay." He looked faintly amused. "So what do you want me to do?"

"Talk to them," Charles said. "You come from there."

Kurok laughed. "Are you really that much of an idiot, or do you just not know that much about my past?"

Doss cut Charles off with a stiff arm gesture. "Daniel, they'll listen to you. It doesn't matter about your past."

Kurok stood up abruptly and put his hands on his hips. "Screw you," he said. "It's not my project, not my screwup, and I'm not going to talk to a posse of jackasses from the other side who will know more about me than you do and probably shoot me on sight."

"Daniel!" Doss shouted. "Be reasonable!"

Charles pushed past him and thrust the blaster forward. "Listen, you jerk! You're going to do what we tell you to do or... blup!" He reeled backwards as Kurok came over the desk at him, flailing his arms as the gun was taken out of his grip, and he was whacked in the head with it. "Ahh!"

"Stop it," Kurok hissed, safing the blaster and tucking it into the front pocket of his harbor shirt. "Idiot!"

Charles pushed off the wall he'd stumbled into. "Don't you call me an idiot you—"

"Just shut up, the lot of you." Kurok removed the blaster again and unsafed it, aiming it at them with casual skill. "Before I blow your heads off."

Doss stepped back in shock, holding his hands up. "Daniel, we just want to do what's best for the station! We have to deal with these people!"

"You," Doctor Dan shoved him back into the room and away from the door, "are an idiot, and you two are bigger ones. You have no idea what fire you're playing with. Have any of you sent a message down to Interforce that we've got an invasion?"

Charles leaned over, holding his head. "No. They took our systems offline."

Kurok sat down on his desk. "Okay I'll have Dev relay it. She can hack them." He put the gun down on the desk and folded his arms. "Because the problem is, oh my colleagues, we don't have anything to give them."

"We can..." Doss started, then paused. "They think we developed a growth medium."

Doctor Dan stared at him. "Why would they think that? Did you tell them that?"

"I did," Charles said. "They were ready to offer us anything." He lowered his hand, and there was blood on it. "You cut me you little bastard."

Kurok went back around his desk and sat down in his chair, scrubbing his hands in his thick, pale hair. "Sit down, all of you." He leaned forward and propped his elbows on the desk, then pulled the blaster back across it and shoved it in his pocket again. "What kind of shuttle is locked onto us?"

Uncertainly, Doss sat down in one of the chairs across from him. "Well, I don't really know," he said. "After they locked on, the systems went down, and besides, Daniel, we really don't know much about all that. Can't you just talk to them?"

They felt the grav shift, and Doss clutched at the desk. "What was that? Maybe the systems are back up."

Kurok slid his entry pad over and tapped it, reviewing the results. "No." He pressed a few keys and then started inputting. "Let me see if I can try something else." The auth pad lit up and he put his hand on it, the pad turning from pink to teal immediately.

There was a light tap on the door, and then it opened to reveal Jess's tall form filling the opening. "You got problems," she said without preamble. "You've got a T300 series military shuttle clamped on and three dozen troops coming down the hall."

"And then again, who needs systems when we have a Drake around." Doctor Dan pushed the console away from him. "These idiots told them we've got a growth medium to sell," he said. "They want to talk to me about it." He glanced past her. "Hello,

Dev. Are you feeling all right?"

Dev produced a whole hearted smile as she came up to join Jess. "Yes, Doctor Dan. Thank you."

His eyes twinkled a little.

"Why did you tell them that?" Jess asked Charles.

"Because they were willing to pay anything for it. For him." Charles pointed at Kurok. "They're dying. Something happened months back that sent them into a spiral and now they're desperate. So, yeah, I told them we'd gotten something working."

"See, Daniel? You have to talk to them," Doss said. "I'm sure the security is just to keep themselves safe. They know we're no danger to them." He stood up. "I left them in the rotunda. Let me go tell them you're coming."

Jess pushed him back into his seat. "He's not going to talk to them," she said. "If they figure out who he is, they'll blow him into bits. We've got to figure out how to get them out of here before they break something we can't fix."

"But..." Doss protested.

"Or before they figure out the person they actually have to talk to is you," Kurok said in a dry tone. "On the other hand, maybe the sheer irony of that will make their heads explode and solve our problem."

The station lurched, and a moment later the power went off, and they were in complete darkness.

"Welcome to the frying pan," Kurok said. "The sound you hear all around you is the fire."

DEV HAD A panel apart, and her head stuck inside of it, a small worklight poking out of her mouth. It was pitch dark around them in the lab, and she could hear the buzz of worried chatter from the bio alts behind her.

She was looking for a way to cross connect the lab systems into emergency power. Her hands moved in automatic motions, sorting through the cabling and boards inside the console as her mind tried to encompass the knowledge that her collar was gone.

If she pulled her head out of the cabinet and looked around, she would see a hundred LED traced rings on a hundred bio alt necks, but if they looked back at her, they'd see nothing.

Even if she took down the neck of her Interforce uniform, still, nothing.

It was such a strange feeling, Prickling and new and strange and amazing and really, really distracting.

"Anything, Devvie?" Jess's voice rumbled behind her.

"Not yet." Dev forced her concentration back on the traces. There was a bus there that she could almost... "Ouch!" she yelped, as she touched a live lead, then almost put her head into it as the cabinet was suddenly full of Jess crowding in anxiously behind her.

"What happened?" Jess said. "Are you okay?"

"There is power here." Dev shook her fingers a little and flexed her hand. "I touched it."

"Oh." Jess cautiously withdrew. "Be careful, Rocket." She bumped against Dev's hip.

Dev turned her head and flashed the light behind her, catching the twinkle of it on Jess's eyes and savoring the feeling that caused inside her. She returned the light to the boards, then almost dropped the light when Jess gave her calf a friendly squeeze.

And all of that was okay. She felt the resonance of that as she carefully put the power on bypass then rerouted the leads over and clamped them on. All of that was okay. She took the light out of her mouth. "Please take care. Power on."

Doctor Dan had told her it was okay, in that deep twilight that was being down, a gentle reassurance she could feel even now, and knew she would never experience again.

"Go." Doctor Dan's voice came from another console some distance from her. "Shunt the power, Dev."

"Yes." Dev removed the bypass and got her hands out of the way as, with a crackle and pop, systems started to come live around her. She backed out of the cabinet and was lifted to her feet by Jess, as lights started to come on across the lab.

Doctor Dan appeared, a screwdriver behind one ear and a pair of cutters in his hand. "Good job, Dev. Let's see where that gets us."

"Doctor Dan, the outer ring hatches are still locked," An AyeBee reported, his head poked through the propped open inner door to the lab. "I can see emergency lamps in the core."

"Yes, thank you, AyeBee. Stay calm. We'll sort this out," Kurok reassured him.

"Yeah, chill," Jess added somewhat helpfully. "Ya got the two best wrenchers in the history of the planet here. If they can't fix this, it ain't fixable."

Kurok chuckled softly, shaking his head.

Doss was pacing. "This is unthinkable." He went to the panel and leaned over it. "This is restarting. You think it will come up?"

he asked Kurok. "Can we get comms?"

Dev had her scanner out and was tuning it. "There is a lot of power flux going on," she reported. "I think the grid's offline," she said to Doctor Dan. "Someone's trying to cut in the reserve systems, but they are not really being successful."

Kurok had a panel open on the console top with wires trailing inside it. "Yes, well, we have to get that sorted before we stop being able to cycle air." He glanced at the door. "It must be pandemonium down below."

A blast of sunlight came through the upper levels, looking strange and harsh. "Cover your eyes." Doss turned and ordered, almost automatically. "All of you! The photo shielding is down. Don't look at the sun."

Jess shut her eyes in reflex as the light poured into the lab, feeling it bathe her face and show blaring and white through her eyelids, and she spared a moment to wonder what it would be like if they could see the sun from downside.

"Systems are booting," Kurok said in a mild tone. "Then maybe we can get comms, get the outer ring open, and find out what the hell is going on."

"It feels warm, doesn't it?" Dev asked.

"Yeah, it does." Jess held her hands out and felt the warmth against her skin. "Like the rad in Market Island."

"Yes." Dev half turned to shield her scanner and eyes from the sunlight, recalibrating it slightly. "Hopefully we will not experience the cold water."

Jess felt the light move off, and she opened her eyes, looking around to see the bio alts lowering their hands from their faces and the two other scientists getting busy at some of the returning systems. Soon they would get things going, and then she could go out and do something far more useful than hanging around here.

She shifted her pack and tightened the straps, wandering away from the consoles and out into the outer chamber where twenty or thirty of the bio alts had settled down. Mostly the pilots and the guys who did mech she realized. "Hi."

They looked at her nervously.

Jess went over to the hatch seal and poked at it. She saw it was on override, the station's systems designed to keep sections sealed when there was some problem out there, keeping as many people safe in one area as it could.

Made sense.

Dev came over to her and fiddled with her scanner. "There's pressure and breathing air in the next section," she said.

"Good thing since they're trying like crazy to open this door. Hate to have it pop open if we're just going to explode."

Dev eyed her. Then she smiled. "You're really funny sometimes."

"Only sometimes?" Jess kept poking at the controls. "How are ya feeling?" she asked. "Neck still hurting you?"

"It's sore," Dev admitted, "But I feel amazing." She kept her voice very low. "Don't talk about it here, though, with the sets around us. I think it would make them feel unhappy and possibly incorrect."

Jess left off messing with the panel and put her arm around Dev instead. "Anything you can do to speed this up, Devvie? I got a feeling I need to be doing something." She felt a certain tension coming into her body.

Dev sighed a little and glanced behind her. "I really don't think so, and if I did, I would cause the director a lot of discomfort. He's really agitated."

"And?"

"He will get upset and start yelling again," Dev said in a slightly confused tone.

"And?" Jess watched her cock her head to one side in bewilderment. "Why care? He can't do anything to ya."

Dev frowned.

"He can't do anything to ya for three reasons," Jess said. "One, you ain't got a leash no more. Two, cause the doc back there is going to whack him if he does, and three, because he knows if he messes with you I'm going to kill him."

Dev considered that. "Hmm." She turned and headed back into the lab, leaving Jess to chuckle behind her and go back to jabbing the controls.

"What are you doing?" a KayTee asked, watching Jess poke at things.

"Trying to annoy this thing enough that it will give up and let us out," Jess replied cordially. "Got any ideas on how to hack it?"

The KayTee regarded her with a serious expression. "We are not programmed to do that."

"Dev wasn't programmed to fly through a mountain. C'mon. You all want to be like her? Think outside the box."

Another KayTee came up next to them. "What box? There are no boxes here." He observed the pad. "The safety systems are secure, and we do not have access to them." He sounded regretful. "But I don't think hitting them will do useful things."

Jess exhaled and rolled her eyes. "What'll happen if I blast it?"

Both KayTees stepped back at once.

"Okay. Clear enough." Jess moved over and opened a panel instead, studying the mechanics behind it. They were thick and appeared pneumatic, huge struts designed to keep the circular seal closed. "What about that?"

DOCTOR DAN WAS standing over one of the consoles and Dev went over to join him. "Is there something else I can do to help you?" she asked, giving the scientists hovering nearby a wary look. "Jess seems to think there is something urgent to attend to outside this section."

"Oh she does, huh?" Kurok smiled. "Well, we probably should pay attention then because that never meant anything good when I used to be in that business."

Doss was hovering. "Is it ready yet, Daniel?"

"Not yet." Kurok edged to one side. "See if you can get your hand in there, Dev. Mine's too big." He indicated the control panel. "It's the intersection crossconnect, I think twenty-four B."

Willingly, Dev set her scanner down and got her light back out of her pocket, directing the beam into the hatch where there was a ripple of colored circuits. "I can," she said. "What is...oh, I see." She put the light between her teeth again and reached inside, setting the board switches with a confident touch. "There. Is that it?"

"Perfect." Doctor Dan ran a routine and the console booted, this time with a rising hum as boards on either side came to life. "Good job, Dev."

"Daniel," Doss said. "There is no way this unit was given that."

"No." Doctor Dan said in a quiet tone. "Dev wasn't given that. She just knows how to do this. Just like I do." He closed the hatch and pulled an input pad over. "And stop calling her the unit, or I'll kick you in the groin."

Doss jerked backward a step. "Daniel. That's uncalled for."

"Yes, probably. Kicks in the groin are seldom called for since they're so damned uncomfortable," Kurok muttered as he worked over the console. "Oh, hell. They took central offline. For crying out loud, Randall, couldn't you at least keep them in their damn ship?"

"Daniel, they just wanted to talk to us!" Doss's voice lifted in frustration. "I don't know what's wrong with you!"

Kurok pulled the hand blaster out of the pocket in his jacket. "Let's go, Dev. Maybe we can get that hatch open now and let your friend out before she damages something." He looked back at Doss. "Stay here. Keep the hatches shut when we leave. You'll be safe in here."

"Where are you going?" Doss asked in a somber voice. "Daniel, please. Let's just go talk to them. I'm positive this is just a misunderstanding."

Kurok regarded him. "Randall, I can't go talk to them. They'll shoot me. Just like they'll shoot Agent Drake if they find her, and for more or less the same reason."

Doss looked disturbed. "I don't understand. You're a scientist. Why would they want to shoot you? What aren't you telling me?"

"This needs to wait," Jess said, coming up on the other side of the console. "C'mon, Doc. We're outta time. I can hear blast return outside and your name's all over this lab. They come in the door they're gonna splat your buddies, so we need to scram, like now."

Kurok sighed. "Later," he said. "If there is a later." He started for the door, and Dev and Jess joined him. They went out into the outer chamber again and went to the door. "Look out folks. Let us through."

His name was whispered and carried back as the emergency lighting brightened. "All right now, just let me get at...ah, yes you have it open." He went to the panel. "Okay let me just make sure we don't have ammonia on the other side of this."

"It's clear," Dev said. "Standard atmosphere mix, nothing toxic."

He smiled his gentle smile at her. "Thank you, Dev." He started the manual process to open the hatch. "Stand back, everyone. Get behind me. In fact, everyone go back inside the lab. I don't want you getting injured."

The bio alts clustered around them instead. "Doctor Dan, can we go with you?" a KayTee asked. "We want to help and do good work."

Kurok turned, his hand hovering over the access pad. "Lads, this is going to be dangerous, you could take harm. Stay behind. Be safe."

"That's okay. We understand," a second KayTee said, immediately. "We could be made dead, but we want to help." He waved the others forward. "We saw the vid of what NM-Dev-1 did. You said it was very good work."

Jess chuckled, low and inside her throat. "Hoisted."

"Yes, it was." Kurok lifted a hand. "But that is not what we're doing here."

"We want to do good work like NM-Dev-1," a BeeAye insisted. "Please let us help you." He turned as the rest of the bio alts in the outer chamber pressed closer. "Please, Doctor Dan?"

"Let 'em," Jess said. "If nothing else we can use them for camo."

"Jesslyn."

"Doc, all three of us are pretty distinctive. Having some native cover might help." Jess stared at him, her tone serious. "Everyone on this thing's in danger right now."

It was true. He knew it. There was also something still inside him that responded to the leadership of someone dressed in that black suit, gun held so casually in one hand. To someone who had this just as firmly built into who they were as any of the bios begging to join them.

Ah, hell.

Doctor Dan sighed then put his hand on the pad. "All right. Come along with us, but stay behind us and keep quiet."

The big lock clicked and shuddered as the pad turned green and slowly retracted, revealing a quiet, empty tube beyond and the sound of blaster fire and screams in the distance.

Jess started to move. "Let's go. Devvie, start scanning."

"No bio targets next thousand meters."

THE UPPER LEVELS of the station were empty. Only emergency lighting was visible, save the blast of regular light from the lab they'd left behind them. The drop tubes were red lit and locked off.

"No null," Kurok said as they passed one. "That means you step inside you drop the distance."

"Nice." Jess looked at it. "How do we get down?"

They approached the inner core of the station through cross paths and tubes that were eerie in their silence. Only creaks and craklings sounded around them, the station protesting its disruption.

"There are service access hatches in the core." Dev said. She adjusted her scanner.

"Yes," one of the KayTees said. "We use them."

Kurok looked at him in surprise. "You do?"

"Over here." Dev pointed at the hatch. "That one goes to central if I remember correctly."

"Yes," the KayTee said. "I have a manual key." He pulled something from the belt at his waist and went to the wall. "Please watch for anyone," he asked the rest of the bio alts who spread out and started looking around.

Kurok looked at Dev. "I think I'm about to get some unexpected education."

The KayTee opened the hatch and pulled it back. "That will take us to central, and we can also access the crèche. We should go quickly."

"Yes," Dev said. "There are non-station biologic approaching." She slung the scanner over her shoulder. "Everyone should go inside and start down." She ducked inside the hatch and disappeared. The rest of the bio alts immediately moved after her.

Jess grinned. "After you, Doc."

He sighed and shoved the blaster into his front pocket. "We should have gone first. We've got the guns."

"Been trying to impress that on Dev for six months now." Jess pulled the hatch closed after her as they moved inside the core of the station, finding a metal ladder leading downward that was the twin of every ladder in every human built system she'd ever been in.

The bio alts moved down quickly, some just using hand grips and letting their legs dangle. They were all adept, and Jess moved to the side of the ladder fitting her tall form between it and the mechanism in the core. "Lemme see if I can get up in front."

Before Kurok could answer, she started dropping down the side of the ladder faster than even the bios could manage, snaking past them as she let gravity pull her body downward.

Ahead of her, at the front, she saw Dev pause and reach for her scanner. Jess responded to instinct and just let go of the ladder to plummet downward, her hand already pulling her blaster from its holder at her hip.

DEV REACHED THE central level and stepped off the ladder, moving onto the metal grid flooring that led toward the hatches that would let them back out into the main part of station. She heard a knocking sound and pulled her scanner off her shoulder and brought it around.

With a startling boom the hatch opened ahead of her and a

figure entered, outlined in the emergency light from outside. She saw a blaster.

She started to drop to one knee when she saw the pre-aim splash, but then there was a sense of motion and a loud boom as Jess landed in front of her. The energy release from Jess's blaster impacted the intruder before they could get a shot off.

The figure rocked backwards, then a moment later Jess pounced on them. The gun in the intruder's hand was knocked free and tumbled down through the central core to clatter on impact far below.

There was a cracking sound, and the intruder followed, a limp body that tumbled past the grid and slammed into structural support on its way down.

Jess went to the hatch and peered cautiously through it then stepped back and pulled it closed. "Must have heard us in here."

One of the KayTees went to the edge of the grid and looked down. "You made him dead? That was a security guard."

"I made him dead. He was pointing a weapon at the wrong thing." Jess holstered her blaster. "Let's wait for the rest of the gang to get down here, and then we can go out." She glanced behind her. "You okay, Devvie?"

"Excellent, thank you." Dev joined her. "I think that person was going to shoot me."

"He was." Jess jumped up and down a little, shaking her arms to loosen up her muscles. "Stupid little bastard. Probably had no idea what he was aiming at. Thought you were a bad guy."

"You made the guard dead because he was potentially going to harm NM-Dev-1?" one of the BeeAyes asked. "Even though he was a natural born?"

Jess turned to him. "Yes. In my world there are good guys, bad guys, and innocent bystanders. We're supposed to protect the good guys, kill the bad guys, and try to avoid splatting too many innocent bystanders."

"I see," the BeeAye said.

Jess smiled at him. "You volunteered to be a good guy."

The platform was getting crowded as the dozen bio alts and Kurok made their way down. Jess backed up until she was at the hatch.

"Okay." Kurok eased his way between the bios and caught up to them. "Now, when we go out there, we'll be in view. So I'd like everyone to be very careful, and if I tell you to lie down, please do that at once."

Jess eyed him.

"Not you." Kurok chuckled wryly. "Dev, can you please confirm if we have anything out there?"

Dev was already scanning and stepped to the edge of the platform near the hatch. She tuned the scanner carefully, getting a wiremap of the area outside the core. "There is security there," she said. "They appear to be searching."

"Our security?" Doctor Dan came over and examined the screen. "Hmm."

The bio alts just waited quietly, most of them watching Jess with interest as she warmed up, making little boxing motions with her hands.

"Let me pop out there and speak with them," Kurok said. "It's just possible they'll tell me what's going on."

"It's also possible they'll plug ya," Jess said. "Depends what bozo up there told them."

"Well, we can't just stay in here," Kurok said, "and all the systems we need to bring us back online are in central so..." He went to the hatch and listened then unlatched it and pushed it open before Jess could stop him. He stepped outside and closed the access just as she reached it.

"You little..." Jess paused and went silent, holding her hand up. "Quiet." She pressed the side of her face against the metal, sealing her ear as she used the surface to amplify the sound outside.

Quiet voices. "Yes, Doctor Kurok, we know but—"

Kurok's response wasn't audible. But they hadn't shot him on sight, and that she considered a good sign.

"Can you come with us to security control? My captain said—"

"I have some sets with me." Now Kurok's voice was audible. "They're frightened. Let me bring them out and we can go to control."

"Jess, energy uplift," Dev said, urgently.

"Yeah." Jess opened the hatch and hopped outside. She let her senses sweep the area, her blaster in her hand as she pushed Kurok down, found her targets and was shooting.

"Get down!" she yelled at the guards, sensing motion at her back. "Dev, stay in there!" She got in front of Kurok and dropped to her knees, finding and shooting targets as fast as she could once the security guards bowed to better judgement and dove for the ground.

Fire came back at her, but she intercepted it with skill. She heard one body tumble to the deck and the crunch of armored plate against metal.

"Six of them, Jess." Dev was on the ground behind her. "Three in the upper mesh, now two in the hallway to central at your ten."

Kurok crouched, one hand on Dev's back. "BeeAyes and KayTees stay where you are," he bellowed behind him. "Stay down!"

But the door bumped open and the sets poured out, surrounding them as they crouched there. "Doctor Dan! There is venting!" one of the KayTees pointed to the clear surface of the station wall. "Look!"

"Shit." Kurok ducked as a blast got past Jess and hit the railing. "Jess! We got problems!"

"Let me get rid of these then." Jess hauled up and bolted forward, coming up to speed as she headed for the hallway where fire was emerging. She ducked and hopped as she ran, bolts hitting the walls and floors in an attempt to stop her.

Halfway across she let out a yell, laying down fire ahead of her path as she came around the curve and saw the two enemy agents, already standing up and getting ready to run as she came at them.

They were in fully armored suits, and she got one brief look at one eye widening before she blew the helmet off one of them and his head disintegrated. He slammed back against the corridor wall and slid down it, his entire body shuddering not realizing yet it was dead.

The second lifted his blaster, but she was already on him. She slammed into him and smashed the gun against the wall as he tried to free his hands to grab her.

She holstered her blaster and went at him, catching the edges of his armor with her fingertips and prying it open, letting out another booming roar as her forward momentum took him to the ground.

He tried to kick out, but she had her knee on his chest as she ripped the armor off and got her hands around his neck. She clamped down and her fingers closed like a vise around his windpipe.

Cartilage crushed under the force like it was light plastic, and then she felt the convulsions as he stopped being able to breathe.

Yells behind her.

Jess yanked her hands back and felt skin and trachea come free. She shook her hands to clear the blood from them as she turned and surged back into the central area.

Three enemy heading for where Dev was.

Jess yanked out her blaster and started firing. They turned, diving behind a console.

"Jess! Don't shoot that!" Kurok bellowed at the top of his lungs. "Everyone stay the hell down!"

One of the enemy came up over the console and braced his arms on it, aiming his blaster at Jess and firing point blank as she came barreling at him.

She launched into the air and the blast went under her. She tumbled into a twisting target that edged and avoided three other bolts that came from the other soldiers, and then she was among them, fighting close in with a scramble of arms and legs and guns being used as hammers.

Jess disappeared under the enemy and Dev put her scanner down and rose up, evading Doctor Dan's quick grab as she bolted across the floor toward the console.

She ducked around the console and started grabbing hold of whatever she could.

A moment later Doctor Dan led the sets to join her, and they were all in the midst of a flailing, dangerous melee.

Jess had one in a headlock and the sets piled on a second that Dev had yanked clear. Doctor Dan knelt on the third's chest, his blaster pointed right between the soldier's eyes.

The security guards came running over.

Then there was a sodden crack, and Jess climbed up over a dead body with a broken neck. She pointed her blaster at the guards. "No zaps!" she warned them. "Anyone touches a weapon, you code as bad guys, and I kill you."

The guards went still and held their hands out, empty. "Okay we got it," the nearest one to her said. "You're Interforce ops. We got it."

"Good." Jess holstered her blaster and turned in a circle, sweeping the area with her senses, looking for moving shadows, waiting for that sense to prickle.

The sets had their target immobilized, mainly with sheer bodyweight, and one of the BeeAyes was sitting on the arm of the soldier with his hand braced against the gun, pressing it flat to the floor. After a moment Jess came over and retrieved it.

Kurok removed the blaster from the man he was kneeling on and safed it. "Smart move," he told the soldier, who stared up at him with wide eyes. "So let me ask you, punkta, you know who I am?"

The man remained silent for a long moment. "The traitor," he finally said, licking a bit of blood that trickled from his lips. "The director said you would come here." He smiled without humor. "Not so much friend, eh?"

"Did he mention I had Jess Drake with me?" Kurok smiled back with equal venom, watching for the reaction. "Not so much friend, eh?"

Dev came over and showed him the screen of her scanner. "Doctor Dan," she said, "this doesn't seem very optimal." She glanced at the soldier then back at Kurok. "I don't think they can hold grav much longer."

"Ah, yes. Back in the day we used to call this a clusterfuck." A low, wailing sound started up, and the station lurched again. "Well, that was a bit of fun." Kurok stood up, dusting his hands off. "Tie them up, lads. Use the hold down straps in the cabinet there. Let's get into control before something really unfortunate happens."

The bio alts hurried to do as he asked. "Is it good, Doctor Dan?" one of the KayTees asked. "We did good work?"

"You did spectacular," Kurok assured him. "Well done, everyone."

Jess checked the tie downs and then she rambled over. "That's all six. You got more, Devvie?"

Dev turned. "No. But we should hurry. Systems are shutting down."

The lights flickered and the air had a faint musty smell. "What's that out there?" Jess asked, pointing at the fog outside. "Is that what the venting is?"

"That's some gas." Kurok pointed up a ramp. "Something is leaking out into space. Could be ammonia, could be carbon, could be oxygen, could be coolant...but the life support systems are offline and we're only going to be able to breathe in here for so long." He glanced at Jess. "Unless your little party trick works without water."

"Don't want to try it." Jess checked the charge in her blaster and started toward the ramp, with Dev trotting at her heels, scanner working. "Cmon."

"Doctor Kurok, we were told to bring you to security," one of the guards said. "You should come with us."

"How about you boys staying here and guarding those bad guys, hmm?" Kurok was already moving away. "Come along, KayTees and BeeAyes. We've got work to do."

"Good work," a KayTee said, in a satisfied tone. "Let's go!"

"Doctor Kurok!"

JESS PUT HER back against the corridor wall and held her hand up to stop the caravan of craziness following her. They were near the control center and she could hear chaos inside, the outer door to the chamber half open and leaking a pungent scented light fog.

When she was sure everyone was going to stay still, she skulked forward, pausing in the entrance with the fog bathing her before she could get a clear sight inside.

Six more armored bad guys. Jess sighed. But they were watching the group of men in the center, two of them hammering at the console, the rest of them yelling at each other with sharp, arm thrusting gestures.

Jess took a deep breath, pausing in case the fog was going to make her cough, and exhaled, willing the jumpy tension to dissipate. Then she clipped her blaster to its hard point and walked on, crossing a metal grid floor and down two steps so quietly none of the men inside noticed.

She picked a spot then put her hands on her hips and let out a shrill, loud whistle.

The soldiers whirled, the scientists and mechs whirled. A tall man in a deep red jumpsuit straightened up behind the main console and grabbed for a sidearm as he spotted her and recognition flared.

"Ah!" Jess barked. "Shooting in here is only gonna make it worse." She kept her hands on her hips as the soldiers brought their long blasters up and aimed them at her, splashing her chest with lurid green dots.

"What are you doing here?" The man in red snarled. "You son of a bitch."

Jess smiled. "Daughter of a bastard, actually. Hello, Darren." She flexed her knees as the station lurched, the sirens morphed to klaxons, and a set of red lights started to flash. "You done screwing this place up?"

The man in red leaned both hands on the machinery. "Nothing would make me happier than to die here knowing you died with me, Drake. My whole family died at Gibraltar."

Jess shrugged. "I have no intention of letting a little bit of vengeance kill off a thousand innocents."

Doctor Dan came up behind her and walked past, ignoring the soldiers, the man in red, and the scientists, who looked utterly relieved at his presence. "Move."

"Doctor Kurok, thank goodness the director found you," one of the mechs said. "Please help us."

"All the stinking fish in one pile," Darren said. "Don't touch that console."

"Don't touch him," Jess said. She caught up with Kurok, and they walked straight to the center, Jess's body collecting tension as they neared the enemy force. "Get away from the tech, and let him alone. He's probably the only one who can keep this thing spinning."

Darren pulled out a small hand blaster and turned it sideways to shoot, finger triggering the blast in a breath.

Jess shoved Kurok out of the way and toward the console, the blast missing both of them by just a hair. She leaped sideways as the man in red reacted, kicking the gun out of his hand then just letting her momentum take her over the railing to crash into him.

He was at her with a knife in a heartbeat. Her semi armored jumpsuit turned the blade, but only barely, and she elbowed him in the stomach as she felt its edge scrape against her skin. She got her arm around his above the elbow and applied pressure, as the knife flickered into her vision and came at her face.

Then chaos erupted behind her, and she heard shouting voices and then the sound of blasters. She had to focus on this opponent, though, because this one meant something and was her equal. She tuned out the yelling and caught hold of his wrist, and they arched into a grapple in tense silence.

Then someone kicked him in the head. He jerked and released the knife, it was picked up, and then Jess twisted him around and got his arm behind him and her knee wedged beneath it. She looked up to see Dev rolling past and coming up against the base of the console.

"You bastard! You bastard!" Darren screamed as she pulled his shoulder out of its socket. "Shoot her! Screw the databank! Let's all die! Shoot! Shoot!"

Jess sincerely wished she had an antipersonnel mine to throw. Instead, she smacked Darren's head against the console to knock him out then lunged forward and threw herself over Dev as all hell broke loose.

She curled her arms and legs around Dev and rolled under the lip of the console. The light around her went from red to white with an almost pain, then went dark.

Gravity came off, and only a quick grab at the bar that went along the bottom of the cabinet kept her and

Dev, from floating up. "Ah boy."

"Severely non-optimal," Dev said into her ear. "Really, really."

"I liked the floating thing right up to this second." Jess twisted them both around so she could see above them. She smelled burnt electrical, blood, and an acrid thin stench. Frightened gasps could be heard nearby. "Doc!"

No answer.

A crunching boom sounded in the distance.

"That's the crèche sealing," Dev whispered. "If they lose grav and atmo, they purge them first."

"Ah," Jess said, after a moment. "Not a good day."

Chapter Nine

THERE WERE BOOMS, thuds and crackling bangs. Far off, a low alarm started howling.

Jess hauled herself upright. "Hang on."

Dev briefly wondered if she was meant to hold on to Jess, but she reluctantly reasoned not and grabbed the bar on the console instead and started along the side of it as Jess moved up and over the top, her body tensed and ready to react.

To whatever.

Situational analysis. Jess extended her senses, aware of a prickling of danger at the sounds and smell of chemicals in the air.

When you were in the moment, it wasn't so much reason as instinct, experience and training that drove reactions that could take a life or save yours. And in which you had to trust.

Trust deeply and she did.

Darren drifted into the air, blood dripping from his face. His eyes were closed, his limbs limp. Jess kept hold of the top of the console and rotated in the air, looking quickly around the room to determine their relative safety.

The armored figures were drifting near the ground, motionless, their bodies contorted.

There was blood all over the control center console, and just past it, she spotted a figure in familiar colors near the ground.

The bio alts were clustered near the entrance hatch, holding onto the bars fastened to the wall. Their eyes were huge and afraid, as they stared around at the carnage and at her.

"Dev, can you get to the middle there?" Jess hand over handed herself across the top of the machinery toward the end of it. "I'm gonna check out the doc. Someone zapped the bad guys."

"Zapped?" Dev drifted up so she could see over the machinery and grimaced at all the blood over it.

"Like an antipersonnel mine," Jess called back over her shoulder. "Automatic maybe?"

"As far as I have programming on it that would only affect," she paused briefly and glanced at the sets clinging to the wall, "us."

"Something zapped 'em."

Dev got herself into the controls seat. After a moment's

inspection she got the restraints clipped around her. She brought up the input pad and keyed it, aware of the dank and musty smell growing around her. "BeeAyes," she called out. "Can you assist please?"

Three of the BeeAyes detached from the hold and kicked off the wall toward where she was seated. They caught the edge of the rack and came around it, taking seats down the row next to her. "Yes," the first one said. "NM-Dev-1, this is not excellent."

"No," Dev said "This is severely non-optimal. There is a lot of damage to station." She glanced to her right. "Jess, is Doctor Dan all right?"

Jess got to him and hooked one leg around the console substructure, gently turning him over to inspect his still form. He was breathing, and his color was relatively good. But there was a big bruise on the side of his head and no indication of consciousness. "He's not dead," she called back. "But I ain't a medic, and he's got a big ass bump on his noggin."

Dev exhaled unhappily. She turned and focused on the console though, since she knew it was probably more useful for her to. "Let's see if we can bring up the diagnostics."

The KayTees came over and the rest of the BeeAyes followed. They floated past the still bodies and reached control, finding places to sit.

"There is much damage," one of the KayTees said, reviewing the console. "Atmosphere is compromised."

"Yes," Dev said. "Let's see if we can do anything about it."

Jess took hold of Kurok and pushed them both across to the other side of central control where there was a small work area with seats and a couch behind it. She bumped up next to the couch and got her patient settled on top of it, clipping two hold down straps over him.

There. At least if grav came back, he wouldn't fall on his ass. Jess then went over to one of the armored soldiers and inspected him. He was dead, his eyes bulged out of their sockets, his facial muscles twisted.

Zapped. Definitely. Neural disrupters that were keyed very specifically to them like the mines back in her carrier were, like the ones they'd used at Base Ten during the attacks.

Emergency controls?

She turned and floated back over to the couch and studied Kurok, then picked up one of his hands, finding it closed around something. She prised his fingers away from it and found a small piece of electronics tucked inside.

She took it and carefully turned it over, ready to snap her eyes shut if it flared. It remained inert, and she could see delicate tracings across the surface that led around to the button seated on the front, flush with the curved edge.

Thoughtfully she put it inside a pocket on her thigh and then turned and pushed herself through the air back to where Dev was working on the systems.

On the way she passed Darren, his eyes half open, his tongue swollen.

Did she do that? Or the zap? Jess pulled the body close and examined his head, the lump under his ear, swollen and tight. She frowned. "Damn it," she muttered under her breath. "I needed to talk to you, ya bastard."

But now, too late. Whether she'd done it or the zapping had, no sense in worrying about it.

She shoved him away, sending the corpse toward the outer wall, the backward momentum causing her to flip in the air and catch a chair back to pull herself down.

With a grunt she came down next to Dev. "Can ya fix it, Devvie?" She peered over her shoulder to see a screen full of blinking red and flashing lines of errors. "Looks crunchy."

Dev looked at her then she went back to studying the readouts. "I'm not sure what we can do," she admitted, after a moment. "I don't really know where to start. There is so much broken."

BeeAye next to her shook his head. "This is not good. Could we try bypassing the upper array? It's shorting out, and we can't get any intake to the grid," he suggested. "We also can't log into most of this."

Dev slid over a little and peered at the screen. She took a breath, then a second, then she reached out and tapped out a code on the pad, pausing, then tapped a second. The screen cleared of its challenge. "See if that is better."

The BeeAye regarded her. "You know the codes," he said. "This is good."

"Yes. That should clear the whole main console." Dev went back to the screen she was working on, aware of Jess floating nearby. "Let me see what I can work here." She triggered her own screen and began sorting through all the alarms.

The consoles themselves were on emergency battery. As she accessed the levels she drew a short, uneasy breath, staring at the levels. "Ah."

"Draining," Jess said. "Up here, down there, it's all

the same. Power to batts."

"True," Dev said. "And this indicates we have possibly fifteen minutes left." Dev called up the diagnostic routines, her fingers moving in almost automatic motions, only the faintest of hesitations indicating the source of the knowledge that drove them.

Programming. A deep pocket of it, gentle and elegant and surely Doctor Dan's. She could almost hear the faint whisper of his voice in her ear as she started a recovery, booting the lowest level of the power drive systems.

Details and instructions about the systems that ran the very heart of the station. Not something she'd been given before she left. Something he'd done today, given to her before he removed the collar. There was an urgency about it, and she responded to it as she scanned and rescanned, trying to retrieve systems in crisis.

Why did they shut them down? What was the purpose? Surely even the downsiders realized the station systems were critical for life support. She shook her head. "This seems so incorrect."

"What, wrecking the joint?" Jess merely watched, having no skills to contribute to the effort. "Probably wanted to force your buddy up here."

"By putting everyone in danger?" Dev saw the routine fail. She made a small sound under her breath and ran it again with a different parameter. "Jess, that makes no sense"

"Maybe it did to them. They couldn't get what they wanted, maybe they wanted to make sure we didn't have access to it either."

A KayTee approached. "NM-Dev-1, we think we have found an incorrectness. Please look."

Dev unfastened the restraints and moved down the row of chairs in an odd, bouncy motion to where three of the KayTees were clustered around a panel.

Jess took over the seat Dev vacated, wrapping her long legs around the base rather than using the straps. She placed her elbows on the console and studied the screen. The fifteen minutes were clocking down in the back of her head, but she felt no sense of urgency over it.

Would they die? Maybe. Jess tapped her fingers on the metal surface. The routine finished and came up with a query. Continue or Abort. Well, Dev had been doing it for a reason, so she probably didn't mean for it to be aborted. Jess touched the continue, and a few seconds after that she felt a vibration run through the console she was seated at.

No clue whether that was positive or negative, Jess turned to her left and saw Dev making her way rapidly back toward where she was seated, and she got up and moved around the chair to make space for her.

Dev pushed herself down in the seat, starting a little as Jess wrapped the restraints around her from behind and clicked them on. "Oh. Thank you."

"That thing came back and asked if it should continue. I told it sure." Jess rested her chin on Dev's shoulder. "Hope that didn't send it to crap."

"No, that was correct. I think I understand why they did all this damage. The craft they came in does not work correctly with the systems here."

"Yeah, the lock ons are coded to the shuttles on our side," Jess said. "They won't let one of the other side dock except in an emergency, and that sends a sig downside."

"So they wanted to stop the rotation so it would not come apart." Dev tapped in a few commands. "It seems the control people here could not explain why that was a bad idea."

Jess frowned. "Dev, no one's that stupid. Even those bimbos from the other side. So can you fix it now? We still have what, five minutes left?"

"The power intake baseline is coming up. I don't know if it will come up in time," Dev said. "If it does not, we cannot recover station as there will be no battery power to run the routines."

"Does that mean we will be made dead?" the BeeAye next to her asked.

"Yes," Dev said. "Eventually. We will not be able to bring life support or systems online." She glanced back at Jess. "I'm really sorry, Jess."

"Don't be." Jess looked at the screen then wrapped her arms around Dev and just held onto her. "We all have to croak sometime. Glad I'm here with you, Devvie. Dying alone is a bummer."

"You are not afraid of that?" the BeeAye said. He turned in his seat to watch them. "Of being made dead?"

"No," Jess said. "It's one of our little quirks. There have been times in my life when I was so damn hurt it would have been a relief to die. Pain does that."

It got quiet as they all watched the screens or the tall agent, stretched out in mid air, holding on to the seated Dev.

"But I'm glad I lived long enough to hook up with my

partner here." Jess gave her a bit of a sideways and uncomfortable squeeze. "All of us live such crappy lives. Finding a friend is good."

Dev was caught in perfect balance between delight and horror, as she watched the racing seconds matched against the sequence running with what seemed to her unreasonable slowness behind it. Did she feel the same way Jess did? Was it okay to be made dead?

She felt the warmth of Jess's cheek against hers, and she had to admit that if one was to be made dead, it would be nice to have the last thing you felt something like that. "We get nearly made dead a lot," she said. "So when you can feel good and nice things, you should appreciate that."

"Hmm." the BeeAye grunted thoughtfully.

"And also," Dev said as the counter cycled down through thirty seconds, "all of those things they told us about sex," she regarded the intently watching sets, "they lied. They lied about a lot of things."

Jess started laughing silently, her breath puffing against Dev's ear.

"Ten seconds." Dev turned her head and twisted her body around so she could kiss Jess, and that felt wonderful.

Seven.

Five.

Two.

The countdown finished, and with utterly anticlimactic blurps two of the alerts went off. The station remained mostly nonfunctional, but relatively in one piece, the emergency lighting still on. Dev finished her kiss then turned and resumed her entry, keying in two more diagnostics. "That was unexpectedly excellent."

Jess licked her lips. "I sure thought so." She ruffled Dev's hair. "C'mon, Devvie. Lets not croak just yet, huh? I want to spend more time with ya."

Dev smiled. "I will do my best. I want to spend more time with you, too."

"We did not get made dead," the BeeAye next to her said. "But that is very valuable information, NM-Dev-1."

"Can we try that, too?" a KayTee asked, looking at Jess with a lot more interest.

Dev's hands paused on the input pad as she gave them a sideways look. "The sex thing?"

"Yes."

"No." Dev went back to her screen as Jess started laughing again, this time audibly. Systems were starting to inch back online, but only the basics and wiremaps. "The power sump is online, but the grid is down," she said. "Jess, the vehicle is drawing current." She pointed at the screen. "It seems they are trying to withdraw from the data banks."

"Of course they are," Jess said. "They want that info." She pushed herself up. "I'll go sort them out." She went to the map on the wall. "This where they are?" she pointed. "Yeah, I can see the outline. Keep trying to fix it, Devvie. I'll be back."

One of the BeeAyes timidly approached. "Agent, if you put these on your boots, you'll stick to the floor." He held out a set of wraps. "May we help you?"

Jess tumbled through the air toward him and retrieved the covers. "Not this time kids." She tucked the covers into a thigh pocket. "Stay here and help Dev." She kicked off from the console and headed for the door. "And keep an eye on the doc!"

Dev half stood behind the station. "Jess! Take care. Please."

Jess turned and grinned at her, giving her a wink before she tumbled in the air and headed out through the half open hatch.

A KayTee started entering on a pad. "All of the sectors are sealed. Should we try to bring up comms?"

Dev resumed her seat. "Not yet," she said. "They will all just start calling and asking questions we do not have answers to."

"Yes. That's true."

A BeeAye looked over. "Should we unseal the crèche?"

Dev considered. "Not right now. The seal works both ways."'

A KayTee nodded. "They are safe there from the natural borns."

JESS ZOOMED DOWN down the hallways, bypassing the floating debris and kicking off against the surfaces that came into range. Movement didn't generate forward motion she'd come to find, not like it did in the water as there was nothing to push against.

So she had to go in a direction until she found something she could shove against to send her in a different one or sling herself along where she wanted to go.

It was slower than running would have been. But also much quieter. Jess reached a crossroads and bumped against the edge of a tube that started outward, its color stark and dark gray. She caught the grab bar on the side of it and pulled herself along, noticing the air around her becoming colder. A little thinner.

Her heartbeat sped up a trifle, and her lungs worked harder for a few minutes, then her body adjusted and her metabolism shifted gear just as it would have if she'd been in high altitude downside.

The tube tilted downward, and she could see through the occasional open panel the world turning in gray shadows below. Ahead of her she saw a bulkhead seal. She reached it, looked back at the core of the station, and saw the next level down, eerie yellow light shining from inside it.

Faces looking out.

Scared.

The crèche, she realized, where all the bio alts were trapped.

Jess paused, momentarily pondering why that bothered her as much as it did. She studied the faces and thought about Dev being in that space, being with those scared people who were people.

Were they people?

They were people, Jess decided. Innocent bystanders.

"Hang on kids," Jess muttered then turned and went to the hatchway. She opened the clearance pad and put her hand on it.

She hoped the other side had air, realizing as her skin hit the metal it might not. The pad went green, and the seal unlocked, a thick chunking sound as the three leaves that made the round surface split and parted.

She sailed through, and her ears caught warning yells ahead of her. Her heartbeat sped up again and she got ready to fight. She got to the shuttle area and went from a tube into a larger, open space.

The enemy shuttle was latched on with a makeshift gangway, full of flexible round conduit and tie downs. The vehicle itself was bumping against station, not quite connected, and there were coils of cables stretching out from it to consoles nearby.

Two techs were holding on to a bar and trying to manipulate controls. Four agents stood by, two of them turning toward her as she entered.

Jess released the edge of the entry and unholstered her blaster. She held it in front of her and squared her body to present the smallest surface to them. They responded, their bodies unused to the lack of gravity and the first two shots at her were wild.

Wild and crackling against the surface of station. She fired back as they tried to get behind metal stanchions and clipped one of them in the arm, sending his gun flying across the room.

One of the techs threw a hand tool at her. Jess aimed not at him, but at the console, and concentrated her fire on the cables running back to the ship.

The two other agents were sailing her way. They were young, but the look in their eyes said they knew who she was and that made Jess smile. She tucked her arms into her body and dipped down a little, blasts of fire coming over her head so close it almost singed her.

She released return fire, aiming carefully as her shots intersected theirs and sizzled to either side of her head.   She closed in on the console, so she flipped forward again and released one hand off the gun, ready to engage.

With a day more experience in null, she had the advantage. She twisted in mid air, grabbed a blaster and wrenched it toward her, pulling its owner and herself into a mashing collision as she aimed between her own knees at the console they were now sailing over. The shot went clean though and bisected the cables.

Hands grabbed her, and she hauled the gun in and mounted it so she could keep fingers from closing on her throat.

A blast hit her in the back armor, but it only served to spin her around and expose her attacker to the second blast that smacked him in the back of the neck and blew the back of his head off. "Thanks!" Jess yelled, using the now inert body as a weapon as she pulled it in a circle and slammed it into the second agent.

An alarm started howling, and the agents shooting at her whirled as two figures came out of the tube and yelled in alarm.

"You stupid bastard!" the second agent yelled at her. "That was the stabilizer!"

"Too fucking bad!" Jess yelled back. She caught hold of a support spar and scaled down it toward the deck, ducking behind it as the agent fired at her. "You're idiots for being here!"

She got to the deck and squirmed through the cables, yanking them clear of the systems with one hand while holding on with the other.

"Drake! Stop it!" the agent yelled. "You're going to undock the shuttle!"

"No shit!" Jess kicked out at one of the clamps holding a makeshift circuitry box to the railing. It spun off, spitting sparks and the acrid smell of burning electrical as it bounced and drifted. "You fucking morons latched on where you don't belong."

"Drake! Drake!" The man scrambled down the support strut and caught up with her. "Stop! Wait!"

Jess got her back to the bulk of the console and turned toward him, body poised to attack. "No," she said in a calm, even voice. "I want you out of here."

The man held a hand out, palm up. "This isn't an attack."

Jess looked around the station and cupped her hand to her ear as the alarms proliferated. "Really?" She recognized the agent, vaguely, as someone she'd encountered in an emplacement sometime, but his name escaped her.

Hers hadn't escaped him. "Drake, we didn't know you were here," the man said. "All we want is the process. You know what I'm talking about. We're just here to keep people from starving." He waved off the others. "Fix the tie downs! I've got this!"

"It's breaking loose!" one of the other agents yelled. "It's gonna blow out!"

Jess lunged forward and caught the young agent, hauling him around against the support strut. "You're a bunch of idiots."

He took a grip on her wrist. "Do you know what you did to us?"

"Doesn't matter," Jess said. "What I did was what I did. The process you're looking for ain't here."

He stared at her for a long moment. "It's here. We know the plants came from here."

"They did," Jess agreed. "But that's all. It's not here. These people don't have it."

He was young, with curly red hair and freckles and green eyes almost the color of Dev's. He shook his head at her in denial. "We know it's here. Otherwise why would you be? They told us you came here for it."

"They?"

"Station."

"Idiots." Jess sighed. "Listen, kid. It's not here. I'm not here for it." She swung them both around to watch the others, who were now working furiously on the tubes. "The rest of your bunch is dead. Go home."

"You're lying, Drake. You always lie," the kid spat back. "Damn you."

She shoved him away from the strut, toward the entrance to the shuttle. "Get out of here! What you're looking for isn't—" She snapped her jaw shut as she felt the impact from behind and let her body go limp as she turned with the momentum.

Her hands hit the deck and she ducked her head and pushed

backwards, shooting under the heavy body that landed in front of her. A backwards somersault brought her feet back under her and freed a hand for her blaster.

This, a face she did know. "Stop it." She had the gun out and pointed. "There's someone at the controls of this thing who's going to suck you out headfirst if you keep on, Peter."

He had his gun out, and it matched hers. "No one on station's friends of yours." He fired at her point blank, and just as he did grav surged into being, just long enough to send his aim deckward and long enough for Jess to brace and fire back. "A Drake? You shoot their moppets for fun and they know it."

Jess hit him square on the chest and his arms flung out sideways, his body skewing to one side. "My partner's driving," she said as he scrambled to get back into position. "Get the hell out. I've got work to do."

He stared at her. "Partner...then it is true. You scraped so low you ended up with one of THEM?"

"Ah screw it." Jess fired again, this time hitting him in the face before he could get his gun up. At the range she was at, there was no surviving it. She bounded forward and took aim at the kid. "Move."

"Red, c'mon!" one of the techs called out. "We need to get clear."

The kid looked around.

"They're all dead. I toldja." Jess splashed her pre-aim on his forehead. "Get out. "

He looked back at her. "I will kill you," he suddenly roared and shoved away from the console right at her, faster than she could fire. She got the blaster down into its hard point as he reached her and a knife headed her way.

Curved and jagged. Triangular teeth.

Her vision went sharp and black and white, and she focused on that scruffy bearded face as the memory surfaced where she knew him from.

Just a flash. Just a profile. A half turned body in Quebec City, hand raised in farewell as Joshua came back over to her, shopping bag in hand.

Little bastard. Jess met his lunge with a grip on his wrist and hooked one leg around a support bar as she leveraged them both into a tumble. His other hand got her throat and she managed to suck in a deep breath before her airway was cut off.

He clamped down, but the null grav robbed him of the pressure his weight would have brought to bear, and she got her knee up against his chest and straightened out her spine, using her height to force him away from her.

The dalknife hovered in her peripheral vision, and he gripped desperately as they struggled in relative silence.

The alarms cut off. The techs from the other side yelled a warning.

Her own hand got to his throat and grabbed hold, and she shoved him backwards, her arms longer than his, and she saw the realization of that in his face.

He released her, grabbed the knife with his free hand, and swung it at her.

She kicked forward and slammed her head into his, the blade going up and over the back of her neck. She ducked her head, opened her jaws, and sank her teeth into his throat.

He jerked hard in surprise and went to grab her, the knife floating free as she tensed and bit down hard, shaking her head as she forced her bite through his skin.

She caught the knife and released her jaws, grabbing hold of a rail as she got both feet up against him and kicked out as hard as she could. It sent him tumbling toward the tube, droplets of blood flying from his throat to spray out and dangle in mid air.

"Go, go, go!" one of the techs screamed. "Grab him!"

The second hauled the kid's flailing figure back with him toward the tube. "Let's blow it! She'll die!"

They shoved him back up the white, ribbed tube and followed behind him.

A shudder went through the station, and Jess kicked off in the other direction, heading for the seal and its triple leaves that had sealed behind her when she'd entered.

She could feel something bad happening. The stresses against her body were suddenly radical, not so much returning gravity, but gravity in flux. It made her tumble through the air, and she reached out to grab the edge of some structure.

Behind her, she heard an explosion.

Then gravity was back with a vengeance, and she was slammed to the ground with stunning force. She heard the sound of a crack and a bang, and then she scrambled for the lock as the very air started to change shape around her.

The hair on her skin lifted, and she felt an icy cold touch her. She had no idea what it was, but her brain hammered urgency, and instinct drove her forward as fast as she was capable of.

The leaves opened as she reached them, and she rolled through. They closed with explosive force. A deep red light came on and bathed the hallway in blood tinge. A hooting alarm started up that rattled her nerves.

She was breathing hard and let her hand relax, dropping the dalknife on the deck as she lay back for a moment, hot and cold flushing through her. "Fuck."

Her skin felt itchy and tight, and she shook herself, an uncomfortable sense of almost pain slowly releasing. Even her eyes felt dry. She blinked repeatedly until the sting faded.

That section had decompressed. She'd been that close to being exposed to vacuum.

Check that off the bucket list. Jess rolled over and shoved herself up, pausing to retrieve the knife as she headed farther inward to station, not stopping until she was at the edge of the inner core, where she could look back through one of the clear panels.

The shuttle was drifting free.

The section she'd been in was imploded, and bodies were floating out of cracks in the skin, exposed to the nothing of space.

She slowly exhaled. "Space is freaking creepy." She licked her lips, tasting blood on them, then turned and spat the taste out of her mouth. She turned and started back toward control. A few steps on, though, she paused and looked down through the clear plas, down at the crèche.

Now the walls were full of faces, staring up at her. After moments hesitation she waved at them then held one hand up, a gesture to wait. Even from where she was she could see the relief.

Jess then went to the core center, kicked open the hatch, and ducked inside.

"STAND BY FOR grav," Dev called out. "Hold! Hold!" She triggered the relays, punching through grid power, slowly amping up.

Everyone grabbed and settled, and the station rotation kicked in, shoving them into their seats as the power grid lurched back into service and control was returned to consoles across the breadth of central.

"There is a breech," a KayTee said. "The vehicle has torn open the bay wall."

A BeeAye shook his head. "That is not good. What should we do now, NM-Dev-1?"

Dev's eyes locked on the command screen, her fingers moving insistently over the surface. She didn't hear the request, didn't even acknowledge she was in the room with others. All she cared about was the unlocking of a locked seal that required level upon level of override because there was danger.

Danger to station. A section was breeched, and they were in danger of explosive decompression, and seals were designed to stay sealed to protect the rest of station when that happened.

It took the ultimate code, Doctor Dan's code, to override it, and she got it typed in just as Jess's hand touched the seal. It had to open or Jess would die.

It opened. Alarms sounded. The bio alts around her gasped.

She got the seal closed again as the pressurization alerts hovered at danger, and the entire structure of the station flexed.

Sweat stung Dev's eyes, and she paused to wipe it away. "Seals are back in secure," she said. "I'm going to release the section blocks." She set the code in work. "Please try to bring comms up now."

"Yes." A BeeAye next to her tapped confidently. "That was a great danger."

"It is secure now." Dev ran a quick scan then closed off the master ring lock leading to the shuttle bay and secured it with a vaccum warning. "KayTee, please ask for damage control to report."'

The KayTee nodded. "Yes. I will release the lock to the crèche as well."

The door to central opened, and a moment later a squad of security ran in, with stun sticks ready, hands going to chests.

Dev stood up. "Stop! We are doing work for station!"

The guards hesitated. Then a captain entered and pointed. "Take them down," he ordered. "Until the proctors can get up here. Hurry."

The guards acted without questioning, slapping the activators on their chests as Dev sucked in a breath to protest, her body already arching to protest an attack that never came.

The rest of the bio alts dropped and tumbled out of their chairs. Dev had only a second to decide what to do, and she did, remaining where she was, standing behind the console, her hands resting on the controls.

One of the guards took a step forward, faced her, and lifted his hand to his chest.

Dev stared at him. "I would not do that," she finally said. "My partner is not going to think it's correct, and I am the only one with command codes here right now." She pointed at the console. "Station is unstable. It's not safe."

The captain looked around. "Where are all th—" He spotted the limp figure on the couch. "What happened to Doctor Kurok?"

Doctor Doss came gasping to the door. "Oh!" He stared at the carnage. "What has happened? Where are the...our visitors?"

The captain was glad of the new arrival. "Doctor Doss! Should we take her down? That one."

Doss looked at Dev. "No." He shook one hand rapidly. "There's too much in chaos right now. Leave her alone. Let's not get Interforce angry at us, too."

"But—"

"Just stop!" Doss yelled at the top of his lungs.

Dev sat back down and started inputting to the console again, her head shaking slightly back and forth, wishing fervently that Jess would return and take charge of things.

And then, like magic, she was there, coming in the entryway, limping, with flash burns across her face, and to Dev's eyes the most beautiful thing imaginable.

She'd risked all of the station to see that face again.

It had felt nothing but correct.

"DEVVIE." JESS CAME around the console and stopped next to her. She put her hands on her hips and looked around. "You okay?"

Dev thought about that. "Yes," she replied. "It's excellent you are here." She half turned. "Unfortunately we were interrupted in our work."

Jess looked at all the slumped bio alts. "Can I ask what the hell is wrong with you people? We're supposed to be the jerks who fire before we think." She pointed at herself. "These guys were keeping it all together up here and you zap them?"

Doctor Doss stood up from examining one of the BeeAyes. "It's very confusing," he murmured. "Captain Branks, why did you fire? Were the units misbehaving?"

"You told us they were dangerous," the guard captain protested. "You told us!"

"I told you they were dangerous." Doss pointed at Jess. "And the other visitors." He looked around, spotting the bodies against the wall. "And I don't know where they all...oh."

Jess looked amused. "I splatted them," she said. "So I guess you're right. I'm dangerous." She eased over next to Dev and put her hands on her shoulders. "Devvie's pretty ferocious, too."

Dev smiled. She folded her arms over her chest, enjoying the warmth of Jess's hands on her. She felt tired and let herself relax a little, leaning back against Jess's body just slightly.

She glanced to the right where Doctor Dan was still lying still on the couch. Too much too fast, and she didn't really know what was going on now.

An alert flashed, and she looked at it. "The master lock at the crèche," she said. "There is something wrong."

Doss hurried over. "Is it sealed? Oh yes, good." He seemed relieved. "I heard the decompression alert, thank goodness alpha sector was secure." He paused, belatedly awkward. "I mean—"

"They gonna get hurt?" Jess asked casually. "Dev's buds, I mean?"

"We better make sure the central seals are good," Doss said. "Good point, Agent. If that seal goes, it could penetrate into central." He sat down and accessed the pad.

Jess reached over and logged Dev out. "We'll go take a look," she said. "C'mon, Devvie. Let's go walk about."

Doss looked up at them. "Oh! Yes, thank you, Agent. We don't really have comms up to all the watch stations yet. Yes, thank you very much."

"No problem," Jess drawled.

The guards stared at them as they went around the console to the half open hatch, slipping through and disappearing from sight.

"Those men were incorrect," Dev said, as soon as they were out of hearing range.

"The guards?"

"Yes. And Doctor Doss. I feel bad for the KayTees and BeeAyes. They were so happy to do good work."

Jess pulled her to a halt around the first bend and wrapped her up in a hug. "They'll be okay," she said, in a reassuring tone. "Let's go get all your buddies out and see if we can get comms downside going. I need to get us a ride."

Dev returned the hug. "Are you okay?"

"Me? Sure." Jess chuckled. "I'm tough as old boots. They just clipped me a few times." She carefully removed the dalknife and showed it to Dev. "See that? That's what made that hole in my back."

"That?" Dev looked at the blade in askance. "It looks awful."

Jess turned her hand, the obsidian blade with its triangular shape reflecting the lighting faintly. "Yeah. Makes a good souvie." She carefully put the knife back into one of her pockets. "Bet April'll appreciate it."

Dev looked up at her. "The section blowout was dangerous," she said. "Really dangerous, Jess."

Jess leaned against the station wall. "Where the shuttle was?"

Dev nodded.

The pale blue eyes twinkled. "You get that hatch open for me?"

Dev nodded again. "I did. I had to override the lock out. I was..." She paused and put her hand on Jess's arm. "I was really worried about you. The section went to vacuum."

"I felt it."

Dev grimaced. "That must have been very unpleasant."

"I wasn't worried. I knew you'd take care of me." Jess bumped her gently. "But yeah, it was creepy. Sort of felt like...I walked outside in the white once, when it was maybe down fifty, and it felt like that. Like you're being flash frozen."

"I just barely got grav on," Dev said. They turned and started walking again, side by side. "I had to use Doctor Dan's codes to open the hatch." She added, a little unhappily. "I think it was incorrect. He could get in trouble."

"He was lying out cold as a seal's butt."

"Still."

"I'll make sure he's okay," Jess said. "He'd have done it. He's that kinda guy."

"I hope so."

Jess guided her down toward the service tube to the crèche, already familiar with the station, remembering exactly how to get there. "He gave ya the code, didn't he?" She glanced at Dev, who nodded. "He knew you'd use it if you had to."

"That's true."

They climbed down the ladder on the inside of the service tube, the grav still locked. The air was moving a little, though, Jess felt the faint brush of it against her skin and smell ions in it. She also felt the vibration against the soles of her feet of machinery in motion. It reminded her a little of what it felt like when the turbines were going down at base.

Or at home.

Jess paused at the bottom and waited for Dev to join her, examining the echo that word was making in her head, given she hadn't considered the Bay home for a very long time.

Just a word?

Dev went to the huge, sealed lock at the base of the lower levels that held the crèche. She opened the access panel and tapped in a request, the area around them eerily quiet. It was too thick to hear any sound from within, and the desk that usually held security was abandoned.

Jess came over and waited quietly as she worked.

"Someone has altered this," Dev said after a moment. "It wasn't comp that sealed it."

Jess peered over her shoulder. "They think all your buddies are scary?"

Dev kept tapping. "There are a lot more bio alts than natural born here," she finally said. "But they have the deactivators."

"Mmm." Jess looked up at the lock as it groaned and clicked, the sound echoing through the lower hall. The round hatch unsealed, and both halves rolled aside, exposing a large crowd of bio alts behind it.

"Be easy," Dev said and held her hand up. "We are safe, for now."

The crowd shifted and then Gigi ran out toward her. "Oh! Dev!" Her eyes were wide and frightened. "They were going to space us!" She hugged herself with both arms. "We heard them. They recalled us all to the crèche and then locked us in!"

The bio alts surged forward, peering around. "Where is security?" Gigi asked. "What happened? Do you know? We saw the ship break loose in the dock."

Dev opened her mouth to reply when there was a stir in the crowd, and then a small figure squirmed through it, and bolted for them. "Jess!" She reached out to Jess and touched her arm. "Look!"

"I'm looking." Jess put her hands on her hips. "As if this needed to get any more complicated."

"Auntie Jess!" Tayler bawled, dashing over to her and throwing his arms around her legs. "Auntie Jess!"

He was dressed in a bio alt jumpsuit, his hair trimmed neatly and close to his head like theirs were. Jess went down on one knee to return the hug. "Hey, Tayler." She patted his back. "Whatcha doing up here, huh? Where's your mom?"

"Dunno." Tayler looked up at her. "They wouldn't let me go to school, Auntie! They made me come here." He sniffled a little. "I don like it. Wanna go home."

The bio alts all watched quietly. Now that the hatch was open, they had calmed, and many of them came out into the central hall and looked around the security stations with some curiosity.

Jess sighed. "Don't worry, Tay. We'll get you where you need to go." She felt a little awkward now about what she'd done to

Jimmy. Not because he hadn't deserved it, but because she now had to explain to this little moppet he wasn't going to go back home in any meaningful sense.

"Glad you're here, Auntie Jess," Tayler said then paused and looked up at the quietly watching Dev. "I member you. You had the bear vid."

Dev smiled at him. "Yes, I did. Have you had fun on station, Tayler? When you saw the bear vid, we were at your home. This is where I came from."

Tayler was immediately distracted, and he released Jess, coming over to stand next to Dev instead. "Yeah?"

"He is your relation, Agent Drake?" Gigi asked.

"My nephew. Son of my brother." Jess stood up. "How long has he been here, you know?" She asked in a casual tone.

Gigi considered the question. "One and a half months I think?" she said. "He arrived on shuttle, and Doctor Doss said it was a new program, to study the differences between natural born and bio alt children."

Jess's eyes narrowed a little. "You have natural born kids up here. Why bring one up from downside?"

Gigi answered readily. "Doctor Doss said it was because downside natural born have a much different way of learning and growing up. Except it wasn't very successful." She looked a bit embarrassed. "This subject was not very obedient."

Jess smiled. "No, he wouldn't be. He's a Drake."

"He kept trying to get out of the crèche. The security guards were always having to run around and find him." Gigi said. "Doctor Doss was very concerned when he found out you were going to visit. He said he didn't want to disrupt the study."

"He did, huh?" Jess looked over past Gigi to where Dev watched her, a noncommittal expression on her face. "I guess that's why he didn't tell me Tayler was here. Huh?"

Gigi nodded. "Yes. He said it would disrupt things. He was actually a little upset with Doctor Kurok for having you and NM-Dev-1 arrive when you did." She looked a little apologetic. "But it seems correct, and I am glad you have found him well."

Jess regarded little Tayler, who should be getting his indoctrination sessions out at the Interforce Basic school, and was unaccountably here, in space, dressed like a bio alt. "Yeah," she said. "No problem. We'll get him sorted out." She reached over to ruffle Tayler's hair. "He come up here by himself?"

"Yes," Gigi said. "We thought he was really brave."

Tayler turned and grinned at her, recognizing the word and

its direction at himself. "Where I'm from, everybody's like that."

Dev rubbed the bridge of her nose. "I think we should all go out and see where we can help repair things," she said to the watching sets who nodded. "Now that grav and power are back."

"Yes," Gigi agreed. "Please move to stations." She turned and lifted her voice. "We need to help."

"The tubes are down," Dev warned.

The sets nearby heard her, and passed the word along, and the flood of bodies started to move out and into the branching corridors.

Gigi watched them go. "What are you going to do now?" she asked Dev.

"We're going to go up to the doc's lab," Jess answered. "I think we left something up there when we all rushed down to help out."

"Yes," Dev said. "Tayler would you like to come with us?"

"Sure," Tayler said. "I'm gonna stay with Auntie Jess." He reached up to take hold of Jess's hand, and they slowly backed away from the entrance to the crèche as the flood of bio alts increased, all intent on getting back to work.

"This seems incorrect," Dev said as they started for the tubeway to the upper levels.

"Ya think?" Jess said wryly. "Let's go get a message sent then go pick up the doc. Less he's near that rotter the better."

"Yes."

DOCTOR DAN'S LAB was very quiet. Dev felt relieved when they went inside, and the doors slid shut behind them. She watched Tayler run over to the models and stand on his tiptoes to look inside. "He looks a bit like you."

Jess was behind the main console, pecking at the control surface. She looked up and over it at Dev. "Yeah." She looked back down. "This is crock, Devvie. I can't do anything with it."

Dev came over and joined her and took the stool next to her. She leaned on the console. "The transmitter is down. See, here." She pointed at the screen. "All those pending messages are waiting in queue."

"Fix it?" Jess slid out of the seat and offered it to her.

"I don't think we can from here." Dev took over the input pad. "The transmitters need the station to be on exact sync to go online. With all the disruption, that will not happen in the short term."

Jess frowned. "You can't do it manually?"

Dev looked at her. "Position station? No. I don't think even Doctor Dan could do that."

"Crap. I should have taken over that shuttle." Jess sighed. "With my luck when they arrived no one triggered the emergency recall because that bastard Doss is in with them."

"I'll check." Dev got busy at the console.

Jess watched her for a minute then went over to where Tayler was climbing on the table next to the models to get a better look. "Hey, Tay."

He had both hands on the glass and looked inside. "What's this?"

"That's the inside of someone's head," Jess said. "You want a drink?"

"Oh, yeah!" he answered immediately. "Don't like the stuff they have here."

"Nah me neither." Jess went over to the drink dispenser and looked inside. There were small, sealed cannisters of kack and she smiled in surprise, recognizing them. "And neither did the doc." She took out three of them and opened one, handing it to him. "There ya go."

Tayler sniffed it suspiciously, then took a gulp, with evident approval.

"Jess," Dev said, suddenly. "I think you should see this."

Jess sighed. "Words like that never end well. Something going to blow up again?"

"No. It's a message for you." Dev looked over at her. "From your home place."

THE FIRST THING he was aware of was a hell of a headache. Despite that, training surfaced before instinct just as it was supposed to, and he kept his breathing slow and even, his eyes closed. He was lying on a somewhat yielding surface. Under the pads of his fingertips he felt the synth fabric of station furniture.

The air smelled stale, but there was a hint of chemical on it. A stirring that brushed it across his face told him the life support systems were not quite dead yet.

He was under gravity, and that meant the grid was engaged with station rotation.

He could hear the tap of fingers against input pads and motion in the air.

His proximity sense told him there was no one nearby, but he cautiously cracked open one eyelid partway just to be sure.

He saw the back of a guard, stun stick cradled in his arms. Beyond that, the central control console with a bunch of agitated bodies around it.

He opened both eyes, but didn't move, waiting for his vision to clear and come back into focus, which it did very reluctantly. He spent a moment trying to remember what the hell had happened. Then it came back, and he instinctively closed the fingers of one hand, finding it empty.

Well. Something had gone right because the techs around console were station techs. He saw Doss messing about with a screen, and in his visual periphery there were the bodies of the other side, still and stiff.

He could also see bio alts on the floor curled in a down position. But neither sight nor ears detected the presence of either Dev or Jess.

Mixed bag. With a sigh, he reached up and undid the hold down, which crossed his chest and went over one shoulder, clearing both arms for action and an indication that he'd been put here by someone who understood that concept.

He sat up carefully, grimacing at the vicious pounding in his head, and upon inspection, discovered the lump on one side of it. Gingerly he twisted his neck in both directions, feeling the pops and crackles as his spine moved back into proper alignment.

A weight fell onto the top of his legs, and he realized the blaster was still in place, inside his front shirt pouch. He quietly removed it, and slid it into the small of his back before he stood up.

"I just don't understand what happened." Doss said in a peevish voice. "We have nothing, nothing I tell you that would do that to those men."

Maybe it was the knock on the head, but Kurok suddenly felt himself in a different space, his eyes seeing the people around him in a completely different way. "I can probably explain," he said quietly.

Doss whirled. "Daniel! You're awake!"

"Brilliant of you." Kurok moved slowly forward, easing past the guard who stepped aside for him, hand hovering over his stick. "Thank you, Charles."

"Daniel, look at this." Doss pointed at the bodies. "There's been terrible damage, and our guests..." He paused as Kurok's eyes met his. "What happened?"

Kurok shooed aside the techs around the console and sat

down behind the master station. "Our guests were extremely busy trying to destroy the station," he said. "Something stopped them." He keyed in one of the pads and entered his codes.

"Something," Doss said slowly. "Was it that agent?"

"Oh, probably not." Kurok smiled. "I'm going to have someone from the crèche come up here and bring these sets up. We could use them, and I see now it's been unsealed." He reviewed the screen. "Yes, it has."

"The special unit and that agent went there," Doss admitted. He sat down in the seat next to his colleague. "Daniel, did you hurt those men? They just wanted to talk to you. Please. I don't understand."

Kurok studied him. "Randall, those men aren't our friends." He saw the movement of muscles across Doss's round face and knew there was shifty in play, and he wasn't completely in control of the situation.

But no mind. He would play the game a bit longer. "Attention." He reached over and keyed comms. "This is Doctor Dan. I need salvage and repair teams to report to their stations and a medical team to central operations with a biometric kit."

He released the comm lock and a moment later a voice answered. "Yes, Doctor Dan. We are deploying."

"Thank you." He was relieved to hear Dev's voice, and he suspected the feeling was mutual. "Now, Randall." He rested his elbow on the console and then pushed the sleeve of it up, exposing the skin of his arm. "Do you see these?"

Doss eyed his skin, which was patterned in old, brown lines. "Yes."

"When I was fourteen years old, I was living in a science center on the other side." He rolled his sleeve down again. "Interforce attacked it and killed almost everyone inside, leaving myself and perhaps one other person alive."

"So the captain of the vessel was correct?" Doss asked. "You were from their side."

"I was," Kurok said. "I was taken to the Interforce labs, and they made a valiant attempt at brainwashing me. I let them think they'd succeeded."

Doss shifted away from him. "I see."

It made Kurok smile. "I would have been a perfect mole, eh? I was a moppy little blond haired kid. They put me through field school, and when I was eighteen they paired me with an enforcement agent and put me into service. And unfortunately, for them and perhaps for me, I found in that enforcement agent someone I could, and did, pledge allegiance to."

"I see," Doss repeated.

"Do you?" Kurok's eyes twinkled a little. "Remember I told you about Interforce agents? Justin was as good a psychopath as the best of them."

"Well. Perhaps not." Doss said, stiffly.

"Mmm. Well between us, me and Justin, we did dozens of emplacements and missions and probably ended up wiping out thousands of people, some of which I probably was related to," Kurok said. "So you see, Randall, talking to them would not have been very successful."

"You were really Interforce," Doss said. "That's why you stayed there, all that time, those months." He shifted slightly. "I knew from your records of course, but I thought you were perhaps a scientist for them."

Kurok shrugged. "I stayed last time because I saw an opportunity to get into the other side's clutches, and if I was lucky, I'd get my hands on the little stinker who had Justin killed. And I did." He smiled at Doss. "Justin was Justin Drake. Jesslyn's father."

"Yes," Doss said in a faint tone. "His son James did approach us, Daniel. I think you must realize that." He slowly lifted his eyes and stared at Kurok. "It was a three part deal, very lucrative. We would send him seed, and in return, he would send us what was priceless to the other side, the means to make agents like his father and sister."

Kurok stared back at him. "What?"

"They don't have any like that, you know." Doss went on in a surreally calm voice. "It would take us to create them, and of course, I knew I couldn't tell you about it. I just told you it was a study. I knew you'd believe that."

"Despite what I told you, you were going to make genetically imprinted psychotics anyway?" Kurok kept his voice equally calm. "Really, Randall?"

He nodded. "Yes. After I saw agent Drake, I understood why our customer wanted that so badly. It's really quite a different genetic set. You pointed that out yourself, Daniel. Don't you realize just how lucrative this will be for us? I hope I'm not making a mistake telling you this. I'm sure you understand."

Kurok sighed.

"After all, it will be many years before we hand them over." Doss seemed to take encouragement by his colleague's lack of response. "Plenty of time to perfect the set. And you proved how successful it could. be, really, Daniel, with your next generation model. So intelligent! So efficient. I can't believe I didn't see it earlier."

"Dev's not..." Kurok paused and sighed again.

Doss patted his arm. "I knew it'd be all right once I explained it to you. You're such a smart man and very logical."

"Mmm. With any luck I'll be dead before the first one of them grows up and kills everyone on station." Kurok shook his head. "It's like breeding saber tooth tigers. But what the hell." He lifted a hand and put it back down. "After all, it's no different than what the Drakes themselves are doing downside. They know what their target endpoint is."

Doss literally beamed at him. "Exactly!" He then frowned "But now, with all this damage..." He looked around at the bodies on the floor. "I suppose I can tell them it was an accident."

Kurok pinched the bridge of his nose hastily.

The hatch filled with figures, and then a flood of bio alts entered, a half dozen of them with med kits over their shoulders. "Over there, lads." Doctor Dan pointed. "Just bring everyone up, will you please? They were put down for safety."

"Yes, Doctor Dan." The TeeBee in the lead nodded confidently. "NM-Dev-1 advised us of the situation."

So many levels of meaning and so unexpected. "Excellent." Kurok smiled at him. "Carry on."

The medical team went over to the down bio alts and started to work. The security guards standing around relaxed and looked longingly at the drink dispenser. The rest of the bio alts split into groups and went to various stations, pulling out tool kits and opening side panels.

Doss watched them for a moment. "Did you teach them all the station mechanicals, Daniel?" he asked, after a long pause. "I wasn't aware."

"You probably just weren't there when we went over that module," Kurok said blandly. "It was in the extended technical section. I think twelve B." He tapped out a few commands on the input pad. "I hardly had a chance to show them today."

"No." Doss acknowledged. "I suspect you have made a long and careful plan."

Kurok tapped steadily. "Oh you can always count on me for that." He keyed in a set of inputs and did a double tap with his thumb, apparently focused on the screen.

"Daniel, I think you should stop what you're doing." Doss's voice got louder. "In fact, I think these guards should escort you to your quarters. Until we sort out what happened."

"What happened was I created a keyed neurotransmitter and activated it." Kurok sat back and let his hands drop to his lap. "I wasn't going to let them take apart the station, Randall. Really."

"You killed them?" Doss's eyes were curiously focused.

"Yes, I did." Kurok folded his hands together and simply sat, waiting. "I'll be glad to go to my quarters if you wish," he added in a mild tone. "But that's not going to change what happened."

"I see."

"They were going to kill us all, Randall. They almost had the station at null. Did you want to die? They had no idea what they were doing."

Doss sighed. "No, of course I don't want anyone to die."

The guards looked uncertain. "Sir." One of them edged a step closer. "I'm sorry, did you need us to do something?"

Doss half turned towards them. "Oh no, Captain. We were just discussing things. In fact," he licked his lips, "I think you can go back to your office. Everything seems all right here."

The guard nodded in some relief. "Okay, sir, we'll do that." He motioned to the other guards and they started for the door as the first of the bio alts began to come up. "We'll send a report."

"Yes, you do that." Doss waited for them to leave then turned back.

"I've asked for med to come and pick up the bodies," Kurok said. "My guess is you'll have until that shuttle ends up downside before you start getting called by your clients."

"I'll have to tell them what you did."

Kurok shrugged. Then he stood up. "Matter of fact, I think I'll go by med myself. I have quite the headache. And then I'll go to my quarters." He started around the console when Doss put his hand up to stop him, moving slightly into his path. "Randall, don't."

"Will you kill me, too?"

"I'd rather not," Kurok said in a kindly tone. "So get out of my way." He started forward and moved past Doss as his colleague moved out of the way. He headed for the door as his head started to pound harder.

A TeeBee intercepted him. "Doctor Dan. May we go with you? You said you needed med."

"Sure." He waved the TeeBee and two restored KayTees after him. "Let's go get everyone settled, shall we?"

"Doctor Dan, what should we do here?" One of the BeeAye's was back behind the console. "May we start repairs?"

"Start repairs." Kurok paused at the doorway, looking back at Randall Doss who was there, alone, with the bio alts still staring at him. "Don't get in their way, Randall. Be a good fellow, will you?" He waved and slipped through the hatch with the bio alts hard at his heels.

"We're glad you're okay, Doctor Dan," the TeeBee said, timidly. "We were worried about you."

"Thank you." Kurok glanced around. "Now can you tell me where NM-Dev-1 and Jesslyn Drake are?"

"In your lab, sir," the TeeBee said. "There are several sets with them."

"Excellent, let's go there."

JESS STUDIED THE screen for the nth time, aware of just how far away she was from being able to do anything useful about the message she was staring at.

Dev was buried in the screen next to her, the pale light from it washing her face in blue as her eyes flicked over the contents with some intensity.

Behind them, four TeeGees and an AyeBee were playing with Tayler, tossing a ball back and forth to keep him entertained.

"So what do you figure, Dev?" Jess finally asked. "Akers turn rogue or did those bastards who shot at the nomads decide to band up and attack or did the nomads finally gain critical mass?"

"I don't know." Dev had all ten fingers moving over the pads. "There is something blocking the transmitter, Jess. It must be physical. Maybe the shuttle hit it when it was going out.

"So can ya fix it?" Jess asked.

"It's outside," Dev said. "I can inspect it, but we can't reach it without a self contained suit."

"We got those?"

"They exist." Dev's gaze went inward. "I don't have any programming on them."

One of the TeeGees heard her and came over. "NM-Dev-1? I have programming on the exosuits," she said. "We just got it just last month."

"Really?" Dev peered at her. "I didn't know your set was mech?"

"They were giving us maintenance," the TeeGee said. "Of the hydroponic tanks. They have a part outside."

Dev nodded. "We should go inspect the transmitter. Jess, do you want to attend?"

"Sure." Jess got up and glanced behind her, watching the game for a moment before she led the way to the door with Dev and the TeeGee at her heels.

Outside, it seemed the station was getting back to normal, the hallways filling with people and jumpsuited technicians moving from panel to panel adjusting things. They gave the two dark Interforce uniforms a wary look, and twice proctors looked like they were going to interrupt them, moving into their paths and holding a hand up.

Jess waved them off and soldiered on past.

They made their way along the edge of the station to a platform mid way between two rings that gave them a view of the top of the structure.

"Hmm." Dev edged along the clear space. "I can see the solar array is out of line."

"Yes," the TeeGee agreed. "It's not in sync, the lower one is." She pointed as the sun blasted through the station again, highlighting the several shades of gold in her curly hair. She was taller than Dev and had a larger body. "I am surprised they did not send mech out to fix it."

"I think someone wants it to remain offline," Dev said in a mild tone. "There are many incorrect things going on."

The TeeGee nodded "Yes. We know this. They locked us in the crèche, and we saw the controls being set to space us. They wanted to save the air and power for natural borns."

"That is normal." Dev folded her arms over her chest. "There's programming on it."

"There is programming on it, but it still feels very incorrect," the TeeGee said.

"Yes," Dev said.

Jess had been listening. "Hey, we're not all assholes. At least, not that kind."

Dev turned and smiled, putting a hand on her arm. "No, not at all, Jess," she said. "I'm sorry." She looked at the TeeGee. "They gave Jess an award for saving everyone and being brave," she explained. "She's very special."

The TeeGee studied Jess with interest. "That is excellent."

Jess was glad the sun blast hid the blush she felt heating her face. She changed the subject. "Okay. So if they fix the solar stuff, then the radio'll start working? Devvie, we gotta get out of here."

"Yes." Dev pointed along the hall. "Let's go to the maintenance and see if we can encourage them to fix the array."

"Would my blaster be encouraging?"

"Let's try asking first."

THE MECH STATION was in chaos. Dev, Jess, and the TeeGee paused at the entry, letting the hatch slide closed behind them.

The large pod was full of people and repair kits with natural borns yelling orders and bio alts scrambling around.

"This seems suboptimal," Dev said.

One of the bio alts, carrying a mech pack on his back, was protesting. "Sir, Doctor Dan ordered us to begin repairs!"

"I don't give a shit what he said. You go where I tell you!" the natural born yelled at him. "Stupid piece of fluff brain!"

"Good place to start." Jess headed for the pair.

The TeeGee and Dev exchanged looks then followed her over. The bio alts around them realized they had entered. Activity slowed. Bodies straightened up and turned to watch them go by.

A mech supervisor realized it as well and started to hurry over.

Jess came to a halt next to the yelling man. "Hey, what's your problem?"

The man turned and then took a step back away from Jess's tall form. "Who the hell are you?"

"Jesslyn Drake," she responded amiably. "So listen. If Dan Kurok said to do something, you should let them get on with it."

"Hold on here," the supervisor said. "I don't think you understand..."

"I understand if you don't let them start fixing things, I'm going to kill you. So get the fuck out of their way."

Both men stared at her in silence.

"Seriously," Jess said. "Leave them alone and come with me because we found something you need to fix right now." She grabbed them by the shoulders and turned them around, shoving them toward the door. "Move it."

Given little choice, the two men complied. "Get things moving, Devvie," Jess said as she kept hold of her hapless captives. "I got this."

The TeeGee folded her arms. "Are all downside natural borns like that?"

"No." Dev headed for the cluster of bio alts. "From what I have observed none of them at all are anything like Jess. She is unique."

"As are you."

Dev paused and smiled. "Yes, that is true. But I am unique on purpose. I think that's just how Jess turned out."

"Hello, NM-Dev-1," one of the ArBees said. "Are things nominal?"

"No, the upper grid is offline and the transmitter is blocked," Dev said. "That is where my partner is taking the two supers to. We will need to get it fixed."

"Yes," the ArBee agreed. "It is known to central. It will need external work, but they refused to assign any of the externally trained mechs to it. I do not know why. It is necessary."

"I have the programming," the TeeGee said, confidently. "We know about the suits. I can go with you to assist in this."

The ArBee turned to look at the central station then turned back after a hesitation. "May we do this?" he asked Dev. "It seems like good work."

"Yes," Dev responded. "Can you proceed? There is an urgency to get the transmitter working again."

"Yes." The ArBee picked up his backpack. Two others of his set came over, watching Dev alertly. "Should we wait for the supers to come back?" the ArBee asked. "They were having a difficulty in assignments."

"No," Dev said. "I am sure it will be fine. This is necessary and good work, and Doctor Dan knows about it." She added for good measure.

The ArBees nodded and got kitted up. "You will come with us?" one asked the TeeGee. "We do not have programming on outside."

"I will." The TeeGee agreed. "I am looking forward to using this programming. I enjoyed getting it."

Dev felt the tiniest pang at that, remembering suddenly that she would no longer be able to experience that moment of pleasure. That exploration of new depth and knowledge that came with being given programming to do good work.

It made her sad, a little. For her, more than most, the programming had been necessary and critical. "Do you have comms?" she asked. "If not, we will get you one so you can advise on progress."

One of the ArBees held up an earpiece. "We are Mech three." He inserted it into his ear, and the group started off, heading for the door, just as one of the other mech supers came around the console and hurried over to where Dev was standing.

Casually, she put a hand out to stop him. "Please wait."

He stopped, but more in shock than anything else. "What did you say to me?"

Dev regarded him. "Were you going to delay the mech team? They are doing important work." She lowered her hand to her side. "I don't want them delayed."

His jaw dropped. "You don't want them delayed? Who are you to assign them?" he spluttered. "You are nothing but one of them!" He looked around. "Where are those other damn supervisors?"

"My partner took them to see the arrays that need to be fixed," Dev said. "I am NM-Dev-1. I am assisting Jess in achieving this. It would be good if you do not try to prevent it." She paused. "Please do not cause me to have to attempt to stop you."

"I'm calling security." The man retreated and headed for the center console. "This is nuts."

Dev remained standing where she was, hands clasped behind her back. One of the ArBee mechs came over to her and regarded the supervisor. "He should not do that," he said. "It will prevent the work."

"Yes." Dev sorted out her options. "Let's see if I can persuade him not to."

Chapter Ten

JESS SHOVED THE two mechs up against the plas. "There." She pointed up at the array.

"We know," the supervisor said. "We could tell that from back there. We didn't need to see it. We know it's down."

"So why aren't you fixing it?" Jess asked. "Seems like that's an important piece of your biz."

To her surprise, they both shook their heads. "No, not really. Lot of more important stuff to check first, like grav and life support." He watched her warily. "Why is it your business, Agent?"

"Yeah. You're just keeping us from getting onto it," the second man said. "But hey, you know what's going on? Mind letting us in on it?"

Jess regarded them, her bright gaze moving from face to face, allowing her senses to take in their body language and scents. Her nostrils flared a little, and she flexed her hands, waiting a moment to see their reactions.

Rough edge of truth. "The other side's shuttle locked on. They wanted some merchandise someone here promised them." Jess said. "Didn't care what they wrecked getting it."

Both were expressionless for a long moment. "Fucking Doss," the supervisor finally said. "Scum sucking whore pig would sell his liver to anyone for a brownie point."

"Could be," Jess said. "He's got a lot of lucrative stuff to offer up here."

"Got the board chasing his ass all rotation," the second man said. "Bios ain't selling so good these days. Looking for cred in other places."

"Who told you that?" The other supervisor demanded.

The man shrugged. "Heard it in the dayroom."

Truth. Not truth. Jess regarded them. Truth.

"So what's your piece in all this?" the second man asked Jess. "What's Interforce all up in our business about?"

Jess felt her nape hairs lift as her body detected approach from behind. She affected relaxation though, crossing her arms and leaning against a support strut. "We're customers," she said. "You're growing some techs for us."

"That's not really true is it?" the supervisor asked. "I heard that in the dining hall, but I don't believe it."

"Sure it's true." Jess felt her breathing slowing down and she focused on keeping her body relaxed, every sense tuned behind her. "My partner's from here. She's kickass."

The supervisor studied her. "The developmental unit?" he said in a surprised tone. "Kurok's little project?"

"Dev." Jess watched him shift as the air pressure changed at her back, and she felt her instincts cut loose. There was no need to decide what to do, her body did it for her automatically, turning and dropping to one knee as a dagger came past her shoulder, hitting the mech supervisor as he gasped and staggered backwards.

"Bad luck." Jess brought her blaster up and braced her hands. "I'd fall down if I were you mech buddy," she called over her shoulder. "There's more where that came from."

The other man had already dived behind a console and was caterwauling into comms. Her opponent was a small man, dressed in dark clothing covering his entire body, including a hood on his head. She could see his eyes watching her, his hands held out to either side of his body, waiting.

"What's another death to you, Drake?" he asked, in a mild, almost mocking tone.

"Nothing," Jess answered in the same vein. "Pointless question. What brings you here, Hector?"

"Killing you." The man smiled at her. "Shuttle left me behind once they realized you were here."

Jess knew Hector. They'd been stuck on an island together for three of the longest days of her life, and even now, watching him, she could smell sea washed rock in the back of her throat. Hector was a hitman, a loner, the kind of operative who simply sat and waited with a finger curled around a trigger or with a dagger in his fingers.

Or with a dart in a pipe.

She actually sort of liked him. He had a slice of honor, in his own way, but not enough to have stopped him from spending those three days alternately trying to screw and then kill her.

Hadn't succeeded in either, and she'd mutilated his genitals on that last day before she spotted a watcher craft coming over head and decided to swim for it.

Forty cold, turgid miles breathing water, evading their search until they'd convinced themselves she was dead, not seeing any bubbles or signs of life.

"You haven't changed any, Jess," Hector said. "Kind of disappointing."

Jess stood up and put her blaster back in its hard point. She then extended her hand out. "Ya never know, Heck. Maybe I have."

She caught him completely offguard. He took a step back, lifting his hands again as though his body wasn't sure what to do. He was a little younger than she was, with thick, curly black hair and a copper tan colored skin.

There was a thunder of bootsteps on the metal grid flooring. "Better decide quick." Jess's blue eyes twinkled a little. "'Cause there's going to be a bunch of mad space dorks with zappers here in a minute, and they already know I'm a lot better friend than enemy."

Hector exhaled then scrunched his face up and extended a hand to hers, clasping it with all the jerkiness of a man testing a hot plate to see if it was really hot.

The guards came around the corner with a group of bio alts wearing medic jumpers, hauling up when they saw the two black clad figures shaking hands.

"Relax boys," Jess said, releasing Hector and turning to face them. "Just a misunderstanding. He ended up in the wrong place at the wrong time." She indicated the mech super. "Took a knife meant for me."

"You need to come to central, Agent," one of the guards said. "It's ordered."

"No I don't." Jess said. "Don't even think about it unless you want to be dead, too."

The medics started to work on the mech supervisor. The other mech had disappeared, and the guards looked undecided, hands shifting from their stun sticks to their comms.

"Let's let them do their thing." Jess pointed down the corridor. "See ya."

The guards' bodies shifted, but they ended up staying quiet and letting them pass. From the corner of her eye, Jess saw an airlock at the apogee of station where she could see some activity.

"So, Jess." Hector walked at her side, every muscle tensed. "Tell me how you got off the island. Been the mystery I've wanted to ask you about for years."

Jess chuckled. "I can breathe water," she said. "I swam out of there and got to Drougas point."

"Asshole." He shook his head. "You grow fins, too?"

"Takes one to know one," she responded in a mild tone. "Did you stay back on purpose just to kill me? Really?"

"I can breathe water," he sniped at her.

The irony of it made her laugh, and then a moment later they were grappling as he swerved and got her in a hold.

The corridor was empty, and they thumped against the wall, fighting in silence save the scuff of boots against the metal and the rasp of the heavy fabric they wore against the walls.

Hector yanked himself sideways, slamming his head into her ribcage with sudden force, and Jess got her elbow down against the side of his neck and pushed away keeping his teeth from clamping down on her.

He went with the motion and got her knees in a grip, twisting savagely to one side to bring her down. Jess crouched against the motion and then kicked away from the ground, taking both of them up into the air a few feet and then back down to the deck with a rolling thumping bang as her boots hit the metal.

He lost his hold and shifted quickly, rolling clear and then coming right back at her in a snakelike motion again at her knees.

Jess hopped into the air again, this time higher since she had only herself to lift, and tumbled into a somersault, twisting to the side as she landed to let him fly past her.

Off in the distance, the sound of light boots coming at them.

Jess reached up and grabbed a support strut as he turned and lunged, lifting herself up and kicking out at him, one boot missing, the other nailing him in the head. He flew backwards, slamming against the wall, and she released her hold, landing lightly and rolling forward over her center of balance as he pushed off the metal panels.

Jess brought her hands up, curled into fists. "C'mon, Heckie." She grinned, cocking an elbow back, waiting for him to come at her. "Let's get in a few more rounds before my partner gets here and cleans your clock."

He paused in mid motion. "Your tech?" he asked. "Cut the bullshit, Jess."

She chuckled. "C'mon." She motioned him forward. "Still mad at me for cracking your nuts?"

"Bitch."

"Oh yeah." Jess ducked and they came together in a wrestling hold.

DEV BOUNDED AROUND the curve of the hallway and spotted the two figures fighting ahead of her. "That's not correct," she said to the KayBee and BeeAye with her. "That man is incorrect."

"He is a natural born," the KayBee said.

"He is doing damage to my partner," Dev responded as they neared the two fighters, and she prepared to do something about it. "We must help."

"Yes," the BeeAye agreed. "Jess helped the children. We must help her." He came up even to Dev as they reached the bend and jumped into the fight.

"Get that retractor," she told the BeeAye. "I will distract him." She grabbed Hector's suit, hauling backwards with all her strength. He came away from his grapple and turned on her, eyes widening.

"What the h..." He twisted to get at her, but Dev just kept backing away, pulling him from behind. "Stop that you little..."

"Strike him on the cranium." She yanked him farther, and then the BeeAye hit him over the head with a spar that had been laying against the wall.

He never even saw it coming, his eyes having glossed over the pale jumpsuits of the bio alts in a frantic bid to fend off an impending attack from Jess. "I said stop it you...augh!"

"Excellent!" Dev released him, and he went down hard. She took a step back and looked at Jess. "Are you all right?"

Jess was grinning, her hands planted on her hips. "You're such a little rock star," she said. "I'm fine, Devvie. We were just scrapping."

Dev frowned. "He was not trying to damage you?"

"Sure he was. Woulda killed me if he had the chance." Jess dusted her hands off. "But scrapping's fun, in a twisted, psycho kinda way."

"That was much simpler than I had anticipated," the BeeAye observed. "Even without any programming." He nodded. "It was excellent that you knew what to do, NM-Dev-1."

"I have had some practice," Dev muttered. "Please secure him with that wiring harness there so he cannot do any more incorrectness."

"Yes." The BeeAye put down the retractor and got to work with the wiring.

"Who is that, Jess?" Dev edged around the limp body and joined her. "Is he from the other side?"

"He is. That's Hector Montserrat," Jess said. "He's an assassin from the other side who doesn't like me. We're enemies from way back."

The KayTee joined them. "That seems very incorrect," he observed. "He could have damaged you?"

"He'd have tried," Jess smiled, "but I'm pretty good at what I do."

"Jess is amazing," Dev told them. "But still people should not try to hurt her." She folded her arms over her chest. "I have some unfortunate news about the array. It's damaged past where they can fix it without additional parts."

"So no messages downside."

"No," Dev said. "That seems to have been the purpose of the damage."

"Uh huh." Jess nodded. "I figured. Okay, then we need to find a way off this thing." She regarded the three of them. "What are our options?"

Dev, the BeeAye, and the KayTee looked back at her. Then the two men looked at Dev. "We need a spacecraft," she said after a pause. "The maintenance craft on station are not made to go downside."

"This is true," the KayTee said. "We pilot them. The station craft do not have the shielding needed to enter the atmosphere." He pondered. "But we could reprogram the guidance comp to do it."

The BeeAye pursed his lips a little. "We could add shielding. There is some in the construction bay. But I don't think the maneuvering jets could allow us to land."

They both looked at Dev.

Jess looked at Dev.

Dev cleared her throat. "I could probably land the craft if it survived entry," she said. "There are planar surfaces on the maintenance models that would allow some lift."

Jess smiled at them. "Doc should get some kind of damn award," she said. "Seriously."

"What?" Dev's brows creased.

"Doctor Dan?" the KayTee asked. "He's very smart."

"Also kind." the AyeBee added. "When it is time for our natal dates he always sends a treat."

"Yes that's true." Dev smiled, distracted. "Usually a sweet of some kind. But what does that have to do with anything, Jess?"

"Fill ya in later." Jess glanced up and past them as the hall filled with guards and several proctors. She eased her way past the bio alts and Dev, putting her body between them and the guards. She let her hand rest on her blaster as they came to a halt, blocking the way.

The KayTee looked at her back. Then he moved up to stand at her side, and the BeeAye came up next to her on the opposite side, the three of them filling the tube.

"What is going on here?" the guard asked, looking at the body on the floor, well and fully trussed up in cables.

"He knifed the mech down the hall. We caught him," Jess said. "Do we get a prize?"

The guard and one of the proctors were staring at them visibly in disbelief. One of the guards put his hand on the zapper at his chest and curled his fingers around it.

"Don't do that," Jess warned softly as the BeeAye and KayTee stiffened next to her. "Won't do a damn thing to me, and I'm the one who's going to punish you for using it."

The guard looked at one of the proctors then slowly lowered his hand. "They told us there were some bio alts causing trouble here," he said. "Doctor Doss sent us."

"They're with me," Jess said. "So leave them alone."

One of the proctors edged forward. "Agent Drake, you have no authority here. You're a guest. We have responsibility for these units, so please let us do our jobs," she said. "Don't interfere, please. It could be dangerous for everyone."

Jess chuckled. "A lot more dangerous for you than for me," she said. "My authority here rests in the fact I am willing to kill everyone who gets in my way. Got something to beat that?"

"That's not..." The proctor's eyes widened in horror. "You can't do that!"

"Sure I can. And I will ya know," Jess assured her. "I just don't care about anyone I don't care about. I know the doc must have toldja all about that."

"Proctor Jan," Dev said. "In this circumstance, you are incorrect, and there is danger. Go back to the crèche, please."

The woman stared at her. "You may not speak to me that way," she said, turning her eyes away from Jess. "Stop it!"

Jess chuckled again, low and almost under her breath.

"I am afraid I can," Dev said in a somewhat regretful tone. "My assignment allows it, and I do not wish to see you damaged."

"The director was right," Jan said. "Doctor Kurok has done something very wrong to you." She touched the zapper at her chest and after a silent pause where no one moved, did it again. "Oh my god."

The KayTee and BeeAye looked at each other and then at Dev. "It is malfunctioning. Maybe the system took damage," the BeeAye suggested. "Which would be suboptimal and yet excellent at the same moment."

Jess started laughing.

The proctor took a step back.

Then the entire station rocked, and there was sound of an explosion. Everything started to move and shimmy, and alarms and sirens started to go off. They felt the gravity shifting, and as Jess went to the nearest clear panel, she saw a large shadow coming nearer and saw a blast of energy hit the edge of the solar panel.

One of the proctors slammed against the wall. "What is that? What's happening?"

"It's another shuttle." Jess started making her way along the rail. "One of ours this time."

"Why's it shooting at us!"

The station shuddered again and the lights went out, the hallway plunging into darkness broken by spears of sunlight as they whirled around in orbit. "Guess we need to go find out." Jess reached behind her and found Dev already at her side. "Let's go, Devvie."

The proctors and guards were hanging on to the railing, but the bio alts scrambled after them. "May we come?" the BeeAye said. "We would like to help."

"Yes," the KayTee agreed. "Let us."

Jess waved them forward, and they left the station staff behind without regret, holding on to the rail along the hallway as gravity started to flex.

"You will get into trouble!" Jan yelled after them.

"Hope so," Jess yelled back. "We need some trouble!"

"Is that good?" the BeeAye asked Dev.

Dev shrugged. "It depends. We will need to find out. Sometimes trouble can be good." She stuck to Jess's back like a tick. "I think it depends what side of the trouble you're on."

THE LAB WAS relatively quiet as Kurok entered, and he paused inside the hatch to look around. Several bio alts spotted him and hurried toward him, but at the back of the section he saw a small boy playing ball. "Ah."

A small boy, dressed as a bio alt who was no such thing, and he had a sinking feeling he was about to get yet another unpleasant surprise.

A GeeBee looked relieved to see him. "Doctor Dan. I am glad to see you well."

"Thanks," Doctor Dan said. "Who do we have here?" he

indicated the child. "And can you tell me where Jess and Dev are?"

The GeeBee nodded. "That is a natural born child who was brought to station by Doctor Doss. His name is Tayler."

"Tayler."

The boy heard his name and came trotting over, carrying a ball under one arm. "Hi. Who're you?"

He was tow haired and lanky, already showing an unusual breadth of shoulder. "Hello there. My name is Dan Kurok." He extended his hand out.

The boy accepted the grip. "My auntie Jess was here, but I don't know where she went."

Auntie Jess. "Ah, Auntie Jess. Well, give me a moment, and we'll see if we can find her, how's that?" Kurok said. "When did you get to station, Tayler?"

He shrugged. "Dunno. I was sleepin, then I woke up and I was here. I was supposed to go to school!"

Kurok sighed a little. "Your auntie Jessie's school?"

He nodded. "Mamma didn't like that."

"Well I can't imagine why not. I went to that school myself, you know," Kurok said, with a wry smile. "We'll sort it all out for you, Tayler. Don't worry."

Tayler looked pleased to hear that. "Said I would go to school here but I don like it."

"No, probably too much reading and not enough activity. Right?"

The boy nodded. "I like the flying," he admitted. "That's cool."

"Doctor Dan, Agent Drake, and NM-Dev-1 went to mech central," the GeeBee told him. "They wanted to see if they could get the transmitter working."

"I see. Well, let me get some painkiller for my head, and we'll see what we can do to sort things out." He headed for his private, inner office. "Since some things have become a lot clearer to me in the last few moments."

Inside his office, with the door closed, he sat down behind his desk and cradled his head in his hands. "This is so god damned out of control," he muttered. "How did we get here? Bloody hell, me and Doss running games at each other in two completely separate directions."

A knock. "C'mon in." Kurok straightened up a little, leaning back and opening a drawer in his desk to remove a bottle.

The door opened and one of his lab assistants entered. "Oh,

Doctor," she said in relief. "Thank goodness I found you."

"Hello, Cathy." Kurok swallowed a pair of tabs dry and regarded her. "Whatever you're going to ask me I probably can't answer I'm afraid."

She sat down across from him, her curly red hair bouncing slightly. "No, Doctor, I don't want to ask you anything, I need to tell you something." She drew in a long breath then exhaled. "They know about the programs."

He pondered that for a moment. "Tell me exactly what you mean, Cathy. Which programs and who they are."

"Okay." Cathy paused to order her thoughts. One of his brightest assistants, an orphan who happened to be in the right place at the right time. "I was in med, helping out," she said. "There were a lot of people who got banged up during the null, you know?"

"I know." Doctor Dan smiled wryly. "I was one of them."

"We heard that. We were very worried," Cathy said. "Anyway, I was in one of the exam rooms, and I heard Sub-director Braedon come in and ask the desk how much trank they had on hand. He said they might need it, might need to apply it to all the sets."

"Mmm." Doctor Dan made a low sound deep in his throat.

"So the desk asked why not just use the biometric blocks," Cathy said. "And the sub-director said they might not work."

Kurok let his head rest against the back of his chair. "They could just be referring to the power outages."

"They could." Cathy agreed. "But then he said there had been changes made, unapproved changes, and they weren't sure how far that went."

Rats. "Well, that's a bit more clear."

"Yes," his assistant agreed. "So I was with Douglas and Pam, and we figured we better come here and find you and let you know, and figure out what we're going to do because, sir, we're not just going to let them put all the sets down."

"No, certainly not," Kurok said. "I think it would have come to this anyway, Cathy. I had noticed the sets, the older ones in the sets, were starting to demonstrate thought independence and it was just a matter of time."

"Yes." She nodded in agreement. "The proctors have been talking. And then, they met NM-Dev-1 when she came back, and everyone realized."

"Mmm."

"At first, everyone wondered, why you were treating this

unit as a natural born? And then after they interacted with her, it was, oh, that's why. She's really good."

That, despite everything, got a smile from Kurok. "Thank you, Cathy. I put a lot of hard work into Dev, and it's personally very gratifying to me to see her success."

"But she scares them," Cathy said. "They think you deliberately made her to be like them."

"Well I did." Kurok's eyes twinkled gently. "Matter of fact I made her to be better than us, and that, Cathy, is what is scaring everyone. Because when you meet Dev, and realize her potential, it's terrifying."

Cathy looked worried. "If they figure out how long you've been making changes, it could be dangerous for the sets downworld." She looked across the desk at him. "And really dangerous for the crèche here. They were going to vent the crèche to space, Doctor Dan."

"They were going to try," Kurok said. "They would have found that they couldn't. A mechanical error." He rocked forward and put his elbows on his desk. "I disabled the explosive unlocks on the clamps that hold the crèche to rest of station."

Cathy looked a little surprised. "The sets didn't know that. They thought they were going to be—"

"Made dead," Kurok said. "Which is a lesson unto itself, Cathy. You never put a value on your own life until you understand what value others put on it. Or lack of value, as it were."

They were both silent for a few moments. "So what are we going to do now, Doctor Dan?" Cathy finally asked. "It's all changed, hasn't it?"

Part of his mind wanted to deny that. Part of him wanted to think that he could, through some political footwork and lies, keep things as they were, but even as he sounded the words inside his head, Kurok knew the truth.

Everything had changed. Time to plan had ended. Time to sculpt the change was done. "Yes, I'm afraid it has," Kurok said. "Now we have to move forward, ready or not." With a sigh, he stood up and grimaced at now stiffened aches. "Call our lab staff back here, and we'll get a plan in place."

Cathy looked relieved. "Absolutely, sir." She got up and tapped the comms unit in her ear. "Open side channel, code Delta please." She intoned as she headed out his door into the main part of the lab.

Ah well. Kurok rolled his head around to loosen the cricks in his neck. His input screen beeped, and he glanced at it. He watched in bemusement as the systems came up and reported attempts to disable his access.

C'mon. Really? He put his hand on the auth plate. "Systems, control code twenty-seven, authorization beta twenty, twenty-six, confirmed."

He felt the scan against his palm, and then another screen popped up. He watched lists of systems starting to scroll past, now locked under his personal credentials. A relatively simple process, especially for someone with his training.

Doss's voice erupted in private comms, the one reserved for the scientists. "Daniel, security is coming to take you somewhere safe. Please don't resist them."

"Oh, Randall." Kurok mock sighed. "It's too late for that."

"Daniel, please."

"Don't send them," Kurok said. "I've locked the access into my lab and quarters, and if they insist, I will react accordingly. It's too late, Randall. It's done."

He heard chaos in the background as Doss held the transmit open, hesitating. Then the key closed and he cut off his end, heading out into the lab proper.

Bio alts were pouring in, excited and alert.

Cathy called him over. "Doctor Dan, there's something approaching station. Look!"

"Doctor Dan!" another of his assistants yelled. "Someone's attacking the lab! They're firing on the lock doors!"

He heard screams. "All right, people. Stay calm." He picked up a comms set and put it in his ear. "Let's get to work."

THE LIGHTS FLICKERED on, then off, then dimly on again, and they were bouncing through the halls as the gravity fluxed. The shuttle bay was sealed off, and they squirmed through a maintenance tube access way as the KayTee led their way upward.

"Oh!" the BeeAye said, suddenly. "Doctor Dan's on comm!"

"Excellent." Dev pulled herself up the maintenance ladder with Jess bringing up the rear. "I'm glad he's okay."

"I think he's in a fight!" the BeeAye said after a moment's listening. "He's calling everyone to his lab!"

"Hmm," Jess rumbled under her breath. "Shit is starting to rapidly roll downhill."

The KayTee and BeeAye paused and looked back at her.

Dev bumped them with her head. "Please proceed. Jess means incorrect things are starting to proliferate."

Power went out again, and a moment later they were shooting upward as gravity cut out. "Well, that makes it easier," Jess said as she had to hold herself back, her larger mass wanting to overrun her companions.

They got to the top of the accessway and faced a hatch. "Hold on." Dev brought her scanner around and tuned it. "Stepping out into vacuum would not be optimal."

"No," the KayTee agreed. "But this is the service way inside the mech station. It should be pressurized."

"It is," Dev said. "Take care. The scanner shows some movement on the other side of the hatch." She regarded the screen. "Null return. It cannot resolve."

The KayTee reached for the unlock, but he was gently bumped aside. "Let me." Jess got her hand around the latch and started undogging it. "If the moving something has a gun, I'll do better with it."

The bio alts drew back, watching her with respect.

Dev secured her scanner and got ready to move with Jess as she cranked the hatch open and flowed gracefully through it, one hand out and ready as she cleared the hatch door and emerged into the small, cramped mech station.

There was nothing outside, but Jess knew better than to trust that, deferring rather to Dev's scanner. She cleared space for the rest of them to come out after her, but squared her body to them to intercept anything unfriendly.

Her ears twitched, hearing odd and discomfiting sounds as the station twisted around her, the consoles abandoned in the center axis as she turned in a circle.

Outside through the thick windows she saw the spaced chamber, bodies still floating aimlessly now that gravity had released them again, the cleanup having bypassed them in favor of mechanical concerns.

"Be careful," Jess said as she pushed herself toward the workstations. "There's something in here."

Dev held a wall pole and got her scanner out again. She swept it right and left around her. "Nothing...no persons." She read the scan returns, now echoing more clearly outside the central core. There was just a hint of a void in motion, and she recorded it to look at later.

It was cold. They could see the rip in the fabric of station where the enemy shuttle had torn out, and a sheen of ice was forming on the metal consoles that filled the mech station.

Jess felt the chill against her eyeballs and blinked. She shoved herself over to the other side where she could see the edge of the shuttle bay, with a shadowy form past it outlined against the stars.

Shuttle, ours. She recognized the outline immediately, and now that it had stopped shooting at station, she could also see the faint puff of maneuvering jets. "Can we talk to it?"

"No transmitter," Dev responded. "I can try with this." She drifted down to one of the seats and wrapped her legs around it to keep still while she fiddled with the settings.

"Why did it shoot?" the KayTee asked. "That's the gamma shuttle. It's for supply."

"Doctor Dan is calling you, NM-Dev-1," the BeeAye said. "Would you like comms?"

"I'll take it." Jess extended her hand. "He won't mind talking to me instead," she added, with a wry smile as he hesitated. "Promise."

He handed over the comms and she put it to her ear. "Hey, Doc."

A soft crackle. "Ah, Jesslyn."

"Glad to hear your voice," Jess said. "Dev's tied up trying to talk to the shuttle that was trying to kill us."

"Ah, excellent," Kurok said. "When you're done sorting that all out, perhaps you could stop back by here since they're working hard to space us with cutting torches and massive amounts of idiocy. I have shields up on emergency gen here, but they won't last forever with the power in flux."

"See what we can do about that, Doc," Jess said. "Spread the word I'll be blowing heads off on my way back, huh?"

One of the hatches behind them thumped to and they all turned, Jess sailing over to get in the way as a figure entered and came toward them. "Ah." She tumbled around in mid air. "Sorry, what was that, Doc?"

"I've locked out pretty much all the systems under my code. Not much going back to be had from here."

"Gotcha." Jess caught hold of the ceiling grid. "One of your kids just came in."

It was the TeeGee out of breath. "I found you!" she said. "Comps down. You were right about the transmitter. I found the lock out. Dev, they did it on purpose."

"Yes." Dev looked up briefly then went back to her scanner. "All kinds of incorrectness."

"Talk to you later, Doc," Jess said. "Wish us luck."

"No luck needed, just a Drake," Kurok said, gentle affection clear in his voice. "Check in when you can."

He clicked out.

"Glad you found us," Jess told the TeeGee. "'Cause things are heading right for the crapper."

The TeeGee turned to stare at her.

"Sanitary unit, rudimentary." Dev forestalled the question. "KayTee, is it possible to achieve supplemental power to the mech comp?"

The KayTee drifted over to the comp access and peered at it. "It seems dormant. I will review the interlock."

"Jess, I have comms with the shuttle," Dev said, half turning. "But it's only text flash." She showed the screen with it's blinking data. "They're damaged. Said they were hit by the other shuttle on its way out. "

"They're drifting." The BeeAye observed. "They can't dock?"

"They can't dock they need assist," Dev said, typing on the screen. "Rotation's down. There's no way to guide them in on auto."

"We could manually dock them," the TeeGee suggested. "There's two exosuits in the lock right on the other side of that hatch."

"What does that get us?" Jess asked.

"Power," Dev said. "We can draw it from the shuttle and regen the systems. And," she added, "they have a transmitter." She started to drift toward the lock hatch. "I will go with you, TeeGee."

"No." Jess hooked her arm in mid air and pulled her back. "My job."

The TeeGee regarded her. "I'm afraid the suit won't fit you, Agent Drake. It's made for someone my size, or a bit taller."

"A bio alt," Dev said. "It's dangerous."

"All the more reason. I'll figure it out," Jess said. "You see if you can get the widgets twirling." She pushed herself toward the hatch.

The bio alts watched her with deep interest. "You would go in NM-Dev-1's place?" the TeeGee asked. "You could be made dead, Agent Drake."

"Absolutely," Jess said. "I'd croak for Dev in a millisecond. She's the brains in this outfit."

There was a little silence. "That's really excellent," the KayTee finally said. He looked at Dev. "You were right. I've never heard a natural born say anything like that ever."

Dev gazed affectionately at Jess, reaching out to catch her arm and give it a squeeze. "I told you Jess is amazing," she said. "But really, Jess, the hard suits don't stretch."

"I will go," the BeeAye said, joining the TeeGee at the hatch. "I have programming for the shuttle, anyway." He bumped the TeeGee through the opening and slid after her, shutting the hatch before Jess could get herself loose and prevent it.

The KayTee seated himself at the console and opened the front of it, looking inside. There was just enough emergency power to see, and he removed a probe from his jumpsuit pocket and poked at things.

Jess felt the blush fade, and she turned to look at Dev. Dev's eyes lifted and met Jess's, and for a long moment Jess just forgot what the hell was going on around her.

If someone had come in and shot her, she'd have just exploded into bits. It felt bizarre. Then Dev gently pressed her knuckles against Jess's cheek, and she found she really just didn't care.

Really just didn't.

It just felt so insanely good to see that look in those eyes focused totally on her. Who the fuck cared if the entire world was blowing up.

"You really are amazing, Jess," Dev said softly.

"Devvie," Jess rumbled softly. "We should be doing something useful."

"Like what?" Dev turned and looked out the thick plex. "We're lucky we found a spot that has atmo, right now, and a small amount of power. We really cannot do that much until they dock the shuttle and release the grav wheel."

"So that's what kicked off the floating again? They didn't damage this thing, it just stopped because they are bumping around out there?"

"Yes," Dev said. "It's for safety."

They heard the hatch cycle, and then the two exosuits came out of the front of the airlock, guided by gentle jets from the rear of the units encasing the two bio alts inside.

"They are brave," the KayTee commented. "That is very dangerous." He turned to look at the two dark clad forms. "But you also did brave things, NM-Dev-1. I saw on the vid Doctor Dan showed us." He smiled a little. "It really scared the proctors."

"I didn't think of it that way at the time." Dev said. She

pondered. "I think I was just too busy. It was my first mission and a lot was going on."

Jess chuckled. "You never do think about that when you're in the zone. It's only when you see yourself on vid afterward that you throw your hands up and say — what the hell?"

"What's a hell?" the KayTee inquired.

Dev held up a hand at Jess. "Don't." She turned to the KayTee. "It starts with some story about a hole in the ground and then it will turn into all kinds of things about asses and really, KayTee, you do not want to know."

Jess's laughter was a fun, surprising sound in all the danger around them. She reached out and put her arms around Dev and pulled her close, hugging her while they drifted in mid air, watching the station rattling itself apart.

"PUT THAT CONSOLE up against the wall," Doctor Dan instructed, holding on to a support bar with one hand as the bio alts around him swirled in reaction. "Quickly please."

The lab, as it were, was something of a bunker. He'd had it built that way, casual, gentle suggestions at this time and that time, adding a layer here and a layer there, but it wasn't designed to survive the entire station coming to pieces.

"Please have care," a KayTee said, welding torch clutched in one hand. "I must make this area very hot."

In a wan, kind of catastrophic way, he was so proud of all of them. None of the sets were panicking, they all moved around doing whatever they could to keep others safe and stabilize the area of station they were in.

Could you program courage? "That's right." Doctor Dan nodded. "Yes, right there, KayTee. Tack it in place." He glanced behind him to where Tayler was turning somersaults in the null, the motion so much like Jess's he had to smile.

Sometimes it was inbred. That light, bold lack of caring about personal safety and security and ability to live completely in the moment that was expressed as courage, but really was more about just not caring about the future.

Justin would have loved the null.

Kurok sighed and studied the entryway that had been reinforced as best he could manage it and now was protecting the several hundred bio alts who had come at his calling and were prepared to share whatever fate it was he'd arranged for.

"Doctor Dan, the shuttle is trying to lock on," a BeeAye said, studying the console they were in front of. "There is danger."

"There is." He floated over and looked at the screen, bare wiremaps driven by the emergency power supply to the lab.

The sounds outside had faded a little, but he still heard the sound of steel cutters in the outer hall, an insanity in the fragile spider web of station supports. He tapped the comms in his ear. "Jess?"

"Here." The warm, slightly burring voice came back at once. "Shuttle said they've got damage."

"Are you trying to dock it?" he asked. "That could be something catastrophic."

Jess responded calmly. "Dev said the thing has power and a transmitter, though. She thinks it's worth the try."

"Mmm." Doctor Dan shifted the basic scan. "Other shuttle's gone?"

"The other shuttle's particles. That's what this one was aiming at."

Ah. Unexpected. Usually the shuttles maintained a kind of space brotherhood kind of idiocy, respecting each other regardless of side. Perhaps the pilot had a history. "Okay."

"Doctor Dan, there is penetration," a BeeAye yelled out, pointing at the wall.

"No rest for the weary." He sighed. "Thanks, Jess." He cut off the comms and drew the blaster from the small of his back, checking the power setting on it. "Everyone please get clear."

Kurok wondered if he should tell Doss he had nothing to worry about, since the shuttle with all the witnesses was toast. Would that make him stop shooting at them? He retuned the comms from the secure point to point link with Jess. "Hello, Randall? Randall, are you there?"

No answer.

Oh well. He kicked off the wall and sailed toward the entryway where the sets reluctantly backed off at his approach. "That's right, friends, give me some space."

He saw the penetration then and heard the thumps of the wall pounders behind it. He got a position with his arm through a support, holding him still in the air. "All of you get back, please, into the main area of the lab. I don't want you all to get hurt."

"But what about you, Doctor Dan?" one of the CeeEms asked. "We should help you!"

He looked to his left and saw them drifting toward him. "No, please stay back. They'll be shooting at me, and I would rather not have you get in the way."

Hesitation.

But then the square of penetration imploded inward, and he was out of time. Security came flooding in and he aimed and fired in short bursts, as he'd been taught in field school.

Head shots.

Eye shots.

Three bodies drifted, arms outflung in shock before they realized. Then they started yelling and the flood became a scramble to get back past the wall, blood flying as they scraped and cut themselves on the raw metal they'd cut.

Kurok released the spar and kicked toward them, feeling the resistance to motion that the blaster caused as it sent energy in counterpoint.

Two of them got bearings and lifted blasters, that were not even supposed to be on station, to shoot back at him and then all hell broke loose as the bio alt sets reacted, all of them pouring toward the guards with arms outstretched.

Fully willing to take shots for him. To be made dead, and by the looks in their faces, Kurok knew they knew that.

Idiots. He ducked under a set and twisted, finding an alley to shoot down as another body squeezed into the irregular square and aimed at him. A mass of bio alts arrived in a swarm of flailing arms and legs and everyone collided.

Civs. Doctor Dan shoved the blaster back into his front pocket and ducked a swipe as the guards swapped unfamiliar blasters for stun sticks and the chest mounted zappers, which they realized in short order were having no effect. "Bastards!" one the guards yelled. "They were right!"

One of the bio alts slapped him, more or less accidently, and he went tumbling off. Kurok grabbed hold of the wall support, using this firm attachment to allow him to punch a guard with his balled fist. "This way, friends!"

Eyes watched him intently, then the bio alts fell to, copying his motion as they engaged the guards, dodging the stun sticks wielded in wild sweeps since the guards were unused to the null.

Kurok twisted a stunner out of a hand and then slammed it into one of the guard's faces, knocking him backwards into the wall.

"Hey, stop that!" a captain bellowed. "Damn you Kurok!"

Kurok laughed. "Call me DJ." He pitched the stun stick at the man and watched it smack him in the eye. "You all better enjoy this party before the Drake gets here." He shoved another guard back out through the opening. "'Cause let me tell you there's going to be blood everywhere after that."

A blast of plasma hit the wall next to him, and he closed his eyes in reflex and shoved away from it, bumping into several of the bio alts and knocking them out of its line of fire. He ducked past a guard who wasn't so lucky.

Hands grabbed him and pulled him to safety, and then a solid, ominous thump sounded next to his ear on the other side of the metal wall.

His ears buzzed.

The station shifted, and he felt grav tug at him. "Hang on! Hold! Hold!" he shouted and scrambled for a handhold. "Bloody ass timing!"

DEV HUNCHED OVER her scanner, a frown on her face as she studied the screen.

Outside, the two bio alts in their exosuits maneuvered a manual lock over a long tube with shackles at the end that would fasten to the shuttle's airlock and make it part of station.

Jess watched this intently, given that she was tumbling idly in null all the while. "Hey, Dev."

"Yes?"

"If they hook that thing up, will the station start turning again?"

Dev looked up and out of the plas. "It might. The interlocks are designed to cut out if they detect something coming in that will collide, like the shuttle. That's why we're in null right now. "

"Yes." The KayTee was busy with his head inside the console, a small glow light stuck to his head as he worked on the grid. "We would feel that sometimes, but they always warned ahead." He set a switch and regarded the wires then removed another. "This shuttle is early."

Jess paused in her flipping. "Yeah? How early?"

"Two days. It's very unusual," he said. "I didn't hear it was supposed to be early and we usually do because we help with the offloading of the supplies."

Jess drifted down and paused at Dev's shoulder. "Devvie, type in this sequence into your little gizmo. 35,4,2003, Graph."

Dev obediently tapped it in and waited. "What is that?"

The screen updated. "Pineapple," Dev read it out.

"Hhmp." Jess looked up and watched them attach the lock. She could hear the long, grinding thump as the manual ring locked onto them. A moment later the shuttle was turning with the station, and they felt the rotation start up. "Where does that leave out? That tube?"

"There, but—" Dev felt herself shift as the station ring engaged. "What does the pineapple mean, Jess?"

"Hopefully, something good." Jess drifted to the floor and started for the large, heavy lock that separated the mech station from the large central core. "Wait for me here, just in case it ain't."

Dev got up and slung her scanner over her shoulder. "I should go with you."

Jess paused at the hatch. "Do me a favor and just hang out a few minutes?" She reached a hand out before she could really think about it, grabbed the rotating lock, and gave it a wrench. "Not sure what's on the other end of this."

Dev frowned.

"Just for a minute," Jess said. "If I start yelling come after my ass." She ducked through the hatch and slammed it behind her.

"That really is an interesting natural born," the KayTee remarked then went back to his task. "I'm glad grav is back. These attachments kept floating away."

Dev perched on the edge of a console and looked at the hatch unhappily. Then she stood up and went to the hatch and gave the locks a decisive spin, and the door opened. "If incorrect things start, please try to warn us, KayTee."

"The agent said for you to stay."

"I did not say I would." Dev yanked the door back. "Doctor Dan gave me the programming to make up my own mind. So I'm going to. Be safe." She ducked through the hatch and closed it behind her, dogging it shut and taking a breath of the cold, space smelling air of the emergency lock.

Peculiar smell, a mixture of ions and dust that got up into her nose and tickled it. Jess was already far ahead of her and out of sight. Dev scrambled quickly to catch up, the tube flexing under her steps as she kept to the center, balancing easily.

She got to a bend in the tube and brought her scanner around, tuning it as she bounced through the joint and found herself coming up on Jess somewhat unexpectedly as she heard a throat cleared in front of her. "Oh!"

Jess stood there, hands in her pockets, a faint smile on her face, just watching her.

They looked at each other for a long moment. "I really wanted to go with you," Dev said, apologetically.

Jess reached up and scratched the bridge of her nose then she held a hand out. "Hope you always do," she said, as Dev scrambled over to join her. "Techs are supposed to listen to us, but you know what, Dev? Do what your gut tells you and it works out most times."

"Is that what you do?"

"Always."

They heard a bang ahead of them and shouting. Jess broke into a run, letting out a yell of her own.

The floor of the tube flexed under their steps and they could only see a few feet ahead, but then the sound of something hitting flesh came through with complete clarity, and as they bounded around the last part of the lock they got a good look at the entryway.

The emergency lock was fastened to the shuttle and there were struts clamped onto the station structure holding it in place. Past it, the rotation ring was in motion, and a blast of sunlight suddenly lit everything up as they came around to the day side of the planet.

It made everyone blink and Jess put a hand up to shield her eyes as she fought to see what was ahead of them.

The shuttle door was open and two figures stumbled out, blasters forward, hopping over a body that tumbled limply out in front of them while a roar of sound rose at their back. The lead figure saw something shadowy approaching and lifted their blaster, pointing it.

"Hey!" Jess shouted. "Don't shoot!"

"Drake!" The second figure said at the same time. "Don't shoot!"

"Doug!" Dev yelped in surprise. "What are you doing here?"

They came together in a rush and heads poked out behind them. "Let me get the trash out of the way first," Doug said. "April, get off this guy's hand, woudlja?"

"Shut up." April caught her breath, her face decorated with several cuts, mostly healed. "Son of a bitch, Drake, thank the piss ass we found you."

"Drake!" Voices behind her called out. "It's the Drake!"

"I hoped it was you." Jess looked past her. "You bring half the Bay with you?"

"Yes."

"Bad?"

"Fucked up beyond belief," April said. "Where do I start? Never mind that. Get in here so we can go back and kick some ass everyone told us you had to be with us for."

"What?" Jess peered past the two Interforce agents. "Jake?"

"Jess." Her brother Jake came out of the hatch, looking white around the eyes. "The fucking bastards shut us down. They fucking came in and shot people. What the fuck? We spilled blood for them for a dozen generations!"

"Hold on a minute." Jess watched Doug drag two bodies clear of the shuttle. "What's that all about?"

"Fucking pilots," April spat. "Fucking sleezy bastards who were on the take from the other side and nearly fucking killed all of us." She kicked one of the bodies viciously.

Jess put her hands back in her pockets. "So Interforce came in and took over the Bay?"

"Yes," Jake said. "I can't fucking believe it. We gave them what they asked for, and they brought a crapload of guns in and started shooting."

Jess suddenly got very serious. "They killed people?"

"Two hundred." Jake glared at her. "Two fucking hundred, Jess! Like it was nothing! What the hell!"

"Money does things to people," Jess said in a remote tone. She glanced at the entryway that was full of big bodies in Bay colors. "How many people ya got?"

"Fifty," April said. "I rounded them up, and we ambushed the shuttle when it landed. Fuckers had them all ready to load on all that plant crap and take it somewhere."

That sounded horrible. Dev wasn't sure what to do or say, she was just aware that there was much uncertainty, and much incorrectness going on and that Jess was very angry.

Doug came and stood next to Dev. "Aside from that, how's it been Rocket?" He folded his arms over his broad chest. "Don't mind April. She's been upchucking since we left downside, and it's pissing her off."

"It's been really suboptimal actually," Dev said. "I am glad to see you and April, however, and it's excellent that you obtained a shuttle. We were going to do something highly incorrect to a working craft from here and probably be made dead in the process of returning to downside otherwise."

Doug pointed at the shuttle. "Can ya fly that? Cause April offed everyone inside who might have been able to."

"I see." Dev studied the shuttle and hiked her eyebrows. "This could get interesting as I have absolutely no programming on that at all."

"Oh boy."

"So like I said, Drake, let's get to getting. I can't wait to splat those fucking bastards," April said, "before they take off with everything on another shuttle."

"Right," Jake said. "Jess, it needs you to release all the locks. Because Jimmy's no longer around."

"Okay, hold it." Jess put her hands up. "I can't just go on there. We've got some civs we have to get clear."

"Jess, we don't have time," Jake said. "They're gonna just tank the whole place." He grabbed hold of her arm. "What here's worth more than that?"

"Right," April said. "Leave 'em. What I hear everyone up here's a fucktard anyway."

Jess looked at them. "I've got to go get Kurok out of here," she said, seeing the protest. "He's family."

"Shit." April wiped the sweat off her forehead with her sleeve. "I have no idea what that even means," she said. "Can we just get the hell out of here?"

"What do you care about family, Jess? You said, and the old woman said, no one was family to you anymore. I just want to save enough patch to not have to live on the beach," Jake said bluntly. "So get your fucking ass on the shuttle and clean up your mess."

"My mess?" Jess's body posture shifted. "Tayler's here, Jake."

He went quiet. "Tayler?"

"That was the price," Jess said. "He was the merch our brother sold to this place for the green stuff. They were going to make more of me to sell the other side."

"For real?" One of the figures in the hatch moved forward. "The kid's here, Drake?"

Dev took a step forward and turned her scanner around to display the screen. It showed Tayler playing ball in the lab.

Everyone went a little quiet. "Compounded fuckedupitness. Screw it," April finally said. "We're out of time."

"You're wasting what time we have." Jess motioned the crowd forward. "Everyone got a bat? Knife? Something? C'mon with me." She started back down the accessway, guiding Doug and Dev ahead of her. "Devvie, how many people'll fit in that thing?"

"It's a storage shuttle," Dev said. "Not sure it will be comfortable for people."

"Better than croaked?"

"About two-hundred." Dev reached the hatch first and opened it, shoving it inward to clear space for the crowd behind her. "KayTee?"

"Watch out!" the KayTee choked out. "W—"

Dev instinctively dove for the ground as a rush of bodies came past her, swarming over the two guards holding KayTee down.

The guards actually screamed in terror and very quickly were made dead.

"Booya!" One of the Bay fighters laughed. "Now that's more like it." He twirled the large, curved knife he'd cut the guards open with and returned it to a sheath at his belt. "Good stuff."

"C'mon." Jess hauled Dev up and started through the core space. "Sooner we go, sooner we leave."

THE SHIELDS WERE failing. Kurok knew it was a losing cause as he got another box in the way and the KayTee tacked it down with the heat torch. Half the front of the entrance was crumpled, and he heard the sound of a mech moving outside, getting ready to ram.

A BeeAye came over to him. "Doctor Dan. There's a hatch over there. You can escape with the little boy. We'll make them stop long enough."

"Thank you, BeeAye. But I don't want to escape, and there's nowhere for me and young Tayler to go." He patted BeeAye on the arm. "If things are going to go so terribly wrong and you all are in danger, I want to be here with you."

All around bodies paused and turned toward him, eyes in every shade of humanity focused on his face. "Well," he said into that momentary silence. "Of course. You all are my children, after all."

"Kurok!" A loud and mechanical sounding voice echoed against the crumpled metal. "Surrender, and the rest of them will be allowed to go back to the crèche."

"No they won't," Kurok yelled back. "You're going to kill all of us, so what's the point? Keep hammering. Maybe I'll get annoyed enough to decompress the section."

"I think that will cause us a lot of discomfort," a CeeDee murmured.

"Only for a moment," he answered, gently. "As far as ways to die go, it's pretty painless. I promise." He limped over to where the cracks were starting in the edge of the doorway and then touched the comms in his ear, again without response.

Maybe Jess and Dev had gotten hurt.

Likely they had gotten hurt. Perhaps they'd gotten terminally hurt and they were drifting in vacuum. Kurok sighed, his face tensing in discomfort. "So damn pointless." He put a piece of steel against the cracks. "Tack it here, would you, KayTee?"

"Yes." The KayTee came over, looking very discomfited. "I'm sorry we couldn't do better work, Doctor Dan. This feels very suboptimal."

"Yes, it does, doesn't it?" Kurok regarded the crumpled entryway, its padlock flashing a dull, repeating red. "What's your crèche name, KayTee?"

The KayTee put the torch down. "Kevin," he said. "I haven't used it in a very long time, though."

Kurok clasped his shoulder. "Thank you, Kevin. Now all of you please go back to the back of the lab. I'm going to go outside and see if I can talk to these people who are trying to hurt us."

A burst of objection rose immediately. "Doctor Dan, they'll do bad things to you," the CeeDee said. "Don't go."

He turned to face them. "Yes, they will. But I would like to try talking to them first. Please be safe here." He gave them all a smile then went to the hatch and put his hand on it, feeling the vibration as the shielded entry started to cycle.

THEY SQUEEZED THROUGH the central core entry hatch, the space that was already somewhat tight for bio alts becoming breathless and overwhelmed with the fifty residents of Drake's Bay making their way through.

"Hah. Like the eject tubes," Dustin said as he followed Jess closely. "Sup, cuz? Major cluster, huh?"

"Major," Jess responded shortly. Already her mind was casting ahead, getting past the task on station, past the uncertainty of returning, past to the driving need that made her heart thunder.

Protect the homestead. Jess knew a sense of personal horror at the knowledge that she'd, without question, brought this on them. Despite what she'd said to Jake, this was her mess.

Her mess. Thoughtless stupid monkey brain.

"More fun than limpet collect," Dustin said. "S'allright."

Monkey brain like her cousin Dustin, who was a big, stupid, simple minded man that thankfully had a good humored personality that let him move past the taunts and jabs of his family.

Dev was at her heels and now, and for some reason reached

up and touched Jess's arm. Just a single, simple squeeze and release as though Dev heard the thoughts going through her head.

Could she? Jess glanced at her then went back to reviewing the ladder she was climbing. No time for that.

Despite the crush, they all moved as quietly as they could, the rustle of Bay outerwear and the rasp of boots against the rungs of the close pinned ladders. It smelled of salt dusted cloth, and as Jess took a breath of that, it brought back a single, vivid memory of some long ago time, back in the Bay.

A brief rumble of phantom thunder tickled her ears and the echo of her father's voice.

Around them, the station was in shuddering motion, a thick, uneasy vibration they could feel through the internal structure they were climbing. "Don't kick anything," Jess said after a few minutes. "Thing's made of tin foil and goat spit."

The bio alts with them frowned a little. "That is not actually true, Agent Drake," the BeeAye said in a timid voice. "Tin is a naturally occurring element not easily synthesized and not much used on station. We mostly use steel alloy."

The Bay residents rumbled in low laughter. Jess remained silent, speeding up her motion as they reached the centerpoint in the core and were near an exit. "Quiet," she ordered in a low voice, and they all hushed.

She reached the platform and held a hand up with her fist closed, and everyone went still behind her, either voluntarily or not, as the fighters took hold of the bios and brought them to a halt.

Jess moved to the big hatch and put her hands against it and leaned close. Then she straightened and undid the locking mechanism, pausing before she disengaged it. "Bios are friendly. Anything else is up for grabs."

Dustin eased onto the platform next to her, his tall form matching hers and more in breadth. "What're we after, Jess?" he asked as two more Bay fighters eased up next to him.

"The doc and Tayler," Jess said.

He nodded.

"Bios that are with the doc," Jess said with a note of finality.

Dustin looked at her. "We want bios? Don't much think we do, cuz," he said, his wiry, dark eyebrows contracting. "Don't got time for that, yeah? Lot of dead to do back home."

"We want these," Jess said. "Let's go." She yanked the hatch inward and slid out, into the bisection of passageways that was

the station's center. "There'll be time enough for killing."

Jake had squirmed his way up to the front lines. "If there's anything left."

"There'll be." Jess grabbed him and shoved him ahead of her. "If nothing else they know I'll be coming back there and they know, better than most, about my kind of vengeance."

Behind her, the fifty fighters emerged and got their weapons out, forming up in an automatic squad.

Bit of born in, bit of training as part of the domestic defense. Jess motioned them forward and took lead point, with April at her side. Doug and Dev followed with scanners out, the bio alts behind them looking intimidated and unsure.

"Stay next to us," Dev told them. "If loud and bad things start happening, lie down."

A KayTee nodded.

The central hall was empty. They heard loud sounds from ahead, though, and Jess's ears pricked as she caught a familiar voice. "Ah."

"That's Doctor Dan," Dev said. "He sounds mad."

Desperate, Jess silently disagreed. Furious, desperate, and grandstanding, and without hope of rescue.

"We should go help him," a KayTee said.

Jess smiled grimly. "Oh, we will."

Chapter Eleven

KUROK GOT THE entry sealed behind him before anyone in the passage beyond realized he was there.

Two big mechanical donks were in position to smash the walls. Beyond them all the security forces the station had were poised, and with them a group of dark clad forms that made Kurok's very blood boil.

No taking that out of him.

Doss was behind a shield. "Daniel! Don't resist!"

He took the blaster from his front pocket and took the safety off, squaring his body to the entryway and lifting his head. "Kiss my ass, Randall!"

"We have to stop you. We know what you did." Doss yelled back.

"What I did?" Kurok bellowed. "Do they know what you did?"

A blaster shot blinked into his eyes, and without thought he brought up his own weapon and fired, intersecting it and sending the energy against the nearby wall. "What you did? Randall? That you sold us out for a little boy?"

Doss came out in the open with a repeater. "They don't care. Daniel, you don't understand. You never did understand. They want money. They want credit. They want things they can sell to let them build up beautiful places to live and to have good things to eat." He took a breath. "They don't care at all how we get it to them."

No, that was true. "So that makes it okay?" Kurok drew in a breath and prepared himself. It was going to be ugly and painful and hopefully, short. "Okay for you to buy a little kid to make killers? Really, Randall?"

"Better than programming bio alts to take over." Doss looked at him in angry triumph. "Which one of us is the bigger bastard, Daniel?"

A moment of silence. Then Kurok smiled. "Me." He lifted the blaster, and before Doss could even move, he targeted and shot, the energy blast hitting the director between the eyes and blowing his head off.

Then he turned toward the defense forces. "C'mon and get me you little stinkweeds!" he roared, facing them all and feeling

that wonderful, fatalistic ferocity, that rush of throwing the future to the winds.

He'd learned that from Justin. One the hardest lessons of all.

"Take him!" the security chief bawled. "He killed the director!"

A surge of bodies started toward him, and he brought the blaster down and gripped it two handed, finger on the release as the roar of the security troops suddenly was intersected by a deeper roar that threw the certainty into abrupt doubt.

He knew that yell.

He looked to his right, to the recently empty hallway leading to central that was now filling with surrealisticly large bodies holding makeshift weapons, dressed in downside clothing. "Son of a bitch. Never thought I'd be glad to see them."

Them was an undisciplined, raw, slightly mad-eyed bunch of hulksters, each with a bludgeon to hand, all ready to create mayhem. As unexpected and outlandish a scene as ever seen on the station in its history.

Outnumbered six to one, but it didn't matter. Jess and April were in the lead, with mil issued blasters that came around and started targeting, leaping past the startled guards, returning shots as they moved into an attack.

The guards really had no idea what was hitting them. Unused to the blasters they were now armed with, they didn't have the instinct or the stomach for a hand to hand battle, and they started going down by the dozens.

April and Dev were almost lost in the group. Jess herself looked average amongst them, her near seven foot frame just notable for the silverstrike motions and the speed, as she led troops from the Bay right into the clustered body of security.

Rambling and ferocious, bearing bats, knives, and just the strength of their bodies, those fifty people started ripping apart the station guards with glee, savoring the conflict in an odd and very dysfunctional way.

Fearless. Uncaring. Exulting in the violence. The legacy of Drake's Bay Interforce had tapped into, shaped and focused and released out into the world.

Dev and Doug raced toward him. Kurok put the gun away, setting aside the need for sacrifice for the moment. "Well, that was unexpected," he said as they arrived. "I take it you all came on the shuttle?"

"Something terrible happened downside, Doctor Dan," Dev said. "People hurt a lot of the natural borns at Jess's place." She

hesitated. "People from our assignment."

Kurok blinked. "People from Interforce?"

"Yeah," Doug said. "So we kinda need to get you and get outta here so they can go fix that." He turned and regarded the bloodshed. "They need Jess, and she wouldn't leave without ya."

Kurok clapped his hand to his forehead. "Jesus." He turned and headed for the hatch. "I can't just go." A step from the entry and it opened, and bio alts started pouring out of the lab, all of them carrying some piece of structure, looking terrified yet determined, ready to fight.

Surprised to see him, they paused, seeing the carnage. "Doctor Dan," Cathy said. "We were so afraid you'd gotten hurt." She had a hammer in her hand, apparently ready to use it. "What's go...oh." She paused. "What is that? Who are those people?"

Kurok looked back at the melee. "Those people are what Randall Doss wanted to sell to the other side, actually. But there's really no time to talk about that. You'll get to see them close up soon enough."

"Doctor Dan, Jess said to bring you and Tayler and the people here to the shuttle," Dev said. "We have to go quickly."

"Yeah," Doug agreed. "Before the yonks start tearing apart the station once they're finished with those guys, y'know?" He glanced past into the lab. "We got room for two-hundred."

It was all happening too fast. "Cathy, let's get everyone from the lab to the shuttle zone." Kurok said, in a determinedly calm voice. "I have to shut down the systems."

"Understood, doctor." Cathy ducked back inside, calling to the two other lab assistants as she squirmed through the now excited bio alts. "Everyone line up! We're going to go with Doctor Dan!"

He got through the crowd and went to his office and sat behind his desk. Dev and Doug had followed him in, and were now seated across from him, just waiting. They had oil smudges on them, and Doug was bruised and hollow eyed.

"Anything we can do to help?" Doug asked, pointing to himself and then at Dev. "Or really," he pointed at Dev again.

"Not really." Kurok called up all the schemas. "Most of this is scripted. It's not like I hadn't thought about coming to this moment."

Dev had her scanner out and was focused on it. "There are power fluctuations going on."

"Yes, I know," Kurok murmured. "Damn it."

A moment later, Jess was filling the doorway, bringing a scent of blood with her. "Gotta move, Doc."

"Yes, just getting rid of any evidence." Kurok was busy with his pad. "Thank you, by the way. I was about to get definitively squashed in a particularly grandstanding way."

"Heard ya." Jess looked behind her. The crowd of bio alts were rapidly depleting, and Tayler had already been picked up by a cousin and carried out. The guards were taken care of, the outer area scattered with bodies and the rest escaped into passageways screaming in fear.

Truly screaming. Running as fast as they could to get away from the butchers lunging after them.

She was aware of time ticking. "Doc?"

"Finished." Kurok got up and then paused. "But you could go on with out me, Jess. I still have responsibility here."

"No."

"Jesslyn."

"They'll kill you. What would the point be?" Jess said. "They've got six monitors from the other side here. Ya see them? They probably got comms off before they were ripped apart by my cousins." She motioned them all forward. "Let's go. "

Dev and Doug moved outside. Jess remained in the doorway. Kurok hesitated behind his desk. "Doc."

He sighed. "All those children I'd leave behind," he said quietly. "I don't know if I can, Jess."

Jess regarded him in silence for a moment then extended her hand. "You gave them the best chance you could. We killed most of the witnesses," she said. "Come with us, we're taking some kids, too. They'll need you down there."

He sighed again.

"Besides, you probably know how to fly the shuttle." Jess went on. "April skunked all the pilots. It's kinda up to Dev." She wiggled her fingers. "C'mon. She could use a hand."

"Shit." He reached into a small cabinet near the desk and removed a large, patched, well worn pack that he slipped onto his back. "I hope I got all the vid. Especially of me blasting Doss's head off."

"That was a nice shot," Jess said. "Bastard deserved it."

Kurok sighed. "No one ever deserves death, Jesslyn. They're just in the wrong place at the wrong time."

Jess put a hand on his back and guided him to the door. "You know better than most," she said. "That's horse shit."

They left the lab and crossed the floor of the now empty

space, and as they reached the edge he turned and looked at it, then shook his head and followed Jess out and into the central hall.

Carnage. There were bodies all over the floor, all in security jumpsuits. Some interspersed with the neutral clothes of station operations and two of the dark figures that were the monitors from the other side, who really weren't anything of the sort.

Spies. But they had a business relationship, and Kurok figured that was who had brokered the deal, and he barely glanced at them as he and Jess passed them by. The troops from the Bay were already gone, and now all that moved were a few bio alt sets, looking at all the mess in deep confusion.

Despair really.

"Take them all to the disposal stations, lads," Kurok said. "Don't worry. Things will be back to normal soon."

"Thank you, Doctor Dan," one of them said, with a wan sort of wave. "Goodbye. We will try to do good work. Please be safe."

They knew. "I will, and you, too." Kurok put it out of his mind but he, too, knew. He knew horrible things were going to happen to these sets, all of them under the taint of his machinations. "Wish I could take all of them with me."

"Yeah." Jess glanced at them. "Sucks."

They walked side by side up the hall. "Anxious to get home?" he asked, finally.

"Anxious to unfuck my fuckup," Jess responded tersely. "They offed around two-hundred."

"Dev told me. Sorry, Jess."

She shook her head. "Let's just get the hell out of here."

Kurok was glad the halls were empty. Everywhere he looked was just space, empty tubes, no sound at all of work or motion or people. He really didn't know if they were all just in lockdown, or what, since he'd deactivated pretty much everything including internal comms.

He remembered, suddenly, his arrival on station. All those years ago when he'd traded one life for another, half his thoughts on the future and half on the past.

Now an echo of his past walked alongside him, and those two lives were coming together again, and he tried to decide exactly how he felt about it.

Torn. He had to admit to himself. Torn between the agony of leaving behind everything he had created here and the almost shameful relief he felt in the sense he was going home.

Home was downworld. Home was storms, and water, and the

harshness of icy wet air, and in some way Drakes and Drake's
Bay, even though he'd been hated there for being one of the
enemy.

Even being a tech and Justin's friend, it was written so deep
in them. He glanced at Jess. In them, but not in her, because Jess
trusted wholly in her father's judgment.

Ironic.

They reached the shuttle area and found April waiting, her
gun resting on her shoulder.

"How we doing?" Jess asked.

"All onboard," she said. "You done?"

"Done." Jess said.

"Y'know bringing those bios with us is jackass," April said.
"Should not have. Don't appreciate it since I broke my ass getting
that thing up here."

Jess pushed past her. "Let's fight about that later." She half
turned and looked past them, finding no sign of anyone looking
back at them. "Let's just see if we can make it back." She
continued down the tube toward the shuttle.

April looked at Kurok, who had turned to take one last scan
of station. His eyes met hers. "They're worth something, you
know," he said. "And I suspect you believe Dev is."

"You're worth something. She is." April conceded. "The rest
of them will probably be chum by the time that thing gets down.
If it does." She pulled the gun down as they followed Jess.
"Jackass." She shook her head.

"Wouldn't bet on that," Kurok said. "Drakes are many
things, but they're neither sentimental nor stupid."

"Mmph." April grunted.

DEV SPENT SEVERAL minutes just sitting in the seat of the
control station in the shuttle. The position was large and far more
padded than the one in the carrier, and it was tilted just slightly
back. It was comfortable, but she took no comfort from it, since it
was all very strange to her eyes.

She had, she realized, zero programming about the craft, and
Doug seated next to her was wide eyed and staring. "Hmm."

"Fuckin' hmm," Doug said. "You even know what to start
with?"

"They never give bio alts any programming about shuttles,"
Dev said. "I think they're..." She paused. "They didn't want us to
know about them." She drew the restraints down and fastened

them around her and angled the seat forward so she could reach the controls. "But there has to be some logic to it."

"Are you just going to start punching buttons until something lights?" Doug asked in a mildly alarmed tone. "Like a rocket, Rocket?"

"Possibly." Dev rested her hands on the control surfaces. She looked at him. "Unless you have a more efficient suggestion?"

Doug shook his head and folded his arms over his chest. "Not me. I got top marks in wrenching, but I had to take flight dynamics three times to pass. Not my gig."

Dev figured that was the case. She inspected the panels, then watched alertly as one of the red lights on the one near her left hand went out. "I think they have sealed the door," she said. "I hope that is a positive event."

"I'll go see if everyone's on or if someone did something stupid. I'm not leaving April in a tube." Doug scrambled for the door and ducked outside. "Much as she'd prefer not to ride back." He closed the hatch behind him and it sealed, compressing the air a little.

Now that Dev was alone with the shuttle, she tentatively pushed a button. After a moment, the panel to her right lit up and she heard the faint whine of systems coming live. "Fortunate guess," she muttered.

There was a helmet, not an ear cup, and she settled it onto her head, hearing the murmurs of various things reporting. She pressed another key, and the board to her left lit up. Then the seat she was in shifted and the restraints tightened.

"Another fortunate guess." Dev studied the results, carefully reviewing the control surfaces and deciding she did, in fact, know which controls were for the maneuvering jets.

She hoped.

Plasma ignitors entering prestage warmup, the vehicle whispered into her ear. *Stand by to test seals. Energy levels to twelve point two, section seals in work.*

She was tired. They hadn't gotten any rest in many, many hours, and she was hungry. She wanted to be gone from the station, no matter that returning downside promised nothing but more trouble, and there were still parts of her a little tender where her uniform rubbed the back of her neck.

Everything seemed very incorrect. So many people had gotten hurt, or made dead, and they had a little over two hundred of the sets onboard, all crammed into a space, all nervous.

All wanting to go but not go. Afraid of the change, but

holding on to the notion that they were there with Doctor Dan, and he'd make it right. Dev exhaled. If he could. If she could, with this strange craft she was poking at.

"Okay, we're all onboard. Doc and Jess just closed it up." Doug returned to the cockpit and resumed the other seat. "April's really pissed off."

"Well, this would be easier if we had pilots," Dev said. "So I am sorry if she is not pleased, but that did not make it better."

Doug grunted. "Yeah, probably," he said. "But they were skunks, and we'd probably have had to put a gun to their heads to get them to do anything anyway."

"I see."

"They were talking to that other shuttle and trying to figure out how to screw us up," Doug said. "They said they got paid better by the other side."

Dev regarded him with some surprise. "For the supplies?"

"Nah. For contraband. Had a good market here."

The door to the cockpit opened and Jess stuck her head in. "Hey."

"Hello." Dev cautiously activated the pre-start for the maneuvering jets. "Did someone disconnect this vehicle? I don't want to attempt to move otherwise."

Jess had taken a breath to say something, now she just grunted, turned and left again, slamming the door behind her.

"Guess everyone's pissed off," Doug said. "What happens if they have to do it from the outside like they did when we came in?"

"I can make the shuttle break loose." Dev responded. "But it will do a lot of damage and possibly cause some for us—" She heard yelling outside the door and she and Doug exchanged glances. "That doesn't sound good."

With an abrupt motion Dev released her restraints and got up, leaving the helmet on the seat before going to the door and shoving it open.

Outside there was an argument going on. Jess and April were facing off with one of the people from Drake's Bay and one of the lab assistants from Doctor Dan's lab. Dev went over to Jess and touched her arm.

Jess paused and looked at her.

"What's going on?" Dev asked. "I thought we wanted to leave quickly?"

"Well we can't, as you reminded me." Jess said. "We're still tied up to this damned thing."

"I can rip free," Dev said, quietly. "But it might be dangerous."

"More dangerous than being in a tin can hanging off a busted station in the creepiness of space?" Jess asked. "G'wan. Risk it."

"And kill all these poor bastards you waited so long to save?" April grumbled. "Why not just blow the whole damn thing up?"

"Enough," Jess barked loudly. "Let's wait to get out of here before we all start acting like assholes." She turned to Dev. "Do what you have to, Dev. I'm going to go make sure everything's tied down."

Doctor Dan appeared, looking as tired and upset as Dev felt. "I think I can help. Let's go to the control room, Dev. If I can communicate to station, I can get the locks released. Since they're so locked down they can't."

"Thanks, doc." Jess pressed against the bulkhead to let him and Dev pass, then moved off in another direction.

"Thanks, Doctor Dan." Dev led him back to the cockpit, leaving the rest of them behind. "I'm not really sure of how to do this," she admitted. "A lot of this is really strange."

Kurok patted her on the back. "We'll sort it out, Dev. Anything to keep my mind of leaving everyone back there."

More unhappiness. Dev got back in the seat and put the helmet back on. She moved to one side to let Doctor Dan get to the machinery. "I have the engine systems started," she said. "And the plasma ignitors in prep."

"So you do." Kurok sat down on a jumpseat next to the comms board. "I know some of the boards here, Dev. We'll do it together."

Doug got up. "Want to sit here?"

Kurok waved him back. "Let's take the opportunity for everyone to learn, shall we?"

Doug sat back down. "Sure." He put on the restraints. "Might as well learn something before we blow up getting down."

THE CARGO HOLD was a disaster waiting to happen. Jess glared dourly at the interior of it, filled with terrified bio alts and Bay personnel.

April was right. This was idiotic. She shouldn't have done it, and what made it worse was she couldn't actually articulate why she had.

The cargo area wasn't meant for passengers. It had a multitude of strapping and tie downs, though, and they had

made the best of that, bios snugged in groups next to each other
with the sturdy plas over them to keep them in place. Those from
the Bay in makeshift restraints.

The homesteaders were in a pretty good mood, given
everything. Most of them were talking about the fight. When they
looked up and saw her, they waved in cheerful good nature.

Jess lifted a hand and waved back

There was a small area for riding crew and an even smaller
area for critical cargo. That was about it. "Fuck."

Jake was at her side. "Clusterfuck."

"Yeah," Jess said. "Let's just get it over with."

Jake didn't respond to that. He just took a breath and
released it. There was a lurid bruise across his left cheek, and he
held his arm at an awkward angle. "There a point?" he finally
asked.

Jess shrugged.

Jake also shrugged. "Ah, couple of hours won't make a craps
difference anyway," he said. "What the fuck. At least we got Tay
back and had a good fight."

"They knew you all took the shuttle?" Jess asked after a long
pause.

He nodded. "Oh yeah. I got that stupid bastard you left in
charge in the eyeball with a fish pike on my way to the ramp." He
reflected on that. "Felt pretty good actually."

Jess managed a wry, tight smile. "Finally came into that
Drake heritage, huh?"

He considered that for a moment, then smiled back. "Yeah,
maybe. I was just so mad I forgot to worry about anything else."
He kicked the edge of the cargo entryway with the toe of his boot.
"Felt like...I don't know."

"Felt like riding a wave down into the rocks and not caring,"
Jess said. "We all have it, Jake. In or out just a matter of degree."

"Mmm." He shrugged one shoulder. "Didn't feel bad. I liked
it. Got my frustration out anyway."

"Why come get me then?" Jess asked, as she felt a rumbling
vibration start under her boots. "Fucking finish it on your own,
Jake. Maybe that's your place anyway." She folded her arms. "I'd
have probably splatted up here."

Jake looked at her. "You really don't know?" He sounded
honestly surprised. "Fish pikes against long rifles? WTF, Jess?"
He turned to face her. "You need to kick that off. Did you really
not know that? Not know it has to be the Drake who does that?"
He watched her face. "Oh shit you really didn't."

"No," Jess said after a long awkward pause. "Why the hell would I? No one ever told me."

The shuttle shifted gently. "I better go see if we're going to kill ourselves now or a little later." She pushed back from the doorway. "At least Dev figured out how to make this thing move."

He followed her. "That's at least one useful jelly onboard."

Jess stopped and looked back at him.

He met the stare for a moment, then he lifted both hands, shoulder level, palms out. "Okay. There's Drakes and then there's Drakes. I like your tech. I just don't understand why you brought the rest of them."

"Neither do I," Jess responded honestly. "But sometimes, with my kind of Drakes, little voices in our heads make us do things." She walked over to the cockpit and went inside, closing the panel firmly behind her.

"OKAY, WE'RE LOOSE." Doctor Dan rested his elbows on his knees. "Back off, Dev."

Dev gently triggered the maneuvering jets and felt the motion as the craft responded, pulling back away from station at a surprisingly fast clip. In the front screen the stanchions and supports of the shuttle bay moved away and got smaller, and they could see more of the area.

The next bay, where the enemy shuttle had been was full of damage. Frost covered lumps were caught on the platforms and bays, and in some cases had drifted out of the station rotation and were in their own independent orbits now.

The rest of station seemed surprisingly intact. Dev could see the arrays, the upper still inactive, but the lower fully articulated and turning to catch the rising sun coming up over the edge of the planet. Her body likewise lifted as they lost grav and were in null.

"Uh, oh," Doug muttered. "Hope April has her chuck bag." He tightened his restraints and watched what Dev was doing. "How in the hell do you know how to do that?" he asked. "You told me they didn't tell you guys anything."

Dev was busy scanning all the panels, watching the readings. "Well," she said, "it is flying, sort of."

Behind her the door opened and a quick glance in the reflection of the screen showed Jess entering. That made her feel better, even though Jess still looked upset.

Jess edged up behind her chair and found a jumpseat lashed up against the wall. She unfolded it, sat down, and pulled the restraints over her tall frame and fastened them.

All in silence.

"Okay, now, thrust forward, Dev." Doctor Dan's voice sounded sureally normal. "We want to come around the station and take a course counter to the planet's rotation."

"Yes." Dev made the adjustments with only a bit of hesitation. "Would you prefer to do this, Doctor Dan? I really don't have any programming for any of this."

Kurok shook his head immediately. "I have a good handle on the theory, Dev, but I'd rather trust your instincts with the actual reality."

"Me too," Jess said.

"Me three," Doug offered.

Dev gave all of them a quick look. "Thank you." She cleared her throat. "I think." She paused then looked around as she felt a warm pressure on her shoulder, only to find Jess just resting her cheek there.

Jess looked so unhappy. Dev felt like she wanted to hand off this shuttle thing to someone else and just concentrate on resolving that unhappiness. "Jess?"

Those pale blue eyes looked up at her and for a long moment the shuttle was on it's own. Then Jess's lips quirked and she winked one eye, exhaling audibly.

"Dev?" Kurok said quietly.

"Yes?" Dev returned her attention to her mentor. "Twenty-seven degrees to the angle of planetary inclination. Acceleration point two four."

"That's not bad for not having any programming, Dev," he said.

"I am spooling the checklists into my comms." Dev glanced at her screens. "They have been somewhat helpful."

It was right then, Jess decided, that Kurok got a gut shot look at what he'd actually done with Dev. She could see the look in his eyes and the faint motion as he kept his jaw from dropping, and she was glad. It took her mind of her own troubles.

He'd known, at an intellectual level. Now he knew from being smacked in the face with it, and it almost made Jess smile, that look on his face. "That's my Devvie," she said. "I've got more guts than brains. Good thing you made her the other way around."

Dev cleared her throat again. "I suggest we wait to see if I can successfully do this before continuing with this type of discourse."

That did get a smile from Jess. She reached over and gave Dev's bicep a squeeze.

Slightly comforted, Dev went back to her input pad, listening to the instructions in her headset. Just bare pilot's checklists, but as she scanned the vast array of controls, some of the names started to match.

Much more complex than the carrier. Two sets of engines, one for space and one for atmosphere, and thousands of systems readouts she wasn't familiar with.

She felt uneasy and squirmy in her guts as she acknowledged how much responsibility was on her shoulders. Her throat was dry and she licked her lips, wishing for a cold container of kack.

The shuttle dropped below the station. It was now in it's own orbit above the planet. She reached over and tapped an inquiry into the pad, the systems requiring no login. "We can allow three orbits with the existing fuel."

Kurok sat over another pad, scrunched up in the jumpseat, tapping rapidly. "Hang on there, Dev. I'm trying to remember my basic astro navigation to figure out when we need to retro." He studied the results.

Jess looked out the viewscreen. "Are we supposed to be upside down?"

"Yes," Dev said. "I have to fire the rockets to slow us down and bring us out of orbit. That has to be at a pitch angle against our forward momentum. It's not like air. There's nothing to push against."

Jess eyed her. "You really are scary sometimes." She reached for her restraints. "Do I have time to go check and make sure no one's freaking out?"

Dev scaned the controls, an unusual pucker between her brows.

"Devvie?"

Doug unbuckled his restraints and let himself float up over the chair. "I'll go check. I got used to this no gravity thing on the way up." He maneuvered his big body toward the hatch. "Doc you really can take my seat. I'm not gonna touch any of that stuff."

Kurok waited for him to clear out then unbuckled and shifted into the other chair, which had more space and better access to the panels.

Dev inspected the aerodynamic controls, her shoulders

moving in relief. The planar surfaces and the in-atmosphere engines were more familiar to her, though the size of the shuttle was almost overwhelming.

After a moment, she glanced to her left to see Jess just sitting there, looking down at the console. She reached out and put her hand on Jess's knee and slowly those blue eyes lifted and met hers. "Are you..." Dev paused. "Okay?"

"Not really," Jess responded. "I feel like crap in a handbasket."

Dev made a face. "Me too," she admitted.

Jess sighed and stretched herself out a little, drawing back when her boot impacted a bag strapped to the side of the pilot's seat. She edged to the side and reached out to open the bag. "Maybe there's an instruction book in here for ya, Devvie."

Dev looked down into it. "I don't think so, but there is something more useful." She dug into it and removed something. "Two protein bars." She handed Jess one. "It's too bad there isn't a drink."

"Thirsty?" Jess refocused her attention to something she could potentially do something about. "On it." She released the straps and pushed herself up. "We all could use something wet."

"Probably in the section between this and the crew strap downs," Kurok said. "Thank you, Jess."

"Thank me after I find some." Jess maneuvered out of the hatch and then it was quiet.

Below them, the planet turned in it's gray roiling way.

JESS FOUND THE water canisters in a slim space to one side of the cockpit. It wasn't quite where she'd been told, but close enough. She was glad to find a relatively large supply. She picked up three and sorted through the rest of the supplies.

Not a lot. The water, some more protein bars, some powdered seaweed for tea. Jess kicked off the edge of the wall and headed back for the cockpit with her burden. She got to the hatch and bumped it open with her shoulder, just as Doug returned from the other direction. "Water back in there," she said.

"Yeah, found it." He indicated a tube in one of his pockets. "This floating stuff is all right." He followed her into the cockpit, and they both settled on jumpseats to either side of the pilot console.

Jess found a drink holder and pushed one of the water tubes

into it. "There ya go, Devvie. It's just water."

"Excellent." Dev removed the container and opened up the sip tube. "Thank you, Jess."

Jess looked out the window, still seeing the planet turning beneath them. Near the top of the spinning globe she saw a huge twisting cloud, and it churned across the surface in a circle. "Look at that."

"It's what a cone looks like from the top, I think," Dev said. "I am glad we're not flying through it."

"Wow." Jess watched the storm. "Me too."

Kurok looked over from his screen. "Okay, Dev. To get back in the right area, we need to retrograde for twenty seconds, twenty minutes from now."

"Excellent," Dev said. "There is an autonomic routine for that. It will start the return from orbit."

"So we have twenty minutes to just hang out here?" Jess asked. "Nothing else to do?"

"Yes." Dev sucked at her water tube, washing down a mouthful of the protein bar. It tasted of seaweed and honey and had a chewy substance at its core that tasted like plants. Just swallowing some of it made her feel better.

"Okay." Jess rotated onto her back and just hung there in space, holding on to the back of Dev's seat with one hand. "Warn me before you push the button."

Kurok spared her a brief wry smile. Then he unclipped himself and pushed up from the seat. "Let me see how everyone is doing." He tucked and rolled and went to the hatch. "Likely to be a bit of a rough landing."

"Likely?" Doug stayed where he was in the second jumpseat, his long legs extended. "Lucky that pad near your place is clear area, Jess."

Jess regarded the ceiling of the shuttle that was covered in instrumentation softly blinking and shifting in her vision. "Yeah."

"Do we have a plan?"

"Yeah," Jess answered after a moment. "After Devvie lands us, I'm going to surrender." She glanced around after that was answered with absolute silence, to see both Doug and Dev staring at her. "Fastest way to get me into Bay ops," she explained.

"What does that get us?" Doug said.

"I see," Dev said at the same time. "Is that the location we could not get scan of?"

Jess nodded. "Interforce shielding technology comes from there."

"Really?" Doug said. "I don't remember hearing that in school."

"No, you didn't. In fact, I didn't," Jess said. "But you didn't learn about the military genetics programs there at the end of the world in school either did you?"

"No," Doug answered, after a pause. "Um...did you?"

Jess smiled grimly. "The hard way, yeah." She watched a tie down string drift past her peripheral vision. "No time for that story now." She glanced at him.

"Good," he said, with a wry smile. "I'm already scared shitless."

DEV FLEXED HER fingers and settled herself into the seat. "We're a minute from firing," she announced, giving Jess a little nudge in the ribs. "You said to warn you." she added as Jess opened an eye and peered at her.

"So I did." Jess reversed her position and settled back down on the jumpseat, using her knees to keep her in place until she fastened the restraints. "Didja warn everyone to sit their asses down?"

"I did." Kurok said. "Ground is trying to contact this shuttle. I recommend ignoring them."

"Yes," Dev agreed. "I am sure discussing what we are doing will be pointless and also non-optimal." She reviewed the controls and settled her hands on the pads. "I am ready." She took a deep breath and let it out.

Jess squared herself in the seat and pressed her shoulders back against its surface. The ride up had been less than eventful, rumbles and shaking, and at the end, the surprise and delight of null gravity. This, she understood, would be something else.

"Heat shields are online," Kurok announced. "Let's hope we didn't damage them at station."

"Light the rockets, Rocket," Doug said. "Let's go home."

"Stand by." Dev hit the pre-ignitors, and they heard a soft, ethereal whine through the cockpit along with a soft rumble. "Engine bells are clear of residual gas. The firing script has started."

A moment later, they felt the motion as the rockets fired and the vibration went through every surface in the cockpit. It went on for what seemed like a very long time and then trailed off, as the shuttle altered its position, swinging in an arc as they flipped end over end and traded a view of clouds for stars. "Burn is complete," Kurok said. "We should start insertion momentarily."

A faint buffeting started. "That's the atmosphere," Dev said. "I hope."

"Bye space," Jess said. "You sure were creepy."

"Got that right." Doug took hold of his seat. "Never diss the ground again."

"I THINK WE'RE on target," Kurok said, after a long period of silence, as the buffeting got worse and the forward view was obscured with a thick haze of pinkish cream.

Dev's hands were still on the console as she watched the automatic processes work. It seemed very strange to just be a spectator, though she was happy enough to let the systems work on their own for the moment.

She took a breath and picked up her water, sucking at the tube and then putting it back into the holder at her side. She glanced to her left to see Jess with her hands folded over her stomach, her eyes closed.

Amazing, and excellent really, how Jess could rest when she was able to. Dev expected there would not be much of that going on once they were back downside. Much incorrectness was in their future unless she was very much mistaken.

Stand by for inception of gravity.

The voice in her helmet intoned the words. "I am going to activate the atmospheric systems. We are expecting grav," Dev said, touching the pads and tapping several keys. Thirty or forty seconds later she felt the first tugs of weight on her.

"Yes, here we go," Kurok snugged his restraints a little closer.

The pressure against the craft increased, and they were moving in a side to side motion. Dev got her hands on the controls and watched the status boards for the in-flight engines. She took a quick look to her left and found one blue eye open watching her.

It winked, and then Jess pushed herself back into her seat and tightened the belts around her. Then she let her hands rest on her thighs, her thumbs tapping against the thick black fabric of her suit. "We have scan?"

"Not yet," Doug said. He had his scanner in his hands. "Too much interference."

Stand by for engine cutoff.

Dev almost jumped, then realized the voice meant the space

engines, and she looked at the status board for them, seeing the intermittent impulses cutting in and out. She could sense enough air around them to act against the surfaces of the shuttle.

She took control of the planar surfaces and made some small adjustments, feeling the craft shift faintly around her in response and felt that little bit of exhilaration that came with flight. With more confidence she altered the angle of descent just slightly, and the mist around the cockpit cleared.

Now beneath her she could see clouds, much closer, and knew them for the upper level she occasionally flew the carrier up through, if only very briefly. "Stand by for scan."

"Got it," Doug said. "We're clear, Rocket."

There were a few thumping noises, as gravity took full hold, and she prepared to ignite the standard engines while listening to the systems checklists in one ear. "Environmental systems are switching over."

"Yes," Kurok said, in a bemused voice. "The air intakes just opened." He looked over at Dev then shook his head a little.

They could smell it, suddenly, the sterile nature of the created air invaded by a fresh, clean, cold scent that held bits of cloud and rain in it.

"Mmm." Jess rumbled softly. "Tell everyone to hold on back in the back."

They dipped into the cloud layer, and as they sank through it, Dev triggered the engines, a deep and skin tingling rumble that passed through the cockpit, a thrust that altered their forward motion, and she felt the craft come alive around her as an aerodynamic construct.

"Devvie?"

"Yes?" Dev didn't turn her attention from the controls.

"You truly are a rock star."

"Thank you," Dev responded. "At some point. You will need to educate me on what a rock star is. But I always assume you mean that as a compliment."

"I do. But do us all a favor and don't fly this thing upside down," Jess said. "Those yonks in the back are gonna turn into a people parts milkshake with a scrambled brain topping."

In the silence that followed, they heard the rising hum of engine power clearly from outside. "That's actually really gross," Dev finally said.

"It is," Doug agreed. "Like really."

Jess chuckled.

"But an accurate request," Kurok said. "The tie downs will be very damaging, if they even hold. So please do take care, Dev."

"This is not a carrier. I had no intention of flying it upside down," Dev said in a dignified kind of way. "Especially since I have no way of knowing if these restraints we are wearing will hold."

Jess bumped her with her head, "Sorry Devvie." She folded her hands together. "Didn't mean to diss ya."

Dev shifted her hands on the controls as the craft broke through the high cloud layer and they were between that and the lower. It was dense and dark beneath them, and she could see arcs of lightning in the middle distance.

The shuttle leveled out, then she got a handle on its flight dynamics before she nudged the throttles forward. "I think it is best to remain at this altitude until we are closer to our destination."

"Yes, some bad weather down there," Kurok said. "Jess? Directly to the Bay?"

Jess remained silent. "Yeah. No sense in waiting."

"I have the coordinates for that." Doug produced his scanner. "Since you got your hands full there, Rocket." He turned it on and tuned it, then straightened. "Hey we got something coming at us. Fast, from below."

"Suboptimal." Dev pushed the throttles forward and felt the large craft respond.

Jess unclipped and moved over to look at the scan. "Bad guys." She jumped back to her seat and strapped in. "This thing got any guns?"

"Nothing to speak of," Kurok said with a grim look. "Shields are decent, but mostly because it goes orbital."

"Suboptimal," Dev repeated, snugging her restraints a little tighter. "What is chasing us?"

"TR-12s," Doug said. "Six of em. About to break the clouds."

Dev regarded the scene outside, then she pitched the shuttle forward and down and headed rapidly toward the cloud layer, glancing to one side at the wiremap that now clearly showed the approaching attackers.

She saw the energy readings peaking on them and knew they were about to fire. She tipped the shuttle to one side, not quite on its side, and accelerated.

"Um. Dev."

"Yes, I know I am heading at them," Dev said, just before she got too busy to talk about it as the lead three crafts came out of the clouds into their path and came right at them.

Blaster fire lit the forward screens and washed out real vision. She looked immediately at the wiremap, as the enemy craft split and came around them, still firing.

Suboptimal. She watched them react, their plasma blasters raking the side of the shuttle as alarms and alerts started going off.

"They're going to turn and come at the shuttle from the back," Jess said. "They know the shields are lighter there."

"That's not good," Doug said. "We've got nothing to fight them with."

Dev got the shuttle leveled out as the flare faded from the forward screens, and she saw the wiremap acquire the three enemy ships, who were, just as Jess said, coming at them from the rear.

She started a bit of evasive motion, but the shuttle didn't have the speed or the maneuverability of the carrier, and the response was sluggish at best.

Alarms flared. "Damage on the left rear wing," Doug called out.

Kurok tapped a key. "Sending silica wash out there."

The enemy came right up the center, tucking themselves in behind the space engine bells, firing at will at them. "Blind spot!" Doug called out, watching the wiremap.

Dev considered her options. Then she scanned a mostly dark panel and tapped a few keys. "Please hold on. I am going to try something, and I do not know what the result is going to be."

"Oh, crap." Doug closed his eyes, and Kurok half turned to watch as she grabbed the throttles with one hand and tapped a few keys with the other. A high pitched whine erupted into their ears.

"Damage to right rear," Doug blurted. "They're going to—"

He never got to finish because at that moment Dev tapped another key and pitched the nose of the shuttle down as she triggered the space engines, which roared unexpectedly to life.

Rocket fire was everywhere as the shuttle almost turned on its nose as the engines interacted and two of the enemy craft were caught in the blast before they could spin away. She cut off the rockets and let the shuttle drop, hearing a huge bang and explosion as she came down on top of the third.

Doug was holding on for dear life. "Holy shit."

Jess just laughed. "Nice," she said. "You're gonna get a prize for that one if we ever land in this thing."

Dev accelerated away, going groundward again as the other

three enemy craft arced away and turned back at high speed.

"We just hit the continental plate," Jess said. "We're in home territory."

"Whatever that means," Kurok muttered.

"Point," Jess conceded.

They ripped through the cloud layer and were under it, inside a dark and windy storm with blasts of lightning rippling through the sky around them. The alarms kept going off and a moment later they were inside a rainstorm, almost obscuring the window that wrapped around the shuttle nose.

Repellers. Dev scanned the controls quickly and then went back to the wiremap, flying by its information as the view was washed out. "Doctor Dan, does this craft have rain shields?"

Kurok was busy at the console, punching things furiously. "Looking for them, Dev. Bear with me."

"Oh crap." Doug covered his eyes.

"You want to try this?" Kurok snapped.

"Everyone relax." Jess's voice was low but crisp. "Dev's got this."

Dev risked a sideways glance, but remained silent. She felt the surging of the shuttle, its responses so slow to her. The wiremaps showed the terrain that abruptly appeared under them and she could see mountains and valleys.

There were many alarms showing on the boards, but she didn't know what to do about them, so she let them flash, sparing a moment to reflect that this must be what it was like to be a natural born, having to learn everything the hard way.

Suboptimal, indeed.

"Okay, we're over the white," Jess said. "At this speed we're gonna come over what's left of North in about ten minutes and be in range of Ten. "I have no idea what they're going to do."

"If they saw what Rocket did to those three they'll keep their asses inside that mountain," Doug said. "That was crazy."

Kurok smiled. "Yes, but it worked. What made you think of that, Dev?"

Dev frowned as she studied her displays. "Does something have to make you think of things?" she asked. "I am not sure what that means." She spotted a control and depressed it. Like magic the forward screen cleared. Now they could see outside, which was awash with violent rain. Visible beneath them was the thick, reflective ice of the white.

It made her feel surprisingly relieved to see the earth beneath her and she wondered about that, but not for long because the shuttles steering was troublesome.

"Crossing over Quebec City in two," Doug said.

"Someone is trying to hail us," Kurok said

"Answer it," Jess said. "If it's Ten, I'd like to know ahead of time if they're going to engage us."

Kurok eyed her, then put the comms helmet on. "This is Shuttle Eleven Beta. Who's calling?"

"Shuttle Elbet, Quebec City control. Comms it?"

Kurok looked at the board in some perplexity. "Go ahead," he said, after a brief pause.

"Overshot. You going around? Market needs what you got."

"Ah." Doctor Dan grunted. "Sorry, Quebec, emergency run, coastwise. Catch you on the back."

Jess nodded. "Nice."

"No no, Elbet! You must c'mon in!" The hailer responded, audibly upset. "You got drugs we need! No scams!"

"I think we have some approaching vessels," Dev said in an undertone. "From the west."

"No scams, Quebec, we got damage. Attack over the white," Doctor Dan said. "Can't land there. Will come back soon as we can."

"Fuck!" The comms intoned in a very frustrated voice. "Who attacked?"

"TR-12s, a half dozen," Kurok said. "We splashed three."

"Huh." The Quebec comms grunted. "You go Base Ten?"

Jess and Kurok exchanged looks and Jess nodded. "Yes," he said. "Endit."

He put the comms down and frowned. "Drugs?" He half shook his head. "What else in hell was going on there I had no clue about? I feel like such an idiot."

The comms lit again, flashing harshly. "Bet I can guess who that is," Jess said. "Dev, you answer that one."

"Yes." Dev keyed the comms. "Shuttle Eleven Beta. Go ahead."

There was a harsh crackle and she almost removed the comms from her ear, then a soft clicking noise. "Eleven Beta, this is Interforce Base Ten. Identify please."

Dev looked at Jess and lifted her eyebrows.

"Go ahead and tell them who you are," Jess said. "They'll pick up scan in a few minutes anyway." She shifted a little. "That sounds like reg comms."

"Base Ten, this is Dev. I am in control of this shuttle."

Jess leaned forward with her elbows on her knees, honestly at a loss to know what was going to come next. "I think that's Roger," she commented. "One of the new techs."

"You've stunned them speechless," Kurok said. "That's a first."

A crackle. "NM-Dev-1?"

"Yes. That's me."

Another crackle and the sound of fumbling. "Rocket!" a different voice erupted. "Son of a bitch!"

Dev winced and moved the comms a bit away from her eardrum. "Hello."

"It's Jason. Is Jess there?"

"Yes. She is here next to me." Dev offered the comms to Jess. "It's Jason." So far, it didn't sound too incorrect, and she was glad to hear Jason's voice, and in the background she was fairly sure she'd heard Brent.

"Drake," Jess said. "Jase?"

"Dude." Jason sounded utterly relieved. "Don't stop here, you heading for home?"

"Yes."

"Go," Jason said. "Long story, tell ya later, see ya soon."

"Endit." Jess cut off the comms and handed it back. "Best news I could've gotten. We're not going to get blown up on the way."

"At least not by Base Ten," Kurok said, but looked relieved himself. "No telling what we'll find at the Bay."

No, that was true. Jess settled back in her seat and flexed her hands. "We'll know in a little while. How ya doing, Dev? Want me to dig up another bar for ya?"

Caught thinking of exactly that, Dev blushed. "Actually I was thinking of those shrimp in Quebec. But a bar would be nice, too."

Jess reached out and gave her neck a knead then unclipped her restraints and stood up. She stretched her body out and shook herself a little. "We made it back from space at least." She eased past the pilot's station and went to the hatch. "Let's see how far we get now."

Dev got herself re-settled and reviewed as much of the controls as she could, only then looking up to see Doctor Dan watching her. He was smiling, and she smiled back. "This is really somewhat difficult."

He leaned on the arm of the chair. "I don't think anything is too difficult for you, Dev. You're amazing."

"Hell yeah." Doug got up from his jumpseat and stretched

his long body out. "I hope we got vid of you torching those TRs. That's gonna be on replay for a month." He looked over at Kurok. "Too bad you made these guys sterile, doc. Those genes could do for spreading."

Kurok regarded him with a wry expression. "Interesting thought."

Doug waited, but there was nothing else forthcoming. "Well, I'm gonna go find the head." He started out the hatch, pausing to glance back at them, then going on and closing it behind him.

JESS FOUND THE little mess dispenser occupied as April was rummaging in the supplies as well. "Hey."

April glanced at her. "Hey. Nice to have my feet stuck to the deck again. We long off?" She seemed to have regained her equilibrium and stolid attitude, without a sign of the angry sarcasm she'd exhibited before.

Jess was glad. She wasn't really in the mood for a fistfight. "No. We just passed Base Ten." She picked up a water and two bars. "The bang you heard was Dev knocking three TR-12s out of the sky."

"Really?" April tucked a bar in one pocket and took a water. "With what? These aren't armed for crap. Believe me I checked. All they have is that repulsor gun to push meteors out of the way they were using to shoot at station." She paused. "She use that?"

Jess chuckled. "No. Two of them she splatted with the space rockets and one she just smacked down on top of. Rest of them took off when we crossed the line inbound."

"Really?" April frowned a little. "Those are battle tactics. Where'd she get that, Drake? Not that I mind, but was that the plan? You coach her?"

Interesting question. "Instinct?" Jess said. "It never even crossed my mind to do that. I sure didn't tell her to. She even freaked out the doc."

"So did you contact Ten?" April asked. Jess nodded. "What did they say?"

"Jason contacted me. Something's going on there, said he would catch up with me later." Jess half shrugged. "Told me to get through the Bay first."

"What? That's nuts." April frowned. "It was Interforce that attacked the Bay. I saw them. Saw the damn carriers come in shooting, Jess. No bullshit." She crunched the bottle in her hand a little. "So what the hell?"

Jess shrugged again. "We haven't talked to anyone since you left. No telling what's going on there. My damn family could have blown up the place by now and maybe Interforce moved on already."

"Makes no sense," April said. "Whole thing makes no sense. I mean yeah, great, growing plants, cred, I get it. My tribe would have sucked the souls out of everyone in the place for it, but it's just one cave. Tank a homestead for that? Really? 'Specially yours?"

Jess folded her arms over her chest and leaned back against the bulkhead. "Maybe the scientists found something else after we left. I saw a couple of them out on the beach looking around," she said. "Sorry I went now."

"Me too," April said. "Everything got a little sideways after you and Dev left. Political shit going on we could tell, but we stayed clear."

Politics, yeah. Jess felt tired and annoyed. "Fucked me up."

"Did," April agreed. "No going back from it, Drake. You go kick their asses, you're seriously screwed. Don't go? More screwed."

"Sucks to be me," Jess said.

April nodded. "Does. No win there, unless you want to go civ. Not sure they'd even let you do that." She opened a water and sucked at it. "Nearest nomad family we bumped into, those ones on the plains, went to ground near the caves you smoked that night. That's trouble."

"Why not go with your people, April?" Jess asked unexpectedly. "Why stick on my side? You know I'm going to end up fish food."

April studied her for a long moment in silence. "You win a lot," she finally said. "I like that." She turned and started back to the seats. "And we all have to croak sometime. That's what my mater used to tell me." She paused at the door. "I'm going to go strap in if Rocket's driving. Falling down now'd hurt."

Jess smiled and pushed off the doorway and went back into the shuttle's corridor, now level since Dev was flying in a relatively even configuration. She went over to the cargo hold and turned the latch, opening it to look inside.

Her family was in good spirits. A few had gotten knocked around, but it was mostly just bruises and cuts. Now that she had a chance to look, she realized the fifty assorted men and women in sea stained clothing were all youngers.

No seniors, no heads of households. Just singles and

youngsters, looking to make a mark.

"We almost home?" Dustin asked. "What's left of it maybe?"

"Almost," Jess said. "Going to be fighting when we get there."

"Hope so," he said. "Seriously not cool them elders and all getting whiffed. Wasn't their fault, cuz. We were all whupping up and they took it out on the noncoms." He was seated on a console, kicking his booted legs back and forth. "Fuckers."

Jess leaned against the wall. "So you started it?" she asked. "Not them?"

"Sure," Dustin said. "Assholes were grabbing what was ours. No way we were gonna let that go on. Mika got all in their faces, Seldon, too, and they started trying to kick people around."

"Ah."

"That stuff was ours," Dustin said. Two others next to them nodded. "We don't let people come take shit from the Bay. You get it, right? You wouldn't have let them just grab stuff, would you?"

"If they were blowing up my old uncle, maybe I would have," Jess said. "What was that crap worth? And I'm active duty, so I don't know what the hell I would have done. Probably not started a fight with Interforce."

Dustin looked profoundly disappointed. "But you're the Drake."

Jess regarded him. "I'm an enforcement agent," she said. "Except for a quirk of my father's, I would have been on the other side shooting at you."

Silence.

"But now? Yeah. Fuckers. I can't let that stand. They can't shoot my old uncle and trash the homestead. I'm the Drake. I'm going to have to kill them." Jess sighed. "Some days it really sucks to be me."

Dustin nodded relieved. "You get it."

"I get it." Jess now saw the situation in a whole range of other colors. But it didn't matter really because in the end it would be the same thing. "Anyway, let me get back to the cockpit. You'll know when we're landing when this thing stops shaking."

She walked among the bios, who watched her with quiet trustfulness. "Your guy, the Doc, is being rock star up there," she told them. "Just relax. Between him and Dev we're golden."

The KayTee who'd stuck with Dev smiled at her and waved a little. "I'm glad we went," he said. "This will be different, even if it's hard." He settled back into his cargo restraint. "We will get to see downside."

"We will," a BeeAye agreed. "Maybe NM-Dev-1 will take us to see a bear, like on the vid."

A bear. Jess sighed internally, feeling that day now a lifetime behind her.

Cathy, the lab assistant, gently intercepted her. "Agent Drake."

"Yeah?" Jess regarded her. "Walk and talk." She indicated the passageway. "I gotta get back to the front." She turned and walked with Cathy beside her. "We got a spare seat up there. Want to come join?"

Cathy smiled. "Yes, I would, thank you. That's what I was going to ask. It's so strange to be going downside. And all the others that came..." She looked behind her, and her face crinkled a little in reaction. "They're a little strange." Cathy looked embarrassed. "I'm sorry, I think they said you come from the same place?"

Jess chuckled. "I do. Don't worry about it. No one's more aware of how strange Drakes are than I am." Jess bumped the hatch open. "How we doing, Dev?"

"Nominal for now," Dev responded. "I estimate ten minutes to the outer range where your home place is. I assume you wish me to land this ship where it took off from." She turned and took the bar Jess held out. "Thank you."

Doctor Dan half turned in the other pilot's seat. "Hello, Cathy. That wasn't too bad an entry, was it?"

"Not at all, sir." Cathy settled on one of the jumpseats against the back wall of the pilot's compartment. "I didn't even realize until we came back under grav." She looked forward out through the viewscreen. "Oh. We're under the gray."

"Yes," Dev said. "That is the ocean, under this craft. We have already crossed the arctic, and soon I will turn the shuttle toward our destination."

Jess dropped into her seat and extended her legs. "Any hails?"

"Nothing," Kurok said. "I can't decide if that's good or bad."

"We'll find out soon enough."

Chapter Twelve

THEIR ARRIVAL WAS, in fact, uneventful. The shuttle approached Drake's Bay from the north, aiming for the pad off to one side of the homestead. The only oddness was the lack of comms, and Jess's insides roiled as they slowed for the approach. "Dev?"

"Yes?" Dev glanced from one panel to the other with a hint of indecision.

"You know how to land this thing?"

"Theoretically," Dev said. "I am glad the place to set down is not near anything fragile." She made an adjustment. "I just hope we do not drop excessively."

Both of Jess's brows lifted and she tightened her restraints a little. "Remember no upside down. Okay?"

"Yes." Dev shifted the controls and the shuttle jittered sideways. "Please hold on."

Jess curled her legs around the seat base and eyed Kurok. "Anything on the wire?"

Kurok shook his head. "Nothing. Not getting a scan on anything at all."

There were no flyers around, nothing on patrol, and when they'd crossed the half circle bay, it was empty. Like there was nothing left. Jess took a tighter hold and leaned forward a little as the shuttle got lower to the rocky ground and slowed.

Dev was sweating. Her blonde hair damp at the temples, her breathing a little fast, aware of her role in trying not to get them killed.

"Easy, Devvie." Jess bumped her calf against Dev's leg. "Just set her down."

"Yes." Dev hunted and found the landing jets and triggered them, just as she felt the engines reach their stall limit. The pad was under them, rocks broken and scattered, and as the jets blasted out air beneath them it spewed bodies out in all directions, rolling across the wet ground.

"I've lowered the landing skids, Dev," Doctor Dan said. "You can set down."

"Yes." Jess took a careful breath behind her. "Fifty feet." She got the engines secured and let them lower, the wet now turning to steam as they hovered, then landed on the cracked pad with a rock and a thump, the hiss of the jets loud and distinct.

Dev turned off the power to them,and the shuttle went mostly silent, just some dings and beeps from the console audible. "We are down," she said, relaxing just a bit in her seat.

"Good job, Dev." Jess stood and leaned over and gave her an unexpected kiss on the top of her head. "You got us home."

Dev enjoyed the moment. She folded her arms over her chest and glanced over at Doctor Dan, who was smiling his gentle smile at her. So many incorrect things, and then, at this moment, a bit of contentedness she was human enough to savor. "Thank you, Jess."

Behind them, on the other side of the hatch, they heard voices and motion.

Doug loosened his restraints. "Rocket rocks another one. So now what? Looks like a graveyard out there."

Everyone looked at him.

"Yeah okay, sorry." Doug got up with grimace. "When we left, we were being shot at from every direction. I don't really know how this thing actually made it up, so everything being equal it was a hella better landing."

The cockpit hatch opened and April entered. "Plan?" she asked brusquely. "Better open the hatch before your family dents it."

Jess shook herself and glanced out the front of the shuttle. The carved path to the homestead was full of rubble and bodies, and it was starting to rain. "Let's go. No sense staying here. Dev, you got anything on your babbler?"

Dev tuned her scanner, and after a moment she looked up. "The area is shielded," she said, with a note of surprise. "I cannot detect anything past that far entry door."

Jess went over to her, crouched down, and reviewed the screen. "Huh." She stood back up. "Let's go. You, me, April, Doug." She settled her blaster at her side. "Doc, keep everyone else inside here."

Kurok regarded her. "No offense, but you're going to have to give that order to your kinfolk, Jesslyn. They're not going to take it from me."

Jess nodded and went to the hatch. "Yeah, probably." She sighed. "Let's hope they listen to me."

"What's the pitch?" April asked.

"We go see who's in charge," Jess said. "If anyone is." She pushed through the opening and edged into the corridor. "Hey," she called out.

It was full of Bay residents, who turned and looked at her. "Get the door open, cuz," Dustin said. "It's cramped in here."

Jess squeezed through the crowd and got to the outer hatch. She turned to face them. "You'll be crowded a while more. We're going out there to see what the deal is. You stay here."

A chorus of dissent rose.

"Stop!" Jess's voice boomed. "If anyone's going to croak here, it's going to be us. Stay put." She went to the hatch and worked it. The hatch opened and the ramp extend. It reminded her suddenly of that moment when she'd first seen Dev.

That dark, cold day, her sitting on the bench outside the base, with nothing but a future of rock scraping ahead of her. Now? Jess felt a bit of black humor. Well, at least then she'd contemplated being a live rock scraper.

"Jess's right," Jake said. "We did our part. Now's her turn."

"Nice." Doug grimaced.

Jess shrugged. "He's right." She flexed her hands and gave herself a little shake. "Let's go do what we do."

"Still no readings," Dev said as the cold air blasted inward, with a stench of cold, damp death roiling over it. "Except deceased persons and rain."

"Yeah." Jess pulled out her blaster. "So I see." She looked at the group from the Bay, who were now silent, noses twitching. "Stay here," she reiterated. "Let them take their spleen out on me." She turned and started down the ramp with Dev and the other two at her heels.

THE WIND HOWLED past them, yanking at clothes and hair as they walked down the sloping rock path toward the narrow cleft between the stone faces that protected the homestead from the back blast of the shuttle. They slowed as they reached the gap. Jess lifted her hand with her gun in it, going still just as she got to the edge.

She listened hard, discarding the whistling of the wind along with the rattle of small stones being driven across the ground and the hiss of the shuttle offgassing behind her. She put aside the knowledge of where she was and what she might likely find past this crick in the rock.

"I do not see anything," Dev said softly. "There is too much rock for me to get a signal past this wall."

"I don't see anything either." Jess eased through the entrance, a crookback kink in the rock that would let a loaded pallet through, but only just. She got herself clear of the second angle and swept the area carefully. She saw nothing but stone with dead bodies scattered over it. Some had crabs eating them. They scattered as the four of them approached, but not far, lifting armored claws up and clicking them.

She edged forward and got to the first of the bodies which was in black. "Scan," she said, since the face and features were nothing but mulch.

"He has a chip." Dev said. "From Base Ten."

"Okay." Jess moved on to the next, aware of how exposed they all were. "This one's from the Bay." She didn't stop to examine the body, getting an angle and seeing the entrance to the Bay past the long stretch of wet stone. It was closed. Beside it the square indentation that was the bio lock flashed a faint, faded red.

The bodies got denser as they approached, roughly half and half between Interforce and the Bay. Jess stepped over the last of them and reached the entrance as Dev came up next to her.

"Crap chance which way this went," April said.

"Crap chance," Jess agreed, and put her hand on the pad. "But I lose either way."

"You do."

The door remained closed. Dev eased over and ran her scanner over it. "This seems defective."

"Ya think?" Jess examined the wires coming out of back of the indent pad. "Someone blasted it." She holstered her gun and pulled the panel out toward them. "All that hurry up here we are."

"Let me see if I can help." Dev set her scanner down and stuck her head into the panel, removed the small light clipped to her suit and turned it on.

"This the only way in?" April asked.

"You can climb the cliff." Jess leaned against the rock to watch what Dev was doing. "They put the shuttle pad here for a reason."

"Didn't trust it," April said.

"Please stand clear," Dev said suddenly. "I am going to apply power and the result could be unexpected."

April went to the door and braced herself against the side of it, her blaster cradled in both hands. After a moment Jess joined her. Doug tucked himself on the other side of Dev and lifted a hand to cover his eyes. "Go on, Rocket."

Dev routed a wire to her scanner and applied the connection.

For a moment she didn't think it was going to do anything. Then there was a loud crack that almost made her drop her device.

"Watch your paws, Rocket."

Then the rock panel shifted and Dev quickly pulled back and disconnected the wire. She looped her scanner over her head and felt the wind start to come through the opening as the surface slid aside.

More death smell.

"Go," Jess said, and she and April flowed through the gap. Doug and Dev went after them, busy with scanners.

"Getting stuff now," Doug called out. "Watch it! Ten targets!"

Dev was through the gap and into the mountain cavern, her own scanner out. She walked along the edge of the wall as she tried to keep Jess and April in sight, the two agents already at the end of the long passage and against one wall.

"Drake!" A voice called out. "Hold it!"

"That's Alters," Doug said as he and Dev moved quickly along the wall. "All interforce targets."

"Yes," Dev agreed.

"It's Drake," Jess responded. "What's the deal?"

The stench was almost overwhelming. Dev resisted the urge to cover her mouth as she got up next to Jess, who had her back pressed against the wall as she listened.

"Jackass," April said.

"It's Bensen Alters. If it's just you, we're clear," he responded. "Come over and let's talk."

Dev tuned her scanner. "They do not have active energy weapons."

Jess cocked her ears and listened for a minute. She heard shifting of limbs and the rustle of fabric, and behind the stench of death she detected fear and cold sweat.

"Okay." She put her gun back on it's hard point. "This is my gig." She looked at the rest of them. "Stay here." Her eyes went from one to the other and paused as they met Dev's. "Please."

Dev's nose twitched, and she kept a very noncommittal expression on her face. "This does not seem nominal." She said. "But I will remain here if you say so."

Jess's lips quirked.

"And of course, if you don't think I could be helpful."

Jess held a hand up. "Give me a couple minutes," she said. "Honestly if they're going to start blasting, better it be me they're aiming at." She didn't give them any more time to protest and moved out from the corridor into the big cavern where the shuttle would deliver and pick up supplies.

There were shadowy figures in the gloom, only one of the several lights up in the roof being on. Jess walked forward with an even pace, avoiding the bodies on the ground as she angled toward where the small group stood waiting.

Alters, yes, with a thick bandage around his head, obscuring one eye, a bloodstained jacket over his jumpsuit. He looked exhausted, and that made Jess feel a little proud despite everything. "So." She came to a halt a bodylength away from them. "Talk."

He indicated a side corridor. "Let's go where we can sit." He was limping, and he didn't try to hide it as he walked away, leaving her at his back.

Jess regarded the rest of the bunch, who all watched her warily, all newcomers to Base Ten, all bearing the signs of a big battle.

It made her feel proud that her homestead hadn't sat down to be taken advantage of. No matter it was against Interforce. She gave them all a brief nod. "Three more at my back. Don't screw with them." She started after Alters and crossed from the storage intake hall into a back corridor where he was standing near a doorway.

Jess walked inside and waited for him to enter and close the door. She sat down in an old, wooden chair and put her elbows on the arms of it. "So."

He sat down facing her. "I understand a hell of a lot more about you now than I did a week ago, Drake." He leaned his weight on his elbows. "Wish you would have warned me."

Jess didn't smile. "Interforce knows all about this place," she said. "My assumption was you knew what you were getting into. And wouldn't be stupid enough to try and rape it."

He didn't deny it. "The idea was to secure this resource. We're out of the habit of asking, and since you are active duty we didn't really have to." He regarded her. "Everyone paid for that arrogance."

"I heard," Jess said. "Two-hundred was the number they gave me."

He nodded. "Something like. Maybe half that on our side that we can't afford to replace. So." He shifted a little. "Now I need you to make these people stand down, get the hell out of the way, and let me do what I came to do."

"Steal what belongs here?"

He stared at her. "That really how you see this, Drake?"

Jess shrugged. "It's the truth. So yes." She moved a little and saw him twitch in response. "It was paid for. Jimmy bought it. You have no right to take it." She lifted her hands and rested her chin on her interlaced fingers. "It wasn't a scam from the other side. At least that part wasn't."

He looked at her in silence. "You don't know that's true."

"I do. I know the price. I found the collateral up on station," Jess said. "I stopped it. Reclaimed the price." She smiled faintly. "My brother sold my nephew to the geeks so they could make more of me to sell to the other side." She watched him carefully and saw the twitch of surprise that, in fact, surprised her. "So yeah, you've got no claim on it."

"Son of a bitch," Alters said, softly, almost under his breath.

"He was, matter of fact," Jess said. "But he kept his part of the bargain, and it wasn't with them. Station made the deal with the other side. I'd say take it out on them, but the doc blew the head off the guy up there who did it for ya."

"Kurok?"

Jess nodded. "I'll get them to stand down, but you're not going to take a damn thing from here."

"Are you rejecting a direct order, Drake?"

"Yes." Jess felt a sense of calm settle over her. Of decisions made and paths chosen. "Because you don't have the right to give me that order, and you know it." She stood up. "I'm the Drake of Drake's Bay. So let's go to ops, and I'll clear the halls."

"Fuck." He stood up as well, sighing wearily. "We can't get into ops. They sealed it."

"I can." Jess went over and pushed the door open. Outside the security guards were waiting, hands on blasters. Their eyes went past her to Alters. Jess drew in a breath of the cold, fetid air and knew herself to be walking along the knife's edge.

She walked past them and headed for the inner door, ignoring the threat and the flickers of motion that might be guns coming up to level.

Would they shoot her? Was Alters really that stupid?

Or that smart?

Would April take vengeance on her, or just join the crowd? If she did, what would Dev do? Would Dev get all crazy and try to stop her?

Jess didn't look behind her but sensed Dev's eyes watching her. She could almost see that frown and the little pucker between her eyebrows.

Suboptimal, was that what she'd call it?

Incorrect?

The guards formed a watch behind her and followed along, and Alters caught up to her as they neared the inner section. Just past the entry, she saw a body move out of the way. Incorrect. She exhaled, and then her ears twitched as she heard the faintest footfalls coming along behind them.

There would be no waiting behind for Dev. She listened intently, and then very faintly smiled.

DEV REMAINED STILL until the last of the agents took up point guard as they followed Alters and Jess. Then she moved out after them, surprising both April and Doug.

After a second, they followed, and the three of them carefully padded out across the rock floor that was dotted with darker shadows of still bodies they skirted.

Dev kept the scanner poised, getting readings now that they were inside the homestead. She found she was almost used to the smell of death, able to move past it as she followed the crowd.

They had sealed the outer door again, so maybe the guards weren't worried about being followed, or they figured they had them outnumbered.

Which they did. Dev paused inside the opening, peering cautiously out and then emerging into the hall where she found their quarry had already vanished. She tuned the scanner and retuned it, picking up only residual markers from Jess.

"Where'd they go?" Doug asked, in a whisper.

"I don't know." Dev angled toward the wall. "I don't see an..." She stopped. "Oh."

April immediately looked at the scanner. "Oh shit."

The flood of armament was unmistakable, and Interforce security quickly filled the end of the hall and headed toward them.

"Hey." A whisper caught their attention, and they looked down corridor to find Jess's uncle Max in a narrow opening. He gestured furiously at them, and after a moment, they raced toward him, ignoring the shouts from security as they reached the opening and went through. Max slammed the door behind them.

"C'mon." Uncle Max limped quickly ahead of them. "We gotta be in place when she pulls the trigger."

"What trigger?" April asked. "You mean Jess?"

"Who else?" Uncle Max snapped. "Took you long enough."

He moved down a long corridor that had grates periodically in the floor and even, squared off walls.

"We had to go into fucking space," April said. "And break into a space station. So shut it, huh?"

Uncle Max glanced over his shoulder at her, and then briefly grinned. "Good job," he said. "Didn't really expect to see ya back." He looked over at Dev. "Hey there, Rocket."

"Hello," Dev responded. "April and Doug did an excellent job bringing a space ship up to let us return."

"Bet those pilots loved it," Uncle Max said.

"I killed them," April replied

He paused. "Out on the pad?"

"Up on the station. They pissed me off." April pointed at Dev. "She flew it back. Where are we going?"

"Here." Uncle Max pushed open a door and gestured them forward. "The shitheads think they scared us off, or killed us off but really — "

"They just pissed you off," April said. She walked out onto a stair landing and looked over it.

They were in a large cavern with a ceiling extending far up into the darkness. There were steps carved into the wall about halfway up. Below them were thousands of people, arranged in groups, dressed in the rough work clothes of the Bay, but with a sense of organization April immediately recognized.

"Yeah." Uncle Max started down the steps. "Let's hope this doesn't take too long."

JESS WAS AWARE of the eyes watching her, and she knew behind her was nothing now but trouble. The halls were full of Interforce security. There was no sympathy in the faces watching her being marched toward the operations center.

The idea that Jason had sold her burned. The knowledge that there were no friendly ears at her back clenched her guts, and not knowing what had happened to Dev, after that rush of running boots made her crazy.

She put on a good face, though, concentrating on remaining relaxed and confident, leading the group around then through the passageways and halls toward the protected section where they kept all the systems that ran the Bay.

Where Interforce had been born, really, the checks and structure very much like what Base Ten had. Many of the weapons and computer systems they all used had been developed right here in this old rock escarpment.

Did Alters realize that?

Jess went down through a crossroads and then through an arch, and she was at the entrance to ops, sealed and solid with nothing but the oldest of old school ident pads protecting it.

She paused and put her hand on it. After a moment, the pad shifted color. Then a long low clicking sound happened, and the rock wall in front of them slid aside

"Son of a bitch," Alters said. "We've been trying to get into here for a week. Thanks, Drake."

Jess started to walk forward and then hands pulled her back. "Hey!"

"Get her in restraints," Alters said as security poured into the space. Figures stood and turned toward them. "Just kill the rest of them."

Jess blurred into motion. She kicked backwards against the guards, dodging a set of shackles. She lunged to the right and then ducked under a blast as she was grabbed again. She used her forward momentum to grab a console and haul herself forward. Then she felt blows and the stunning force of a zapper against her spine.

Other hands grabbed her and pulled her forward. She twisted and half fell over a console as the ops watch came scrambling over at them.

"Stop!" Alters yelled. "We're taking charge!"

Jess flexed her body and yanked one hand loose, suspended between competing forces that were pulling her back and forward. She hauled herself down and slammed her hand down into an indentation in the very center of the control set, refusing to let the forces haul her backwards until she felt the bone deep tickle against her nerves.

The panel flickered and there was a crackle of comms opening. "Drake!" Jess yelled into it. "GO!"

"Foxtrot Ultra!" One of the ops cons yelled. "Go, go, go! Release!" They dove for the floor and ducked behind the consoles.

A low siren wailed, and all around them they heard the sound of motion, of rock and steel shifting, and thick, heavy booming thumps that shook the very air.

The guards turned Jess over and put a gun to her throat. They grabbed her blaster from its holster as the sound got so loud it made ears buzz.

"Drake! What in the hell did you just do!" Alters was at her side, a knife in his hands, his one good eye vivid and wild.

Jess smiled at him. "I loosed the dogs of war." Her heart started to beat more powerfully, and color started to leach out of her vision. "Or maybe the wolves of war." She heard the rasp enter her voice and knew they did as well, and then it all went crazy. "And If I were you I'd run."

THEY BARELY HAD time to get down to the rock floor before the lights changed, morphing from bluish white to red, as a low bonging tone started to sound.

"Didn't take her long at all," Uncle Max said, with an exultant tone in his voice. "All Drake, all the way."

"You have any idea what's going on?" April asked Dev as they felt the room start to move around them. Everyone stood up, an electric excitement rising.

"No idea at all," Dev said. "I just hope Jess is all right."

"Probably not," Uncle Max said. "They'll kill her once they realize what she just did. Damn shame."

April slid in front of him and poked him in the chest with her knife. "What did she just do? I don't really have time for games, old man."

Uncle Max stopped and looked at her. April's expression didn't change, and she didn't pull back. "That's a nomad knife."

"Earned one."

A faint smile appeared on his grizzled face. "There's an armory here at the Bay. Last time we opened it, Jessie's grandpappy took a nuclear missile out of it and blew up ten thousand people and a crap ton of land they can't use no more."

"That's what that is?" April sheathed her knife as the rock wall to their left slid open. "She just picked a side?"

From the gap in the wall rolled a wall of air, full of the scent of old oil and mechanicals. "Nah," Uncle Max said. "There's no picking for her. She's all Drake all through." He regarded them seriously. "But you all will need to decide to shoot at us or shoot at them."

"Already did," April responded tersely. "Before I got on that fucking shuttle."

Max nodded.

"Excuse me," Dev said suddenly. "Did you just say they were going to make Jess dead?"

The crowd started moving forward, excitement rising. "Let's go." One of the men nearby slid a pack onto his back.

"Let's get rid of these bastards."

"They will, Rocket." Uncle Max waved them forward with him. "Soon as they figure it out. Their fault, the idiots." He shook his head and limped faster. "Lemme get my hands on a launcher, can't wait to take one of those asses out of the air."

Dev felt like she was caught in a violent windstorm, bits of programming coming up into her consciousness, only to be blasted aside as the knowledge hit that she might not see Jess again.

That Jess might, in fact, already be made dead.

"C'mon Rocket." Doug patted her gingerly on the arm. "Don't believe the worst until it happens."

Comms crackled into her ear as she followed him by rote, moving with the mass of bodies into a chamber that opened their view as they cleared the door and she touched it with a mechanical gesture. "This is Dev."

Maybe it would be Jess?

"Dev, it's Doctor Dan. We heard the alarm go off. Can we help?"

"I don't know, Doctor Dan," Dev said as she got a good view of the room, full of devices she didn't have any real knowledge of. "Jess did something...and now they think maybe she's going to be m..." The overwhelming sense of despair came over her without warning and it made her have to stop speaking."

Doctor Dan understood anyway. "I'm coming. Hold on, Dev. I'll do my best."

The comms clicked off, and Dev found a piece of rock to put her back to, staring out over a cavern now alive with people picking up devices and full of a rising emotion. The man she remembered was called Mike, who was security for the homestead, stepped out and threw his hands forward.

"FORM UP!" He bellowed. "Make sure everything's energized!"

Men and women were throwing aside covers and tops of boxes. They pulled what were, apparently, weapons out of storage crates and started up vehicles that quickly turned out to be hovercraft, with rough seats and heavy blasters forward and aft.

Doug shook his head. "Fuck it. I'm going." He headed for one of the vehicles, where April was already jumping aboard. "Short career!" he yelled back over his shoulder.

All Dev could hear in her head were echoes. Flashes of memory, clips of Jess's voice. She had no desire to join the Bay staff. No desire to be part of the force that was gathering. All that mattered to her, right now, in this moment was Jess.

A breath, and she turned and bolted back the way they'd come in, through the outer cavern and toward the tunnels that led from it.

JESS TWISTED VIOLENTLY as the zaps drove pain through her body, and she was back, suddenly in the enemy station knowing herself betrayed. That brought a surge of rage, and she used that to throw off the hands of Interforce security who were trying their best to contain her.

The Bay station ops were shooting from behind their consoles and ducking the responses, somehow keeping the agent's back from the controls Jess had triggered with her biometric presence.

"Shit!" She heard Alters yell. "This is unresponsive!

"Fuckin A, you chicken masterbater!" One of the ops yelled at him. "Wait till they get to those disintegrators! You're gonna be fuckin fish chum!"

Alters grabbed Jess and forced her to look at him. "Is that true?"

Jess merely turned her head and clamped her teeth in his arm, ripping her head back and forth as she fought to get free.

"These people are crazy," one of the security men said. "Out of their damn minds."

"Sir! Someone's gone through the landing bay with our chips!" Another guard yelped. "Going for the carriers! Sir it's the bio alt!"

"Blow that damn thing when she touches it!" Alters yelled back, wrenching himself free of Jess's teeth then hauling himself backwards as Jess suddenly went from raging to explosive in a heartbeat. "Shit!"

Two security guards went flying as Jess got her feet on the ground. Then she went for the third, brushing past his hand to hand guard and going right for his throat. He grabbed her, but it wasn't enough, and she had her teeth in his jugular and her jaws closing before he could stop her.

Before anyone could stop her. She shoved his body away from her as she scrambled on top of a console and launched herself at Alters who was trying to move fast enough to get away from her.

She let the hate take her. He was nothing but a target. His Interforce uniform meant nothing to her. All she could hear was his voice...giving that order.

Blow Dev up? Jess felt herself go over a threshold as her hands reached him and her head slammed into his. She closed her eyes to keep the blood from obscuring her vision as she felt his nose break under the impact. She grabbed his jaws in her hands and changed motion in mid air, using momentum and the strength of her fingers to snap his head around and break his neck.

Then she was on the security guard with his portable operations console, his fingers rattling hurriedly at the keys as he backpedalled away from her. "Stop! Help! Stop her!"

All the security guards headed for him, two of them blasting at Jess as she reached him and took the console from his hands.

She turned at the last moment and the blasters hit the console, sending blue flares through it. She kept going around too fast for them to stop firing as the console cleared the guard holding it, and his head was blown off his body.

"Go, Drake!" Ops yelled from behind her. "We got 'em!"

Jess would have gone anyway. She came around the corner into a squad of security heading the other direction and didn't even pause an instant before she threw herself at the first of them and got his blaster from him before he could react to the blood and burn covered figure coming at them.

She wrenched the blaster around and started shooting, the gun recognizing her as Interforce and agreeably blew apart her erstwhile colleagues. She saw them realize who she was, and the fifth and sixth of them threw their hands up and fell to the ground.

She jumped over them and hauled herself down the hallway, spitting bits of skin and blood out of her mouth as she ran.

Sirens were going off incessantly. In the distance, she heard concussive fire, and she knew the long kept weapons of true war had been broken out.

She left that to her homestead. All her mental energy was diverted, focusing on the landing bay and the overwhelming need in her guts to protect Dev. She felt it as a mania, a burning in her that pushed aside duty and honor and she didn't really care.

A flicker in her peripheral vision. She turned and fired with little thought, the blast bouncing off the rock walls and sending the oncoming body diving to the floor to escape it. Who was it?

She didn't care. Ahead of her was the main entryway of the stakehold, and as she cleared the space the whole world fell in on top of her.

DEV PUT HER back flat against the wall, breathing hard as she waited for the hall entry to clear of Interforce personnel. They were all running in the direction she'd come from, all wearing armor and carrying weapons, all in the dark blue of security.

Security. Dev ducked around the corner of the corridor and got between the staircase and the wall. She reached up, grabbed the wrought iron, and quickly pulled herself upward.

They might have the stairs in scan. But she used the bars to climb in the shadows, trying to ignore the horrible clenching in the pit of her stomach and the constant barrage of thoughts of Jess.

She wasn't really sure why she was trying to get to the carrier, except that was the one thing she knew well, knew of herself, as well as from programming. She thought if she could get to it, maybe she could do some good work.

Maybe Jess would need her to do something.

She hoped Jess would need her to do something.

She hoped Jess hadn't been made dead.

She had to stop climbing and held on for a long moment, her chest hurt so badly. It was hard and confusing, and she pulled herself close to the bars as tears burned her eyes.

So hard. She felt so bad, thinking something had happened to Jess, even though part of her knew they could always be made dead at any moment. She got a boot up on one of the ornate curls and took a few breaths then continued upward.

At the seventh level, she pulled herself up and over the rail and raced down the corridor, this one bare and empty, the end, half blocked by a shattered stone door. She went over and listened past it, not wanting to reveal her presence by opening a scan.

It was quiet, she could hear rain outside. After a moment she slipped inside and looked around. The landing bay was empty. Only two carriers were inside, and the rest of the floor was full of rubble and discarded parts.

As she took a step forward, she felt the tickle of a scan, and froze. Then she burst into a run, pelting across the floor toward the carrier with her name on it. Across the floor she saw motion and ran faster, a half dozen guards running in her direction.

They had an angle, but she was faster. She got to the carrier and triggered the unlock. She dove inside and hit the retract just as they reached the pedestal the carrier was crouched on. They slammed into the outside and then hammered on it. She got to her feet and got into her chair, pulling it close as she started up the systems.

The shields powered just in time as they started blasting at her, the long battery soak giving her plenty of power to bring the boards online. They came around to the front and shot directly at the forward screen.

She hit the retract to close the hard shield, and it slid into place. The restraints retracted around her as all the systems came online.

She started a deep scan as the sound of blaster fire exploded around the carrier. Her hands were poised over the pad, but she stared at it, unable to force herself to put in the codes that would find Jess in all that chaos.

What would she do if it returned neg? Was there any point in doing anything? Dev stared at the controls blankly. Would she then just...her eyes tracked to the door. She was sure the guards would make her dead, and the idea came to her that maybe if Jess was gone that would be okay.

It was odd and very confusing, and she suspected very incorrect.

With a breath she tapped in the commands and executed, forcing herself to stare at the screen. She ignored the pounding and crackling outside as the scan reached out through all the rock, past the guards and the weapons and some very odd returns from inside the Bay, and came back with the only thing she actually cared about.

Blinking dot, wiremap, Drake, J.

Dev hit the jets and the carrier lifted. She rotated it, watching the big screen wiremap of the area around her. The room filled with people shooting at her with blaster rifles that did nothing much to the carrier's heavy shielding.

Then the scan alerted, and she saw the map redraw with an onrushing clump of bodies carrying something that came back red on the boards. She hit the mains without thinking about it, filling the cavern with energy as she aimed for the opening and felt, rather than heard, a huge disruption behind her.

The carrier lunged forward. She barely kept control as she unlatched the forward screen so she could see realtime, every surface rumbling and shuddering as she shoved the throttles forward and was in clear air, rocketing away from the cliff wall as she picked up an energy release coming at her.

She got altitude, sending the carrier skyward at a radical angle and then going half null as she brought the craft in a circle and saw the entrance to the landing bay disintegrate as it blew outward, followed by a fireball flaring out with a bombastic roar.

Everyone inside, she realized, had been made dead. Dev banked the carrier and ducked behind the cliff face, running a quick scan for anyone in the area. The system caught a lot of debris, and as she flew along the rock, she saw small figures beneath her running for cover and damage all along the homestead.

Jess was in there. Dev felt a sense of relief and it surprised her to find her hands shaking. Jess was not made dead. Yet. Jess was possibly depending on her to help. Dev was not entirely sure what she was supposed to help do, or who was in the right, or what was correct.

But she would figure it out.

"PSST."

The shaking finally dragged her upward and out of the swirling confusion of darkness, and Jess became aware again of her surroundings.

Water hit her face. That sped up the process, and by the time the second wave headed toward her she opened her eyes and tried to lift a hand to defend herself.

That was painful.

"Get back!" A voice sounded nervously near her. "Oh crap did we screw up!"

Jess blinked at that, and the blurry world around her slowly came into focus, and at the same time she became aware of the fact she hurt like hell.

Six small faces peered nervously back at her. "Cuz, we're sorry," the nearest said. "We didn't mean to drop it on you."

"No, we was trying to get them," a second said.

Jess found herself on the ground next to a heavy anchor lying on the floor of the central stairs, a lot of rubble around it. She tried to sit up and then stopped as the darkness threatened to overwhelm her again. "Shit."

"Cuz, we gotta get you in the safe area," the first youngster said. "Them guys find you they're gonna splat you for sure."

Jess covered her eyes with one hand then they all jerked as they heard a sudden and violent explosion not that far away. The blood drained from Jess's face as the sound profile became something she recognized.

A carrier had imploded.

Everything got very quiet inside her head. She stared up at the skylight far above her as a rain of rocky debris rushed into the central hall and began to cover them, the six adolescents holding their arms over them in wide eyed alarm.

"Dev," Jess whispered.

DEV FELT A sense of familiar confidence settle over her as she got all her controls settled and started up long range scan from the carrier. It was a relief to feel programming settling solidly in place and to know exactly what she was doing.

Not like the shuttle at all. Everything there had been in question, and she knew a moment of discomfort at the notion that everything in her life now might be just like that. Was that how natural borns felt all the time?

Dev turned her attention back to the boards and adjusted the trim of her craft as she brought the carrier back around from the north to approach Drake's Bay again. She needed to find Jess now and find out how she could help her.

It was raining hard, and she heard the impact against the roof of the carrier along with the low rumble of thunder overhead. She tuned scan and directed it outward, finding six craft inbound toward her, too far as yet to identify.

Coming from the direction of Base Ten, though. Dev aimed her course down behind the rock walls of the homestead, searching for an opening she might be able to take advantage of. Finding Jess now was the most important thing, as there was no way for her to defend the carrier aside from flying it.

No way to trigger the weapons from her station, even if she knew how to use them, which she didn't. No way for that matter for Jess to drive the carrier from her weapons position aft. It needed both of them.

Both.

Dev checked the scan and saw Jess's code, buried inside the rock wall. She quickly built a wiremap around the area pulled from her portable scanner. She realized Jess was inside the void that was the huge stairwell, and she tipped the carrier and went up the cliff face at top speed.

She opened the outside sound monitors and heard the rush of the waves beneath her and a booming thump along with the far off sounds of impacts.

Then she was at the top of the cliff and she slowed, coming up over the space in the wall where she'd seen light coming in when inside.

Several things happened. The alarms in her scan went off,

and her shields activated, just in time to disrupt a heavy blast from two security defender craft coming right at her.

At the same time, she hit the lights on the bottom of the carrier and lit up the plas surface underneath her. Comms crackled into her ear, urgently yelling.

The oncoming security craft kept up a barrage, and after a moment she turned off the lights and shoved the throttles forward, building up speed quickly as she headed right into the fire.

Her shields held and she went head on to the nearer defender, getting close enough to see the helmeted pilots who swerved out of her way at the last moment.

She went over them and then reversed course, tumbling around one-hundred-eighty degrees and boosting the engines to send her carrier right over the top of the one who'd swerved, as they twisted frantically unable to outrun her.

She felt the scream of metal and a thumping crunch as the shielded bottom of the carrier scraped over the defender, and it pitched and headed for the deck, trailing smoke.

"Holy shit, did you see that!" Comms erupted into her ear piece as she tuned in to Interforce bands. "What the hell!"

"Who is...oh fuck!" the voices chattered on the wire. "That's 270006!"

Dev dodged the second defender who was trying to get a line on her. She tuned the comms and searched for an open line to Drake's Bay. "BR270006 to Drake's Bay control." She dumped and went sideways as she detected a blast coming from the side of the mountain and saw blue clad bodies on the ledge overlooking the sea.

Nothing but static answered, and she frowned. She heard an alarm and looked to her right to find the other defender coming right at her, firing all of its guns. She boosted the shields and inverted, curving around and flying under the defender as its guns thumped against her lower shields.

Comms went out. She glanced over to see the channels now closed to her. Then another alert went off, and she saw the six incoming signals resolving, wiremap tracing them out as craft just like hers.

Suboptimal. The defender crafts were less heavily shielded and had smaller guns than hers did, but the six incoming figures were her equal, and they had gunners inside who could target her.

She was running out of time. But first there were these

gunners on the platform, and she cut power to the engines and let the carrier tumble down the side of the cliff toward them. At the last possible moment, she cut the mains in again and struggled to retain control as the booming roar against the rocks shook loose a thick ledge and sent it plunging downward.

A twist and a roll, and she was at sea level, headed away from the cliff. Behind her the scan showed still falling rocks, and there were no more blasts from the ledge.

She curved around and started back, now seeing an opening at the bottom of the mountain just at the waterline. Was that where the ships went? She aimed for it and ran along the tops of the waves as the six targets came into close scan proximity and she started to get pinged.

Scan alert detected inbound fire. A second later full strength blasters erupted on either side of the carrier, impacting the water and sending it boiling, and her own draft lifted waves on either side of her passage.

Very suboptimal. She aimed for the opening and hoped there was something large enough on the other side of it. The shields started to react just as she cut mains and hit the landing jets, sensing something passing over her head as the carrier flashed inside the cliff face, and she went from the rains roar to inky darkness that lit up suddenly as she turned on the carrier's external lamps.

Proximity alarms, loud and urgent and she automatically compensated, reflexes trimming the carrier and turning it sideways as solid surfaces loomed up in her vision.

Too close. Too small. She got control of the carrier just in time to weave through massive pillars that subdivided the cavern, scraping past stone on either side with a squeal of tortured metal.

Motion. Panic. She ducked the carrier down and got her forward momentum stopped, skids extended to land on a tiny patch of clear rock in the only place possible that could take her.

Big double thump and a bounce, and then she let go of the throttles, their surfaces slick with sweat as she caught her breath.

She heard running boots and yelling outside. She looked up over the console to see a crowd of figures entering the cavern from the inside, all carrying large, extended barreled guns she had no programming at all for. They started to haul up and point the guns at her, when one of them pointed at the side, and then they all raced past her and started firing past the carrier.

Confusing. But better than being shot at. Dev focused her eyes on the scan console, anxiously looking at the readouts and searching for Jess's bio marker.

Yes. There it was, surrounded by others. A quick adjustment showed them to share that distinctive pattern that was from this place. She let out a little breath of relief then looked outside the windscreen, trying to decide what to do next.

The carrier seemed to be in a relatively safe place. She got up and went to the hatch, glad it was on the side away from the opening where many people were now shooting. After a pause, she took her service pack from the storage hatch and put it on.

She studied the weapons rack. Should she bring Jess her big gun? She hefted it experimentally then slung it over her back.

It hit the back of her legs and made it difficult to move, so she reluctantly put it back. Then she triggered the hatch and hopped out, wincing at the sudden barrage of loud sounds all around her. The carrier shielded her from view, and she started for the entryway at a purposeful trot.

JESS WASN'T REALLY sure how she'd gotten where she was. She'd faded out in the hall, and now she lifted her head and found herself in the family kitchen, sprawled on the floor, alone.

She put her head back down and looked up at the kitchen ceiling, aware of booms and roars outside, the pale light of a stormy midday coming in the small window carved in the rock wall to her right.

Her back felt like it had been dragged over stone, and a slight look left showed tracks leading to the closed door to the interior that probably were from her boots.

She lay there breathing quietly. She considered making an effort to do something about the situation, but found little desire to do so.

It was a strange feeling.

She slowly rolled over onto her side and caught the edge of the table. She pulled herself up onto her knees and felt the lingering pain of the zapping she'd taken. Her skull also throbbed from the kid's misguided attack on her.

Really misguided. Jess tentatively released one hand off the table and reached back to touch the back of her head where a large lump was still present.

Anchor would have killed anyone non Drake she suspected. She thought about that huge explosion and wished it had put her out of her misery. Nothing was going to come out of this worth being alive to see, not the destruction of the homestead, not the killing of her kin.

Not Dev.

Jess's breathing shortened, and she turned and slid onto the ledge of stone the window was cut into, staring past the battered plas at the half circle bay full of rain and whitecaps, very surprised to find a stinging in her eyes and tears coming for the first time since she'd been a small, confused child.

It was strange and it hurt. This was something they bred, beat, and trained out of them, and yet, here in this moment, Jess knew sadness and a pain of the heart she hadn't been aware she was actually capable of.

She let her head rest against the stone and stared out over the bay, without really looking at anything. She remembered bits and pieces of her childhood here in random sepia toned images that brought flashes of phantom sounds only she could hear.

Aunties yelling in the kitchen.

A cousin crying from a bumped head.

Her father singing to her.

A booming roar shook the wall, and her eyes tracked outside, recognizing the distinctive boom of a carrier arriving out of the speed of sound and then finding a flicker of motion that moved right across the front of the bay.

Chased by others.

Jess blinked and sat up a little, seeing the first carrier swerve and change direction in evasion and speed away, chased by two others. Who and what? The craft were too far for her to see any hull markings, only the distinctive shape of them identifying Interforce.

Rogue?

Then she saw the craft reverse course without warning and zip between its chasers, and her heart pounded as the craft rotated to accept fire on its bottom shields before heading for the deck at top speed.

Could there be two pilots that crazy skilled? She slid to the other side to follow its course, eyes widening as she realized it was going for the ship cavern, which had no entry space for it. Two pilots that studiously insane?

The carrier disappeared into the cavern opening and she held her breath, waiting for an explosion that didn't come. The two chasers veered wildly and only barely avoided the rock face, one plunging into the water and coming to an abrupt halt as it hit bottom.

No. That could only be one pilot. Jess felt a sudden flush of emotion she really didn't have a word in her head for that nevertheless made her lightheaded and brought back some energy to her aching bones.

That fluid flight path born in space, that could only be Dev.

Dev, Dev, Dev.

"Fuck." Jess shoved herself upright and stood a moment to catch her balance before she started for the door. She ignored the horrific pain as training reasserted itself. She paused to pick up a fish pike to use as a weapon, its spear barbed point rising higher than her head.

She pushed the kitchen door open and headed up the hallway to central then paused before she headed out.

Blaster fire. Concussive explosions in return.

She wanted no part of it.

A fuzzy memory surfaced, and she turned and went down a side corridor, unlocking and pushing aside a metal hatch that exposed a long, round hole in the rock with a rusted, fragile iron ladder sunk into its surface. She let the spear fall down its length and then took hold of the bars to follow.

A rush of air brought moisture and the sea to her, bathing her skin in salt tinged with the faintest hint of the offgassing of an Interforce carrier.

"OKAY PEOPLE." DOCTOR Dan finished hot wiring the entry, and it slid open, emitting a gust of death tainted air. "Let's go." He glanced behind him to the waiting crowd, quiet and intent.

The fifty kids from the Bay were with him, holding their sticks and bats and whatnot, vibrating with excitement, even though they knew the odds they were facing.

"Let's see now." Kurok led the way into the outer cavern, a storage point full now of dead bodies and scattered plas boxes.

"Other side's locked," one of the kids said, knowledgably. Can ya crank it, Doc?"

"Give it my best." Doctor Dan moved through the big cavern and heard concussive shocks from the outside he didn't recognize. "Wonder what that is?"

"Mortars," a second kid told him. "Cuz musta gotten the armory open."

"Yeah!" Voices lifted in excitement. "Hurry before they get 'em all and we ain't got a chance!"

Armory! Kurok put a hand on his head in realization. Of

course. That's what they needed Jess for, to open the locks on all those old weapons. "Holy crap." He sped up and they got to the inner lock, a solid red across the board.

He tossed a scanner down on the surface and started it up. "Anyone got an alternate way in they'd like to tell me about before I start hacking?" he called over his shoulder, not really with much hope. "Aside from not using the main entrance and getting blown up?"

One of the kids squirmed forward, a red haired moppet with a heavily freckled face. "There's a surf tube," he said. "You handle that?"

Kurok glanced over his shoulder at the waiting kids and the quiet bio alts behind them. "Where does that put us?" He asked after a pause.

"Ship base. But if we get a surge we're fish," the kid said. "Comes in from there, out near the wall to water release."

Kurok calculated the relative risks. Then he shook his head and went back to the panel. "Let's keep that as a bad second choice. With my luck today it's high tide."

The kid grinned in acknowledgment. "Got caught once and broke my leg coming back out here. But it's a good ride sometimes."

"Good ride," the other kid next to him agreed, shifting the harness he was wearing that held Tayler to his back. "Right Tay? You done that, huh?"

Tayler nodded silently, looking around at the dark, death filled cavern with an uncomfortable expression. "Stuff's bad."

"Yes, it is, lad," Kurok said, tuning the scanner carefully. "Just try to keep steady, will you? We'll try to get everyone out of this."

No real hope of that, and he knew it. Likely they'd all end up dying in some massive pointless crossfire. There was no compassion here. No one would care about any of them because that was the nature of who they were.

No win situation. Kurok sighed. And yet, here he was hotwiring a door that would let them right into it. All the justification he'd ever convinced himself of was as bogus as he'd always suspected it to be. With a shake of his head he bent his attention over the boards.

A sudden explosive shock rumbled underfoot and threw them against the wall. He grabbed the scanner with one hand and caught his balance on the panel with the other, by chance hitting his palm on the center of it. "What the hell was that?"

"Dunno, Doc, but good job!" Dustin pointed at the hatch which was creaking open. "Something big went boom." He peeked through the widening opening. "Hope it was them!"

Kurok looked in bemusement at the now green lock panel. Around him the Bay kids were already slipping through the opening ahead of him, into an open space full of sounds and reverberations, holding arms over their heads to ward off falling shards of rock.

He squared his shoulders and followed, a long line of bio alts hastening after him.

JESS REACHED THE bottom of the shaft and released the bottom rung. She landed on a slick rock surface that jarred every bone in her body. She swept around and pressed her back against the nearby wall, stooping to retrieve the spear lying nearby.

She was in an irregularly shaped tunnel that sloped downward to her left and upward to her right. She started downward, reaching up to touch her head as she heard a distinct ringing in her ears. Concussed, probably. She resisted the urge to shake her noggin and hoped the ringing would stop.

Hard to hear past it. Hard to concentrate on what she was doing with all that noise, and the nausea, and the pain elsewhere. Though she'd been trained well to ignore all that, right now she was finding it rough. It was even hard for her to remember the last time she'd...

Oh, no. She remembered now her brief rest up in the shuttle, trusting Dev not to drive into something catastrophic.

Dev. Who took on that shuttle and sweated it down, and who must be even more tired than Jess was. She leaned against the wall and considered that then focused her intent on finding Dev and getting a nap. Screw everything and everyone else.

This far down the noise from the fighting had faded, and she shoved off against the wall only to pause again as a brief spell of dizziness almost made her stumble.

Not good. She took a breath and forced her body to settle then started off again more confidently in the direction she knew would lead her to where she'd seen the carrier disappear.

Ahead of her she heard the sound of the sea. That and the salt smell drew her insistently, speeding up her steps as she reached the end of the ramp and entered the ship cavern.

There she halted and stared, her eyes widening at the destruction in front of her.

Six ships were half sunk in the harbor, overturned and full of holes while dead bodies floated nearby. The edge of the cavern was still dropping debris into the water, and one side of the space looked like a bomb had hit it.

Between two granite columns, a little sideways, was an Interforce carrier where no such thing belonged. Jess looked at the angle and then at the carrier. "Son of a bitch."

If she'd had any doubt, now she didn't. No other pilot on the planet could have landed that damn brick where it was in one piece, and in fact she had no real idea how they were going to get it back out because there wasn't even clearance to turn.

She made her way along the edge of the ship dock and came up to the carrier, circling it and leaning against the engine, cowling long enough to look at the painted names on the outside of the craft.

Her carrier.

Their carrier. She went up next to the skin and bumped it with her shoulder, leaning over and kissing it where the block letters DEV were stenciled then resting her head against the cool surface for a long moment.

Then she unlocked the door and stepped inside, letting it close behind her.

She could still smell Dev's presence, and she stood a moment, taking in a breath of the air inside and tasting it on the back of her tongue as she set the spear down. What now? She was aware that thoughts were coming more slowly to her than usual, but bangs on the noggin did that.

She wished she could sit down for a while in her nice, padded chair, but she forced herself to keep standing, as she removed the jumpsuit she was wearing and traded it for her half armored battle suit that would at least give her a small bit of protection that her duty suit hadn't.

She took a wipe from the dispenser and ran it over her face. It came back covered in soot and blood and bits of bone. She carefully avoided looking at her reflection in any shiny surface after she dropped the wipe into the garbage bag.

Damn, her head hurt. Jess finished fastening up her battle suit and peered around the carrier. She reached into the drink dispenser and removing a container of kack that she opened and drained. It didn't do much for her roiling stomach but at least brought a flicker of energy behind it.

Dev's pack was gone, she noted.

The med kit was also gone.

Jess finished the kack and tossed it then went to the arming rack, noting her long blaster was slightly out of place. She studied it for a minute then lifted it up and examined it before she seated it along her leg on it's hard points.

She added two more heavy blasters and a long dagger then turned to the hatch and put her hands on the edges of it, waiting for the dizziness to fade again before she hit the hatch to let it open.

Salt air hit her in the face and then death almost did as a flicker of motion made her half turn. Facing her were two blue clad security guards. Before she could react they fired at her point blank.

She twisted and lunged to one side as one blast hit her half armor. It spun her around enough to miss the second and she slammed into the side of the carrier and then headed for the rock floor.

Ow.

She got her hand blaster out and fired back as she hit the ground, a bump in the rock giving her enough cover to survive to shoot again and then again. Instinct took over in a wash of relief, and she stopped trying to think and just gave over to it.

One of them dove behind the engine and took a shot then as she watched him aim at her, in almost slow motion, something hit him in the side of the head and blew his skull apart.

The other guard dove for the ground, glancing around frantically. Jess got a line on him and shot him, and then she scrambled to her feet and ducked behind the engine, glad of its solid bulk under her hands.

"Drake!"

"Here." She kept the blaster in her hand as a tall figure came around the carrier and spotted her, and they looked at each other for a very long moment. "Mike."

"Fuckin A." The Drake's Bay security chief wiped his forehead off. "Ops ops," he said into a comms. "Found the Drake. Secure."

Jess pushed herself upright. "What's the deal?"

"Got carriers coming in," Mike said. "Saw this one come in the cavern. Son of a fucking bitch."

Jess patted the skin of the carrier. "Dev," she said. "You know where she went?"

Mike shook his head. "Fighting's up near the stairs. We got 'em pinned down. Maybe she went that way to all the noise? Figure she's looking for you."

"Probably," Jess said. "Got my bell rung."

"Looks it," Mike said. "Got a lot of blood there." He took a step back. "Maybe you should stick here in that crate? Safest place in the joint at the mo."

Jess moved past him toward the long sloping rampway that led from the cavern up to the processing rooms where fish became food, or items to sell. Here the rock never really lost the scent of that, and she circled the carrier and started upwards.

Mike caught up with her. "Okay, so not." He fell silent and kept pace with her. There were far off sounds of shots and yells and, more distant, the scream of the wind. "Storm's comin. Ground those bastards."

Jess nodded. "Until reinforcements get here from the west. We can only do this so long. They got more and bigger bombs than we do."

"We's we now?"

"Yeah. Maybe always was," Jess muttered.

Mike smiled grimly and just nodded.

They heard running steps coming at them and they drew apart, going to the walls of the passage and bracing, Jess with her blaster and Mike with an old style rocket launcher he lifted to his shoulder.

A running body came around the corner and spotted them, skidding to a halt. She threw her hands up. "For fucks sake I surrender. Don't shoot me! I'm done!"

Red cropped hair and security blue. Jess stepped away from the wall but kept the blaster in focus. "Rusty," she said. "No shooting yet."

The woman stared at her. "Drake?" She took a very cautious step forward. "Holy shit." She looked surprisingly relieved. "Listen, I'm null. I'm not under orders. I just want to stay alive." She got the words out quickly. "Don't kill me."

"Okay," Jess said after a moment. "Who's in charge now?"

"No clue." Rusty slowly lowered her hands to her sides. She was unarmed and had blood over the front of her uniform, now visible to Jess. "There's an insanity here, Drake," she said. "We walked into a buzz saw."

Jess almost smiled. "Insanity that Interforce has been tapping for a long time now." She pointed back the way Rusty had come from. "We're going that way."

Rusty stared at her. "Are you good guys or bad guys, Drake? What side am I on if I go with you?"

Jess shrugged. "Side that probably lives. But no guarantees."

She moved past the security guard and picked up the pace, hearing echoing sounds and shots ahead of her.

DEV PRESSED HER back against the wall and felt both salt and moisture as she carefully peered around the corner. She heard screaming and a quick check of her scan showed a lot of people, mostly Interforce ahead of her. She swept around and behind her, searching for Jess's bio.

Hard with so many people around that had that. But she persisted and after a moment the wiremap resolved and she spotted Jess on the move heading... "Ah."

Dev blinked and looked behind her, a moment later spotting a familiar figure stalking her way. She stepped out away from the wall and into the dim light from the overhead. Jess's eyes tracked to her and they locked on.

Jess looked horrible. She had blood all over her head and she was limping, almost staggering with one hand lightly brushing the wall. But when her eyes met Dev's her face broke into a grin, and Dev knew a brief sensation of floating on air as she exhaled in relief.

It made her knees weak.

"Devvviiieee!" Jess warbled softly as they met and without hesitation pulled Dev into a hug. "Nice landing back there, you Rocket Raccoon you."

Dev gently hugged her back, noting the odd stare from the short figure behind her and the brief nod from the tall man. "Hello," she said. "I'm really glad I found you. There's so much incorrectness here I don't know where to start."

A loud roar interrupted their reunion, and they threw themselves against the corridor wall as rocks started coming down from the ceiling.

"What the hell!" Mike bawled. "They get so pissed of they blew themselves up?"

"Wouldn't put it past 'em," Rusty said. "End game." She braced next to him. "No real thinking going on." She shielded her head with an arm. "Is that a rocket launcher?"

"Yeah." He ducked a thick blanket of stone that detached from the ceiling and covered them. "Real Bay issue."

"Holy crap. Last time I saw one was in history class at Rainier Island."

Jess closed her eyes, her body braced and arms lifted over both of them to shield them from the debris. Dev reached up to touch her face. "You are not well."

One blood shot blue eye opened and peered down at her. "I'm absolutely fan-fucking-tastic right now," Jess said. "I thought you croaked. I was really bummed there for a minute."

Dev gave her a brief smile. "I felt the same way. I was thinking if that was true, and you were not here anymore, that it would be okay if they made me dead, too."

"Really?"

"Yes of course," Dev said. "You're my reason for being here."

Jess felt a little prickling against her skin, and it got very quiet in her head, just for a minute there as those words echoed through her ears and traveled down to her heart in a spread of warmth she could actually feel.

It felt so amazing. It made the headache, and the pain, and all the crap they were dealing with just a secondary consideration. She got an insight into herself she hadn't really expected. Amoral sociopaths weren't supposed to give a shit about anyone else, and right up to now, this one hadn't.

Not really. Not even for her father, who she'd liked as much as someone like her could.

Jess looked past Dev's head and saw a cloud of dust heading their way, most likely full of vaporized relatives. So maybe there was a little bit of her that wasn't all that craziness. "Thanks, Dev. I was kinda feeling the same way, too."

"Excellent," Dev said. "I hope everyone can stop shooting now."

"Me too." Jess almost chuckled. "Let's go see what blew up," she finally said, aware of the stares and the discomfort of it all. "And see if there's anyone left to surrender."

She put her arm across Dev's shoulders and shifted her gun to her other side, starting forward as the cloud hit them and peppered them with stench, stone, and dust that made her slit her eyes and clamp her lips shut as her black half armor was covered in debris.

Dev ducked her head and pressed her face against Jess's side, allowing the suit she was wearing to block some of the dust.

It was suboptimal, stinky, dangerous, horrible, and yet, absolutely excellent, all at the same time. Crazy and sad and good. And in that moment, with Jess's arm around her, for the very first time Dev felt a sense of herself as a person.

It felt strange but awesome.

They made their way through the cloud and at the end of the hallway, where Dev had first paused, they found utter destruction. The arch had collapsed and the spot Dev had been standing was gone, the hallway half obscured with rubble.

Mike climbed up the rubble and sprawled across the top of it, peering past. "Hey!" he yelled into the darkness beyond.

"Mike?" A voice yelled back. "Holy shit, man! Whole fucking mountain fell down in here!"

Jess sighed.

Mike squirmed up through the open space at the top of the debris and slid down the other side. Jess reluctantly released Dev in order to follow him. Rusty brought up the rear and they carefully climbed up and over the rubble and emerged into the large central hall of Drake's Bay.

Ghostly figures were everywhere. Lights started to come up, highlighting lumps and piles of bodies and stone on the floor. As they came to the center with the overhead plas opening above them, lighting blasted overhead and lit everything in tarnished silver.

"We give up," a quiet, dark clad figure came over, hands up, exhausted. "Drake, you win." It was one of the Western Interforce seniors, barely known to Jess except as a face in the hallways just before she'd left Base Ten. "Please just stop killing people."

"Get the bats going!" a voice called out. "We beat their asses!"

Jess looked around and saw all the bodies, all the death, the destruction of her stakehold, and knew it all for a lie. "Tell everyone left to put their weapons down," she said to the senior. "Let's see what we can salvage from this."

The man nodded. "I'm sorry, Drake," he said. "We should have refused orders." His face was white and creased in pain. "We didn't know what we were getting into."

The boom of thunder rolled through the rock. "Yeah." Jess sighed. "Me either."

Chapter Thirteen

THEY MANAGED TO get inside one of the service corridors. Kurok was in the lead, the kids from the Bay at his heels, and the bio alts clustering behind them. It was an outer pathway he vaguely remembered from years past that wound its way through the storage areas in the lower levels of the stakehold.

"That one there," Dustin said. "That'll come up through the mess and we can get to central ops from there."

"Yah. We take the garbage out this way. To the grinder," another youth said. "Damn, I'm hungry."

"Maybe later, lads," Kurok said. "Let's get out of some trouble first, hmm?"

They entered a niche that held a doorway, and Dustin took hold of the latch and hauled it backwards. Before Kurok could react, six of the Bay kids were inside, sticks, rocks, and random weapons held at the ready. He got inside with the next group, glad he'd left Cathy, Taylor, and Jake back in the shuttle.

No argument from Jake. "Might end up being the last Drake after all," he'd said.

And well he might. Kurok could smell gunpowder and flash, and yes, the cloying scent of death as he shouldered his way through the moving crowd and got to the front. He remembered this room. He remembered walking through it at Justin's side and sitting at table surrounded by members of the homestead amidst the smell of fish stew and beer. Accepted because to not would be risking Justin's hair trigger wrath, and they all knew it.

Like swimming with sharks, he'd told Justin later, and Justin had laughed and laughed.

If he'd seen this room now, Justin wouldn't have been laughing. The betrayal of his birth home would have put him so deep in the zone, Kurok didn't think any of those stop words would have pulled him out of it.

They moved through the mess, going between the tables and stepping over bodies in the dim light. "Them mostly," Dustin commented. "We kicked ass."

Security uniforms, largely. Kurok pondered that as they got to the front of the room and the big folding old school doors that were actual wood and smelled of antiquity and dust. "Hold up," he said and pressed the side of his head against the warm neutral surface.

"C'mon." One of the kids pushed gently against the door.

It yanked back without warning, and in the next breath, blasters and heavy duty weapons were raised and pointed.

Kurok spread his arms out. "Get back!"

"Kill them!" The shout came from those dark clad figures, stripped of reason and desperate as they faced off against the Bay kids, who bristled instantly, full of hormones and inbred instinct and responded in kind.

The rage around Kurok built, and as fingers tightened on triggers he managed to shove his way forward and raise both hands. "STOP!" he bellowed at the top of his voice. "STAND DOWN!"

For just an instant there was an afterflash. He almost saw them fire, almost felt the wash of rage as the youngsters next to him moved in response. Yet when the echo of his voice faded, incredibly, they listened.

No one fired.

"Who the hell are you?" a man in an Interforce uniform asked. "What are those kids?" He lifted the muzzle of his blaster up. "I don't care. Even the damn babies in this place are screwball, so you better get out of our way buddy. We're getting out of here."

Kurok took a step forward. "My name is DJ Kurok," he said in a calm tone. "Senior field tech, retired." He half turned. "And yes, these are some juvenile members of Drake's Bay homestead." He paused. "Along with several sets of biological alternatives under my direction."

He was aware of the vibrating tension in the young bodies next to him, their eyes focused on the security force, fingers curled around pikes and poles they'd picked up on the way in.

The Interforce agent studied him intently. "Peter, contact centops again. See if they're answering," he said to a shorter man in green next to him. "If not you're all just going to get out of our way."

"Sure," Kurok said. "You're welcome to leave. But if you go out that way, you'll just end up in the outer passageways."

"No answer, John," the tech said. "I don't hear anything on any channel."

Kurok took another step forward. "We heard some explosions. I don't know if anyone's left that way." He indicated the central hall. "May not be anyone left to answer."

The agent was young. Kurok saw him lick his lips, and suddenly he felt sad for all of them. "You're from Tempe? Or

Juneau?" he asked. "I was stationed Base Ten, back in the day."

They looked shell shocked, on the edge. Unsure of how to move forward, afraid of retreating. Holding tight to a twisted normality. But he could see some of them listening to him, blinking, soothed by the familiar words.

"John, I'm not getting any returns," the tech said. "We should go see what happened." He glanced at Kurok. "Or get out of here. Anything but just stand around."

There were twenty of them. Ten agents and ten techs. Kurok didn't know any of them. They were all young, probably just graduated from field school, new recruits after the last disaster.

"We're from Juneau," the agent finally said. "They sent us to help."

Kurok sighed. "My advice to you is to just go into the mess there and sit down, or come with us to see what happened. Put the guns down. Don't try to damage these young people because they just came back from Bio Station Two in space. It's been a long day for them, too."

Dustin straightened up next to him in visible pride. The rest of the kids joined him, bearing their wounds and scars proudly.

The agent licked his lips again. "They brought Drake back," he said. "With the shuttle."

"Bet your ass we did," Dustin said. "My cuz." He pointed his thumb at his own chest. "My pop was her pop's bro. I'm Drake, and this place is Drake, and you ain't got no damn right to be here." He rocked forward a little. "No right to snuff out them olders, no right to be taking nothing from here."

Kurok watched the agents carefully. "He's right," he said in a gentle tone. "For the entire history of Interforce, the backbone of everything it is, came from here. This place has bled more for it than any other place on earth."

The agent hesitated, clearly on the edge, clearly poised on the brink of that slide into the zone. Then the agent's body posture changed. His shoulders relaxed. Hand slid off the blaster. "Yeah. How do we get out of here?" he asked. "We left our carriers on the next ridge."

"C'mon." Kurok waved him forward. "You'll need to get up to the upper levels to get out that way. Follow me."

And they did. This odd assortment of Bay rats, Interforce ops, and stolidly following bio alts.

NIGHT HAD FALLEN, and now the flashes of lightning were

almost continuous, lighting the central hall in gold washed silver as power came back and what was left to return did also.

Jess sat on a box, her hands resting on her knees, allowing Dev to clean some of the blood off the side of her head as Mike read off statistics from a plas clipboard.

Old as the hills. Older than she was. A sheet of beaten and gouged material that had been used by men in Mike's position for as long as Drake's Bay had existed.

"Still findin' bodies," Mike said. "Told everyone to just drag everything to the processor and start pumping. Gotta get them out of the halls."

"Yeah," Jess agreed.

She wasn't really sure if it mattered. Interforce would come back at them with everything they had soon as the storm ended.

She paused and thought. Wouldn't they? "Any word from the shuttle?" she asked Dev.

"No. I can't raise them." Dev finished cleaning the deep cut under Jess's ear and gently wiped off the lump on the side of her head. "That looks very sub-optimal."

"Feels like that," Jess agreed. "We lost a thousand people here, Dev." She shook her head very faintly. "For what?"

Mike was scribbling on the plas, and he answered. "For the Bay, our side. Been building to it, Jess. Everyone's trying to make this place like all the other homesteads. Blood can't handle it." He looked up at her. "Pretending we're not different."

"Yeah," Jess said after a pause. "We are different."

"We," he repeated.

"We," Jess echoed. "Me more than many. They only take the most different. Make us Interforce. Let us kill as much as we want. Rest of you are stuck here wanting to beat kittens to death, and you have to just scrape limpets. Sad." She blinked a few times. "Not enough people left to breed it out of us."

"They tried." Mike folded his broad arms over his chest and the clipboard. "Got them babies off anyone they could."

"Never worked. Doc saw it upside. What did they call it, Dev? Sticky?" Jess sighed. "Flipped a bit. We all got it. Just mattered what degree."

Mike nodded. "You got it." He studied the board. "That's why the first ones down were the elders. They wanted to bleed for the Bay. I saw old Uncle get it. He took out one of them with a kitchen knife in that one good hand." He smiled a little. "Bastard was laughing his head off."

Old Uncle. Jess remembered seeing him at that dysfunctional

lunch on the occasion of her mother's processing. "Good on ya, Jessie," he'd said on hearing of her slaughter of the other side. Good on ya.

"Yeah I can picture it," Jess said. "He had a right to it. They skunked him."

"They did," Mike agreed. "He took it back from 'em."

"Jess?" Dev was there, holding something out. "Would you like some hot tea?"

Jess took the cup and held it, feeling it warm the palms of her hands. "Didja get some yourself, Devvie? You must be whacked." She looked at her partner, who did in fact look exhausted.

"Yes, I did, and also this." She handed over a fishroll.

Jess shifted her cup to one hand and took the roll with her other. "Glad everyone stopped shooting for now." She took a sip of the tea, hot and pungent. "Better than the stuff up on the station."

"It is." Dev sat down next to her and took a sip from her own cup. "I'm glad we're back here."

"We're going to get toasted, Dev. There're not gonna let me survive this," Jess said, in a tired tone. "Either Interforce'll eliminate me or the family council will. I did this." Jess gestured to the battered hall with her cup. "My fuck up. "

Mike stood there, listening. "Nope. You just did a sitch. Jimmy did this and that crackerhead director." He leaned against one of the crates that had been dragged into the central hall. "Sides, nothing left of the family, Jess. You're it."

"Jake's in the shuttle with Tayler," Jess said after a long pause.

Mike snorted. "One's worthless, the other's taken. Like I said, you're it."

"I'm taken."

Mike shook his head. "You're old enough to have sense. Like Justin was." He looked up as a buzz of voices suddenly rose. "Now what?"

Arms rose, bodies straightened and turned and came to order as the far hall filled with figures, some black and green clad. But at their head was a short, scruffy form in a Bay jacket. He lifted both hands and let out a sharp whistle.

Dev stood up. "Doctor Dan."

"Doctor Dan." Jess had to smile, seeing him as he herded a handful of Interforce along with his battle group of Bay rats and bio alts. "Relax, Mike. He's a friend." She managed to get to her feet and lifted one hand to catch his attention.

"He's not with friends," Mike said. "Where the hell did those bios come from?"

"Space," Dev said. "They came from the space station. They helped us get away from there."

Mike looked at her. "Don't much care for you all."

Jess swung her head around to stare at him.

"Give me the stink eye all you want, Drake," Mike said. "I'm gonna say it. I don't like the jelly bag brains. We don't here. Never have." He studied her shrewdly. "Justin didn't."

Jess was too tired to really get mad. "He never met Dev," she said. "She's us." She indicated the bios who were all turning in a circle, looking up at the huge hall. "Don't diss them, Mike. My head hurts too much to kill ya."

Mike snorted softly. "Where'd he get the Bay coat?"

"I gave it to him." Jess watched Kurok approach. He looked almost as tired as she felt. "He was my pop's tech back in the day."

"Huh." Mike's expression shifted a little.

Kurok reached them with his crowd. The Interforce agents looked sullen and nervous. "Excuse me." He edged past Mike. "Are you all right?" he asked them both. "Dev told me you got into some trouble." He came close, grimacing when he saw Jess's face.

"Probably never been out of trouble." Jess sighed and sat back down. "I figure we've got 'til the storm clears before we're ass over teakettle again."

Kurok opened the med kit Dev put next to her. "Let's do what we can until then." He half turned and motioned to the crowd. "Frank, settle your group over near the wall there with the others."

Without a word, the Interforce agents and their techs went over to where there were a half dozen surviving others, all seated near the wall with drinks and fishrolls."

Kurok watched them then turned back around to Jess. He paused when he saw them all look at him in bemusement. "I was a senior," he said with the faintest of smiles. "That's trained in, too."

"It is." Jess leaned back and held onto the edge of the box with her fingertips. "For all the good it's gonna do us."

"Ah, you never know, Jesslyn." Kurok motioned the bio alts over, and they slowly surrounded them, watching Jess with interest. "Now, my friends, you're going to see an old fashioned technique called stitching."

Jess grimaced. "Ugh."

"Oh, it'll only take a minute."

MET WAS ON their side for a change. Jess felt a sense of utter relief as she lay down flat on her back on the bed in the quarters they'd been assigned. She felt raw around all the spots Kurok had attended to.

That had hurt. But now the painkillers had kicked in, and she'd been forced to lay down, the violent weather allowing for nothing else. Everything would wait now for that nonstop rumble and flash of lightning to end.

In the distance she heard April and Doug recounting their part in the battle. The laughter and the clink of mugs let her relax a little.

No one was going to try and kill her yet, though that was coming.

The bio alts were settled in one of the storage areas with rations and padding to sit on while the storm raged overhead, and according to met it would remain that way for another six to eight hours.

Nothing could fly. Even comms was disrupted. One of the bad ones that for once, for her, meant nothing but good. She could rest.

So here she was in a big bed, with Dev curled up next to her, already showered, and in a fresh green jumpsuit from her kit and out like a light.

It felt so nice to just be still. Jess had her eyes half closed, one arm draped over Dev's compact body, not really giving a crap what anyone else thought about it. What the hell did it matter? She had no future. Neither in the force nor in the Bay. Now it was just a matter of waiting it out.

She felt peaceful about it actually. Jess let her eyes close and immediately felt that sense of dislocation that meant sleep was coming at her fast. Maybe when she woke up it would already be over.

Maybe someone would overpower the guard and kill her in her sleep.

Dev stirred and snuggled closer to her. It brought a soothing warmth to her right side, and the gloomy thoughts faded, leaving her in just that moment of the present. And with that, she just let it go.

Maybe she'd dream about space, and stars, and tumbling in the null.

IT WAS THUNDER that woke her. Dev lifted her head and looked around, confused for a moment where she was. She didn't

354 Of Sea and Stars

recognize the rock walls at first or the loud sound of rain, much louder than she'd become used to in the Citadel.

Then she remembered and she settled back down in the bed next to Jess. Aside from the thunder it was quiet, the voices she recalled before sleep were silenced, though far off she thought she heard footsteps echoing softly against the stone.

She was in Drake's Bay, where terrible things had happened.

Jess was breathing deeply, sound asleep next to her. Dev closed her eyes again. She wasn't on that ragged edge of exhaustion that had barely let her finish her shower and tumble into bed, but she felt she could still get more sleep.

It had felt so amazing to be able to rest. She'd been so tired. To be able to curl up next to Jess and know for at least a little while she was safe was excellent.

Now she had a piece of time to sit quietly and think about everything that had happened in the last few days, from their flight to station, to her losing her collar, to the escape back downside.

She lifted a hand and touched her neck, slipping her fingers under the edge of her jumpsuit to feel again the smooth skin that was covered so long with metal. The back of her neck was no longer even sore, and she barely felt the small scabs over where Doctor Dan had removed the synaptics in her brain.

Good and bad. The good being she no longer could be controlled, and the bad being everything she learned from now on had to be the old fashioned way. She would never again wake up with new knowledge effortlessly inserted into her head.

Dev thought about that. Then she shrugged just a little. After all, that's how Jess did everything, right? And the rest of the agents and techs.

That pushed her thoughts to Interforce and what might happen with that since all the bad things. Were she and Jess still part of it?

Did they still hold her contract?

Did her contract actually mean anything now that she was no longer able to be programmed?

So many questions. Dev was more awake now, and she was aware of being thirsty. She rolled carefully away from Jess, got up, and felt the rough surface of the seaweed mat rugs that covered the stone floor through her socks.

She ran her fingers through her hair and slipped out of the room into the hallway, pausing to look out the plas round windows in the side of the cliff.

Complete darkness outside, rain lashing against the surface, only the barest hint of whitecaps outside the Bay. She continued on and pushed the door open between the hall and the outer central space, careful to close the door softly behind her.

Here it was also quiet. There were guards near the walls and they glanced at her as she proceeded through the open central space toward where she remembered there being a drink dispenser. To one side she saw the other Interforce agents and techs, the ones she didn't know, lying down on some pads, asleep.

Wasn't that strange? They had been the enemy, and defeated, and now they slept in trust of the guards from the Bay standing against the walls with old fashioned guns and quietly proud expressions.

One of them saw her watching and gave her a little nod. Was that acceptance? Approval? Dev retrieved a bottle of water and opened it. She took several swallows, almost sure the sound of her gulping was echoing across the hall. Then she removed another bottle and walked over to the guard, offering it to him.

His face creased into a smile, and he took it. "I saw you fly into the cavern," he said without preamble. "Freaking awesome."

They stood together drinking for a moment. "I had to get away from the people who were chasing me and, also, to find Jess," Dev said. "I think I did some damage to the vessels there however."

"They blew up that other one," the guard said. "Jerks. Take forever to get that bay cleaned out."

"Yes, I felt the explosion as I was exiting," Dev said. "It seemed somewhat pointless to me."

"They was trying to get you," the guard said. "That old jerk, yeah? He said they should blow you up, and the Drake went and broke his neck for it."

"Commander Alters?"

He nodded. "Broke it like a stick. Pissed her off." He took a swallow of the water. "I'm Bruce. They call you Dev, right?"

Dev nodded. "Right. Yes, I think that would have made Jess very upset. I know if someone said that to me I would have been really mad."

Bruce looked around and made a small grunt under his breath. "Cleared out a lot here. Things'll be diff now I betcha."

The sound of footsteps made them both look to the right, to see Kurok emerging from a side hallway, pulling his bay shirt over his head as he walked over to join them. "Hello, Doctor

Dan," Dev said.

"Hello, you two," Kurok responded. "I see it's still raining outside."

"Like crazy," Bruce agreed. "Ops said another two, three." He crushed the water bottle in one hand and tucked it into a pocket on his rough Bay garb. "They got all the boards back up. Ready if those bastards come back at us."

Kurok got his shirt settled and gave himself a little shake. "Never thought I'd be so glad to see weather," he said. "Seems like they cleaned up in here, too. Now it just smells like fish and the sea."

"Yup." Bruce leaned against the wall. "Finished chewing 'em all out 'bout two hours ago. They got Jake and the kid from the shuttle, too." He pointed to one of the hallways. "Got the mess back up."

Dev's ears perked up. "I could bring a snack back for Jess. Would you like a meal, Doctor Dan?" She started off in the direction Bruce pointed. A moment later Kurok caught up with her. They walked together in silence until they were some lengths down the hall.

The lights were back on, and all the way down the tunnel-like passage the inset lamps were glowing with a steady golden illumination. Now they could hear sounds of mechanicals echoing softly through the rock and a few voices from the mess ahead.

"I'm sure you realize this whole thing isn't over," Kurok said.

"I had, yes," Dev said. "But Jess has taught me to appreciate the current moment because you really never know what's going to happen next."

"In her type of life, that's very true, Kurok said. "Come to think of it, in my life lately that's pretty true as well."

They entered the mess, and the few people inside looked up at them. One of them was the security chief, Mike. He waved them over to a table where April was also seated with a very sleepy looking Doug.

Doug brightened when he spotted Dev, however. "Rocket!"

"Hello." Dev sat down next to him while Doctor Dan took a seat across from her at the table. "Did you get any rest?"

"About ten minutes." Doug gave April a dour look.

"Suck it up, buttercup," April replied with a droll expression. "And you got more than that. We just got up here." She leaned on the table as one of the mess workers came over with a tray of fishrolls and steaming cups of sea grape tea.

Dev took two rolls and a cup of the tea. Two more she set to one side. The tea was richly pungent, almost spicy, and it cleared her head as she sipped it. Very different than the leaf tea they drank on station, and she thought it was better.

The fishrolls were fresh and full of water grains along with the tiny fish. She munched it appreciatively, enjoying the taste. "Have there been any comms?"

"Nothing," April responded. "Nothing from Ten, nothing from any other homestead. It's like the bands are just shut down. I was in ops, and they didn't even hear any weather squirts from Quebec City."

Kurok grunted under his breath.

"Could be weather," Doug suggested. "The spectrum is off the charts. Almost like it was when we were up against that stuff from the other side."

"That was shut down," Kurok said. "I wonder if this is people not responding because they can't or because they just don't want to. Interforce attacking a settled homestead, especially this one, is a political situation to say the least."

April nodded as she chewed.

"Got that right," Mike agreed. "The fuck were they thinking?"

April swallowed thoughtfully. "Possible Alters was rogue? Hell, the old man was." She glanced at Kurok. "How deep did that scam go?"

Kurok's eyes narrowed a little, and his face twitched.

"Most of the ones who came here were from the west," Doug said. "Not from Base Ten. But Jess said Jason didn't warn her off, so..."

"Yes." Doctor Dan swallowed. "So maybe people didn't think this was right, but no one wanted to stop it. I bet there are homesteads out there waiting to see what they can scavenge after this is done."

Mike eyed him, his head moving up and down. "No one's friends. Everyone wants a piece of this." He lifted a hand and circled his finger to indicate the Bay in general. "They ain't getting nothing. Don't care what they think they got to throw against us."

April chuckled without much humor. "I'm sure plenty of reports went back to HQ to support that," she said. "We going to send those westies out of here after it stops raining? Or keep them for barter?"

A little silence fell after that. "So, you us now, too?" Mike asked in a quizzical tone. "Seems like that induction doesn't mean much these days."

Doug covered his eyes with one hand, but April just regarded him benignly. "That goes both ways," she said. "Right's right, wrong's wrong. I wasn't raised to follow anyone without knowing what's best for me." She winked at Mike.

Dev started on her second roll. A few more people entered, and she saw a color difference and focused past the wandering guards to see a space suited figure peering inside hesitantly. "Doctor Dan." She indicated the door. "I think the sets may be hungry."

"Bet they are." Kurok waved the bio alts forward. "Hope I don't have to fight the wolves for some food for them." He stood at his place as the group came timidly toward him, four AyeBees and two KayTees, with Cathy, his lab assistant, trailing behind them.

The Bay people all stared at them. But they didn't do anything to prevent their passage, and the mess worker, after a glance at Mike, brought over a tray of rolls.

It was a tipping point. Kurok knew it, even if his table companions didn't. "Thank you," he told the mess worker. "It's as strange for them to be here as it is for you all to have them." He gestured for them to sit at the table next to them. "I appreciate the courtesy."

Some of the Bay people eased around them, with curious expressions, and sat down nearby. "These are real ones," one of them said. "Not like her." He pointed at Dev.

Kurok didn't bother to argue. "These are AyeBees, and KayTees, service workers and pilots from the space station." He was glad to see a tray of hot tea added to the table. "That's sea grape tea, lads. And the items on the plate there are fishrolls. Try them."

Cathy came to his side. "I didn't want to bring all of them," she said in a low tone. "Someone told me...they said the sets weren't really welcome here."

Kurok sighed. "It's complicated." He pointed her to a seat next to Dev, who had taken the opportunity to consume another of the fishrolls. "Cathy is one of my lab assistants from station."

Mike gave her a brief smile. "Welcome to the nuthouse," he said in a cordial tone. "What's it like living in space?" He offered her a mug. "Cathy's your name? I'm Mike."

She nodded and took the mug. "Thank you." She sipped it gingerly then her brows lifted a little. "That's really good," she said. "What's it made of?"

"That's sea grape. It's a type of seaweed that grows off the coast nearby. The fishermen bring it in with the catch," Kurok said. "They boil it to make tea then they eat the sea grapes as a vegetable."

Mike studied him intently. "You do know."

"I do." Kurok sat down and picked up his mug. "I came here a few times with Justin on the odd day off or so." He leaned back a little and looked around the mess. "Enough to know the drill."

Mike tilted his head a little. "Justin Drake?"

"Yes. He and I were partnered in Interforce together. So now that we've done with history, has anything happened while we've napped?" he asked. "Should be getting light soon."

"Thought you looked a little familiar," Mike said. "Justin had a still vid of you in his office before he bought it." He stood up and drained the contents of his mug. "Rain is all that happened. I'm going to ops to see if anything's on scan."

One of the KayTee's looked up. "This is good." He held up the fishroll.

Dev stood up and gathered up a cup and the fishrolls she'd set aside. "They are," she agreed. "I like them and so does Jess, so I will bring her some now." She stepped around the table and started for the door, confident that Doctor Dan would make sure things were all correct.

A moment later April caught up with her and Doug belatedly followed.

IT WAS DARK in the room. Not even a shadow preceded the figure slipping through the door, and there was no sound when it was pushed closed behind it.

The figure paused and slowly scanned the space, eyes hidden behind night glasses that outlined everything in shades of blue and gray. The bed only held one occupant, and that was a clearly defined heat map, burning an almost white against the silvery surface.

Long and lean, arms outflung, one palm turned upright and relaxed.

After a moment the figure moved forward silently, lifting a blaster and releasing the safety with equal lack of sound. Took position, and a breath, ready to level, aim, and fire. One more look at the body on the bed revealed only a gentle regular rhythm of breathing.

Easier than planned.

Brought the blaster down and aimed and only then realized there were eyes looking back at him, with a smile. "Oh shit."

Jess moved with the speed of a long lost species of snake, rolling off the bed and lunging forward to slam into the figure with a solid sound of bodies impacting.

One hand to the wrist of the hand holding the blaster, breaking that with a snap and boxing the gun away with a quick motion to hear it impact the wall across the room and drop to the ground.

The smell of steel. Jess unlocked her elbows and dropped to the ground as she felt the pass of a knife near her ear. She came up under it and butted the attacker's chin with the top of her head, as her knee snaked up and pinned the arm wielding the weapon to the floor.

She lifted up and let her eyes focus as the room came into clear vision in silver and gray. "Stop." She caught the other arm swinging across and shoved it back down onto the ground, putting her other knee across the attacker's torso. "Enough of us haven't died?"

The soft thunk of a head falling back to land on the floor. "Fuck." Her brother let out an exasperated breath. "Finish it then."

"No," Jess responded. "Believe it or not, I don't randomly kill people, even if they're stupid enough to try to kill me." She got up and lifted him with her, shoving him into one of the chairs, then went to put her hand on the light plate.

She walked back and yanked the night glasses off his head and tossed them into the corner. "What was that for? Don't tell me you were taking revenge for Jimmy." She glanced briefly around the room. "He was no friend of yours."

Jake cradled his broken wrist in one hand, blood dripping from his nose where he'd impacted his sister's head. He was dressed in a black jumpsuit with a hoodie. "No. I don't want anything for him. I just want all that's left of this place for me."

Jess sat down on the bed and rested her hands on her knees. "You know something? I'm going to have to castrate you because you really are too stupid to be allowed to breed. It's one thing to want that Drake heritage, Jake. It's a completely other thing to try and take it from someone like me."

"At least me they'd all treat with," Jake said. "You? This won't stop until this place is nothing but sand and dead bodies. Tell me that's not true."

"Probably," Jess said. "Doesn't change me not letting you

take it."

"Bitch."

"Absolutely," she said. "Alpha bitch, get of an alpha dog, who didn't want you to have it either." Jess smiled humorlessly at him. "This is mine until they splatter my insides all over it, Jake. Don't try that again."

"Whole place die with you not matter?"

"No." Jess folded her hands and tapped her thumbs together. "I don't care. That's the whole point of being an amoral sociopath. You really, truly do not give a fuck in the slightest."

The door opened and at once the room was rather full of agitated techs and a nomad with a gun. Dev quickly emptied her hands of her supplies and came over to Jess while April drew a bead on Jake with very little humor in her expression.

Jess eyed them. "Is that food?" She got up and went to the desk Dev had dropped her burden onto. "Nice." She picked up a fishroll and turned, leaning against the furniture. "Thanks, Devvie." She munched contentedly on it. "My brother thought he'd grease the skids of Bay ownership."

"When you see the whole region coming at us at light, you'll wish I'd succeeded," Jake said. "Hope you enjoy croaking, Sis. I'll enjoy watching."

Jess continued chewing. "You really think you won't die first?"

"How about now?" April asked with a brief smile. "We might be busy later. Scan picked up bio readings coming in."

Jess picked up the second roll. "Party time," she said. "Tie him up. Don't want a rotting corpse in my bedroom." She winked at Dev and took a bite. "Then let's go do what we do."

THE STORM STILL raged outside, but central ops had been cleaned out and re-manned. When Jess got there, she smelled the astringent scent of antiseptic sea foam soap that was used to scrub up pretty much everything at the Bay.

The smell was imprinted in her brain, and a brief flicker of memory inserted itself into her mind's eye as she brushed past the broken door into the large room.

Morning. Early. The family kitchen still bearing that smell after being cleaned the night before. Herself stealing fishrolls from the night hearth meant for the guard.

Jess smiled briefly and straightened then looked quickly around the room to evaluate the attitudes of the ops watch.

"Hey, Drake," the captain of the watch greeted her casually. "Good fight."

Eyes looked up to see her, faint smiles flickered over faces before they went back to the screens and pads, looking closely at metrics since the big screens on the wall had been blasted into carbon charred bits.

"Good fight," Jess agreed. "Got another coming?"

"Got something." The captain turned a screen to face her. "Bio readings all up and down the ridgeline here near the caves."

Jess put her hands on the console and studied the readout. "Jake said the whole region'd be coming down on us. Guess he was right."

"Smarmy little gitwad," the chief said. "No offense, Drake, but you had a skank family."

"No offense taken. Had no control over it." Jess straightened as a flicker of motion caught her attention, and she half turned to watch Dev enter, her flight pack on her back. "What do you think you're up to, Rocket?"

Dev smiled. "I am going to try and get the carrier out of where I landed it," she said. "I think it will be more useful if I do that." She moved aside as April and Doug entered behind her, both of them carrying packs and April armed to the teeth.

"Looks like the neighbors have come calling." Jess indicated the screens. "I'm going to go out to the back fence and see if they'll talk."

"Us too," April stated flatly. "In case the stupidity gets to crazy level."

"They know you don't got much to bargain with, Drake," the captain said, but in a commiserating tone. "Everyone around knows we got thumped."

"Did we?" Jess eyed him. "I don't see Interforce in charge here."

A little silence fell as the ops team regarded her in some silent surprise.

Jess got that. She was in Interforce colors, with a tech, and another team at her side, and Interforce had arrived at her request. They had no actual reason to trust her, save that she'd come back, walked the gauntlet and thrown herself at the unlock code that would allow the Bay to defend itself.

These ops watchers knew that. They'd been here. The one near the back wall was the one who'd grabbed her arm and hauled her forward across the console and fired over her head in her defense.

But still, she was Interforce.

Wasn't she?

"What's the scan on the Bay side?" Jess asked after the silence had gotten awkward. "Empty?"

"Empty," the ops watch replied. "No one's stupid enough to come in there with ships."

Jess drew breath then exhaled, finding herself in a very odd moment of indecision. She was trying to tell everyone to get going to the back entrance, send Dev to get the carrier, and in that moment, she realized she couldn't.

Could not. Could not send Dev off by herself. Even though it was the right decision. To have Dev get that carrier out and go herself to distract what seemed like an oncoming mob.

She was aware everyone was watching her.

Fuck.

"Carrier'll be a better negotiating platform," she finally said. "Let's go use that." She pointed at the door and was relieved when she saw not only April, but Doug nod in agreement. "If Dev can fly it out of there."

"Drake," the watch captain called out, and Jess turned at the door. "You're not just going to fly off are ya?"

Jess didn't even have the energy for offense. "And go where?" she asked simply. "Where else but here?"

The captain lifted a hand in acknowledgment and dropped back into a seat. "Kill 'em all then. We'll take vid."

IT WAS A relief to get to the carrier. Dev settled into her station, with Doug in the jumpseat next to her, and April strapping herself into the drop rig as Jess settled behind her console.

"How in the hell are you going to get out of here?" April asked with mild curiosity in her tone. "Don't get me wrong, Drake. I was as glad to get into this thing as anyone was."

That was actually a good question. Dev had the front shield up and the nose of the carrier was right up against the rocks with stone pylons on either side of it. There was no room to turn, and the overhead was so close there was no room to hover.

Outside, a few Bay workers halted their efforts to salvage some of the ships she'd literally ripped in pieces on entry to watch.

Dev got her ear cups settled and started up systems, bringing on a distinct sense of pleasure.

Jess leaned back in her seat. "Dev'll figure it out."

Dev glanced at her in the reflector. Faintly amused blue eyes looked back. She smileed in response. "I hope so," she said, "or this will be an extremely short expedition."

"Just glad to be in here," Doug said. He rested his big hands on his knees. "Jess, no offense, but your family's a dozen devils worth of fierce." He exhaled. "Holy crap."

"They are," Jess agreed in a mild tone, as the whine of applied power started to rise around them. "Like a whole pile of enforcement agents...and wannabees. Which is exactly what they are." She put her elbows on the arms of her chair and hiked one knee up. "It's only the craziest of us that get put into service."

April nodded. "I like it," she said. "Fighting with those kids up on station—nice." She tugged her straps a bit tighter. "When I was with my family, I felt like a fish with wings. No one was like me. Here? Everyone is."

Doug grimaced a little.

"S'true," Jess said wryly. "Ready, Devvie?"

Dev regarded the control panels and the wiremap that showed the enclosure of rock all around the carrier generating proximity warnings echoing into her ear. "Yes." She flexed her hands and made a picture in her head of what she wanted to do.

Getting the carrier to actually do it would an interesting process.

She put her hands on the controls and triggered the landing jets, stilling the alerts as the top of the carrier immediately almost impacted the stone cavern roof. She adjusted the multiple thrusters, lowering the force in the aft jets just slightly.

The forward jets pulsed, releasing and returning power in a quick flicker of her fingertips, and in reaction the carrier backed up. The stone columns closed in on either side and they felt the jostling shock as the sides of craft hit them.

Dev pulsed the front jets a bit more, grimacing a little at the scraping squeal.

"I can blow out those things if you want," Jess said.

"Thank you. But I believe they are holding up the ceiling." Dev gritted her teeth. "Please hold on."

"Uh oh." Doug grabbed for a handhold. "Please don't tell me you're going upside down." He curled his legs around the jumpseat supports.

"I don't know why everyone always assumes I am going to invert this craft," Dev muttered, adjusting the power to the side jets to tilt the carrier to one side. There was a soft pop and crunch as stored items in the cabinets shifted and she increased the power to the forward thrusters, rocking the carrier back and forth as it wiggled backwards.

"No one in the world's ever driven one of these like that I bet," April remarked.

"No bet." Jess watched the scan intently, reaching up to kill the alarms as they were dinged and dented by the hard stone that made up Drake's Bay.

Dev adjusted the jets, tilting the carrier over a little more as the restraints contracted around her and the carrier engine pods came loose from the hold of the rock. Quickly she righted the craft and boosted the rear landing thrusters as they came free of the narrow spit of stone and emerged over the docking area.

In free air.

Jess clapped her hands, and after a moment April and Doug joined her. Dev gave them all a bewildered look from the pilot's station. "Is there something wrong?"

"No." Jess settled into her seat. "I told you all Dev would work it out."

Natural borns. Dev shook her head and gently rotated the carrier, sweeping the scan around as she did. She picked up several people standing on the far end of the cavern. She keyed in vid scan and put it on the screen. "We are being observed."

Jess glanced at the screen. "You are being observed. Let's go, Devvie. Before they think I'm going to take off and start shooting at us."

Dev eased her way through the destruction she suspected she caused, avoiding the masts of the sunken at dock ships as she approached the cavern entry, lit faintly from the outside. There were fallen rocks half obscuring the opening, and beyond that the scan picked up an Interforce carrier, sunken and lifeless where it crashed on chasing her.

She wondered briefly if she'd known the pilot and tech. It made her feel sad as she cautiously emerged from the cavern into the blowing rain.

It thundered down on the roof of the carrier, and she adjusted the thrust against it, setting up a scan that covered all of the half circle of Drake's Bay. The storm was still overhead but moving off and the lightning blasts were now only occasional rather than constant.

She started up the mains and cut off the landing jets, feeling the little thump as she was shoved back in her seat. Beside her, Doug was half turned in the jump, watching the boards and the forward view.

There was just enough light for the outline of the cliffs to show against the dark gray sky. Below them the Bay was ruffled slightly from the wind, the edge of the cliffs showing fresh scars of blast damage, the shoreline littered with fallen rock.

The bay itself was empty. The docks to one side that usually held skiffs and work boats were barren, the pens that held the catch showing empty and broken sided.

"Mess." Jess sighed. "They're gonna blow my brains out for this."

"Who is?" Dev asked.

"The Bay." Jess put her hands behind her head. "C'mon, let's get over the top of the cliff to the back side. See what's waiting for us there." She slid closer to her console and keyed up the weapons systems. "Gimme some juice."

Dev did, as she increased speed and started upward, over the cliff as the sound of the rain increased and a roll of thunder rumbled overhead. She topped over the forward cliff and flew up and over the bulk of the mountain, aiming for the pass between two tall crags that angled down toward the small plateau that eventually sloped down to the barrens beyond.

"Scan is showing large bio mass," Dev said into the quiet. "Also picking up high energy weapons."

April had unhooked herself and edged over to get a view of Jess's console. "Holy crap. Where did those grubbers get that?"

"Same place they got the guns they fired on that caravan with." Jess dialed in settings. "People'll sell anyone anything for enough cred." She pulled down her triggers and flexed her hands. "Does it pay to talk to them?"

April held on to a roof rack spar. "Can we outgun them? Not with those metrics. They'll blow us out."

"If they can catch us." Jess's eyes twinkled wryly. "They've never seen Dev fly."

"Jess, we're being hailed," Dev said. "Signal is originating from the bio mass. Open frequency. They do not know who we are."

Jess studied the scan. She saw energy points that were tucked behind rock walls, and the smaller flares that were heavy blasters.

Someone had armed her neighbors. She drummed her thumbs on the console. Probably end up a no win. "Go ahead and answer them, Devvie." Jess retrieved her own comms set and put it inside her ear. "Let's see what this is."

"Yes." Dev nodded. "Calling station, this is Interforce flight BR270006. Please identify," she responded crisply, as though she was answering central ops. A brief look at the comms board showed it with normal readings, and she was just a little too distracted to evaluate what that meant.

"BR270006, this is a rep from Cooper's Rock. What's your intention?" a female voice answered with loud sounds of other voices and the thrumming of rain in the background.

"I got it." Jess keyed in comms. "Dee, better question would be what's your intention."

"Is that the dumbass with the kid?" April muttered. "That feels like a damn year ago."

Dev was happy enough to leave the communications to Jess as she guided her way through the granite spires, the rain repellers clearing the windscreen as the light grudgingly grew brighter given the clouds. She could now see the steep, craggy mountainside, and as she crossed over the landing caverns, she saw three of them at least were completely destroyed.

"Jess, come down and let's talk," Dee Cooper said. "I'm sure we can do a deal."

There was a rough, desperate edge to the voice, and Jess evaluated that as she tapped her fingers together. "They thought they could do a deal with the Bay, too, Dee. Didn't work out for them. Sure you want to try?"

Silence.

Dev slowed the engines as they came up over the plateau. Between the next fold of the mountain she could see the faint outline of the shuttle, abandoned on its pad. The caves were in the valley before it, and she saw a lot of black charring across the surface of the rock and wagons filling the passage with lots of bio around them.

Finally, a sigh, then Dee's voice came back. "Let's try talking, Jess. What choice do you really have?"

Jess lifted her hands and then put them back down in a shrug that the other woman had no chance of seeing. "Sure." She folded her hands around her hiked knee. "Be there in a sec." She cut off the comms. "Dev, put it down right on that crossroad there in the center."

"This is going to be a bitch," April said. "They want that rock. Space station wanted that rock. Other side wanted the rock, and Interforce half killed itself for it." She went back and perched on the drop rig again.

"The Bay wants it," Jess said after a pause. "They don't really even know why they want it, they just know no one should take it away from them. There's no logic there. I can't fight that." She sighed and leaned back in the seat. "Protect whats ours. It's in here." She thumped her chest.

Dev angled the carrier into the valley and dropped down to ground level, skimming over the wet, racing runoff and coming head on to the caravans. Scan showed her big energy weapons pointed their way from inside the caves, and this close she could now see the armed bodies behind the blockade.

She set the carrier down in the center of the crossroads, extending the skids and settling onto them, cutting the thrust from the engines but keeping the power up for shields and weapons.

Scan beeped softly. "Jess, there is a flight inbound." She half turned "A dozen carriers of this class."

Jess sighed. Then she released her restraints and got up. "Let me get some grandstanding in while I can then." She went over to the arms rack and set her long blaster into its hard points. "Want to come along?" she asked April.

"Positively." April checked her hand blaster. "Sorry I left my guns on that damn carrier they blew up." She frowned. "Shoulda taken them with."

Jess put her knives into the sheaths at her back and then paused as her fingers brushed something inside the pack she'd brought with her "Oh." She carefully withdrew it. "Here. Brought you a souvenir from station." She reversed the knife in her hand and offered it hilt first. "Figured you'd do better with it than I would."

April paused in mid motion and blinked, glancing at Jess first and then at the knife. "Wow." She gingerly reached out and took the hilt of the dalknife, lifting it to the harsh inside light of the carrier to see it's reflection. "That is wicked."

Jess felt an unusual sense of pleasure, watching the reaction. "And hey I owed you for coming up to fetch my ass." She finished arming. "Took it off the scum bastard who turned my last tech."

April paused and looked up at her, the knife held between them. After a moment, she smiled. "Nice. I'll try to reclaim its honor in yours."

Jess grabbed her jacket from the locker and shrugged into it. "You two—"

"Stay here," Dev finished for her. "But we may assist if things do not go well."

Jess turned her collar up and produced a wry, faint smile. "If they end up killing me, take it out on them, wouldja, Devvie?"

Dev didn't even twitch. "Yes, I will."

Jess turned and slapped the hatch release and walked down the ramp that extended from it. April smiled and slid the dalknife into her pocket, keeping hold of the hilt. "Wicked," she repeated, then hopped out of the carrier to follow Jess.

Dev triggered the hatch and it closed, shutting out the sound of the weather.

DEV SWITCHED ON the outside vid, giving them multiple shots of the outside of the carrier. One screen she focused on the line of the wagons and then another on the two dark clad figures walking away from them toward the enemy lines.

"That was seriously right on target with that knife," Doug commented. "Never seen April light up like that before. Not even when she's killing people."

"Yes," Dev agreed. "I thought she seemed pleased. Jess often gives excellent gifts."

Doug digested this for a long minute in silence. "Would not have figured that. Even for an ops agent, she's kinda scary."

"I have never found her frightening," Dev said. "Even from the moment I came downside and met her, she's always been very kind to me."

Doug wrinkled his nose up a little. "I think you're an exception. She really likes you."

"This is true."

"Enough to want to give you presents."

Dev smiled. "The most excellent thing I have gotten from her is a piece of clothing that has a lining and is very warm."

"Oh. That snazzy jumpsuit."

"It's really comfortable. Jess got it for me when we were at the trading island on the other side." Dev wished she had it with her now, in fact, since the pervasive chill of downside was making her shiver a little. But the suit was back at Base Ten, and it was impossible to know at this moment if she'd ever see it again. "She understood I was not really used to the cold downside."

"That's cool. I think the only thing April ever gave me was a head cold." Doug grinned wryly at her. "You had much better luck."

Dev considered that in silence. "Yes." She concluded. "I believe in fact I have been quite fortunate." She glanced at the screen and leaned closer to it. "Hmm."

"Hmm?"

"Yes." Dev turned around in her seat. "Do you know how to use the weapons in this vehicle?"

"Theoretically," Doug answered in a wary tone. "Why?"

With a nod, Dev stood up and moved around the pilot's position. "Please take my seat." She went back to Jess's console and sat down, studying the control surfaces. "I am not sure my knowledge is more than theoretical either, but I want to be able to do something useful if this situation gets incorrect."

Doug didn't argue. He hopped from the jumpseat into the pilot's chair and pulled over an ear cup to settle in as the restraints contracted around him. "No problem, Rocket. I got this."

"Keep an eye on the approaching vehicles. I suspect they are suboptimal." Dev tentatively selected a few controls and activated them, hearing the reaction as the weapons boards on either side of her lit up. She, too, had theoretical knowledge about this station, but there was a depth to it that meshed as she studied the boards and felt programming overlay them. "Ah. Yes. I have programming for this."

"That must be so cool," Doug said.

"What?"

"Just waking up knowing stuff. I had to study so damn hard to get anything to stick." He glanced at her in the reflector. "Good thing you brought the doc with you, huh?"

Dev met his eyes in the mirror, evaluating the straightforward friendliness and tasting the truth of it. "I am glad we brought Doctor Dan because I like him a lot, and he can do many useful things." She unzipped the neck of her suit and pulled the edge of the collar down. "But I can no longer take advantage of his programming skills." She pointed at her own neck, visibly sans collar.

Doug's eyes went wide and he turned around in the pilot's seat. "Wow! They took it off?" His voice rose in astonishment. "Really?"

"Doctor Dan did." Dev sealed the neck of her suit and returned her attention to the console, turning on the targeting metrics. "I agreed to it. I did not want to be subject to someone else getting inside my head."

Doug was still staring at her. "That's smart," he finally said, turning back around. "Makes you more like the rest of us."

"Yes." Dev smiled. "It pleased Jess as well. It also bypassed the synaptic shutdown that could have affected me, which she found quite non optimal."

"Yeah I get that. Like if someone did it when you were flying this thing. But you can't just get stuff anymore."

"No, I will have to do it like you do," Dev said. "Doctor Dan advised he'd equipped me to be able to do that, though there is no doubt it will be more difficult than just accepting new data." She rested her hands on the metal surface. "But on the other hand, I don't have to wonder if the data is trusted."

"That's really smart, too. 'Cause I can see where they'd want to go in there and look around, you know? Like how'd Rocket get so rockety."

"Yes. Exactly."

Doug got the engines tuned and adjusted the pilot's seat a little to accommodate his larger frame. He got his hands settled on the throttles and focused on the scan as April and Jess crossed the edge of the slope that headed toward the line of wagons. "Power's jumping."

"Yes." Dev got her own seat adjusted and paused then she stood up to pull the triggers down so she could reach them. "BR270006, Tac one."

"Go ahead, Devvie," Jess's voice answered.

"They are preparing weapons," Dev said. "Energy levels rising at your eleven and two."

"Thanks. Tac out."

JESS UNHOLSTERED HER long blaster and released the safety. "This is gonna be ugly."

April nodded and got her hand blaster into her grip. "Hopefully ugly and short." She tugged her hood a little closer against the cold wind now sweeping through the valley.

They reached the edge of the road and stopped, going brace legged and still as they waited for a reaction.

Two people stepped around the edge of the wagons and approached, dressed in the waxed sealskin of the better off homesteads. The one in the lead was Dee Cooper, a tall red haired woman with a thick scarf around her neck and a blaster in a holster at her side.

The second figure was the nomad Jess remembered talking to on a day that felt years in the past, but at least he was someone who owed her a mark.

They came to the edge of the road, edge of the line that marked where the land that was part of Drake's Bay started, the road that went up to the craggy rock escarpment and gave entrance to the Bay from landside.

"Jess," Dee Cooper said after a moment. "This isn't what it looks like."

Jess laughed. "You have two thousand people there with guns and two big truck mounted blasters you got from the other side. You coming to shop?"

Cooper lifted a hand and let it drop. She boldly came across the road within reach of Jess's long arms, sparing a glance for the shorter agent next to her. "You have something we need."

"I have something that's mine," Jess responded. "That you have no part of, that Interforce had no part of, that Drake's Bay considers its own."

Cooper regarded her seriously. "Who's in charge in there? You? Really?"

"Me. Really. So if you want to bring that rag tag in here, take what's mine, you'll need to come through me to do it." She shifted her hold on her long gun. "And then you'll have to deal with the Bay, who took down Interforce, and have in their hands the good old tools from the old days, and they want to use them."

"So they beat the black and greens?" Dee asked. "Really?"

"Really."

Dee let her hand drop to the handle of her blaster. "Then why are you still wearing that uniform, Jess? Why have this scrub next to you, or that box behind you with guns aimed?"

April's eyes narrowed. "Big talk from someone who lives in a tin can." She ran her fingertips over the hilt of the dalknife.

"Because it provides a lot more body protection than a Bay shirt does," Jess answered straightforwardly. "I'm not an idiot, Dee. You think I'd leave behind the firepower of a carrier to make a point? C'mon."

The nomad just remained there at Dee's side, listening.

Waiting to pick a side, April thought, with an inward smile.

But then Dee relaxed a little. "Jess, no one wants to tangle with you. We all have a stake. We want to buy into this, if you're still the Drake and you run things. The guns were for Interforce."

Lie? Not? Jess breathed out slowly, a long stream of vapor coming out of her nose. "Do I want to do a deal with people stupid enough to think they could outgun Interforce?"

"You did." Now Dee Cooper smiled. "Fish or cut bait, coastie."

What was the truth here? Jess found herself unable to decide. "I didn't outfight Interforce. The Bay did." She made a slight gesture behind her. "I was either up in space or out like a light courtesy of some little cousins who couldn't tell one black suit from another."

April nodded. "S'true," she said. "That's a whole stack of bad news back there with her family name on it."

"Someone unlocked the armory," the nomad standing next to her stated. "We heard it."

Jess nodded. "That was me. I am the Drake. But that just put the nail on it," she added after a moment of silence, then paused and touched her comms as she heard the frequency open. "Dev?"

"Incoming targets, locked on to this location," Dev informed her. "I am going to try to hail them."

Jess shrugged. "Sure, why not? They know who we are anyway. That bus has a distinctive signal." She looked at Dee. "Interforce inbound. A dozen carriers."

"Pissed 'em off, did you?"

"They don't like to lose," April stated. "So if I were you, I'd start blasting this place so they don't take it out on you, too." She looked straight at the nomad. "Truth."

"Truth," he agreed.

"No response to hail, Jess," Dev's voice sounded quietly in her ear. "They will be in range in five minutes."

"Warn Bay ops," Jess said. "This isn't going to be pretty." She reseated her long rifle. "April's right. Start shooting," she told Dee. "They figure the whole region's coming up and we won't have anything left to bargain over."

Dee stepped forward and put a hand out to delay her as she started to turn to head back to the carrier. "Are you going to go against them, Jess?"

"Yes." Jess felt a wash of both relief and sadness. "I have to protect the homestead. It's in here." She patted her chest. "Maybe if I die in some spectacular way it'll make up for the colossal fuckup of bringing them here to start with."

She turned and headed back to the bus and April turned and matched her steps. "You could stay with them."

"No I couldn't," April said.

"Hey, nomad!" the man called after them. "What family? For the book?"

"Fuck the book," April muttered. "He can kiss my ass."

Jess triggered the hatch and turned as the ramp extended, looking back over the nose of the carrier at the two of them, still standing there. "Drake," she yelled back. "Couldn't you tell?"

Then she entered and closed the door to find April staring at her and Dev getting up out of the gunner's seat where she'd apparently been prepared to shoot things. "Wish we had time to talk. Tie yourselves down. Devvie, light the rockets."

Doug scrambled out of the pilot's seat, and a moment later Dev lifted them with a flare of the shields and a blast of steam.

"THAT'S NOTHING GOOD." The ops captain said, glancing warily at the sandy haired man standing with crossed arms next to him. "Dozen of those are going to make a big hole."

"Undoubtably," Kurok said. "The older weapons you have here don't have the frequency range to disrupt their shields."

The captain studied him.

"Justin gave me the tour back in the day." Kurok correctly interpreted the look. "And of course I know the other side from somewhat recent experience." He caught a brief bit of motion at the doorway and turned to see a KayTee and a BeeAye entering. "Ah."

"Doctor Dan." The KayTee came over to him. "They told us it will be dangerous here soon."

Kurok was aware of the hostility around him, he could almost smell it coming off the people sitting at console, glaring at the bio alts. "That's right, lads. I'll find you some place to take shelter in."

But the KayTee shook his head. "Doctor Dan, we want to help. We want to do good work here like we did up on the station. You showed us." He held up his hand, balled into a fist.

"You're gonna croak," the captain said. "You know how to fight like I know how to cook."

"We know," the BeeAye said. "We know we'll be made dead, but we want to help anyway."

Kurok held up a hand and started to talk but stopped when the captain got up and came over, staring intently at the two bios.

"So wait," the captain said, addressing the KayTee. "You're saying you know you're going to die and you want to do it anyway?"

KayTee nodded. "Because we'll have done good work," he explained earnestly. "And if we are made dead, but doing something for the people here, we want to do that."

Kurok drew breath in to speak again, and then, again, halted because he saw the expressions of the watch change and felt a prickle across his skin as they all focused, a sudden intensity of interest that was as potent and intent as blaster fire.

It was strange, and then familiar, as he remembered seeing that expression on Justin's face, the two of them newly paired cadets in a mock melee with live fire when he'd all unthinkingly stepped in front of a blast to take it on his new partner's behalf.

Just a moment. Just shoving Justin out of the way behind a rock and feeling the impact against the armor he wore across his back, and looking up to see that expression looking back at him, primordial and inbred, coming up from underneath the sophisticated intelligence that was Justin Drake's arrogant outward armor.

"Idiot." Justin had said. But he hadn't meant it.

"Idiots," the captain of the watch said, but he, too, didn't mean it. Now the ops watch relaxed and returned to their consoles, and just like that it was okay because the bio alts, with no real understanding themselves, had used a language these anachronistic throwbacks would respond to.

Absolute migraine inducing genetic insanity. But in this place and time, again, it worked.

"Okay, well. Now that we've got that settled. I'll go find some place for them to guard," Kurok said. "Is there some place we can make a hideously pointless last stand? Relieve some of the others, perhaps?"

"Yes," the captain said. "Here," he pointed to a map on the wall. "Non coms, what's left of 'em, are bunked out there. Kids and all and med."

"Ka...Kevin," Kurok addressed the KayTee. "Take everyone, and go to that location. Protect everyone there as best you can."

"Yes." Kevin nodded. "We will do that, Doctor Dan." He turned to the captain. "We will do our best work for you," he added, and then he and the BeeAye left, heads high.

The captain watched them then regarded Kurok.

"Surprised?" Kurok asked in a wry tone. "Yeah, me too. But let's move on."

"Got troop carriers behind them," one of the ops watch muttered. "Ain't playing."

"No," Kurok said then cleared his throat a little. "Mind if I helped out here? I'm better with a keypad than a gun."

Everyone regarded him in wary silence.

"Justin was the best friend I ever had," Kurok added gently. "I feel I owe it to him to do what I can. He'd expect it of me because this was his place."

One of the older watch looked at him, eyes slightly narrowed. "You were his."

"I was," Kurok said. "We bled for each other."

Silence.

"And I went back and snapped the neck of the guy who got him," Kurok added with the faintest of wry smiles. "However unlikely that may seem now."

And that, too, there was magic in, as they cleared an ops console for him and waved him forward, and the captain extended a hand to him. "I'm Johnathan."

"DJ," Kurok responded, returning the clasp as he sat down. "Let's see how much boom we got left."

Chapter Fourteen

"TAKE A POSITION, Dev." Jess swept her board again, flexing her hands. "Want the aux comp?" she asked April, who was sitting on a small ledge near the weapons console, a pair of tie downs crossing over her shoulders to the panel behind.

"Sure." April pulled the swinging inputs over so she could reach them. "If I'm going to blow up, I want to be shooting when I do it."

Jess understood that at a gut level and nodded. "Any response yet, Devvie?"

"Negative."

"New target," Doug said. "Coming from the west. Looks like two dozen inbound and a big transport." He dialed in the board. "All heavy weaponed."

"Nice." Jess sighed. "Hope Dee takes that advice."

"Bet she doesn't," April remarked, seeming more cheerful than usual.

Dev got herself settled. "Do you want to approach them or let them approach us?"

Jess found herself suddenly very tired of waiting. Tired of everything. "Take it to them, Dev. Fly the hell out of it, and let's see if they've got anyone who can do more than just get out of your way."

"Yes." Dev took hold of the throttles. "Please hold on."

"I get chills whenever she says that," Doug said, "but I'm as hung on as I can be."

"Same here," April said.

"Go." Jess pulled down her triggers and let the tension wash out of her. "Let's go do what we do."

A moment later they were all slammed back in their seats as Dev took the carrier from idling to full speed, going through the speed of sound in seconds as she aimed toward the phalanx of carriers coming in from the north.

Comms was still silent, though she could hear the open frequencies with their faint white noise in her ear cup. They still were a minute out from being in range, and she set her boots on the side thrusters and fit her hands around the engine controls.

They were in visual. She saw the incoming craft and plotted a course in her head, then without warning she executed it.

"Oh crap." April grunted.

The carrier tilted and went sideways then she angled for zenith and rotated as she dove between the first and second line of carriers, hearing the thumping as Jess let loose with the plasma cannon.

She wove a line between the carriers who belatedly reacted, dodging frantically as she skimmed close to them, pushing the engines to the red line as she rotated between two other craft so closely she could almost see the faces inside the other cockpit.

One carrier smoked and headed for the deck. She twisted and circled upward, shooting for the clouds as suddenly, shockingly, comms erupted into her ear.

"ROCKET ROCKET ROCKET!" A familiar voice bawled. "STOP STOP STOP!"

"Jess, that is Brent." Dev brought the carrier around and to even, in a long curve to bring them back into engagement. "Request for sideband."

"Grant." Jess didn't take her hands off the guns.

"Sideband six, connected." Dev finished her curve and was facing them. "This is Dev."

"Stop shooting!" Brent said. "Holy for craps sake hold up! Wait! Is Jess there?"

"Gimme." Jess hit the accept. "Drake, J," she said. "Talk fast."

"Jess. It's Jason," A deeper male voice answered. "Hold on. We're not...we're with you," Jason said. "Please, no shit, okay? We're the last of us at Base Ten, and we can't afford to lose anyone else."

Dev held the ship steady, still heading directly at the now scattered formation.

"Twelve left?" Jess asked after a long pause.

"There was fighting. We won," Jason said. "Got Elaine here in my bus, she knows the scoop. We need to talk."

"Twenty minutes for the inbound west targets," Dev said quietly.

"You see what's coming, Jason? They for you or against you?" Jess said. "We got about six teams tied up at the Bay."

"Land and talk, Jess. Five minutes."

Five minutes. Jess regarded the scan output. Five minutes in the long scheme of things was insignificant. "Sure," she said. "Follow us." She muted the input. "Dev, land on that little escarpment over there, near the —"

"I see it." Dev swept them around in a half circle and then

went into a mild dive, waiting until the last minute to reverse power and come back around to land on the rocky point, nose facing the carrier that was following them. She secured the systems and waited.

April untied herself and got up, going over and standing by the hatch in silence.

Jess stood and shook herself a little then glanced over as Dev got out of her seat and walked back. "Hey."

"I would like to come with you," Dev said in a straightforward kind of way. "The carrier is set up to move quickly if needed."

Jess studied her for a long moment.

"And also," Dev tossed her second card on the table, "bio alts are very familiar with being lied to. I might be able to provide useful input."

Now Jess smiled.

Dev smiled back. "And also, I just want to be with you."

Jess lifted both hands and turned them up, laughing a bit. "Let's all go." She waved Doug forward. "This is going to end one of two ways, and only one is going to require any pilots."

April hit the hatch release and they exited in a close cluster as the hatch opened on Jason's carrier. Once down the ramp they separated a little, and Jess took the lead.

Jason and Elaine hopped out of the other craft, Brent and Tucker right behind them, Tucker with a bandage across the side of his face.

No one else. Dev hadn't brought her scanner, she merely watched all four of the natural borns and responded with a little smile as Brent waved at her, examining the relaxation across his shoulders as he caught up to Jason.

The eight of them came together in a group, and after a swift evaluation of both Jason and Elaine, Dev herself relaxed. They were not going to be made dead. At least not at the very moment. She reached out and touched Jess's arm, giving it a little squeeze.

"I don't have time for the whole story," Jason said without preamble. "But I've learned more about internal politics in the last week than I ever wanted to know."

Jess nodded. "Alters was a faction."

"You knew?" Elaine asked. "Only one of us he couldn't fake out onto some long term mostly terminal mission was Jase because he was on med."

Jason nodded. "Started bringing in his people right after you left for the Bay," he said. "Half the base got sent west."

"I guessed," Jess said who hadn't done anything of the sort. "He was bucking to put me at the Bay to run some scam, then pushed me upside when it looked like I was going to make trouble."

"Were you?" Elaine asked.

Jess smiled and issued a small, self deprecating shrug.

Jason nodded. "What threw it up was that thing you found here." He gestured vaguely at the Bay. "Anyway, we turned it around. That's what left in flight, and maybe down, now that we had to face off against Rocket for like ten seconds."

Dev put her hands behind her back and assumed a diffident expression.

"So what's the deal with the incoming?"

"Unfriendly," Jason said. "I sent a relay back to Rainier, told them we were invoking intervention. And that we'd rather have the Bay as allies than enemies."

Jess sighed. "Oh nice."

Elaine nodded. "Insurrection. Their choice. You probably never got that far in the rule book, Jess. Jason had plenty of time in med to read."

The entire situation turned. Jess exhaled. "According to Dee Cooper, that ragtag gang of rock scrapers with guns was all ready to fight off Interforce on the Bay's behalf."

"Because they wanted that seed stuff," April said. "Don't give them any credit."

Jason chuckled. "So now it's scrapers and the Bay and us against them. Sucks to be them."

"And Doctor Dan," Dev said. "He sent a message that he's in the operations center."

Elaine smiled. "Cherry in the sundae. This is going to be like shooting fish in a tide pool."

Jess took herself into a bit of head silence and shut out the world for a moment. She could sense a tickle of what felt like sandpaper, or the rough skin of a shark against her perceptions as she forced herself to stand still and look at the situation from the outside.

"Jess?"

She held one hand up and slightly turned her head to one side, focusing her eyes on the ground as she silently assembled the pieces in her mind, the seeds, the station, her brothers. Where were the threads? Where were the little sticky bits that would bring them together...if they even existed?

Was she trying to put two and two together to get six?

Doug's voice echoed into her concentration. "Ten minutes. We should get moving."

"Jess." Jason put his hand out and touched her shoulder. "C'mon. Let's take this. We got it."

Her family, the Bay, the legacy that lived inside her. What would happen if the Bay was the center of an insurrection...and the irresistible pull of the seeds?

Step out. Step back. Jess dissected the emotion of the situation out of it, removing the knowledge of her own part in this hideously technicolor clusterfuck.

What was the goal? Whose goal was it?

"Jess, let's go. We take these guys out, they'll think twice before coming at us again once the word about the rest of them getting tanked gets to them."

"Wait a moment," Dev said, moving closer. "Jess is thinking." She put her own hand up. "Please be quiet."

And Dev. New Model Developmental number one. Who started out a biological alternative thrown into an insanity and now...

And now spoke with a steady authority and was so brilliant and so...Jess let out a slow breath. So made for her.

Made for her. Had she been? What had the end stage been in the mind of Daniel Kurok?

"Listen, we're out of time," Elaine said, but in a gentle voice. "If they catch us on the ground we're toast."

Jess straightened up and returned her eyes to the group surrounding her. "It's a scam," she said in a low tone. "It's them."

"Meaning?" Elaine asked, cautiously.

"Them?" Jason echoed a moment later. "The other side?"

"Why waste your resources fighting us when you can get us to fight each other," Jess said. "Perfect plan. Get us to destroy each other then they come in and take the pickings. Get revenge for Gibraltar with no loss on their side."

The agents looked at each other in a sudden, charged silence.

"Destroy the station, destroy the Bay, destroy the trade over the whole east," Jess said. "Deplete Interforce by shoving them up against the one place they can't win against because the Bay..." She took a breath. "The Bay is where the heart of Interforce comes from."

"Holy shit," Jason finally said. "For real?"

"We were designed for killing," Jess said with a faint smile. "We Drakes and the long timers at the Bay. You all are the one offs, Jase. The exceptions. We're the rule."

April nodded. "It's all tail and no scorpion. No lie."

Elaine half turned to look west then turned back and looked at them. "Going to be a moot point in a minute," she said. "They're going to come in shooting. We're not going to talk them down. They don't have the benefit of personal knowledge."

"But we have to stop this," Jess said. "Or we'll lose everything."

Dev took a breath and looked at the assembled pieces Jess showed them. But she too could see the incoming force. "Jess." She hesitated. "We should get inside the vehicle."

"How do we stop this?" Jess repeated. "Anyone left we can talk to?"

Jason and Elaine exchanged looks. "I think it's past talking, Jessie," Jason said. "Maybe if we knock these guys out of the sky they'll stop and listen."

"Jess, what about those agents from the west in the hall?" April said suddenly. "They came from there. Can we leverage them?"

Jess stood there in silence for sixty seconds, face tense and still. Then she exhaled. "All of you, take your carriers and get into the landing bays, lower level," she said. "Keep out of sight until I signal."

Jason eyed her. "What are you going to do?"

Jess smiled. "Be a Drake." She started for the carrier, waving them back. "Go go. Get behind the Bay shields on the water side. They won't see you there." Her boots hit the ramp to the carrier as April, Doug and Dev scrambled after her. "Let's give this one shot."

Dev got into her seat and got her comms on, hearing now the open channel as Brent relayed the order and the protests filtered down. She opened the frequency for Bay control and tuned it. "Drake's Bay, this is BR270006, do you copy?"

A burst of static then Kurok's voice replied. "Hello, Dev."

"Some carriers will be coming into the area in front of you. Jess would like you to leave them undamaged." Dev got them airborne.

"I see," Kurok said. "Well, we will of course unless they start shooting at us. I don't think I can prevent the good folks here from shooting back."

Jess chuckled. "He's such a hoot." She got her boards ready. "Dev, go right at 'em, and see if we can intercept before they cross Bay boundary."

"Yes." Dev brought the carrier around, and they blew past

where Dee Cooper's force was camped, going between the high mountain passes that separated the Bay from the inland plateau behind it.

It was dark, barren, and rock strewn land. On the far side of a long black lake they could now see the approaching carrier force clearly outlined against the granite terrain.

"Broadcast our ident," Jess said.

"Broadcasting." Dev triggered the looping alert. She shunted full power to the forward shields and tirmmed power to the engines, sorting through the battery cells and segregating a section of them for the weapons systems behind her.

"Hail them." Jess folded her hands over her stomach and watched the screen.

It was a reasonably large force, given the circumstances, but as she studied the formation she saw the configuration shift, become less of an arrow and more of a box, and she recognized that in some deep and root memory way.

"They're scared," April succinctly summed up the observation herself. "Nice."

"Someone," Dev remarked, "possibly showed them that vid."

Jess laughed out loud. "Hail them again, Devvie."

Dev keyed the mic. "Approaching vehicles, this is Interforce carrier BR270006. Do you copy?" She waited, hearing only silence. "Approaching vehicles. Please respond or this carrier will regard your approach as hostile."

"They're idiots if they don't answer." April snugged her restraints tighter.

Jess sighed and reached up to pull down her targeting triggers. "Probably going to have to get their attention before they'll talk."

"That means shooting them, right?" April swung the boards around that controlled the plasma bombs. "I gotta remember not to release these if we're upside down, right?"

The radio crackled. "BR270006, this is BR56003. Dalton Arp in command," a male voice echoed softly through the speakers. "Please identify yourself."

Dev keyed the mic without hesitation. "Certainly. This is Biological Alternative, set 0202-164812, instance NM-Dev-1," she responded. "But you may call me Rocket."

Doug snickered and gave her a thumbs up.

"You will land the craft and deactivate weapons, immediately," Arp's crisp command came back.

"No, I don't think so," Dev responded. "That would be

suboptimal. I suggest that you do not proceed further as you will upset Agent Drake, and that does not seem to cause excellent results for anyone in any way. At any time."

"This flight is going to attack if you do not comply."

Dev tightened down her restraints. "I would recommend separating into a larger profile in that case," she said. "Otherwise you will likely shoot each other trying to shoot us."

Jess was laughing so hard she was crying.

"Please hold on," Dev said suddenly. "They are going to fire, Jess. I am taking evasive action."

And they went.

"ARE WE IDIOTS to do this?" Elaine regarded Jason over the drop rig's profile.

"Are we idiots to hide behind the cliff while Jess plays chicken?" Jason had both big hands resting on his knees as he sat in his weapons console seat. Brent and Tucker up in the nose of the carrier muttered together, "I dunno, El. Could be she has a plan. Could be she just doesn't trust us at her back."

Elaine sighed. "This is so fucked up."

"Sixteen different kinds of seagull vomit fucked up," he agreed. "Shit, look at that blowout."

They had come around the edge of Drake's Bay and now could see the sea frontage of the stakehold, black scarring all down the side of the landing bays.

"Holy, crap." Elaine twisted in place to see the screen. "Are those bodies down there? That pile...they are." She blinked. "Tanked carriers to the right there."

Jason exhaled. "What the hell."

"They crushed it," Brent said. "We're on hail, Jase," he added. "Local sideband, Bay ops."

"I got it." Jason put on comms and accepted the call. "Go."

A soft crackle of the circuit opening, something they could have long ago digitally removed and never had. "This is Drake's Bay control."

Familiar voice. Jason almost smiled. "Hello, Doc. This is Jason, A. Jessie told us to wait here."

"Yes, we heard," Kurok said. "If I were you, I would land up on the top level and come inside."

He and Elaine exchanged glances.

"There are some colleagues of yours here," Kurok added. "And of course, if we have to start shooting it would be good not to hit someone accidentally."

Brent chuckled. "Point."

Jason shrugged in a tired kind of way. "Sure, why not." He flicked over to a different frequency. "Flight, this is Blue lead, follow to land."

"Ack." Multiple responses, sounding as tired as he felt.

"He in charge there now?" Elaine wondered. "This is so freaking twisted." She leaned back against the rig as the carriers started to move, crossing the ruffled waters of the half circle bay and heading toward the large flat open space at the top of the homestead.

Big and rough and raw, Drake's Bay. Never an effort to make the place look like anything other than it was. She regarded the pile of bodies, swarmed with seagulls chewing at them, as they crossed over a mixture of civ and the distinctive dark that matched the suit she and Jason wore. "Ever been here, Jase?"

"No." Jason shook his head as his hands moved over the weapons board, safing it. "You?"

"No." Elaine watched the ground as they neared it, seeing tall figures standing in the entryway, long rifles of some kind cradled in their arms. Disciplined stance, training evident, but wearing the rough woven cloth of the stakehold draped over them.

The carrier landed, and without speaking they all unbuckled and stood up. "Arm," Jason said after a moment of silence.

"You think it's a trap?" Elaine paused, in the act of adding her blaster. "Really?"

"No." Jason put his long gun on its hard point. "Just want to be on equal footing." He hit the hatch unlock and walked down the ramp. "They won this war."

"They never really stopped fighting the last one." Brent fastened his jacket up as they followed. "That's what I heard."

DEV DOVE FOR the rocky escarpment as the fire came inbound, tipping the carrier onto its side between two jagged rocks and then reversing her course so close to the ground they could hear the reflectivity of the jets against the stone as they shot straight up into the attacking formation.

"Firing." Jess pulled her triggers with a sense of fatalistic inevitability, bracing herself against her seat and holding her breath as they took on heavy G, and her muscles worked against it as the carrier swerved and went into rotation.

Dev carved a path through the lines of carriers and then headed toward the big personnel transport. It realized her intent and started to turn aside. She kept the line they were drawing in constant motion, ducking and swerving as fire erupted on all sides of them.

Too crowded. Several of the carriers peeled off and started to come around farther out, but she was under and then behind the transport. "I am going zenith," she warned.

"Oh crap." April grunted.

She hit the mains full and shot from under the transport straight up and over the top of it, flying upside down and taking a barrage on the bottom shields.

"Shunting the alarms." Doug was braced hard, hammering the repair boards. "All repelled."

The carrier went sideways, falling rapidly in a spiraling tumble as Dev cut power to the engines and two of the opposing force shot each other, sending a rumble of engine recoil through the skin of their craft as she went past and cut the engines in again. The blast flashed across the front nose of one, sending it to the deck.

"Plasma." April ejected a handful as they came to level again above a cluster. The explosions as they hit rocked them side to side. "Got 'em!"

Jess finished a three-sixty blaster barrage then she cut in the comms. "You fuckers done?" she snarled into the radio. "Or do we have to destroy the whole lot before you'll talk?"

"Ident!" A harsh response.

"Drake!" Jess yelled back. "Who the fuck did you think it was? Some fucking sea lion? You morons done destroying the corps yet?"

"Firing stopped," Doug reported. "Good job, Dev!"

Dev came to level and swept around the lead carrier, seeing the transport limping to the side, black char of fire crumpling its hull. Her heartbeat settled as she brought their flight line to come in nose to nose.

Everyone was moving, things were shifting all around them, but she held position in mid air, watching the scan closely as Doug tapped on the pads next to her.

"Well?" Jess snapped into the mic. "You want more of that?"

April pinched the bridge of her nose. "Hope they don't," she said. "I left my bag of gummies behind."

"Drake," the voice came back.

"Yes," Jess answered in a calm tone. "You ready to talk now

that we kicked you in the ass? Because you're not coming any closer to the Bay."

"Should I land over there near that water?" Dev asked, pointing down and to the left.

"You get out of this thing, they'll target you," April said. "Keep the talk to the radio."

"Drake, you don't understand what the situation is here," Arp said. "There's more at stake here than you know."

Jess flexed her hands and put them back on the triggers. "I understand more of what's going on here than you would if you spent ten years with your head up my old dead uncle's ass. If you want to discuss turning around and leaving or going under guard to the Bay we can."

The sigh came through clearly. "Do you really think that's how this is going to go?"

Jess pondered that for a minute. "Yes," she then said, "that's exactly how it's going to go. We're not going to put up with you trying to either take what's ours or hurt any more of the people at Drake's Bay." She glanced up into the reflector to find Dev's pale green eyes looking back at her. "And to be honest, Arp, there's more going on here than you realize. Let's land and talk."

"Mmm..." April grumbled.

Jess sighed. "Yeah. I know. Dev, go ahead and put her down." She got up and gestured April to take her seat. "If I fuck this up, kill everything you can." She went to the arming locker. "I want to see if I can convince this guy we're all being gamed."

April slid over and slowly closed the restraints around her. "What if he doesn't buy it?"

Dev turned the carrier in a gentle glide and landed it on the ridge, watching the wiremap as the single command carrier followed her over. She kept the shields up at full and waited as the other carrier landed. "Jess, I think it would be more optimal if you asked this person to come into this vehicle."

Doug immediately gave a thumbs up.

"She's right on." April agreed at once. "Make the bastard come in here, and if they try anything at least I'll have the satisfaction of cutting his heart out of him."

Jess regarded them both with a mildly bemused expression. "What in the hell is going on here that I'm the optimist in this crate?"

"Jess, those people can do great damage before it could be prevented." Dev unbuckled herself and got up. "I think there is less chance of that if they were here." She touched the comms unit in her ear. "This is BR270006. Please present yourself at our hatch for this discussion."

Jess felt a prickle of surprise as she realized what had just happened, and she saw April's brows lift as she did as well. Techs weren't supposed to do that, neither the regular kind or hers. She took a breath to object then internally her psyche shrugged its shoulders and her body followed suit. "All right, Devvie. Have it your way." She went to the back equipment rack and hitched herself up onto it.

Dev had her hand still on the comms, holding it into her ear. "They are coming." She sat back down in in her seat and activated scan, focusing on the other craft and the ones now circling overhead, aware of how vulnerable they were sitting there.

"Nice," Doug muttered under his breath. "Not that I'd have tried it."

"What?" Dev whispered.

The hatch opened at that moment and drew their attention to the back of the carrier, where hesitantly, two dark clad figures slowly entered. The man in the lead was about April's height, with curly brown hair and a very muscular body.

The man behind him was taller and had straight black hair with a lighter build and angular face.

They stopped. "Drake?" the man in the lead asked, half turning to face Jess. "Dalton Arp. Senior agent, Northwest." He turned his head slightly. "This is my tech, John Feld. You've got about five minutes to pitch your gig at me."

Jess regarded him. "Or?"

"Or what?"

"Five minutes or what are you going to do, try and get past me to run into the buzz saw that's waiting for you over the ridge?" Jess remained relaxed, her arms folded over her chest. "All the surviving from Base Ten are being held there. We did a great job killing each other."

Arp looked around the inside of the carrier then back at her. "Okay," he said. "What's the game?"

Jess got up and walked over to him, studying the square, hard face, and the arrogant lack of fear she understood at a gut level. He was what she was and had as many years behind him. She imagined herself in his place, coming into this situation and considered what anyone could say to her that would get past the automatic assumptions she knew were going through his head and would have been through hers.

It took brass ones to walk into her carrier and face off. Jess had to smile. "No game. Just answer this question. Who gains?" she said. "Who wins from this?"

Arp's hazel eyes studied her. "If you sell that growing tech to the other side? You do," he said in a straightforward tone. "Whoever gets it wins. Whoever gets it can be self-sufficient. Owes no one. Drake's Bay's been trying that route for generations. We all know it, Drake."

Jess shook her head. "You're looking in the wrong place. It's not about the plants. Never was about the plants. That was just the bait."

"Jess," Dev said. "We're being called." She got up and faced them. "Long range scan at the Bay has detected a large force approaching from the east."

Jess took a breath. "End game," she said. "They make Interforce fight each other. Make Interforce fight the Bay. Then when all that's left are bodies, they come and take over." She met Arp's eyes. "Finish what the old man started and get their own back for what we did to Gibraltar."

"What you did," Arp said. "So maybe the target's just you. Maybe we realized how dangerous you are, Drake, and we want you dead as much as they do. Consider that?" He cocked his head to one side. "Maybe we all meet over that pitstop on the way to hell and end up getting a drink and going home, with all of you gone."

"Good luck with that," April remarked. "If that's the game from Interforce, glad I stayed on the side I did. What a bunch of wankers you are."

Arp smiled. "Looking to die, nomad?"

April shrugged. "We're in the game of dying. Now? Later?" She shrugged again. "Best I ever hoped for was a good, juicy death taking as many people with me as I could. I'll settle for you, though." She wiggled her fingers. "We done talking, Jess?"

"You collect a lot of riff raff, Drake." Arp took a step toward the ramp. "So no, I don't buy your game. We're going to keep on mission. Maybe we'll take some shots for them at your ass when you run from us." He glanced over at the pilot's seat. "Your five minutes are up."

"Dev, get ready to rumble." Jess shook her head. "When they ask, I can say I tried."

"Yes." Dev thumped back into her seat and started up the power gen. "Stand by."

The tech, John, had edged inside and now he walked up behind Dev and stepped over Doug's sprawled legs. "Pilot," he said in a low, rumbling voice.

"Don't be mean to Rocket," Doug warned as he was taking the scan results and updating the targeting system. "She'll bump something with her elbow, and your ass is going to be thumping its way down that slope backwards. She doesn't mess around."

"C'mon, John." Arp stepped backwards and down off the ramp. "We've got company we have to meet."

"You really on their side?" Jess asked in a very mild tone.

"I'm not on your side," Arp said. "So if that means I play their game long enough to get rid of you, then maybe I...John!"

Dev felt the motion start behind her and reached up to release her restraints as she heard Doug draw breath to yell. Instinctively she dove over the arm of her seat and heard the sound of a knife puncturing the surface of it. She ended up tangled with Doug as something big and fast moving hit the chair from the opposite direction.

"You motherfucker!" Doug's yell erupted.

A flash of steel reflected the blue and green power leds and Dev twisted around to see a blade plunging down toward Doug's chest as he threw himself in front of her. Her eyes widened as she got her arm up and around him and grabbed for the knife wielder's wrist.

"John, no!" Arp scrambled back into the carrier only to haul up as a knife blade pressed up against his stomach, and he threw his hands back. "No!"

"Stay still," April warned. "Drake'll handle him."

Jess had vaulted over the weapons console and a second later hit the pilot's chair, reaching around it to grab for the attacking technician who was stabling wildly after Dev's form. She latched on to him just as Dev caught his arm and pulled him down.

The knife stopped at the edge of Doug's jumpsuit and its tip just cut through the fabric as Dev got her knee up under her forearm to brace it.

The man stared at her, panting. Then his body was gone, and the arm was ripped out of Dev's hand. He disappeared backwards over the top of her chair, and there was a horrible cracking sound along with a growling roar.

Dev grabbed the arm of the chair and untangled herself from Doug. "Are you okay?" She hauled herself up into the pilot's position and looked over the back of it to see Jess dragging the limp tech toward the hatch of the carrier. "Jess!" She let out a yell of alarm, seeing past her. "Watch out!"

"Better get this thing going, Rocket." Doug strapped himself down as April dove at Arp and they crashed to the ground of the carrier. Jess ejected the body she had in her hands, and it cleared the hatch just as it slammed down, the barrage of blaster fire thumping against it.

"Get out of here!" Jess yelled, jumping over the two fighting agents. "Go go go!"

Dev wasted no time. She lit the engines and exploded away from the ridge, the backwash from the engines flaring out over the now sodden body lying on the rocks and the empty carrier they left behind them.

"Oh boy." Doug braced his legs and watched his partner anxiously. "Gonna be a rip long day."

JASON WALKED THROUGH the huge central hall, its monstrous grandeur still evident despite the damage. "Whoa," he muttered to Elaine, as they both glanced at their tall, scrub overalled escorts, gangling and tousle haired and young.

"Whoa," Elaine echoed. "They trashed this place."

"They did. Crapola." Jason shook his head. "I think maybe Jess has something in that whole attack each other thing. It's just a variation on the theme, right? What the old man was trying to stir up."

"Mmm. Maybe it was bigger than he was."

"Maybe."

They went down a hallway full of gun toting hulksters and into a blasted open door that revealed a set of old fashioned ops consoles and a wall full of blaster scar. In the center room, at one of the main consoles, sat a familiar blond haired figure, dwarfed by the Bay residents around him. "Hey, Doc"

Kurok glanced over at him. "Hello there." He leaned on the edge of the console. "Want the good news or the bad news?"

"Oh oh," Elaine muttered. "There's good news?"

The rest of the agents and techs that had come with him filed in and took spots against the wall. Mike Arias, and Chester, Jorge and his partner Sal among them. Everyone had battle scars. Uniforms were torn, and there were blood stains and shadow rimmed eyes.

"Hey, Doc," Chester spoke up.

"There's a force coming in," Kurok said.

"We know, from the west coast," Elaine said. "Jess's screwing with them."

"No, not those." Kurok tapped a pad and indicated a screen,

half cracked, being held up with plas. "Those."

"Oh crap," Jason said. "She was right."

"Jess?" Kurok asked. "It's a trademark of the Drakes in general, but she knew about those?" He looked skeptical. "Behind the ridge I didn't think they'd make good scan."

"No." Elaine folded her arms over her chest. "Something she said before she told us to come hide here."

He got up and approached them. "I assume you turned out to be good guys."

"We did." Mike half smiled. "I owed it to April."

"Jess said she thought this whole thing was a scam of theirs to make us all kill each other. Save them the trouble," Elaine said. "When she said it, my guts just started nodding along. Said it was a set up, all of it, bringing in the Bay and pitting them against the force."

Kurok cocked his head slightly to one side as he considered that, and his gaze shifted off them into the distance. "Could be," he said after a brief pause. "More likely they just wanted her dead. She's too damn wildcard for them."

"Not all this for one person," Elaine said.

"One person? Actually two persons did them enough damage to put them back fifty years," Kurok reminded them. "Same person, somehow, comes into ownership of the most dangerous force on the continent, and through a bizarre set of circumstances gets hooked up with an experiment that outreached even my admittedly biased high expectations."

"Dev." Jason leaned against the wall, one eye on the screen with the incoming force.

"Dev," Kurok said. "Biological Alternative, set 0202-164812, instance NM-Dev-1, likely my last contribution to science."

Elaine regarded the screen with a furrowed brow for a moment. "Maybe not." She went to the console and leaned on it, ignoring the wary looks of the console operators who nonetheless made space because that black uniform was what it was.

"Got a squirt from Jess's bus," someone on comms said. "Coming in, warning what's following."

"That didn't work," Jason said. "Okay, everyone back to the line. Let's get this over with and blast them before we're fighting two fronts." He pushed off the wall and started out the door. "You coming, E?"

"Let me suck this." Elaine was shuttling through data. "Blow something up for me."

"Lots of something," Jason said, hauling up when he cleared

the entry and came face to face with a half dozen men dressed like he was. Instinct threw his hand to his blaster, and he went into a crouch as Mike Arias came past him and leveled a muzzle just past his ear.

The agent in front threw his hands up though, palms out. "Hold it, Jason!"

"Derek." Jason lowered his gun, but left it in his hand. "What's the game?"

Derek shook his head. "No game, bro. We're done on the dark side. You going to fight? We want to go, too." He glanced at his companions. "We're all from either Juneau or Rainier Island. "

Jason cocked his head and stared at him. Stared through him. Derek was young and new and had the idealism brutally beaten out of him in the last few days. Before he could say anything though, Arias came past him all the way and went nose to nose with Derek.

"I remember you in class," Mike said. "You're a marginer."

Surprisingly, Derek nodded. "True. My parents paid to have me taken in. I was a pain in their ass and it was worth their cred to get me off their back and leave them with my perfect little sister and brother." He looked around the Bay. "I never figured to have to understand this."

Mike smiled. "They lied. April knew."

Derek nodded. "She knew."

"C'mon. We're wasting time." Jason abruptly made his decision and holstered his blaster. "Those your carriers on that ridge? We'll drop you on 'em. Take care of the bunch that's chasing Jess, then die pointlessly blowing ourselves up in front of the bad guys."

"Nothing left to go back to anyway," Derek said. "Let's go, call the wrenchers."

DEV WASN'T SURE if they were going to be attacked immediately, but she wasn't going to take a chance. She shot for the high horizon at a steep angle as Jess got herself into the gunner's position and ratcheted her restraints down with one hand while reaching out to punch the agent April was fighting with, feeling her knuckles impact something as she got her triggers down.

Arp was very strong but April had just that much more experienced in half grav and took advantage of that. Dev hit the top of an arc and curled over, and they came off the floor of the carrier. She flipped him over, aiming an elbow at his throat when Dev started to dive, and they slammed back down.

"Go for the Bay, Dev." Jess released the rear plasmas as they came across the flight line of two of the carriers, and a moment later they were in a very hard arc to the left as Dev evaded the return fire. "Warn 'em!"

"Yes." Dev was busy fighting the throttles. "Doug, could you possibly do that?"

"Sure." Doug got the comms into his ear. "BR270006 to Drake's Bay control, copy?" He reached over to tune. "Hope you copy. We're incoming with enemy following, take action."

A crackle. "DBOPs, got it," a low, growly voice answered. "Got ya on scan."

Dev whipped the carrier in a circle in mid air, cutting out the mains and letting them drop two full lengths before she boosted them forward, shooting right back at the cluster of chasing carriers at full speed, the only thing out racing her the blaster fire from the big guns on either side of her window.

She chased it, the new engines in the carrier giving her more speed and better maneuverability than the ones she was facing. She went through them at a steep angle and saw they couldn't react fast enough.

Jess released plasmas on either side of them, and one of the carriers frantically tried to get away by a hair, her engine cowling coming with inches of scraping theirs.

There was a bang behind Dev, and then Doug ripped the comms from his ear and the restraints from his body and dove into the back of the craft as she heard Jess let out a warning yell.

Halfway through a maneuver, she had no options but to keep her hands on the throttles and her eyes on the screen. She caught a brief glimpse of motion behind her before she heard the distinct sound of Jess's belts retracting.

A wordless yell from April, and Dev put them into a rotation, then a steep dive, feeling the gravity yank against her body and throw her into her own restraints as she heard a cracking sound and then thumps and bangs. "Jess!"

"Keep flying!" Jess shoved herself away from the floor against the pressure and finished coming around and pulling Arp's arm around and right out of his shoulder socket. "Get back!" She yelled at Doug, who was dragging April away from the melee.

Dev was going right at the cliff, and she got to the narrow gap a blink ahead of the enemy, twisting the carrier onto its side and bolting between the sheer rock faces that fairly scraped either side of the carrier.

"Ow, shit!" Jess somehow kept ahold of Arp and slapped her knee over his wrist as he tried to shoot her in the head with his good hand. "Dev, other side!"

"A moment." Dev angled them downward as the boards picked up an explosion behind her. When she barely gained enough space, she rotated them one-hundred-and-eighty degrees. "Jess?" She looked anxiously into the reflector, relieved to see Jess's tall form braced against the weapons console.

"Can ya straighten us up?"

They had airspace, and she did, the carrier now running almost at ground level, the engines sending up blasts of steam as the energy impacted the wet ground. "We are not being pursued any longer."

Jess dropped into her seat, blood running down one arm, blinking against the burn of a blaster that had creased her face. Doug had April secured near the back of the carrier, near the weapons rack, her eyes closed and a line of red, heavy blood leaking down from her ear.

Arp was out cold, sprawled near the hatch with one arm at an impossible angle.

"Imagine what they look like," Jess commented, after a minute. "Get us back over the landing bays, Dev. I need to take the trash out before we have to turn around and fight again."

"Yes." Dev risked turning around in her seat. "This vehicle is undamaged."

Jess leaned on her console and blinked bemusedly at her. "They didn't hit us once?"

Dev shook her head. Then she smiled and turned back around, adjusting her boards and resuming the comms unit Doug had dropped as she used the mottled skin of the carrier to hide against the mottled rocks.

"Wow."

"HOLY SHIT, DID you see that?"

Bay ops were on their feet, staring at the cracked, but working screen. On its surface was displayed a mass of motion and the flare of blaster fire.

One blip was moving faster than the rest, and the square, boxy outline of BR270006 was mostly a blur as it ducked and spun in impossible motion, spinning in a nexus of plasma outbound from it.

"What the hell?" Johnathan had his hands on his hips.

Kurok regarded the image, and held his breath a little, as the carrier seemed to stop in mid motion and tumble, then erupt into a new path as belated fire impacted the air that it had occupied only fractions of a second before.

Brilliant. Physical aptitude beyond anyone's expectations. "Dev's quite a good pilot," he remarked, suppressing a smile.

"Wow." Elaine looked up from her data dump. "I've seen her fly, but that's nuts. She's going to run those bastards right into each other or that wall."

Kurok wasn't sure if he should feel sad, or gratified, or a little of both. "That wasn't really programmed," he admitted. "I mean yes, the control surfaces and so on, sure. But not that flight instinct."

Johnathan sat back down. "You made that thing?"

Kurok didn't even feel insulted. Not even on Dev's behalf. "I designed the genetic structure that resulted in Dev, yes." He sent another query into the Bay's old systems.

Elaine looked up again. "Did you key her to Jess? On purpose?"

There was a small silence as Kurok finished typing in his request, giving himself a moment to think about what to answer. Finally, he tapped enter and looked back at her. "Depends what you mean by that. I had in my head some vague idea of what an Interforce tech should be, having been one myself. And I had some idea of what they expect of an enforcement agent."

Elaine continued staring at him. "I thought it was real convenient for something like her to show up right when we thought Jess was a goner."

Kurok gave her a wry look and rested his elbows on the console. "Thank you for crediting me with that level of both skill and prescience. Unfortunately, I deserve neither," he said, aware of the closely listening Bay ops. "At best I'll cop to trying to design Dev as best I could to serve as I had to an agent like the ones I was familiar with."

"Why'd you muster out?"

They heard a booming crack and eyes went to the screen to see a carrier coming across the ground at speed, and behind it, a bloom of dark, gray smoke and the flash of flames.

"Here they come." Johnathan reached up and triggered an alarm, a deep bonging sound that echoed in the chamber and then far off. He adjusted the comms on his ear. "Ops JoJo. Stand by to repel invaders. Close the doors ya can."

Jason's voice came thorugh the speakers. "This is Jason A., BR37309. We're assembling to overfly and attack. Everyone keep your heads down please."

"Stand by, BR37. This is BR88 and five coming to join," Derek's low tone chased after. "Someone tell the hotshot we're friendly, huh? Do not want to get in their way."

Kurok reviewed the results of his query and settled into his seat. "I think you're going to have to risk that external battery." He tapped a few keys. "Let's just hope we don't blow up half the mountain."

"THERE ARE FIFTEEN craft coming toward us over the Bay ridge, Jess." Dev was hastily sucking at a water container, her eyes darting between the panels in front of her. "Idents are Base Ten and Western."

Jess had just finished tying up Arp and now dropped back into her seat. "That could be good or bad." She settled into her chair and glanced behind her. "How's things?"

April had regained her wits, and was spitting blood out onto the floor. "What the fuck hit me."

"The side of the carrier," Doug informed her. "He smacked you against it, just before Jess yanked his arm out of its socket."

April looked around and realized she was leaning up against Doug, and her nostrils flared. "You couldn't have done that a little earlier, Drake?"

"Sorry, I was shooting things," Jess said. "Dev, put a hail out on one of the encrypted subchannels."

"Yes."

"Where'd the rest of them go?" April asked, as she slowly pushed herself upright and sat down on the back shelf. "You kill them all?" She gave Doug a brief nod as he got to his feet and dusted his uniform off. "Thanks."

He paused in mid motion and eyed her, his mouth quirking into a grin. But then he just went back to his jumpseat and settled into it, drawing the repair boards over.

"We got a couple, I think," Jess said. "Got comms, Devvie?"

"One moment." Dev set up the side band. "Go ahead, Jason. Jess is on com." She passed the call back to Jess's console and finished her water, wishing fruitlessly for a hot meal and some rest.

It would be so excellent to be able to lie in bed. So excellent to be able to have a small space of time to just relax, and have a snack, or maybe read a page or two of her book.

Or go swimming with Jess.

A small space of time to stop almost being made dead and making others that way.

"Okay, Jase. We'll join up with you coming over the ridge and go into formation," Jess said. "Maybe when they see all of us they'll just stop."

"You got Arp?"

"Tied in my bus."

"Better odds for us," Jason said. "Relaying that to the rest of them."

Jess nodded and smiled. "Heard that."

"See you on the other side."

Jess put her hand on the comms pad. "Yeah," she responded softly. "Hope there is one."

"HERE THEY COME." Brent adjusted his seat. "Down the ridge there."

Jason glanced at the vid. "Any scan past them?"

"No," Brent said in a calm tone. "Bet they scared the assholes back to Juneau." He tapped the input pads, and the carrier shifted slightly under them. "Nice soak. They got good power there."

"Yeah." Jason frowned a little. "A bit too familiar."

They watched as the oncoming carrier suddenly bolted almost straight up, slowing and coming through the speed of sound with a booming crack as they reached the same flight level and did a lazy rollover to come nose to nose with Brent and Jason's bus.

"Wow." Brent sighed. "That's some flying."

Jason shook his head a little. "I've watched every minute of vid we got on her flying and you know, it's more like watching a bird fly than a machine."

"'Specially in one of these," Brent said. "Hey, Dev," he spoke into his comms as the sideband came up with the proximity of the recently arrived carrier. "It's Brent. What's the deal?"

Dev's slightly burring tone answered. "We engaged the vehicles approaching from the west. Jess did some excellent work on them. But we also took onboard the person leading the attack, and he is now secured."

Jason snorted a little. "What in the hell are we doing here? They don't need any help."

"Jason," Jess's deeper voice emerged. "Got anything behind

us coming? Heard a big boom, and the rear screen's a little scratched."

"Nada, Jessie." Jason tuned his screen. "Oh, wait. Crap. Sorry. Here they come." He flicked the comms. "Form up!" He braced his boots against the deck. "All hail, Brent. Give me comms over the whole range."

"Go." Brent flexed his hands as the carrier facing them slid sideways then arched around, coming into line next to them with a small rocking motion. They were close enough for him to see the block lettering on the side, and through the forward canopy Dev's profile was just visible.

A moment later, she looked over and then gave him a little wave. He took his hand off the throttles and waved back, suppressing a grin.

"What are you doing?" Jason asked.

"Nothin'." Brent focused on the scan. "They're not at attack speed," he said. "You calling?"

Jason cleared his throat. "Oncoming Interforce flight. What are your intentions?"

Silence.

"Fucktards," Brent muttered. "Ass end of a seagull."

"Oncoming Interforce flight, speak up or we're going to tank you," Jason said in a slow and deliberate tone. "There's an invasion force coming over the water, and we don't have time for this."

"Ident," a voice erupted.

"Jason Anders, Base Ten," Jason said. "Ident."

"Jason, Elaine's calling on sideband ten," Brent said. "Urgent."

"Sure it's urgent. Whole fucking world is urgent and gone the hell to crap." Jason switched inputs. "G'wan, El."

"You all better turn around and get back here. There's already an advance group on the ground, and we have heavy incoming."

"Jess." Jason switched to sideband.

"I heard it. Let's go," Jess said. "If they come up our asses, blast them."

"Who us?" Brent asked.

"That was to the Bay," Jess said. "They just activated the topside guns."

No choice. Or, to be real, out of choices. "Got it." Jason switched back to broadcast. "Listen, jackasses. We're going to go fight the real bad guys. If you're smart you'll come with us and earn your pay," he said. "Anders out." He pulled down his triggers and flexed his hands into them. "Let's go do what we do."

ARP REGAINED CONSCIOUSNESS, much to his dismay. "Fuck. You're killing me!"

Jess glanced over at him. "No, if I'd wanted that you'd be dead. Shut up or you'll wish even more you were." She flexed her hands. "Dev, go for the closest ground forces."

"Yes." Dev drew in a breath and released it. "Stand by to maneuver. Brent, we are going to thirty degrees your horizon and pitch down."

"Got it," Brent answered. "Good luck! We're executing a spread Gamma. Try to keep out of your way."

Arp was arching his neck to look at the screen. "What is that?"

"Your allies, invading." Jess pulled her restraints tight. "Go for it, Devvie!"

Arp stared in silence as the view abruptly changed, and the carrier went into an attack dive, with the rest of the flight splitting up and dividing around them. They swept up and over the ridge, barely skimming the ground and then dove across the curved frontage of the homestead, heading toward three small craft firing against the entrances.

Jess didn't hesitate an instant as the attack against the Bay got into her guts and her back arched in pure reaction. She came down on the triggers in a full on barrage as Dev swept them in a tight arc, their backs to the cliff.

Two of the enemy diverted and came around, but a moment later they were under fire as Jason's craft came in from the other direction and with two booming thumps obliterated one of them.

"Bay's hailing them," Doug said, busy with the repair boards. "Just got tagged by their targeting." He keyed off an alarm. "Hope that means they won't shoot us."

"I am going for the sea entrance," Dev said. "There are anomalies there." She curved the carrier around and ducked under the remaining small craft as Jess pounded them with plasma bombs and heard the searing crack of penetrated shields.

Then they were at sea level, coming across the wide curve of Drake's Bay, toward the ship cavern at full speed. "Drake's Bay operations, this is BR270006, we are inbound firing," Dev said into comms. "Please tell everyone to take care."

"Thank you, Dev, we see you," Kurok answered calmly. "There is some fighting going on in the halls here. Take care yourself."

"Shit," Doug said. "Where did these bastards come from so fast?" He reset the scan and sorted the results. "Body landers, at water level."

"See 'em." Jess redirected her guns at the entrance, and a moment later the water was boiling as she slammed fire into the opening. Bodies went flying as a half dozen light personnel carriers dove at her in a frantic attempt to cut them off. "Get me right in there, Dev."

"Yes." Dev kept one hand on the throttles and put her other on the engine controls, counting in her head the microseconds before reversing course would not be an option. "Three, two, hold on please." She shoved the engines into reverse and hauled up on the directional controls as the carrier plunged toward the rock wall in a shudder of competing forces

Jess dropped two plasma bombs just as the carrier changed direction in mid air, dropping almost into the water as Dev cut the mains and turned them with just aerodynamic motion. She engaged power again and released a blast that sent up a ferocious spray of water behind them as they went sideways and then upright as she sent them on a tight parabola along the cliff wall.

A swarm of attackers plunged at them. Dev got the carrier around and was starting up when a voice erupted into her ear.

"Dev, stay down!" Kurok yelled. "Down! The battery is about to fire!"

Instinctively she sent the carrier back down to the water. Over head they all heard a cavalcade of thunder and then explosion after explosion as the Bay's barrage guns let loose. "Wow," Dev muttered, her ears buzzing painfully from the loudness of it. "What was that?"

"Plasma cannons," Jess said. "Old school ones. They're lucky they fired and not blew the hell up." She reset the targeting arrays. "What a freaking backwash."

The carrier was buffeted, a wash of plasma across the forward screen tinting it orange and pink. They emerged from the wash and were at sea level again, and a light spray of water abruptly hit them from a falling chunk of metal plunging past.

"Doc's hailing them again," Doug said. "That just took out like a dozen of them. They're falling in pieces...oh crap, watch out!"

"Incoming!" Jess said at the same time. "Devvie get us out of here!"

Dev jerked them abruptly to the right, then she pitched up and cut in the mains full power as they rocketed up the side of the mountain through a wall of fiery debris coming down on either side of them, smaller pieces impacting their outer hull.

Hatches were open in the wall, huge and dark and smoke rimed, barely seen as they flashed past.

"Watch it!" Doug yelled as alarms blared over the system showing them being targeted. "They're live! Dev! Look out!"

A momentary flash of a barrel and a flare of energy released. It was too late to avoid it, but then there was no need to. It stopped long enough for the carrier to come across it and started up again as they cleared.

"Lucky." Doug was sweating. "Holy crap."

April opened her hastily closed eyes, and grunted. "Buh."

Jess smiled faintly. "Drake's luck. I felt it scan me." She got her hands back in the triggers. "Come over the top and get around, Dev."

"BR270006 to flight," Dev said. "Please stay clear of the guns in the wall." She curved them around, and they came up and even and could see the Bay, now full of flaming debris.

"Gimme comms, Dev." Jess looked around for targets and saw only wreckage and landed troop carriers, and on the screen the inbound force.

"Go ahead," Doug answered, setting up the relay. "You're live."

"Attacking force," Jess boomed. "This is Jesslyn Drake. Drake of Drake's Bay. Put down your weapons and surrender!"

Silence.

"We will never stop killing you," Jess said. "We will never give up an inch. You will all die. Give up."

Silence.

The Interforce flight formed up in a line with them, intact. "This is Jason Anders, Base Ten," Jason's voice cut in. "We are with Drake."

"This is Dustin Kirk," another voice broke in, "Juneau Base. We are with Drake."

"This is Dee Cooper, representing Eastern stakeholds, here in Drake's Bay Ops. We are with Drake," Dee's voice unexpectedly added. "We're not in their class, but we'll fight, too."

April reached out and kicked Arp's boot. "You better pick a side," she said. "Actually pick a better side. No percentage here for you to stick with whatever plan you think you had."

Arp smiled. "You really think all those people are really on her side?"

"No," Jess answered. "They're just smart enough to know a losing cause when they see one." She triggered comms again. "Thirty seconds, and we start attacking again," she said. "And believe me, you ain't seen nothing yet."

Dev took a moment to wipe the sweat off her hands and forehead and flexed her fingers. "Did the repair routine run?" she asked Doug. "I think I might have clipped one of the engine cowlings."

Doug just laughed.

"Was that funny?"

"WE GOT ABOUT another blast left in those things," Johnathan said, leaning on the ops console. "Mofos." He glanced around, keeping an eye on both Elaine and Kurok, both crouching over the same datascreen. "What's up in the hall?"

"Shooting," a guard told him, "standby." He ducked out of the broken door and took off at a run with a yell.

Johnathan sighed. "Not good. Fuckin' hell."

More yells, and then the sound of firing, up and close in. "Ware!" One of the ops watch scrambled to his feet and pulled out a blaster. Instinctively Elaine did the same, shoving Kurok down as she braced out over the screen. As bodies shoved past the edge of the door she fired.

Them. No question. She pulled the blaster trigger again as the door filled with them. She recognized a face, and then another, and bolted past the chair and went for the fight. They spotted her, and she heard the warning call and grinned in fierce response.

A knife and she kicked it. Her own knife in her fist, she slashed in a backhanded motion as she shoved her gun into a throat and triggered it. A head came off in a splatter of blood and burned skin.

The next thing she knew she had tall figures at her back and sticks and hammers were beating back the attackers, driven by a strength that made them as deadly as the weapon in her hand. She was then part of a wall that moved forward, step by step, driving them back.

Then a surprise as a crowd appeared behind them and started pounding on them with fists and cast iron pans, all dressed in space jumpsuits and all yelling for Dan Kurok.

Melee. Insanity.

Then she saw one of the bios pick up an enemy soldier twice

his size and throw him against the wall. The enemy turned and started firing at them, and then a figure let out a yell and threw himself between them and the bios.

So stupid. Elaine braced and fired, ducking behind a piece of twisted steel and targeting the bad guys implacably as they fired into the oncoming bios. She saw Kurok disappear beneath a crush of bodies.

Then a bio stepped in front of a Bay rat, a kid just past childhood, and took one for him, body parts exploding across the room and hitting everyone in range. Elaine got the one who got him, her blaster fire getting him right between the eyes. It sent him flying back into his comrades in a flailing of twitching arms and legs as his brain disintegrated.

Everything stopped for a moment, and then Johnathan was there at her side, bellowing in bass rage. Then from the side corridors, from every direction, Bay residents came running, bringing a wash of seawater and blood with them. Elaine saw the enemy squad leader's face. His eyes met hers and she knew.

He knew.

"Kill 'em all." She aimed and fired. "No one lives today."

Chapter Fifteen

"JESS, THEY ARE hailing us," Dev said. "Asking for you."

"Gimme." Jess straightened up a little in unconscious reaction as she heard the faint popping in her ear before the link opened. "This is Jesslyn Drake," she stated, then fell silent.

She clearly heard an indrawing of breath. "Drake," a voice answered, low and slightly raspy. "What is your pitch?"

Jess rested her elbows on her console. "Give up, or I'll kill you," she said in a mild tone. "That's all I got."

April leaned back against the wall of the carrier, eyes blinking in pained exhaustion, and smiled. "All we got." She repeated softly.

"And..." the voice paused, "we fight to nothing." It sounded wryly resigned. "Die, die, die, soon nothing but seals and gulls left."

"Probably," Jess said.

Arp listened in silence. Now he spoke up. "That's Brudegan."

Jess nodded. "Josten, turn around and go home," she said. "Or stay and we fight. Pick one. I'm hungry, and I can tell my pilot wants a break."

Another sigh. "You talk? This is your homeplace. We sit down and talk before die?"

"Why?" Jess asked.

"Why not?" Brudegan answered with the same offhand mildness. "We have never met face to face. I have never looked into the eyes of a Drake. I want to before die," he said. "But maybe you say yes, and I die anyway your guns shoot me."

Jess considered that. "If I say yes, my guns won't shoot you. Word."

"And what is that worth?"

"You tell me." Jess smiled. Brudegan was their ace of aces. Overage now, her father's vintage, but a strategist without peer and a legend even Interforce respected. Careful, rational, and often incapable of coping with the madness that was what Jess was sometimes.

Most times.

"What is it with all the, let's talk, crap today?" April grumbled. "Yak, yak, yak."

Dev tapped a pad next to her, regarded it, then grunted softly under her breath. "That is a somewhat attractive animal."

"What?" Doug leaned over. "What is that?"

"A yak."

It was an oddly poignant moment and they both produced pained grins over it. "I don't think that's what she meant," Doug said.

"What will it be for us, Drake?" Brudegan sounded faintly amused. "I have heard you have heart. Come show it to me."

"Sure," Jess said with a faint shrug. "Land at the top layer there, near the cave entrance. Flight, stay in position."

"Jessie," Jason's low tones rumbled. "Guy wants to plug you."

Jess got up as the carrier started to move, Dev bringing them around in a gentle curve. "Yeah I know, Jase." She opened the sideband. "Everyone wants to plug me. Maybe I can get a straight answer out of them for once and it'll help some poor intel bastard someday."

"Jess, the other flight is holding back beyond the ridge," Dev reported. "I just got them on scan as we elevated over the ridge." She held the carrier in place, waiting for the enemy light speeder to land. "I have tried to inform Bay ops but they are offline."

Not good. Jess held on to the overhead rigging as the carrier set down and faced the possibility this was an end game. "Come with me, Devvie. Everyone else stay here."

April's eyes slitted.

"Someone has to have their hands on the guns." Jess correctly interpreted it. "Jase is probably right. They're probably going to try and skunk me."

"Why take Rocket then?" Doug asked, unexpectedly. "Point to get you both skunked?"

"Yes, actually," Dev answered. "The point would be there is so much unpleasantness it would be incorrect in the extreme to have to deal with it without Jess here." She stood and shrugged into her sharkskin jacket, closing up the front of it as she joined Jess at the door.

As no one put forth any further protest, Jess hit the hatch and stepped backwards through it, then stood with her hand on her blaster as Dev followed her out.

The enemy speeder was crouched nearby, rough and blocky architecture, as ugly and utilitarian as their own craft with slightly more angular lines. A man in a long jacket stood outside, with thick, windruffled gray brown hair and a blaster fastened across his chest.

"C'mon." Jess put her hand on Dev's shoulder.

They walked across the rocky ground, scoured by a stiff wind and as Jess blinked a few times to clear it from her eyeballs. It occurred to her that right now life wasn't good. She wished she was weeks back in Base Ten, having lunch with Jason and listening to Dev make sonic booms overhead.

She slowed to a halt an arms length away from him, studying his lined, weathered face just as he was studying her, his hazel eyes revealing nothing.

"So you are Drake," Brudegan finally said. "You much resemble your father."

Jess nodded. "And grandpappy Jack," she said. "We all look like gargolyes with no sense of humor."

He shifted his eyes to Dev. "And this is the prodigy?"

"Hello," Dev responded before Jess could. She held a hand out. "I'm Dev." She waited for him to take her hand and then she squeezed down and released him. "I am Jess's partner."

Jess smiled. "Also known as Rocket."

"Yes," Dev admitted. "Also known as Rocket."

Brudegan studied her. "You did not learn this flying from them."

"No," Dev said. "My technical instruction was given to me as biologic programming prior to my arrival." When he didn't respond, she continued. "Dev is short for NM-Dev-1. I am a biological alternative."

"We ordered a bunch more." Jess smiled lazily. "But I was lucky enough to get the original." She watched his face and read the twitches and unconscious reaction without effort. "You were hoping it wasn't true, weren'tcha?"

He moved his head a trifle. "What you purchase, so can we."

"In time," Jess agreed. "But you'll never have this one."

"In time we can do better." The enemy flyer was behind him, and he leaned back against it, perching a little on the wing. Though tall, he was shorter than Jess, and he relaxed a little, reviewing her angular form. "A force is coming, Drake, that you cannot defeat. You know it."

"I don't," Jess said, "know it. I'll know I'm defeated when I'm dead." She gestured faintly at the wall. "You know what we are, now."

"Monsters," Brudegan said. "Yes."

"Yes." Jess wasn't offended. "Designed and bred monsters. You think the barrage was bad? Go inside. I have ten-year-old cousins you won't be able to stop." And it came home to her, that lifelong sense of difference that had nothing to do with her as an individual but had dogged her all her career.

She felt a little idiotic, really, not having put that together.

He remained silent for a moment. Jess merely waited and watched, her body relaxed, stained with blood, all the preceding hours of effort leaving no mark.

Everywhere else, they'd been able to make inroads. Insertions in the west had been easy, his overarching plan a success. "I found a leverage point here," he remarked with a little smile.

Jess smiled back. "And I killed him. But if I hadn't, someone else would have." She laced her fingers together, her thumb rubbing idly at some dried blood across one knuckle. "It's part of our crazy."

He looked at Dev, who watched him with an intent, sober stare.

"It would be excellent," Dev said, "if you would explain what you want." She blinked placidly. "Because I do not think anyone is having an optimal experience here." She paused. "And it would be interesting if there was an alternative to having everyone made dead."

Brudegan's bushy grizzled eyebrows lifted a little. "So we have the speech of a construct but perhaps not the mind of one, eh?" His eyes flicked to Jess. "Perhaps you were leveraged more than you knew."

"As in she comes from your side? Nah. The guy who made her is a lot smarter than you are."

Brudegan's lips twitched. "And if I said he was ours?" He folded his arms over his chest. "Never Interforces'."

"Half true." Her blue eyes twinkled just a little. "Neither yours, nor Interforces'."

Dev straightened up a little, but remained silent.

Jess sat down on a nearby uneven rock. "So what do you want? All of us dead? All of us, and all of us. Everyone dead, so that we run out of spirals and it all ends with a seagull eating our guts?"

He nodded. "Yes."

"Because of Gibraltar?"

"No. Because if you exist, and continue to exist, you will eventually make all this side of the world in your image, and when the wolves run out of rabbits to eat, then what?" Brudegan asked. "We cannot let you exist. Your own side cannot let you exist. You are a sickness with no cure."

"Probably true." Jess folded her hands over one knee, her ears picking up motion behind the craft and knowing it. *You're right, Brudegan. We are wolves. You can't defeat us.*

He straightened as he now sensed the motion, and from the landing bay to the right of them emerged a drifting crowd of armed figures, coming around the side of the flyer to stand and watch.

Covered in blood and dust and in the working coveralls of the Bay.

"But wolves know their own," Jess said with a faint smile. "And they defend their territory."

"Cuz." It was Dustin, blood covering half his face. "We got 'em all inside." He stared insolently at Brudegan. "Want me to get this one for ya?"

"No, he's flagged," Jess said. "My chit."

"Too damn bad." He winked at Dev. "But they put some hurt on the non coms, cuz."

Dev felt a sense of apprehension and she looked at Jess.

"Tried to get at the kids, but the spacies whacked at 'em," one of the youngsters with Dustin added. "Pretty cool."

"Cool," Dustin agreed.

Jess stood up and moved closer to him. "I told Interforce about your scam. I told them how you wormed your way in and were setting us against each other. Games up." Her voice hardened a trifle. "They're hands off."

Brudegan looked over at the line of waiting carriers outlined against the clouds and faintly shook his head.

A faint crackle in Jess's ear and she touched the comms. "Jase?"

"Heard the channels open up," Jason said with wry calmness. "Westies ordered to stand with us against the incoming."

April's voice chimed in. "Yeah, the jackass here heard it, too. Bitching."

Jess's eyes went to Brudegan's face, studying it. She could sense the coming fight, and like a mist of rain coating her skin, her body responded, flushing out the exhaustion and replacing it with the subtle buzz of excitement and anticipation.

"Ops says they're gonna have to farm out the bodies if the rest of them come on in here, cuz." Dustin glanced up at the thickening clouds. "Gotta sharpen the process blades."

Jess saw the faintest of flinches in her enemy's face. Just the minutest of contractions, and she felt time slow as she took another of those minutes out and stepped back in her head, coming out of the moment into that gray place of no emotion.

Where really was the win? She replayed and considered the last words Dev had said, their clear tones echoing in the back of her head. Everyone expected the battle now. Wanted it. She could even sense the taste for blood in her kinfolk standing nearby, denied them for so long.

Where was the win? Was there a win? Or just the lesser of two losses?

She drew breath and came back in. "You want to see what this whole scam was about before you die for it?" she asked. "See if it was worth it?"

She'd startled him. She read it in his eyes, in the flicker of reaction, in the sudden shift of his body he couldn't quite control. "You talk big. Walk it. I'll show you." She gestured to the bay opening across the rocks now full of fighters.

He shook his head. "I can die here as well in the clean air," he said. "What protects me in there? The word of a Drake?"

Jess looked him in the eye. "My father told me once the only thing you come into and out of the world with is your honor. And that you can't have it taken. You can only give it away." Her lips twitched a little. "Jimmy died for giving his."

Brudegan shifted his gaze off hers just long enough to see the crowd nearby unconsciously nodding their heads in agreement. He lifted one hand and let it drop. "Go. I will follow," he said, with the faintest of shrugs. "Death is death."

They walked across the rocky ground that moderated and became flat and regular as they approached the cliff opening and entered, the worksuited figures inside slowly drawing aside to let them pass.

JASON STARED AT the screen. "What the hell is she doing? Are they going inside?" He triggered comms. "Jess!"

"Ack." Jess's voice came back at him. "Standby tac. Ops G1."

"Got a game on," Brent said.

"What kind of game...oh. Gonna leverage the bastard," Jason said. "Insurance."

"Jason."

He flicked comms. "Go, El."

"Had a bad mix up here. Doc's down," Elaine said. "Need to get him to the tank."

Jason straightened up. "No med there?"

"TP bandages," Elaine responded. "He's in countdown."

"Crap." Jason considered a minute. "Bring up the sidechannel to April, Brent."

"Sideband up."

"April, this is Jason."

"Ack," April responded promptly. "Sup?"

"Need you to take a med run back to Base Ten."

Dead silence for a moment. Jason figured it could go either way. "It's the doc," he added in a card. "Took a hit."

Still silence.

"Pissed," Brent said. "Don't want to miss the fight."

"Ack," April finally answered. "Going in."

A moment later a carrier broke out of formation and pitched down, heading for the cliff face. "El, the kids are on the way in for a pickup. Jess's bus."

"K, ack." Elaine cut off and the channel went offline.

Jason leaned back in his seat and folded his hands over his stomach. "Least they get to do something." He sighed. "Wish I knew what she was up to."

THEIR BOOTS SCUFFED on the cut stone floors and then rang as they reached the circular iron stair. They started downward bathed in gray light from the cap at the apogee of it. Below, they heard shots and shouting and a low booming roar.

"I have heard of this place," Brudegan said after a long silence. "This hall."

Jess nodded as they climbed down past the residential levels, all doors closed and sealed, red light that bathed the landings in warning. She was in the lead with Dev at her side and Brudegan a step behind. The fighters from the Bay followed in an unruly clump, a dozen of them at her heels.

They reached the bottom, and now there were bodies evident, growing more numerous as they skirted them and headed down a corridor.

Bay security chief Mike emerged from the ops area. "Jess! All sealed." His eyes went to Brudegan and his hand to his gun in the same motion.

"Stop." Jess lifted a hand. "Let him alone."

Mike stared hard at her and him. "Some like him just blew out some worth a lot more then him," he said. "Including your buddy from space."

Jess hauled up sharply. "Kurok?" She saw Dev's eyes widen and she gasped.

Mike nodded. "We just hauled him into your crate and that nomad lit out for the base."

"Ah," Brudegan said. "Best news I could have had. The traitor dead." He barely got the words out when he was lifted up bodily and slammed against the rock wall, held there with solid force. He reeled and his head went back and forth before it dropped down to see furious green eyes looking up at him.

"If Doctor Dan is injured," Dev said, "or made dead, it is not at all good news."

Jess exhaled, letting the momentary shock fade. "Easy, Devvie." She patted her back. "Let him down. I'll find out what the score is. They're getting him back to med."

Dev released the unpleasant man, and he fell to his knees on the rock from the force of it. It took a lot of concentration, more than she'd expected, to resist hitting him.

She wanted to. There was no sense in her that it was even wrong for her to do so. She glanced up and found Mike looking at her. He nodded at her in understanding.

Which she in no way understood. But she could feel Jess's hand still on her back, the tips of her fingers making little scratching motions.

"Big mix," Mike said. "Bunch of his buddies got in the lower hall, and the doc's kids heard it and came to help. He jumped in front of a blast and they went nuts and tore those bastards apart. We hardly had a chance to get in on it."

Brudegan slowly climbed to his feet.

"Yeah, they did good," Dustin added. "They're all right." He extended a fist to Dev, who stared at it until Jess picked up her hand and guided it to bump knuckles. "Booyah."

Dev exhaled. "Severely non optimal," she muttered.

Jess grabbed Brudegan's arm and started forward. "Let's get this over with," she said. "I got things to do."

Mike stood in her way. "What's 'this'?" he asked bluntly. "Besides something else to kill?"

"Not yet," Jess said. "Not damn yet."

DEV'S HEART STILL pounded as they crossed into the ops area. Abruptly she was barraged by a crowd of anxious sets who spotted her.

"NM-Dev-1!" voices chorused. A KayTee rushed over. "Something terrible happened to Doctor Dan!"

Dev was caught between wanting to find out what happened

and following Jess and the bad guy. Jess seemed to realize this because she half turned and gestured her to stay.

"Be right back, Devvie," Jess said. "Take charge here, huh?"

Obey? Not obey? Dev slowed, allowing the sets to catch her up. "What happened, AyeBee?" she asked as she was surrounded. The fighters from the Bay also paused, but Mike followed Jess, a gun gripped in one hand.

"It was very incorrect," the Kaytee said. "There were incorrect people here, and they came in the same way as we did, where the shuttle was."

A CeeBee nodded. "We saw them. Some of them tried to make dead the children."

Dev frowned. "That's terrible. So incorrect!"

"We stopped them," The Kaytee tried not to sound proud and completely failed. "They ran away from us." He added with widened eyes.

"We chased them here, and then they were trying to make dead the people in operations, where Doctor Dan was," a CeeBee said. "And then they tried to make us dead, and Doctor Dan came out to fight with them to make them stop!"

Yes, Doctor Dan would have done that. "He is brave," Dev said. "And he cares very much for us."

The sets around her nodded. "He does," the CeeBee said. "He said we were like his children. It was so excellent."

"Yes," the Kaytee agreed. "But they made him very damaged, and we got angry about that." He paused. "And then we had to make them stop hurting him and we did."

Dev studied them and understood. "Yes. That was a correct thing to do," she said, in a quiet voice. "I hope he is okay. Jess said they were taking him back to our base, to med."

"Yes. Cathy went with him also. Will we go there, too?"

She looked around and saw the sets, working alongside the people from Jess's home place to clean things up, some of them in burned jumpsuits and covered in blood. As she watched, one of the Bay workers went up to a Kaytee and offered him a coat.

The Kaytee took it gratefully, and put it on over his shredded jumpsuit, rubbing his arms from the cold. The person from the Bay smiled.

"I don't know," Dev finally answered. "We did good work here."

"It was hard," the Kaytee near her said. "And two of us got made dead," he added. "Many of us were damaged."

"Yes," Dev said. "Downside is hard, and damage is frequent.

Even for the natural borns." She watched as one of the sets helped a limping Bay worker move to an area where there seemed to be some med. "It is not like the station."

"No," the Kaytee said. "It is not like the station." He considered. "But maybe that is not all incorrect for us." He folded his arms over his chest. "It is good to help and do work and be brave, like Doctor Dan."

"Yes, it is," Dev agreed.

"NM-Dev-1, this place is called Drake's Bay," the CeeBee said. "Like the name of your partner."

"This is her birthplace," Dev responded. "She came from here, like we came from the station." She considered a moment. "I know she appreciates the good work we have done here...ah." She spotted Elaine at the same time the agent spotted her and Elaine changed direction and came over to her. "Hello."

"So these are more of your kind of bio, huh?" Elaine said. "I figured there were more." She glanced around. "Where's Jess? Someone said she was just here."

"Yes." Dev decided to leave the first question alone. "She was taking an enemy person to show them something. She said she would be right back."

"Enemy person?" Elaine said. "Who? What the hell'd she bring one of them in here for? We killed enough of them already!"

"I think she is trying to avoid everyone being made dead," Dev said placidly. "I will go find her and see." She ducked out of the group and started down the hallway she'd seen Jess disappear through, reasoning that she'd stayed in the location Jess had indicated just long enough.

She was tired, and hungry, and she wanted the fight to be over. It had been more than enough for one day.

THE DOORS TO the cavern were solidly shut, but they opened to Jess's handprint, and she shoved the portal open to allow them to pass.

Brudegan had fallen silent and remained so as they entered the cave, and the rich scent of growing things washed over them. The large door boomed shut behind them, and then all the sound heard was the soft hiss of the water misting system cutting on and off.

"The fuck you showing him this for?" Mike said bluntly.

"Shut up," Jess replied. "This crap is where it all started."

Brudegan slowly turned in a circle, looking at all the greens and colors. "It is real," he finally said. "I never thought it was."

Jess walked over to one of the plant areas and touched a leaf. "You thought it was a scam."

"I did." He came to join her and reached out to touch the plant himself. "I knew this was possible on the stations, yes? I have seen it. I have eaten it. We provision ourselves much better than you."

It was true. Jess merely nodded.

"It was a well done game. To destroy your trustworthiness and also gain us a lab rat." Brudegan turned to look at her. "And it succeeded." He smiled. "So now, Drake, what's your offer? You brought me here to make one." He wandered a step down the walk and sniffed one of the plants. "Despite your big talk, we both know the force coming here is going to obliterate you."

"Then why even bother offering you a deal?" Jess leaned against the wall. "If you're so sure you'll win, why not just wait. Though, we both know I'm going to kill you anyway."

He looked at her. "You promised me safety."

"From them." Jess smiled at him, a frank and full expression of glee. "Not from me."

He went for his gun but Jess was full seconds ahead of him, and she ripped it off him before he could touch it. She flung it far off before it could recognize her as an enemy and explode.

All in a breath.

Then she leaned against the wall again. Mike did likewise, with a grunt of approval. "You're not going to win," Jess said. "If I have to kill every single one of you coming in here, I will." She folded her arms over her chest. "And I can, y'know." She watched his face carefully. "Of course you know, or you wouldn't have made my nephew your price."

He shook the hand she'd slammed into. "The price you paid. You who have no price."

Jess smiled again. "Not my price. I took what belonged to me back on that station. You just don't know it yet, Bruddie."

He stopped in mid motion and let his hands fall to his side.

The sound of the outer door opening made them turn to see Dev making her way into the cavern, her issue boots rasping softly on the ground.

Mike turned to watch her but didn't move to intercept her slight form. She moved past him with just a brief sideways glance.

Jess was between Dev and Brudegan, but she gently pushed

off the wall and brought her center of balance up over the balls of her feet, her senses focused on him as Dev arrived. "Hey, Devvie. You stayed there longer than I thought you would."

Dev frowned. "The agent Elaine was looking for you," she explained. "There is some data they would like you to review, and I said I would come find you."

"Coulda called me."

"Yes."

Jess saw the furrows of worry on Dev's cute face. "Any word on the doc?"

"No. The sets said he was really damaged." Dev lifted her eyes to Jess's. "He was trying to defend them."

Yes, he would have. "'Sa'll right, Dev. I'm about done here. Just wanted this clown to see what he's going to die for," Jess said. "They get the power spooled up to that laser disrupter on the ridge?"

Dev caught her eye for a long moment. "Yes."

Brudegan stirred. "A long lost technology," he said warily. "We know it."

"Not here. Everything here's a throwback. You forget that? Left in the past? Isn't that why you want to have us kick the bucket, you, and maybe Interforce? You ain't got nothing to match us anymore."

"Got that right," Mike said.

A rumble moved through the walls. "Yep, there's the energy pumps now," Jess said. "Fish are gonna get a damn good meal." She chuckled. Off to the rear of the chamber she detected a faint sound, and her fingers flexed. A rough play put in work far too fast, but then, it had often been like that in her life

She casually reached over and pried off a bit of the glowing rock, turning it in her fingers and examining it. "Good thing the doc got to suss this. Got all the scoop in the carrier." She glanced up at Brudegan whose face had gone still. "Kickass scientist, that Kurok."

Her senses came alert as she gently juggled the rock in one hand, her breathing slowing as she shifted slightly. In reaction, Dev reached out and put a hand on her back in an unconscious motion. Jess half turned and smiled, letting the rock drop to the ground at her feet.

Brudegan's hand clenched. His face twitched, starting a grin of triumph that froze solid. His hand clenched again, and again, and they heard the faintest of clicks coming from his closed fist.

Dev watched him with a puzzled expression, then her eyes

widened as Jess casually reached over and undid the fastenings at Dev's uniform neck and peeled it back.

"Like I said, kickass scientist," Jess smiled. "Drop it, Brudegan. It's useless." She leaned closer to Dev, and with a wink she kissed the spot where once there had been a metallic band around her neck.

Dev stood stock still, unsure of what reaction to have. Her body reacted to the touch though, a pleasant flush of response that cleared the exhaustion out some. She took a breath, and then many things happened.

Blaster fire, and then she was pushed flat to the ground with Jess crouching over her, returning the fire. The man, Brudegan, bolted across the floor. Mike was on his knees, his big old rifle aiming past them, a yell coming from his throat.

They heard boots in the outer corridor. At that moment Brudegan reached the gun Jess had thrown across the chamber and dove for it. He grabbed it and tumbled into a turn and shot back at them right at the floor where Dev was.

And then she wasn't as Jess picked her up and lunged into the opposite direction, to a curve in the cavern wall that blocked the fire and dusted them with glowing backsplash.

Mike landed next to them and fired over Jess's head. "They're getting out!" he yelled. "He got that rock piece!"

"Let 'em." Jess spat a bit of dust out of her mouth.

"What?" Mike stared at her in shock.

"Just keep your fucking head down and let them go," Jess repeated, wiping the back of her hand across her face.

A portal boomed in the far end of the cavern and the firing stopped. They were alone.

"Let's go." Jess got to her feet and pulled Dev with her. "Ops." She holstered her blaster and started off at a lope that became a run.

"WHAT THE HELL'S going on?" Elaine thumped down in the ops seat and yanked a board over. "Penetration?"

"Sig!" the next ops yelled. "Got sig from the back! Josh send a crew back there!"

"El, two armored fliers by the shuttle pad," Jason's voice erupted in comms. "Target?"

"Target!" she confirmed. "Take 'em out!"

"On it."

The ops next to her grinned. "Nice to have an air force

again," he said, both thighs moving in convulsive twitching as he
set and reset parameters.

Elaine looked at him and their eyes met, she had to grin back.

The carriers holding off outside went into attack formation
and spun off into a dive, aiming at the narrow cleft that would
open to the plateau where the shuttle pad was that was now the
focus of the enemy.

"'Bout twenty for the rest of that crowd," Johnathan said
from the master ops console, half its lights out and covered in
dust from the roof. "Gonna cover us like gull shit."

Boots in the hall, coming fast. They turned to find Jess
entering, slowing so as not to take out a few people who didn't
get out of the way in time.

"There you are," El said. "We just went for the back there.
Jason's going to take those bastards out before the rest of them
get here and we're screwed." She indicated a board. "Those are
all Szenge class, Jess. Just got the intel. We can't take that, not
even if all the coast were here fresh fueled."

Dev came in with Mike behind her.

"Move." Jess took over a console. "Gimme comms to Jason."
She saw Dev sit at an empty board then start tapping surfaces.
"Dev get our net up."

"Yes." Dev put a comms in her own ear.

"What's up?" Elaine asked.

"Gotta stop them tanking those flyers." Jess got a headset on.
"Jase! Jase!"

"What?" Elaine stood up. "The hell are you doing?"

"Jason is on channel twelve," Dev said. "I am trying to
contact Base Ten or our vehicle."

Jess heard the channel open. "Jase!"

"Busy!" he yelled back. "Shooting bad guys in a barrel!"

Jess took a breath. "Stop," she said emphatically into the
comms. "Stop firing. Let them go." She felt the shock around the
room and saw Elaine stand up at her station and turn. Only Dev
remained where she was, eyes on the boards, fingertips moving.

"What?" Jason answered. "The fuck, Jess?"

"Let them go," Jess repeated. "My order."

Dead silence for a long moment. "You asked me to trust you,
Jase. Return the favor," Jess finally said. "Let them go. Let them
get back to their fleet."

"You've gone nuts," Elaine said. "Must be that crack in your
skull because I know enough about Drakes to know you haven't
gone over."

"Thanks, El." Jess leaned on the console. "Nicest thing you ever said about me." She touched the comms. "Jase? You gonna listen or not?"

"Ack," Jason answered. "Heeling off."

"Better have a good reason for that, Drake," Mike said from behind her. "If you just sold us down the river I'm gonna shoot you myself." He shifted his gun then paused as Dev got up and got between him and Jess's back. "Shoot you, too, jelly bag."

"That is possibly true," Dev said. "But I will do my best to prevent it."

Jess leaned back, her body coming to rest against Dev's as she let her head rest just between her shoulder blades. "Pretty funny when a bio alt from an egg in space is standing guard over me against my family and the force, y'know?"

The screen showed the enemy fliers bolting across the sea, one of them singed as they passed the line of Interforce carriers that had started to break off. Two of the carriers bent into a tight turn and sped after them but held fire.

As they all watched the two intersected the oncoming force, and the carriers peeled off to run parallel to them, shields up. The attack never came.

Instead, as they all stared at the monitor, the force from the other side first slowed, and then broke apart, turning in formation as the two fliers joined them.

"Guess they got what they came for," Elaine said in a dry tone. "What's up with that, Jess? What's the game?"

"They got what I wanted them to get." Jess relaxed her shoulders. "Not sure there was a game. Not sure I had time for a game. Not even sure yet what their game was."

"Everyone is not going to be made dead," Dev said. "That seems optimal."

"Maybe that was my game." Jess propped her chin up on her fist. "Dev wanted to know if there was a way to end this in something other than mutual slaughter."

Dev regarded her in slight bemusement.

"That's fucked up." Elaine nevertheless sat back down at the console. "You have a lot to explain to a lot of people, but yeah, maybe it's not the worst thing not to croak today. Because I've lost track of who the hell the players are at this point."

Johnathan looked at the console output. "They're really turning around and hauling ass away." He sounded surprised. "Maybe that means we can finally get some food in here. I'm fuckin' starving."

Jess had to laugh just a little. "I bet Dev is thinking the same thing."

Dev cleared her throat a little.

"So." Elaine looked at them. "Is this over?"

Jess just shrugged.

"I mean, what the hell?"

THE FAMILY TABLE didn't have much family around it, and the bowls of edibles on top of it were nothing fancy. But Jess was happy to sit with her hands curled around a cup of rich fish broth and savor, however brief, a moment of peace.

A moment of survival anyhow.

The Interforce carriers from Base Ten had landed. Jason and Elaine were seated at the table with Johnathan and Mike resting bloodstained elbows on the scarred wood surface.

There was no Uncle Max. No old uncles or aunts, and no brothers or any of their family. Jake was still in lockup, and Tayler was somewhere, bewildered, bereft of his own family in a place now very strange.

Not really his home anymore.

She was tired. Now, after it all, her head hurt like crazy again, and she knew if she peeled off her uniform there would be lots of bruises under it, and for what, really?

No win, anywhere. At best, she'd kept them from being obliterated by a much superior force that despite her bravado could not have been stopped.

Jess thought about it. Was that a win? She looked around the table. Fuck.

Dev was in ops, persistently trying to get information from Base Ten. Horribly worried about Kurok. Jess lifted her eyes and saw a bio alt enter. "Hey."

"Hello." The bio alt came over to her. "We would like to bring some food to the operations center. Is that all right?"

"Sure," Jess said. Dev had shared a plate of seaweed rolls with her, but she figured more couldn't hurt. "Take that basket over there."

"Thank you."

CeeBee? BeeTee? "What's your name," Jess asked.

"I am AyeBee 354."

Right. "How about I call you, Abe?" Jess said. "I'm not good at remembering numbers."

The bio alt regarded her with surprised interest. "My crèche name was Alvin," he said, after a pause to retrieve the basket. "Would you like to address me as that?"

"Alvin. Sure." Jess watched as he left the kitchen with the basket, taking the task of someone who probably died in some pointless way in some corridor and was now fish food.

"This is profoundly fucked up," Jason said after a pause.

"Yeah," Jess agreed. "What do we do now? Go back to base?" She sucked at her soup, then straightened a little as Dev entered. "Any luck?"

Dev came over and sat next to her on one of the kitchen stools. "I got through to our base. They have put Doctor Dan in some mechanical device. They do not expect he will...he was very damaged."

Aw. Jess put her cup down. "Sorry to hear that, Devvie."

"Yeah," Elaine said. "He's the one who figured out how to set off those guns on the roof. He's good people."

Dev remained silent for a few moments. "May we go see him, Jess? April and Doug have just returned with our vehicle."

"We should all go back," Jason said. "I'm sure there's some coded message somewhere telling me to go shoot myself that I should probably read and ignore."

"Or shoot me," Jess said. "Or shoot them. Or shoot ourselves in the head."

"I don't feel like shooting anything right now," Elaine admitted. "But I'd love a hot shower and a nap."

Jess studied Dev's face. "Sure, lets go." She put down her soup and pushed herself to her feet. "I don't think the gooneys are coming back. Not if they think we've got a laser disrupter all ready to make them atomic particles."

"Yeah what was that all about?" Mike asked, turning and standing up as she neared.

Jess paused. "A laser disrupter is a piece of old school technology that basically grabs whatever energy it sees and multiplies it into a really big boom. Used against the big troop transports and stuff like that. Could take out a base."

Mike's jaw dropped a little. "We got one?"

Jess yawned and rubbed the side of her face. "No."

Jason started to laugh. "But you told them we did."

"Yeah. Figured, what the hell? We had a thermonuke. We're certified crazy. We got barrage guns on the roof. Why not?" Jess half shrugged. "We coulda."

"Those guns nearly blew up on us," Johnathan said. "Doc guy said it wouldn't take another round."

"But they didn't know that," Elaine said. "Crap I didn't know that. After what I saw here, if you'd have told me you had a disrupter in the basement, I'd have believed it."

Mike moved over a little, into her way. "So that's it? You just leaving now?"

Jess was too tired to even take offense. Actually, she reasoned he had a point. "I'll be back."

"Might not want you back," he said straightforwardly. "A lot of people died being in your target range."

Jess considered that for a minute. "Move out of my way or I'll kill you," she finally said in a mild tone. "Maybe it was me who almost got splatted because the target was this." She pointed at the ground then drew her gun from its hard point and had it at his neck before he could stir. "Move."

He stared at her for a long minute, and they all wondered. Then he stepped back with an almost smile. "Not going to call that bluff, Drake." He sat down at the table. "But someone will."

Jess put the gun back and continued on her way, with Dev silently moving at her side. After a pause, Elaine and Jason followed, and the kitchen fell silent as the two Bay men regarded each other across the table.

"She'd have done it," Johnathan said. "She's Drake both sides. There's just no end to the jackassery in that." He sipped from his mug of soup. "Could end up net plus, Mike."

"It could," Mike agreed. "Cleared out a lot of the useless round here. Finally get to move my fuckin' quarters where they should be."

"Mmm."

IT WAS EXCELLENT, really excellent, to be sitting back in her pilot's seat in the carrier, going through the now familiar steps to bring the big vehicle online. Dev slid her comms helmet on and plugged into the inputs, anxious to be on their way.

Behind her Jess was speaking with April. To Dev's left, Doug sat in the pilot jumpseat, his long legs sprawled across the floor of the carrier. "Sorry about the doc," he said after a bit of silence.

Dev drew a breath then released it. "Thank you for trying to bring him to safety," she said. "I know that must have been difficult."

Doug blinked a few times. "Truth? I thought April was going to kick up when they asked, but she didn't. Just told me to get my ass moving. "I was glad to. She was glad to. He bled for us."

He bled for us. Dev had heard that a lot in the last few days. "Yes." She pre-spooled the engines. "Jess? We are about to maneuver."

Without comment both agents sat down and strapped in.

Dev lifted the carrier and slid it sideways on its landing jets, turning the vehicle and easing out of the landing bay door to emerge above the cliff that held Drake's Bay.

Below, in the half circle bay, there were already small work boats afloat, gingerly moving toward the debris from the fight, towing it out of the way.

It started to rain.

"Base seemed okay." April continued the conversation she'd been having with Jess. "Got me in and out, all reg, no real grilling or nothing."

Jess sighed. "Hope that's still the case with my ass on board."

Behind them the rest of the Base Ten carriers emerged from the bays and made up formation as Dev waited there for them. Then she started forward, hoping the same thing Jess hoped.

She wanted a chance to see Doctor Dan.

They flew along the coastline, unmarked and unremarkable in its rain lashed and ruffled gray blue surface. Waves crashed up against the cliffs and covered the isolated small beaches full of small rocks and sand.

"This is Interforce flight BR270006, inbound to Base Ten," Dev said into the silence after it had gone on for a long while. "Requesting approach and landing assignment."

Just like nothing had happened. Just like they were coming back from a training run.

"BR270006, acknowledged," Base Ten ops answered. "Stand by for pad assignment. Welcome home."

"Did they actually just say that?" April said. "Really?"

Jess lifted her hands in a shrugging motion and put them down. "Insanity."

Surreal. Dev merely shook her head.

They approached the imposing cliff face that was the Citadel to where the new landing doors had been installed recently and yet seemingly a lifetime ago.

The bay was already open for them, and the carriers behind them. Dev saw mechs moving into position, and she slowed the carrier as it crossed into the bay, which bore signs of recent battle.

"BR270006, pad six," Ops said. "Please clear quickly so the rest of the flight can land."

"Yes." Dev headed for the pad. She could already see a group of bio mechs standing by. She cut power as she extended the landing skids, feeling the faint jar as they hit the pad surface and then the thump and pop as the jets cut out and they were down. "BR270006, secure," she reported to comms.

Jess was up and out of her seat. She opened the hatch and stood full in its breadth as the small ramp extended. Her eyes swept the interior of the big cavern, but nothing seemed out of place. Then she saw Cliff heading her way, his arm in a sling.

Across the cavern the rest of the carriers were landing, the noise in the room rising to include all their offgassing and the clanks and pops of the umbilicals being attached.

All normal.

"Jess. Welcome back," Cliff said. He mounted the raised pad. "Everyone okay?"

Jess stepped aside to let the rest of them out, sensing Dev at her back. "Yeah. Dev needs to get to med. We can all talk later."

Cliff nodded in understanding. "Hey, at least you all made it back in one piece. We heard the comms. They multiplexed it all call." He moved aside to let them exit then followed along as they came down off the pad and walked across the cavern floor.

Dev felt sick now that she was here. She kept her hands in the pockets of her jacket, responding to the quiet greetings of the mechs and techs as they passed.

The rest of the agents and techs quickly caught up to them, and they went into the long corridor together, a vague flash of memory coming to Dev of her return from her first mission here, where everything really had changed.

She wished briefly that she was back in that time, on that walk to the briefing room, everything so new and fresh again. It was sad and tiring to be surrounded by so much pain and death, where nothing seemed like it would be optimal and all choices appeared wrong.

They passed a glowing blue ring, and she almost didn't notice, just felt the brief tingle under her skin, and the soft chorus of chimes as they all were scanned, recognized and allowed.

There were marks of fighting on the walls, but mostly the base seemed to be as normal as she remembered it to be. Some mechs in the hall, some security, all moving aside to let the operations group pass.

Soft tones, standard announcements, ops reports all moving past her as they moved from gray to green to the blue of operations and then off one corridor to the white of med.

Jarad was in the hall, and he paused as he saw them. "You're back." He had one of the tough fabric med jumpsuits on, liberally splattered with blood and the yellow and green blood stop and pain cream they used for triage.

"Busy day." Jess said.

"Could say." The chief medic glanced at Dev then back at Jess. "Guess you're here for the tank." He paused, but they all just looked at him. "C'mon." He waved them to follow. "I told ops I'd keep the lights on until you all got here."

Dev didn't understand what that meant, but she saw the expression on Jess's face and her heart sank. She knew her partner understood, and it wasn't good. She took a breath, and they went through a pair of double doors that opened for them, and then she was in a room she hadn't been in before.

Inside there were six big units, all filled with thick green liquid. In three of them there were naked human forms with tubes and leads snaking from them.

Jared led them to the last one, near the back wall. Inside, they saw a stocky form that had old, faded marks on its arms, and the tab readouts over the tank were all red. Jared turned. "As I told the agent here." He indicated April. "He took a neural right in the head."

"Fuck." Jess exhaled in pure reaction.

"He walked in front of it," Elaine said in a somber tone. "Had a half dozen of the dirty firing. He just took it."

Dev walked closer and put her hands on the surface of the tank. Doctor Dan's eyes were closed, and he wasn't moving. She could see the damage.

She exhaled a little, her breath fogging the surface of the tank and felt a very deep sadness. There had been so much she'd wanted to talk to him about.

Jared regarded the form then swiveled back around. "If anyone had any doubt he was one of us, that killed it." he said. "And it killed him." He looked at Dev. "I just kept the machines on so you could...um." He paused and faltered as Dev's eyes filled with tears. "Ah, sorry," he ended in a mutter.

People died in here all the time. Jared wasn't used to anyone reacting to it, even when long time friendships were lost and partnerships ended. Their lives just didn't allow for that.

Much.

"Gosh I'm sorry, Dev," Clint said in a small voice.

Most of the agents looked down or away. Most of the techs moved closer. Doug reached over to pat her on the arm. It was a little uncomfortable.

Embarrassing. Dev felt hideously alone there. She hastily wiped at her face and tried to think about something else.

But then Jess moved closer and put her arms around Dev, pulling her close in a hug and she turned and buried her face into Jess's chest to get away from all those watching eyes.

"Ah, Devvie," Jess said in a sad and resigned tone. "Only thing I can tell ya is if he had to pick a way to go, you know he'd pick this one."

"I know," Dev said softly. "But I'll miss him so much."

"Yeah, I know. Me too." Jess rubbed her back. "You want some of your other buddies to come up here, too? Maybe we'll sing him a song, something like that, huh?"

Dev had to struggle to understand what Jess was asking. "Oh," she finally murmured. "Yes."

"I'll go get some of them," Clint muttered. He turned and shoved his way out of the room.

"Damn, that's a real shame," Jason finally said, awkwardly. "No shot, Jared?"

The doctor shook his head, looking uncomfortable. "It was a crapshoot even getting him here." He gave April a little nod. "They redlined it."

Jess could feel Dev sniffling against her and felt a sense of deep sadness herself. To have come as far as he had, and escape all that they all had, to end like this?

A waste and it was making Dev really unhappy. Jess remembered what she'd felt in those minutes she'd thought Dev had blown up and her brow creased.

A man who had lived and died by his own rules. Who had worn his honor on his sleeve, literally.

Who had given his loyalty and love to her father. Now she'd never get a chance to ask him why, though she thought she knew.

There were sounds behind her. She looked over her shoulder as some bio alts entered, eyes wide with shock and horror. Cathy came in with them, her eyes unapologetically reddened with tears.

His dying mattered. Jess exhaled. His dying made a difference to all these people, herself included and it was a shame he wasn't there to see it. "Okay." She took the lead because she had to. "We'll sing him out. Then Jared can get his work done."

They gathered close, all of them mingled together in common silence.

THEY WAITED UNTIL the bio alts stopped coming in, and Jess figured everyone who wanted to be there was. The bios were nervous, sad, scared, and a little afraid to approach the tank. She waved them forward with what she hoped was an encouraging look.

Okay, possibly not. Jess frowned when the bulk of them froze in place, averting their glances.

Dev wiped her eyes and walked to the tank and pressed her hands against the surface. "Come here," she said to her crèchemates. "We have to say goodbye. Doctor Dan was very damaged. This machine is just keeping him from being made dead until we can."

"Oh, no," a KayTee moaned softly.

One of the BeeAyes whispered, "Now I see why they told us to come."

"Yes." Dev turned her head and looked at him. "He was our teacher. He cared for us. So come and look and say farewell."

And so they did, slowly filing in behind Dev and around the tank. The agents and techs came in behind them and Jason and Elaine got next to Jess and exchanged looks with her.

April and Doug edged their way closer, and Brent came around to the other side of Jason, near the wall.

Cliff came back into the room last of all, standing somewhere between the bios and the agents as though he couldn't decide where he belonged, then after a moment joined three of his bio alt mechs in the back row around the tank.

The room was full. It felt like hearts inside it were, too.

Jason put his hands behind his back. "Jesslyn Drake, the first words are yours," he said, as Jared went to the med console, visibly glad to be hidden behind his responsibilities. "Start the end."

Yes, it was hers. Jess stood up a little straighter. "They are," she said. "He was kin to my kin." She paused. "His blood was shed for us. He died in honor, giving his life for his friends." She regarded the bios who watched her wide eyed. "For his family. His children he shaped with his own hands."

The bio alts held their breaths, listening hard.

"He was brave when he didn't have to be," Jess continued, thoughtfully. "Not because it got him anything, just because it was part of who he was. He was one of us. Always."

She stopped speaking and the crowd around her started. "He is our brother in arms," agents and techs said in unison. "He goes where all the brave hearts go to join the long line of those before him and us who will follow."

"Go with the wind." April spoke up. "That touches everything, always as you touched us." She clasped her hands behind her back.

"Thank you for teaching us," Cliff added softly. "And for creating good people."

A KayTee spoke up timidly. "Thank you for taking care of us."

Dev drew in a breath and laid her hands flat on the tank surface, peering into the green, misty liquid. "Thank you for making me."

Another silence and eyes shifted back to Jess.

"Give my regards to Dad." Jess set herself aside from the emotion of it and drew in a breath, then she started to sing, the first part of a very old hymn taught to everyone who came through the field school.

It had once been a religious song, when there were still religions. It had almost no meaning now, but the force had used it to sing out their dead when there was a chance and they hadn't just had to keep on moving. She'd only sung it twice in her career, but this was the first time it was hers to lead.

She'd missed singing it at her father's ceremony, and now here, at this one, she held the notes true on this song they had once called "Taps" and hoped somewhere, in some spectral echo, he'd hear it.

It was difficult, singing. But she bore down and concentrated, closing her eyes as she worked to fill the room with the sound of the song, trying to make sure it was right and perfect.

The last note of the first part faded, and then the rest of the agents and techs joined in for the rest, filling the space with multivoiced harmony that sent its vibration through surface and bodies, reflecting off the stone walls and the plas of the tanks.

Deep male voices and lighter female ones, but all in tune, all knowing their part in the whole.

Dev felt like it was impossible to breathe, the sound behind her made the hair stand up on her skin, and her heart was filled to overflowing. It was so horrible and so beautiful at the same time, and she could see the awe in the faces of the rest of the bio alts standing near her.

She so wished Doctor Dan could hear it. There was so much respect and honor in it, and as she thought that she cried in earnest, tears silently rolling down her face. In all the violence and horror they'd been through, to have to come to this beauty for the worst of reasons broke her heart.

A KayTee put his hand over hers, resting on the glass. He was crying, too, silently, they all were, and shivering from the emotion of the sound that touched them in places they had no programming for as it vibrated through them and marked, in an aural bloodstain, this moment.

And then the last of it faded, the softest of echoes reflected against the glass, and there was silence. Then Jared shifted a little, and lifted his hands to turn off the mechanical systems. As he did, Dev turned to watch him and her eyes flickered over the status panels overhead.

And because she was what she was, and she was programmed how she was, that part of her that had been so painstakingly designed, registered the surface of them with even that passing glance and she gasped in reaction without even really understanding why.

But her sound made Jared stop. He looked where she was looking and his hands went still as he blinked.

The status was mostly still red. Mostly.

Mostly.

But there were flickers there now that had not been before. "Son of a bitch." The doctor swung around and hit some inputs. "What the hell? He was flatline."

"Hey." Jason's voice sounded more than a little bemused. "We sang him back a little, Jessie. Good job!" He clapped Jess on the back. "Must've been your voice. You always had a nice set of pipes."

Dev turned and looked at Jess, who was still standing there behind her, eyebrows lifted a little, in patent, silent surprise. "Did you do that?" she asked, sniffling back the tears.

Jess turned her hands upmost just a bit and shrugged, then was nearly bowled off her feet as Dev launched herself at her and hugged her fiercely. "Oof."

"Can it do that?" Elaine asked, glancing at the now very busy Jared. "That was just a quirk, right? We didn't actually do anything."

Jared looked up at them. "He still could go. He's maybe just not ready to yet." He frowned at them. "And no, your singing, pretty though it was, didn't do squat. Want to clear out now? Apparenty now I've got work to do."

The KayTee came over, bewildered. "What happened? Is Doctor Dan not going to be made dead?"

"Dunno," Jason answered him. "Life's fucked up like that

sometimes, y'know? Let's go eat."

"Hmm," Jess grunted. "What a fucking way to end the day." She looked over everyone's head at the panel, and at Jared's frown, and at the figure in the tank that now, wasn't actually just fish food yet.

Freak chance?

Pure cussedness?

"Oh, Jess, thank you," Dev whispered, still hugging her.

"No problem," Jess said. "Anything for you, Dev."

Chapter Sixteen

THE OPS MESS was busy. Everyone in the room had found a reason to come over and talk, however briefly, with Jess as she sat at one of the back tables.

She was in a fresh uniform. She and Dev had shared a shower, and though they could have eaten in quarters, both had elected not to.

They were still jointly freaked out about what had happened in med. Dev sat with a withdrawn expression, her hands folded on the table in front of her as Jess poked around in her tray's contents, letting the sound in the room go by them.

No messages from HQ. Arp and his cronies had returned to the West. She felt like a whole years worth of the other boots were going to drop on her any minute. But for right now, she had a tray of fishrolls and seaweed in front of her and a tall glass of kack, and it was okay.

"Hey, Jess." Elaine put a tray down next to her. "Jase finally got through to HQ."

"And?" Jess swirled her drink in its cup and sipped from it.

"And nothing. Jase said it was like no one knew what the hell to do now." Elaine chewed her seaweed salad and swallowed. "Probably that's exactly what's up."

"Probably," Jess said. "Hope they put Jason in charge and just leave us the hell alone. There's no win in anything else. Even those idiots have to realize that."

Elaine regarded her in some surprise. "You don't want the bump?"

"No," Jess said, in a definite tone. "I've had enough of being in charge of crap. It sucks." She forked up a bit of seaweed and chewed it. "Way overrated."

Elaine bit the end off her fishroll. "I thought you had all these ambitions," she remarked in a mild tone. "Didn't you want Bricker's job? Or Stephen's?"

Had she? Jess considered that as she chewed. "Aren't we supposed to?" she responded. "Everyone wants to be in charge sometime I guess. Mostly just so you can be in a space where no one tells you what the hell to do."

Elaine pointed a fork at her. "Point."

"But I don't know. I'd rather be in charge of myself. Not

other people," Jess added after a long pause. "Too much bull."

Elaine chuckled dryly. "You going back to the Bay?"

"Not tonight." Jess felt herself relax. "I'm going to go bunk out." She glanced at Dev. "Sound good to you?"

"Yes," Dev answered at once. "I'm really tired. I'm going to fall asleep right here if we don't go elsewhere soon."

"Let's go." Jess abandoned what was left on her tray and stood. "Let tomorrow be whatever it is." She lifted a hand in Elaine's direction as they headed for the mess door, and Elaine returned the wave with a faint smile.

The lighting was dimmed for night shift, and it was a relief to approach the curve in the corridor that held their quarters, and even more so when the doors to Jess's closed after them.

It was quiet and dim in there. The lights came up a little as Dev headed across the floor toward the inner doors that led to her own space. "Hey, Dev?" Jess called out, feeling surprisingly hesitant.

At the door, Dev turned and looked back. "I hope you are not going to suggest surfing," she said, in a wry, plaintive tone. "Please."

Jess smiled. "No." She walked forward and joined Dev at the portal. "You doing okay?"

"I have no idea," Dev said, honestly. "I'm so tired I can't even think." She leaned against the metal. "It's just so much to think about, and I don't want to think about any of it."

Jess understood that at a gut level. "Okay if I share your bunk?"

The thought of cuddling up to Jess in bed almost made Dev cry again. "Yes." She managed to get out. "That would be really excellent."

Jess patted her gently on the cheek. "Go change. I'll be in there in a second." She stepped back to let the door close and then turned and went over to her dressing cabinet, opening it to expose her gear locker. "Yeah, that sure would be excellent, huh?"

It felt like it had been a week since she'd slept. She could hardly even remember being on station or what had led up to it. She remembered the null, a little.

Space, a little. The sun, blazing in and hitting her.

She took off her uniform and hung it up, then got into her sleep clothes, avoiding looking at herself in the mirror so she wouldn't bum herself out. She could feel all the hurts.

Then she closed the cabinet and walked back to the doors,

palming them open without a glance behind her.

DEV CHANGED INTO her tank top and shorts and then went into her sanitary unit, pausing as she caught sight of herself in the reflector there.

A faint shock jerked her upright.

In reflex she lifted her hand to her throat and traced the skin across the front of her neck, then around to the back where she still felt the faintest bits of scab where the wires had been removed.

She heard the inner door open, and a moment later Jess was in the doorway, arms braced against it. "I forgot about this." She touched her throat. "I didn't remember until right now."

Jess entered the unit and gently touched the side of her neck. Then she removed her hand and put her lips there instead, nibbling the skin softly. After a moment she peeked up at Dev. "That make you forget it again?"

Dev had to smile. "Yes. But I think I'm too tired to practice sex right now."

"Me too." Jess held her hand out. "Let's just go to bed." She led the way into the main chamber of Dev's quarters. They both paused when they spotted Doctor Dan's gift sitting on the desk.

"Oh," Dev murmured. "I wanted to ask him about that." She looked pensively at Jess. "Do you think I'll be able to? I didn't really understand what happened before."

Jess sighed. "What happened in med? Me either. That was really weird." They tumbled into the big, soft bed, tangling together as they relaxed on its surface. "Usually when someone is flatline like that, it's kinda permanent. But you know...Doc's a fighter."

Dev nodded. "He used to tell us in class that a bad result was just a reason to find another way to a good result." She snuggled up to Jess and knew a moment of absolute bliss at the full body contact. "But do you think he's going to be okay?"

"Dunno," Jess answered honestly. "Last thing I am is a medic. Jared's a good one though, and the tank's pretty good tech. Saved my ass after that last insert. No one thought I'd make it."

Dev couldn't keep her eyes from closing, she was that tired. "That thing you did was so pretty," she murmured. "I never heard anything like that."

"Mmm." Jess sighed a little. "One class we all hated in

school. Choir. You'd come out of the field covered in turtle guts and grime, wash down, put on a smock, then sit and sing. Used to be for morale, now it's just for processing out."

"But it was beautiful." Dev touched her side and moved closer. "Your sound especially."

"Thanks." Jess smiled into the dimness and let her eyes close. "Someone once told me I could break glass with it. Who knows? Maybe the doc heard it, and it juiced his noggin."

"That's really good." Dev gave her a little hug. "I hope it works out."

Jess pressed her lips against the top of her head. "Me too. I sure as hell don't want to have to do that again."

THE FAINT ILLUMINTION that indicated dawn woke Jess up. She opened her eyes to see the gentle outlines of the walls of Dev's quarters around them.

It was very quiet. She was grateful to have gotten some rest in a place her body instinctively trusted.

But should it have? Jess pondered that. She really had no idea what the hell her status was, what Base Ten's status was, or what the future held.

And yet, she felt secure inside this place, where she hadn't either on station, or in the Bay. Safe as she often felt inside the carrier. What did that mean? Just indoctrination? Jess glanced down at her still sleeping companion. Programming?

Peh. She rolled out of the bed in the other direction and stood up, stretching and feeling renewed energy from her rest. She quietly went to the doors and paused to let them slide open, then stepped through and continued across her own quarters.

She used the sanitary unit and then made herself a cup of hot seaweed tea. She brought it with her to her workspace and sat down behind it.

The display was dark. She reached out and put her hand on the input pad to activate it. It flickered and brightened, bringing up her dashboard and all of its metrics.

There were messages waiting, but they were old and she ignored them. She tapped on the latest ops reports and after looking at the first one, pushed it aside and drank her tea instead.

A moment later, her comms chimed. She looked at the incoming, then accepted. "Hey, Jase."

"Morning." Jason rested his chin on his fist. "HQ came in

overnight. Want to talk to you. I told them it had to wait for you to wake up."

Jess leaned back and sipped at her tea. "Do I want to talk to them?"

"Probably," Jason said. "They came in humble. Asked nicely."

"Ah."

"Surprised the crap out of me." He smiled a little. "We've seen so much jacktardness I figured it would go on, but no."

"Okay," Jess said. "Let me put a suit on, and I'll come down to ops. I assume that's where they are?"

Jason shook his head. "I refused to let them in." His eyes twinkled a little. "I said they weren't being jackasses. Didn't say I wouldn't be one. They're in the conference center, level six. After you're done look me up and we can talk."

"Sounds good." Jess signed off and finished her cup, enjoying the pungent astringency that seemed to clear her head. She got up and went to the closet, trading her sleep clothes for an offduty suit and a pair of indoor boots.

About to head for the door, she paused and went back to the workspace and sat down. After a brief hesitation, she reached out and activated comms. "Med. Jared, you there?"

He answered after a few moments. "You think everyone here wakes up when you do, Drake?" He glared blearily at her. "What?"

Jess smiled. "Sorry. Just wondering how Kurok was. If it's bad news, I'd like to give it to my partner first myself."

He ran his fingers through his hair, his expression mollified. "Hang on." He clicked off and Jess waited patiently, tapping the sides of her thumbs against the desk's plas surface in idle rhythm.

Abruptly Jared was back. "Fucking bag of miracles," he muttered. "He's level two."

Jess exhaled in relief. "Glad to hear it."

"Can I go back to bed now? I was thrashing the tanks all night."

"Yeah, thanks, Jared," Jess said in a sincere tone. "We'll be by later." She disconnected and stood up, detouring to the sanitary unit to wash her face and run a brush through her hair, twisting it back into a tail and regarding her reflection for a long moment. "Peh."

She shook her head and headed for the door and her meeting with HQ.

DEV WOKE UP and looked around in confusion before she recognized her surroundings. She rolled over onto her back, listened for Jess's nearby presence, and found nothing but silence.

It was morning, and she felt better for the long sleep, but all the things that had happened in the last while came flooding back to her, and she hopped right out of bed with a sense of anxiety over it.

Also, that Jess was missing. She went around to the work surface in her unit and peered at it, checking comms for messages. There were three. She sat down to consume them, finding one from Jess from just that morning. It was short, but the first words made Dev almost slide down out of her seat with relief.

        Doc's okay. Having a meet with the big shots.
    See you for breakfast.

"Excellent." Dev sighed. "Just really excellent." She tapped the others, finding one note from Cliff about some new mods, and an older one from general ops about the construction.

The disruption and the test flights seemed a lifetime ago. She sat back in her chair and looked around at her space, finding a curious sense of comfort being here in these quarters she'd come to feel as home.

They weren't, really. No more than the small closet she'd been assigned to on station, that tiny bit of privacy that had marked her advanced status, but always with a sense that it could be taken away at any moment. But here it felt different because...

Well, she wasn't sure why it felt different. Maybe because this was her assignment and she'd proven value to it. Dev turned her chair a little and regarded the little piece of space that had come from station, resting on the surface of the desk.

A view of space from station. It had charmed her, but now that she'd had a chance to see it again for real, she was glad to be downside, rumbles of thunder overhead, with downside's consistent gravity around her.

She spent a moment looking at Doctor Dan's gift, then she got up and went up into her recreation area, sitting down on the couch. She picked up her book, left lying on the surface nearby. Dev regarded it and wondered if she could one day have the chance to maybe write a story.

Could she put down the things she'd seen and done? After a

period of time, perhaps years, where she could use her and Jess's experiences to make a story that she could tell other people?

She put the book down. Probably not. She leaned back in the couch and touched the controls of the screen overhead, calling up the outside views of the Citadel, noting that it was once again raining.

Raining hard, in fact, the sheets of water falling down past the cams, down the front face of the base, down toward the sea that crashed directly against the mountain wall.

It felt good to be back in the base, she decided. Here she had a long list of things she could do, from checking in mods for her carrier, to doing gym, to getting rad. She stood with a smile and decided she'd get busy doing any one of those things.

Maybe she'd stop by and visit Doctor Dan first.

JESS ENTERED THE conference room and regarded the two men seated at the table with a noncommittal look. She took a seat across from them, rested her elbows on the table, and folded her hands together.

They were roughly her age, and as she studied them in silence, she had a sense that maybe one of them was a relative at some degree since he had that Drake angularity and Justin's sharp gray eyes.

He confirmed it a moment later. "Hello, cousin," the man said. "We've never met, but I'm Tomas Santander. A Drake bastard from a couple gens back."

"Hi," Jess responded equably.

"This is Elliot Brack," he introduced his companion, who delivered a brief nod to Jess. "We're the new directors of Juneau and Rainier Base, respectively."

Jess regarded them. "Changes there?" she asked after a pause. "Before or after?"

"After," Brack said. "Shoulda been after Bain. No one wanted to think that went any deeper than him."

"It did," she said.

He shrugged. "So we kind of performed the unclusterfuck goods in the west, and now we're here to figure out what to do next."

"What does that mean?" Jess asked.

They exchanged glances. "Well." Brack shifted a little in his seat. "A bunch of us took a step back from the craziness and decided killing each other was just shitass dumb. We didn't want to do it." He paused, thoughtfully. "I'm a senior at Juneau. My partner comes from Cooper's Rock."

"Ah." Jess nodded. "So you...you refuse orders, shoot people, or what?"

Brack smiled thinly. "Yes. We started getting comms back from the fight here and figured either we put a stop on the deal or we'd all end up losing everything. Pure self interest."

Jess perked up a little. "So what's the scam?" she asked. "They didn't all of a sudden wake up one day and realize they'd been intaking maniacs. They knew."

The two of them exchanged glances, then Tomas shrugged and leaned forward. "What did Arp tell you?"

Jess leaned back in her chair and hiked up one knee, wrapping her arms around it. "That we were a target."

"We?"

She indicated herself then him. "That they realized we were getting to a tipping point."

Tomas nodded. "He was right. On both counts. They did a bio study and started collecting spirals, maybe two, three years back. Turns out ours are more pervasive than most."

"Sticky," Jess said. "They thought they were trying to breed it out of us, and it turns out we were breeding it into them." She gestured outward. "All of them. Never diluted."

Brack nodded. "Surprised to hear a field agent knows it."

Jess smiled. "I hang around with scientists and bios," she said. "It's in me. I know what I am." She pointed her thumb at her own chest.

Tomas nodded again. "So Arp was right. That genetic signature is a crazy nightmare. It's going to drag this part of humanity into chaos."

"It's already chaos. You been to the outlands lately?" Jess asked.

"We have," Brack said. "The engineered DNA is making it worse. It makes people hard and pitiless and very uncaring."

"Amoral sociopaths, in fact," Jess said. "Don't expect me to feel bad about that. I didn't make me."

Tomas smiled. "I was the test subject of the study," he said. "Once they tested me and found all that engineered kickass, I got hit with every crackpot idea on how to stop it there was. Every drug. Every freaking electrical manipulation." He lifted his arm and pulled back his plain black jumpsuit sleeve, exposing a wrist circled with scars.

Jess regarded him. "Better you than me," she finally

commented. "For everyone."

Tomas started laughing. "True." He rolled is sleeve down. "I failed the battery. I was just enough crazy to be a lab rat. I've seen what you can do when people annoy you, Drake."

"So you see the problem," Brack said.

"I do," Jess said. "I just don't see a solution. Because if you intend on castrating my entire homestead, I have news for you." Her eyes twinkled gravely. "There aren't enough of you to even try."

"We wouldn't if we could. It's spread too far. We would end up depopulating the whole eastern half of Atlantia," Brack stated. "It really wasn't about that, and it's a double edged sword. We need those spirals. Keeps us even with them, even if they have more resources and better tech."

Jess regarded him. "And if Interforce keeps taking all the natural leaders, it keeps a lid on Drake's Bay."

Brack nodded. "True. You do get it. Interforce got it. No one really knew what to do about it, no one wanted to lose that edge. And then after the whole thing with Bain..." He cleared his throat. "But now there's a complication."

"Seeds."

Tomas nodded. "Put it over the top. Made everyone west crazy." He flexed his hands. "Literally all they could think of was this resource in the hands of... um..."

"Amoral sociopaths," Jess said. "Not in the pay of Interforce ones, I mean."

"Not just that," Brack said. "It changes the whole landscape of the east." He cleared his throat. "Makes it independent from the west, and that's where all the admin is. You know that. You went to school." He laced his fingers together. "Life in the west is relatively cush. We control trade, all that. This is the wild hinterlands."

"So yeah, the want made them crazy. Knowing someone else would have the edge," Tomas said. "A little of us in that, too, cousin."

"Ironic," Jess said after a minute's reflective silence. "My brother sold his son to the other side so they could breed us. I wonder if they realize what that would mean."

"Tayler?"

"Tayler," Jess confirmed. "I found him up on station. They were figuring out how to make more of them and deliver them for a price."

Both men were silent, blinking in some surprise at her. "Holy shit," Tomas finally said. "So Station Two did turn."

Jess shrugged. "It was a business deal to them. No one really has that — us and them — thing all the way down except maybe us," she said. "Was about cred. Other side was offering a lot of it."

"Money talks," Brack said. "Old, old history."

"Pointless and stupid. There were already copies of Drake DNA up there," Jess said. "Whole thing for nothing. This whole thing for nothing because the Bay's not going to give up that cave," she added. "We're going to figure out what to do with it."

"We're not going to try and stop that, Drake," Tomas said. "They sent the science samples back. They're going to try and replicate it of course."

"Of course," Jess said, dryly. "After all, you got all the brainiacs out there. We just have maniacs here."

Both of them looked a little uncomfortable. "A success at this could help everyone y'know," Brack said. "Not all of us are complete assholes."

Jess and Tomas exchanged looks, a brief flash of shared understanding that excluded the other man.

"Anyway, we need to figure out what to do about this base. They took sides."

Jess smiled. "They took my side."

"They did. We heard the comms. Everyone knows what that cave means. They want a piece of you." Tomas's lips quirked. "Except no one really wants a piece of you, Jesslyn. You're just an obstacle to everyone's plans, including Interforces'."

"Sucks to be me."

"It does," Tomas said. "Just like it sucked to be me, being fried and doped for years and then finding out half the Interforce agents in the west were intakes for cred." He looked as disillusioned as he sounded, a slightly detached, unfocused look to his eyes.

They regarded each other in silence for a long minute. "Call in Jason," Jess finally said. "Let's sort out the options. No one's going to take a hit for taking up my part if I can help it." She paused. "Except maybe me."

DEV FASTENED THE neck of her lined jumpsuit and attached her creds to the pocket before she made her way out her seldom-used quarter doors and into the hallway.

She immediately encountered several mechs who greeted her

with smiles as they went in the opposite direction. The halls were almost empty, though, and she was aware of how few people were around as she made her way through the operations levels and up to med.

Med was also quiet, and she hesitantly poked her head into the room with the tanks, pausing as a technician looked up to see her.

The tech greeted her with a brief smile. "Hello, Dev. That was really something last night, huh?"

"Yes." Dev took this as an invitation to enter and she did, walking over to the last tank where now the screens above it were alive with motion and color. Inside, the liquid seemed to have changed shades, and she could see the tips of Doctor Dan's fingers twitching. "He's moving."

"Yup." The tech came over and joined her. "Usually that starts up when the nervous system realizes it's in a tank. Good sign. Last night I figured..." He paused and shrugged. "He was gone."'

"Yes." Dev put her hands up against the glass. "It was really sad."

"Been a lot of that lately," the tech mused. "But I never heard the field song before. That was something to hear." He peered into the tank with her. "Made my hair stand on end."

"Me too," Dev said. "Do you think it helped Doctor Dan?"

The tech thought about that for a minute. "Never heard of anything like that before," he said. "But hey, who knows, right?"

"Why would it make you feel like that?" Dev asked, curiously. "Prickly?" She rubbed her hand over one arm.

"Don't know." The tech leaned against the console. "Something about the sound, and the echoes in here, maybe. Or the fact it means someone kicked off." He shrugged. "Usually the ops people get konked in the field and just sink to the bottom or end up crab food."

Dev grimaced a little.

Jared entered, stifling a yawn. "Oh. It's you," he said to Dev. "Your agent called this morning to check up on things. Didn't you believe her?"

Dev frowned and took a step back from the tank. "Of course I did. I just wanted to say hello." She indicated the figure floating in the liquid. "Thank you for taking such good care of Doctor Dan."

Jared chuckled."He took care of himself. Wasn't anything I did." He swung a console around and started it up. "I hear we've got nabobs in. Guess we'll find out what the plan is after we told them to get lost." He sat down and tapped a few inputs. "And anyway, I..."

He paused and looked up at Dev.

Dev looked back at him in question.

"Brad, excuse us," Jared said, after a pause. He waited for the tech to leave and the door to close before he leaned on the console and squinted at Dev. "Something happen to you?"

Dev's brow rose. "Quite a lot of things have happened in the last while."

"I'm not getting any synaptic return from you," Jared said. "That closer?"

Dev hesitated then shrugged. "I had my collar removed," she said. "The synaptics are no longer embedded inside my brain. So I suppose that is why you do not see them."

Jared looked surprised. "I didn't think that was possible. But wait. That's right you and Jessie went up to the space station, didn't you?"

"Yes," Dev said. "It was done there."

"Why?" he asked. "I thought the whole point with you is that they could keep giving you new stuff. Without that, aren't you just like one of us?"

"Yes, actually, that's true." Dev smiled. "It will be difficult, but I'm glad I had it removed." She turned as the door opened and waved as Doug and Brent entered, both in offduty suits. "Hello."

"Hey, Rocket." Doug glanced at Jared. "They said you were in here. Want to come see my new bus?"

Brent grinned a bit ghoulishly. "Had lots to choose from."

"Sure." Dev was glad to get away from the questioning. "And then I have to go find Jess and have a meal." She backed away and joined them at the door. "Goodbye. Thank you."

Jared watched her in silence as they left, a speculative expression crossing his face.

"DID WE WIN or lose in there?" Jason asked as he followed Jess out of the conference center and down the hall. "Holy crap."

"Who the fuck knows. At least you got the bars." Jess's stomach growled. "Let's find the wrenchers and get some chow."

"Yeah, but after what you said do I want them?" Jason sighed. "Oh hell, I do. I like what it felt like taking this place over. I won't lie."

Jess smiled, unseen. "You did a damn good job. Of course I wouldn't be saying that if you went the other way."

Jason made a face. "And gotten my ass kicked."

"Maybe not. I think we were about out of circus tricks," Jess admitted. "Could have gone either way there. I think I just got lucky."

"You're still senior," Jason said, after a little silence. "Or are you? What the fuck are you gonna do about the Bay? All that seed crap? That needs a politico. That's some big time admin jackassery."

"Don't want that," Jess said. "Had my share of being the Drake. That one damn council meeting did it for me. I don't have the patience for it, and everyone knows that. I won't talk. I'll just shoot people who annoy me."

"True," Jason said. "But if not you then who? Needs someone in charge."

"Doesn't need me, so we'll have to figure something out." Jess fit a comms into her ear and tapped it. "Dev. You there?" The line opened and she heard a lot of background noise, and she loosened the comm unit with a grimace. "Oof."

"We're in the landing bay," Dev said. "Doug is examining his new vehicle. Brent is here as well."

Normal. Sounds of mechs. Sounds of rain on the roof, now firmly sealed. The hiss of offgassing.

Home. "C'mon in for chow," Jess said then shut the line down. "Wrenchers."

Jason smiled. "Guess I have to break the news to Brent," he said. "See who I can get him assigned to. He's a good tech."

"Not as good as mine." Jess led the way through the corridors toward the mess.

"No." He made a face. "That why you didn't want any part of a promotion, Jess? Everyone in the Citadel knows you're stuck on her."

Jess stopped and turned, he stopped behind her, his hands coming up automatically palms out, chest level. But she just smiled at him. "Maybe," she admitted. "She matters to me."

Jason lowered his hands.

"She's a mech. She's a flyer," Jess said. "I don't want her going out with someone else, and I don't want her to have to hang out at the Bay fixing boat motors if I chuck this joint and take her with me."

His face tensed and shifted. "Interforce owns her contract," he said. "Is it an option for her to just walk out with you?"

Jess merely smiled.

Jason's eyes widened a little, and he drew in a breath and let it out. "Wow." He glanced around. "Maybe we should finish this over a drink?"

"Or over some mushroom cakes." Jess indicated the hallway and started along it. "I'm buying. Did I thank you for coming to save our asses yet?"

He caught up to her, and they crossed the main hall where a trickle of jumpsuited figures were moving and entered the mess.

DEV PAUSED IN the entry to the mess and looked around, spotting Jess at a back table. She waved and went to the line and grabbed a tray. There was an AyeBee behind the counter, and she smiled in greeting. "Hello, AyeBee."

He smiled back. "Hello, NM-Dev-1." He offered her a glass of kack. "I am glad you are back. We have heard many stories about your good work."

"Thank you." Dev selected from the dispenser and waited for it to produce a plate. "It was difficult."

"Yes," the AyeBee said. "But good. Things are optimal now. Things are changing." He glanced past her, and in reflex Dev turned her head to look behind her to find two mechs in jumpsuits. She had to look twice to realize one was bio alt.

Bio alt, and though a little hesitant and shy, sitting at a small table with his workmate, having breakfast here in the operations mess just like she'd be doing in a moment with Jess. He looked up and their eyes met, and Dev smiled at him.

After a brief, startled moment he smiled back and lifted one hand with its thumb upraised.

Interesting. "Excellent." Dev moved down the line with Doug and Brent behind her, picking up several packets of seaweed crackers before she took her meal back to the table Jess was sitting at with April and Jason. "Hello."

Jess bumped her with her shoulder. "Gull's eggs. Must be my birthday." She indicated the trays. "Yum."

Dev regarded the contents of hers and forked up some of the egg. It tasted completely different than the eggs she had consumed on station, but she liked them. "These are good," she said. "And actually, it is my natal date in fact. So it's nice but probably not related."

"What?" Jess half turned and stared at her. "It's your birthday?"

Dev paused chewing and nodded.

"How come you didn't tell me?" Jess demanded. "Dev!"

Dev swallowed and took a sip of the fizzy drink. "Why would I tell you?" she asked in some confusion. "It's in the records. Did you need to know that information? I am sorry."

Doug chuckled. "I sense a frustrated present opportunity." He winked at Dev. "Nice suit."

Dev grinned and went back to her tray.

"Just for that, I see surfing in your future," Jess mock growled.

Brent had taken a seat next to Jason. They were conversing in low tones, heads together. Dev caught the change of expression on Brent's face, going from casual to startled and then dismayed. She wondered what was going on.

A sideways glance showed Jess to be relaxed and at her ease, though, so she went back to consuming her meal and made a mental note to ask Brent later what was so disturbing.

"So how's the new bus?" April asked Doug. "Are the seats actually attached to the deck, or are we going to go flying the first time you put the brakes on?"

Brent got up, put his tray in the dispenser, then walked out in silence.

Jason exchanged looks with Jess and shrugged a little. "Backhanded compliment," he said, going back to his tray. "I guess."

April glanced from one of them to the other then at Doug in question. Doug shrugged his shoulders and shook his head. He looked over at Dev, who likewise produced a bewildered look.

Jess belatedly realized all this silent WTF'edness in her presence. "Jason's been promoted to Station Director," she said. "Means he's got to hook Brent up with someone else as a tech."

"Oh," Both April and Doug said at the same time with the same inflection. "Hey, congrats." April added to Jason. "Glad they went local and didn't bring in yet another jacktard from the other coast."

Jason eyed her mildly. "I'm a Rainier Islander," he said.

"Not recently," she responded.

"True," he acknowledged. "They couldn't get Jessie to take it, so I did." He drained his glass and stood up. "So I guess I should go start doing something useful." He glanced at the outer door. "Fix Brent up." He carried his tray up to the line and deposited it then headed out.

"That true, you turned 'em down?" April asked Jess in a

straightforward kind of way.

"Uh huh. Had no desire to sit in a chair dealing with all this political bullshit." Jess glanced over at the attentively listening Dev. "Plus I'm not an idiot. Only place I'm going to add unlimited glory to my blood spattered name is with Dev." She smiled at the hiked eyebrows. "Why would I stay here in the Citadel when I can terrorize the entire other half of the planet just with her carrier call sign?"

Dev's eyes widened perceptibly.

"Nice." April nodded approvingly. "Also, truth."

"Truth." Doug agreed.

"Yeah. Now I just have to tell the Bay and not have them shoot me," Jess said. "Or maybe they'll be relieved if I put someone else in charge there. Deals won't get busted by me randomly gutting people."

Doug and April regarded her. "Truth," Doug said again. "But I think they kinda like you like that. It's that whole bloodthirsty vibe there." He picked up his tray. "See you back in the mod trench, Rocket?"

"Yes." Dev watched the two leave then she rested her elbows on the table and regarded Jess. "So everything is correct here?" She selected her words carefully. "We are going to stay at this facility?"

Jess sat back in her chair. "That okay with you?"

"Of course. As long as I am with you, it doesn't really matter to me what we are doing. But I am glad I will get a chance to use my programming and also that you think my results were excellent."

Jess bumped her shoulder again. "You don't mind me being a limpet on your fame?"

"I don't really think that is accurate."

"Hah."

JESS WALKED THROUGH the night darkened halls on her way through ops to Med. She felt rested, finally, and healed. All the bruises faded to normal skin tone and a regular Citadel schedule giving her a chance to re-sort out her plans for the future.

She glanced at the bio alt minder at the Med central desk and waved.

"Hello, Agent Drake," the bio greeted her. "Are you going to visit Doctor Dan?"

Jess grinned. "How'd you guess?"

The bio alt just grinned back.

Jess went past the desk and back into the convalescent area, bypassing the tank room that was now, thankfully, empty. She paused at the door to one of the doors, pushed it open, and poked her head inside.

The med tech on duty spotted her. "Hello, Drake."

Jess entered. "How's he doing?"

The tech nodded. "He's close to coming out of it. He's responding to physical touch, and his latest scan shows a lot of activity." He leaned on the console. "How about you sing to him again and maybe he can just get up and leave."

Jess rolled her eyes and walked past three or four half shielded areas with other recovering figures in them. Kurok was in the one at the rear. The largest one with the most equipment, with a big screen on the wall showing a view of the sea.

He was lying on his back, on the body cradling couch that periodically shifted position. His eyes were closed, and he had a light cover over him, his chest moving steadily under it.

Jess approached the mechanism, eyeing it warily as she edged closer. It blooped and pinged at her, and she paused to regard it, having no real understanding of what it meant.

But after a moment, she turned her attention to the figure on the couch. After a moment, as if knowing and understanding that, he opened his eyes and looked back at her.

IT WAS LIKE waking up completely covered in glue. A singularly unpleasant sensation. But he recognized it. Had known the tank enough times to know what that grudging release into consciousness felt like.

Consider the alternative, Justin had always advised him.

So there was that. He could faintly hear the sounds of the room around him, the monitors and thumping of the pumps, and far off, the rumble of the tunnels and their power generation. It fit an old pattern he knew, and so he knew where he was, though not how he'd gotten there.

Last memory? A fuzzy blare of yelling and the afterimage of a blaster in his eyes. Sets around him. And ah. The booming roar of the Bay battle yell.

Bay ops. Leaping over the console like an idiot and...

Protecting the innocent bystanders, who were also sets, and his...

His children.

Chaos. Seeing a BeeAye fearlessly step in front of a shot meant for one of the Bay kids, taking a stand with equal fearlessness and seeing that shot returned by an Interforce long rifle.

Then pain.

Then nothing.

Then this.

He heard his own breathing and felt the just perceptible movement of blood inside his body, that concussive double thump against his inner ear drum.

Far off, he thought he heard the door open, and then the sound of someone approaching. There was no rustle of a med smock, or the mechanical clank of equipment, just a presence coming near, and then the faintest motion as hands were put on the edge of his med couch, a kinetic vibration transferring residual energy.

He felt no threat. But he wanted to know more. Find out what happened. So he opened his eyes and found steadfast blue ones looking back at him with extraordinary clarity.

With that Drake understanding that went past knowledge. That difference he'd seen and codified in Justin as a counterpoint to what he'd always described as his little family insanity problem.

Except it wasn't. Not really. He blinked a few times and tried to clear his throat.

"Hey," Jess said. "Glad you're back. I got an idea I want to run by ya."

"Uh oh." He managed a croaking whisper.

DEV SHOULDERED HER carry bag and left the gym. She felt pleasantly tired from her recently completed exercise. The halls of the Citadel were quiet, and along one wall, a bio alt was polishing the newly finished sections from the last construction.

Things had settled. Sort of. Everyone still seemed a bit wary, but daily operations had moved back into a more normal schedule and there was a general sense of relief in evidence. Dev was glad.

She detoured to the engineering lab and ducked into one of the mod pods. She settled behind the console with a grunt of satisfaction.

"That you, Rocket?"

She looked up from the pad. "Yes, it's me," she responded. "I wanted to see if comp had finished some metrics I asked for."

Cliff came around the pod partition and sat down on the second stool inside. "Whatcha making now?"

Dev cleared her throat a little diffidently. "I was thinking about how to refine the altitude and attitude jets. To increase the precision. When I had to remove my vehicle from Drake's Bay cavern, it was difficult."

Cliff folded his arms over his chest. "What was the clearance?"

"There wasn't any. That's why it was so difficult."

The tech chief started laughing.

Dev smiled sheepishly. "I did not really have time to evaluate the ingress. And I had to park in a very narrow space." She indicated the panel. "So I submitted a mod request for the control surface."

Cliff tilted his head a little. "Under your own name this time?" he asked.

"Yes," she said after a pause. "I think it will be all right."

The door opened again, and they looked up as Brent appeared. "Hey, Brent." Cliff waved, casually. "Got your console set up there, row B."

"Thanks." Brent hesitated, then waved at Dev. "Hey."

Dev waved back. "Hello."

Brent went into the second row of the pods and disappeared from sight, though they could hear him rummaging around.

"Did you hear all the craziness, Dev?" Cliff said. "They lost so many people they raised up the senior ranking to three." He eyed her meaningfully. "That's a lot of positions for the taking."

Dev had heard. It seemed sad that this opportunity was extended to compensate for the violence they'd all been through. "Jess told me," she answered simply. "She thinks I should do the test for it."

Brent came back around the partition. "Why the hell they have to test you for it?" he asked. "You write the damn nav programming. They got mech sups can't do that."

"You can't do it," Cliff said, stiffening a little.

"No I can't, but I ain't no mech sup," Brent said. "I aint never going to be senior either." He glowered at them. "Don't even know if they'll pair me up with anyone." He turned and went back to the other pod, slamming down in his chair.

Dev and Cliff exchanged looks.

"He has a point," Cliff said softly. "We lost a lot

more agents than techs."

Dev considered that in silence. Jess had once told her that was the way of it because the agents did the fighting and stepped into the line of fire. She remembered all those black clad bodies in the Bay, being dragged out to the processor station, like so many sacks of rocks. "Yes."

"Takes a long while to restock," Cliff said. "And the newbies come in pairs, you know?"

Like April and Doug had. "Maybe they could get some new agents right from Drake's Bay," she suggested. "I think they like fighting."

Cliff looked around somewhat wildly then put his finger to his lips. "Don't even suggest that!"

"Why not?" Dev cocked her head in question. "I saw them on station. They are really ferocious."

Her comms chirped, and she touched it. "Dev."

"Hey." Jess's voice had that faint tone that indicated something pleasant was in store. "C'mon to med and say hi to the doc. He's tired of my jokes."

"Excellent." Dev stood up and palmed the console, sending the output to her quarters for later review. "I have to go, Cliff. Maybe we can talk about this later?"

Cliff looked wryly at her. "Let's not talk about this later. One Drake around is enough, you know what I mean?"

Dev considered that. "No, actually, I don't." She smiled and moved past him, heading for the door.

DEV SAT CROSS-LEGGED in front of her workstation, tapping on the input pad. She was in her sleep clothes, an expression of contented happiness on her face.

Her screen was full of messages, and she was busy returning them. Some were from other techs, responding to the new mod she'd proposed. Some were from the dorms below, the relatively newly created message accounts for her fellow bio alts.

So excellent to have gotten to talk to Doctor Dan. He was still mostly down, but he'd smiled at her and said he was glad to see her and that things would end up all right.

So excellent. She typed in the message and sent it. She was so relieved. She would be able to tell all the sets at Drake's Bay as well since Jess told her they would visit there tomorrow to finish up some things.

She heard Jess enter her quarters and felt a brief buzz of

anticipation as she detected the sound of footsteps, and then the door between them opened to admit Jess's tall form. "Hello."

"Hey." Jess came over and dropped into the chair next to her workstation. "Know what I heard in the mess?"

Dev focused her attention on Jess. "You were in the mess?"

"I was." Jess removed a packet from her thigh pocket and put it on the table. "They had these. New ration bars."

Dev picked it up and sniffed it. "That smells excellent." She unwrapped it. "Would you like a portion?"

Jess chuckled. "Had two. You want to hear what I heard?" She looked pointedly at Dev, who was now munching on the bar. Dev watched her with that noncommittal look that meant she probably already knew. "Wrencher queen?"

Dev swallowed then washed her mouthful down with a sip of tea. "Was it about the class?" Dev asked. "I just got confirmation a moment ago. So many of the instructors were damaged I guess."

"So many instructors can't tell their asses from a sea turtle, I guess," Jess said. "They'd rather get taught by Rocket Racoon."

"I am sure it's only for the moment."

Jess reached over and ran her fingers through Dev's hair. "Don't be so modest, my friend. Don't diss yourself. Wasn't easy for them to ask you."

Dev put her cheek down on Jess's leg. "I know that. I just want to be...I just want to fit in."

"Aw." Jess gave her neck a little scratch. "Yeah. But sometimes you can't. Like I can't, y'know? I figured that out."

Dev enjoyed the contact. She closed her eyes and listened to the words, understanding them at some deep, base level. "They know about my collar," she said after a pause. "Med found out."

"And Med told everyone," Jess said. "But if they hadn't, the other techs would have. They know." She leaned over and nibbled Dev's ear. "They think that's good. That they'll be able to catch up to you now, but you know what? That's not true."

Dev, at that moment, really didn't care if it was true or not. Tingles were working their way down from the side of her head into her middle. It was so excellent to be able to relax and enjoy it. She gently stroked the inside of Jess's thigh in response and heard a faint, low purring sound right in her ear.

It was awesome. She felt that insistent burning in her guts increase, and she pressed closer, savoring the throaty chuckle Jess produced. "Can we discuss the class later?"

"C'mon." Jess got up and extended her hand out.

Of Sea and Stars

"Let's go scare the seals."

Dev's eyes narrowed a little, and a furrow appeared between her brows.

"Don't think about it."

Dev took hold of her hand, and they walked across the floor to the big bed in her quarters and tumbled into it. She started to undo the catches on Jess's duty suit.

There were a lot of them. It was very difficult to work them out because Jess began to nibble her way down Dev's neck, making her brain go somewhere else. It felt amazing, and they'd had so little opportunity to practice sex in a while.

It was in the carrier the last time, and though she really liked her vehicle, it was much more optimal to do this in bed.

Jess softly moved her shoulders in a sinuous wave as Dev managed to get the suit's fastenings undone. She slid Dev's tank top off, and then their bodies brushed lightly against each other, skin to skin.

A surge of blood and sensation rushed to her skin, negating the typical chill in her quarters. The heat felt wonderful. She put her practice to work. Her lips meeting Jess's in a very optimal way.

Jess's hands slid down Dev's body in a hesitant dance, removing her sleep shorts as she kicked off her own suit. She then settled on her side to continue her sensual exploration.

Gentle yes, but experienced. She seemed to always know just where to kiss and touch and tease, and Dev felt that breathless tension start to grow inside her, a craving that always surprised her.

They both smelled a bit like the sea foam soap from the shower and a bit from the stone dust of the Citadel. Dev inhaled deeply of it as she traced a line around Jess's breast and felt the faint uneven line of a scar. Jess had so many of the marks. Dev never found them anything but interesting, and she'd learned to find her way along Jess's very long body almost using them as a guide. She traded touch for kiss, for nip, for stroking while they curled around each other across the center of the bed.

Jess moved upward and gently nibbled her pulse point, then slowly kissed her way around Dev's neck, the sudden prickling of memory almost making her hiccup as she forgot, and then remembered why that touch was so sensual to her of all people.

She took a deep breath and felt no constriction. And then Jess started working her way down her body and she lost the ability to think about anything at all, letting the craving take her over and make her breathe hard as Jess brought that desire to the breaking point and she started to convulse.

It was wave after wave of pleasure and then a gentling of the touch and a soft stroking that continued the pleasure without overwhelming.

It was the best feeling in the world, and Dev took a moment to savor it before she shook the sweat out of her eyes and went to return the favor.

All thoughts of sleep were gone, all the long trials of the day forgotten. All she was focused on right now was this sharing of pleasure, where all her knowledge had come not from programming but from Jess's playful, gentle lessons.

And so she gladly used what she'd learned, finding and teasing those places on Jess that made her tense and surrender and release herself to the pleasure with gasping abandon.

She ended up in a hug, and she exhaled in satisfaction, taking a moment to rest before they'd start the practice all over again.

Excellent.

"CENTOPS, THIS IS BR270006, requesting flight status and permission to depart." Dev released comms and adjusted her power levels, bouncing around a little in her seat as she watched the reflection of Jess relaxing in hers.

"Centops to BR270006, flight status is go, clearance given. Good flight."

Dev lifted off the pad. "Stand by for departure," she said to her passenger, who opened one eye and regarded her. "I will try to avoid going upside down."

"Thanks." Jess closed her eye and folded her hands over her stomach, "I'll just be taking a nap back here since I didn't get any sleep last night."

Dev chuckled a little.

"Not that I'm complaining," Jess added. "Been a long time since I've had that much fun."

Dev maneuvered the carrier out of the cavern and into dark gray cloudy, but at the moment rainless, weather. She observed the wind metrics and set her course, taking the vehicle up and over the escarpment that held the Citadel and along the coast heading for Drake's Bay.

Familiar route, now. She ran scans along the ground and saw little organic return, save some clusters of seagulls and what she thought might be a whale offshore. "We didn't bring our packs," she said.

"We're not staying."

"I see." Dev glanced in the reflector and saw Jess just sitting in her station, arms folded over her chest. "You seem discomfited."

Jess looked up and their eyes met. "Time to pay the bill, Dev." She got up and came forward to the pilot's station, pulled down the jumpseat, and dropped onto it. "Bay wants to know what my intent is." She rested her head against the console. "So I need to go tell them I'm not going to be the Drake for them. Not now at any rate."

"They will not be pleased," Dev said.

"I don't know," Jess mused. "Something Jake said was right. Hard for the rest of the coast to make deals with me in there. They don't have much leverage. I remember the yelling matches when my dad was doing it."

Dev considered that. "I believe," she cleared her throat, "they do not have much leverage now in any case. Your birthplace has something all of them want." She adjusted an engine trim. "Can they continue the seed project? It's quite technical."

"Good question."

"It would have been excellent work to assist with that if we had remained there," Dev said. "I have both the basic and the secondary programming for it." She turned the carrier a little to follow the coastline, already spotting the promontory that was the outer edge of the half circle of the Bay on the far horizon. "Some of the other sets who came there do also."

"Drake's Bay doesn't care for bios," Jess said, but in a musing tone. "Devvie. You're so damn smart." She watched Dev's profile tense into a faint grin. "They just didn't have the time or energy to kick up when we were in the middle of a firefight."

Dev counted down the moments as they sat there together in quiet peace, waiting until she saw the initial stages of the long range scan from the Bay reach them. "Drake's Bay operations. This is Interforce flight BR270006, inbound."

A long pause, then the comms channel opened. "BR270006, welcome. You're expected," a male voice answered. "Top dock, pad one."

Jess sighed. "All that's left."

"Copy that, Drake's Bay," Dev said then closed comms. "Maybe it will be okay, Jess."

"Maybe a whale will fly up out of the ocean and sing."

HE WAS MANAGING to stay more aware. There was a positive and negative to that. The positive being his brain was healing and negative in that there wasn't anything to do or look at most of the time when his eyes were open.

Roughly squared rock walls. The robust security of being inside the mountain. Inside the Citadel, a place he'd stayed long enough at a vulnerable enough time in his life for it to become home in a way station never was.

Weird little crick in the psyche. He'd collected just enough moments of happiness here for it to have set solid. He realized it when he'd been here last, had known he'd brought it back up to station with him, setting that soft far off sound of fake thunder around him and the gentle patter of rain.

Ah well. He regarded the slightly uneven ceiling. Now it was his reality again. He tried not to think too much about what was going to happen next. That just got him into a whole circular thought pattern about what he'd left behind up on station, and what was the point?

Really. What was the point? Justin always said forget the past, don't worry about the future, just focus on now, and at this very moment he understood.

Finally.

The bed moved a little under him, and he shifted with it, grimacing at the stiffness and the phantom pains that were healing nerves. He could only imagine what horrific state he'd been in before he'd been put in the tank, and he flexed his hands, too uncomfortable to go back to sleep.

He couldn't focus enough to read a screen, and he wasn't really sure what he would look at if he could. Sometimes being unconscious had its points.

Sometime after noon, as he was counting the striations in the ceiling for the nth time, the outer door opened and Jared came in.

"Hello," he greeted the senior medic, ready to be mildly entertained. "Been a bother for you I'm sure."

"Highlight of the shift." Jared treated him with respect, as a peer really, since he understood his background. "How's the head?"

"Still attached," Kurok replied. "Got anything to play on the screen? Underwater cam from the turbines? View of the repair pads?"

Jared smiled. "I'll see what I can rummage up for later." He checked one of the input pads. "You cook your own spirals, Doc? You've got healing metrics I've never seen before."

"Yes, well, you'd have to dig into my Interforce records for that, I'm afraid. They shot us up with all kinds of things in field school back in the day."

"I'll have to do some research on that," Jared said. "But right now, before it gets too long after, I'd like to ask you some questions about something that happened here. Drake tell you?"

One of Kurok's blond eyebrows hiked up a bit. "Tell me what?"

Jared considered. "Easier to show you." He pulled a screen around so Kurok could see it. "I wouldn't usually do this, but I doubt you're shockable."

Kurok chuckled just a little. "My scans?" He hazarded a guess.

"I'll show you that too since you probably know a lot more about what that looks like than I do," Jared said. "But no, this first. So basically, you were flatline."

"Ah."

"So everyone was coming in to say so long."

"Oh." Kurok's tone changed. "That bad? What the hell am I doing here then?"

"That's what I want to know." Jared triggered the vid. "See what you think."

Kurok watched the screen come live in front of him and saw a wide angle view of the tank room, with one occupied and the room filling up with a mix of bios and Interforce, horrified faces of sets, and the stolid lack of expression of the agents and techs.

Jess, stood square in the middle, her arms around a visibly upset Dev, as though it were the most natural thing in the world and apparently not caring if it wasn't.

Dismay. The gasps and moans from the sets when they realized what was going on.

Dev went to the tank and called the sets over.

He could see Jared's back, waiting near the life support gear, ready to remove it.

The room was full.

A sudden memory and then Kurok knew what was coming. A brief, vivid flash of field school surfaced, standing next to Justin at the end of a long day, wanting nothing more than to be released to mess and bunk.

A phantom pressure on his shoulder as Justin rested his forearm on it. In his mind's eye he could even see the smudge of dried blood on the side of the hand just in his peripheral vision.

Jess spoke. Standing as family to him in the old tradition and giving him what eulogy she could on short notice, as it always was. "He was kin of my kin."

Kurok's fingertips twitched as he felt a mixture of embarrassment and horror, listening to the accolades he should never have heard, awed at the honesty of them, doubting their truth until the last, Dev's quiet, "thank you for making me."

That, there was no doubting.

"Give my regards to Dad."

Then Jess stood up a little straighter, drew in a deep breath, and started to sing. For a moment he forgot what the song was for in the beauty of her voice.

He held his breath, almost. Then he had to inhale as the rest of the ops group joined in, a mixture of voices in harmony that made his skin prickle and his eardrums itch, and in pure reflex his lips moved along with them as he felt the echo of that memory again and imagined he heard the ghost of Justy's voice alongside, deeper and male but that same tonal quality.

Then it faded and he didn't want it to.

Jared was pointing and talking, and he had no real choice but to listen.

"So right there? See that? You went from flatline to this. What I want to know, Kurok, is how. Why? How did that happen? You know better than I do what the odds were of that."

Kurok still heard that song in silent echoes. "Yes," he finally said, "I know the odds." He studied the readouts. "Is this where I'm supposed to tell you about some out of body experience, floating around touching clouds or something like that?"

"I don't know. Is it?" Jared asked simply. "You were dead. Then you weren't."

Kurok shook his head. "I don't know what happened," he answered honestly. "The last thing I remember was doing some damn fool thing and falling in front of a blaster. Then I woke up here yesterday. Jess didn't mention anything about that."

"It's weird," Jared said.

"It's weird," Kurok agreed. "But I don't know." He studied the now dark screen. "Mind leaving that here though?"

"No, go ahead." Jared pushed it a little closer. "They were joking, you know? With Drake. About that singing doing something."

"Not possible," Kurok said. "No auditory response possible in that state. But I have to admit it's quite stirring. I remember learning to sing that in school." He paused. "And once in assembly, but there aren't many voices like hers."

Jared grinned. "Surprised me," he admitted. "You don't expect that from one of them."

Echo of the song again. "She inherited it," Kurok said. "When he was particularly frustrated, her father used to go down into the turbine cavern and about bring the roof down singing."

"Justin Drake?" Jared asked, his eyebrows hiking up to his hairline. "Really?"

"Really."

Chapter Seventeen

JESS SHRUGGED INTO her jacket and ran her fingers through her hair as they exited the carrier into the top flight deck at Drake's Bay. All the flyers left to the stakehold were there in various states of repair, and several others she reckoned were from their neighbors.

One, conspicuously, from Quebec City, its pilot seated on a skid, looking out over the sea from the shelter of a wing.

The entry to the cavern was open and there were some stone workers there, fixing the battered metal that once closed it, barely sparing them a glance as they walked by. Once inside they were hit with a barrage of sound from repair stations.

"Jess." Dev touched her elbow. "Look."

Across the cavern there were three figures intent on one of the power stacks, two tall Bay homesteaders, and one shorter with sandy blond hair in overalls like theirs. "That one of your buddies?" Jess asked in an undertone.

"Yes, that's a BeeAye," Dev whispered back as they passed, watching the three working together intently.

"Huh." Jess grunted softly. "Interesting."

They walked to the top level of the big central staircase and started down the circular stairway amidst echoes of hammers and the smell of plasma cutters.

At the bottom, Jess saw a group of figures waiting for them. A mix of Bay and outlanders, long rifles cradled in arms. "That looks friendly."

"Does it?" Dev kept pace with her as they continued down.

"No."

"Oh."

Jess had deliberately left her weapons behind, but aside from that she was dressed as reg Interforce in her blacks with their green piping. Dev was in her tech greens, only her sharkskin jacket non reg.

But that was okay because Rocket had earned that difference, Jess reckoned, and it fit her much better than the reg parka did.

They reached the bottom of the stairs and walked across the floor they'd both last seen covered in bodies toward the waiting group. Jess recognized both Dee Cooper and Jean Argnaut from Quebec City, mixed in with what was left of the leadership of her homestead.

She slowed and stopped as she reached them. "Morning."

"Morning, Jess," Brion greeted her. "Council chamber."

"Let's go." Jess made a motion with her hand.

"Just you." Brion said.

"Fuck off," Jess responded without hesitation. "Dev stays."

They regarded each other in silence. No one moved. "You really want her to witness this?" Brion finally asked. "Could get ugly."

Dev cleared her throat. "I am a biological alternative who was born from an egg in space. After what I have seen this past half year, I do not think there is anything you could have me witness that would overly disturb me." She paused. "Unless you intend to do incorrect things to Jess, in which case I will react as my programming allows and it could get discomfiting for everyone."

"Besides, for all you know I made her my heir," Jess said mildly amused. "And you'll have to deal with her owning Drake's Bay if you splat me." She watched the eyeballs widening. "She's Interforce ops. Has a citizen cred."

There were now large clouds of "oh shit" floating over the group. Brion stepped back and swept his arm out in the direction of the family quarters. "Shall we?"

They walked down the hallway past the room Jess had been born in and turned left down the slope past the kitchen and the family living space, all empty. At the bottom of the passage was a large door. Brion pushed it open and then walked in.

Inside was the large space that the Bay councils had been held in forever. A large unevenly shaped table was in the middle, surrounded by chairs, some of which had been fixed, refixed, and patched a dozen times. A reproduction of the homestead's crest was nailed on the wall, and all around the walls were plas cabinets full of records.

Jess went to the head of the table and sat down in the largest seat. Dev settled next to her, and the rest spread out around the table. The four big Bay guards went to the corners, cradling their weapons, and Jess just smiled at them.

"Okay. Let's get this straight," Jean spoke up.

"Shut up," Jess cut him off. "Let me get what I have to say said, then you all can talk." She stood up and put her hands on the table. "First thing's first. There's five hundred thou cred transferring into Bay accounts from Interforce. Should be in tonight."

Dead silence. "W..what?" Brion finally said.

"Compensation," Jess said, "for damages and unlawful attack on a homestead in contraindication of official orders."

More silence.

"So whatever scam you all did with Quebec or with Dee is null," Jess went on. "And it's null anyway because I didn't sign off on it." She slowly scanned the table. "Because you can't make the inconvenient fact that I am the Drake, go away." She paused. "Where's Jake?"

"We killed him," Mike said from down the table. "Processed him out the other day."

Jess nodded. "I figured. You waste Tayler, too?"

"No," Brion responded. "He's a minor. You can't proxy to him."

Jess sat down. "I wouldn't anyway. He's going to Interforce." She sat and folded her hands on the table.

"So who runs the place, Jess?" Brion asked. "We killed off everyone we thought you could put in your place. Fish or cut bait. You can't be the Drake and be Interforce, and we've decided which way we want that to go."

Jess studied all of them. "You want to force me to stay here?" she asked after a long pause. "Is that what you're saying?" Her voice lifted in disbelief.

They nodded. "Good contracts at hand, Jess," Brion said. "That's why Jean and Dee are here. Not because we did a scam with them. They want to partner."

"But we want someone we can trust," Dee said. "And that's not some half assed cousin of yours who can't spell his name."

Jean nodded. "I have seen the product. Without question, you will get top dollar and cheaper for us since we don't have to buy from station. Win win."

Jess leaned back in her seat, hiked up one knee, and clasped her hands over it. "Interesting. I thought you were just going to try and kill me." She sounded bemused. "Instead, you killed everyone else you thought I could get to stand in for me. Make me come back here. Flattering." She paused. "I think."

"Interesting," Dev remarked next to her.

Mike nodded. "Jake was the only one blood close enough to do a handover to. Screw that." He shrugged. "We want you, Drake. Real Drake. Drake both sides who took up with us against Interforce. Surprised they didn't just kill ya. That's how they covered it? Said it was non reg?"

"Something like," Jess said. "You people seem to forget that I was the one who brought Interforce in here and gave them the keys."

Brion shook his head. "No. You just done what we wanted to. Jimmy was dealing with the other side. We knew he was."

"We knew," one of the collections supervisors agreed. "Saw them come in twice. Saw him go dark. We knew." He shifted a little in his seat. "No one had the guts to report it."

Ben folded his hands on the table. "Truth. But then you came in for council and we didn't have to."

Jess studied all of them. "I felt it," she said after an uncomfortable moment.

Brion half smiled. "We know you did. You went to the mess. You were us, not them. Jimmy was so scared he sent his family out to Quebec, and then when you knew the scam he did with the scavengers you proved it. You were more Drake in that ten seconds than he'd been his whole life."

"Hmm." Jess grunted.

"Yeah," Mike spoke up again. "Just one thing we need to square with you, Drake." He stared hard at her. "You let them go, I saw it. That needs explaining." He leaned forward on the table. "'Cause that, we're thinking, we might need to kill you for."

Silence.

"Suboptimal," Dev finally said. "And not so interesting."

NOW IT WAS just Drake's Bay in the council. Two remaining elders had joined them. They looked apprehensive and confused. Six more scarred and banged up fighters, with the biggest guns they could carry, stared at Jess to let her know they meant business.

Jess ignored them. She rested her hands on the table, her brow furrowed, as she listened to the uncomfortable conversation around her.

Dev leaned closer to her and lowered her voice almost to inaudible. "Jess. Is there something I can do? Do you need records or something from the carrier? I have my scanner with me."

"No," Jess said, absently. "I'm not worried about this." She jerked her head a little at the council.

"You aren't?" Dev murmured.

"Nah. Wasn't expecting their other pitch."

Dev thought about that. "That they want you here?" Jess nodded. "I actually understand that part."

Jess's dark eyebrows lifted.

"Of course," Dev said placidly. "I always want you, so of course I understand that."

Jess covered her eyes and stifled a laugh.

"Was that amusing?"

Brion re-entered the chamber and put a pad down on the table. "Okay. I've got the cam output so let's just review it, and then Jess can explain herself."

"Or not." Jess rested her chin on her fist as they all stared at her. "Kids, you can have me be Drake or not have me be Drake. There ain't no middle ground. I'm not a homicidal maniac only when it's convenient."

The guards all shifted.

Jess looked at them. "Let's be clear," she said. "I'm going to kill all of you before you kill me, so put those stupid things down before you drop one and it blows your foot off."

Everyone regarded her in reflective silence for a few minutes. Then Brion cleared his throat and started up the output, giving the screen a thump as it refused to focus.

Dev got up and went to the display and adjusted the controls, bringing the picture into clarity. Then she went back and sat down.

"Thanks," Brion muttered.

They watched the vid from the plant cavern twice. When it was over the second time, everyone quietly turned and focused on Jess. "Seems pretty clear," Brion said.

"It is. I let them go," Jess responded. "I wanted them to take intelligence I gave them back home with them."

"What intelligence?"

"That's my business," Jess said. "and Interforces'."

There was a truth to that, and they knew it. "Can't have it both ways, Drake," Mike finally said. "You were shooting at them. Now you say you were doing something for them at the same time? That's crock."

"Sure I can." Jess stood up to relieve the stress building in her body. "I'm active Interforce. Even if I was shooting the bastards, that didn't change." She leaned on the table. "You go in with an oath, y'know. You swear you're going to act in their best interests, but the kicker is, it's left in your hands to figure out what that is."

"What?" Mike and Brion asked at the same time.

Jess straightened up again and folded her arms over her chest. "Yeah. There's a twisted comedy to being in service. But you only know that after you go in." She smiled."It's a game. You try to get one up. Sometimes that means you engineer what they're supposed to think they found out from you."

"Oh," Dev said. "Like you let them think there were those terrible weapons here."

Jess nodded. "And sidetracked them from focusing on bio alts by letting them think you weren't one." She regarded Dev. "They were sure the doc made a breakthrough."

Mike looked hard at her. "Dying wasn't better than sending them back with that?"

"Not that one. Brudegan goes back and delivers that message, they'll all listen to him." Jess shook her head. "Now he knows that cavern is a success, and it's behind some catastrophic weaponry he knows I'd use on them in a heartbeat. Because after all," she shrugged deprecatingly, "I'm Grandpappy Jack's, in service, grandkid."

Brion now smiled a little. "And you blew up Gibraltar. There's no weakness here." He glanced around the council room and saw comprehension showing on the faces at the table. "You showed them the crazy."

"I did," Jess acknowledged. "And tried to convince them they didn't really want to buy the crazy and breed it." She eyed them. "That's the message I wanted Brudgan to deliver, and he will. He has no choice because he saw what he saw."

"They took a piece of that rock with them," Mike said. "I saw it."

Jess nodded. "So did I."

Silence.

"They replicate that, you lose big, Jess," Brion said. "No more exclusive."

Jess half shrugged.

Dev shifted a little and put her folded hands on the table. "Plants take a long time to grow, and you need the proto soil. That comes from station. They did a lot of damage to station, so I am not sure they will be able to get more easily."

"We heard that," Mike said. "Kids said."

"Will we be able to get more?" Brion mused. "This could just be a one off, yeah? Besides, we don't know jack about all of that, and you shot the only guy left who did, Mike." He eyed the security chief. "Interforce don't know how to grow plants any better than we do."

Ah, Jess felt a sense of relief relax her shoulders as she spotted a way out of the suddenly insistent desire of her birthplace to keep her around. "That's true," she said. She reached casually over to put her hand on Dev's wrist when her bio alt partner looked like she was going to speak up again. "They're sure not going to talk to me after what I did up there."

"Shit," Mike said, after a pause.

"But you know who they might talk to?" Jess said after a pause of her own and in a musing tone as if she'd just thought of it. "The doc."

The silence lengthened. "Kurok?" Mike said finally. "I thought he croaked." He looked around the table. "That's what ops heard, on the wire."

"Truth," Ben said. "Blew his head off practically. We saw it."

Jess shrugged again. "Tough kill."

"Doctor Dan is recovering," Dev said. "I spoke with him last night. In fact, I am looking forward to letting the sets here know he's getting better."

There was an uncomfortable shifting around the table. "He's all right," Mike said. "What's his gig going to be now? Back to Interforce? He's reg. You could see it. He ain't gonna go shopping for us, and by the by we need to talk about those bios you brought."

Jess sat down and folded her hands on the table again. "I'm not going to stick around here," she said in a flat voice. "Not now. Not yet." She took a breath and let it out. "I can't."

Silence.

"I can't," Jess repeated. "I'm not ready for that. You're not ready for me, and what I'd do here would only fuck things up worse."

"So what the fuck are we supposed to do?" Mike asked standing up. "We gotta live here!"

"I know." Jess stood up as well. "So here's what I got. I'm going to put Kurok in here as my proxy because it's the best thing to do for Drake's Bay."

"Jess, wait—"

"He's smart. He knows how to mess with those plants," she said over Brion. "And he'll figure out what to do with those bios because they're staying here." She let her voice lift on the last few words. "We lost enough bodies for them to have space."

Everyone looked back at her. "Fuck yeah," Mike said. "Straight out they're staying here. Most useful fucking things to come in the place in decades. We like 'em. We want more."

Jess felt like a singing polar bear had just entered the council room and started dancing. "What?" She put her hands on her hips. "You're the asshole who told me you wanted to shoot them."

"Yeah. Sucks to be me," Mike said. "Never had anything to do with them before. What the hell did I know?"

"None of us had," Ben said.

"So what the hell?"

Ben shrugged. "They know stuff. They do stuff that's useful like fix things."

"Screw that." Mike waved them off. "They're nice," he said. "They're not assholes like the rest of us and holy crap that's a relief." He put his hands on the table. "So yeah I was wrong, Drake. Sucks to be me."

Jess looked at Dev, who smiled a little. "Yeah. I was wrong, too," she admitted.

Brion nodded, and the two men next to him nodded, too. "That might work. Kurok, I mean. He knows all about those bios. And he knows the plant stuff. Yeah." He eyed Jess. "And he doesn't have the crazy. But what's going to make him agree? He's not stupid. He knows what this place is."

Unbelievable throw of the dice coming up right for a change. "I think he'll be okay with it," Jess responded in a mild tone. "He's kind of over the station. Looking for a place to land." She sat back down. "Don't think he wants it to be Interforce."

"So, good," Brion said. "You rig that, Jess? Make it happen?"

"I will," Jess said, having already done so.

Dev cleared her throat. "The sets that came here. They have programming for the plants. We all do. They know how to work the systems in the cavern. We all took a turn on station doing that."

"Even better," Ben said. "We done now? I'm hungry. Let's let the outlanders know and we can get some chow."

"Done," Mike said. "Good deal, Drake." He paused and grinned. "Still want you here though. That's gotta happen."

Jess grinned back. "Some day. When I'm a little less crazy."

Everyone stood and started to file out of the room. Dev got up and shook her head as if to clear it. "That turned out rather optimal. Did you expect that?"

Jess just laughed.

THE WERE IN the mess hall. The sets were gathered around Dev, intently listening to her while Jess relaxed at a table nearby with Cathy.

"Doctor Dan is getting well, and soon he will be coming here," Dev said.

"Excellent," a KayTee said. "NM-Dev-1, does this mean this will be our assignment?"

Dev regarded him. "I am not sure if it will be like what an assignment has been, but you will live here and work with the natural born here."

All the sets nodded in agreement. "This is good," a BeeAye said. "We like it here. It's not like station at all. They gave us nice quarters, and the meals are excellent. "

"We were given these coverings and also things to keep in our quarters," a KayTee added. "We have a sleeping space to ourselves! And it's always the same one."

"Yes. They do not have a crèche or space for a dorm here," Dev said. "It is excellent to have your own space. I do have the same at the Interforce base." She smiled. "One of the things I really enjoy about downside is the water showers."

"Yes!" a chorus of voices lifted.

Ben took a seat next to Jess. "They took over guest quarters on five," he said. "Holy crap. You would have thought we'd given them a million creds."

"Literally different world for them," Cathy said. "It's hard for them to believe they've been given so much. Honestly, this is an assignment most of them would only dream of."

"They talk funny," Ben said.

"We talk funnier to them," Jess said. She straightened up a little as she saw the mess crew bringing in chow. "About time."

Dev could see the sets were happy. That made her happy. "Do you have the hammocks to sleep in? I found they reminded me of the crèche a little."

"Yes," the KayTee said. "They are very comfortable, but they don't move. And we can do many things here! There is a lot of equipment to fix, and we can use our pilot programming as well. It's very good."

"It's good work," the BeeAye agreed. "And the natural borns like when we do things for them and help them in any way."

"They are not used to biological alternatives here," Dev said. "It is new for them as well. You are new to them like I was new to Interforce when I started my assignment there. Biological Alternatives had never done the tasks I was doing before."

"You performed them with excellence," the KayTee said, "and now we will do the same."

Dev smiled. "I know you will." She spotted the mess crew

coming in. "And now I think we can have a meal. I have to tell you that of all the places I have been downside, this place has the most excellent meals."

Everyone stood up to go to the dispensers, but the KayTee edged closer to Dev. "NM-Dev-1, may I ask you something?"

"Of course." Dev saw Jess approaching from the corner of her eye.

"They wish to give us different names," the KayTee said. "Is this permitted?" He eyed Jess with a little apprehension. "They want them...they want us, I think, to be different from each other."

"Yes." Dev nodded. "It's a special thing with natural borns. You would be surprised what they end up calling things. And people." She cleared her throat a little. "At the base, I am referred to as Rocket Raccoon."

The KayTee stared at her in puzzled disbelief.

"Doctor Dan will explain it." Dev edged toward the line. "But it is fine, KayTee, really. If you want, you can give them your crèche name. That also will be fine, and I think some of us have done that already."

The Kaytee looked relieved. "Excellent. Did you have a crèche name?" he asked as he fell into line behind her. "I never heard if you had."

"No." Dev saw Jess's ears twitching. "I did not need one as I was the only instance in my set."

"One of a kind," Jess said, as she passed back the rough edged, well worn, plas plates. "My one of a kind."

Dev grinned and considered the day proceeding well.

"Devvie, I see shrimp on the line," Jess said from her higher vantage point.

Well, and getting better by the moment.

Chapter Eighteen

TIME HAD PASSED, and the launch bay had regained much of the loud and random noise common to it. On a pad near the entrance a carrier was perched, hatch open, several umbilicals attached.

"I dunno about those new tunings," Doug said from his position seated on the floor with a board in his hands. "It feels a little laggy when I turn starboard."

Dev was lying on her back, her head inside a panel in the carrier. "I did not find the same," she said. "Would you like the diagnostic outputs from this vehicle to compare?"

"Nah." Doug traced at silver lead. "April thinks I'm just a ditzball driver." He picked up a tool and examined the surface. "Maybe I'll ask Brent to take a drive in it."

Dev peeked out of the panel. "He would like to give an opinion, I think."

"He's still bummed with no gig," Doug said. "Sucks."

Dev considered that then just shook her head and pulled herself back inside the console, and they worked along in silent companionship for a while.

She'd just finished installing the part when she heard footsteps approaching. She peeked out from under the metal grate and saw Jess through the open hatch, and she squiggled out and rolled onto her side as her partner climbed up inside. "Hello."

"Devvie." Jess dropped into her seat, her hair a little windblown. "This crate okay to fly?" She was dressed in one of her standard on duty suits, but had her outdoor jacket with her. She tossed it onto the back shelf as she passed. "Hey."

"Hey." Doug picked up his toolkit and stood. "I'm gonna go put this thing back into my bus." He winked at Dev then sauntered down the gangway whistling softly under his breath.

"Yes, we're fine." Dev sat up and crossed her legs under her. "I was just making some adjustments to the new nav mod."

Jess's pale eyes twinkled. "The one you designed?"

Dev made a little face in response. "Yes," she said. "Are we going somewhere?"

"Yep, we're up to take Doc to the Bay and then pick up Tayler and take him to school," Jess said. "And when that's done,

I'm released to standard ops again." She did a little dance in her seat to Dev's muted amusement. "Hot damn."

"Excellent." Dev got up and brushed herself off. "When will this take place?"

"Now." Jess glanced out the hatch. "Here comes the doc, so get the hamsters scrambling." She settled into her seat. "I'll plug into the coordinates for the school."

Dev went to the front of the carrier and got into her pilot's seat. She heard a second set of footsteps and glanced in the reflector to see Doctor Dan entering.

It had been several weeks, and though he still seemed pale, he winked at her as he came into the carrier. "Hello, Dev." He put a backpack down on the back shelf. "Try to be gentle, will you?"

"Of course," Dev assured him.

"You got enough kit?" Jess asked. "They fill that sack up for ya?"

Kurok came up and gingerly sat down on the jumpseat next to Dev. "They did. I have what I brought from the station, and they added the basics." He clipped restraints over him. "And frankly, I'm glad to be getting away from med here. Too many questions I can't answer."

"Jared?" Jess hazarded a guess.

"He's convinced I should be a study project," Kurok muttered. "I told him to go find some starfish or something."

Jess chuckled. "Yeah, he tried that on me back in the day. I had to slug him to get him off it." She pulled down her restraints and fastened them. "They won't ask those kind of questions at the Bay."

"No." Kurok smiled wryly. "That they won't."

Dev clipped comms on. "BR270006, requesting flight access." She hit the hatch retract. "I will miss having you here, Doctor Dan. But I know the sets at Jess's birthplace will be very glad to see you."

"Mmm." Kurok made a low noise in his throat. "I'll be glad to see them, too, especially after what you told me about the Bay's sudden reversal of generations of rampant hatred of bio alts. I'm not quite sure I buy that." He eyed Jess. "Based on past experience there."

Jess regarded him from behind her console. "Thanks for taking them on," she said.

Dev lifted and turned the carrier and gently glided out the cavern opening into a fog dense, but rain free afternoon.

"Mmm." Doctor Dan made the same low noise again and met

Jess's eyes. "Not really sure how many other options I have," he admitted, with one of his gentle smiles. "Or you, for that matter."

"Truth." Jess leaned back in her chair. "Though they'd have put you back in service if you'd wanted it." She jerked her head back in the direction of the Citadel. "Jase okayed it."

"I know." Doctor Dan extended his legs out along the floor of the carrier. "But I think I'd do better at the Bay. More challenges and fewer complications."

Jess got that. She triggered her boards and ran the checks, though she hoped she wouldn't have to use anything on them today. Then she pulled the navigation input over and coded in the coordinates for their second destination.

THE BAY WAS full of ships, unlike the last time they'd been there. The foggy air drifted over the water, revealing craft crossing from the sea entrance to the cavern, the debris from the war dragged clear out of the way. Along the cliff face there were also signs of repair, and the doors to the big ancient guns were closed and sealed.

They saw teams outside working. Small moving figures busy and flyers overhead with hooks and cradles moving things.

Dev curved the carrier around in an arc and aimed for the landing bays, two of which were now operational. "Stand by, Drake's Bay control," Dev spoke into her input. "I copy station two, pad one."

"Welcome, Dev," Ops responded. "See ya down."

Kurok's lips twitched. "That was friendly."

"They think Dev flies sexy," Jess said. "And they've never really been formal."

"Mmm."

Jess deactivated her boards and folded her hands over her stomach. "They got a lot of fixing done," she said as Dev brought them in for a landing, using her jets to ease them into the bay and onto the pad as gentle as soft rain.

"They did," Dev agreed. She shut down systems and glanced outside to see a Bay mech hooking them up to power. She gave him a smile and wave. He waved back and winked at her, and she realized it was the young man who'd inspected the carrier way back when they'd first come.

A Bay rat he said? Now he was a mech, and he'd been one of the ones who'd gone to station. So many changes for so many people.

She opened the hatch, extended the ramp, and he stuck his head inside as they were gathering themselves up. "Hello."

"Hey, Rocket." He winked again. "Yo, Drake."

"Yo," Jess returned the greeting. "How's it?"

"Bitchin'," he responded. He backed out of the way to let her exit, with Doctor Kurok and Dev behind her. "Waiting for you up in the hall," he informed her. "Whole bunch."

"Thanks, ya scrub." Jess, nevertheless, smiled at him.

"Yo, like level two mech scrub." He pointed at the patch on his overalls. "I got a promo since they processed half the half, you know?"

"I know." Jess did a fist bump with him. "Congrats."

They walked through the cavern and through the halls, accompanied by the far off sounds of hammering and the screech of cutting steel, but without seeing any other living beings.

It seemed creepy. Jess pushed that thought out of her mind though and squared her shoulders as they emerged onto the landing, hauling up a little as she detected the presence of a lot of people. "Whoa."

The entire floor of the hall was filled. As they entered, all the people there fell silent and turned to face the stairs, heads tilted back.

"Mmm," Kurok grunted softly. "Could be welcome, could be lynching. You never can tell with the Bay."

Jess went to the balcony and looked down at them, her hands resting on the wrought iron railing. "Let's find out. I'm not in the mood to be lynched today." She paused then drew in a breath. "Hai!" She let out a bellow, the echoes reflecting from the rock walls.

A moment of silence and then. "Hai!" The yell came back from a thousand throats.

"Meh. Should be okay." Jess turned and started down.

Dev and Kurok exchanged glances. "Programming really did not cover all of this natural born stuff, Doctor Dan."

"No," he agreed. "I never really envisioned this particular scenario." He took hold of the railing and started down after Jess. "Really, I never envisioned being inside this place again. Or leaving station. Or having you be as breakout a success as you are." He sighed. "Failure all around on my part."

"I'm sure it will be okay." Dev walked quietly next to him. "They really liked the idea of you coming here. I was there and heard them. And of course the sets were really happy."

"We'll see," he replied. "It is what it is, I suppose, and

certainly could have been far worse."

They reached the fifth level. "This is where they have the sets living," Dev commented. "They said they liked it."

Kurok paused and regarded the corridor. "Guest quarters?" he said after a moment. "Or it was, at any rate." He noted the newly affixed designation. "Hum. Spacer quarters."

Dev studied it with interest. "Spacers," she mused. "So that is what they decided to call us? Interesting."

"Interesting," Kurok agreed. "Let's see what else we have in store." He started down again. "This might not be as horrific as I'd imagined."

There was a space cleared at the bottom of the steps and the three of them stepped into it. Jess felt it as soon as she stopped walking. That ephemeral, extrasensory energy that was the Bay. Was all it's history, and the self knowledge of what it was.

What it had been.

Who they were. Who she was. For a very long moment she almost reversed it all. Chucked up Interforce. Gave up the oath and the crazy.

Almost wanted to just come home because in that moment she breathed it in and understood that this was hers, and home, and where she belonged.

She knew it.

They knew it.

If she stepped back now, the odds were a million to one she'd ever come to this place again, to have this, to own this place and be wanted by these people because all those odds were against her staying alive long enough to claim it again.

Was she an idiot for turning her back on this? Jess glanced aside to see Dev standing next to her, hands clasped behind her back, head up, jaw forward, ready to stand by her regardless of what fool thing she did next. Dev would stand by her.

Would fly into danger with her. Would risk the insanity that was insertions and single team entries into dangerous places and likely, likely die alongside her in some ultimately pointless way.

Then the time for reflection was over and several slighter figures ran forward, sets and Cathy, to greet Dan Kurok, and the crowd moved toward them.

One of the bios reached him. "Doctor Dan! It's so excellent to see you!" he said. "We have so much to show you, and the natural borns here have been so good to us!"

Mike, and Brion and Dan were moving forward, and it was a little chaotic. "C'mon back to the council room so we can hear ourselves think," Brion said. "Time enough for a party when we're done with everything."

Jess exhaled and moved forward, touching Kurok on the shoulder and indicating the way.

DEV LET THEM go off and decided to stay with the sets and listen to their excited stories. Cathy was there as well, and she came over to Dev.

Dev smiled. "It's very different, isn't it?"

"I thought it was going to be terrible," Cathy confided. "It was so rough and so horrible at first. But really they've turned out to be good people." She glanced to the side and lifted a hand to wave slightly.

Dev was aware of the kid from the cavern standing nearby, arms crossed, a grin on his face, watching Cathy. "I find many of the people here quite interesting," she said. "I understood a lot more about Jess after I met some of them."

Cathy nodded.

"Do you want to see where we live now, NM-Dev-1?" one of the BeeAyes asked. "Can we show you?"

Dev nodded, and the BeeAye, along with two KayTees, guided her back up the steps toward the fifth level. They were all dressed in the Bay overalls and the woven sweaters covered their collars as she remembered hers being covered when she was dressed as a seafarer during her first mission.

"That's nice." Dev indicated the sign as they went past. "Spacers."

"Yes," the KayTee next to her said. "That is what they said was different about us. That we came from space. From station."

"Not that you are biological alternatives."

"Yes. It's so excellent!" The KayTee opened one of the doors. "This is my housing." He stood back with evident pride. "Only mine!"

It was much the same as the space she'd stayed in when they'd visited. Small, and somewhat shabby, but his. More space than he'd ever had in his whole life before now. A cubby to store things in, the hammock for sleeping, the sanitary unit. On the table and chair there was already a scattering of things.

A shell, she noted and smiled. "Excellent," Dev said. "I know how it feels to have this, in fact. When I was assigned quarters in the base, I was also amazed to have a space all for myself."

She thought, perhaps, that this was likely the least of the

spaces available, and that the natural born had larger, nicer rooms, but given what they had come from and what their expectations had been?

Yes, this was more than optimal.

"Excellent," the KayTee agreed. "And they call us by our names." He took a breath and smiled at Dev. "I never thought an assignment would be this good. And see the coverings!" He extended his arm. "We were so cold when we got here and they gave us these so we would be more comfortable."

The overalls were rough and workmanlike. A thick constructed fabric that provided protection from the fierce wind and a little coated against the ever present rain. The sweater they wore along with it was an off color gray green, but all importantly warm.

And, as importantly, what many others in the Bay wore. Probably these in fact had come from some of the natural born who had been made dead in the fighting.

Dev held out her arm. "This garment was given to me by Jess for the same reason. It is the skin of a fish."

They all crowded into the room on hearing this, reaching out to touch the sleeve of her jacket.

"A fish?" the BeeAye said in an astonished tone. "Really?"

"Yes. A shark, which is a very large fish in the sea. It is lined and very warm." Dev unzipped the front and displayed the inside. "It is good when people take care for us," she said. "And I am very glad the people here want to take care and make this a good assignment."

"It could have been suboptimal," the BeeAye observed.

"Very," Dev said. "There was no time to make a plan."

There was a little silence. "NM-Dev-1, may I ask a question?" the KayTee said.

"Please address me as Dev," Dev responded with a brief smile. "And you are Kevin, correct?"

"Yes, Dev," he said, smiling back. "Is it true you had your collar removed?" he asked. "We heard that from the natural born here."

Without hesitation, Dev unfastened the neck of her tech jumpsuit and peeled it back to show her neck. "Yes. It's true. Doctor Dan removed it on station." She paused thoughtfully. "He did not want anyone who was not correct to add programming to me."

The sets nodded.

"And also my partner Jess was concerned I could be put

down by someone who knew I was a bio alt and not allow me to perform with excellence."

"That is optimal," Kevin said. "Do you think he will do that for us now as well? There are no programming chambers here."

That was an interesting and good question. "I do not know," Dev admitted. "He might want to give you programming about this place or other things. I will now have to learn everything the difficult way."

"Do you think that's non optimal?" the BeeAye asked. "It is good to get new programming."

Dev thought about that for a few moments in silence, while the sets waited patiently for her, as was their way. "It is good to get new programming," she concluded. "But Doctor Dan has told me that one of the things he made different as part of my development was to make it easier for me to figure things out without programming."

"You are new model, developmental," Kevin said.

"Yes," Dev said. "So we will see if that is true, but so far it has worked out okay."

The sets nodded. "Can we ask you another question?" Kevin asked.

"Of course." Dev fastened her suit back up and folded her arms.

"It's about the sex thing."

"Ah." Dev felt her skin heat a little. "Well."

"We were told you are the expert."

JESS SLOWLY SETTLED into a chair and rested her forearms on the table. She waited for the rest of the bunch to take their seats, while Dan Kurok dropped into the one next to her.

"Having second thoughts?" Doctor Dan asked in a mild tone.

Jess eyed him.

"It's not a bad place," Kurok said. "Well, now that they've decided to like my products at least." His eyes twinkled a little.

"Mmph," Jess grunted then shifted her body and straightened up in her chair. "All right let's get this over with," she said. "Here's the chip." She stood and leaned over, putting the plas square on the table. "Interforce signed off. Once I seal the proxy, you get your head of stakehold, and I get released back into field ops."

Eyes shifted to Kurok.

Obligingly, he stood up and put his hands inside the front

pocket of his Bay shirt. "Hello, you lot," Kurok said. "Shall we have a go at this? I'll try not to make too much of a mess of it."

Jess muffled a smile.

"That supposed to be funny?" Brion asked.

"No, just true," Kurok responded mildly. "I have extensive experience at being an Interforce field tech and at being a genetic scientist. Running a stakehold, especially one like this? Not so much." He rocked a little bit on his heels. "But I'm thinking no one else here has much either, so perhaps we can all just march forward together, eh?"

The battered, weathered figures around the table regarded him in somber silence.

Kurok leaned on the back of one of the empty chairs. "Problem maybe being I'm from the other side?" he asked and watched those faces twitch in reaction. "I am, you know. I was born in a research station on the coast of what was once the North Sea. Interforce attacked it. I was one of only two survivors. A fourteen-year-old mop head they brought to Canon City."

Jess shifted a little in surprise. "That name doesn't get tossed around much," she commented.

"No." Kurok smiled at her. "I was too young to be put in the field program, so after they finished trying to condition me, they put me in with the class of agent cadets. Which is where I met Jesslyn's father, Justin. I survived to graduation and was partnered with him on assignment to Base Ten."

"We heard all that," Mike said brusquely. "Everyone knows Justin was all in with you. He spliffed someone here who made a crack and put two more in med for a month. Got it."

Kurok nodded. "We were great friends."

"You quit," Mike said. "Get tired of the game?"

Kurok heard the question behind the question under the anger in the voice and understood. "No." He laced his fingers together and regarded the big security chief. "I left because Justin asked me to." He glanced down at his hands then back at the room.

Mike leaned forward. "And?"

Dan Kurok met his eyes with stolid evenness. "And nothing," he said, a flat tone in his voice. "That's all you get. You just have to know he asked and I went."

The mystery itched at them. Jess could see it. "I said he was family," she said in the same flat tone. "Take it or leave it. Trust me or not."

Mike studied her for a long moment. Then he looked at the

rest of the people at the table. "No fucking choice is there? You got control."

"I do." Jess stood up. "And I give a crap enough about this place and you people not to subject you to me." She indicated the chip. "So let's get this moving. I've got things I have to do today."

And slowly then, all nodded, an odd wave of motion around the table as though heads were tied with strings. Brion picked up the chip and stood. "We go," he said. "See how it works out."

JESS FOUND A plas window and gazed out it, watching the wind ruffle pale green waters in the Bay near the shore. She felt a sense of relief, of some progress however skewed, and now there remained only one task left for her to do to complete the commitments she'd made.

The deal she'd brokered with Interforce, to get what she wanted and do what she wanted that also got them what they wanted, in some way.

She tapped comms. "Dev?"

"Ah, yes." Dev's voice came back with a tone of definite relief. "Is it time for us to go?"

Jess's eyebrows lifted. "You in a rush?"

"Actually, yes."

The brows lifted further. "I'm in the kitchen. C'mon over." She shut down the signal with a bemused look. "Wonder what the hell that's all about."

"Jesslyn."

She turned to find Brion there, looking a bit uncomfortable. Behind him was a short, apprehensive figure. "Hello, Mary," Jess said. She took a seat on the window sill with an almost audible sigh. "You can come in. I'm not going to shoot you."

Jimmy's wife, widow now, edged into the room around Brion, who unapologetically backed out and left them together. Mary had a haggard, haunted look to her, and she rubbed her hands together nervously. "I wanted to talk to you about Tayler."

Jess sighed again. "Okay." She let her hands rest on her knees. "What do you want to talk about?"

"Don't take him," Mary said, getting it out in a rush. "You can make a deal with them. They want what you have here. Leave him alone."

Jess got up, went to the table and pulled out a chair. She sat down in it and gestured to a second one. "Siddown," she said. "I can't leave him. He passed the battery." She rested her elbows on the wooden surface. "He can't stay here."

"He won't," Mary said. "I'll take him with me. I'm going to stay in Quebec City. I don't want my kids raised here in this place." She took a determined breath. "I don't want him becoming a monster like you."

Brave, really. Jess regarded her mildly. Brave, just clueless. "Sorry my suck ass brother never explained it to you," she said. "He's already a monster." She folded her hands. "He was born that way."

Mary stared at her. "That's not true. He's just a child."

"So was I," Jess said. "So was my father, and his father, and my uncle, and my aunt out in the hills, and ten other generations of us." She regarded her sister-in-law without emotion. "School doesn't teach us to be that way. It just teaches us to," she paused a little, "manage the crazy."

Footsteps approached, and the door opened. Dev poked her head in and then pushed the door open. "Hello," she said. "I found Tayler looking for you, Jess." She stood back to let the boy enter. "I told him I would help him get his things together to go."

"Auntie, Jess." Tayler went around the table, ignoring his mother's presence. "There ya are. When we goin'?"

"Soon," Jess told him.

"Tayler, don't you want to stay with your sister and me?" Mary asked. "We're going to live someplace nice."

Tayler looked over at her. "Wanna go to school," he said after a pause. "Like Auntie Jess."

Mary stood up. "Like your loving aunt who killed your father? Why not ask her about that, Tayler? You have no father now. Ask her why she killed him."

He was too young for that crap. Jess sighed internally, as the now six-year-old boy turned and looked at her, and their eyes met. "That's true, Tay. I did kill him," she said.

He put his hand on the table and then his knee on the chair next to her. "How come?"

She heard a faint sound and glanced up across the table to see Dan Kurok framed in the doorway. "How come? Because he broke a promise. And it was a wrong thing." She watched the small face watch her and saw that difference, her difference, looking back.

Tayler nodded a little. "He used to hurt my sister a lot," he said in a thoughtful tone. "He would do things and she'd cry." He looked over at his mother. "S'good." He looked back at Jess. "We go now?"

"Yeah." Jess smiled at him, lifted her hand and offered a fist. He lifted his own hand and bumped his smaller knuckles with hers. "Go with Dev. She'll help you get your stuff and you'll get a ride with us. Okay?"

"Yes!" He turned and ran back to the door as Dev hastily scrambled up to follow him. "Wooo!"

Dan Kurok came and took the chair Dev had been sitting in as Mary just sat there, stunned and without speech. "That's one of the differences," he told her in a gentle tone, "that the battery was designed for. To find that lack of attachment."

"He doesn't care," Mary whispered, her eyes unfocused, not looking at them.

"No, he really doesn't," Jess said. "He'd have gotten Jimmy himself. That's why they take us at six. Before we get hold of old uncle's fishing knives." She leaned forward a little, forcing the woman to make eye contact with her. "Not your fault. You couldn't have changed it. It's what it is to be a Drake, both sides."

Mary pushed herself to her feet and stumbled out, crying.

Jess sighed. "I'll see if Jonton can keep an eye on her." She stood up and went to the old style cabinet and reached inside to remove two fishrolls. "Want one?"

Kurok accepted the offering. "Ah, my favorite kind." He bit into the seaweed wrapped item. "Any last words of advice for me, Jesslyn?"

Jess just laughed.

Kurok chuckled himself after a moment. "Do you want to know why?" He eyed her.

"No." Jess chewed contentedly. "I know." She swallowed and winked at him.

"I see," he mused. "And?"

"And that's all you get."

TAYLER RAN TOWARD the carrier, his eyes going everywhere as Dev followed him with a backpack and a duffel bag, the only things he'd be taking with him to school. "S'cool!" He paused near the engine pod as Dev triggered the hatch.

"Yes, I think so, too," Dev agreed. She watched him go over and trace the names lettered on the outside of the carrier's tough skin. She mounted the ramp, and a moment later he scrambled up it next to her, racing inside and then coming to a halt. "Be careful."

He looked around with wide eyes as she stowed his gear into

one of the lockers then went to her position up in the nose of the carrier. "You can sit there in Jess's seat if you like," Dev said as she dropped into her own and got ready to bring the craft active.

He followed her instead. "C'n I watch?"

"Yes." Dev indicated the jumpseat. "But please do not touch anything. It might cause suboptimal results."

She heard chatter as she settled her comms rig on and tuned it. Bay ops, a young yet confident voice instructing a supply freighter in. She paused, listening, then touched the input. "Drake's Bay operations, this is Interforce flight BR270006 requesting departure clearance."

A pause. Then. "BR270006, you are cleared for exit, please have a care northeast, there is other traffic approaching."

"Understood," Dev answered with a smile. "Thank you, Kevin."

"You are welcome, Dev," her crèche mate answered, a shared yet unshared pride in both their voices. "Please return soon."

So excellent.

Boots on the ramp, and Dev felt the rocking as the carrier deck took Jess's weight. "We are cleared to leave, Jess."

"Hell, yes." Jess took her seat. "You ready there, Tay?" She fastened her restraints. "Get that belt on. You're about to fly with Rocket."

Dev leaned over to help Tayler fasten the jumpseat restraints. "Is everything nominal, Jess?" She glanced into the reflector to see her partner shrugging with exaggerated motions and lifting her hands. "I see."

"Is what it is, Devvie. Let's get moving." Jess relaxed against her padded seat. "School's waiting on us."

"Yes. Stand by to lift."

IT WAS THE first time, really, that she'd flown west. Dev had the external inputs on, and they were cruising over a shallow inland sea, the weather so far holding and only producing some small, scattered showers as they made their way toward the mountain range that held the Interforce school.

She'd seen some birds, and her sensors had detected some fish, but otherwise the trip had been empty of any ground or people.

She had the forward screens on, though, and on the horizon she saw the fuzzed delineation that was an elevation of land. "Are there any settlements in this area, Jess?"

"No." Jess was leaning back in her chair, her hands folded on her stomach. "Some fishing towns to the west on the edge of the water, but that's about it."

Tayler had been napping, but now he woke and rubbed his eyes. "We there?"

"Almost," Jess responded.

He unhooked himself and got up on his knees on the jumpseat, looking through the front screen as the blur of land started to take on structure, the carrier moving toward it at just three times the speed of sound. "Oh we're goin' fast!"

"Yes." Dev saw the comms light up. "We're being hailed."

"Send our ident," Jess said. "You ready, Tay?"

He sat down and looked at her. "I dunno," he admitted. "Is it gonna be weird?"

Jess swung her chair around to face him and leaned forward. "Yeah," she said. "They'll take you and talk to you for a few days. Then you should be able to go with the other kids, and it'll be better." She paused. "The class started ahead of you, but it'll be okay."

Tayler nodded with a slightly doubtful expression. "Okay."

"Canon City control, this is BR270006, Senior Agent Jesslyn Drake in command." Dev said into the comms. "We are on assignment to this location."

They were now within visual range and ahead of them spread a long, sloping plateau of red rock, beyond that towering walls. Atop them were guard stations and the flashback of plasma shields, but in the center of the wall were large doors that were open.

"Roger that, BR270006. Understand you have a delivery for us," a voice, calm and almost gentle, came back. "Please proceed to the intake and processing building on the left."

"Understood." Dev slowed the engines as they came into approach, hearing the rumbling boom as they slowed below the speed of sound and dropped in altitude.

Tayler had turned in his seat again and looked out at the buildings. "Wow. Big."

"Very." Jess felt a mixture of nostalgia and good riddance as she regarded the complex. "Plenty of space, Tay. I think you'll like the classes."

The large central space had people in it. Groups of assorted sized figures, all of whom stopped and stared as the carrier drifted in over them, their eyes following its progress as Dev picked her path toward the rust stained rock walls and structures she'd been directed to.

There were a number of structures spread out around a central area of plateau, with smaller structures and walls crossing it.

To one side of the red building there was a cleared pad, and she set the carrier down on its extended skids, the jets' blast vaporizing the layer of water on the ground.

A group of people, waiting in the shelter of the doorway of the building started toward them. Dev secured the carrier and released her restraints. standing up as the pilot's chair moved back and cleared space for her. She went to the locker and removed Tayler's things.

"Tay," Jess said, as she released her own restraints and he came back toward her. "It'll be okay. You'll make friends and have fun. They'll understand how you feel here."

Tayler nodded a little, his bottom lip poking out just a bit.

Jess hesitated. "But you're always going to be different. Just like I was different. Because we come from Drake's Bay. You know?"

Now he grinned a little. "Yeah."

"That's okay." Jess reached out and ruffled his hair. "A lot of us came here. In some of your classes you'll find us up on the vid, and you can tell people, hey that's my family."

"Will you come see me?" he asked, suddenly the little boy who was scared coming out.

"I will." Jess held her hand out. "Just like my father came and saw me. Let's go get you settled."

Dev opened the hatch and stood back as the ramp extended. She followed Jess and Tayler out to where the group of people were waiting a respectful distance from the carrier's blunt outline. As she looked around, it occurred to her that the place itself was a somewhat forbidding one.

All the guards.

Nearby, a group of older teens were clustered, examining the carrier and pointing. They were wearing the gray suits she remembered the incoming new agents and techs wearing back at Base Ten.

The tallest of the men facing them came forward and offered a hand. "Hello, Agent Drake. It's nice to see you again after all this time."

"Yeah, been a while." Jess clasped his hand and released it. "This is my partner, Dev."

"Oh, we've heard of her." The man smiled and extended his

hand toward Dev. "Welcome to Canon City, Dev. I'm John Callister, director of the school."

"Hello," Dev responded cordially.

"And this must be Tayler," Callister said, looking down. "Are you ready to come to school, Tayler? We've been waiting for you. I heard you had a lot of adventures before coming."

Tayler seemed unsure, but then he released Jess's hand and took a step forward. "Yeah," he said. "I even been in space." He watched as two other people, a man and a woman, came forward. The man reached out to Dev to take his pack and bag.

"Can't wait to hear all about that," the woman said. "I'm Tracy, and I'm going to help get things arranged for you. Ready?" She held her hand out and waited until he reluctantly took it. "Thanks, Tayler."

He looked behind him uncertainly, catching Jess's eye. She waved and smiled, and he relaxed a little, then he let himself be led off. "Bye, Auntie Jess."

"Bye, Tay. Have fun," Jess called back. They watched until the remainder of the group followed Tracy and Tayler as they headed for the door into the processing hall. Jess sighed. "He's gonna have a tough time."

"You all do." Callister said, not without some sympathy. "But you've all ended up walking out that gate." He glanced around. "Want to come in for a drink? I've heard a lot of stories I'd like to get a gut check on from you."

Jess looked past him then shook her head. "Gotta get back. Next time." Without further preamble she turned and headed back to the carrier.

Dev regarded the man briefly then followed, aware of a general sense of incorrectness but not entirely sure where it lay. She entered the craft and closed the hatch. "Was that suboptimal?" she finally asked Jess, who was slumped in her chair.

Jess sighed. "I remember my intake day," she said. "Peh. Get moving out of here willya, Dev?"

"Of course." Dev started that process going. "Jess, what is this facility? Is it just a school? It seems very imposing."

Jess remained silent as the carrier lifted. "Back in the day, in what was then called Colorado, Canon City was where they had all their lock ups." She glanced forward. "Jails. Penitentiaries. Maximum security prisons. So that's what that rock pile is. There are tunnels that connect them, and each one now holds different levels of classes."

"I see," Dev said, who really didn't.

"Kids start in the easier sections. Not as scary. As you get older and more dangerous, they move you into places they can control you in if you let the crazy out," Jess said. "He's right. At least we Drakes end up walking out of there. Not everyone does."

Dev thought about the little boy with the starfish and felt a sense of sadness. "That does not sound very excellent, Jess."

Jess regarded her with a wry smile. "Worse than being a bio alt, huh? I'm hoping the doc'll figure out how to flip our bit before the next generation." She leaned back. "If anyone can, he can."

Dev exhaled slowly. "If he can, he will," she murmured, meeting Jess's eyes in the reflector.

They stared at each other for a long moment. "Maybe he already has," Jess said. "We just don't know it yet."

OTHER MELISSA GOOD TITLES

Tropical Storm

From bestselling author Melissa Good comes a tale of heartache, longing, family strife, lust for love, and redemption. *Tropical Storm* took the lesbian reading world by storm when it was first written...now read this exciting revised "author's cut" edition.

Dar Roberts, corporate raider for a multi-national tech company is cold, practical, and merciless. She does her job with a razor-sharp accuracy. Friends are a luxury she cannot allow herself, and love is something she knows she'll never attain.

Kerry Stuart left Michigan for Florida in an attempt to get away from her domineering politician father and the constraints of the overly conservative life her family forced upon her. After college she worked her way into supervision at a small tech company, only to have it taken over by Dar Roberts' organization. Her association with Dar begins in disbelief, hatred, and disappointment, but when Dar unexpectedly hires Kerry as her work assistant, the dynamics of their relationship change. Over time, a bond begins to form.

But can Dar overcome years of habit and conditioning to open herself up to the uncertainty of love? And will Kerry escape from the clutches of her powerful father in order to live a better life?

ISBN 978-1-932300-60-4
eISBN 978-1-935053-75-0

Hurricane Watch

In this sequel to *Tropical Storm*, Dar and Kerry are back and making their relationship permanent. But an ambitious new colleague threatens to divide them — and out them. He wants Dar's head and her job, and he's willing to use Kerry to do it. Can their home life survive the office power play?

Dar and Kerry are redefining themselves and their priorities to build a life and a family together. But with the scheming colleagues and old flames trying to drive them apart and bring them down, the two women must overcome fear, prejudice, and their own pasts to protect the company and each other. Does their relationship have enough trust to survive the storm?

ISBN 978-1-935053-00
eISBN 978-1-935053-76-7

Eye of the Storm

Eye of the Storm picks up the story of Dar Roberts and Kerry Stuart a few months after *Hurricane Watch* ends. At first it looks like they are settling into their lives together but, as readers of this series have learned, life is never simple around Dar and Kerry. Surrounded by endless corporate intrigue, Dar experiences personal discoveries that force her to deal with issues that she had buried long ago and Kerry finally faces the consequences of her own actions. As always, they help each other through these personal challenges that, in the end, strengthen them as individuals and as a couple.

ISBN 978-1-932300-13-0
eISBN 978-1-935053-77-4

Red Sky At Morning

A connection others don't understand...

A love that won't be denied...

Danger they can sense but cannot see...

Dar Roberts was always ruthless and single-minded...until she met Kerry Stuart.

Kerry was oppressed by her family's wealth and politics. But Dar saved her from that.

Now new dangers confront them from all sides. While traveling to Chicago, Kerry's plane is struck by lightning. Dar, in New York for a stockholders' meeting, senses Kerry is in trouble. They simultaneously experience feelings that are new, sensations that both are reluctant to admit when they are finally back together. Back in Miami, a cover-up of the worst kind, problems with the military, and unexpected betrayals will cause more danger. Can Kerry help as Dar has to examine her life and loyalties and call into question all she's believed in since childhood? Will their relationship deepen through it all? Or will it be destroyed?

ISBN 978-1-932300-80-2
eISBN 978-1-935053-71-2

Thicker Than Water

This fifth entry in the continuing saga of Dar Roberts and Kerry Stuart starts off with Kerry involved in mentoring a church group of girls. Kerry is forced to acknowledge her own feelings toward and experiences with her parents as she and Dar assist a teenager from the group who gets jailed because her parents tossed her out onto the streets when they found out she is gay. While trying to help the teenagers adjust to real world situations, Kerry gets a call concerning her father's health. Kerry flies to her family's side as her father dies, putting the family in crisis. Caught up in an international problem, Dar abandons the issue to go to Michigan, determined to support Kerry in the face of grief and hatred. Dar and Kerry face down Kerry's extended family with a little help from their own, and return home, where they decide to leave work and the world behind for a while for some time to themselves.

ISBN 978-1-932300-24-6
eISBN 978-1-935053-72-9

Terrors of the High Seas

After the stress of a long Navy project and Kerry's father's death, Dar and Kerry decide to take their first long vacation together. A cruise in the eastern Caribbean is just the nice, peaceful time they need — until they get involved in a family feud, an old murder, and come face to face with pirates as their vacation turns into a race to find the key to a decades old puzzle.

ISBN 978-1-932300-45-1
eISBN 978-1-935053-73-6

Tropical Convergence

There's trouble on the horizon for ILS when a rival challenges them head on, and their best weapons, Dar and Kerry, are distracted by life instead of focusing on the business. Add to that an old flame, and an aggressive entrepreneur throwing down the gauntlet and Dar at least is ready to throw in the towel. Is Kerry ready to follow suit, or will she decide to step out from behind Dar's shadow and step up to the challenges they both face?

ISBN 978-1-935053-18-7
eISBN 978-1-935053-74-3

Stormy Waters

As Kerry begins work on the cruise ship project, Dar is attempting to produce a program to stop the hackers she has been chasing through cyberspace. When it appears that one of their cruise ship project rivals is behind the attempts to gain access to their system, things get more stressful than ever. Add in an unrelenting reporter who stalks them for her own agenda, an employee who is being paid to steal data for a competitor, and Army intelligence becoming involved and Dar and Kerry feel more off balance than ever. As the situation heats up, they consider again whether they want to stay with ILS or strike out on their own, but they know they must first finish the ship project.

ISBN 978-1-61929-082-2
eISBN 978-1-61929-083-9

Moving Target

Dar and Kerry both feel the cruise ship project seems off some-how, but they can't quite grasp what is wrong with the whole sce-nario. Things continue to go wrong and their competitors still look to be the culprits behind the problems. Then new information leads them to discover a plot that everyone finds difficult to believe. Out of her comfort zone yet again, Dar refuses to lose and launches a new plan that will be a win-win, only to find another major twist thrown in her path. With everyone believing Dar can somehow win the day, can Dar and Kerry pull off another miracle finish? Do they want to?

ISBN 978-1-61929-150-8
eISBN 978-1-61929-151-5

Storm Surge

It's fall. Dar and Kerry are traveling—Dar overseas to clinch a deal with their new ship owner partners in England, and Kerry on a reluctant visit home for her high school reunion. In the midst of corporate deals and personal conflict, their world goes unexpect-edly out of control when an early morning spurt of unusual alarms turns out to be the beginning of a shocking nightmare neither expected. Can they win the race against time to save their company and themselves?

Book One: ISBN 978-1-935053-28-6
eISBN 978-1-61929-000-6

Book Two: ISBN 978-1-935053-39-2
eISBN 978-1-61929-000-6

Winds of Change

After 9/11 the world has changed and Dar and Kerry have decided to change along with it. They have an orderly plan to resign and finally take their long delayed travelling vacation. But as always fate intervenes and they find themselves caught in a web of conflicting demands and they have to make choices they never anticipated.

The exciting conclusion!

Book One: ISBN 978-1-61929-194-2
eISBN 978-1-61929-193-5
Book Two: ISBN 978-1-61929-232-1
eISBN 978-1-61929-231-4

Partners

After a massive volcanic eruption puts earth into nuclear winter, the planet is cloaked in clouds and no sun penetrates. Seas cover most of the land areas except high elevations which exist as islands where the remaining humans have learned to make do with much less. People survive on what they can take from the sea and with foodstuffs supplemented from an orbiting set of space stations.

Jess Drake is an agent for Interforce, a small and exclusive special forces organization that still possesses access to technology. Her job is to protect and serve the citizens of the American continent who are in conflict with those left on the European continent. The struggle for resources is brutal, and when a rogue agent nearly destroys everything, Interforce decides to trust no one. They send Jess a biologically-created agent who has been artificially devised and given knowledge using specialized brain programming techniques.

Instead of the mindless automaton one might expect, Biological Alternative NM-Dev-1 proves to be human and attractive. Against all odds, Jess and the new agent are swept into a relationship neither expected. Can they survive in these strange circumstances? And will they even be able to stay alive in this bleak new world?

Book One: ISBN 978-1-61929-118-8
eISBN 978-1-61929-119-5

Book Two: ISBN 978-1-61929-190-4
eISBN 978-1-61929-189-8

OTHER REGAL CREST PUBLICATIONS